IAN FLEMING'S
JAMES
BOND

THREE COMPLETE
NOVELS BY
JOHN GARDNER

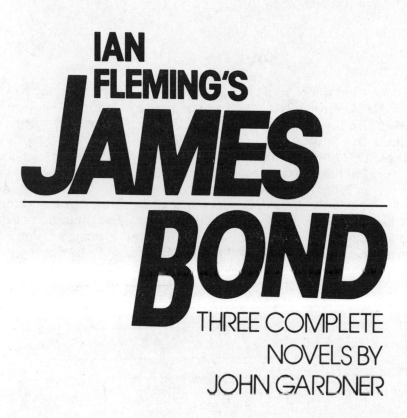

ABOUT THE AUTHOR

JOHN GARDNER was born in England in 1926. He served in the Royal Navy Air Fleet from 1944 to 1946, and in the Royal Marine Commandos in 1946. He then attended St. John's College, Cambridge, where he earned a B.A. in 1950 and an M.A. in 1951.

From 1952 to 1958 Gardner served as a curate in Evesham, England, and then left the church to become theater critic and arts editor for the *Herald* in Stratford-Upon-Avon from 1959 to 1965. After his employment at the *Herald*, Gardner began his full-time writing career, and his work made him the logical heir to the literary tradition of the legendary James Bond. His continuation of Ian Fleming's vision has drawn praise from all quarters. John Gardner currently lives in Ireland.

IAN FLEMING'S JAMES BOND

THREE COMPLETE NOVELS BY JOHN GARDNER

LICENSE RENEWED

FOR SPECIAL SERVICES

ICEBREAKER

AVENEL BOOKS · NEW YORK

This 1987 edition is published by Avenel Books, distributed by Crown Publishers, Inc., 225 Park Avenue South, New York, New York 10003, by arrangement with the Putnam Publishing Group.

Printed and Bound in the United States of America

LIBRARY OF CONGRESS CATALOGING-IN-PUBLICATION DATA

Gardner, John E.
  Ian Fleming's James Bond.

  Originally published in separate volumes.
  Contents: License renewed—For special services—
Icebreaker.
  1. Bond, James (Fictitious character)—Fiction.
2. Spy stories, American. I. Fleming, Ian, 1908–1964.
II. Title.
PS3557.A712A6 1987   813'.54   87-1210
  ISBN 0-517-64293-X

h g f e d c b a

Book design by Cynthia Dunne

CONTENTS

LICENSE RENEWED

ACKNOWLEDGMENTS

I would like, especially, to thank the Board of Directors of Glidrose Publications Ltd., the owners of the James Bond literary copyright, for asking me to undertake the somewhat daunting task of picking up where Mr. Ian Fleming left off, and transporting 007 into the 1980s. In particular, my thanks to Mr. Dennis Joss and Mr. Peter Janson-Smith; also to H.R.F.K., who acted as the original "Go-Between."

We have become so used to James Bond gadgets which boggle the mind that I would like to point out to any unbelievers that all the "hardware" used by Mr. Bond in this story is genuine. Everything provided by Q Branch and carried by Bond—even the modifications to Mr. Bond's Saab—is obtainable on either the open, or clandestine, markets. For assistance in seeking details about such equipment I am especially indebted to Communication Control Systems Ltd., and, more particularly, to the delicious Ms. Jo Ann O'Neill and the redoubtable Sidney.

As for the inventions of Anton Murik, Laird of Murcaldy, only time will tell.

JOHN GARDNER

In memory of
IAN LANCASTER FLEMING

CONTENTS

PASSENGER FOR FLIGHT 154

THE MAN WHO entered the airport washroom had light hair, cut neatly to collar length. Stocky, and around five feet three inches in height, he wore crumpled jeans, a T-shirt and sneakers. A trained observer would have particularly noted the piercing light blue eyes, above which thin brows arched in long curves that almost met above the slim nose.

The man's face was thin in comparison with his body, and the complexion a shade dark in contrast to the color of the hair. He carried a small brown suitcase, and, on entering the washroom, walked straight toward one of the cubicles, stepping carefully past a dungareed cleaner who was mopping the tiled floor with a squeegee, though without enthusiasm.

Once inside, the man slid the bolt and placed the suitcase on the lavatory seat, opening it to remove a mirror which he hung on the door hook before starting to strip as far as his white undershorts.

Before removing the T-shirt, he slid his fingers expertly below the hairline at his temples, peeling back the wig to reveal close-cropped natural hair underneath.

With a finger and thumb he grasped the corner of his left eyebrow and pulled, as a nurse will quickly rip sticking plaster from a cut. The slim eyebrows disappeared—together with what seemed to be some of the flesh—leaving black, untrimmed, thick lines of natural hair in their place.

The man worked like a professional—with care and speed, as though he was trying to beat a clock. From the suitcase he took a canvas corset, wrapping it around his waist, pulling tightly at the lacing, giving the immediate twin effect of slimming the waistline, and an illusion of more height. Within a few seconds the latter illusion was strengthened. Carefully folding the jeans and T-shirt, the man pushed his socks into his abandoned sneakers and pulled on a new pair of dark gray socks, followed by well-cut lightweight charcoal gray trousers and black slip-on shoes, into which were built what actors call "lifts": adding a good two inches to his normal stature.

Adjusting the mirror on the door, he now donned a white silk shirt and knotted a pearl gray tie into place, before opening an oblong plastic box that had been lying—held in place by the shoes on either side—directly beneath the corset, socks, trousers and shirt, in the suitcase.

The plastic box contained new components for the man's face. First, dark contact lenses, and fluid, to change those distinctive light blue eyes to a deep, almost jet, black. Next, he inserted small, shaped foam rubber pads into his cheeks which fattened the face. While they were in place he would not be able to eat or drink, but that mattered little compared with achieving the desired effect.

The pièce de résistance was a tailor-made short beard and mustache, sculpted from real hair on to an invisible, adhesive, Latex frame—genuine bristles overhanging the flexible frame which, when he set it correctly in place on his chin and lower lip, gave the impression of complete reality, even at very close range. The beard had been made specially, in New York, by an expert who dubiously claimed distant kinship with the famous nineteenth-century Wagnerian singer Ludwig Leichner, inventor of theatrical greasepaint.

The man smiled at the unfamiliar face now looking back at him from the mirror, completing the new picture with a pair of steel-framed, clear-glass lensed, spectacles. Leichner's unproven relative apart, the unrecognizable person looking out from the mirror was a makeup expert and disguise artist in his own right. It was part of his stock-in-trade—probably the least lethal part—and he had studied under top men and women in Hollywood, as well as being almost encyclopedic in the personal knowledge he had culled from all the famous works, such as Lacy's *Art of Acting,* the anonymous *Practical Guide to the Art of Making Up,* by "Haresfoot and Rouge," and the other standard works by Leman Rede, C. H. Fox, and the great S. J. A. Fitzgerald.

Now he closed the oblong box, removed a jacket, which matched the trousers, from the case, filled his pockets with an assortment of items— wallet, passport, travel documents, handkerchief, loose change and notes—and took a final look at himself in the mirror. He then packed everything with extreme care, clipped a gold digital watch around his left wrist and removed a final item from a pocket in the lid—a tightly fitting cover, which, when slipped into place over the suitcase, gave it an outer skin: changing the color from brown to a glossy black. Lastly, he closed up, slid the new skin around the case, and spun the numbered safety locks.

Taking a final look around, the man checked his pockets and left the cubicle, completely unrecognizable as the person who had entered. He walked straight to the exit, then out, across the concourse, to the check-in desk.

Inside the washroom, the man who had been engaged in swabbing the tiled floor leaned his squeegee against the wall and left. He also headed across the concourse, passing close to the check-in desk, and going to a door marked Private, which he unlocked with a personal key. Inside the small room there was a table, chair and telephone.

As the man with a new face was preparing to board Aer Lingus flight EI 154 from Dublin to London, Heathrow, the insignificant-looking cleaner was speaking rapidly into the telephone. The time was shortly before eight forty-five A.M.

2

THOUGHTS IN A SURREY LANE

JAMES BOND SHIFTED down into third gear, drifted the Saab 900 Turbo into a tight left-hand turn, clinging to the grass shoulder, then put on a fraction more power to bring the car out of the bend.

He was driving through a complicated series of country lanes—back-doubles as London cabbies would call them—following a short cut through the hedges, rolling fields and cathedral arches of trees threading the byways of Surrey. It was a cross-country route that would, finally, take him on to the Guildford bypass and a straight run, on good roads, into London.

Bond was traveling much too fast. A glance at the display of digital instruments, reflected in the windshield of this personalized Saab, told him the machine was touching seventy miles per hour. Decidedly dangerous for this kind of secondary road. The motor howled as he shifted down again, then accelerated through a series of S-bends. Gently common sense took over, and Bond applied a touch to the brakes, reducing speed to a more realistic pace. He still, however, remained hot and angry.

Already that evening he had made the same journey, in the opposite direction, to his recently acquired and newly decorated country cottage. Now on this beautiful Friday evening in early June, he was driving at breakneck speed back to London.

The weekend had been planned for some time, and, as the builders and decorators had just moved out, this was to have been his first free weekend at the cottage. Furthermore, he had planned to spend it with a girlfriend of long standing—an agile, superbly nubile blonde he had known—as Bill Tanner, M's Chief-of-Staff put it—"on and off for years." The fact that she lived only six miles or so from the cottage had greatly influenced Bond's purchase. On that Friday, he had completed a mound of paperwork in record time, not even leaving the office for lunch, so that he could get out of the hot chaos of London traffic in good time, before the normal Friday evening snarl-up began.

The countryside was at its best; the mixed fragrance of a perfect summer filtering into the car, bringing with it a sense of well-being and content-ment—something rare for Bond these days.

James Bond was not a superstitious man, but, as he neared the cottage that evening, he had noticed there seemed to be more magpies than usual. They flew low, rolling and fluttering across the roads and lanes like black and white dice in a game of craps. Bond thought of the old adage, "One for sorrow, two for joy." There were a lot of single magpies swooping near the car.

On reaching the cottage, Bond put a bottle of Dom Perignon '55 on ice, knowing that it would either be magnificent or the most expensive wine vinegar he had ever tasted.

He then went into the downstairs spare room, discarded the somewhat conservative business suit, and showered, first under a scalding spray, then with ice cold water, which seemed to cut into him like needles. After drying himself with a rough towel, Bond rubbed a small amount of Guerlain's Imperial Cologne into his skin before putting on a pair of lightweight worsted navy slacks and a white Sea Island cotton shirt. He slipped into comfortable soft leather sandals and was just clipping the old and valued gold Rolex Oyster Perpetual on to his wrist when the telephone rang.

It was more of a purr than a ring. The red phone. His heart sank. Both here, at the cottage, and in his London flat off the King's Road, James Bond was required to have two telephones: one for normal use, though unlisted; and a second, red instrument—a flat, angled piece of equipment, without dial or number punches. Called, in his trade, a "wiretap trap," this secure, sterile, unbuggable phone was linked directly to the building overlooking Regent's Park, known as the headquarters of Transworld Export Ltd.

Before he had even put a hand to the phone, Bond experienced his first flash of mild annoyance. The only reason for a call from headquarters on a Friday evening could be some kind of emergency or a state of readiness created by M for Bond's benefit. Bond's annoyance was possibly heightened by the fact that, of late, many emergencies had meant sitting in a control or communications room for days at a time or going through a complex briefing which ended with orders to abort the planned mission. Times had changed, and Bond did not like some of the political restraints placed on the Secret Service, for which he had worked with fidelity for longer than he cared to remember.

He picked up the red phone.

"James?" As Bond expected, it was Bill Tanner's voice on the line.

Bond grunted a surly affirmative.

"M wants you here," Tanner said, in a voice flat as a billiard table.

"Now?"

"His actual words are not for the telephone, but he indicated that sooner than now would be more acceptable."

"On a Friday evening?" Bond mused, the irritation building quickly inside his head as he saw an idyllic weekend filtering away, like an excellent bottle of wine being poured down the drain.

"Now," repeated the Chief-of-Staff, closing the line.

As he reached the Guildford bypass, Bond remembered the sound of disappointment in his girlfriend's voice when he had telephoned to say the weekend was off. He supposed that should be some consolation—not that there was much to console Bond these days. There had even been times, recently, when he had seriously considered resigning, to use the jargon, to "go private." Argot changes. At one time the phrase would have meant defection, but not anymore.

"Changing world, changing times, James," M had said to him a couple of years ago, when breaking the news that the élite Double-O status—which meant being licensed to kill in the line of duty—was being abolished. "Fools of politicians have no idea of our requirements. Have us punching time clocks before long."

This was during the so-called Realignment Purge, often referred to in the Service as the Snafu Slaughter, similar to the CIA's famous Halloween

Massacre, in which large numbers of faithful members of the American service had been dismissed, literally overnight. Similar things had happened in Britain, with financial horns being pulled in, and what a pompous Whitehall directive called "a more realistic logic being enforced upon the Secret and Security Services."

"Trying to draw our fangs, James," M had continued on that depressing day. Then, with one of those rare smiles which seemed to light up the deep gray eyes, M grunted that Whitehall had taken on the wrong man while he was still in charge. "As far as I'm concerned, 007, you will remain 007. I shall take full responsibility for you, and you will, as ever, accept orders and assignments only from me. There are moments when this country needs a troubleshooter—a blunt instrument—and by heaven it's going to have one. They can issue their pieces of bumf and abolish the Double-O section. We can simply change its name. It will now be the Special Section, and *you* are it. Understand, 007?"

"Of course, sir." Bond remembered smiling. In spite of M's brusque and often uncompromising attitude, Bond loved him as a father. To 007, M *was* the Service, and the Service was Bond's life. After all, what M suggested was exactly what the Russians had done with his old enemies Smersh—*Smyert Shpionam*, Death to Spies. They still existed, the dark core at the heart of the KGB, having gone through a whole gamut of metamorphoses, becoming the OKR, then the Thirteenth Department of Line F, and now, Department Viktor. Yet their work and basic organization remained the same—political murder, kidnap, sabotage, assassination, the quick disposal of enemy agents, either after interrogation or as acts of war on the secret battlefield.

Bond had left M's office on that occasion in an elated mood. Yet, in the few years that had passed since, he had performed only four missions in which his Double-O prefix had played any part. A portion of his work was to kill people. It was not a facet of life he enjoyed, but he did it very well in the course of duty. There was certainly no pathological hankering after that kind of work. It was the active life that Bond missed; the continual challenge of a new problem, a difficult decision in the field, the sense of purpose and of serving his country. Sometimes he wondered if he was falling under the spell of that malaise which seemed, on occasions, to grip Britain by the throat—political and economic lethargy, combined with a short-term view of the world's problems.

Bond's four most recent missions had been quick, cut and dried, undercover operations, and, while it would be wrong to say that James Bond yearned for the danger, his life now seemed, at times, to lack real purpose.

He still kept in the peak of condition: each morning going through a rigorous workout of pushups, leg-raising, arm and breathing exercises. There was a "refresher" on combat and silent kills once a month, at the firm's training establishment; the weekly small arms shoot in the sophisticated electronic range far below the Regent's Park headquarters; and the monthly all-weapons shoot at the Maidstone Police Range. Twice a year he disappeared for a fortnight to the SAS headquarters in Herefordshire.

Bond had even managed to alter his lifestyle, very slightly, adapting to the changing pressures of the 1970s and early 1980s: drastically cutting back—for most of the time—on his alcohol intake, and arranging with Morelands of Grosvenor Street for a new special blend of cigarettes, with a tar content slightly lower than any currently available on the market. At this moment twenty of these cigarettes, each one with the distinctive three gold rings just below the filter, lay in the gunmetal case, snug in Bond's breast pocket.

For the rest, the last few years for Bond had been the grind of an executive officer to M: planning paperwork, interrogating, debriefing, analysis, dirty tricks and bugging operations, with his fair share of Duty Officer watches to stand. His only extra joys during this period had come from the purchase of the cottage and the new car.

He had fancied a small country retreat for some time, and found the right place five miles out of Haslemere and a good mile from the nearest village. It fitted Bond's requirements perfectly and was bought within twenty-four hours of first viewing. A month later the builders and decorators had moved in with very precise instructions from the new owner.

The car was a different matter. With fuel costs running high, and the inevitability that they would continue to do so, Bond had allowed the beloved old Mark II Continental Bentley to go the way of its predecessor, the 4.5-liter Bentley.

Some eyebrows were raised at his choice of a foreign car, when all the pressure was on to buy British, but Bond shrugged it off by pointing to the fact that it was a British specialist firm which carried out the particularly complex and sophisticated personalization—such as the digital instrument display, the cruise control system, and several other pieces of magic, made possible by British know-how and the mighty microchip.

He did not mention the month during which the car had been taken over by the multinational Communication Control Systems (CCS) company, who added some of their own standard refinements—security devices that would make Q Branch's mouths water. Bond reasoned that it was his car, and he, not Q Branch—which was under severe financial restraint anyway—would decide what features should be incorporated. On several occasions he had seen Major Boothroyd, the Armorer, nosing around the Saab; and it was now commonplace for him to catch members of Q Branch— the "gee whiz" technicians of the Service—taking a close look. None of them ever mentioned the things they could not fail to notice—such as the bulletproof glass, steel-reinforced ram bumpers and heavy-duty tires, self-sealing even after being hit by bullets. There were other niceties, though, which nobody in Q Branch could detect without bringing out specialist gear.

The Saab now suited Bond's purposes, and was easily convertible from gasoline to gasohol if the fuel situation became even more critical; the consumption was low in relation to speed; while the turbo gave that extra dynamic thrust always needed in a tricky situation.

Only a few people knew about the cottage, so there were no raised eyebrows or jokes about Bond having a country seat.

The London Friday-evening rush was almost over by the time he reached Roehampton, so the Saab was in Bond's personal parking slot, in the underground garage of the headquarters building, before seven-thirty.

Bond would have put money on M having some inane and boring job waiting for him, and even made a mental wager with himself as the lift sped him silently to the ninth floor, at the top of the building, where M's suite of offices was located.

Miss Moneypenny, M's secretary, looked up with a worried smile as Bond entered the outer office. This was the first sign that something important might be on the cards.

"Hallo, Penny," Bond greeted her breezily, shrugging off the slough of irritation over the lost weekend. "Not out with one of your young men? It's wicked Friday night, you know."

Miss Moneypenny cocked her head toward the door of M's office as she spoke: "And he's been wickedly waiting for you. Keeping me here into the bargain." She smiled. "Besides, the only man who could lure me out on the town seemed to be otherwise engaged."

"Oh, Penny, if only . . ." Bond grinned. There had been a special bantering relationship between them for years, yet Bond had never fully realized how much the able and neat Moneypenny doted on him.

"Tell Commander Bond to come straight in," M's voice snapped metallically from the intercom box on Miss Moneypenny's desk.

Bond lifted a quizzical eyebrow and moved toward the door. Lowering his voice, he said, "Did anyone ever tell you that Olga started her business with you in mind, Penny?"

Miss Moneypenny was still blushing as Bond disappeared into M's office and closed the door. A red warning light blinked on above the door as it clicked shut. She stared into space for a moment, her head filled with the afterimage of the man who had just entered M's inner sanctum: the bronzed good-looking face, with rather long dark eyebrows above the wide, level blue eyes; the three-inch scar which just showed down his right cheek; the long, very straight nose, and the fine, though cruel, mouth. Minute flecks of gray had just started to show in the dark hair, which still retained its boyish black comma above the right eye. As yet, no plumpness had appeared around the jowls, and the line of the jaw was as straight and firm as ever. It was the face of an attractive buccaneer, Miss Moneypenny thought, shaking herself out of a slightly improper reverie and wondering if she should have warned James Bond that M was not alone in his office.

As James Bond opened the door to M's office, another door was opening, some five hundred miles to the north of London

The man who had left Dublin so skillfully disguised, early that morning, looked up, rising from his chair and extending a hand in greeting.

The room in which he had been waiting was a familiar place to him now, after so many visits: book-lined, with a large military desk, comfortable leather chairs, the impressive cabinet containing literally priceless antique weapons—a pair of chased silver flintlock pistols, a matched set of American Kentucky handguns, lavishly inlaid, a French wheellock with mother-of-pearl and gold wire stock decoration, a pair of cutlass pistols, and an Allen pepper-box with six revolving barrels. The artist of disguise knew the pieces and lusted after them on each viewing. The whole place had that air of solidity which comes with what is known as "old money."

The person who entered the room was its owner, playing host now to the man from Dublin. They shook hands, almost gravely, the guest waiting in silence until his patron had moved to the large upright chair behind the desk. He did not speak until he was seated.

"It's good to see you again, Franco."

"Good also to see you. But I enjoy working for you; this always makes a difference." The man called Franco paused, searching for words. "You know, after all this time, I never know how to address you—your title, or scientific . . . ?" He made a small gesture with his hands.

The other man chuckled, his bulldog face creasing into a smile. "Why not Warlock?"

They both laughed. "Appropriate," Franco nodded. "Operation Meltdown, with you—its creative and directive force—Warlock."

The man behind the desk laid his hands flat on the leather top. "So be it." He nodded his head in a quick, birdlike, manner. "You had no trouble?"

"Nothing at all. Clean as your proverbial English whistle. The chopper was on time; there were no tails. By now you should know I always have care."

"Good." The birdlike pecking nod again. "Then I trust, my friend, that this will be your last visit here."

Franco gave a quirky little grin. "Perhaps. But maybe not quite my last. There is the question of payment."

The man behind the desk opened his hands, fingers splayed, palms upward. "I mean, of course, your last visit until after Meltdown is completed. Yes, of course there is the question of picking up your share. But first, location and the small detail. That's one of the things we have to discuss; one of the reasons you will be here for a slightly longer period this time, Franco."

"Naturally." Franco's voice took on a cold edge and the word came out in four syllables, spoken curiously like the slow, cautious footsteps of a man testing an ice bridge across a deep crevice.

"There is much to talk about. Europe, I presume, is completely arranged?"

"Everyone ready, yes."

"And the States?"

"Ready and waiting for the final instructions."

"The men . . . ?"

Franco leaned forward. "These *people*, as I've already told you, have been waiting for a long time. They always were the least of my worries. Each of them is dedicated, ready to give his or her life for his separate cause. To all purposes, they consider themselves martyrs already. But the various organizations that have provided the personnel for your operation—organizations outlawed by most Western governments, and regarded as terrorists—are anxious. They want assurances that they will receive their share of the money."

"Which, I trust, you have given them, Franco." From behind the desk the bulldog face had ceased to beam. "Our commitment was clear. I seem to recall that we spoke of this at great length over a year ago. I provide the plan, the—how do you say it these days?—the know-how. I also arrange the means. You are the go-between, the contact man. Now, we have more interesting things to talk about."

3

THE OPPOSITION

BOND BECAME MORE alert when he reached the far side of M's door. He was prepared for his old chief to be seated in his usual concentrated position behind the large glass-topped desk, but he was not expecting to find two extra men in the room.

"Come in, Bond," M addressed him with a small, economic, movement of the hand. "Gentlemen"—he glanced toward his visitors—"allow me to introduce Commander James Bond. I think he's the man to fit the bill."

Bond warily acknowledged the other men. He knew well enough who they were, though it would not do to show it openly.

M allowed the pause to lie for just the right length of time, as though testing Bond's discretion, before completing the instructions. "Commander, this is Sir Richard Duggan, Director-General of MI5, and Deputy Assistant Commissioner David Ross, head of the Special Branch of the Metropolitan Police."

Bond reached out and, in turn, shook hands with the men, noting they both possessed firm dry handshakes. They also looked him straight in the eyes. These were two features Bond had long since come either to admire or guard against—depending on what side he suspected the owners of such attributes to be working.

It was certainly a puzzling situation. MI5 and its executive arm, the Special Branch, constituted what was known officially as the British Security Service—responsible for counterespionage and antiterrorist activities on British sovereign territory.

To Bond's service they were always jokingly known as "The Opposition," and there had always been a keen rivalry between the two organizations: a rivalry which had sometimes led to grave misunderstandings, even open hostility.

It was certainly most unusual for the heads of "The Opposition" to come calling on M, who saw them regularly anyway—at least once a week at the Joint Intelligence Committee meeting.

M motioned Bond into a leather chair and looked—a shade too benignly, Bond thought—first at his two visitors, then at Bond. "Our friends from

MI5 have a small problem, Commander," he began, and Bond noted with caution that M was treating him with almost military correctness. "It is an interesting situation, and I feel you might be able to help; especially as it has all the marks of moving out of MI5's jurisdiction and into our own area." He tapped his pipe into the copper ashtray on the desk. For the first time, Bond noticed his chief had a file lying directly in front of him. It was thick and marked with the red Most Secret: Classified tags. Two small circles, on the top right hand corner of the white binding, denoted that the file concerned both European and Middle East connections, while a small sticker bore the words, which Bond could easily read upside down, "Not for Brotherhood," which meant it contained information not to be circulated to the American service, the CIA.

The fact of the file was enough to alert Bond. M would have had it photostated on a blow-up, direct from its stored microfilm, especially for this kind of meeting. It would be shredded once those instructed to read it had done so.

"I think," M said, looking at the Director General of MI5, "it would be best if the two of you put Commander Bond in the picture. Then we can take it on from there."

Sir Richard Duggan nodded and leaned down to open his briefcase, removing a file and placing a matt ten-by-eight photograph on the desk in front of Bond. "Know the face?" he asked.

Bond nodded. "Franco—to the press, public, and most of us. Code Foxtrot to those in the field—ourselves, GSG9, Gigene, Squad R, Blue Light, C11 and C13." Bond was referring to the German, French, Italian and American antiterrorist squads, together with C11 and C13, of Scotland Yard, who often worked closely with Special Branch (C11 staffs the Anti-Terrorist Squad, in conjunction with C1).

The head of MI5 was not, however, going to let Bond get off so lightly. Did the Commander know anything else about Code Foxtrot—Franco?

Again Bond nodded. "Of course. International terrorist. Wanted in most European countries and some in the Middle East. There is a request for him to be held in the United States, though, as far as we know, he has not operated from, or in, that country. His full name is Franco Oliveiro Quesocriado; born Madrid 1948 of mixed parentage—Spanish father and English mother. I believe her name was something quite ordinary, like Jones, Smith or Evans . . ."

"Leonard actually," said DAC Ross quietly. "Mary Leonard."

"Sorry." Bond smiled at him, and the policeman returned the smile.

He had the look of a modern copper, Bond thought. Almost certainly one of the university types—quiet, with a watchfulness buried deep in his eyes and the sense of a coiled spring held back by the retaining pin of both caution and calmness. A very tough and sharp baby if roused, was Bond's instant assessment.

He turned back to Sir Richard Duggan, asking if they wanted him to continue.

"Naturally." Richard Duggan was a very different breed, and Bond already knew his pedigree—that was, after all, part of his job. Duggan was old school Home Office. Eton and Oxford, then a career in politics, which lasted only a short time before the Home Office snapped him up. Tall, slim and good-looking, with thick light-colored hair, which his enemies claimed was tinted, Duggan looked the part—young and rich, authoritative and in control. The youthfulness, Bond also knew, was an illusion, and the luck of a good facial bone structure.

As the head of MI5 drawled, "Naturally," Bond's eyes momentarily met those of M, and caught the tiny stir of humor. Sir Richard Duggan was not one of M's favorite people.

Bond shrugged. "Franco," he continued, "first came to our attention in connection with a hijacking of two British passenger jets—the airline was BOAC at the time—in the late 1960s. He appears to have no direct political affiliations and has operated as a planner who sometimes takes part in terrorist actions, with groups like the former Baader-Meinhof gang, and is still connected with the so-called Red Army Faction. He has links with the PLO, IRA, and a whole network of terrorist groups." Bond took out his gunmetal cigarette case, glancing at M for permission to smoke and receiving a curt nod.

"He would, I think, be best described as an anti-capitalist." Bond lit his cigarette and gave a small quick smile. "The paradox has always been that, for an anticapitalist, he appears to be exceptionally well-off. There is evidence that he has personally paid for, and provided, arms for a number of terrorist acts. He has certainly committed murder, in connection with two political kidnappings—not to mention those who have died in bomb attacks inspired directly by him. A very dangerous and most wanted man, Sir Richard."

Both Duggan and Ross nodded in harmony, Ross muttering something about Bond knowing his man. Duggan voiced his opinion in a louder voice, saying Bond might well have to know his man even better. He then delved into his briefcase again, bringing out five more matt photographs, which he placed in a row on M's desk, in front of Bond. Each photograph carried a small sticker attached to the bottom right-hand corner. Each sticker bore a date.

Bond immediately noted the dates before looking at the photographs. The most recent was today's. The other four were marked April 4th and 23rd; May 12th and 25th. The pictures were obviously blow-ups from a videotape recording, and he studied each one with great care. The man portrayed was dressed differently in each photograph; and, indeed, looked different—plump, in jeans and denim jacket, with long hair and mustache; clean-shaven, but with shoulder-length blond hair and dark glasses, wearing a rumpled turtleneck sweater and slacks; gray-haired and gaunt in loud check, hung around with cameras, and clutching an American passport as though he expected it to be torn from his hand at any moment; clean-shaven again, but with dark hair, fashionably cut, clad elegantly in slacks and an expensive fur-collared windbreaker.

Today's photograph showed him with close-cropped hair, neat beard and spectacles. He wore a business suit.

The disguises were all excellent, yet Bond had no hesitation. "Franco," he said aloud, like an order.

"Of course." Duggan sounded a little patronizing, going on to point out that all the photographs had been taken at Heathrow.

"Five times in the past three months, and he hasn't been picked up?" Bond's brow creased.

Deputy Assistant Commissioner David Ross inhaled and took over the explanation. At a meeting earlier in the year, it had been decided that certain major "most wanted" terrorists like Franco should be kept under close surveillance if they appeared to arrive alone in the country. "Big fish, little fish," he grinned, as though it explained everything. "When the surveillance teams at Heathrow spotted him in April—the first time—there was, naturally, a full-scale alert."

"Naturally," Bond did a fair imitation of Sir Richard Duggan's condescending drawl. M busied himself loading his pipe, gently kneading the tobacco into the bowl and keeping his eyes well down.

Ross looked a little shamefaced. "Afraid we lost him the first time. Not ready for him. Lost him in London."

Something stirred in Bond's memory. There had been an increase in police activity early in April, and he recalled signals coming in with instructions about being more than normally alert: watching for packages and letters, stepping up embassy security—the usual stuff on a Terrorist Red, as the police and security services called it.

Ross was still talking. "We checked all his possible contacts, and waited. He wasn't detected leaving the country."

"But, of course, he did," Duggan chimed in.

Ross nodded. "As you can all see, he was back again, entering through Heathrow, later in the month. That time we established he moved straight out of London, almost certainly heading north."

"You lost him again," Bond stated. Ross gave sharp affirmative before saying they had better luck during the first May visit.

"Followed him as far as Glasgow. Then he slipped the leash. But on the last trip we kept him in our sights all the way. He ended up in a village called Murcaldy, inland from Applecross, at the foot of the northwest Highlands."

"And we're sure who it was he visited there," Duggan smiled. "Just as we're certain he's gone to the same place this time. I have two officers breathing down his neck. He came in from Dublin this morning—and we were tipped off from there. He went straight to King's Cross and took the first train to Edinburgh—likes to change things around, you know. He'll have reached his destination by now. We expect further reports any time."

A silence fell over the four men, broken only by the scraping of M's match as he lit his pipe. Bond was the first to speak. "And he's visiting . . . ?" allowing the question to hang in the air like M's pipe smoke.

Duggan cleared his throat. "Most of the land, including the village of Murcaldy, is owned by one family—the Muriks. For at least three centuries, possibly longer, the Lairds of Murcaldy have been Muriks. It's almost a feudal setup. Murik Castle, which dates back to the sixteenth century, has had many modernizations over the years, and there is the Murik estate—farms; hunting and fishing rights. The present Laird is also a celebrity in other fields—Dr. Anton Murik, director of many companies and a nuclear physicist of both renown and eccentricity."

"Recently resigned, under some sort of cloud, from the International Atomic Energy Research Commission," added Ross. "And, as you'll see, there's grave doubt regarding his claim to be the Laird of Murcaldy."

Bond chuckled. "Well, Anton isn't exactly a well-known Scottish name. But where do I come in?" He already had a fair idea, but it would not do to jump the gun.

Duggan's face did not change: the granite good looks appeared flawed at close quarters. There was none of the usual smoothness about him as he spoke again. "Franco has now almost certainly made four visits to Dr. Murik. This will be his fifth. An international terrorist and a nuclear physicist of some eminence: put those together and you have a rather alarming situation. On each occasion, Franco has left the country again. Probably—and we can only guess—via a Scottish port or airport. We're banking on the possibility that his business with Murik will take some time to conclude; but our hands are tied from the moment he leaves Britain. Our visit today is to ask the help of your service in tracing his movements outside this country."

This time it was Bond's turn to nod, "And you want me to dash off up to Scotland, make contact, and follow him out?"

Duggan deferred to M. "Only if that is—ah—convenient. But I really don't think there's much time left on this trip. Anton Murik owns a string of racehorses, which he has under training in England. Two are running at Ascot this coming week—one in the Gold Cup. It's his one passion, apart from nuclear physics. Franco will either be gone by the middle of the week or up at the Castle awaiting Murik's return from Ascot."

Bond stretched out his long legs and thought that if there really was a sinister connection between Franco and Murik, the timing indicated this would not be Franco's last visit. But you could never tell.

Duggan was on his feet. "I've passed on all information to M." He indicated the file—which Bond had taken to be one of M's dossiers—on the desk, as he gathered up the photographs and swept them into his briefcase. "Also how to contact my people in the field, and all that. We have come to you for assistance, in the interests of the country. It is time to work in harness and I must now leave the final decision here with you."

M puffed on his pipe. "I'll brief Commander Bond about everything," he said pleasantly. "Be in touch with you later this evening, Duggan. We'll do all we can—in *everybody's* interests."

The two officers took leave of M and Bond quite cordially, and, as soon as the door closed behind them, M spoke—"What do you think, 007?"

James Bond's heart leaped, and he felt a new urgency coursing through his veins. It was a long time since M had addressed him as 007, and it signified that he could well be off into the real unknown again. He could almost smell the possibilities.

"Well, what *do* you think?" M repeated.

Bond lit another cigarette and looked up at the ceiling before he spoke. "I should imagine you'll want me on the way to Scotland tonight." M's eyes betrayed nothing as Bond continued. "Not a healthy mix—an international terrorist and a renowned nuclear physicist. Been one of the nightmares for some time, hasn't it, sir? That some group would get hold of not only the materials but the means to construct a really lethal nuclear device? We suspect some of them have the materials—look at that fellow

Achmed Yastaff I took out for you. At least four of the ships he arranged to make disappear were carrying materials . . ."

M snorted, "Don't be a fool, 007. Easiest thing in the world to construct a crude device. Yes, they've almost certainly got the materials—and don't ask me who I mean by 'they.' You've got to think logically on this one. If any of the existing terrorist organizations wanted to use some crude bomb to blackmail a government, they could do so. But for a man like Franco to be consorting with an old devil such as the Laird of Murcaldy—well, that's a very different matter, and it could mean one of two things."

"Yes . . . ?" Bond leaned forward.

"First," M ticked off the index finger of his left hand with that of his right, the pipe jammed into the corner of his mouth, held tightly between his teeth as he spoke. "First, it could mean that Franco is setting up a very sophisticated operation, and is soliciting Anton Murik's specialist help and knowledge. Second"—the fingers moved—"it could be the other way around: that Dr. Anton Murik is seeking Franco's aid on a little adventure of his own. Either of those possibilities is going to take more than five short visits from Franco."

"And Anton Murik is capable of either of these things?" Bond's brow furrowed. He could read absolutely nothing in M's weatherbeaten face, and that was always a danger signal. There was far more to all this than the information brought to them by "The Opposition."

"Not only capable of it, but also a most likely candidate." M opened a drawer in his desk and dropped another file on top of the one provided by MI5. "We've had our eye on Dr. Anton Murik, Laird of Murcaldy, for some time now." He tapped the two files. "What Ross told you is a slight understatement—the business about Murik resigning from the International Atomic Energy Commission under some sort of cloud. *They* don't have all the facts. We do. Murik resigned, 007, under a damned great storm. In fact the man was kicked out and didn't take kindly to it. He is a man of some brilliance, and very large resources."

M took the pipe from his mouth, looking Bond straight in the eyes. "Even the title—Laird of Murcaldy—is more than highly suspect, as Ross mentioned. No, I don't intend to send you scooting off to Scotland, 007. It's my job to see that you're properly briefed and given good support and cover. The hell with The Opposition and their surveillance team. I want to get you as close to Murik as possible. On the inside; and before we get to that, there's a great deal you should know about the so-called Laird of Murcaldy."

4

DOSSIER ON A LAIRD

IT WAS OBVIOUSLY going to be a long evening, and Bond thought he should not surprise May, his able and devoted housekeeper, by returning suddenly and late to the flat off the King's Road.

Before M could launch into the details of the dossiers which lay, full of secrets, in front of them, Bond asked permission to leave the office for a moment.

M gave one of his irritated old-fashioned looks, but grudgingly nodded his consent for Bond to make a telephone call from the privacy of his own office.

In the end, it was easier for Bond to dial his own number on Miss Moneypenny's extension. May had given up trying to fathom her employer's working hours long ago, and merely asked if he fancied anything special to eat when he did get in. Bond said he would not be averse to a nice pair of Arbroath Smokies—should she have some tucked away. May, being a strict conservative in matters of kitchen equipment, would never in a thousand years have allowed a freezer in her domain. Bond agreed with her, though it was sometimes nice to be able to have delicacies within reach, so they had compromised. With tact, Bond had talked her around to allowing him to buy a large refrigerator with a spacious freezing compartment, which May christened the ice box. She thought, now, that there might be a pair of Smokies in "the ice box," adding, "So I'll see what I can do, Mr. James; but mind you don't get back too late." May had a habit of treating Bond, when the mood was on her, as a nanny will treat her small charges.

The fact that Bond was only out of his office for a few minutes mollified M, who had refilled his pipe and was poring over the dossiers. Caustically he asked if 007 had managed to arrange matters so that they were not interrupted again.

"Yes, sir," Bond replied calmly. "I'm quite ready for the Laird of Murcaldy, Rob Roy and even Bonnie Prince Charlie, if you wish."

"It's not a matter for levity, 007," M spoke sharply. "The Murik family is a noble line. There was a Laird of Murcaldy at Dunbar and another at Culloden Moor. However, it is possible that the true line died out with the present Laird's grandfather. It has yet to be proven, or even properly tested, but it is a matter which disturbs the Lord Lyon King of Arms greatly." He shuffled through some of the first dossier. "Anton Murik's grandfather was well known as an adventurer—a traveler. In the year 1890 he was missing for more than three months in central Europe—searching, it is said, for his brother who had been disinherited for some offense. Their parents were dead, and the village folk believed that Angus Murik— that was his name—planned to return with his brother, shepherding the black sheep back into the fold. When he did return it was with a wife—a foreign woman, the records say. She was with child, and there are also written documents suggesting that the prodigal Laird was not Angus at all, but the brother, Hamish. It is also suggested that the child, who became Anton's father, was born out of wedlock, for there are no records of a marriage having actually taken place."

Bond grunted. "But surely that would only weaken the line, not destroy it altogether."

"Normally, yes," M continued. "But Anton was also born in strange circumstances. His father was a wild lad who, at the age of eighteen, also began to travel. He did not return at all. There is a letter, extant, saying that he had married an English woman of good family in Palermo. But shortly after that a young woman arrived at Murik Castle, in an advanced state of pregnancy, with the news that her husband, the heir to the title, had been killed by bandits during an expedition in Sicily."

"When was this?" It sounded a confused and odd story to Bond.

"Nineteen-twenty," M nodded, as though reading Bond's thoughts. "Yes, there *are* newspaper reports of some 'English' gentleman having been killed in Sicily. The newspapers, however, claim that this gentleman's wife also perished at the hands of the bandits, though the young woman insisted it was her maid who died. The graves, at Caltanissetta, are so marked; but diaries, and some memories, say that the girl who presented herself as wife of the Laird-presumptive was far from being an English lady of good breeding. It's difficult to sort out fact from fiction, or even bigotry. What is certain is the fact that some of the older people on the Murik estate maintain Anton is not the true Laird—though, knowing which side their bread is buttered, they only whisper it privately, and will not commit themselves to either strangers or authority."

"But the baby was baptized Anton and took the title?"

"Baptized Anton Angus, yes; and took the title Laird of Murcaldy, yes," M said with a slight curl of the lip.

"So, whatever else, we must treat him as a Scottish Laird. I presume he is also a bona fide nuclear scientist? We have to take that part seriously?"

"We take him very seriously indeed." M looked grave, repeating, "Very seriously. There is no doubt at all that Anton Murik is a man of great intellect and influence. Just take a glance at the background précis." He passed the relevant sheet from the dossier across to Bond, who took it in with a quick sweep of the eyes:

> Anton Angus Murik. Born Murik Castle, Murcaldy, Ross and Cromarty, Scotland, December 18th, 1920. Educated Harrow and St John's College, Cambridge. First Class Honours in Physics followed by a Fellowship, then a Doctorate. So good that he was reserved for work under Professor Lindemann—later Lord Cherwell—scientific adviser to Winston Churchill; also worked on Manhattan Project (the making and testing of the first atomic bomb); Committee for the Peaceful Use of Atomic Energy; International Atomic Energy Commission . . .

Murik had resigned from this last position just two years ago. There followed a lengthy and impressive list of companies with which Murik was associated. Bond's eyebrows gradually rose higher as he read the list. Among other things, Anton Murik was Chairman of Micro-Modulators Ltd., Eldon Electronics Ltd., Micro Sea Scale Ltd., and Aldan Aerospace, Inc. In addition he sat on countless boards, all of which had some direct application to nuclear power or electronics. Bond also saw that the firms included some specialist contractors with great knowledge of design and building in the field of nuclear reactors.

"You spot the odd man out?" M asked from behind a cloud of pipe smoke.

Bond looked down the list again. Yes, there tucked away among all the electronics, nuclear companies and aerospace conglomerates, was a strange entry, Roussillon Fashions. Bond read out the entry.

"Yes. Damned dressmaking firm," M snorted.

James Bond smiled to himself. "I think a little more than just a dressmaker, sir. Roussillon is one of the world's leading fashion houses. They have branches in London, Paris, Rome, New York—you name it. Ask any woman with dress sense. I suppose Roussillon would come among the top five fashion houses in the world."

M grunted. "And charge top prices as well, I've no doubt. Well, Anton Murik has a majority holding in that firm."

"Don't suppose he just likes dressing up in high-class ladies' clothes or something like that?" Bond grinned.

"Don't be flippant, 007. You have to look at the financial aspect."

"Well, he must be a multimillionaire," Bond said, almost to himself. He was rarely impressed by such things, but, even from the list in front of him, it was obvious that Dr. Anton Murik wielded considerable power. "How in heaven's name did a man with these qualifications manage to get himself thrown out of the International Atomic Energy Commission, sir?"

M did not hesitate. "For one thing he's unscrupulous in business matters. Sailed very close to the wind in some dealings with those companies you see listed. At least two of the chairmanships were gained by stepping, almost literally, over the bodies of other men."

"Most good businessmen are inclined to be ruthless . . ." Bond began, but M held up a hand.

"There was another matter," he said. "Anton Murik is a bit of a fanatic, and he tends to take the view of most of those people you see protesting against the use of nuclear power and the dangers of the disposal of nuclear waste. He mounted a stiff campaign against the use of the major types of nuclear reactor already in service, or planned to go into service. Worldwide. You see, 007, the man claims to have designed the ultimate in reactors—one which not only provides the power but safely disposes of the waste, and cannot go wrong. Calls it the Murik Ultra-Safe Reactor."

"And his colleagues didn't buy it?"

"'Didn't buy' is an understatement. His colleagues say there are grave flaws in the Ultra-Safe design. Some even go as far as claiming the whole thing is potentially a hundred times more dangerous than the current families—the fast-breeders, BWRs, PWRs, gas/graphites and liquid metal fast-breeders. Murik wanted funds from the Commission to prove them wrong, and build his own reactor."

"So they cut off the money."

M said they did exactly that, and Bond laughed again, remarking that a little thing like money should not make much difference to a multimillionaire. "Surely Murik could go out and build his own—in his back garden. It seems big enough."

M sighed. "We're talking in billions of dollars; billions of pounds sterling, James. Anton Murik argued. There were, apparently, some terrific rows, and suggestions that the man's far from stable." He touched his forehead with an index finger. "That's really why this whole business of contact with a fellow like Franco worries me. It is also why I will on no account allow you to go charging into the field without preparation. Could be wrong, of course, but I really don't think a week or so is going to make that much difference. Especially if I can turn you into the ideal penetration agent—establish you within the Murik entourage: and to that end," M began to leaf through his own dossier again, "I think you'd better meet Anton Murik and his household." He drew several photographs from the bulky depths of the file.

"You're going to officially deny Duggan's request, then?" Bond's mind had become completely concentrated on the job in hand by now. Having been inactive for a long time made little difference to him. The job was like swimming or driving; once the rudiments had been mastered, professionalism—when something big turned up—came back like the flicking of a switch. Whatever plot was being hatched—either by Franco or Dr. Anton Murik—Bond would not, now, rest until every end was tied up; no matter how dangerous or arduous, or even plain dull, it turned out to be.

M grunted. "Duggan's got two good people in the field. They've already had four tries at keeping tabs on Franco—plenty of practice. That should, eventually, make them perfect. I have confidence that they'll discover his port of exit this time. We'll put a tail on Franco when the moment comes. Your job's too important . . ." he must have seen the quizzical look on Bond's face, "and don't tell me that I'm putting you in on MI5's territory. I know that, and so do you, but my bones tell me it won't be for long. The action's going to move out of Scotland as soon as whatever it is they're cooking comes to the boil. Now for the pretty pictures."

First, he explained the obvious. With the castle and huge estate, the Laird of Murcaldy had immediate access to manpower. "He's got gamekeepers, wardens, and every imaginable kind of servant up there, from drivers to guards. So, as far as the Laird's concerned, he has no real security problem. There is a central core of family, though. First, the doctor himself."

The photograph showed a pugnacious face, not unlike that of the late Lord Beaverbrook, but without the crescents of humor bracketing the mouth. A bulldog of a man, with cold eyes that were fixed on somebody, or something—certainly not the camera—slightly to his right. The line of the mouth was hard, uncompromising; and the ears, which lay very flat against the head, gave him an odd, symmetrical outline. Photographs can be deceptive—Bond knew that well enough—but this man, captured by a swift click and the activation of a shutter, could have been an inquisitor. He had that slightly puritanical look about him—a stickler for discipline; one who knew his own mind and would have his own way, no matter what lay in his path. Bond felt vaguely uneasy. He would not admit to anything as grave as fear when confronted by a photograph, but the picture said clearly that the Laird of Murcaldy was a force—a power.

The next print showed a woman, probably in her early forties, very fine-looking, with sharp, classic features, and dark, upswept hair. Her eyes were large, but not—Bond thought—innocent. Even in this image they seemed to contain a wealth of worldly knowledge; and the mouth, while generous, was not out of proportion, the edges of the lips tilting slightly upward, in some ways softening the features.

"Miss Mary Jane Mashkin," said M, as though it explained everything.

Bond gave his chief a look of query, the comma of hair connecting with his right eyebrow as though to form a question mark.

"His *éminence grise,* some say." M puffed at his pipe, as though slightly embarrassed. "Certainly Murik's mistress. Was his secretary for ten years. Murik's strong right arm and personal adviser. She's a trained physicist. Cambridge University, the same as the Laird, though not his standard it seems. Acts as hostess for him; lives at Murik Castle. Travels with him, eats . . . and all the rest of it."

Bond reflected that he could have been wrong about the puritanism, but then amended his thoughts. It was quite possible for Anton Murik to have strong moral feelings about what everybody else did while excepting himself from similar restrictions. It happened all the time—like the people who campaigned against certain television programs and films, yet imagined they were themselves immune to moral danger.

"I should think he takes her advice in a lot of matters, but I doubt he would be swayed by her on very large issues." M pushed a third photograph toward Bond.

This time it was another woman, much younger, and certainly, if the picture was really accurate, a stunning girl. Blond hair fell around the sides of her face in a smooth, thick sheen, while the face itself was reminiscent of Lauren Bacall as a young woman. This one had the same high cheekbones, the promise of some smolder in the dark eyes, and a mouth made striking by the sensuality of her lower lip. Above the eyes, her brows were shaped naturally, in a kind of elongated circumflex. Bond allowed himself to relax in an almost inaudible low whistle.

M cut short this reflex reaction. "Anton Murik's ward. Miss Lavender Peacock. The relationship is not known. She became his ward in 1970, all legal—daughter of some second cousin, the court report says. Father and mother both killed in an air crash. There's a little money—several thousand—which comes to Miss Peacock when she reaches her twenty-seventh birthday. That is next year."

Bond observed that Lavender Peacock was quite a girl, though he somehow thought he recognized her—not just from her resemblance to the young Bacall.

"Possible, 007. The girl's kept on a tight rein, though. In some matters the Laird is very old-fashioned. Lavender Peacock is treated like a fragile piece of china. Private tutors when she was a kid, trips abroad only when accompanied by Murik and trusted watchdogs. The Mashkin woman's toted her around a bit, and you may have seen her picture in connection with that dressmaking business. From time to time the Laird allows her to model—but only at very special functions, and always with the watchdogs around."

"Watchdogs?" Bond picked up on the expression.

M rose and strode to the window, looked out across the park, now hazy as the sun dropped slowly and the lights began to come on over the city. "Watchdogs?" M queried. "Oh yes, mainly women around the Mashkin lady and the dressmaking firm." He did not turn back toward Bond. "Murik always has a few young Scottish toughs around. A kind of bodyguard—you know what these people are like. Not just for the ward, but the whole family. There's one in particular: sort of chief heavy. We haven't got a photograph of him, but I've had a description and that certainly matches his name. He's called Caber."

There was a long silence. At last Bond took a deep breath. He had been looking at the triptych of photographs in front of him. "So you want me to ingratiate myself with this little lot; find out why Franco's paying so much attention; and generally make myself indispensable?"

"I think that's the way to go." M turned from the window. "We have to play the game long, 007. Very long indeed. I have great reservations about Dr. Anton Murik. He'd kill without a second thought if it meant the success of some plan with which he's obsessed; and we all know he's obsessed, at this moment, with the business of his Ultra-Safe Nuclear Reactor. Maybe there's some harebrained scheme of investing in one of Franco's endeavors and raking in a rich profit—a quick return—enough money to prove the Atomic Energy Commission wrong. Who knows? It'll be your job to find out, James. Your job, and my responsibility."

"Suggestions on how to do it would be welcome," Bond began, but, as M was about to reply, the red telephone purred on his desk.

For a few minutes, Bond sat silently listening to M's side of a conversation with Sir Richard Duggan. When the call was completed, M sat back with a thin smile. "That settled it then. I've told MI5 that you're ready to move in and follow up any information they care to give. Duggan's left details of his surveillance people here," he tapped the MI5 file with his knuckles. "All the usual cloak and dagger stuff they seem to like."

"And Franco?"

"Is definitely at Castle Murik. They've confirmed. Don't worry, James, if he leaves suddenly I'll put someone on his back to cover you with MI5."

"Talking of cover . . ." Bond started.

"I was coming to that. How you get into the family circle, eh? Well, I think you go under your own name, but with a slightly different passport. We can drum it all up here. A mercenary, I think. You heard what Ross said about Murik's second passion in life—racing. Well, as you know, he's got horses running at Ascot next week. In fact the one he's entered in the Gold Cup has only been in the first three once in its life. Name of China Blue. Our friend, the Laird of Murcaldy, merely seems to like watching them train and run—enjoys all the business of racetracks and trainers."

"Just for the kicks," Bond stated, and M looked at him curiously for a moment.

"I suppose so," M replied at last. "But Murik's visit to Ascot next week should give us the opportunity. Unless there's any sudden change of plan, I think you should be able to make contact on Gold Cup day. That'll give us time to see you're well briefed and properly equipped, eh?"

5

THE ROAD TO ASCOT

APART FROM THE great golf tournaments, James Bond did not care much for those events which still constitute what the gossip columnists—and the drones who pay lip-service and provide morsels for them—call "the Season." He was not naturally drawn to Wimbledon, the Henley Regatta, or, indeed, to Royal Ascot. The fact that Bond was a staunch monarchist did not prevent the grave misgivings he felt when turning the Saab in the direction of Ascot on Gold Cup day.

Life had been very full since the Friday evening of the previous week, when M had taken the decision to place Bond within the heart of the Laird of Murcaldy's world.

Inside the building overlooking Regent's Park, people did not ask questions when a sudden personal disappearance, or a flurry of activity, altered the pattern of days. Though Bond was occasionally spotted, hurrying to or from meetings, he did not go near his office.

In fact, Bond worked a full seventeen-hour day during this time of preparation. To begin with, there were long briefings with M, in his big office, recently redecorated and now dominated by Cooper's painting of Admiral Jervis's fleet triumphing over the Spanish off Cape St. Vincent in 1797—the picture having been lent to the Service by the National Maritime Museum.

During the following weeks, Bond was to recall the battle scene, with its background of lowering skies and the British men-o'-war, trailing ensigns and streamers, plowing through choppy seas, tinted with the glow of fire and smoke of action.

It was under this painting that M quietly took Bond through all the logical possibilities of the situation ahead; revealed the extent to which Anton Murik had recently invested in businesses all connected, one way or another, with nuclear energy; together with his worst private fears about possible plots now being hatched by the Laird of Murcaldy.

"The devil of it is, James," M told him one evening, "this fellow Murik has a finger in a dozen marketplaces—in Europe, the Middle East, and even America." As yet, M had not alerted the CIA, but was resigned to the fact that this would be necessary if Bond found himself forced—by the job he hoped to secure with Anton Murik—to operate within the jealously guarded spheres of American influence.

Primarily, the idea was to put Bond into the Murik ménage as a walking listening device. It was natural, then, for him to spend much time with Q Branch, the experts of "gee-whiz" technology. In the past, he had often found himself bored by the earnest young men who inhabited the workshops and testing areas of Q Branch, but times were changing. Within the last year, everyone at headquarters had been brightened and delighted by the appearance of a new face among the senior executives of Q Branch—a tall, elegant, leggy young woman with sleek and shining straw-colored hair which she wore in an immaculate, if severe, French pleat. This, together with her large spectacles, gave her a commanding manner and a paradoxical personality combining warm nubility with cool efficiency.

Within a week of her arrival, Q Branch had accorded its new executive the nickname of Q'ute, for even in so short a time she had become the target of many seductive attempts by unmarried officers of all ages. Bond had noticed her, and heard the reports. Word was that the colder side of Q'ute's personality was uppermost in her off-duty hours. Now 007 found himself working close to the girl, for she had been detailed to arrange the equipment he would take into the field and brief him on its uses.

Throughout this period, James Bond remained professionally distant. Q'ute was a desirable girl, but, like so many of the ladies working within the security services these days, she remained friendly yet at pains to make it plain that she was her own woman and therefore Bond's equal. Only later was 007 to learn that she had done a year in the field before taking the two-year technical course which provided her with promotion to executive status in Q Branch.

At forty-eight hours' notice, Q'ute's team had put together a set of what she called "personalized matching luggage." This consisted of a leather suitcase together with a similarly designed, steel-strengthened briefcase. Both items contained cunningly devised compartments, secret and well-nigh undetectable, built to house a whole range of electronic sound-stealing equipment; some sabotage gear, and a few useful survival items. These included a highly sophisticated bugging and listening device; a VL22H countersurveillance receiver; a pen alarm, set to a frequency which linked it to a long-range modification of the SAS 900 Alert System. If triggered, the pen alarm would provide Bond with instant signal communication to the Regent's Park headquarters building in order to summon help. The pen also contained micro facilities so that it operated as a homer; therefore, when activated, headquarters could keep track of their man in the field—a personal alarm system in the breast pocket.

As a backup, there was a small ultrasonic transmitter, while, among the sabotage material, Bond was to carry an exact replica of his own Dunhill cigarette lighter—the facsimile having special properties of its own. There was also a so-called "security blanket" flashlight, which generates a high-intensity beam strong enough to disorientate any victim caught in its burst of light; and—almost as an afterthought—Q'ute made him sign for a pair of TH70 Nitefinder goggles. Bond did not think it wise to mention that these lightweight goggles were part of the standard fittings Communication Control Systems, Inc. had provided for the Saab. He had tested them himself—on an old, disused, airfield during a particularly dark night—driving the Saab without lights, at high speed, while wearing the Nitefinder set strapped to his head. Through the small projecting lenses, the surrounding countryside and cracked runway down which he took the car could be seen with the same clarity he would have experienced on a summer evening just before twilight.

As well as the time spent with M and Q'ute, Bond found himself in for some long hours with Major Boothroyd, the Service Armorer, discussing weaponry. On M's instructions, 007 was to go armed—something not undertaken lightly these days.

During the years when he had made a special reputation for himself in the old Double-O Section, Bond had used many hand weapons: ranging from the .25 Beretta—which the Armorer sarcastically dismissed as "a lady's gun"—to the .38 Colt Police Positive; the Colt .45 automatic; .38 Smith & Wesson Centennial Airweight; and his favorite, the Walther PPK 7.65mm. carried in the famous Berns-Martin triple-draw holster.

By now, however, the PPK had been withdrawn from use, following its nasty habit of jamming at crucial moments. The weapon did this once too often, on the night of March 20th, 1974, when a would-be kidnapper with a history of mental illness attempted to abduct Princess Anne and her husband, Captain Mark Phillips. The royal couple's bodyguard, Inspector James Beaton, was wounded, and, in attempting to return fire, his Walther jammed. That, then, was the end of this particular handgun as far as the British police and security services were concerned.

Since then, Bond had done most of his range work with either the Colt .45—which was far too heavy and difficult to use in covert field operations—or the old standby .38 Cobra—Colt's long-term favorite snub-nosed revolver for undercover use. Bond, naturally, did not disclose the fact that he carried an unauthorized Ruger Super Blackhawk .44 Magnum in a secret compartment in the Saab.

Now, minds had to be clear, and decisions taken regarding Bond's field armament; so a lengthy, time-consuming, and sometimes caustic battle ensued between Bond and the Armorer concerning the relative merits of weapons.

They had been through the basic arguments a thousand times already: a revolver is always more reliable than an automatic pistol, simply because there is less to go wrong. The revolver, however, has the double drawback of taking longer to reload, usually carrying only six rounds of ammunition in its cylinder. Also—unless you go for the bigger, bulky weapon—muzzle velocity, and, therefore, stopping power, is lower.

The automatic pistol, on the other hand, gives you much easier loading facilities (the quick removal and substitution of a magazine from, and into, the butt), allows a larger number of rounds per magazine, and has, in the main, a more effective stopping power. Yet there is more to go wrong in the way of working parts.

Eventually it was Bond who had the last word—with a few grumbles from Major Boothroyd—settling on an old, but well-tried and true friend: the early Browning 9mm. originally manufactured by Fabrique Nationale-De Guerre in Belgium from Browning patents. In spite of its age this Browning has accurate stopping power. For Bond, the appeal lay in its reliability and size—eight inches overall and with a barrel length of five inches. A flat, lethal weapon, the early Browning is really a design similar to the .32 Colt and weighs about thirty-two ounces, having a magazine capacity of seven 9mm. Browning Long cartridges, with the facility to carry one extra round in the breech.

Bond was happy with the weapon, knew its limitations, and had no hesitation in putting aside thoughts of more exotic handguns of modern manufacture.

Unused weapons of all makes, types and sizes, were contained in the Armorer's amazing treasure trove of a store, and he produced one of the old Brownings, still in its original box, thick with grease and wrapped in yellow waxed paper. No mean feat, as this particular gun has long since ceased to be manufactured.

The Armorer knew 007 well enough not to have the pistol touched by any member of his staff; calling Bond down to the gunsmith's room, so that the weapon could be cleaned off, stripped, checked and thoroughly tested by the man who was to use it. If Bond had been scheduled to make a parachute jump, both the Armorer and Q Branch would have seen to it that 007 packed his own 'chute. In turn, it was the only way Bond would have it done. The same applied to weapons.

Late one afternoon Bond found himself down in the empty gunsmith's room, with the run of the place, plus the underground range, while he went through the exacting chore upon which his life might depend.

He was, therefore, surprised when, just as he started to clean the grease from the Browning, the door opened to reveal Q'ute, dressed in brown velvet and looking exceptionally desirable. Major Boothroyd, she told Bond, had suggested that she come down to watch the cleaning and preparation of the weapon.

"Why should he do that?" Bond hardly glanced up at the girl, conscious for the first time that her cool manner constituted a direct challenge. He had worked hard over the past days—now a sensual snake stirred in the back of his mind. Q'ute would make a relaxing partner for the evening.

Q'ute swung herself on to the workbench after making certain she had chosen a clean patch of wood. "The Armorer's giving me a weapons course, when I'm off duty," she told him. For the first time, Bond noticed Q'ute's voice had a throaty quality to it. "I'm not very good with handguns, and he says you are. He mentioned that the weapon was of an old type as well. Just thought it would be a good idea, if you didn't mind."

Bond's strong, firm hands moved expertly, even lovingly, over the pistol as he silently chanted the stripping routine.

"Well, do you?" Q'ute asked.

"Do I what?"

"Mind my watching?"

"Not at all." He glanced up at the girl, whose pretty face, behind the large spectacles, remained impassive. "Always best to handle weapons with care and gentleness," he smiled, as the movements of his hands over the mechanism became increasingly erotic.

"With care of course." Q'ute's voice took on a slight edge of sarcasm. Now she repeated, parrot-fashion, from the Service training manual, "'Weapons of all description should be treated with great care and respect.' Don't you carry it a bit too far, Commander Bond?"

Hell, he thought. Q'ute was a good nickname for her. Bond even slowed down the movements of his hands, allowing the process of stripping to become more obvious as he silently repeated the instructions: *Grasp head of recoil-spring guide; push toward muzzle to release the head of the guide from the barrel. Draw out barrel from breech end. Remove stocks, giving access to lockwork. Dismount slide assembly, starting with firing pin and continue normally . . .*

"Oh come on, Commander Bond. I do know something about weapons. Anyway, nobody believes all that stuff about guns being phallic symbols anymore." She tossed her head, giving a little laugh. "Stop playing strip the lady with that piece of hardware, if you're doing it for my benefit. I don't go for those paperback books with pictures of girls sitting on large guns, or even astride them."

"What do you go for then, Q'ute?" Bond chuckled.

"My name's Ann Reilly," she snapped, "not that damn silly nickname they all use around here." She looked at him, straight in the eyes, for a full twenty seconds. "As for what I like and dislike—go for, as you put it—maybe one day you'll find out." She did not smile. "I'm more interested in the way that automatic works, why you chose it, and how you got that white mark on your hand."

Bond glanced up sharply, his eyes suddenly losing their humor and turning to ice in a way that almost frightened Q'ute. "Someone tried to be clever a long time ago," he said slowly. In the back of his mind he remembered quite clearly all the circumstances which had led to the plastic surgery, that showed now only as a white blemish, after the Cyrillic Letter *III*—standing for SH—had been carved into the back of his hand in an attempt by Smersh to brand him as a spy. It was long ago, and very far away now, but clear as yesterday. He detected the break he had made in Q'ute's guard with his sharp cruelty. So long ago, he thought—the business with Le Chiffre at Royale-les-Eaux, and a woman called Vesper—about the same age as this girl sitting on the workbench, showing off her shapely knees and calves—lying dead from an overdose, her body under the sheets like a stone effigy in a tomb.

The coldness in Bond's mien faded. He smiled at Q'ute, again looking down at his hand. "A small accident—carelessness on my part. Needed a bit of surgery, that's all." Then he went back to removing the packing grease from the Browning. All thoughts of dallying with the Q Branch executive called Ann Reilly were gone. She was relatively young and still learning the ways of the secret world, in spite of her electronic efficiency, he decided.

As though to break the mood, she asked, in a small voice, "What's it like to kill somebody? They say you've had to kill a lot of people during your time in the Service."

"Then they shouldn't talk so much." It was Bond's turn to snap. He was reassembling the gun now. "The need-to-know system operates in the Service. You, of all people, should know better than to ask questions like that."

"But I *do* need to know." Calmer now, but showing a streak of stubbornness that Bond had detected in her eyes before this. "After all, I deal with some of the important 'gee-whiz' stuff. You must also know what that covers—secret death—undetectable. People die in this business. I should know about the end product."

Bond completed the reassembly, ran the mechanism back and forth a couple of times, then picked up one of the magazines containing seven Browning Long 9mm. rounds that would shatter a piece of five-inch pine board at twenty feet.

Looking at the slim magazine he thought of its lethal purpose and what each of the little jacketed pieces of metal within would do to a man or woman. Yes, he thought, Q'ute—Ann Reilly—had a right to know. "Give me a hand." He nodded toward a box on the workbench. "Bring along a couple of spare magazines. We have to test this little toy on the range, then work's over for the night."

She picked up the magazines and slid down from her perch as she repeated the question. "How does it feel to kill a person?"

"While it's happening, you don't think much about it," Bond answered flatly. "It's a reflex. You do it and you don't hesitate. If you're wise, and want to go on living, you don't think about it afterward either. I've known men who've had breakdowns—go for early retirement on half pension—for thinking about it afterward. There's nothing to tell, my dear Q'u—Ann. I try not to remember. That way I remain detached from its reality."

"And is that why you clean off your pistol in front of someone like me—stripping it as though it were a woman?"

He did not reply to that, and she followed Bond quietly through the corridor that led to the range.

It took Bond nearly an hour, and six extra magazines, before he was completely happy with the Browning. When they finished on the range, he went back to the gunsmith's room, with Q'ute in his wake, and stripped the gun down for cleaning after firing. As he completed this last chore, Bond looked up at her. "Well, you've seen all there is to see. Show's over. You can go home now."

"You no longer require my services then?"

She was smiling. Bond had not expected that. "Well," he said cautiously, "if you'd care for dinner . . ."

"I'd love it," she grinned.

Bond took her in the Saab. They went into Kensington, to the Trattoo in Abingdon Road, where Carlo was pleased to see his old customer. Bond had not been there for some time and was treated with great respect, ordering for the pair of them—a simple meal: the *zuppa di verdura* followed by *fegato Bacchus,* washed down with a light young Bardolino (a '79, for Bardolino should always be drunk young and cool, even though it is red, rather as the French imbibe their rosé wines young, Bond explained). Afterward, Carlo made them plain crêpes with lemon and sugar, and they had coffee up in the bar, where Alan Clare was at the small piano.

Ann Reilly was enchanted, saying that she could sit and listen to the liquid ease of Clare's playing forever. But the restaurant soon started to fill up. A couple of actors came in, a well-known movie director with crinkled gray hair, and a famous zany comedian. For Ann, Alan played one last piece—her request, the sentimental oldie from *Casablanca:* "As Time Goes By."

Bond headed the Saab back toward Chelsea, at Ann Reilly's bidding. Between giving him directions, she laughed a lot, and said she had not enjoyed an evening like this for a long time. Finally they pulled up in front of the Georgian terraced house where Q'ute said she had the whole of the second floor as her apartment.

"Like to come in and see my gadgets?" she asked. Bond could not see the smile in the darkness of the car, but knew it was there.

"Well, that's different," he chuckled. "I still stick to the etchings."

She had the passenger door open. "Oh, but I have *gadgets.*" She laughed again. "I'm a senior executive of Q Branch, remember. I like to take my work home with me."

Bond locked the doors, followed her up the steps and into the small elevator which had been installed during what real-estate agents call "extensive modernization."

From the small entrance hall of Q'ute's apartment Bond could see the kitchen and bathroom. She opened the main door and they passed into the remainder of the apartment—one huge room—the walls hung with two large matching gilt-framed mirrors, a genuine Hockney and an equally genuine Bratby, of a well-known composer whose musicals had been at their peak fifteen to twenty years ago. The furnishings were mainly late 1960s Biba, and the lighting was to match—Swedish in design, and mounted on supports angled into the corners of the room.

"Ah, period décor," said Bond with a grin.

Ann Reilly smiled back. "All is not as it seems," she giggled, and for a moment Bond wondered if she was not used to drinking—perhaps the wine had gone to her head. Then he saw her hand move to a small console of buttons by the light switches. Her fingers stabbed at the buttons, and in the next few seconds Bond could only think of transformation scenes at childhood pantomimes.

The lights dimmed and the room became bathed in a soft red glow which came from the baseboards. The large, circular, smoked glass table which formed a focal point at the center of the room seemed to sink into the carpet, and from it there came the sound of splashing water as it gleamed with light to become a small pond with a fountain playing at its center. The Hockney, Bratby, and both of the mirrors appeared to cloud over, then clear, changed into paintings of a nature that almost shocked Bond by their explicitness.

He sniffed the air. A musky scent had risen around him, while the sound of piano music gently rose in volume—a slow, sensual blues solo, so close and natural that Bond peered about him, thinking the girl was actually sitting at an instrument somewhere. The scent and music began to claw at his senses. Then he took a step back, his eyes moving to the wall on his right. The wall had started to open up, and, from behind it, a large, high, waterbed slid soundlessly into the room—above it a mirrored canopy hanging from crimson silk ropes.

Ann Reilly had disappeared. For a second, Bond was disorientated, his back to the wall, head and eyes moving over the extraordinary sight. Then he saw her, behind the fountain, a small light, dim but growing to illuminate her as she stood naked but for a thin, translucent nightdress; her hair undone and falling to her waist—hair and the thin material moving and blowing as though caught in a silent zephyr.

Then, as suddenly as it all happened, the room started to change again. The lighting returned to normal, the table rose from the fountain, the Hockney, Bratby, and mirrors were there once more, and Q'ute slowly faded from view. Only the bed stayed in place.

There was a chuckle from behind him, and Bond turned to find Q'ute, still in her brown velvet, and with her hair smooth and pleated, as she leaned against the wall laughing. "You like it?" she asked.

Bond frowned. "But . . .?"

"Oh come on, James. The transformation's easy: micro and electronics; *son et lumière*. I built it all myself."

"But you . . .?"

"Yes," she frowned, "that's the most expensive bit, but I put most of that together as well; and the model *is* me. Hologram. Very effective, yes? Complete 3D. Come on, I'll show you the innards . . ."

She was about to move away when Bond caught hold of her, pulled her close and into a wild kiss. She slid her hands to his shoulders, gently pushing him away. "Let's see." She cocked an eyebrow at him. "I thought you'd have got the idea. You said the place was period décor—1960s. All I've done—and I've spent many happy hours getting it right—is add in a 1960s' fantasy—music, lights, the waterbed, scent, and an available bird with very few clothes on. I thought you of all people, James Bond, would have got the message. Fantasies should change with the times.

Surely we're all more realistic these days. Particularly about relationships. The word is, I think, maturity."

Yes, thought Bond, Q'ute *was* a good name for Ann Reilly, as she scurried around showing off the electronics of her fantasy room. "It might be an illusion," he said, "but it still has a lethal effect."

She turned toward him, "Well, James, the bed's still there. It usually is. Have some coffee and let's get to know one another."

In his own flat the next morning, Bond was awake before six-thirty. The biter bit, he thought, with a wry smile. If ever a man's bluff had been called, it was by the ingenious Q'ute. In good humor he exercised, took a hot bath, followed by a cold shower; shaved, dressed and was in his dining room when the faithful May came in with his copy of *The London Times* and his normal breakfast—the favorite meal: two large cups of black coffee, from De Bry, without sugar; a single "perfectly boiled" brown egg (Bond still affected to dislike anything but brown eggs, and kept his opinion regarding three and one-third minutes constituting the perfect boiling time); then two slices of wholewheat toast with Jersey butter and Tiptree "Little Scarlet" strawberry jam, Cooper's Vintage Oxford Marmalade or Norwegian heather honey.

Governments could come and go; crises could erupt; inflation may spiral, but—when in London—Bond's breakfast routine rarely changed. In this he was the worst thing a man in his profession could be—a man of habit, who enjoyed the day starting in one particular manner, eating from the dark blue egg cup with a gold ring around the top, which matched the rest of his Minton china, and happy to see the Queen Anne silver coffeepot and accessories on his table. Faddish as this quirk certainly was, Bond would have been outraged if anyone told him it smacked of snobbery. For James Bond, snobbery was for others, in all walks of life. A man has a right to certain pleasurable idiosyncrasies—more than a right, if they settled his mind and stomach for the day ahead.

Following the Q'ute incident, Bond hardly took any time off during the preparation for what he now thought of as an assignation with Anton Murik on Gold Cup day.

On most evenings lately he had gone straight back to his flat and a book which he kept between his copies of *Scarne's Complete Guide to Gambling* and an 1895 edition of the classic *Sharps and Flats—A Complete Revelation of the Secrets of Cheating at Games of Chance and Skill* by John Nevil Maskelyne. The book he read avidly each night had been published privately around the turn of the century. Bond had come across it in Paris several years before, and had it rebound in board and calf by a printer often employed by the Service. It was written by a man using the pseudonym Cutpurse and titled *The Skills, Arts and Secrets of the Dip.* It was, in fact, a comprehensive treatise on the ancient arts of the pickpocket and lightfingered body-thief.

Using furniture, old coats—even a floor lamp—Bond practiced various moves in which he was already well skilled. His discussions with M as to how he should introduce himself to the Laird of Murcaldy and his entourage had formulated a plan that called for the cleverest possible use of some of the tricks described by Cutpurse. Bond knew that to practice some of these dodges, it was necessary to keep in constant trim—like a card sharp or even a practitioner of the harmless, entertaining, business of legerdemain. He therefore began anew, relearning the bump, the buzz, the two-fingered lift, the palm-dip (usually used on breast pockets), the jog—in which a small billfold is literally jogged from a man's hip pocket—or the thumb-hitch.

A pickpocket seldom works alone. Gangs of from three to ten are the normal rule, so Bond's own plan was to be made doubly difficult. First he had to do the thing by himself; second, the normal picking of pockets did not apply. He was slowly working up his skill to the most difficult move in the book—the necklace flimp: flimp being a word that went back to the early nineteenth century, when flimping referred, normally, to the removal of a person's fob watch. Toward the end of the period Bond was spending several hours a night perfecting the moves of the necklace flimp. All he could hope for was that M's information, given to him during those long hours of briefing under the Cooper painting of Admiral Jervis's victory, would prove accurate.

Now, a signpost read "Ascot 4 miles," and Bond joined a line of Bentleys, Rolls-Royces, Daimlers and the like, all heading toward the race course. He sat calmly at the wheel; his Browning in its holster, locked away in the glove compartment; Q'ute's personalized luggage in the trunk of the car, and himself in shirtsleeves, the gray morning coat neatly folded on the rear seat, with the matching top hat beside it. Before leaving, Bond had reflected that he would not have put it past Q'ute to arrange some kind of device inside a top hat. She had been very affable, promising any assistance in the field—"Just let me know, and I'll be out with whatever you need, 007," she had said with only the trace of a wink.

Bond allowed her a small twitch of the eyebrow.

Now he looked like any other man out to cut a dash in the Royal Enclosure. In fact his mind was focused on one thing only—Dr. Anton Murik, Laird of Murcaldy, and his association with the terrorist Franco.

The careful, if quickly planned, preparation for the assignment was over. James Bond was on his own, and would only call for help if the situation demanded it.

As he approached the race course, Bond felt slightly elated, though a small twist in his guts told him the scent of danger, maybe even disaster, was in the air.

6

PEARLS BEFORE SWINE

THERE WAS ONLY one part of any race course that James Bond really enjoyed— the down-market public area. Alongside the track itself life was colorful: the characters always appearing more alive and real—the day-trip couples out for a quick fling; tipsters with their sharp patter, and the ebullient, on-course bookies, each with his lookout man watching a partner; the "ticktack" sign language being passed across the heads of the bettors, relaying changes in the betting odds. Here there was laughter, enjoyment and the buzz of pleasure.

For the first couple of races that day, Bond—immaculate in morning suit and top hat—strolled in the "public" crowd, as though reluctant to take his rightful place in the Royal Enclosure, the pass for which (provided by M) was pinned to the lapel of his morning coat.

He even stayed down near the rails to watch the arrival of Her Majesty, Prince Philip and the Queen Mother—stirred, as ever, by the inspiring sight of tradition as the members of the Royal Family were conveyed down the course in their open carriages: a blaze of color, with liveried coachmen and postilions—like a ceremony from another age.

His first action, on arrival, had been to check the position of Anton Murik's box in the Grand—or Tattersalls—Stand (another fact gleaned from one of M's expert sources). The Murik box was third along from the left on the second tier.

Leaning against the rails, Bond scanned the tiered boxes with binoculars provided by Q Branch—field glasses of a particular powerful nature, with Zeiss lenses, made especially for the Service by Bausch & Lomb. The Murik box was empty, but there were signs it would soon be inhabited. Bond would have to keep his eye on the paddock prior to the Gold Cup; but, before that event, there was an overwhelming desire to have a wager on his target's horse. Dr. Anton Murik's entry did not stand much chance. That was patently obvious from the odds being offered.

For the Gold Cup, the Queen's horse was favorite, with Lester Piggott up and odds at only five-to-four on. Other contenders were very well-tried four-year-olds, most of them with exceptional records. In particular, Francis' Folly, Desmond's Delight and Soft Centre were being heavily tipped. The other ten runners seemed to be there merely for the ride; and the Laird of Murcaldy's China Blue—by Blue Light out of Geisha Girl—appeared to have little opportunity of coming anywhere near the leaders. Bond's race card showed that in the last three outings, the horse had achieved only one placing, the card reading 0-3-0.

The harsh facts were borne out by the betting odds, which stood at twenty-five-to-one. Bond gave a sardonic smile, knowing that M would be furious when he put in his expenses. If you're going to plunge rashly with the firm's money, he thought, do it with a little style. With this in his head, Bond approached a bookmaker whose board showed him to be Honest Tone Snare, and placed a bet of one hundred and ten pounds to win on China Blue. One hundred and ten pounds may be a negligible sum, but, to the Service accountants, even five pounds was a matter of arguable moment.

"You got money to burn, Guv?" Honest Tone gave Bond a toothy grin.

"One hundred and ten to win," Bond repeated placidly.

"Well, you know yer own mind, Guv, but I reckon you've either got money to burn or you know something the rest of us don't." Honest Tone took the money in return for a ticket that, if China Blue should—by some chance of fate—win, would yield Bond something in the region of two and a half thousand pounds: taking into account the eight percent betting tax—hence the extra ten pounds stake.

Once in the Royal Enclosure, Bond felt his dislike for this side of the race meeting descend on him like a dark, depressing cloud. As much as he liked the female form, he was repelled by the idea of so many women, young and old, parading in fashionable dresses and outlandish hats. That was not what racing was about, he considered.

Some of them, he acknowledged, would be there for the sheer pleasure of the day, which had turned out to be warm and cloudless. Yet a fair majority attended only to be seen, attract the attention of the gossip columnists, and outdo one another with bizarre headgear. Maybe this aversion was a sign of maturity. A depressing thought; and to quell it, Bond headed for the main bar where he consumed two rounds of smoked salmon sandwiches and a small bottle of Dom Perignon.

On M's personal instructions, he had come into the Enclosure unarmed—the Browning still snug in the car. In case of trouble, Bond carried only the small pen emergency contact device and the replica Dunhill cigarette lighter which contained more dangerous possibilities than Messrs. Dunhill would have approved.

Casually he strolled around the Enclosure, finally settling himself under the shade of the trees which surrounded the paddock. Safe in his pocket was M's other piece of cover—a well-forged owner's pass that would get him inside the paddock and close to the target. He did not have to wait long. The horses were already entering the paddock, from the end farthest from the stands. Bond watched. Within a few minutes he identified China Blue.

The horse looked an unpromising proposition by any standards. The coat was dull and the animal had about him an odd, lackluster look—as though it would take dynamite rather than a jockey to make him perform anything more than a sedate canter on this warm afternoon. Bond gave the animal a good looking over and decided that it was just an unpromising-looking horse. This did not mean that the animal could not show unusual form. Stranger things had happened. Looking at the horse being led around by the stableboy, Bond had one of those sudden instincts—the kind which so often saves lives in his profession—that he would win his money. There was more to China Blue than the eye could tell.

How? He had no idea. Frauds on race horses in England are rare these days. Anton Murik would certainly not resort to unsophisticated risks like doping or substitution when competing against the kind of stock running in the Ascot Gold Cup. Yet Bond knew at that moment that China Blue would almost certainly win.

Suddenly the short hairs on the back of his neck tingled, and he experienced a shiver of suspense. A man and two women were approaching China Blue — the trainer turning toward them, hat in hand and a deferential smile of welcome on his face. Bond was getting his first view of Dr. Anton Murik.

He shifted position, moving closer to the paddock entrance.

It *was* Anton Murik — the face of the man he had seen in the photograph. What the picture had not captured was the high mane of white hair sweeping back from the bulldog face. It came as a shock, until Bond remembered the photograph had been cut off just above the forehead. Also, no still photograph could ever capture the walk or manner. The Laird of Murcaldy was barely five feet tall, and walked, not as Bond had imagined, with the stride of a Scottish chieftain, but in a series of darting steps. His movements — hands, head, fingers and neck — were of the same quick precision. In a phrase, Dr. Anton Murik, Laird of Murcaldy, was possessed with the movements of a grounded bird.

The features, and authoritative way he appeared to address his trainer, however, made up for any other physical deficiency. Even at this distance, the man clearly had a power that overrode physical peculiarities or eccentricities. A born leader, Bond thought; sometimes the best of men, or the worst; for born leaders usually knew of their power early in life, when they chose either their good or evil angel as a guide to success.

The two women with Murik were easily recognizable. Oddly, Bond considered, they were identically dressed, except in the matter of color. Each wore a classic, V-necked, midcalf-length dress in a knitted bouclé. Over the dress was a short, sleeveless gilet.

The elder of the women — obviously Mary Jane Mashkin — wore the ensemble in navy, with white trimming, and a neat, short-brimmed hat in white.

The ward, Lavender Peacock, was taller, more slender, and just as stunning as her photograph. Her identical clothes were in white, with navy trimmings and hat. Bond wondered if their outfits were originals from Murik's Roussillon Fashions.

The younger girl was laughing, turning toward Murik, the gilet flaring away from her to reveal firm and impertinent breasts, under the dress, in splendid proportion to the rest of her body. The sight was breathtaking, and Bond could see why the Laird of Murcaldy kept her on what M referred to as a tight rein. Lavender Peacock looked like a spirited, healthy and agile girl. To Bond's experienced eye, she also had the nervous tension of a young woman unused, and straining at the leash. Left to her own devices, Lavender Peacock might well carve a path of broken hearts—even broken marriages—through Scottish and English society, in a matter of months.

Bond narrowed his eyes, straining and never taking them off the girl. She talked animatedly, constantly glancing at Murik. Concern seemed to pass over her face each time she looked at the Laird, but Bond only took this in as a kind of side issue. He was looking for something more. Something essential to the whole scheme of insinuating himself into the Laird of Murcaldy's immediate circle. Something M had revealed to him in great detail during their hours of planning.

It was there. No doubt. The triple, heavy rope of matching pearls clearly visible around Lavender's neck. From this distance, under the shade of the paddock trees, it was, of course, impossible to tell if they were the real thing, but they would undoubtedly be taken as such. The real thing certainly existed—£500,000 worth of *mohar* pearls, graded and strung on three short ropes, all held by a decorated box clasp and safety chain at the back of the neck.

The pearls had been kept in trust for Lavender until her twenty-first birthday, having originally been a wedding present from her father to her mother, during whose lifetime they had been kept mainly in a bank vault.

Lavender—M told Bond—had broken this habit, against Anton Murik's advice, and now wore them on every possible occasion. In the confines of M's office, Bond wondered aloud if the Laird of Murcaldy did in fact allow the pearls to be worn. Substitution would, for a man of his resourcefulness, be relatively easy. M had snappily told him this was not the point. The Peacock pearls were known to be worn in public. They certainly seemed to be around Lavender's neck this afternoon.

Bond thought they could not be around a prettier neck. If he had been taken with the photograph of the girl, he was certainly dazzled by the real thing. Murik had turned away and was talking to the two women, while the trainer leaned close to the jockey, giving him last instructions. In the background China Blue looked as docile as ever—as spirited as a wooden rocking horse.

It was time for Bond to move. The entrance to the paddock was busy, with people passing in and out. Already he had noticed that the Ascot race course officials were only giving cursory glances at proffered owners' passes. Within the next few minutes, Anton Murik and his party would be coming through this entrance—which doubled as the main exit—out into the Royal Enclosure, through which they would presumably pass on their way to the Tattersalls Stand. The whole of the present operation's future depended upon timing and Bond's skill. With the binocular case over his right shoulder, race card held open, firmly, in his left hand, he made his way into the paddock, flicking the owner's pass quickly in front of the official who seemed most preoccupied.

Horses were being mounted, and two had already begun to walk toward the exit that would take them down on to the course. Bond circled China Blue and the group around him, staying back, seeming to keep his eyes on another horse near by.

At last, with a final call of good luck from the assembled party, China Blue's jockey swung into the saddle. Murik, the Mashkin woman, the trainer and Lavender moved back, pausing for a second as the horse walked away, urged forward by the jockey, who, Bond noticed, looked very relaxed and confident.

Murik's party began to move slowly toward the exit through which Bond had just come. It was now becoming crowded with owners, their families and select friends leaving to view the race. Carefully Bond stepped close to Murik's party. The Laird himself was talking to the trainer, with Mary Jane Mashkin standing to one side. Lavender Peacock was to their rear. Bond sidled between her and the Laird with his two companions, staying behind them just long enough for others to press around him, therefore putting several people between Murik's group and Lavender Peacock, so that she would be reasonably far behind them when they reached the exit.

Bond sidestepped again, allowing himself to be overtaken until he could push in just behind Lavender Peacock. They were five or six paces form the exit, now jammed with people trying to get through as quickly and politely as possible. Bond was directly behind the girl, his eyes fixed on the box clasp and safety chain at the back of her neck. It was clearly visible, and, as he was pushed even closer, hemmed in by the crowd, Bond caught the smell of the girl's scent—Mille de Patou, he thought—the limited edition, and the most expensive scent on the market. So exclusive that you received a certificate with your purchase.

There were enough people around, and Bond was well screened. Allowing himself to be jostled slightly, he now pushed his shoulders forward for added protection and bumped full into Lavender Peacock's back.

The next complicated moves took only a fraction of a second, just as he had practiced and planned them during the past few days. Keeping the left hand, which was clutching the open race card, low down by his side, Bond's right hand moved upward to the nape of the girl's neck. The inside of his first and second fingertips grasped the box clasp which held the pearls, lifting them away, so that no strain would be felt by their owner. At the same time, his thumb passed through the safety chain, breaking it off with a deft twist. Now the box clasp fell into position, held tightly by the thumb and forefinger. He pressed hard, tilting, and felt the clasp give way.

The box clasp is constructed, as its name implies, as two metal boxes — in this case decorated by tiny pearls — which fit one inside the other. When released by pressure they fall apart, but there is an added safety feature. The inner box contains a small hook which slips around a bar in the outer box. Using the thumb and first two fingers, Bond controlled both boxes, slipping the hook from its bar. He then withdrew his hand, glancing down and dropping his race card. Silently the pearls fell to the turf. His aim and timing were perfect. The race card followed the pearls, falling flat and open on top of them. Lavender Peacock did not feel a thing, though Bond caused a minor clogging of the exit as he bent to retrieve his card, lifting the pearls with it, so that they were securely held inside the card.

Relaxed now, and holding the card and pearls, hidden behind the tail of his morning coat, Bond sauntered towards the Tattersalls Stand, following Anton Murik's party, at a discreet distance, as they moved toward the Tattersalls Stand — just as he hoped they would. Lavender had caught up with them, and Bond prayed she would not discover her loss before reaching the Murik box.

Bond slowed considerably, allowing the Laird's party to get well ahead. He knew there was still the vague possibility that some plainclothes policeman had spotted his moves. Any moment one of two things could happen — a cry from Lavender, announcing the pearls were missing, or the firm hand on his shoulder that would mean, in criminal parlance, that he was having his "collar felt." If the latter occurred it would be no use telling them to ring M. Precious time would have been lost.

Murik's party had now disappeared into the stand. Nothing happened, and Bond entered the side door, climbing the stairs to the second tier about two minutes after the Laird's group entered. On reaching the corridor running behind the boxes, Bond transferred the pearls to his right hand and advanced on the Laird of Murcaldy's box.

They all had their backs to him as he knocked and stepped inside. Nobody noticed, for they seemed intent upon watching the runners canter down to the starting line. Bond coughed. "Excuse me," he said. The group turned.

Anton Murik seemed a little put out. The women looked interested.

Bond smiled and held out the pearls. "I believe someone has been casting pearls before this particular swine," he said calmly. "I found these on the ground outside. Looks like the chain's broken. Do they belong to . . . ?"

With a little cry, Lavender Peacock's hand flew to her throat. *"Oh my God!"* she breathed, the voice low and full of melody, even in this moment of stress.

"'My God' is right." Murik's voice was almost unnaturally low for his stature, and there was barely a hint of any Scottish accent. "Thank you very much. I've told my ward often enough that she should not wear such precious baubles in public. Now perhaps she believes me."

Lavender had gone chalk white and was fumbling out toward Bond's hand and the pearls. "I don't know how to—" she began.

Murik broke in, "The least we can do, sir, is to ask you to stay and watch the race from here." Bond was looking into dark slate eyes, the color of cooling lava, and with as much life. This gaze would, no doubt, put the fear of God into some people, Bond thought—even himself, under certain circumstances. "Let me introduce you. I am Anton Murik; my ward, Lavender Peacock, and an old friend, Mary Jane Mashkin."

Bond shook hands, in turn; introducing himself. "My name is Bond," he said. "James Bond."

Only one thing surprised him. When she spoke, Mary Jane Mashkin betrayed in her accent that she was undoubtedly American—something that had not appeared in any of the files in M's office. Originally Southern, Bond thought, but well overlaid with the nasalities of the East Coast.

"You'll stay for the race, then?" Murik asked, speaking quickly.

"Oh yes. Please." Lavender appeared to have recovered her poise.

Mary Jane Mashkin smiled. She was a handsome woman, and the smile was much warmer than the subdued malevolence of Anton Murik. "You must stay. Anton has a horse running."

"Thank you." Bond moved closer within the box, trying to place himself between Murik and his ward. "May I ask which horse?"

Murik had his glasses up, scanning the course, peering toward the starting gate. "China Blue. He's down there all right." He lowered his glasses and for a second there was movement within the lava-flow eyes. "He'll win, Mr. Bond."

"I sincerely hope so. What a coincidence," Bond laughed, reaching for his own binocular case. "I have a small bet on your horse. Didn't notice who owned him."

"Really?" There was a faint trace of appreciation in Murik's voice. Then he gave a small smile. "Your money's safe. I shall have repaid you in part for finding Lavender's pearls. What made you choose China Blue?"

"Liked the name." Bond tried to look ingenuous. "Had an aunt with a cat by that name once. Pedigree Siamese."

"They're under starter's orders!" Lavender sounded breathless. They turned their glasses toward the far distance, and the start of the Ascot Gold Cup—two and a half flat miles.

A roar went up from the crowd below them. Bond just had time to refocus his glasses. The horses were off.

Within half a mile a pattern seemed to emerge. The Queen's horse was bunched with the other favorites—Francis' Folly and Desmond's Delight, with Soft Centre clinging to the group, way out in front of three other horses which stood back a good ten lengths, while the rest of the field straggled out behind.

Bond kept his glasses trained on the three horses behind the little bunch of four leaders who seemed set to provide the winners. Among this trio was the distinctive yellows and black of Murik's colors on China Blue.

There was a strange tension and silence in the box, contrasting with the excited noise drifting up from the crowds lining the course. The pace was being kept up hard, and the leading bunch did not appear to be drawing away from the three horses some distance behind them. The Queen's horse was ahead, but almost at the halfway mark Desmond's Delight began to challenge, taking the lead so that these two horses almost imperceptibly started to pull away, with Francis' Folly and Soft Centre only half a length behind them, running as one animal.

As the field passed the halfway mark, Bond shifted his glasses. Two of the trio following the lead bunch seemed to be dropping back, and it took Bond a second to realize this was an optical illusion. He was aware of Anton Murik muttering something under his breath. China Blue was suddenly being ridden hard, closing the distance between himself and the third and fourth runners among the leaders.

"Blue! Come on, Blue," Lavender called softly. Glancing along the box rail, Bond saw Mary Jane Mashkin standing, taut, with her hands clenched.

The crowd was intent on the four horses battling for position at the front of the field. They were past the three-quarter mark by the time people realized the serious challenge China Blue presented as he came up, very fast, on the outside.

The racing China Blue could have been a different animal from the horse Bond had watched in the paddock. He moved with mechanical precision in a steady striding gallop; and now he was reaching a speed far in excess of any of the lead horses. By the time they reached the straight final three furlongs, China Blue was there, scudding past Francis' Folly and Soft Centre—well up and gaining on Desmond's Delight, who had again taken second place to the Queen's horse.

A great burst of sound swept like a wind over the course as China Blue suddenly leaped forward in a tremendous surge of speed, outstripping both Desmond's Delight and the Queen's horse, to come loping home a good length in front of the pair who had made the running from the start.

Lavender was jumping up and down, excitedly clapping her hands. "He did it. *Uncle Anton, he did it!*"

Mary Jane Mashkin laughed—a deep, throaty sound—but Dr. Anton Murik merely smiled. "Of course he did it." Bond saw that Murik's smile did not light up his eyes. "Well, Mr. Bond, my horse has won for you. I'm pleased."

"Not as pleased as I am," said Bond, quickly, as though blurting out something he would rather have kept hidden. It was just enough to interest Murik—the hint of a man rather in need of hard cash.

"Ah," the Laird of Murcaldy nodded. "Well, perhaps we'll meet again." He fumbled in his waistcoat pocket, producing a business card. "If you're ever in Scotland, look me up. I'd be glad to provide some hospitality."

Bond looked down at the card bearing Anton Murik's address and again feigned surprise. "Another coincidence," he said smoothly.

"Really?" Murik was ready to go. After all, he had just won the Ascot Gold Cup and wanted his moment of triumph. "Why another coincidence?"

"I leave for Scotland tonight. I'll be in your area in a couple of days."

The slate eyes grew even cooler. "Business or pleasure?"

"Pleasure mostly. But I'm always open for business." He tried to make it sound desperate.

"What kind of business, Mr. Bond?"

Bond hesitated slightly, timing the pause. "The contracting business."

"And what do you contract?"

Bond looked at him levelly. "Myself as a rule. I'm a soldier. A mercenary—up to the highest bidder. There—that'll be the end of our acquaintance, I expect. We're a dying breed." He gave a short laugh at his grim little joke. "People don't take too kindly to mercenaries these days."

Anton Murik's hand closed around Bond's forearm, pulling him to one side, away from the two women. "I am not averse to your profession, Mr. Bond. In fact I have been known to employ mercenaries in a way—gamekeepers, people on my estates. Who knows, I may even have a place for a man like yourself. To me, you look tough enough. Come to Murik Castle. On Monday we have a little annual fun. Most of the land and the nearby village—Murcaldy—is mine. So each year we hold our own version of the Highland Games. You know the kind of thing—the caber, the hammer, shot-putting, a little dancing, wrestling. You will enjoy it." This last sentence was almost an order.

Bond nodded as Murik turned toward the ladies. "We must go down, greet China Blue, and accept our just rewards. Mary Jane, Lavender, you will be seeing Mr. Bond again soon. He's kindly consented to come and stay—for the Games."

As they left the box, Bond was aware of a mildly sardonic look in Mary Jane Mashkin's eyes.

"Thank you again—for the pearls, I mean, Mr. Bond," Lavender said. "I look forward to seeing you soon." There was something odd about the way she phrased the parting sentence, as though she meant what she said but was hinting some warning. Lavender, Bond thought, appeared at first meeting to be a woman with some hidden fear below the charming, easy and poised exterior.

The Laird of Murcaldy did not even look at Bond again—leaving the box in his quick, birdlike manner without a word or backward glance.

Bond stood, looking after them for a moment, wondering about Murik's personal version of the Highland Games and the part he might be expected to play in them. Then he went down to collect his winnings from a suitably impressed Honest Tone Snare, before making a short double-talk telephone call to Bill Tanner and another to the Central Hotel in Glasgow, booking himself a room for the following morning—stressing that he would need to use it immediately on arrival, which he hoped would be in the early hours.

The Laird of Murcaldy would doubtless be flying his party back to Scotland. Bond did not want to be far behind them. Neither did he wish to arrive at Murik Castle without rest and time for reflection.

Slipping the leather strap of his glasses case over one shoulder, James Bond walked as casually as he could toward the parking lot.

7

KING OF THE CASTLE

DURING THE FURIOUS night drive north Bond had plenty of time to puzzle over Anton Murik's win with China Blue. Horses for courses, he thought. But that horse had not looked fit enough for any course. How, then, had it romped home at Ascot? The only possible explanation lay in the old trick of having China Blue pulled back by his jockey in earlier races—not displaying his true form until the strategic moment. But perhaps the real answer would be found—with the others he sought—at Murik Castle.

The journey to Glasgow was without incident. Bond went flat-out on the freeway sections, managing to avoid police speed traps and stopping to refuel at a couple of all-night service areas.

He was parked, settled into his room at the Central Hotel, and eating a breakfast of porridge, scrambled eggs, toast and coffee, by nine in the morning. He then hung out the "Do not disturb" sign and slept like a baby, not waking until seven that evening.

After a lengthy study of the Ordnance Survey maps to plan the route, Bond went down and dined in the hotel's Malmaison Restaurant—named after Napoleon and Josephine's reteat, and one of the best French restaurants in Scotland. Bond, however had no desire for rich food that evening, and settled for a simple meal of smoked salmon followed by a filet steak with a green salad. He drank only Perrier. He was determined to do most of the journey by night—traveling like one crossing a desert in secrecy.

He was on the road, with the bill paid, by ten-thirty, heading north on the A82, which took him right alongside the waters of Loch Lomond. Early on the following morning, Bond stopped for a day's rest at a village just short of Loch Garry—having switched to the A87 that would eventually lead him as far as the coastal lochs, and those narrow roads with frequent passing places, around the western seaboard.

He reached a wooded area just to the east of Loch Carron early the next morning, and having parked the Saab well out of sight among trees, remained at rest through a day of pale blue skies and the scent of pine and heather, knowing that as soon as dusk set in, the village of Murcaldy, and from there Murik Castle, would only be a matter of seventy or eighty minutes' drive. He had brought meat pies and some fruit, together with more Perrier, not wanting to chance anything stronger at this stage of the operation.

Having concentrated on making the journey in good and safe time, Bond so far had not been able to savor the views or delight in the beauties of Scotland. Indeed, there had been no opportunity while doing most of his traveling by night. So now he lay back, adjusted the driver's seat, dozing and eating as the sun slid across the sky and began to settle behind the trees and hills.

While there was still light, Bond began to make his emergency preparations, unlocking the trunk and transferring a pack of cigarettes from Q Branch's prepared briefcase to his pocket. Only six of the cigarettes were of any use to a smoker, the remainder being cut short to hide an easily accessible compartment into which four pre-set electronic microbugs nestled comfortably. If Bond was to be a walking surveillance unit within the Murik household, he might well need assistance, and the small receiver for these bugs—complete with tape and minute headset—remained in one of Q'ute's ingenious hiding places in the luggage.

He also made certain that the fake Dunhill lighter—dangerous to the point of immobilizing any grown man for the best part of an hour—was well separate from his own, real lighter.

The rest of his weaponry remained locked away in the safety compartments of the car. The only other tools he required were to hand—the Bausch & Lomb field glasses and the strap-on Nitefinder headset.

As the last traces of daylight vanished and the first stars began to show in the wide sky, Bond started the Saab, turning the car in the direction of Applecross, skirting Loch Carron in the knowledge that his destination was not far away and there was cause for him to be alert. He made good time, and seventy minutes later the Saab was crossing the small bridge at Murcaldy, leading directly into the one village street with its quaint, neat rows of cottages, the two shops, inn and church.

Murcaldy was situated on a small river at one end of a wide glen, the sides of which, Bond could see by the now risen and bright moon, were devoid of trees. Ahead, at the far end of the glen and above the village, the castle stood against the sky like a large outcrop of rock.

The village appeared to be deserted except for occasional lights from the cottages, and Bond calculated that it took him less than forty-five seconds to travel through this little cluster of buildings. At the far end, near the church, the narrow road divided, a signpost pointing its two fingers in a V. Murik Castle lay directly ahead, up the glen; the other sign showed an equally narrow track leading back toward the road to Shieldaig, though Bond considered the track would inevitably meet yet another narrow road, with its inevitable passing places, before one was really on the main A896 to that small town. The track thus marked, however, would have to follow the line of the glen to the east, so would probably lead him to a vantage point from which he could gain a view of the castle.

Pausing for a second, Bond slipped the infrared Nitefinder kit over his head so that the little protruding glasses sat comfortably on his nose. The moonlit night immediately became as clear as day, making the drive along the dry track a simple matter. He switched off the headlights and began to move steadily forward. The track dipped behind the eastern side of the glen, but the upper stories of the castle were still visible above the skyline.

Both village and castle had been built with an eye to strategy, and Bond had little doubt that his passage through Murcaldy had already been noted. He wondered if it had also been reported to the Laird.

At last Bond reached a point which he considered to be parallel to the castle. Stopping the car, he picked up the binoculars and, with the Nitefinder headset still in place, got out and surveyed the area. To his right he could clearly see low mounds of earth, just off the track and running for about a hundred yards, as though somebody had been doing some fresh digging.

He paused, thinking he should investigate, but decided the castle must be his first concern. Turning left, Bond walked off the track and made his way silently toward the rolling eastern slope of the glen.

The air was clear and sweet with night scents. Bond moved as quietly as possible, almost knee-deep in gorse, bracken and heather. Far away a dog barked, and there came the call of some predatory night bird beginning its long dark hunt.

On reaching the top of the rise, Bond stretched himself out and looked around. He could see clearly down the glen to the village, but it was impossible to gain any vantage point above the castle, which lay about a mile away in a direct line, having been built on a wide plateau. Far away behind the castle he could just make out the jutting peak of Beinn Bhan breasting itself almost three thousand feet above sea level.

Taking up the binoculars, Bond adjusted them against the Nitefinders and began to focus on the Murik Castle. He could see that halfway along the glen the track from the village became a paved road, which ended at a pair of wide gates. These appeared to be the only means of access to the castle, which otherwise was surrounded by high granite walls, some apparently original, other sections built by later hands. Indeed, most of the present castle seemed to have undergone vast reconstruction. To the rear Bond could just make out what could well be the ruins of the original keep; but the remainder looked more like a great Gothic-style heap, beloved of Victorians—all gables and turrets.

Three cars stood in front of what was obviously the main door—a wide structure with a pillared portico. The castle seemed to be set in the midst of large formal gardens, and the whole aspect produced a half-sinister, half-Disneyland quality. Craning forward, Bond could just make out the edge of a vast lawn to the right of his view. He thought he could glimpse the corner of a large tent. For tomorrow's Games, he presumed. Well, Dr. Anton Murik certainly had a castle and no doubt acted like a king in it.

Bond was just about to get to his feet, return to the car, drive back and present himself at King Murik's court, when he realized, too late, that he was not alone.

They had come upon him with the craft and experience of professional hunters, materializing from the ground like spirits of the night. But these were not spirits—particularly their leader, who now loomed huge above him.

"Spyin' on Murik Castle, eh?" the giant accused him in a broad Scots accent.

"Now wait a minute . . ." Bond began, raising a hand to remove the Nitefinder kit. But, as he moved, two hands the size of large hams grasped him by the lapels and he was lifted bodily into the air.

"Ye'll come guy quiet wi' us. Right?" the giant said.

Bond was in no mood for going quietly with anybody. He brought his head down hard, catching the big man on the forward part of his nose bridge. The man grunted, letting go of Bond, who could see the butt had been well placed. A small trickle of blood had begun to flow from the man's nostrils.

"I'll kill ye for—" The man was stopped by another voice from behind them.

"Caber? Hamish? Malcolm? What is it?"

Bond instantly recognized the slight nasal twang of Mary Jane Mashkin. "It's Bond!" he shouted. "You remember, Miss Mashkin? We met at Ascot. *James Bond.*"

She appeared, like the others, suddenly as though from the ground.

"My God, Mr. Bond, what're you doing here?" She peered at the giant. "And what's happened to *you*, Caber?"

"Yon man gied me a butt to the neb," he muttered, surly.

Mary Jane Mashkin laughed. "A brave man, doing something like that to Caber."

"I fear your man thought I was a poacher. He—well, he lifted me up, and became generally aggressive. I'm sorry. Am I trespassing?"

Caber muttered something which sounded belligerent as Mary Jane Mashkin spoke again. "Not really. This track is a right-of-way through the Laird's land. We've been doing a little night hunting and looking at the digging." She inclined her head toward the other side of the track where Bond had seen the low earth piles. "We've just started working on a new drainage system. Just as well you didn't wander that way. You could've stumbled into a pretty deep pit. They've dug down a good fifteen feet, and it's over twelve feet wide." She paused, coming closer to him so that he caught the scent of Madame Rochas in his nostrils. "You didn't say why you were here, Mr. Bond."

"Lost." Bond raised his hands in a gesture of innocence. He had already slipped the Nitefinder set from his head, as though it was the most natural thing to be wearing. "Lost and looking for the castle."

"Which I guess you found."

"Found, and was observing."

She put a hand on his arm. "Then I think you'd better take a closer look, don't you? I presume you were coming to visit."

"Quite," Bond nodded. In the darkness the men shuffled and Mary Jane Mashkin gave some quick orders. There was, apparently, a Land Rover up the track a little way. "I'll guide Mr. Bond down and you follow," she told Caber, who had calmly relieved Bond of the Nitefinder set.

"You should have taken the track straight ahead at the village," she said when they were settled in the Saab and moving.

"I gathered that."

The Land Rover was close behind as they swept up to the gates. A figure appeared to open up for them, and Mary Jane Mashkin told Bond they kept the gates closed at night and on special locks. "You can never tell. Even in an out-of-the-way place like this, where we know everybody, some stranger might . . ."

"Come in and ravage you all?" Bond grinned.

"Could be fun," she laughed. "Anyhow, it's nice to know we have a guest like yourself, Mr. Bond—or can I call you James?"

"No need for formality here, I suppose," said Bond as they came up to the main door with its great pillared porchway.

Behind them, Caber and the men called Hamish and Malcolm were climbing down from the Land Rover. Mary Jane Mashkin called out for Hamish to inform the Laird, then turned to Bond. "If you let Caber have your keys he'll take your luggage in, James."

But Bond had carefully locked the door. "I think the luggage can wait." He made a courteous gesture toward the door of the castle. "After being taken for a poacher, or a spy, the Laird might not want me . . ." He stopped, for the small, birdlike figure of Dr. Anton Murik was emerging from the castle. He peered forward for a moment. Then his face lit up.

"Why, it's Mr. Bond. You've come as promised—Good heavens, what happened to your nose, Caber?"

The big man was still dabbing blood away with his handkerchief. "My fault, I'm afraid," said Bond, "Sorry Caber, but you were a little overenthusiastic."

"I thocht yon man was some kindo' spy, or a poacher, Laird. I didna' ken he was a visitor. Mind, he acted strange."

"Get him to bring your luggage in, Mr. Bond," Murik smiled, and Bond repeated that it could wait. He had no desire for Caber to be messing about with the car.

"Fine," beamed Murik. "No need to lock anything here. We'll collect the bags later. Come in and have a dram," and, with a sharp order to Caber and his henchman to look after the Saab, Murik ushered Bond through the gloomy porchway.

Mary Jane Mashkin had already gone ahead, and as they crossed the threshold, Murik gave a small cackle of laughter. "May have made an enemy there, Bond. Caber doesn't take kindly to being bested. You gave him a nosebleed as well. Not good. Have to be careful."

8

VIRGIN ON THE ROCKS

LATER BOND CONSIDERED that in all probability he had expected the Victorian Gothic gloom of the porchway to be reflected in the interior of Murik Castle—Newfoundland dogs and deer antlers. He was therefore greatly surprised by the dazzling sight that met his eyes.

From the brooding exterior he was suddenly transported into another world. The hall, with its vast circular staircase and surrounding gallery, was decorated in shimmering white, the doors being picked out in black, and the matching white carpet underfoot giving Bond the impression that he was sinking into a soft, well-kept lawn.

The lower part of the walls was decorated, with elegant sparseness, by a series of highly polished, mint-condition halberds, *ronchas,* bat's wing *corsèques,* war forks and other thrusting weapons of the fifteenth and sixteenth centuries, which gleamed under the light thrown from a huge steel candelabrum of intricate modern design. The arrangement was in no way cluttered or overdressed.

Murik spread out an arm. "The raw materials of war," he said. "I'm a bit of a collector, though the best pieces are kept in other parts of the house—except, possibly, these." He pointed to a gilded console table on which rested a glass case covering an open pistol box—a pair of dueling pistols with telltale octagonal barrels, the case fitted out with all necessary accessories, brass powder measure and the like. "Last known English duel," Murik said proudly. "Monro and Fawcett, 1843." He indicated the nearest pistol. "Monro's weapon. Did the killing."

Bond stepped back to view the hallway again. There were other illuminations, placed strategically over modern pictures which hung higher up the walls. He recognized at least two from Picasso's Blue period, and what looked like the original of Matisse's "Pink Nude."

Bond caught the smile on Murik's face. "You're a collector of other things too," he said. "That looks like the—"

"Original? Yes." Murik made a little swooping movement.

"But I thought—"

"That it was in the Baltimore Museum of Art?" The Laird nodded. "Yes, well, you know the art world. After all, there is a da Vinci 'Virgin of the Rocks' in the Louvre and in London. The same goes for the de Champaigne 'Richelieu.' Come now, Mr. Bond. You would like a drink." He raised his voice for Mary Jane Mashkin, who appeared as though on cue at the top of the stairs.

"Had to do a quick change." She smiled, making a regal descent and extending a hand which appeared to drip with expensive rings. "Nice to see you, Mr. Bond. It was kind of dark outside." She raised her voice. "Lavender, where are you? We have a guest. The nice Mr. Bond is here. The one who was so helpful with your necklace." She crossed the hall to Bond's right, opening a pair of double doors.

"You will excuse me." Murik gave his birdlike nod. "The ladies will take care of you. I must talk to Caber. I hope he did not treat you too roughly, though you seem to have given him good measure."

"Come." Mary Jane Mashkin ushered Bond toward the living room, in the doorway of which Lavender Peacock now stood.

"Mr. Bond, how nice." Lavender looked even more like a young Bacall, and somehow seemed almost relieved to see Bond, her eyes shining with undisguised pleasure.

Both women were dressed in evening clothes, Mary Jane having done her quick change into a somber black, probably by Givenchy. Lavender glowed in flowing white which was, to Bond's experienced eye, undoubtedly a Saint Laurent. They motioned him toward the room.

"After you, ladies." As they turned, Bond detected a tiny noise on the balustraded gallery above them. Glancing up quickly, he was just in time to see a figure slipping into a doorway on the landing. It was only a fleeting glimpse, but there was little doubt in Bond's mind concerning the identity of the man. He had studied too many pictures and silhouettes of him in the past few days. Franco was still at Murik Castle.

The room in which Bond now found himself was long and wide, with a high, ornate ceiling, decorated in the same bold style as the hall. The walls were a delicate shell pink, the furnishings designed for comfort, and mainly in leather and glass. The wall opposite the doorway had been transformed into one huge picture window. Even in this light, Bond recognized the tint of the glass, similar to that in the Oval Office of the White House, but in a pink shade and not the green of that elegant seat of power. One would be able to see out of this huge window, but, from the outside, the human eye would only be able to note light, without detail. It was undoubtedly bulletproof.

"Well, now, a drink, Mr. Bond." Mary Jane stood by a glass cabinet. "What will you take after all your exertions?" She made it sound coquettish.

Bond had an overwhelming urge to ask for a Virgin on the Rocks, but chose Talisker. "When in Scotland . . ." he explained. "A small one. I'm not a great drinker—a little champagne sometimes, and a well-made vodka martini. But here—well . . ."

Mary Jane Mashkin smiled knowingly, opening the cabinet and taking out the fine malt whisky. "There." She held out the glass of amber liquid which glowed like a precious stone in the light.

Lavender had seated herself on a deep leather sofa. "Well, it's certainly nice to have someone else staying here, Mr. Bond. Especially for the Games." She looked him straight in the eyes as she said it, as though trying to pass a message. Yet, as he looked quizzically at her, Bond saw the eyes alter, the steady look faltering, her gaze shifting over his shoulder.

"They're looking after you, then, Mr. Bond?" Murik had come silently back into the room, and Bond turned to acknowledge his presence. "I have verbally chastised Caber," the Laird continued. "He has no right to manhandle people—even if he does suspect them of poaching or spying." The old, dangerous gray lava lurked in Anton Murik's eyes, and Bond saw that he was holding out the Nitefinder headset. "An interesting toy, Mr. Bond."

"In my profession we use interesting toys," Bond smiled, raising his hands. "I have to admit to carrying out a reconnaissance of the castle. You invited me, but my training . . ."

Murik gave a small smile. "I understand, Mr. Bond. Probably more than you will ever know. I rather like your style."

Lavender asked what the strange glasses and headset might be, and Bond told her briefly that they allowed you to see clearly in the dark. "Very useful for night driving," he added.

"Mr. Bond," Murik cut in, "if you'll let one of my men have your car keys, I'll see your luggage is taken to the guest room."

Bond did not like the idea, but he knew the only way to gain Anton Murik's confidence was to appear unruffled. After all, they would need a great deal of time and some very expert equipment to discover the secrets of both the car and baggage. He felt in his pockets and handed the keys to Murik. Almost at the same moment a burly man, whose tail coat and general demeanor proclaimed him as the butler, entered and stood in subservient silence. Anton Murik addressed him as Donal, telling him to get "one of the lads to take Mr. Bond's luggage to the East Guest Room and then park the car."

Donal acknowledged the instructions without a word and departed with the car keys.

"There now, Mr. Bond." Anton Murik gestured to one of the comfortable leather chairs. "Sit down. Rest yourself. As you see, we're old-fashioned enough to be formal here. We dress for dinner. But, as you've arrived late, and unprepared, we'll forgive you."

"If the ladies don't mind." Bond turned to smile at Mary Jane Mashkin and Lavender Peacock. The Mashkin woman returned the smile; Lavender gave him a broad, almost conspiratorial grin.

"Not at all, Mr. Bond," said Mary Jane, and Lavender followed with a quick, "Just this once, Mr. Bond."

James Bond nodded his thanks and took a seat. He had long ago ceased to worry about being the odd man out on formal occasions—except, of course, when it was some forewarned important function.

In the back of his mind, Lavender Peacock caused niggling concern. She was beautiful, obviously intelligent, and at ease when Dr. Anton Murik was absent, but in her guardian's presence Lavender had about her a certain wariness that he could not readily define.

It should not surprise him, Bond realized. Anton Murik and his castle, with people like Caber and the butler creeping around, would be enough to make anyone wary. There was something eery about this large Gothic structure with its interior which stank of wealth, taste and gadgetry, all set far out in the middle of a beautiful nowhere.

Murik helped himself to a drink and they chatted amiably—Murik mainly interested in Bond's journey north—until Donal, the butler, reappeared to confirm that Mr. Bond's luggage had been taken to his room and that the car was parked next to the Laird's Rolls outside. As an afterthought, and with a look of distinct disapproval at Bond's apparel, he announced that dinner was served.

Bond was led across the hall—automatically glancing up at the doorway through which he had seen Franco vanish—into the long dining room, this time decorated in more traditional style, but still retaining light colors and the same stamp and flair which showed in the hall and living room. None of Murik's weapon collection was on view in either living or dining room.

They sat at a fine long mahogany table, polished and kept in magnificent condition, and ate with Georgian silver from an exquisite dinner service, every piece of which was rimmed in gold. The Lairds of Murcaldy had obviously lived well for many decades. The table silver and china would, Bond considered, have brought a small fortune in any reputable London auction room.

Murik's food matched the outer show: a fine lobster cocktail, prepared individually at each diner's elbow from freshly cooked and cooled crustaceans; a light consommé with a chicken base, followed by rare rib of beef which almost dissolved on the tongue; and, before the cheese board was circulated, there was one of Bond's favorite Scottish puddings, the delicious cream-crowdie—toasted oatmeal folded into thick whipped cream.

"The simplest things are best at table," Anton Murik commented. "You pay a fortune for that in the Edinburgh and Glasgow hotels, and yet it's merely an old farmhouse dish."

Bond reflected on a fact he had noted so often in his travels—that the wealthy of today's world take their so-called "simple" pleasures for granted.

He was not surprised when the port arrived and the ladies withdrew, leaving the two men to their own devices. The running of Murik Castle, it seemed, clung to the fashions of more gracious days. The servants—there had been two muscular young men waiting at table under Donal's eye—withdrew, as did the butler himself, after placing cigars, cutter and matches within the Laird's reach. Bond refused a cigar, asking permission to smoke his own cigarettes.

As he drew out the old and faithful gunmetal case, James Bond's thumb felt the rough section around the middle, where it had been skillfully repaired. The thought flashed through his head that this very case had once saved his life, by stopping a Smersh assassin's bullet. The evidence was in the rough patch, invisible to the eye, on either side of the case. For a second he wondered if he would have need of any lifesaving devices in this present encounter with the Laird of Murcaldy.

"So, you took up my offer, Mr. Bond?" The eyes assumed the gray and menacing lava flow look as Anton Murik faced Bond across the table.

"To visit you, yes." Bond watched as Murik expelled a great cloud of cigar smoke.

"Oh, I didn't just mean the visit." He gave a throaty chuckle. "I know men, Bond. I can scent them. You are a man of vigor who lives for danger. I smelled that the moment I met you. I also felt you have a similar facility—for scenting out possible dangers. Yes?"

Bond shrugged. It was not time to commit himself to anything.

"You must be good," Murik continued. "Only good mercenaries stay alive, and you did all the right things—reconnoitering my estate, I mean. There may well be a job for you. Just stay for a day or two and we shall see. Tomorrow I may even give you a small test. Again, we shall see."

There was a moment's pause, and then Bond asked levelly, "How did you do it?"

Murik arched his eyebrows in surprise. "Do what?"

"Win the Gold Cup with China Blue?" Bond did not smile.

Murik spread out his hands. "I have a good trainer. How else would I win such a prestigious cup race? And I had the right horse."

"How?" Bond asked again. "China Blue's form made him the biggest outsider in the race. He even looked like a loser. Now I know that's easy enough to do, but you brought it off and there were no questions. You have him pulled in his other races?"

Slowly the Laird of Murcaldy shook his head. "There was no need for that. China Blue won. Fair and square." Then, as though suddenly making up his mind, he rose from the table. "Come, I'll show you something." He led the way to a door Bond had not noticed, in a corner on the far side of the dining room. He took out a bunch of keys on a thin gold chain, selected a key and unlocked the door.

They went down a cool, well-lit passage which terminated at yet another door, which Murik unlocked with a second key. A moment later they stood in a large book-lined room. There were three leather chairs facing a wide military desk and a cabinet containing some exquisite pieces of antique weaponry. On the wall above the desk hung the only painting in the room—a large and undeniable Turner.

"Genuine?" asked Bond.

"Naturally." Murik moved behind the desk and motioned Bond into one of the chairs facing him. "My inner sanctum," he commented. "You are honored to be here at all. This is where I work and plan."

Gently Bond drew the chair nearer to the desk. Murik was opening one of the drawers. He removed a small buff folder, opened it and passed two photographs to Bond. "Tell me about these photographs, Mr. Bond."

Bond said they were pictures of China Blue.

"Almost correct." Murik smiled again—a deep secretive smirk. "They are brothers. You see—I will not bore you with the documents—just over four years ago I had a mare in foal, here on the estate. I happened to be in residence at the time, and was in at the birth, so to speak. Happily I have a vet who knows how to keep his mouth closed. It was a rare thing, Bond. Two identical foals. Absolutely identical. No expert could have told them apart, though it was obvious to the vet and myself that the second would always be the weaker of the two. That is usual in such cases."

He paused for effect. "I registered one only. They were from good racing stock. There is one China Blue—the one you saw running at Ascot—with tremendous stamina and the natural aptitude for racing. The other? Well, he races, but has no speed and little stamina. Though still, at four years, you would be hard put to tell the difference in build. Now, I've shared a secret with you. I am attempting to establish a trust between us. But if it ever leaks out, I promise you are a dead man."

"Nobody's going to hear it from me." As he spoke, Bond moved the chair even closer, taking out his gunmetal cigarette case and the package of cigarettes provided by Q'ute. The Laird of Murcaldy had just answered a prize question. The man was a cheat and a fraud. Franco was in the house and for Bond, that was enough. M had been right to send him—this was certainly no panic or fool's errand.

Quickly he removed a couple of the cigarettes from the packet and placed them in his case. At the same time Bond pressed on the side of the packet, expelling one of the small electronic microbugs into his hand. Murik was still chuckling as he picked up the photographs from the desk. As he leaned down to return them to the drawer, Bond slid his hand under the footwell of the desk, pressing the adhesive side of the bud hard against the woodwork. Now the Laird of Murcaldy's inner sanctum was wired for sound.

Murik snapped the drawer closed and stood up. "Now, Mr. Bond, I suggest you say goodnight to the ladies and retire. Your cases are in your room, and tomorrow we must all take part in the Games. After that you may wish to stay, and I may wish to make you a proposition. It depends on many things."

In the living room, Mary Jane Mashkin and Lavender Peacock sat listening to Mozart through hidden speakers. Bond thought he glimpsed the look of friendly conspiracy on Lavender's face as they entered the room. Once again he experienced the feeling that she was trying to warn him of something as they shook hands, bidding each other goodnight.

The silent Donal had appeared, summoned surreptitiously by Murik, and was instructed to show Bond to the East Guest Room.

As he left, Bond caught Lavender's eyes in his, warm, friendly, but with a lonely message hidden within. Of one thing he was certain, she was a living virgin on the rocks—though he admitted to himself that he was being presumptuous about the first part of that statement.

He followed Donal up the stairs, anxious to get at the receiver in his case and set it up so that any further business transacted by Murik in his inner sanctum could be recorded and listened to at leisure.

Donal opened the door, intoning, "The East Guest Room, sir," and Bond stepped into an Aladdin's Cave for the passing visitor.

9

ALL MOD CONS

THE ROOM WAS decorated almost entirely in black, with soft lighting hidden high up behind pelmets, where there must once have been ornate old picture rails. It took Bond a second to realize that there were two rooms and not one; for half of each of the bedroom walls and a large section of the ceiling was made of mirror—difficult to distinguish against the black décor. This gave the illusion of more space; it also had the unnerving effect of disorientation. Donal spoke just as Bond confirmed, to himself, that an archway led from the bedroom into a bathroom.

"You did not leave the keys to your luggage, sir; otherwise I would have had your clothes unpacked and pressed. Perhaps tomorrow?"

"Certainly." Bond turned his back, speaking sharply. "Good night, Donal."

"Good night, sir." The butler withdrew, and Bond heard a very solid click as the door closed. He went over and tried the handle, immediately realizing he had been correct in his identification of the sound. The door was fitted with a remote-controlled electronic lock. He was virtually a prisoner. At least, he thought, setting the roomy briefcase on a side table, he would not be a prisoner who would be secretly watched or overheard.

Unlocking the briefcase by turning the keys twice, he pressed down hard on the catches, which lifted on small hinges, revealing the real locking devices underneath—three wheels of numbers on each side. Bond spun the dials, and the briefcase opened. With this one they had made little effort to hide the equipment inside, the top of the case being a simple tray in which his toilet gear rested. Lifting out the tray, Bond uncovered the few pieces of hardware beneath.

The largest item was the one Bond required—the standard VL 22H countersurveillance receiver, which looked something like a chunky walkie-talkie, but with headphones and a hand-held probe.

Bond plugged in the headset and probe, slipped the instrument's shoulder strap around his neck, adjusted everything and switched on. For the next ten minutes he carefully ran the probe over the entire room, covering every corner and fitting. The built-in verifier would quickly determine any type of bug, differentiate between various signals and even lead him to any television cameras hidden behind the large expanse of glass; or secret fiber-optic lenses, the size of pencil holes, in the wall. He followed a well-learned pattern, completing the sweep with great care. Nothing showed. The note in the earphones remained constant, and the needle in the VU unit did not waver.

Returning the countersurveillance unit to its hiding place, he pulled out the larger piece of luggage. Checking the locks, he once more used his keys to open the lid, throwing the clothes out in a manner that would have made the sinister and fastidious Donal wince. When the case was empty, Bond returned to the locks, turning the keys a further three times in each. At the final click of the right lock, a minute panel slid back in the far left-hand corner of the case bottom, revealing a small, numbered dial.

Bond spun the dial, selecting the code arranged between Q'ute and himself only a few days previously. Another click and he was able to slide a larger portion of the case bottom to one side, disclosing some of Q Branch's special hardware, packed neatly in velvet-lined trays. Removing the tiny receiver/recorder—based on the STR 440, and only eighty-four by fifty-five millimeters in size, complete with a specialized tape cassette and foam-padded minute headset—Bond switched on, set the control dial to the figure 1, and saw a small light glow like a red-hot pinhead. The bug placed in Murik's study was now active. A cassette lay ready, attached to the machine. Now, any conversation or movement in Murik's room would be recorded on Bond's receiver. He looked around and decided that, for the moment at least, it was safe to leave the receiver on the long dressing table that took up the bulk of one wall. He put the small piece of apparatus carefully on the dressing table and started to unpack, first sliding the hidden compartment in the case back to its locked position.

Long experience had taught Bond to pack and unpack with speed and efficiency. In less than five minutes he had shirts, underwear, socks and other necessities packed neatly in the drawers which ran down the outer ends of the long dressing table, and his other clothes hung in the closets built into the walls on either side of the archway leading to the bathroom. He left one or two special items in the cases, which, after locking, he placed at the bottom of one of the closets. Only then did Bond allow himself an examination of the room, which had all the makings of an expensive movie set.

The centerpiece of the main room was a vast bed, made up with white silk sheets and pillows. The visible edges of the bed glowed with light, and the whole was partially enclosed by two high, padded, semicircular panels. Bond slid onto the bed, and found himself in what was almost another bedroom within the main room. The inside of the panels was softly lit; a large console took up the whole of one section to his left, while a television screen was set into one of the paneled sections which made up the semicircle at the bed's foot.

After a few experiments with the console, Bond found that each section of the two semicircles could be moved by remote control; that the bed could be slowly rotated and even raised or lowered at will. The console also had facilities for complete quadraphonic sound, television video-recording, the Ceefax system, a telephone and intercommunication sets. Behind him, in a rack sunk into the black padding of the panel was a whole range of music and video cassettes, plus a pair of expensive Koss headphones. Bond glanced briefly at the cassettes, seeing that Anton Murik appeared to provide for all tastes—from Bach to Bartok, the Beatles to the latest avant-garde rock bands; while the video cassettes were of movies only recently released in cinemas.

Bond recognized the bed as the famous and exclusive Slumberland 2002 Sleepcentre, with some modifications, made probably on Murik's own instructions, He noted that the console provided sound and light programs marked "Peace Mood," "Wake," "Sleep" and "Love." Something Q'ute would have appreciated, he thought with wry amusement.

It took a lot of willpower for Bond to leave the so-called Sleepcentre and investigate the bathroom, which also had several intriguing gadgets, including a sunken whirlpool bath, and even a blood-warm lavatory seat.

"All mod cons," he said aloud.

With a short chuckle, Bond returned to the bedroom. He would try out the communications system and complain that his door seemed to be jammed. As he headed toward the bed, a glance at the receiver on the dressing table showed the tape revolve for a second and then stop. The bug placed in Murik's study was picking up noises. Grabbing the receiver and headset, Bond dived into the Sleepcentre, slipping the phones over his ears.

Someone was in Murik's study. He heard a distinctive cough, then Murik's voice: "Come in, the door's open. Close it and shoot the bolt. We don't want to be disturbed."

The sounds came clearly through the headphones—the door closing and then the rustle as someone sat down.

"I'm sorry about dinner," Anton Murik said. "It was unavoidable, and I didn't think it wise for you to show yourself to my visitor, even though he probably wouldn't recognize you from Adam."

"The message was understood. Who is the man?" The other voice was heavily accented. Franco, Bond thought.

"Harmless, but could be useful. I can always do with a little intelligent muscle. Caber is good, but rarely puts his brains into gear before working. You have to give him orders like a dog."

"This man . . . ?"

"A mercenary out for hire. I shouldn't think he has many scruples. We met by accident at Ascot . . ."

"You have him checked out?"

"You think I'm that much of a fool? He says his name's Bond. I have the number and details of the car—very smart. It'll give us an address and by tomorrow night I shall know everything I need about Mr. James Bond."

Bond smiled, knowing that M had him very well covered. Any inquiries coming from passport number, driver's license, car registration, or other means, would be nicely blocked off. All Murik could learn would come from the cover dossier—the service record of one Major James Bond, a Guards officer who had probably served with the SAS, and performed certain dubious duties since leaving the armed forces—under a slight cloud—six years previously.

Murik was still speaking. ". . . but I smell the need for money. Mercenaries are good earners, if they live, yet they all have that tendency to spend as though tomorrow did not exist. Or they turn to crime."

"You must keep sights on all strangers until they are proved."

"Oh, I'm testing him. He'll give us some interesting sport." The laugh was unpleasant. "At least we'll see what he's made of. But, my dear Franco, you're leaving shortly, and I want to get things finalized."

"Everything in my head. Clear as day. You know me well now, Warlock. The teams are ready in England, France and Germany. No trouble. They are on call. Listening the whole time. There is only America, and my people wait there for me."

"And you'll be in the States by tomorrow night?"

"Afternoon."

There was a long pause and a rustling of paper before Murik spoke again. "You're quite certain of your American people?"

"The same as the others."

"Willing to expend themselves in the cause?"

"Absolutely. They expect death. I have said it is not likely for them to survive. This is good psychology. Yes?"

"I agree. Though as long as they do exactly as they're told, there'll be no risk. That's the beauty of it. First, the fact that we only need to place four men in each station—to secure themselves within the control rooms—and take orders from *me* alone. Second, that they refuse to maintain contact with anyone outside—no hostage taking, nothing to distract them. Third, that I make it plain to the governments concerned that they have twenty-four hours only, from the moment of takeover. The twenty-four hours run out . . . then *Boom*. England, France, Germany and the United States have big problems on their hands for many years to come—problems, if all the scientists are correct, that will not be confined to the four countries concerned. The death toll and damage could cover almost half the world. This is the one time that governments will have no choice but to give in to blackmail."

"Unless they do not believe you."

"Oh, they'll believe me," Murik chuckled. "They'll believe me because of the facts. That's why it's all important that your people go in at the same moment. Now, your Americans. How long will it take to brief them?"

There was another pause, as though Franco were trying to make up his mind. "Twenty-four hours. One day at the most."

"For both lots? For Indian Point Unit Three, and San Onofre Unit One?"

"Both. No problems."

"It's the San Onofre that's going to scare the wits out of them."

"Yes, I've studied papers. Still active, even though the authorities know how close it is to a fault. A seismic fault—is that how you say it?"

"Yes. America will press Europe. They just won't be able to take the risk. As long as your American people know what is expected and do only what I tell them. You must stress—as you have done in Europe—that if they obey orders, nobody can get at them for a minimum of twenty-four hours. By that time Meltdown will all be over anyway. So I see no reason why Meltdown cannot go ahead at twelve noon British Summer Time on Thursday, as planned."

"There's one thing . . ."

"Yes?" Murik's voice, sharp.

"How are you to give the signals—pass on the instructions—without detection?"

A slight chuckle, subdued and humorless. "Your people have the receivers. You have a receiver, Franco. Just use them, and let me worry about the rest."

"But with radio signals of that strength—covering Europe and the United States—they'll pinpoint you faster than you can do your *Times* crossword—which is fast."

"I told you, Franco. Let me worry. All is arranged, and I shall be quite safe. Nobody'll have the slightest idea where any instructions are coming from. Now, Franco, we are on schedule for Thursday, which is ideal. If you can really finish everything in America within twenty-four hours, it means you will be in a position to carry out the other assignment for me on Wednesday night. You think you can make that location?"

"There is time enough. Better I should do it than someone else . . ."

Even with the headphones on, Bond was suddenly distracted by a click from the door. His head whipped around and he saw the handle turn a fraction. In one movement he grabbed the phones from his head, stuffing the receiver under the pillow before launching himself out of the Sleep-centre toward the door.

His hand shot out, grasping the door and pulling it sharply toward him.

"It's okay," whispered Mary Jane Mashkin, "only me." She slipped inside, the door swung to heavily, and Bond heard the locks thud into place again. His heart sank. Mary Jane Mashkin was a handsome woman, but not Bond's fancy at all. Yet here she was, dressed a shade too obviously in a heavy silk Olga nightdress and wrap, her dark hair hanging around her face, a flush to her cheeks. "I thought I should come and see that you're comfortable," she murmured coyly. "Have you got everything you need?"

Bond indicated the door. When Donal had closed it, Bond had realized there was some kind of automatic locking system. The noise following Mary Jane's entrance had confirmed his fear. "How do you get through that system? It's electronic, isn't it?" he asked.

She pushed herself toward him, smiling in a faraway manner. "Some of the rooms—like this—have electronic locks for safety. The doors can always be opened from the outside—and all *you* have to do is dial 'one' on the phone. That puts you through to the switchboard. They'll open it up for you. If Anton agrees, of course."

Bond backed away. "And that's what you'll do? To get out, I mean."

"Oh, James. Are you telling me to leave?"

"I . . ."

She slid her arms around his neck. "I thought you needed company. It must be lonely up here."

Bond's mind scrabbled around for the right actions and words. There was something decidedly wrong here. A carefully orchestrated seduction scene by this American woman—an intellectual, mistress to Anton Murik, and almost certainly in on whatever villainy was being planned at this moment by the doctor and Franco.

"James," she whispered, her lips so close that he could feel her breath, "wouldn't you like me to stay for a while?" Mary Jane Mashkin, fully dressed, made up, and with her hair beautifully coiffured, seemed a handsome and attractive woman. Now, close, with her body unfettered from corset or girdle, and the face cleaned off, she was a very different person.

"Look, Mary Jane. It's a nice thought, but . . ." He wrenched himself free. "What about the Laird?"

"What about him?" It's *you* I've come to see."

"But isn't this risky? After all, you're his . . . trusted confidante."

"And I thought you were a man who was used to taking risks. The moment I set eyes on you, I . . . James, don't make me humiliate myself . . ."

She was a good actress, Bond would say that for her. The whole thing smelled of either a setup or a special reconnaissance. Had he not just heard Anton Murik talk about testing him? Women involved with men like Murik did not offer themselves to others without good reason. Bond took the woman by the shoulders and looked her straight in the eyes. The situation was delicate. A false move now might undo all the good work which had got him into Murik Castle. "Mary Jane, don't think I'm not appreciative, but . . ."

Her lips tightened into a petulant grimace that changed her expression into one of acid, unpleasant hardness. A lip curled upward. "I've made a fool of myself. Men used to flock . . ."

"It isn't like that," Bond began.

"No? I've been around, James Bond. You think I don't know the signs by now?"

"But I'm Anton Murik's guest. A man can't abuse hospitality like . . ."

She laughed—a derisive single note. "Since when did a man like you stand on that kind of ceremony?" She stood up. "No, I just misread the signals; got my wires crossed. You should know by now, James, that a woman can always tell when a man finds her—well, I guess, unattractive."

"I told you. It's not like that."

"Well, I know it is. Just like that."

She was at the door now, turning, her mood changing to one of anger. "I could've saved you an awful lot of hassle, James. You could've avoided much unpleasantness with me on your side. But I could make you regret the last few minutes. You'll see, my friend."

It all sounded very melodramatic, and Bond was becoming more and more convinced that Mary Jane's presence in his room—her thrusting, unsophisticated attempt to seduce him—was an act designed for some other purpose. Her hand reached out to the door.

"Shouldn't I ring the switchboard?" he asked, trying to sound suitably subdued.

"No need. They have warning lights that go on and off when the bolts move, but I have arrangements with them. There's also a way out for the members of this household." From the folds of her robe she produced a small oblong piece of metal the size of a credit card and slipped it into a tiny slot that Bond had not noticed, to the right of the lock. The bolts shot back, and Mary Jane Mashkin opened the door. "I'm sorry to have troubled you," she said, and was gone in a rustle of black silk.

Bond sat down on the bed and looked at the door. Possible friend or eternal enemy? he wondered. The whole business had been so bizarre that he found it difficult to take seriously. Then he remembered the receiver and Murik's conversation with Franco.

The cassette was not turning when he retrieved the apparatus from under the pillow. He put the headphones over his ears and started to wind back the tape. The conversation had finished only a few minutes before. Now he rewound it to the point at which he had left them talking. The voices, through the phones, were as clear as though the two men were with him in the room.

"Now, Franco," Murik was saying, "we are on schedule for Thursday, which is ideal. If you can really finish everything in America within twenty-four hours, it means you will be in a position to carry out the other assignment for me on Wednesday night. You think you can make that location?"

"There is time enough. Better I should do it than someone else."

"It would give me greater confidence to know that it is you."

"And I shall be required to be in the appointed place at . . ."

"At the time we've already talked about. What I need to know, for my own peace of mind, is how you will do it. Will she suffer? What reaction should I expect?"

"No suffering, Warlock, I promise you. She feels nothing—and the onlookers, they imagine she has fainted. The weapon will be high-powered, an air rifle, and the projectile, it has a gelatin coating. She feels a little pinprick but no more. I shall use a . . ."

There was a thud in the earphones, and the conversation became blurred. It took Bond a few seconds to realize what had happened. Either the adhesive on the microbug under Murik's desk had given way or one of the man had accidentally dislodged it with his knee. Gently he wound the tape back, but the whole conversation was now muffled, and he could pick up only a few words. It was not even possible to separate the voices of the two men—". . . very fast . . . catwalk . . . below . . . neck . . . bare   flesh . . .   Warlock . . .   steps . . .   point . . .   palace . . . Majorca . . . coma . . . death . . . two hours . . . heart attack . . . time . . ." and so on. It meant little, except the obvious fact that someone—a woman—was being set up to be killed, probably just before this operation that Murik referred to as Meltdown.

The whole thing was deadly, and Bond knew that M's worst fears were proved. This was no ordinary little plan but a full-scale worldwide conspiracy of great danger. As for the contract killing, he could not even start to think how that fitted in. The weapon would be an air rifle, undoubtedly firing a capsule containing some quick-acting poison. As for the place and target, it was anyone's guess. The word palace had been mentioned, and the victim was a woman. Bond immediately thought of royalty. The Queen, even. Then there was the word Majorca. A meeting place, perhaps? These were things he would have to pass on to M as soon as possible. It even crossed his mind, as he carefully packed away the receiver, to trigger the pen alarm now, inside the house. But that could prove more dangerous than helpful. Murik had him neatly stowed away, and the place was a fortress. Stay with it for the time being, Bond decided.

He was just returning the headset to the closet, packed away in the case, when he heard the click of the door bolts again. His stomach turned over. Surely Mary Jane would not have the nerve—even at Murik's instigation—to return to his room for a second visit? The handle was turning, and for the second time that night Bond moved quickly to the door and yanked it open.

10

DILLY-DILLY

THERE WAS A little squeal as Lavender Peacock half fell into the room, and James Bond's arms. She quickly recovered, snatching at the door, but it was too late to stop it closing behind her, with its ominous electronic click.

"Blast," she said loudly, shaking out her long sheen of hair. "Now I'm locked in with you."

"I can think of worse fates," Bond said, smiling, for Lavender was also dressed in her nightclothes, making a distinctly more desirable picture than Mary Jane Mashkin. "Anyway," he asked, "haven't you got one of those neat little metal things that opens the door from inside?"

She leaned against the wall, pulling her wrap around her, one hand brushing back her hair. "How do you know about those?" she started. Then: "Oh Lord, has Mary Jane been up here? I can smell her scent."

"Miss Mashkin did play a scene of some ardor, but I fear she didn't go away contented."

Lavender shook her head. "She wouldn't expect that. I thought I might get here before they started to play tricks with you. Anton has a warped sense of humor. I've seen him put her on offer before now, just to test people. Have you got a cigarette?"

Bond took out his case and lit one for each of them. His mind had gone into a kind of overdrive. Quite suddenly he had recognized two of the things overheard in Murik's conversation with Franco, via the bug: two names that were familiar—Indian Point Unit Three and San Onofre Unit One. He was beginning to come to some conclusions.

Lavender inhaled deeply, then shook her head again. "No, I haven't the privilege of being allowed to carry electronic keys. In this place I'm usually just as much a prisoner as yourself." She gave a little smile. "Don't doubt that you're a prisoner, Mr. Bond."

"James."

"Okay—James."

Bond gestured toward the bed. "Make yourself comfortable now you're here, Lavender—and you might as well tell me why you *are* here." He did not doubt that this was yet another test.

She moved away from the wall, heading for one of the armchairs. "I think I'd better sit over here. That bed's too much. Oh, and call me Dilly, would you? Not Lavender."

"Dilly?"

"Silly old song—'Lavender blue, dilly-dilly'—but I prefer it to Lavender. You're honored, incidentally. Only real friends call me Dilly. Nobody here would dream of it."

Bond settled himself on the Sleepcentre, where he had a good view of his latest visitor. "You still haven't told me why you're here, Dilly."

She paused for a moment, taking another long pull at the cigarette. "Well, I shouldn't be. Here, I mean. I suppose I'm taking a chance. Don't know if I should even trust you, James. But you've come out of the blue, and I've got to talk to someone."

"Talk away."

"There's something very strange going on. Mind you, that's not unusual for this place. My guardian is not like other men—but you know that already. I should ask you what you know about him, I suppose."

Bond told her he gathered Anton Murik was wealthy, that he was a nuclear physicist of some note, and had half promised him a job.

"I should be careful about the job." She smiled—a knowing, somewhat foxy smile. "Anton Murik hires people to do the dirty work. It's a terrible thing to say, but when he fires them, he does it in a literal sense." She lifted her hand, holding the fingers as a child will play at using its hand as a gun. "Bang!" she said.

Bond looked straight into her eyes. She was the kind of woman who had an immediate appeal for him. "You sure you wouldn't be more comfortable over here?" There was a challenge in her eyes, and Bond thought he detected that familiar charge of static pass across the room between them.

"Probably *too* comfortable. No, James, I came to give you some advice. I said something strange is going on. It's more than that. It could even be something terrible, disastrous."

"Yes? What sort of thing?"

"Don't ask what it is because I just don't know. All I can gather is that it has something to do with the Laird's plans for building a new kind of nuclear reactor. He left the International Atomic Research Commission because they wouldn't fund his idea. He calls it an Ultra-Safe Reactor. There's a mountain of money needed, and I think he plans to use you in some way. But first—apart from the danger of being involved with him— he's going to put you at risk. Tomorrow. I heard him talking to Mary Jane."

"Tomorrow? But he has his Games tomorrow."

She stubbed her cigarette out in one of the large glass ashtrays. "Quite. It probably has something to do with the Games. I really don't know."

"I might get hurt then. It wouldn't be the first time."

"No, but . . . Another cigarette?"

"Smoking damages your health, Dilly. It says so on the packets."

"It's not just smoking that can damage you here, James. Give."

He went over to her, lit her cigarette, then bent down and kissed her lightly on the forehead. She drew back fractionally, putting a hand up to his shoulder. "That wasn't what I came here for, James."

"No?"

Firmly she moved her head. "No. People've already got into a lot of trouble because of me. I just came as a kind of Cassandra, uttering warnings."

"Just uttering warnings? I wonder, Dilly. You said you were taking a risk to trust me; that you were virtually a prisoner like me. I wonder if you came hoping that I'd get you away; that I'd take fright and run, carrying you off on the pommel of my saddle."

"That's not on, I'm afraid. But I think you should get out, and I'm willing to help you."

"So that I can ride back with the Fifth Cavalry and save you?"

"Maybe I'm beyond salvation."

Bond squeezed her shoulder and went back to the bed. For a time they were silent. Did she, he asked himself, have any inkling of what was really going on? Already his mind had latched hard on to the locations of Indian Point Unit Three and San Onofre Unit One. He knew exactly what they were, and the possibilities of Murik's involvement with them carried things into a nightmare world.

He returned to Lavender's last words, "Why beyond salvation, Dilly?"

"Because I am who I am—the Laird's ward, a distant relative, trapped in the outmoded traditions of this place, and by my guardian's intrigues."

"Yet you're willing to get me out?"

"I think you should. Not just you, James. I'd probably say it to any stranger who came here and took the Laird's fancy."

"I can't go yet, Dilly. You've whetted my appetite about what's going on here. If I find that it's something really dangerous, or even criminal, then I'll take you up on your offer. I'll let you give me a hand. If it comes to that, will you ride off for help with me?"

Once more she slowly shook her head. "I was brought up here. It's all I know. Prisoner or not, there are certain responsibilities . . ."

Bond showed surprise. "Brought up here? I thought you had only been his ward . . ." he stopped, realizing he had already given away too much.

"Legally only for a short time. But I've lived here—well, forever."

"And you don't like it, and yet don't want to leave?"

She said that if she ran away now and something went wrong, things could be very bad for her. "At least you can get out now, while the going's good."

Bond said that was the last thing he wanted to do. Privately he also knew that it might be the only thing he *could* do. Triggering off the pen alarm from the castle roof—if he discovered the full extent of Murik's plans—might put a spoke into the Laird's wheel—but spokes can easily be mended. No, he told Lavender, if he discovered something really criminal going on, then he would get out and bring help. He added that he would be happier if she came as well, but she gave a stubborn shake of her head. Bond found it difficult to believe that a girl of her spirit would allow herself to remain in these circumstances. She really was a virgin on the rocks—or a damned good actress.

"Well, for your sake, I hope you find out something quickly." Lavender rose, went over to the door, realized there was no way out, and turned to walk back to her chair. "It'll break this week, I'm pretty certain. We're off to do a fashion show and if he is up to something, that could be the perfect cover for him."

Bond tried to sound surprised at the mention of the fashion show, and Lavender explained what he already knew, that Anton Murik owned the controlling interest in one of the world's leading fashion houses. "Rous-sillon. I am lent out to them for major shows. A clotheshorse with legs, that's me, James—but I can tell you, those shows are the high spots of my year."

"You slip the leash, eh?"

She almost blushed, and Bond slid from the bed, walked over to her chair, sat on the arm and put a hand across her shoulders, drawing her close. She looked up at him, her eyes cold.

"James. No. I only cause trouble."

"What kind of trouble?"

"The kind I wouldn't want to bring on you." She hesitated, indecisive for a moment. "Okay. The first time was years ago. A boy. Worked here on the estate. I was about sixteen or seventeen. Mary Jane Mashkin caught us and sent for Anton. The boy—David—disappeared, and his family were moved. I'm pretty certain Anton had him killed."

"And, if I touched you? What would he do to me?"

"You'd end up the same way. David was just the first. After I began to model for Roussillon there was a guy in Paris. I didn't know anyone had discovered, but he was found in an alley with his throat cut. Yes, I think he would kill you, James. He was once forced to buy someone off, but that was in Rome—one of the modeling jaunts again. The man was from a wealthy Italian family. One day things were fine, the next I had a letter saying he had to go away and wouldn't be seeing me anymore. A year later I heard my guardian talking to Mary Jane. He said it had cost almost a quarter of a million dollars, but it was money well spent."

Bond bent down and kissed her on the lips. "I'm willing to chance it, Dilly. You're . . ."

She pulled away again. "I mean it, James." Then she smiled, putting a hand up to his cheek. "Not that I . . . Well, perhaps I'm being selfish. If something sinister really *is* going on here, you're my one hope—if they don't do for you at the Games tomorrow, I'll get you out, and you can bring in the stormtroopers—rescue the damsel in distress."

"Some damsel," Bond laughed. "How do you get out of this room, then? Or are we forced to spend the night together in separate corners?"

Lavender said she would have to stay now—until early morning, at least, when Bond could ring down and get the locks taken off. "You can say you want to go for a walk or something, when it's light. They'll let you do that because they can keep an eye on you then." She giggled. "We could bundle."

"Aye, we could do that an' all," Bond laughed, thinking of the old custom of courtship by sharing a bed, fully dressed, with a bolster to separate the couple.

"I'm for that. I'm bloody tired as well." Lavender stood up. "I hope there's a spare bolster in that mobile gin-palace the Laird's provided you with."

They made do with pillows, and Bond found it a frustrating experience, being so near and yet so far from this delightful girl. When they were settled, she asked if he really would go for help if anything came to light.

"I'd be happier if you came as well. But I understand your wanting to stay. In the long run you'll be safer. But, yes, if there is something that means taking urgent action, I'll get the hell out as quickly as possible—with your help—and be back to bring your precious guardian to book." Then, trying to make it sound like an afterthought, Bond asked if he was the only stranger in the castle.

She did not hesitate. "There's someone else here, but he's become a regular visitor. Anton calls him Franco, and we're all under instructions not to talk about him. When you turned up he was pushed out of sight, but I think he's due to leave early in the morning."

"You think he's got something to do with what's going on?"

"I'm certain of it. He spends a lot of time closeted with Anton when he's here."

"How does he come and go?"

"In the helicopter. My guardian has a helicopter pad tucked away behind the old part of the castle."

"Thank you, Dilly. You just hang on and we'll sort it out—and thanks for the warning." He reached over the pillows and squeezed her hand.

"If we get out of here, James . . ."

"Yes?"

"Oh, nothing. There might be no need to get out at all. Sleep, eh?"

For a few minutes Bond's mind was in a turmoil of anger, the eye of his personal hurricane centered on Anton Murik: cheat, fraud; a man willing, and ruthless enough, either to kill or buy off his ward's lovers. He was like some Victorian millionaire martinet. Slowly Bond pushed down the anger. It was no good becoming emotionally outraged. Coolness would be the only way to deal with Murik, and he would have to establish himself quickly to gain the man's trust and get him to fill in some of the details of Meltdown. Then he must get word out fast to M—who would have his own problems explaining the source of his information to MI5 and the Special Branch.

With this in mind, Bond set his own mental alarm, which seldom failed to work, and drifted into restful sleep, waking accurately at five in the morning, just before dawn.

He roused Lavender and asked about the electronic locks. She told him the door locks on rooms in the castle were made up of three cylindrical bolts, activated by an electromagnet. When the locks went on, the bolts slid into tightly fitting housings. At the end of each housing the bolt completed an electric circuit, activating an "on" light in the castle's switch-board room.

Would they notice the light flickering? Probably not, Lavender said. They had experienced cases of momentary malfunction: lights going out completely, then coming on again within a few seconds. She had only intended to stay for a minute of whispered warning on the previous night.

"And there's no way in which you can get hold of one of the inside keys—the oblong strips?"

She told him that was impossible. The castle gates were another matter, but the electronic keys were held only by certain people, and there was never any chance with them. Bond nodded. He now had to turn his mind to gaining Murik's confidence.

He went into the bathroom and changed into slacks and a sweatshirt, then dialed the castle switchboard to tell his story about the door being jammed. A detached voice asked why he wanted to leave his room, and he said it was his habit to exercise each morning. The voice told him to wait for a moment.

Within a minute they heard the locks fall back. Bond tried the door and it opened easily. He kissed Lavender on the cheek, and to his surprise she reached up and kissed him quickly but firmly on the mouth. Then she was gone.

Within a few minutes he had checked the room to make certain nothing incriminating was left lying around. With a final cautious look, he left.

The first hint of dawn was touching the sides of the glen as James Bond went along the corridor, down the stairs and out into the castle grounds. As he emerged, the sound of a helicopter came throbbing in from the west. He waited until the machine—a small Bell JetRanger—came up the glen, turned, hovered, and slowly dropped out of sight behind what had once been the keep of the old castle.

Hunching his shoulders, Bond began to jog around the house, heading for the wide lawns where, only last night, he thought he had glimpsed a tent set up for the day's Games. He wanted to give his body the best possible workout. He knew all his reserves of stamina would be needed that day.

11

THE SLINGSHOT SYNDROME

LATER BOND WAS to learn that the four acres of beautifully kept grass which ran down the far side of Murik Castle—bordered with shrubs, gravel paths and topiary work—had been known as the Great Lawn for at least two centuries.

Even at this early hour the estate workmen were out and about, putting the finishing touches to two large tents, a number of small ones, and an oblong arena the size of a small landing strip.

As he jogged past, Bond reflected it would be somewhere in this arena that he would probably face whatever test Anton Murik had devised for him. He used the jogging as an opportunity first to get the lay of the land, and second to settle his mind and concentrate on the numerous problems he had to resolve.

It was obvious, from what he had overheard of the conversation between Murik and Franco the previous night, that they planned at least five terrorist attacks, in Europe and the United States. The two in America, he knew from the names, were connected with nuclear power stations. Logically, the ones in Europe would be similar targets. He also knew that the codename was Meltdown. If his suspicions were correct, Meltdown could mean only one terrifying thing. What intrigued Bond even more was the codename Anton Murik appeared to have adopted for himself— Warlock.

Jogging around the castle, Bond slowly made up his mind. In spite of what he had said to Lavender, there were two clear choices. Either he could get out now and alert M with the information already in his possession or stay, face the test and glean the full details of the plot. If he could make a good showing, it was possible that Murik would put more trust in him, maybe even reveal everything. That this final course of action was dangerous, Bond did not doubt; yet it was the path he had to take.

Again he thought about Murik's conversation with Franco the night before. Meltdown, the Laird had said, would begin at twelve noon British Summer Time on Thursday. That would be noon in England, one in the afternoon in France and Germany, seven in the morning at the place they called Indian Point Unit Three, and four in the morning at San Onofre Unit One. The operation was to be held strictly to twenty-four hours, and it involved the blackmailing of governments. For the time being he put the other problem, the contract killing by Franco, to one side. In time all things would be made clear.

After eleven circuits Bond returned to his room in the castle. Things now appeared to be stirring throughout the building. The morning noises of a house coming alive.

Bond could smell his own sweat from the harsh exercise, but as he opened the door to his room, his nostrils caught another scent. Somebody else had been there during his absence.

Quickly he checked the cases. They were out of alignment, but the locks showed no sign of having been forced or tampered with in any way. Murik was checking him out—on the spot as well as through his own, possibly dubious, outside sources. Bond made a mental note to look at the Saab at the earliest opportunity—not that anyone would easily be able to penetrate its secrets. The car had certainly looked all right as he jogged past it, parked between Murik's gleaming Rolls and a wicked black BMW M1, which was probably Mary Jane Mashkin's speed.

Returning to his toning up, Bond ran through his usual morning pushups, situps and leg raising. Then he cleared a space in the room and started that magic, dancelike series of elegant, deadly, movements which make up the first *kata*—or formal exercises—of Uechi's style of karate—the *Sanchin* which you see men and women performing in parks and gardens, during the early morning or evening, in the East. Bond's body moved in a smooth, prearranged pattern as he went twice through the routine. By the time he had completed the physical·and mental exercises, Bond's body was soaked in perspiration. He stripped, padded through to the bathroom and showered—first under scalding water, then with an ice-cold spray.

After a good rubdown and shave, he changed into lightweight slacks with a matching beige shirt and cord anorak. He slipped his feet into comfortable Adidas sports shoes. Normally he would have preferred the soft moccasins, but, as a possible confrontation was imminent, Bond thought it best to choose reliable athletic shoes that would not slide or let him down.

He filled the gunmetal cigarette case—making a resolution that he would not smoke until after the test, whatever it might be—and put it in the jacket, together with his Dunhill lighter. The pen alarm was clipped into the inside of the jacket, while Q'ute's version of the Dunhill was deposited in his right-hand trouser pocket.

Quietly he left the room. Passing through the hall, Bond heard voices from the dining room. Breakfast was obviously in progress, but first he had to take a quick look at the Saab.

The car was locked. Perhaps they had not got around to running a full check on it. Certainly, once he was inside, he saw that nothing seemed to have been moved or touched. Slipping the keys into the ignition, Bond started the motor. It fired straight away, and he allowed it to idle for a few seconds. When he switched off, Bond found Donal standing on one side of the car, and the man he recognized from last night as Hamish on the other.

Removing the keys, he put on the wheel lock and activated a switch under the dashboard, then climbed out with a curt "Yes?" to Donal.

"Breakfast is being served in the dining room, Mr. Bond." The butler's face showed no emotion, and Bond assumed the man had about as much sensitivity as a block of stone. He replied that he was just going in. Not looking at either of the men, Bond locked the driver's door and stalked into the house.

Lavender and Mary Jane were both seated at the table when he entered the room, where a sideboard almost groaned with dishes reflecting the old-style expensive life lived by the Laird in his castle. Bond bypassed the eggs—fried and scrambled—bacon, kippers, kedgeree and other delights; choosing only two pieces of dry toast and a large cup of black coffee. Breakfast was his favorite meal, but on this occasion he knew it would be unwise to fill his stomach.

Both Mary Jane and Lavender greeted him with seeming pleasure, and Bond had only just seated himself when Anton Murik came in, dressed, as befitted a Scottish laird, in kilt and tweed jacket, his pugnacious face all smiles. He also seemed pleased to see Bond, and the talk was easy, Lavender giving no sign of what had passed between them during the night. All three appeared to be excited about the Murcaldy Games, Murik

himself particularly bouncy and full of good humor—"It's my favorite
day of the year, Mr. Bond. Even tried to get back here for it whenever I
was out of the country. Landowners and people like myself have a responsibility to tradition. Traditional values mean anything to you, Mr. Bond?"

"Everything." Bond looked straight into the lava of the eyes. "I've
served my country and abide by its traditions."

"Even when it lets you down, Mr. Bond? Or should I call you Major
Bond?" Murik let out a small cackle of laughter.

So the Laird had swallowed the bait: followed up the one clue available—the Saab registration—and got the facts back, as M had arranged.
Bond tried to look puzzled.

"We'll talk later, James Bond." Again the laugh. "If you're able to talk.
I think your breath may be taken away by the Games. It's quite a show."

"Quite a show," echoed Mary Jane, smiling. She had said little during
breakfast, but appeared unable to take her eyes off Bond—an experience
which he found disconcerting, for the look she gave him lay halfway
between one of feminine interest and that of a Roman empress sizing up
a gladiator. There was no hint of the malice she had shown on leaving
his room the previous night.

Bond remarked that things seemed to be starting outside. He was
rewarded by Murik, who launched into a complete and lengthy program
of events that would take place throughout the day. "Almost dawn to dusk.
I must get going. After all, the Laird is the host. You will excuse me, I
trust." He turned at the door. "Oh, Mr. Bond, I would particularly like
to see you at the wrestling. My man Caber is Champion of Glen Murcaldy—that's the equivalent to being the Laird's Champion around here—a
singular honor. He takes challengers at noon sharp. Please be there."

Bond had no time to answer, for the man was gone, almost with a hop,
skip and jump. So that was it—a bout with the giant Caber. Bond turned
to the ladies, trying to be gallant, asking them if he could be their escort.
Lavender said yes, of course, but Mary Jane gave her enigmatic smile,
remarking that she would have to accompany the Laird. He would, she
said, have to "make do" with Lavender. Bond could not decide if the
remark was meant to sound belittling, but Lavender hardly seemed to
notice, rising and asking Bond if he would give her a few minutes to get
ready.

"The child doesn't get much company." Mary Jane slid an arm through
Bond's, in a surprisingly familiar manner. "There aren't many of the right
sort around here, and she's impressionable."

"You make her sound very young and unsophisticated." Bond spoke quietly.

"In many ways she is. I've tried—for Anton's sake of course—but I fear unless a good and understanding man arrives in the area, she'll have to go to London or Paris. She *needs* a good course in sophistication." She giggled. "Perhaps if you please the Laird he'll present her to you as a prize."

Bond gave her a cool, humorless, look.

"Oh come on, I was only joking." She laughed again.

"Look," said Bond, trying to change the subject, "I wonder—do you have a library? I realized last night that I came without any reading matter."

"Of course. I'll take you there before I go out to join the Laird. But what a pity, James, that you won't allow other things to occupy your nights. No hard feelings about *last* night, by the way."

"None for my part," said Bond, puzzled by her friendliness

"Pity," she giggled. Then her expression changed, and he glimpsed the face behind the mask. "For my part there are a lot of feelings. I said you could avoid trouble, but you refused, James, and you'll be sorry. I have suggested a small test at the Games. Anton agrees. In fact he thought it amusing. You will be matched up with Caber at the wrestling, and Caber has his blood up. Given his head, he'd kill you." Another laugh. "And just for giving him a bloody nose. How vain men are. But come, I'll show you the library. You may need it, and a lot of bedrest when Caber's finished with you."

The library backed on to the living room and was decorated in light colors. Three of the high walls were covered with books, and there were library steps on fitted rollers for each wall. The fourth wall contained three large bay windows, each provided with a padded surrounding seat.

It took Bond a few moments to get his bearings and work out how the books were graded—moving the high steps along each wall until he found what he wanted. First, he quickly chose a book to cover his story—snatching one of his old favorites, Eric Ambler's *The Mask of Dimitrios,* from its place among the novels. Then he made for his real quarry: a thick, beautifully bound copy of *Webster's Dictionary,* which he dragged out and placed on a large lectern.

Thumbing the volume to the letter W, Bond ran his finger down the lines of words until he came to Warlock. Rapidly he scanned the entry. It gave the usual definition. "1: One given to black magic: SORCERER, WIZARD. 2: CONJURER." Then Bond's eyes slid up to the derivations, and his heart skipped a beat. "Old English—*wǣrloga,* one that breaks faith, scoundrel, the Devil."

One that breaks faith? Bond wondered. Could that be it? Was Murik having his own unholy joke in choosing Warlock as his name for the direction of a terrorist operation he had planned? Was he, in turn, scheming to break faith with the international terrorists he had hired through Franco? A man so obsessed by his own brilliance as a nuclear physicist, and feeling snubbed and cheated of his triumph, might well be forced to such lengths.

He was replacing the heavy copy of *Webster's* when a sound made him whirl round, his hand moving naturally to the hip, where he would normally be carrying a pistol, in the field; realizing a fraction of a second later that there was no weapon there.

Lavender stood just inside the library door, wearing a pink creation which gave her a cool, poised look. In one hand she carried a large matching hat. As Bond approached, he saw she was pale under the smoothly applied makeup.

She put her finger to her lips. "James, he's putting you up against Caber in the wrestling."

Bond grinned. "I know—the Mashkin told me with great relish, Dilly."

"It's not funny. He's asked me to take you out there. He wants us to mingle. Caber knows, and he's after you. The business last night—apparently some of the lads have been pulling his leg. Did you really nearly break his nose?"

"Gave it a butt in the right place. Made it bleed a bit."

"He'll pound all hell out of you, James. I've seen him in action. He's a rough fighter—knows a lot of tricks. He's got the weight and tremendous strength as well. Making Caber look stupid with a nosebleed could drive him wild with anger."

"Let me worry about Caber, Dilly darling." Bond took hold of her hand and squeezed it. "If you get no other message from me, can you come to my room tonight?"

"I can try."

"With a way to let me through the main gates?"

"You're going to run?"

"Only if I've got the full story, and it's bad enough to take some definite action. I'll do my damnedest to have enough on your guardian and his crew to bring the law—or worse—into this place. If not, then we'll just have to do some more bundling."

"You'll be lucky if you're not just a bundle yourself by the end of the morning."

"I told you—just work out a way for me to get through the gates and leave Caber to me. If not tonight, then tomorrow night will have to do. Okay?"

She replied with a worried nod, and he could feel her body trembling close to his as they went out through the hall and into the sunlight.

The band of a well-known Scottish regiment was playing on the Great Lawn and already the Games were in full swing. Bond thought the village of Murcaldy would be a ghost hamlet today, and certainly there were many people who had obviously made more lengthy journeys to the Murcaldy Games. Murik did not stint his guests on this occasion: there was free food and drink for all and plenty of entertainment. Bond was cynical enough to wonder what price the local people had to pay in service—and silence—to the Laird for this one day of blatantly feudal fun.

Groups of men and women in Highland costume were preparing to dance, while brawny young men were at the far end of the arena indulging in the incredible sports of tossing the caber and hammer throwing.

Several people doffed their bonnets or bowed to Lavender, showing great respect. Bond also noticed that they glanced at him with undisguised suspicion. Out of long habit and caution, he tried to pick out the more dangerous of the Laird's private army—the big young men with watchful eyes, quiet and careful, silent and alert as loyal mafiosi. Of one thing he was sure: there were a lot of them. For the next couple of hours he remained with Lavender, watching with interest the traditional sports and dancing.

Eventually a crowd started to gather around an area at the castle end of the arena, and Bond allowed himself to be led toward it by Lavender, who whispered that this was where her guardian wanted him.

Mats had been laid down, and he saw the little figure of Murik talking to a group of men on the far side, his mane of hair slightly ruffled, but a smile permanently set on the bulldog face. He spotted Bond and waved cheerfully before making his way toward the pair.

"Well, Mr. Bond. My champion is almost ready to take on all comers. Do you feel like facing up to him?"

Bond smiled, pretending the Laird was joking. "I mean it, Bond." The trickling deadly lava was back, deep in the eyes. "I want to see what you're made of. If you do well, there may be much in it for you. Can I announce you as the first competitor?"

Now Bond laughed aloud. "I hardly think I'm his weight, Laird. He'd lay me out with one finger."

Anton Murik's face was set, grim as a tombstone. "That's not the point, Bond. I want to see what stuff you're made of—if you've got the guts to go into a wrestling bout with someone as dangerous as Caber. It's not a question of beating him, but standing up to the man, even avoiding him. Guts, Mr. Bond, that's what I'm looking for. Guts."

Bond smiled once more. "Oh, well," he spoke casually, "that puts a different complexion on it. Yes, Laird, I'll take a bout with your champion."

He heard Lavender's sudden quick intake of breath as Murik gave a tough little grin: "Good man. Good man," and disappeared over the mats to the far side of the arena.

In a moment he was back, this time in the center of the mats, holding up his arms for silence. A hush came over the crowd. The pipes and drums played on in the distance, but for a man of his size the Laird of Murcaldy had a strong, carrying voice. "Friends," he shouted. "As you all know, it's time for the unquestioned Champion of Murcaldy—Champion of the Laird of Murcaldy—to offer himself to anyone who wishes to challenge his right. Give your hands to my Champion, Caber."

Caber emerged from the crowd, among which he had been sitting, hidden from public view.

Bond had only really caught a glimpse of the man on the previous night. Now he seemed even larger and more formidable—well over normal height, his chest roughly the size of a standard barrel, and the biceps standing out like miniature rugby footballs. Yet like many big men in peak condition, the Scot moved with a surefooted, almost silent grace, nodding his large but fine-looking head in answer to the appreciative applause of the crowd.

The Laird was motioning for silence. "Friends, there is one who has come to take up the challenge," he announced. Then, with a dramatic pause, "One from over the border."

A buzz went around the crowd. Even though he had not yet been singled out, Bond could sense the hostility. He felt in his right hand trouser pocket to be certain that what he needed was there. Then he quickly slipped out of his anorak, handing it to Lavender.

"Look after this please, Dilly," he said, grinning.

"James, take care. Last night . . . I wish we . . ." she whispered. Her sentence trailed off as the Laird called his name:

"From over the border. A Mr. James Bond."

Bond sprang on to the mats, holding up his hands against the now angry mutterings of the crowd. "Not altogether from over the border," he cried out. "I'll grant my mother did not come from here, but neither was she a Sassenach, and my father had good blood in his veins—a true Highlander—and I take up the challenge, Caber."

"Well done!" The Laird thrust his head forward in his birdish manner. "Well done, James Bond." Then, quietly to Bond, "I didn't know you had Scottish blood. How splendid."

Bond, well-built and tall as he was, felt like a pygmy next to Caber, who merely smiled at him with the confidence of one who knows he has never been bested. There was only one way to deal with the situation, and Bond knew it—keep away from those hands for as long as possible, stop Caber from getting a deadly lock on him, then move at just the right moment.

The two men squared up, and the Laird asked each one if he was ready. Bond nodded and Caber said, "Aye, Laird, it'll no tak' long."

"Then . . . Wrestle!" Murik shouted, ducking out of the way.

Caber came straight at Bond, who sidestepped, attempting a trip with his ankle as he did so. But the huge Caber was very quick. Before he knew what was happening, Bond felt the man's hands grasp his forearms and he was lifted into the air and unceremoniously thrown, hitting the mats square on his back, the wind knocked from his body.

Caber made a dive for him, but this time Bond fractionally beat him to it—rolling clear so that Caber was forced to handspring back to his feet. He rounded on Bond, coming in fast again. Bond weaved, but it was no good. Caber performed a quick cross-ankle pickup, sending Bond sprawling again.

This time there was no rolling free, for Caber had one arm and a good deal of weight on Bond's right shoulder. At the same time, the giant of a man drew back his right arm. Bond saw the motion and in a split second realized that Caber was playing for keeps. The Scot's fist was balled, ready to strike hard into Bond's face. It was time to use science in all its forms.

Bond's left arm was free, and he just managed to roll his head to one side as Caber's blow came hurtling toward him. The fist grazed his ear and thudded hard, and painfully, into the matting beside his head.

Caber was slightly off-balance, but still holding down Bond's right shoulder. Time to use the left arm, and use it on the area of greatest weakness in all men—even a wrestler as strong as Caber. An instructor had once pointed out to Bond that you do not have to hit hard on what he called "the golden target" to be effective. The little nutbrown instructor's voice was ringing in Bond's ears as he brought the left hand up, fingers pointed in a sharp jab at Caber's groin. As he heard the big man grunt with pain, Bond remembered that the move used to be called the "Ganges Groin Gouge." It worked, particularly when followed up by another, slightly stronger attack at the same target.

Caber grunted again, and Bond felt his shoulder freed as the Scot fell forward, rolling as he did so. Bond backed away. Caber was rising quickly, the pain of those two blows showing in his eyes. It was the moment for Bond to be most alert. He had hurt Caber who, like a wounded animal, was now enraged. That he had been willing to maim and mutilate at the start of the bout was clear to Bond. Now the big man would kill if he had to.

Bond let his right hand drop to the level of his trouser pocket, and, as Caber came in for the attack, Bond launched himself forward in a leg dive, the movement covering his right hand, which slid quickly in and out of the pocket.

He hit Caber's legs, though it was like diving into a wall. The big man hardly wavered, but Bond now had Q'ute's special Dunhill firmly clasped in his hand. He twisted, trying to bring Caber down, but the man just laughed and kicked hard, throwing Bond aside, stretching his arms out and diving for Bond again.

This time Bond's right hand came up as though to ward off the certain pinioning by the giant. His right hand moved across the face of his target, and, as Caber's tree-trunk arms caught his shoulders, so Bond readied the Dunhill.

Q Branch's version of the Dunhill lighter was cunning and efficient. It contained no flint or electronic mechanism to spark a light. Neither was it filled with inflammable liquid, though its contents could be expelled, in four specially measured bursts, by activating the fliptop.

The Dunhill was loaded, under pressure, with a liquid containing a high base of the anesthetic Halothane. One burst of Halothane near the mouth or nose should have the desired effect, for the drug—first produced in the early 1950s—is quick-acting, highly potent, and yet produces no nausea or irritation of the mucous membranes. In Q'ute's own words, "They won't know what hit 'em—before, during or after."

Bond's hand was in exactly the right place to deliver the primary burst, Caber's mouth and nose being less than two inches from the hidden

Dunhill as he flicked the fliptop. As he moved his fingers, so Bond prepared to roll clear. He had seen the lighter demonstrated and did not particularly want to get a whiff of the Halothane himself.

Caber simply kept on coming, like an aircraft landing heavily with its undercarriage down but not locked. Bond was just able to glimpse the look of surprise, then the glazing of the big Scot's eyes as he collapsed— Bond rolling clear just in time. As he rolled he grabbed at Caber's now inert arm. To the crowd, the whole thing would look like a clever, or lucky, jab to the face, and Bond had to leave some kind of mark. Twisting Caber's arm, he turned the man over, though it was like trying to move a ton of lead. Once Caber was on his back, Bond dived at the shoulders and delivered two swift blows, using the cutting edge of his hand to the jaw. Caber did not move. Even his head remained rigid.

As he sprang back and away Bond returned Q'ute's useful little toy to his pocket. There were three more shots in that if he needed them.

A hush came over the crowd. Then Murik, looking shaken, was by his side, and two men were leaning over the prostrate Caber. One of them— Malcolm this time—looked up at the Laird. "Yon's oot cold, Laird. Oot cold."

Murik swallowed hard, glancing uncertainly at Bond, who smiled pleasantly. "Shouldn't you announce, or proclaim, or whatever you have to do?" he whispered. "I think I'm your new Champion."

There was a pause lasting only a few seconds. Then the Laird of Murcaldy gave a watery smirk, took a deep breath, and announced, "Ladies. Gentlemen. Friends. People of Murcaldy. You've seen the result of this match. We have a new Champion—I have a new Champion—and you'll treat him with the respect and honor always afforded to the Champions of Murcaldy. I give you, Champion of Murcaldy, Champion of the Laird of Murcaldy—Mr. James Bond."

There was an uncertain silence, then the cheers began, and Bond was lifted shoulder-high to be carried around the Great Lawn with drums beating and the pipes skirling the strains of "Highland Laddie."

David and Goliath, Bond thought, knowing that it would be a good idea to keep out of Caber's way once the former Champion had regained consciousness. He had successfully played David to Caber's Goliath, and Q'ute had provided him with the ultimate in the slingshot syndrome.

Through the crowd he saw Lavender Peacock looking at him with warm admiration in her eyes. Well, if he worked on Murik with speed, Bond might even have all the information he needed to get away before the next morning. Then, once M was alerted, there could even be time to get to know Dilly Peacock really well.

12
___

A CONTRACT, MR. BOND

THOUGH ANTON MURIK had presented the major trophies for the Murcaldy Games, people seemed reluctant to leave. On the Great Lawn, groups still performed reels and strathspeys, while those who had not been good enough to enter the major competitions were now availing themselves of the equipment, and space, to practice or emulate their superiors in the arts.

The tents remained thronged; there would be many a sore head or upset stomach in the glen by the following morning. It was now just past six in the evening, and after an enthusiastic speech amidst much applause and cheers, the Laird had set off in the direction of the castle, motioning Bond to follow him.

Lavender was left with Mary Jane Mashkin, who, Bond noted, was never short of young and well-built male company—a fact that seemed not to upset the Laird. The previous night's experiences still puzzled Bond, who had begun to wonder how genuine the two women were. It could be a case of playing the hard and soft roles, as in a classic interrogation. Yet of the two, he would rather have Lavender on his side.

Murik led Bond through the hall, past the main staircase, pushing open a set of swing doors that led to a corridor, blocked at the far end by the great dividing line between old-style servants and their masters—the green baize door.

The Laird stopped halfway down the corridor, bringing out the ever-present keys—this time from his sporran—to unlock a solid oak door strengthened with steel grilles. Bond followed him down a wide flight of stone stairs. Tiny guide lights gleamed, throwing vague shadows in the darkness. Halfway down, Murik turned toward him. With his mane of white hair, against the face in darkness, the visage took on the appearance of a negative. When he spoke the Laird's voice echoed eerily. "You've already seen my inner sanctum. We're going to the most interesting part of the castle this time. The oldest remaining relic of my heritage. Now you are my Champion, Mr. Bond, you should know of it."

The air smelled dank, and the stone stairs seemed endless, descending deeper and deeper underground until they came out into a flagged open space. Murik reached out to a switch hidden in the wall and the place was suddenly flooded with light. Huge arches supported the vaulted ceiling, which Bond thought must be as old as the original castle. There were two more doors, one on each side of the flagged space, while ahead of them another narrower passage continued. Murik nodded, "That way leads to the old dungeons." His jowl moved in a twitching smile. "They are occasionally useful. To our right, a room which I do not like using. The old torture chamber." He pushed open the door and Bond followed him in,

At one end of the room Bond identified a rack, bolts and chains set into the walls, a flogging frame, brazier, and all the old and sinister instruments—from whips and branding irons to pincers and gouges. Murik pointed out other devices: "You see, Mr. Bond, all the old Scottish pleasures—the thumbikins and pilniewinks, and, of course, the boots. Very nasty things, the boots. Having your feet gradually crushed with wedges is not the way to ward off fallen arches."

"Nor deal with your corns." Bond shuddered in spite of the lightheartedness. In his time, he had suffered much physical torture, and its instruments were not unknown to him. Yet when he looked toward the far end of the room his blood ran cold. The walls there were tiled in white, and in the center was an operating table. Cabinets along the far wall were of modern design, and Bond guessed they would contain more terrifying instruments than the brutal weapons of pain—hypodermics and drugs to send the mind reeling to the very edge of madness, and possibly even the means of inflicting agony through electrodes attached to the most sensitive areas of a man or woman. A man, well-trained, might withstand the exquisite pain that could be inflicted by the crude implements of torture, but few would keep truth or secrets for long in the more sophisticated part of this, Murik Castle's chamber of horrors.

"Very occasionally this room is put to use, Mr. Bond. Have care. All who serve me are given a guided tour. It usually does the trick, as a salutary warning. You defeated the good Caber, so you automatically serve me. Let your glimpse of this place act as a warning. I demand complete loyalty."

Murik led the way out and across the flagged area to the door facing that of the torture chamber. He turned, smiling before he opened the door. "My operations room."

The contrast was staggering. They were in a long, low, vaulted chamber. Its gray walls were covered with weapons ranging, at the end nearest the door, from artistic and obviously valuable broadswords, rapiers, dirks and knives, through magnificently engraved crossbows decorated with inset stones, to wheellock, snaphance and flintlock pistols and muskets; and finally, on the far wall, there were modern rifles, carbines, pistols and automatic weapons.

"The most valuable part of your collection?" Bond recalled that Murik had already told him the best pieces were elsewhere in the castle.

Murik smiled, and Bond could not resist one gibe. "No thermonuclear devices to bring it right up to date?"

The Laird's face darkened, then cleared into a seraphic smile. "We have no need. The world provides them. They are all around us, sitting there ready and waiting to wreak disaster at the right moment."

Murik reached up, touching a large broadsword. "A *claidheamh mor,*" he said. "A two-handed sword that once belonged to an ancestor of mine." Bond nodded. He was certainly impressed, but his gaze had moved beyond this unique collection of weapons to the far end of the vault which, indeed, looked like some kind of operations room, with its long console desk, computer monitors, radio equipment and a large transparent map of the world covered in chinagraph markings.

Murik motioned him to the console table, gesturing to one of the comfortable leather swivel chairs behind it. He took the other chair himself and gave a throaty laugh. "From here, Mr. Bond, I control the destiny of the world."

Bond, uncertain whether Murik was joking or not, laughed with him. There was an uneasy silence for a moment, giving Bond the opportunity to glance up at the map. Quickly he took in the fact that Indian Point Unit Three and San Onofre Unit One were both plainly marked on the American map. As he turned his gaze back to Anton Murik he knew that another couple of glances would probably give him the names of the targets in Europe. At the moment, however, it took all his willpower to drag his eyes back to the Laird. Don't seem too eager, he told himself, willing relaxation, even disinterest—into his brain.

"You know who I am?" Anton Murik was asking, and Bond replied that he was Dr. Anton Murik, Laird of Murcaldy.

Murik laughed. There was far more to him than that. "I am probably the greatest nuclear physicist who has ever lived," he said in an alarmingly matter-of-fact way.

Nothing like modesty, Bond thought. Aloud he tried to say "Really?" with a convincing gasp.

"Let me tell you . . ." Murik launched into his own version of his brilliant career. Most of what he said corresponded with what Bond already knew, deviating only when the Laird started to talk about his final disagreements with the International Commission. In Murik's version, he had resigned out of protest. "Those who fight for the abolition of nuclear power stations in their present form are right," he said in a voice that had slowly been rising in agitation. "Note, Mr. Bond, I say in *their present form*. They are unsafe. Governments are keeping the truth concerning their potential dangers from the general public. Government agencies have tried, again and again, to muzzle people like me. Now they deserve a lesson. They say that the only way out of the energy crisis is to use nuclear power. They are right—but that power must be made safe. How is electricity made, Mr. Bond?"

"By turning a generator."

"Quite. And the generator is operated usually by a turbine, in turn operated how, Mr. Bond?"

"Water, in hydroelectric plants; boiling water producing steam in other types of plant."

"Good. And the steam is produced through boiling the water, using coal, oil, gas—or the core of a nuclear reactor." He gave another little laugh. "An expensive way to boil water, don't you think? Using nuclear power?"

"I hadn't thought of it like that. It's always struck me as being one of the few sure ways to produce energy and power without using dwindling supplies of oil and fossil fuels."

Murik nodded. "In many ways I agree. I do not go along with Professor Lovins when he says that using nuclear power to boil water is like using a chainsaw to cut butter—though he does have something on his side: wasted heat. No, the problem, Mr. Bond, is one of safety and control. Nuclear reactors, as they now stand throughout the world, put our planet and its people at risk . . ."

"You mean the problem of radioactive waste?"

"No, I'm talking about unavoidable accident. There have already been incidents galore. If you're an intelligent man you must know that: 1952, Chalk River, Ontario; 1955, Idaho Falls; 1957, Windscale, England; '58, Chalk River, Canada; '61, Idaho Falls; 1970, Illinois; '71, Minnesota; '75, Alabama; '76, Vermont. Need I go on? Or should I mention the Kyshtym catastrophe in the U.S.S.R. when an atomic waste dump exploded in the Urals? Spillage, partial fuel meltdown. One day, with the kind of reactors we have at the moment, there will be catastrophe. Yet governments remain silent. The Carter Administration almost admitted it . . ." He rummaged among some papers. "There. 1977 — 'Between now and the year 2000 there *will* be a serious core meltdown of a nuclear reactor, but with proper siting such accidents can be contained.' Contained? Proper siting? Do you realize what a core meltdown means, Mr. Bond?"

"Is that something to do with what they call the China Syndrome? I saw a movie with Jane Fonda . . ." Bond continued to play innocent.

Anton Murik nodded. "A nuclear reactor produces its enormous heat from a core — a controlled chain reaction, and as long as it's controlled all is well. However, if there is a failure in the cooling system — a ruptured pipe, a shattered vessel, the coolant lost — that's it. The core is just left to generate more and more heat, create more and more radioactivity . . ."

"Until it goes off like a bomb?" Despite Anton Murik's fanaticism, Bond found himself absorbed in what the man was saying.

Murik shook his head. "No, not quite like the big bang, but the results are fairly spectacular. One of the great American-born poets wrote, 'This is the way the world ends; not with a bang but a whimper.' The whimper would be a kind of tremor, a rumble, with the earth moving, and one hell of a lot of radioactive particles being released. The core itself would become so hot that nothing could stop it, right through the earth — rock, earth, metal — nothing could stand in its way. Right through to China, Mr. Bond; the Peking Express — and that could happen in any one of the nuclear reactors operating in the world today. The trouble is that *I* could make it safe for them." He gave a long slow smile, then a shrug. "But of course, as usual, the moneymen won't pay. My system is foolproof, but they won't allow me to build it or show them how." He paused again, looking hard at Bond. "Can you blame me, Mr. Bond? I'm going to demonstrate how unsafe the present systems are and at the same time show them just how safe they could be."

Bond shook his head. "No, I wouldn't blame you for doing that if your system *is* as safe as you say."

For a second he thought the Laird of Murcaldy was going to lash out at him.

"What do you mean?" Murik screamed. "What do *you* know, Bond? *If* my system is safe? *If* my system is as safe as *I* say? I'm telling you, I have the only positively one hundred per cent safe nuclear reactor system, and because of grasping economists, because of contracts and profits, because of self-seeking politicians, they've tried to make a laughing stock of me." He seemed to relax, drawing back into his chair.

During the long speeches about nuclear reactors, Bond had managed to steal two more glances at the large map. The American targets were ringed in red chinagraph. Now he had managed to identify the English and French locations. Heysham One and Saint-Laurent-des-Eaux Two. What was this man going to do? Was his brilliance so unhinged that he was prepared to expose governments or organizations he hated by sending suicide terrorists into nuclear reactor sites to manufacture disaster that might affect the entire world? Would his madness carry him that far? Meltdown—of course.

Murik was speaking again. "I have prepared a master plan that will do both of the things I require." He gestured toward the map, giving Bond the opportunity to take another look, his eyes moving unerringly to Germany. There it was, marked in red like the others.

Bond experienced a sinking deep in his stomach when he realized that there were two targets marked in the German area, one in the Federal Republic, the other in the East—in the D.D.R. So, even the Eastern Bloc had not been left out of Anton Murik's plans. In the East it was Nord Two-Two. The site in West Germany could be identified as Esenshamm. Now Bond had them all locked in his brain. The job would be to lead Murik on to reveal the bulk of his Operation Meltdown; though, even without further information, Bond considered the mission complete. If he could get out that night, MI5 would be able to track down and isolate Murik and with luck collar Franco through the American security agencies. Meltdown could be blown, and with it the instigator, Warlock: Anton Murik.

"My little plan will alert the world to the horrific danger that exists through the nuclear plants already built and working." Murik gave another of his chuckles, rising to a full-throated laugh. "It will also provide me with the necessary capital to build my own safe plant and demonstrate to those cretins and profitseekers that it is possible to use nuclear energy without putting the human race at risk."

"How?" Bond asked, convinced that a straightforward question would produce a reflex answer. But Anton Murik, in spite of the hysterical outbursts, was not easily trapped.

"It's a complicated business. But you will play your part, Mr. Bond. Ours was a happy meeting; a pleasant coincidence."

"What sort of part?" Bond dropped his voice, sounding wary.

"There is one essential piece of the operation: to ensure no legal action will be taken against me. It is something that has to be done so that nobody ever knows I have had a part in what will happen. Your job is to kill one man. A contract, Mr. Bond. I am giving you a contract—that's the right terminology, I believe?"

"You think I'll just go out and kill someone—"

"I see no reason for you to be squeamish. From what I gather, you are not a man who values human life very highly. Also, the job pays well. According to my information you need around £20,000 quite soon. I'm offering £50,000, which I'm certain is more than your usual basic fee. It should also serve to keep you silent."

"I don't know what you mean," Bond said flatly. Inside there was a mild sensation of elation. Anton Murik had been fed the entire cover story. "I mean, you know nothing about me . . ."

"No?" Murik's eyes clouded, the old dangerous lava flow hot in their depths. "I think you will find I know far more than is comfortable for you."

"How . . . ?"

"There are ways, Mr. Bond. *Major* Bond. Who won the Sword of Honour for your year at Sandhurst?"

"Fellow called Danvers . . ." Bond tried to make it sound spontaneous.

"And you used to call him Desperate Dan, yes?"

Bond allowed his face to take on a puzzled expression. "Yes, but . . . ?"

"And you went into the Guards, like your father before you, like the late Colonel Archie Bond? Correct?"

Bond nodded silently.

"You see, James Bond, I have my informants. I know about your career. I also know about your heroism. I have details of the great courage you displayed while assigned to the SAS. . . ."

"That's classified information!" Bond blurted out.

Murik nodded, unconcerned. "Like the name of all officers seconded to the Special Air Service—yes. But *I* know. Just as I am up to date with your failures: how they allowed you to resign rather than face a court martial after that unfortunate business with the Mess funds; how you have lived by your wits and skill ever since. I have details of the small jobs you have performed in Third World countries, and I also have a record of the unpleasant gambling gentlemen who would like to get their hands on either you or the £20,000 you owe them."

Bond allowed his shoulders to slump forward, as though he had been defeated by some clever policeman. "Okay," he said softly, "but how do you know all this about me?"

"By wits and weapons, James Bond—that's how you've lived since the Army let you go," Murik went on, ignoring the question. "Apart from mercenary engagements, I can make an informed guess concerning the contract killings you've performed."

M had certainly placed the information well. Bond wondered exactly how Murik's informants had been manipulated as channels for Bond's mythical past. He sat up, his face impassive, as though Murik's knowledge of his supposed profession as mercenary and contract artist was something with which he could deal. "Okay," he said again. "I won't deny any of it. Nor am I going to deny that I'm good at my job. It's not a profession of which a man can be proud, but at least I do it very well. How's Caber?" There was a tinge of malice in his voice. Bond had to show Murik he was unafraid.

The Laird of Murcaldy was not smiling. "Bewildered," he said coldly. "Nobody's ever really beaten Caber until today. Yes, you are good, Mr. Bond. If you were not, I wouldn't be offering you a sum of £50,000 for a contract killing now."

"Who's the lucky client?" Bond assumed a straight-forward, professional manner.

"A man called Franco Oliveiro Quesocriado."

"I don't think I've had the pleasure."

"No. Probably not. But at least you'll have heard of him. Hijackings, bombings, hostage-taking: his name is often in the papers—his first name, that is. He is said by the media to be the most wanted international terrorist on the books."

"Ah." Bond opened his mouth, allowing a flicker of recognition to cross his face. "*That* Franco. You're putting out a contract on him?"

Murik nodded.

"How do I find him?"

"By staying close to me. There will be no problems. I shall point you in the right direction. All you have to do is remove him—but not until you're told. You will also do it in a prescribed way. The moment will come, in the operation I am about to set in motion, for Franco to disappear. Vanish. Cease to exist, leaving no trace."

"For that kind of money I might even throw in his birth certificate."

Murik shook his head. In a chilling voice he said, "That has already been taken care of. *You* will be his death certificate." Both men were silent for a moment. Bond looked down and absently fingered a knob on the console in front of him. Then he looked Murik straight in the eye.

"And the money? How shall I receive it?" he inquired firmly.

"You will be free to collect £50,000 in bank notes of any currency of your choosing a week from today at my bank in Zurich. I assure you it is the most respectable bank in Europe. I shall arrange for you to call them from here tomorrow—on the public telephone system, of course. I have no private connection. I shall leave you alone to ascertain the number from the Swiss telephone directory and verify the arrangement personally. But I can allow you only one call to Switzerland."

"Sounds fair enough," Bond said, wildly thinking that here was a heaven-sent opportunity for getting word out to M. But he knew full well the call would be monitored and intercepted the moment he tried any sort of bluff. It was on Bond's lips to ask what would happen should he fail and Franco escape, but he remained silent.

Murik stood up and began to walk calmly down the long room. "I think we should get ready for dinner now, Mr. Bond. Then I would suggest a good rest. It is likely to be an active and taxing week." There was no suggestion that Bond might like to consider the proposal, no polite inquiry as to whether he would accept. Murik had already assumed the terms were agreed and the contract sealed.

Bond started to follow Murik toward the door and as he did so, caught sight of one of the weapons on display in the Laird's collection. On a small shelf display among grenades and other devices stood a cutaway German S-Mine, from the Second World War—a metal cylinder with its long protruding rod housing the trigger. Bond knew the type well, and the display version showed clearly how deadly the mine could be. You buried the thing until only the tip of the slender trigger showed above the ground. An unlucky foot touching the trigger activated the mine, which then leaped about seven feet into the air before exploding to scatter fragments of its steel casing, together with ball bearings loaded into the sides of the device.

The cutaway S-Mine had been so arranged as to show the ball bearings in position, and also separately. A small pile of these steel balls, each about a centimeter in diameter, lay beside the weapon. They looked just the right size for Bond's purpose. Loudly he asked—"You're tied up with this Franco fellow? In this scheme of yours?"

Before Murik had time to stop and reply, Bond had quietly reached out his hand and scooped three of the ball bearings from the display, slipping them into his pocket, out of sight, as Murik turned.

"I am not going into the finer points, Mr. Bond." Murik stood by the exit as Bond caught up with him. "There are some things you should know, I suppose." Murik's voice was low, with a rasp like the cutting edge of a buzz saw. "Yes, friend Franco has contacts among all the major terrorist organizations in the world. He has provided me with six suicide squads to infiltrate half-a-dozen major nuclear power stations. They are fanatics—willing to die for their respective causes if need be. For them, if my plan works, it will mean vast sums of money set at the disposal of their several societies and organizations. Terrorists always need money, Mr. Bond, and if the plan does not work, it is of no consequence—to the suicide squads, at least." He gave another of his unpleasant chuckles before continuing.

"All these men are willing to sit in nuclear control rooms and, if necessary, produce what you have called the China Syndrome. If they have to do that, a very large part of the world will be contaminated, and millions will die from radioactive fallout. I personally do not think it will happen—but that is up to me. I have provided Franco with the means to get these squads into the reactor control rooms. I have, through Franco, trained them so they can carry out destructive actions at my command. At the end of the day there will be a huge ransom. Franco is to get half of the final ransom money, which he will split with the groups according to his prior arrangements. It is up to Franco to come to me in order to collect his share. He has even tried to tell me that the terrorist groups are pressing for assurances that the money will reach them. Lies, of course. It is Franco himself who needs the assurances. He will get none."

They were now back in the main flagged hall. Murik quietly closed the door to the armory.

"You will understand, Mr. Bond, that I do not intend Franco to collect anything. For one thing, he is the only living person who would be able to tie me into this operation—identify me—when the security forces of several countries begin to question the terrorist squads. For the other"—he shrugged lightly—"I need all the money myself in order to build my own reactor, to prove that I am right. It is all for the benefit of mankind, you understand."

Bond fought down the desire to point out the terrible risk that Murik would be taking. The facts of Operation Meltdown were like a kaleidoscope in his mind, but of one thing he was certain: hired and fanatical terrorists are unstable in conditions of stress. However strongly Anton Murik felt about the ultimate threat, the situation might well be out of his control once the terrorist squads were in place.

More than ever, Bond realized that he must make a bid for freedom. They made their way slowly, side by side, to the foot of the stone stairway.

"There is one thing," Bond said calmly, hands clasped behind his back.

"Go on," Murik encouraged him. The two men might have been discussing new staffing arrangements at a respectable company in the City of London.

"If you want Franco removed," Bonds continued politely, "to—ah—protect your little secret and to save on expenses, why should I suppose you'll not have Caber and his men similarly dispose of me as soon as I've done the job? And why not anyway simply put something in Franco's nightcap and get Caber to dump him in the loch?"

Murik stopped in midstride and turned to beam at Bond.

"Very good, Mr. Bond. You show yourself to be the man of wits I'd hoped for. You are right to question my trustworthiness. It would be all too easy for me to arrange matters as you prognosticate. Except, of course, your last suggestion. I would not wish Franco's remains to be discovered on my doorstep."

Murik said this in a tone of mild parental shock. They resumed strolling back to the stairs.

"As to your own well-being," Murik continued, "it is by no means assured by my proposal. One false move would certainly bring about Caber's longed-for revenge. He is a savage man, Mr. Bond, but I can control him. All the same, I should point out that neither could you be sure, had you declined my offer, that I would not be able to make your future life—or death—very unpleasant. The choice remains yours. Even now you can walk out of here freely, without a penny, and spend every minute of the days to come wondering where and when I might catch up with you. No one would believe the cock-and-bull story you might think of imparting to the police—or anyone else. So you have only my word for good faith. But remember, much greater risks lie on my side of the contract."

"You mean," Bond interjected, "that you are gambling on my not taking up with Franco at the last minute, instead of killing him, so as to aid him in collecting a much larger sum even than the generous fee you have suggested for me?"

"Precisely." Murik flicked the switch and the vault was once again plunged in gloom. They mounted the stairs in silence.

13

NIGHTRIDE

THE NAMES OF the six nuclear power stations were in the forefront of Bond's mind for the rest of the evening, running like a looped tape in his head. His knowledge of nuclear power, and the location of reactors throughout the world, was sketchy, though, like his colleagues, he had done a short course on the security of such power plants.

Indian Point Unit Three was somewhere near New York City—he knew that because of a remark made during a seminar. A serious accident at any of the three Indian Point plants could cause grave problems in New York itself. It was the same with San Onofre One, situated a hundred miles or so from Los Angeles. There had been criticism of the siting of that plant so near a possible offshoot of the San Andreas fault, he recalled.

Heysham One was in Lancashire, near the coast, and only recently operational. Saint-Laurent-des-Eaux Two, in France, he knew was in the Orleans area. As for the East and West German reactors—Nord Two-Two, and Esenshamm—Bond had no clues.

At least he had the names, and the knowledge that they were subject to terrorist squad takeover on Thursday. Small squads in the control rooms, the Laird had said. Get out, Bond's experience told him. Get the information to M and leave the rest to the experts. Sir Richard Duggan's boys from MI5 almost certainly had Murik Castle under surveillance, and it would not take long for troops to move in. If they were on the ball, Franco would already be in the FBI's sights in the United States. It should not require much to take him, and if part of Meltdown was already under way, strict security at the target points would mop up the suicide squads.

Bond did not have time to start thinking of the delicate intricacies of Murik's plan. Already there was enough on his mind, and it was essential for him to appear completely relaxed in front of Murik, Mary Jane Mashkin and Lavender Peacock.

The old adage about the best form of defense being attack might not be either tactically or strategically sound on a battlefield, but here, around the Laird of Murcaldy's dinner table, Bond knew it was his only salvation. He drew the talk around to his favorite subject of golf, and took over the conversation, launching into a long and amusing account of a game he had recently played. It was, in fact, a highly embellished description of a round with Bill Tanner, and Bond felt it was perfectly within the interests of the Service to slander M's Chief-of-Staff outrageously.

Even Murik appeared to be amused by the long tale, and Bond was so caught up in the telling that he had to pull himself from the half-fantasy when the ladies withdrew, coming down to earth as he faced Anton Murik alone over the table.

Little passed between the two men except an explicit warning from the Laird, who obviously felt he had already told Bond too much about his plans. As they finally rose, he placed a hand on Bond's arm and said, "Stay alert," the note of command clear in his voice. "We shall probably be leaving here in a day or two, and I shall want you on hand all the time before you go out and earn your money. You understand?"

Bond thought of the old English word *wǣrloga*—one that breaks faith— and knew that, if Murik was going to break faith with desperate men like Franco's terrorists, there would be little likelihood, had Bond really been a contract mercenary, of any money coming his way. Franco's death would undoubtedly be followed quickly by Bond's own demise, whatever Murik said about his good intentions.

As he said goodnight to Murik and the ladies, Bond took heart from Lavender's quick, conspiratorial look, guessing that she would come to his room as soon as the castle was quiet.

Back in the East Guest Room, Bond heard the telltale thud as the electronic lock went on after the door was closed. Murik was not a man to take chances: great care would be required once Lavender arrived.

He now moved with speed, packing only the essential hardware and clothes into the larger case, then laying out other necessary items on the bed: the fake Dunhill, the pen alarm—which he would use to put M on alert once he was clear of the immediate vicinity of Murik Castle—and a small flat object that looked like a television remote control. This last he placed next to the car keys. When the moment came, speed would be essential. He wished now that there had been the opportunity to smuggle the Browning into the castle. He would have felt a small edge of confidence in being armed, for in the clear light of logic he should trust no person in this place, not even Lavender Peacock. But, as far as M was concerned, 007's job was complete—the basic information was to hand and ready to be reported. Maybe the Saab would have to run some kind of gauntlet, but if his luck held and Lavender really was the girl he thought, it would only be a matter of hours before M would have a special unit—maybe the SAS smashing their way into the castle.

Last of all, Bond laid out a pair of dark slacks and a black turtleneck sweater, together with the dullest-colored pair of moccasins he possessed. Then, after placing the three steel ball bearings, filched from Murik's control room, near the door, he showered, changed into the dark clothing, ototohed out on the Sleepcentre, and lit a cigarette. Near his right hand lay the last piece of equipment, a wide strip of thick plastic, one of many odds and ends, screwdrivers, wires and such, provided by Q'ute.

Time passed slowly, and Bond occupied himself by working on the remaining pieces of the Meltdown puzzle—should he not get through, it would be best to have some operational diagram in his head.

Six nuclear power stations were to be taken over by small suicide squads. Murik had stressed that the squads were small, and would occupy the control rooms. This probably meant that Anton Murik himself, with his many contacts in the hierarchy of worldwide nuclear power, had been able to supply identification and passes for the terrorist groups.

From what little Bond knew of nuclear power stations, the control rooms were self-sufficient and could be sealed off from the outside world. With desperate and determined men inside, the situation would be tense and fraught with danger.

If Meltdown did happen, and even if troops and police were brought on to the six sites, it would take time to break into those vaultlike rooms. Besides, the authorities would be loath to precipitate matters, particularly if they knew the terrorists were prepared to die—and take a lot of people with them—by cutting off the cooling systems to the nuclear cores.

Logically, Anton Murik would be making demands at some very early point. From what the little man had said, the demands obviously concerned money or valuable convertible items alone. It would be a lot of money, and, if Murik was as shrewd as he seemed, the time limit had to be minimal. Whatever the governments of countries like Britain, the United States, France and Germany had said about never giving in to terrorist blackmail, Meltdown would present them with the gravest dilemma any country had yet faced.

With hostages, aircraft, embassies, and the like, governments could afford to gamble and sit it out—establish a dialogue and find a way to still matters. Yet if this situation arose, the governments would be left with no option. The hostages would consist of large tracts of land, cities, seas, rivers, and millions of people—all caught in a deadly pollution that would be devastating, and could even alter the whole course of the world for decades to come.

It was, Bond decided, the ultimate in blackmail—worse even than the threat of a thermonuclear device hidden in the heart of some great city. For this very real threat meant—technically at least—that six nuclear cores would not only wreck six plants, throwing their radioactive filth over large areas, but also bore their way, gathering heat, through the earth itself—possibly producing radioactive expulsion at other locations on the way, and certainly at the final point of exit.

Anton Murik was thorough. He would have worked out every move, down to the smallest detail, from the takeover by the terrorist squads, and the making of his demands, right down to the collection of the ransom, and the point where Bond would rid him of Franco—and he would rid himself of Bond.

Yet there was still one factor for which Murik had not accounted: the circumstances Bond had considered earlier—the trigger-happy, death-wish uncertainty of any terrorist group under pressure. This thought—above anything else—strengthened Bond's commitment to get out and back to M as quickly as possible.

It was almost one in the morning before he heard the click of the electronic lock. Bond sprang like a cat from the bed, the strip of plastic in one hand, the other scooping up the trio of ball bearings. Gently he pulled back on the door, allowing Lavender to enter the room. Raising a hand, he signaled silence, then slipped one ball bearing into each of the circular bolt housings, softly tapping all three, so that the bearings rolled gently to the far ends of the housings. If Bond's thinking was accurate, the metal bearings would make contact at the bottom of the bolt housings. By rights the "on" lights would be activated in the castle switchboard room. If luck was with them the flicker as Lavender unlocked the door would have gone unnoticed.

Bond then inserted the thick plastic strip over the bolt heads, to prevent them locking back into place. Only then did he partially close the door.

Lavender was still in the dress she had worn at dinner. In one hand she carried what looked like a pocket calculator, and gingerly in the other, one of the dueling pistols, which Bond recognized as coming from the valuable set in the hall.

"Sorry I'm late," she whispered. "They've only just gone to bed. A lot's been happening. Caber came up to the house with some of the men. The Laird's been giving them instructions, Lord knows what about, but Caber's in a fury. I heard them talking in the hall. It's a good thing you're going, James. Caber is threatening to kill you; but I heard Anton say, 'Not yet, Caber, your turn will come.' Have you any idea what's going on?"

"A fair amount, Dilly—enough to call in help. Yes, it *is* serious, I'd be foolish not to tell you that much. While I'm away, I want you to keep to yourself as much as possible. If things get bad, try and hide somewhere—and would you please not point that thing in my direction?" He took the dueling pistol from her.

She told him it was safe—the hammer was down. "I just thought you should have some kind of protection—some weapon—and I know how to load these. Anton showed me years ago. There's a ball in it, and powder, and a percussion cap."

"Just hope it doesn't blow up in my hand if I have to use it." Bond looked with some misgivings at the piece.

Lavender said it was fine. "The Laird tests them regularly—about once a year. He told me once that he shouldn't, but he seems to enjoy it. That one's Monro's pistol, by the way. The man who won."

Bond nodded, trying to hurry her along by asking about the main doors and the best way out. She told him there was a red button high up on the top right-hand side of the main door. "You'll find a small switch just beneath it in the down position. Move it up, and the alarm system'll be disconnected. then just press the button and the main door locks will come off. They'll know in the switchboard room straight away, so you won't have much time. I've checked, and your car's still in the same place outside."

"And that?" Bond pointed to the flat black object.

"The main gates," she told him. They apparently had a permanent guard on the gates, which were also equipped with electronic locks. "Both

Anton and Mary Jane carry these in their cars." She demonstrated that the flat box had two controls, marked Open and Close. The rest was obvious. If you started to press the Open button at around fifty yards from the gates they would unlock and swing back of their own accord. "That's about all the help I can give you."

"It's more than enough, Dilly, darling. Now I'm going to let you have about three minutes to get well clear, and back to your room, before I start. If everything goes to plan, I'll have help here, and there'll be some unmasking to do. I fear your guardian could end up in the slammer for a long time."

"Just take care, James. Dear James." She put her arms around his neck and he kissed her. This time there was no doubt about her intentions as she pushed close to him and their mouths locked. It was no way, Bond considered, to start out on a wild dash to safety. "Take care," she whispered again, and he opened the door—holding the plastic strip in place—wide enough for her to get out.

Bond slipped the remote control for the gates into a hip pocket, then slid the hard barrel of the dueling pistol into his waistband, making sure the hammer was down, and thinking of the dangers he would be running if it wasn't. Next he picked up his car keys and the flat box of his own. This was also a remote operator—one of the many extras provided by Communication Control Systems for the Saab. With this, he could turn on the ignition and have the motor running almost before he was out of the main castle doors; that was unless somebody had wired a bomb to the ignition—the true security reason for having a remote starter anyway.

Taking several deep breaths, Bond clutched the car keys, remote ignition control, and the suitcase in his left hand, leaving the right free. Opening the door, he allowed the thick plastic to fall and pulled the door closed behind him. The bolts shot home, and he waited anxiously to see if the mechanism would jam against the ball bearings. It didn't.

For a few seconds Bond stood in the darkness of the corridor, letting his eyes adjust. Then, slowly, he moved toward the gallery.

A low wattage safety lamp burned at the top of the stairs. Bond stopped, peering down into the hall and along the gallery. The old building creaked twice. Quietly he made his way down the staircase, keeping to the side of the steps, where the wood is always more solidly based and unlikely to make any noise.

Once he got to the hall there was the normal desire to move too fast, an overwhelming need to get it all over. But long discipline made Bond cross to the door at a slow, tiptoe pace. He could see the small panel with the red button and switch quite plainly. Reaching up, he flicked off the alarm and pressed the button. There were three heavy bolts on the main door, and the whole trio clunked back in unison, like a pistol shot. In the night silence of the house it was enough noise to waken the dead, he thought; and, at that very moment, with the door swinging back and the fresh air carrying the unique scent of the gardens and Glen Murcaldy into Bond's nostrils, all the lights went on and a voice told him to put his hands up.

It was Donal. Bond recognized the voice, and judged the butler to be somewhere just to the left of the stair bottom. Trusting his own experience and intuition, Bond's hand grasped the dueling pistol, cocking the hammer as he drew it from his waistband. He whirled round as the end of the barrel came clear.

It was a risky shot, and the pistol made far more noise than he had bargained for, the metal jerking in his hand like a trapped snake and a cloud of white smoke rising from the explosion. But Bond's senses had been accurate. Donal was just where his ears had placed him. A pistol of some kind clattered over the floor as the butler wheeled in a complete circle, clutching his shattered shoulder where the ball had struck and whimpering in a high-pitched squeal, like a terrified animal.

Of this Bond had only a brief and blurred picture, for he was already out of the main door, pressing his own remote ignition control and dropping the dueling pistol so that he could grasp the keys to the Saab. He had the impression of lights coming on and the shadows of running figures rising from the lawns near the great gravel sweep and heading toward the Saab as its motor sprang to life.

Almost dragging the case behind him, Bond sprinted to the car. The motor was ticking over gently as he thrust the key into the door lock. The key turned in the lock and came away as he pulled at the door. Throwing the case into the rear, he slid behind the wheel, slamming the door and flicking down the lock.

The click of the lock came almost at the same moment as one of the shadowy figures closed on the car. It was time to test CCS's special fittings. Working quickly, Bond unlocked the two hidden compartments, threw the Browning onto the ledge above the instrument panel and grasped the spare set of Nitefinder goggles.

There were at least five men around the car now. Even before he had the goggles in place, Bond could see two of them carried what looked like machine pistols, pointing toward him. He thought Caber was there in the background, but he was not going to hang around to find out. One of the men was shouting for him to get out of the car. It was then that Bond hit the tear gas button.

One of the safety devices—standard equipment in the CCS "Supercar," as they call it—consists of tear gas ducts placed near all four wheels. At the press of a button, the gas is expelled, enveloping the car and anyone attempting to assault it.

Bond heard the thud and hiss as the canisters opened up, then saw the effects as the five men began to reel away and the angry white cloud rose around the windows. There was a portable oxygen unit, with masks, within reach, in case the gas penetrated the car or the air ran out, but Bond was more concerned with getting the Nitefinder set around his head, slipping the remote control for the main gates onto his lap and putting some distance between himself and the castle. He snapped on the seat belt, slammed the machine into gear, took off the handbrake. Holding down the footbrake, he slowly pressed the accelerator, building up power. Then, suddenly taking his foot off the brake, Bond let the car shoot forward, skidding wildly on the gravel. Straightening as he gained control, he drove at breakneck speed away from the castle. Through the rearview mirror he could see the men coughing and reeling about, shielding their eyes, bumping into each other, and and one huge figure—it could only be Caber—lunging into their midst as though reaching out for a weapon.

He did not see the flashes, only felt the heavy bumps as a burst of automatic fire hit the rear of the Saab. Best not to be concerned about that: there was enough armor plating and bulletproof glass around him to stop most kinds of weapons. Maybe an antitank gun would have some effect, but certainly not automatic fire.

Bond shifted gears, still with his foot hard on the accelerator. Then, touching the brake, he took the turn in the drive too fast and sent up a great spray of gravel as he slid outwards, before regaining control. There were two more heavy thuds. One of the tires, he thought. No problem there: Dunlop Denovos—puncture and split-proof.

He could see the gates in the distance, and one hand went to the locking device on the gun port built in just below the dash. A turn and slide, and the port was open. Bond removed the old and unauthorized heavy Ruger Super Blackhawk .44 Magnum, pushing it into a spot where he could easily grab the butt.

He changed to third, the gearshift moving with comforting, firm precision. The gates were coming up fast, and Bond's hand now went to the remote control given him by Lavender. It flashed through his mind that this might not work and he would have to run at the gates full-tilt, relying on the stressed steel ram bumpers fitted to front and rear. After the experience with Donal and the waiting men in front of the castle, Bond had begun to doubt Lavender and her instructions. So far, the events had all the marks of a setup; so it was with some relief that he saw the gates start to move as he pressed the control button.

Then, from the right, he caught sight of a figure running toward the gates, one arm raised. A small yellow flash, followed by a thud; then another. The gatekeeper was firing at him. Bond went for the Blackhawk and, still keeping his eyes on the opening gates, thrust the muzzle through the gun port, twisting the weapon to the right to allow himself the most extreme field of fire.

The gates, still opening, came up with alarming speed as Bond let off three shots in quick succession, the noise and smell of powder filling the car and battering at his eardrums. The figure of the gatekeeper was now out of sight, but the slowly opening gates were on him. He felt both sides of the Saab scrape against the metal. There was one long ripping sound and he was free, shifting again, and hurtling along the paved road away from the castle.

The speedometer showed well in excess of 85 mph; there was no moon, but the view was clear as day through the Nitefinder. In a moment the Saab would be off the paved road and on to the wide track leading to the village. Time, Bond thought, to give M some warning. He reached for the pen alarm.

At first he imagined it had merely slipped inside his pocket, so often had he checked it. More than thirty seconds passed before he realized that the alarm was missing—dropped outside the castle, or rolling around somewhere inside the Saab. As the stark fact penetrated Bond's mind, he glimpsed the lights of another car, far back toward the castle. Mary Jane's BMW, he would guess, crammed with Caber and the boys, carrying machine pistols and automatics.

Bond had to make up his mind in a matter of seconds. The village would have been alerted by this time. He reasoned that the most dangerous path lay straight ahead. The answer would be to take the Saab around, doubling back, following the track which ran parallel to the castle—the way he had come to reconnoiter the previous night. Without lights, the Saab would be difficult to follow and he figured that, even on the rough track, it would not take long to make the road to Shieldaig. At some point there would be a telephone. A call to the Regent's Park building would bring all hell down upon Murik Castle in a very short time.

The car was bucketing badly along the uneven road, but Bond held his speed. In the mirror, the twin beams of the chase car did not seem to have grown any larger.

Keep the speed up, he thought. Hold her straight and try for a feint at the village, which was now visible, and appeared uncannily close—the bulk of the church and other houses sharp against the sky, standing out like fists of rock. Would they be waiting? Bond tried to picture the junction near the church, with its little wooden signpost. Watch for the signpost and drag the car around.

Without warning a light came on, then another—twin spots from near the church. The reception committee. The spots wavered, then homed in on the Saab like spotlights following the demon king in a pantomime. Bond started to pump the brakes, shifting down, slowing, but still traveling at full speed. Slow just enough to let them think you're going to run straight through. Make them think the spots are affecting vision. That was the godsend about the Nitefinder.

Bond took in a gulp of air as he saw the first flicker of automatic fire from near the church, coming from between the spots. Then the slow, colored balls curved toward him. Tracers—lazy but deadly. Once again he shoved the Blackhawk through the gun port, stood on the brakes and wrenched at the wheel, slewing the car to one side and blasting off two more rounds as he did so. Then one more shot. That was the Blackhawk empty. He reached for the Browning, clawing it from the shelf as he saw, with some elation, that one of the spots had gone out.

Now his subconscious seemed to yell: *Now—drive straight at them!* The Saab kicked and jarred on the rough heather and gorse as Bond spun the wheel to right and left in a violent Z pattern.

The remaining spot lost him, then caught the Saab again as a second burst of tracers began its arc toward him. Bond squeezed the Browning's trigger in two bursts of two, loosing four shots through the gun port as it came into line with the spot. For a second the firing ceased and he realized he was driving flat-out toward the village, ears bursting with the noise and the car filled with the acrid reek of cordite. Get it as near as you can, then skid-turn onto the other road. In his mind he saw the pattern as a hairpin with himself traveling fast along the right-hand pin. He had to negotiate the bend onto the left pin, and there was only one way to do that while still leaving the reception party wondering if he was going straight on—presumably into a second roadblock in the village itself. At top speed it was a dangerous confidence trick. One sudden or misjudged action and he could easily run right out of road or spin the car over onto its back.

He saw the little wooden signpost almost too late. There were figures of people running, as though afraid he would smash into them. Wrenching the wheel and doing an intricate dance between brake and accelerator, Bond went into the violent skid turn. The world seemed to dip and move out of control as the Saab started to slew around, the tires whining, as though screaming because they had lost their grip on the rough surface of track, or heather. For a second, as the car spun sideways on, Bond knew that all four wheels had left the ground, and he had no flying controls. Then he felt a shudder as the wheels took hold of the earth. He spun the wheel to the right, put on full power, in a speedshift, and began to slide, broadside on, toward the signpost.

The car must have torn the post straight out of the ground. There was a teeth-jarring bump as the door hit the sturdy sign. For a second Bond knew he was at a standstill, then he had his foot down again, heaving the wheel to the left. The Saab plunged like a horse, shuddering, shaking its tail violently, then smoothly picked up speed again. Briefly, in the midst of the noise, Bond thought he heard another engine running in time with his own.

He sighed with relief. He was now moving fast up the track which he had followed with such caution the night before. At least the dirt track was minimally smoother than the one he had just negotiated. There was no sign of the following lights, which he had assumed to be the BMW. He shifted up, feeling confidence grow with every second. He needed as much speed as possible to cover the ground parallel to the glen and Murik Castle. He would not be happy until he was completely clear of the castle area, away somewhere to his left, on the far side of the rise.

For reassurance he felt down, touching the butt of the Browning, and at the same time glancing toward the dashboard—something he rarely did. But with the lights off and instruments dimmed right down, the dials were not as clear as normal.

He looked up again and immediately knew he was in trouble. A shape showed through the Nitefinder goggles, above and just ahead. Automatically, he shifted down and pumped the brake. Then the shape moved, splaying a great beam of light across his path and he heard the engine noise he thought he had imagined back at the turn near the church. The helicopter. He had not counted on the helicopter. But there it was, backing away slowly like some animal gently retreating, uncertain of its prey.

Well, if he hit the damned thing it was too bad. Bond did not slow down. Again he reached for the Browning, pushed the barrel through the gun port, pointed upward and fired twice. The helicopter was dangerously low, yet remained directly in front, still backing away. Then, without warning, it lifted and retreated fast. From directly in front of the Saab came a massive flash and boom — like a huge version of the SAS "flashbang" stun grenade. The Saab shook and Bond felt the inertia-reel harness clamp hold of him. Without it he would have been thrown across the car. He slammed a foot onto the brake as he felt, with the intuition of experience, that another grenade would follow the first. Certainly the helicopter was coming forward, and low, again. Bond prepared to haul the wheel over and put power on the moment he saw the chopper alter altitude.

It came just as he expected — the same maneuver, a dipping of the nose, a fast slide up and back. Bond swung the wheel to the right, shifted into second, and allowed his foot gently to increase pressure on the accelerator.

The Saab changed course, going off the track to the right just as the second large "flash-bang" exploded. His mind was just starting to grapple with the strategy he would need to use against the chopper when the Saab began to lift its nose.

With the horrific clarity of a dream over which one has no power, Bond realized what had happened. He had been fool enough to do exactly as the helicopter had wanted. The little metal insect had probably been watching his progress — on radar, or by other means — almost from his moment of escape. The sudden appearance of the machine, dropping its large "flashbangs" in his path, was a lure. They had wanted him to go to the right, and at full speed. Had not Mary Jane Mashkin told him about the digging? A new drainage system? Had he not seen the evidence of it on his visit to this spot?

All this flashed through Bond's head as he applied the car's brakes too late. The nose of the Saab reared up, and he was aware of the Mashkin woman telling him the size and depth of the pit. The wheels clawed at empty air, then the Saab began to drop forward, tipping to one side, bouncing and bumping in a horrible crunching somersault.

In the final moments Bond was buffeted around in his harness, and something, possibly the Blackhawk, caught him on the side of the head. He felt the numbness, but neither fear nor pain as the red mist came in, with ink in its wake, carrying him floating off into its black impenetrable sea.

Out on the track, the lights of the BMW could be seen in the distance as the helicopter slowly settled on the heather. "Got him," said Anton Murik with a smile.

The pilot removed the Nitefinder goggles taken from Bond the previous night. "They work well, these," he said. "Clear as sunlight up to over five hundred feet."

14

HIGH FREQUENCY

THERE WAS A blinding white light. James Bond thought he could hear the noise and for a moment imagined that he was still in the Saab, rolling into the ditch.

"The bloody ditch," Bond muttered.

"I told you it was dug for drainage, James. Fifteen feet deep and over twelve wide. They had to get you out with oxyacetylenc cutters."

Bond screwed up his eyes and looked at the woman now coming into focus. It was Mary Jane Mashkin, standing above him.

"Nothing much wrong with you, James. Just a little bruising."

He tried to get up, but the harness held him tightly. Bond smelled the dampness, and turning his head, he saw where he was—in Murik's white-tiled torture chamber.

They had him strapped down on the operating table, and Mary Jane Mashkin stood beside him wearing a white coat. She smiled comfortably. Behind her, Bond made out the figures of two men—a couple of the Laird's heavies, their faces sculpted out of clay and no expression in their eyes.

"Well." Bond tried to sound bright. "I don't feel too bad. If you say I'm okay, why don't you let me get up?"

Anton Murik's voice came soft, and close, in his ear. "I think you have some explaining to do, Mr. Bond. Don't you?"

Bond closed his eyes. "It's getting so a man can't even go out for a night drive without people shooting at him."

"Very witty." Murik sounded anything but amused. "You killed two of my men, Mr. Bond. Making off in secret, with the knowledge you have about my current project, is not the way to keep me as a friend and protector. All previous contracts made with you are canceled. More to the point, I would like to know your real profession; for whom you work; what your present aim in life happens to be. I may add that I know what your immediate future will be: death; because I am going to bring that about unless you tell us the absolute truth."

Bond's head was almost clear now. He concentrated on what was happening, feeling some bruising on his body and a dull ache up the right side of his head. Memory flooded back—the night ride, the helicopter and the trap. He also knew what was going to happen, realizing he would require all possible reserves of physical and mental strength.

Start concentrating now, Bond thought. Aloud, he said, "You know who I am. Bond, James, 259057, Major, retired."

"So," Murik purred, "you accept work from me and then try to blast yourself out of Murik Castle and the glen. It does not add up, Major Bond. If you *are* Major Bond—I have people working on that, but I think we'll probably get to the truth faster than they will."

"Got jumpy," Bond said, trying to sound tired and casual. In fact he was fully aware now, his mind getting sharper every minute, though he knew the stress of that drive would already have played havoc with him. The fatigue had to be just under the surface.

"Jumpy?" Murik sneered.

"Fear is not an unknown failing in men." Concentrate, Bond thought— get your head into the right condition now. "I got frightened. Just thought I would slip away until it was all over."

Murik said he really thought they should have the truth. "There is so little time left." Bond saw him nod toward Mary Jane, who stepped forward, closer to the table.

"I'm a trained psychiatrist," Mary Jane Mashkin drawled. "And I have one or two other specialties."

Like being a nuclear physicist, Bond thought. Anton Murik's partner in nuclear crime. "Proper little Jill-of-all-trades," he muttered.

"Don't be frivolous, Bond. She can make it very unpleasant for you." Murik leered at him. "And you should know that we've been through your luggage. As a mercenary and retired army man, you carry very sophisticated devices with you. Interesting." He again nodded toward Mary Jane Mashkin, who rolled up Bond's sleeves. He tried to move against the restraining straps, but it was no good. His mind began to panic, casting around for the right point of mental focus, trying to remember the rules for what one did in a situation like this. A thousand bats winged their way around his brain in confusion.

Bond felt the swab being dabbed on his arm, just below the bicep: damp, cool, the hint of its smell reaching his nostrils. The panic died, Bond conquering the immediate fear of what would come. Focus. Focus. Bond; James. 259057, Major, retired. Straight. Now what should he keep in the forefront of his consciousness? Nuclear power: Murik's own subject. Bond had only an elementary knowledge, but he concentrated on the reading M had made him do before going on this mission. Blot out M. See the book. Just the book with its drawings, diagrams and text. Bond, James. 259057, Major, retired. If they were to use the conventional truth drugs on him, Bond had to remain alert. There were desperate mental countermeasures to interrogation by drugs, and 007 had been through the whole unpleasant course at what they called the Sadist School near Camberley.

"A little Mozart, I think," Murik's voice called, away from the table. Mary Jane Mashkin moved, and Bond winced slightly as he felt the hypodermic needle slide into his arm. What would they use? In their situation what would he use? Soap—the Service name for Sodium Thiopental? No, they would risk a more toxic substance. The book: just keep the pages turning. Lazy. The pages. Probably a nice mix— Scopolamine with morphine: twilight sleep, like having a baby.

Bond felt his whole body slowly become independent of his mind. The book. See the pages. Far away an orchestra played. Violins, strings and woodwinds, a pleasant sound with a military rhythm to it; then a piano—all far away.

Walking in a park on a summer Sunday, with the band playing. Lavender was there. Holding hands. Children laughing; the ducks and water fowl. People. Yet he felt alone, even in the crowd, with Lavender—with Dilly—as they floated over the grass near the Mall to the sound of music.

Bond heaved his mind back. Bond, James. What was the next bit? The band played on, and he could smell the expensive fragrance of Lavender's scent as she held his hand tightly. No. No. Bond, James. 259057. Major, retired. The book. Nuclear power plants derive their energy from the splitting—or fission—of the uranium isotope U-235.

The music had changed, more gently, like Dilly's touch on his hand.

Drag your mind back, James. Back. Don't let go. Then Lavender was asking the questions. "James, what do you really do for a living?"

"Bond, James. 259057. Major, retired." He knew that he should not have trusted her.

"Oh, not that rubbish, James, darling. What do you *really* get up to?"

Fight, James. Fight it. Even from outside his body. The echo in his own ears was odd, the speech blurred as he said, "In a nuclear plant, steam is produced by the heat coming from the controlled chain reaction occurring inside the uranium fuel rods within the reactor core . . ." then he was laughing and the band played on.

"You're talking scribble, James. Did your nanny say that when you were little? Talking scribble? You've got something to do with nuclear power, haven't you? Are you from the Atomic Research? The International Commission? Or the International Atomic Energy Agency in Vienna?"

Think, James, there's something very wrong here. Pull yourself up, you're dreaming and it's getting worse. Feel your body; get into your own mind. Be determined. Beat it. "Nuclear power is a very expensive way to boil water." That was what the book said; and there was a diagram next. Fight, James. Do everything they taught you at Camberley.

"Come on, who are you really?" asked Lavender.

"My name . . ." It wasn't Lavender. The other one was asking the questions. Yet he could smell Lavender's scent; but it was the American woman. What was her name? Mary Jane? That was it, Mary Jane Mashkin. Maybe Dilly was straight after all.

In a drowning pall of dark smoke, Bond shouted loudly, "Bond, James. 259057. Major, retired. That what you want to know, Mary Jane? 'Cause that's the truth." He fought hard and stopped there, knowing to go on talking in this floating cloud of uncertainty would lead him into babbling on like a brook. Brook. Babble. Book.

Another voice cut through, loudly. "He's resisting. Increase the dosage."

"You'll kill him. Try rewards."

"Yes."

Bond's body seemed to tilt forward. He was sliding down an invisible slope, gathering speed. Then something was pressed against his ears. Headphones. Music poured in on him. Beautiful liquids that slowed up his descent, soothing him. Lord, he was tired. Sleep? Why not? The voice again—"James Bond?"

"Yes."

"What are your duties?"

"I am . . ." No, James, fight, you silly bugger. "I am 259057 . . . Major, retired . . ."

The soothing music was still there in his head, and the voice snapped back, "I want the truth, not that rubbish. When you don't speak the truth, this will happen—"

Bond probably screamed aloud. The noise filled his head. The terrifying blinding noise, the screech and wail. NO . . . No . . . No . . . As suddenly as it started, the horrific, bursting blaze of sound stopped. It had been counterproductive, for Bond felt the nerve ends of his body again and was quite clear for a few seconds about what was happening. If he gave them evasive answers they would pour the sound into his head again. The sound—high-frequency white noise: waves of sound; waves on a nonuniform pattern. They brought pain, distress, and worse.

The soft music had returned, then the voice again. Murik. Anton Murik, Laird of Murcaldy. Bond had regained enough sense to know that.

"You were sent on a mission, weren't you, Bond?"

"I came here. You invited me." His body started to slip away, the mind floating.

"You made sure I invited you. Who sent you here?"

Slipping. Watch it, James. Air brakes; slow up; slow up. The Saab's wheels clawing at the air and the crashing somersault . . . Then the agony, the screech of noise filling his head, bursting the brain, red in his eyes and the pain sweeping between his ears: great needles of noise against the screams—which he could not hear—and the faces of evil glaring out from the terrible high-pitched cacophony. His brain would burst; the soundwaves rising higher and higher. Then silence, with only the echoes of pain leaving his head the size of a giant balloon: throbbing.

"Who sent you here and what were your instructions?" Sharp. Orders, like the crack of a whip.

No, James. Control. Concentrate. Fight. The book. The page. Bond knew what he was saying, but could not hear it. "A nuclear plant's reactor core is suspended inside a steel vessel with thick walls like a giant pod . . ."

The white noise came in—a flood that swept away his cranium; whining, clawing, scratching, screaming into his very soul. This time it seemed to go on in an endless series of red-hot piercing attacks, not falling or letting up, but rising, enveloping him, filling the brain with agony, bursting at his eardrums, inflating him with its evil.

When it finally stopped, Bond was still screaming, on the very edge of madness, teetering on the precipice of sanity.

"Who sent you, Bond? What were you supposed to do?"

"The twelve-foot-long fuel rods are inside the core . . ."

The madness covered him again, then stopped.

Whatever drug they had used was now ineffective; for the ache in his great, oversized, head had taken over and all Bond knew was the terrible aftermath of the noise.

"Tell me!" commanded Anton Murik.

"Screw you, Murik!" Bond shouted.

"No." He heard Mary Jane shout, so loudly, so close to his ear, that he winced—as though the whole of his hearing and the center of his brain had been branded by the white noise. "You'll get nothing now."

"Then we'll take him along for the ride. Dispose of him after the girl."

Bond found it hard to understand what Murik was saying. The words were there, clear enough, but his concentration was so bad that he seemed incapable of sorting out the meaning. Each word had to be weighed and understood, then the whole put together.

"Get Caber," he heard. Then:

"Quite extraordinary," from the woman. "His mental discipline is amazing. You'd normally expect a man to crack and blurt out everything. He's either for real—an adventurer of some kind who got frightened—or a very clever, tough professional."

"I want him kept safe; and well away from the girl. Does she suspect anything?"

Mary Jane Mashkin was answering. "I don't think so. Went a little white when I told her Mr. Bond had met with an accident. I think the silly bitch imagines she's in love with him."

"Love! What's love?" spat Murik. "Get him out."

"I'd like tae do it fur permanent." It was Caber's voice, and they were Caber's treelike arms that picked Bond from the table. Bond could smell the man close to him. Then the weakness came, suddenly, and he felt the world zoom away from him, as though down the wrong end of a telescope. After that the darkness.

The next time he opened his eyes, Bond seemed to be alone. He lay on a bed that was vaguely familiar, but as soon as he shut his eyes, all consciousness withdrew itself from him again.

Some kind of noise woke him the next time, and it was impossible to know for how long he had slept. He heard his own voice, a croak, asking to be left alone, and, louder, "Just let me rest for a minute and I'll be okay," before he drifted off again. This time into a real dream—not the nightmare from the torture chamber—with music: the band playing light opera overtures and Lavender close to him among the trees of St. James's Park, with a cloudless London sky above them. Then an inbound jet stormed its way overhead, lowering its gear on a final approach to Heathrow, and he woke, clear-headed, with the pain gone.

He was in the East Guest Room, but it had been changed greatly. Everything movable had been taken out—tables, chairs, floor lamps, even the fixtures in the Sleepcentre, on which he was lying, had gone. Bond's final wakening, he realized, had come because of another noise—the clunk of the electronic locks coming off. Caber's bulk filled the doorway. "The Laird's seen fit tae feed ye." He moved back, allowing his henchman, Hamish, to enter, carrying a tray of cold meats and salads, together with a thermos of what turned out to be coffee.

"Very good of him." Bond smiled. "Recovered, have we, Caber?"

"It'll be a gey long time afore ye recover, Bond."

"Might I ask a couple of questions?"

"Ye may ask; whether I answer'll be up tae me."

"Is it morning or evening?"

"Ye daftie, it's evening."

"And what day?"

"Tuesday. Now tak your food. Ye'll no' be bothered agin this night." Caber gave him a look of unconcealed hatred. "But we'll all be off early on the morn's morn." The door closed and the locks thudded into place again.

Bond looked at the food, suddenly realizing he was very hungry. He began to tear into the meal. Tuesday, he thought; and they were leaving in the morning—Wednesday. That meant something. Yes, on Wednesday Franco had a date with someone who was to die. Catwalk . . . palace . . . Majorca . . . high-powered air rifle with a gelatin-covered projectile. Murik's words in the torture chamber came floating back into his head. "Dispose of him after the girl." Could Murik have meant after Lavender, of whom Bond was not entirely sure? The pieces of the Meltdown puzzle floated around in his head for most of the night. He dozed and woke, then dozed again, until dawn, when the door locks came off and Caber threw in a pile of clothes, telling him to get dressed. There would be breakfast in half an hour and he should be ready to leave by eight.

* * *

High up in the building overlooking Regent's Park, M sat at his desk, looking grave and concerned. Bill Tanner was in the room, and "The Opposition" had come calling again in the shape of Sir Richard Duggan.

"When was this?" M had just asked.

"Last night—or early this morning, really. About one-thirty according to our people." Duggan reported some kind of firefight, a car chase and a couple of explosions—a very large form of "flash-bangs," near Murik Castle. "They say your man's car was taken back to the castle this afternoon, and that it looked like a write-off."

M asked if they were still keeping the place under watch.

"Difficult." Duggan looked concerned. "The Laird's got a lot of his staff out—beaters, people like that. They're making it look like some routine job, but they're obviously combing the area."

"And Franco?"

"FBI lost him. Yesterday in New York. Gone to ground."

M allowed himself a few moments' thought, then got up and went to the window, looking down on the evening scene as dusk closed in around them. 007 had been in tight corners before; worse than this. If it were really desperate there would have been some word.

"Your man hasn't made contact; that's what I'm worried about. He was supposed to be in touch with my people. I hope you're not letting him operate on our patch, M."

"You're absolutely certain he didn't follow Franco?"

"Pretty sure."

"Well, this can only mean he's being detained against his will." M allowed for a little harsh logic. 007 knew the score. He would make some kind of contact as soon as it was humanly possible.

"Do you think Special Branch should go in with a warrant?" Duggan was probing.

M whirled around. "On what grounds? That an officer of my Service is missing? That he was sent to take a look at what was going on between the Laird of Murcaldy and an international terrorist? That your boys and girls have been watching his place? That's no way. If Anton Murik is involved in something shady, then it'll come to light soon enough. I would suggest that you try to keep your own teams on watch. I'll deal with the FBI—tell 'em to redouble their efforts and keep a lookout for my man as well. I may even talk to the CIA. Bond has a special relationship with one of their men. No," M said with a note of finality, "no, Duggan, let things lie. I have a lot of confidence in the man I've sent in and I can assure you that if he does start to operate, it will either be to warn your surveillance team or take action out of the country."

When Duggan had gone, M turned to his Chief-of-Staff. "Didn't like the sound of the car being smashed up."

"007's smashed up cars before, sir. All we can do is wait. I'm sure he'll come up with something."

"Well, he's taking his time about it," M snorted. "Just hope he's not loafing around enjoying himself, that's all."

15

GONE AWAY

As HE WAS sitting toward the rear of the aircraft, it was impossible for Bond even to attempt to follow a flight path. Most of the time they had been above layers of cloud; though he was fairly certain that he had caught a glimpse of Paris through a wide gap among the cumulus about an hour after takeoff.

Now, hunched between two of Murik's muscular young men, he watched the wing tilt and saw that it seemed to be resting on sea. Craning forward, Bond tried to get a better view from the executive jet's small window—the horizon tipping over, and the sight of a coastline far away. A flat plain, circled by mountains; pleasure beaches, and a string of white holiday buildings; then, inland, knots of houses, threading roads, a sprawl of marshy-looking land and, for a second only, a larger, old town. Memories flicked through the card index of his mind. He knew that view. He had been here before. Where? They were losing altitude, turning against the mountains, inland. The jagged peaks seemed to wobble too close for comfort. Then the note of the engines changed as the pilot increased their rate of descent.

Lavender sat at a window, forward, hemmed in by one of Murik's private army. The Laird had brought four of his men on board, plus Caber acting as their leader. At this moment Caber's bulk seemed to fill the aisle as he bent forward, taking some instructions from Murik, who had spent the entire flight in a comfortable office area with Mary Jane, situated just behind the flight deck door. Bond had watched them, and there seemed to have been much poring over maps and making of notes. As for Lavender, he had been allowed no contact, though she had looked at him with eyes that seemed to cry out for help—or beg forgiveness. Bond could not make up his mind which.

The journey had started on the dot of eight o'clock, when Caber and his men arrived at the East Guest Room. They were reasonably civil as they led Bond down into the main building, through the servants' quarters to the rear door, where Caber gave instructions for him to be handcuffed— shackled between two men. Outside what was obviously the tradesmen's entrance a small man loitered near a van, which looked as if it had been in service since the 1930s. Faded gold lettering along the sides proclaimed the van belonged to Eric MacKenzie, Baker and Confectioner, Murcaldy.

So. Anton Murik was taking no chances. The baker's van; a classic ploy, for the baker would, presumably, call daily at the castle. Any watchers would regard the visit as normal. Routine was the biggest enemy of surveillance. Simple and effective; the ideal way to remove Bond without drawing any attention. He was dragged quickly to the rear of the van, which was empty, smelling of freshly baked bread, the floor covered with a fine patina of flour.

Caber was the last of Bond's guards to climb in, pulling the doors behind him and locking the catch from the inside. The giant of a man gave a quick order for Bond to stay silent, and the van started up. So the journey began uncomfortably, with Bond squatting on the floor, the flour dust forming patches on his clothes.

It was not difficult to detect that they were making a straightforward journey from the castle to the village, for the direction was plain, and the changes in road surface could be felt in the bumping of the van. Finally it started to slow down, then made a painful right-hand turn as though negotiating a difficult entrance. Eric MacKenzie, if it was he, had problems with the gearbox, and the turn was orchestrated by many grinds and vibrations. Then the van crawled to a stop and the doors were opened.

Caber jumped down, ordering everybody out with a sharp flick of his massive head. The van was parked in a small yard, behind wooden gates. The telltale smell of bread pervaded the atmosphere outside, just as it had done in the van. Bond thought you did not have to be a genius, or Sherlock Holmes, to know they were in MacKenzie's yard, somewhere in the middle of Murcaldy Village.

Parked beside them, facing the wooden gates, was a dark blue Commer security truck with the words Security International stenciled in white on both sides. The Commer looked solid and most secure, with its grilled windows around the driver's cab, the thick doors, reinforced bumpers and heavy panels along the most vulnerable points.

Bond was now bundled into the back of the security truck, Caber and his men moving very quickly, so that he only just caught sight of a driver already in the cab, with a man next to him, riding shotgun.

This time Caber did not get in. The doors closed with a heavy thud, and one of the men to whom Bond was handcuffed operated the bolts on the inside.

There were uncomfortable wooden benches battened to either side of the interior, and Bond was forced onto one of these, still flanked by the personal guards. These well-built, stone-faced young men did not seem inclined to talk, indicating they were under orders to remain silent. Bond admitted to himself that Murik really was good on his security, even ruling out the possibility of their prisoner starting to build some kind of relationship with the guards. When he tried to speak, the young heavy on his left simply slammed an elbow into his ribs, telling him to shut up. There would be no talking.

The journey in the security van lasted for almost six hours. There were no windows in either the sides or the front—connecting with the driver's cab—and it was impossible to see through the small grilled apertures in the rear doors.

All Bond could do was try to calculate the speed and mileage. All sense of direction was lost within the first hour, though he had some idea they were moving even farther north. When they finally stopped, Bond calculated they had come almost two hundred miles—a slow, uncomfortable journey.

It was now nearly three in the afternoon, and when the doors of the truck were unbolted and opened, Bond was surprised to see Caber already waiting for them. A sharp breeze cut into the truck, and Bond felt they were probably on an area of open ground. Again it was impossible to tell, for the rear of the truck had been backed up near to a small concrete building, only a pace or so from a pair of open doors. The view to left and right was screened by the truck's doors, now fully extended. Nobody spoke much, and almost all the orders were given by grunts and sign language—as though Bond were either deaf or mentally deficient.

Inside the concrete building they led him along a narrow passage with, he noted, a slight downward slope. Then into a windowless room where, at last, the handcuffs were removed and the freedom of a washroom was allowed, though this too had no windows, only air vents fitted high, near the ceiling. Food was brought—sandwiches and coffee—and one of the guards remained with him, still impassive, but with his jacket drawn back from time to time so the butt of a snubnosed Smith & Wesson .38 was visible. It looked to Bond like one of his own old favorites, the Centennial Airweight.

From the moment of departure from the castle, Bond's mind hardly left the subject of a possible breakaway. This, however, was no time to try anything—locked away in what seemed to be a very solidly built bunker, in an unknown location, kept close with armed men and the giant Caber. He thought about Caber for a moment, realizing that, if they had been through all his effects, the huge Scot would know the secret of Bond's success in the wrestling match. Caber was going to be a problem, but at least things were moving, and Bond had been heartened by one item of his clothing they had returned to him—his thick leather belt, the secrets of which he had checked, to find they had not been discovered.

In his luggage there were three belts of different design and color, each containing identical items of invaluable assistance. Q Branch had constructed the belts in a manner which made their contents practically undetectable—even under the most advanced Detectorscope, such as the sophisticated J-200 used extensively by Bond's own service. With everything else—watch, wallet and the rest—removed, he at least had this fallback.

Bond sat looking at his guard, giving him the occasional smile, but receiving no reaction. At last he asked the young Scot if he could be allowed a cigarette. The man merely nodded, keeping his eyes on Bond as he withdrew a packet of cigarettes and tossed one towards 007's feet. Bond picked it up and asked for a light. The man threw over some book matches, telling him to light up, then drop the book onto the floor and kick it back. There would be no blazing-matches-in-the-face routine.

At around four o'clock there were noises from above—a helicopter very low over the building, chopping down for a landing. Then, a few minutes later, Caber entered with the other guards. "Ye'll be joining the Laird now." He was ordering Bond, not telling him. "It's only a wee walk, so ye'll not be needing the irons. But I warn ye—any funny business and ye'll be scattered to the four winds." Caber sounded as if he meant every word and would be more than happy to do the scattering personally.

Bond was marched up the passage, between his original guards, and through the door. The security truck had gone, and they were standing on the edge of a small airfield. It was clear now that they had come out of the basement of what must be a control tower.

A couple of Piper Cubs and an Aztec stood nearby. Away to the left Bond saw the helicopter, which he presumed was from Murik Castle. In front of them, at the end of a paved runway, a sleek executive jet shivered as if in anticipation of flight, its motors running on idle. It looked like a very expensive toy—a Grumman Gulfstream, Bond thought—in its glossy cream livery with gold lettering, which read "Aldan Aerospace, Inc." Bond recalled the company's name in the dossier on Anton Murik which M had shown him.

Caber nodded them toward the jet and, as they walked the few yards—at a smart pace—Bond turned his head. The neat board on the side of the control tower read "Aldan Aerospace, Inc. Flying Club: Private."

Anton Murik and Mary Jane Mashkin were already seated, as was Lavender with her guard, when they climbed into the roomy little jet. The pair did not even turn around to look at their captive, who was placed with a guard on either side, as before. A young steward passed down the aisle, fussily checking seatbelts, and it was at this point that Lavender turned to lock eyes with Bond. During the flight she repeated the action several times, on two occasions adding a wan smile.

They had hardly settled down when the door was slammed shut and the aircraft moved, pointing its nose up the runway. Seconds later the twin Rolls-Royce Spey jets growled, then opened their throats, and the aircraft began to roll, rocketing off the runway like a single seat fighter, climbing rapidly into a thin straggle of cloud.

Now they were reaching the end of the journey, with the sun low on the horizon. The mountains were above them, seeming to lower over the bucking aircraft. Bond still peered out, trying to place their location. Then, suddenly, he recognized the long, flat breast of the mountain to their left. The Canigou. No wonder he recognized it, knowing the area as well as he did. Roussillon—that plain circled with mountains, and bordering on the sea, hunched against Spain. They were in France, the Pyrénées Orientales, and the old town he had spotted was the ancient, one-time seat of the Kings of Majorca, Perpignan. He should have spotted the towers that remained of the old wall and the vast fortress which had once been the palace set among the clustered terracotta roofs and narrow streets.

Roussillon? Roussillon Fashions. The blurred and sporadic conversation, overheard after the bug had been dislodged from Murik's desk, came back to Bond. It was down there at the ancient palace, dating from medieval times, when the area had been an independent kingdom, ruled over by the Kings of Majorca, that Franco was to administer death: through a high-powered air rifle on Wednesday night—tonight—the day before Operation Meltdown. The target? Bond knew with fair certainty who the target would be. The situation was altered beyond recognition. Whatever the risk, he must take the first chance, without hesitation. More than at any time during the whole business, Bond had to get free.

Of course. They were on the final approach to Perpignan airport, near the village of Rivesaltes, and only three or four miles from the town itself. Bond had even been here in winter, for the skiing, as well as spending many happy summer days in the area.

The engines flamed out and the little jet bustled along the main runway, slowing and turning to taxi away from the airport buildings, out toward the perimeter of the airfield.

The aircraft turned on its own axis and finally came to a halt, the guard next to Bond placing a firm restraining hand on his arm. The top brass were obviously going to disembark first.

As Murik came level with Bond, he gave a little swooping movement and his bulldog face split into a grin. "I hope you enjoyed the flight, Mr. Bond. We thought it better to have you with us, where we can keep an eye on you during this most important phase. You will be well looked after, and I'll see that you get a ringside seat tomorrow."

Bond did not smile. "A hearty breakfast for the condemned man?" he asked.

"Something like that, Mr. Bond. But what a way to go!"

Mary Jane, following hard on Murik's heels, gave a twisted little smirk. "Should've taken up my offer when the going was good, James." She laughed, not unpleasantly.

Murik gave a chirpy smile.

"We shall see you anon, then," and he was off, doing his little bird hop down to the door.

For the first time Bond was one hundred per cent certain about Lavender. He looked up, giving her a broad, encouraging grin as she passed down the aircraft, her brawny escort's hand clamped hard onto her arm. A flicker of nervousness showed in her eyes, then the warmth returned, as though Bond were willing courage and strength into the girl.

They were parked alongside a huge hangar, with adjacent office buildings, topped by a neon sign that read "Aldan Aerospace (France), Inc." Bond wondered what had prompted Murik to choose this Catalan area—the Rousillon—as his headquarters for this part of Europe. Roussillon Fashioners, for sure, but there had to be some other reason. Bond wondered how much of it concerned Meltdown.

The guards acted like sheepdogs, closing in around Bond, trying to make the walk from the aircraft look as natural as possible. The hangar and offices were no more than a few yards from the perimeter fence of the airport, where a gaggle of ancient Britannias rested, herded together like stuffed geese, each with the legend "European Air Services" running above the long row of oval windows. The fence was low, and broken in a couple of places. Beyond, a railway track with overhead wiring ran straight past; behind that, a major road—the Route Nationale—slashed with cars, moving fast. Going to, or coming from Perpignan, Bond thought; for in this area all roads led to that town.

At full stretch he could be away and through that fence in a matter of thirty seconds. Thirty seconds: he actually considered it as they neared the offices. The muscular Scots around him would be prompt in their reaction. Yet Bond was almost hypnotized by the idea of escaping this way through the fence, should opportunity present itself.

It was to happen sooner than he expected. They were within a few paces of the office doors when, from around the corner, in a flurry of conversation and laughter, there appeared a small group of men—four in the dark blue uniforms of a commercial airline. They were close enough for Bond to make out the letters EAS entwined in gold on their caps. European Air Services. A fragment of English floated from the conversation, then a quick response in French, for the aircrew were accompanied by two young French customs officers—the whole group strolling lazily towards the Brittanias.

Murik and Mary Jane were almost at the office door, accompanied by one of the guards; behind them, Lavender was being led firmly by her guard, and Caber walked alone between her and Bond, still flanked by his two men.

It would be one of his biggest gambles. The odds flashed through his mind: putting everything you owned on the turn of a card; on one number at the roulette table; on the nose of a horse. This time it *would* be everything he owned: life itself. If Murik's men could be so shocked into holding fire or chase, even for a few seconds, he might just do it. In this fraction of time, Bond weighed the chances. Would Murik wish to call attention to himself and his party? Would they risk other people being hurt, killed even? It was a matter of audacity and nerve.

Later, Bond thought the appearance of the train probably made up his mind; the sound of a horn in the distance, and the sight of a long railway train snaking its way along the tracks, about a mile off.

He slowed, dropping back a couple of paces, causing one of the guards to nudge him on. Angrily, Bond shoved the man. "You can stop that," he said very loudly. "I'm not interested in your bloody meeting." Then, looking toward the group of aircrew and customs men, he raised his voice and shouted "Good grief," already taking one step away from the nearest guard, who moved a hand to grab him. Bond was quick. The bet was laid. *Le maximum: faites vos jeux.*

Bond had stepped away and was moving in great long strides, his hand up, toward the group of uniformed men. "Johnny," he shouted. "Johnny Manderson—what the hell are you doing here?"

The uniformed men paused, turning toward him. One smiled broadly; the others looked puzzled.

"Get back here." Caber tried to keep his voice low as he started forward; and Bond heard Murik hiss, *"Get him. For God's sake. Take care."* But by this time Bond had reached the group, his hand stretched out to one of the aircrew, who in turn put out his hand in a reflex action of cordiality, while beginning to say something about a mistake.

"It's good to see you, Johnny." Bond pumped his hand wildly, still talking loudly. Then he pulled the man toward him, spinning around to put him, as a shield, between Murik's people and himself. Caber and two of the guards were advancing warily, hands inside their jackets and, doubtless, on the butts of their weapons. Behind them the others were moving slowly into the building, Murik glancing up, his face a mask.

Bond dropped his voice. "Terribly sorry," he said, grinning. "A little problem about nonpayment of dues. I should watch out for those blokes. Hoods, the lot of them. Must dash."

Using the group of uniformed men for cover, he was off, going flat-out in a low crouch, weaving toward one of the jagged gaps in the fence. There were shouts from behind him, but no shots. Only the sound of pounding feet, and an argument of sorts, between Caber's men and the aircrew and customs officers. Bond dived through the gap, sliding down the small embankment onto the railway track—the train now bearing down on him, its roar shaking the gravel, the sound covering everything else. If there was going to be shooting, it would happen in the next few seconds, before the train reached them.

The big engine was coming from his right—from the direction of Perpignan, he thought. There was no time for further reflection. It was now or never, in front of the train looming above him. Bond chanced it, leaping in two long strides across the track and doubling his body into a ball, rolling as he reached the far side; the engine almost brushing his back as it passed with a great *parp* of its horn.

The horn sounded nothing like that unmistakable *too-too-too-too-toot* of the hunting field, but, for a second, Bond was transported, hearing the noise of hooves heavy on grass, the baying of hounds and the huntsman's horn, "Gone away." He had never cared much for fox hunting, and now—casting himself in the role of the fox—he liked it even less. How the hell did you go to earth in a foreign country with Murik's hounds at your heels?

In an instant Bond was on his feet running down the far bank toward the Route Nationale, his thumb already up in the hitchhiker's position. But luck was still with him. As he reached the edge of the road he saw a small, battered pickup truck pulled into the side. Two men were being dropped off, and there were four others in the back, shouting farewells to their comrades. They looked like farmworkers going home after a long backbreaking day in the vineyards.

"Going into Perpignan?" Bond shouted in French.

The driver, a cigarette stuck unlit in the corner of his mouth, nodded from the window.

"A lift?" Bond asked.

The driver shrugged, and one of the men in the back called for him to jump up. Within seconds they were edging into the traffic, Bond crouched down with the other men—thanking providence for his own facility with the French language. He sneaked a peep toward the airport side of the railway tracks. There was no sign of Caber or the others.

No, Bond thought, they would be running for cars—Murik would be well organized here. His men would already be taking short cuts into Perpignan to head Bond off.

Cars already had their headlights on, as the dusk gathered quickly around them. Bond asked the time, and one of the workmen told him it was after nine, holding out his wrist with pride, to show off a brand new digital watch, explaining it was a gift from his son. "On my saint's day," he said. The digits showed four minutes past nine, and Bond realized that they were in a different time zone, an hour later than British time. "We'll have to move if we're going to see the fun," the man said.

Fun? Bond shrugged, explaining he had just come in on a flight, "with freight." He was very late and had to meet a man in Perpignan.

"All men are in Perpignan tonight. If you can find them," laughed one of the workers.

Bond scowled, asking why. "Something special?"

"Special?" the man laughed. It was Perpignan's night of nights.

"Fête," one explained.

"Vieux Saint Jean," said another.

A third gave a bellow, lifting his arms histrionically: *"La Flamme arrive en Perpignan."*

They all laughed. Bond suddenly remembered that he had been here before for the fête. Every town in the Mediterranean had its own rituals, its battle of flowers, processions, carnivals—usually religious. In Perpignan it was the great feast of St. John; when the whole town was crammed to the gills, and there was dancing in the streets, singing, fireworks, spectacle. The festivities started when bonfires were lit by a flame brought, with Olympian ceremony, by runners from a high point in the Canigou mountain itself. He could not have arrived in this ancient place at a better time. There would be crowd cover until the early hours— with luck, enough breathing space to find a way of making contact with London and M.

16

FÊTE AND FATE

THEY DROPPED HIM off on the corner of the Place de la Résistance, which was already full of people standing shoulder to shoulder, pushing along the pavements. There were plenty of police in evidence, directing traffic, closing off streets, and—presumably—keeping an eye open for troublemakers.

Bond stepped back into the crowd. It was some years since he had been here, and first he had to get his bearings. In the middle of the crush of people, Bond realized, with a sudden stab of fear, that his legs were shaking. Directly in front of him there were three great bonfires ready to be lit. To the left he saw a bridge spanning the well-kept canal, banked here by green lawns and flowers, which runs, above and below ground, through the town—a tributary of the river Têt.

A platform had been built over the bridge and was even now crowded with musicians. A master of ceremonies spoke into an uncertain microphone, telling the crowds about the next *sardana* they would be playing, keeping things going until the flame arrived to ignite both bonfires and excitement. The musicians burst into that music, known to anyone who has passed even briefly through either the French or Spanish Catalan lands: the steady bray of pipe, drum and brass in 6/8 time to which the *sardana* is danced. The groups of dancers, some in traditional costume, others in business suits or jeans and shirts, formed their circles, clasping hands held high, and launched into the light, intricate, foot movements: a dance of peace and joy; a symbol of Catalonia.

On the far side of the bridge, other circles had taken up the dance in front of the towering red Castillet—the old city gateway, still intact, glowing russet in the light from the street lamps; its circular tower and battlements topped by what looked like a minaret.

The crowds began to thicken, and the music thumped on with its hypnotic beat and lilting melodies, the circles of dancers growing wider, or re-forming into smaller groups—young and old, impeccable in their timing, and dancing as though in a trance. It was as if these people were reaching back through the years, linking hands with their past.

Bond thought that if there were to be any future for them—or at least a chance of one—he had better move fast. Telephone London. Which was the best way? Call from a telephone box on the direct dialing international system? For that he would need money. It would have to be quick, for telephone booths—particularly on the Continent—are highly unsafe, and Bond had no desire to be trapped in a glass coffin, or one of those smaller, triangular affairs which would preclude keeping an eye on his rear.

The first move was to lose himself in the swelling throng, which rose and fell like a sea. Above all else, he had to be watchful, for Murik's men could be already among the crowds, their eyes peeled for him. And if they saw him Bond knew what he could expect. Most likely they would use dirks, sliding the instruments of death through his ribs, covered by the crowd, in the middle of the celebrations. There was no point in going to the police—not on a night like this, without identification. They would simply lock him up and perhaps tomorrow, when it was too late, telephone the British Consul.

Bond took a deep breath and began to move through the crowd. It would be best to keep to the fringes, then disappear into a side street.

He had just started to move when a large black Mercedes swept into the Place, only to be halted by a gendarme, who signaled that it should turn back. The road was about to be closed. The driver spoke to the policeman in French, then turned to the occupants of the car. Bond's heart missed a beat. Next to the driver sat Caber, while the three other big Scotsmen were crammed into the rear.

Caber got out, two of the men joining him, while the gendarme made noises suggesting they get the car out of the way as soon as possible.

Bonds tried to shrink back into the crowd as he watched Caber giving orders. The men dispersed—Caber and two of them crossing the Place, the last diving into the crowd a little to Bond's right. The hounds were there, trying to spot him or sniff him into the open. Bond watched the big lad shouldering himself away. Then he moved, taking his time, along the fringe of the crowd, going slowly out of necessity, and because of the density of the shouting, laughing, chattering people.

Bond kept looking back and then scanning the way ahead and across the road. The band had stopped and the master of ceremonies was saying that the Flame, carried from near the summit of the Canigou by teams of young people, was now only a few minutes from its destination. A few minutes, James Bond knew, could mean anything up to half an hour.

The band started up again and the dancers responded. Bond kept to the edge of the crowd, slowly making his way across the now sealed-off road, toward the towering Castillet. He was looking for a street he recalled from previous visits: an ancient square almost entirely covered by tables from the cafés. They should be doing a roaring trade tonight.

He reached the Castillet and saw another bonfire ready and waiting to be lit. A great circle of dancers around it was going through the intricate patterns, slightly out of time to the music, which was distorted on the night air. On the far side of the circle he spotted one of Caber's men turning constantly and searching faces in the throng.

Bond held back, waiting until he was certain the man was looking away from him; then he dodged nimbly through the crowd, sidestepping and pushing, until he found a clear path through the archway of the Castillet itself. He had just passed the café on the far side and was about to cross the road, when he had to leap into a shop doorway. There, walking slowly, scanning both sides of the street, head tilted, as though trying to catch his quarry's scent, was the giant Caber. Bond shrank back into the doorway, holding his breath, willing the Scot not to see him.

After what seemed an age, the giant walked on, still constantly scanning faces with his eyes. Bond edged out of the doorway and continued up the street. He could already see the intersection for which he was searching, marked by the bronze statue of a nude woman who looked unseeing down the wide road to his right. Crossing over through the thinning crowd, Bond arrived at his goal—Perpignan's Loge de Mer, once the great financial center of the town: its Rialto. Indeed, many people felt the street contained many an echo of the glories of Venice—particularly the old Bourse with its gray stone walls, high arched windows and intricate carving. Right on the corner of this building the original weathervane—a beautifully executed galleon—still swung gently, but the Bourse itself like the buildings opposite, had been given over to a different kind of financial transaction, for it was now a café. Here it was hard cash for hard liquor, coffee, soft drinks or beer. The old marble pavement was a litter of tables and chairs and people taking refreshment before joining in the festivities.

Bond walked straight into the corner Bar Tabac and asked for the *toilette*. The bartender, busy filling orders and being harassed by waiters, nodded to the back of the bar where Bond found the door marked with the small male symbol. It was empty, and he went into the first *cabinet,* locking the door behind him and starting work almost before the bolt slid home.

Quickly his hands moved to his belt clasp—a solid, wide U-shaped buckle with a single thick brass spike, normal enough until you twisted hard. The spike moved on a metal screw thread. Six turns released it, revealing a small steel knife blade, razor sharp, within the sheath of the spike. Bond removed the blade, handling it with care, and inserted the cutting edge into an almost invisible hairline crack in the wide U-buckle. With hard downward pressure the buckle came apart, opening on a pair of tiny hinges set at the points where it joined the leather. This was also a casing—for a tiny handle, complete with a thread into which the blade could be screwed. Equipped with this small but finely honed weapon,

Bond pulled the belt from his waistband and began to measure the length. Each section of the double-stitched leather contained a small amount of emergency foreign currency in notes. German in the first two inches, Italian in the next, Dutch in the third . . . the whole belt containing most currencies he might need in Europe. The fourth section was what Bond needed: French francs.

The small, toughened steel blade went through the stitching like a hot knife laid against butter, opening up the two-inch section to reveal a couple of thousand francs in various denominations. Not a fortune—just under two hundred pounds sterling, the way the market was running—but ample for Bond's needs.

He dismantled the knife, fitted it away again, and reassembled the buckle, thrusting the money into his pocket. In the bar he bought a packet of Disque Bleu and a book of matches, for change; then sauntered out into the Place, back along the way he had already come. His target was the post office, where he knew there would be telephone booths. A fast alert to M, then on with the other business as quickly as possible.

Music still thumped out from the other side of the Castillet. He continued to mingle with the crowd, keeping to the right of the circling *sardana* dancers. He crouched slightly, for Murik's man was still in place, his head and eyes roving, pausing from time to time to take in every face in the ever-changing pattern. Bond prepared to push himself into the middle of a group heading in his direction. Then, suddenly, the music stopped. The crowd stilled in anticipation, and the amplifier system crackled into life, the voice of the French announcer coming clear and loud from the hornlike speakers, bunched in little trios on the sides of buildings and in trees.

"My friends"—the announcer could not disguise the great emotion which already cut in waves through the gathered crowds—"the Flame, carried by the brave young people of Perpignan, has arrived. The Flame has arrived in Perpignan."

A great cheer rose from the crowds. Bond looked in the direction of the watcher by the Castillet, who was now searching wildly for signs, not of Bond, but of this great Flame. The fever pitch of excitement had got to everyone.

The loudspeakers rumbled again, and with that odd mixture of farce and sense of occasion which besets local feasts—from the Mediterranean to English country villages—the opening bars of Richard Strauss's *Also Sprach Zarathustra* climbed into the air, shattering and brilliant, associated as it was with the great events of the conquest of space.

As the opening bars died away, so another cheer went up. A group of young girls in short white skirts came running, the crowds parting at their approach. About eight of them, each with an unlit brand held aloft, flanked the girl who carried a great blazing torch. Taking up their positions, the girls waited until the torch was set to a spot in the middle of the bonfire. The tinder took hold and flames began to shoot from the fire, rising on the mild breeze. The girls lowered their own torches, to take flame from the fire before jogging away in the direction of the Castillet entrance.

The crowd started to move, backing off to get a better view. Bond moved with them. It was only a matter of turning to his left and he would be at the post office within minutes.

The bonfires in the Place went up, other groups of girls having jogged down the far side of the canal to do their work. Another roar from the crowd, and the band started up again. Before he knew what was happening, Bond was seized by both hands a girl clinging to each, giggling and laughing at him. In a second, Bond was locked into part of the large circle of *sardana* dancers which was forming spontaneously. Desperately, and with much help from the girls, he tried to follow the steps so as not to draw attention to himself, now an easy target for Caber and his men.

Then, just as suddenly as it started, the *sardana* stopped, all eyes turning towards the Castillet, where the girls, with their blazing brands, occupied the spaces on the battlements, holding the torches high. A rocket sped into the air, showering the sky with clusters of brilliant fire. There followed three more muted explosions, and a great flood of light appeared to rise from the battlements on which the girls stood, their brands flickering, making a breathtaking spectacle. The effect was as though the whole of the Castillet was on fire, gouts of crimson smoke rising from the turrets, battlements, even the minaret; and from this more rockets pierced the darkness of the night, exploding with shattering sound and shooting stars.

Bond at last freed himself from the two girls, looked around carefully, and set off again, pushing and shoving through the wall of people whose eyes could not leave the dazzling spectacle of starshells, rockets and Roman candles.

The entire area around the Castillet was tightly packed with shining faces—old men and women, who probably could remember this fête when it was not done on such a grand scale; children getting their first view of something magical; tourists trying to capture the experience for their home movies; and locals who entered into the spirit of the fête.

Bond saw all these faces—even teenagers aglow and delighted, not blasé, as they might have been in Paris, London or New York. He saw none of the enemy faces and finally pushed through the crowds, walking fast toward the less-populated streets and in the direction he remembered the post office to be.

The noise, music and fireworks were behind him now, and the streets darker. Within a few minutes he recognized the landmark of the Place Arago with its palm trees, shops and attractive bars. On his last visit Bond had often sat at the large café occupying the center. The post office was only a minute away, in a street straight ahead to the left of the canal.

The street was narrow—buildings to his left and trees bordering the canal to the right. At last Bond saw the line of open telephone booths, each dimly lit and empty—a row of gray electronic sentries beside the post office steps. He drove his hand into his pocket, counting out the one franc pieces from his change. Six in all. Just enough to make the call, if the duty officer allowed him to speak without interruption.

Swiftly he dialed the 19-44-1 London prefix, then the number of the Regent's Park building. He had already inserted one of the franc pieces into the slot from which it would be swallowed when contact was made. In the far distance he was aware of the whoosh and crackle of the fireworks, while the music was still audible through the noise. His left ear was filled with clicks and whirrs from the automatic dialing system. Almost holding his breath, Bond heard the sequence complete itself, then the ringing tone and the receiver being lifted.

"Duty watchman. Transworld Exports," came the voice, very clear, on the line.

"007 for M . . ." Bond began, then stopped as he felt the hard steel against his ribs, and a voice said quietly, "Oot fast, or I'll put a bullet into ye."

It was the watcher who had been standing near the Castillet. Bond sighed.

"Fast," the voice repeated. "Put down yon telephone." The man was standing very close, pushed up behind Bond.

Primary rule: never approach a man too close with a pistol. Always keep at least the length of his leg away. Bond felt a twinge of regret for the man as he first turned slowly, his right hand lowering the telephone receiver, then fast, swinging around to the left, away from the pistol barrel, as he brought the receiver of the telephone smashing into the Scot's face. Murik's man actually had time to get one shot away before he went down. The bullet tore through Bond's jacket before ricocheting its way through the telephone booths.

Bond's right foot connected hard with his attacker's face as the man fell. There was a groan, then silence from the figure spreadeagled on the pavement outside the open booth. The blood was quite visible on his face. A telephone, Bond reflected, should be classified as a dangerous weapon. He had probably broken the fellow's nose.

The receiver was wrecked. Bond swore as he rammed it back onto the cradle. He bent over the unconscious figure to pick up the weapon. Cheeky devil, he thought. The gun was Bond's own Browning, obviously retrieved from the Saab.

In the distance, among the noises of the fête, there came the sound of a horn. It could well be a fire engine, but someone might have heard the shot or seen the scuffle. There had to be another place from which to get a message to M. The last people Bond wished to argue with tonight were the *flies*. He pushed the Browning into his waistband, turning the butt hard so that the barrel pointed to the side and not downward, and then set off at a brisk walk, crossing the road and returning in the direction from which he had come.

At the Place Arago he stopped for traffic, looking across the road at an elegant poster prominently displayed on the wall of the large café. It took several seconds for the poster to register: ROUSSILLON HAUTE COU-TURE. GRAND SHOW OF THE NEW ROUSSILLON COLLECTION ON THE NIGHT OF THE FESTIVAL OF OLD ST. JOHN. PALACE OF THE KINGS OF MAJORCA. ELEVEN P.M. There followed a list of impressive prices of admission which made even Bond wince. Eleven—eleven o'clock tonight. He gazed wildly around him. A clock over a jeweler's shop showed it was five minutes past eleven already.

Franco . . . the catwalk . . . air rifle . . . death with a gelatin cap-sule . . . Now. M would have to wait. Bond took a deep breath and started to run, trying to recall from his previous visits the quickest way to the ancient Palace and the easiest clandestine way into it. If he was right, the girl would die very soon. If he was right—and if he did not get there in time to prevent it.

17

DEATH IN MANY FASHIONS

THE PALAIS DES Rois de Majorque stands on the higher ground at the southern part of Perpignan, and is approached through narrow sloping streets. The original Palace was built on a vast knoll, in the eleventh century, and was later walled in with the citadel—which rises to a height of almost three hundred feet and is wide enough at the top to accommodate a two-lane highway. On the inside, the walls dip to what was once the moat, making the whole a near-impregnable fortress.

Bond had visited the Palace several times before, and knew that the approach is made from the Street of the Archers, up flights of zigzagging steps which take the normal sightseer underground, to the main entrance, and then into the large cobbled courtyard. Above the entrance is the King's Gallery, while to the left are apartments closed to the casual visitor. On the right stands the great and impressive Throne Hall, while opposite the entrance runs a cloister with a gallery above it. Behind the cloister stands the lower Queen's Chapel, and above that, off the gallery, the magnificent Royal Chapel, with its series of lancet, equilateral and drop arches.

Above the two chapels the keep climbs upward to a small bell tower. This is the extent of the Palace usually on view to the public. Bond knew, however, that there was a further courtyard behind the cloister, gallery, chapels and keep. This area was still used: the yard itself as a depot for military vehicles and the surrounding buildings as billets for some of the local garrison, the bulk of whom lived below the citadel, in the Caserne Maréchal Joffre.

On his last visit to the area—some three years before—on a skiing holiday in the nearby mountains, Bond had fallen in with a French army captain from the garrison. One night, after a particularly lively après ski session, the gallant captain had suggested drinks in his quarters, which lay within the second courtyard of the Palace. They had driven to Perpignan, and the Frenchman had shown Bond how easy it was to penetrate the barracks by entering through a narrow alley off the Rue Waldeck-Rousseau, and from there follow the transport road which climbed steeply to the top of the citadel. It was not possible to enter the rear courtyard through the main transport gates, but you could squeeze through a tiny gap in the long terrace of living quarters forming the rear side of the courtyard. It was on that night Bond also learned of the archway through the rear courtyard, which leads straight into the main Palace area.

So it was to the barracks, the Caserne Maréchal Joffre, that he was now running as if the plague was at his heels. He knew there was little chance of gaining admittance to the main courtyard by following the normal route. Concerts were held there, and he had few doubts that this was where the Roussillon fashion show was being staged, under bright illuminations, and with the audience seated in the cobbled yard or occupying the windows in the old royal apartments, the King's Gallery, and the gallery in front of the Royal Chapel.

It took nearly fifteen minutes for Bond to find the alley that led into the barracks, then another five before he could start the grueling climb up the dusty, wide transport track. Bond forced himself on—heart pumping, lungs strained and thigh muscles aching from the effort required to move swiftly up the steep gradient.

Above, he could see the burst of light from the main courtyard, while music and applause floated sporadically down on the still air. The fashion show was in full swing.

At last he reached the rear of the buildings that formed the very end of the second courtyard. It took a few minutes to find the gap, and, as he searched Bond was conscious of the height at which he now stood above the town. Far away fireworks still lit up the night in great starbursts of color, shooting comets of blue, gold and red against the clear sky. Squeezing through the gap, he hoped that the bulk of the garrison would be away, down in the town celebrating with the locals on this feast of feasts.

At last Bond stood inside the dimly lit courtyard. Already his eyes were adjusted to the darkness, and he easily took in the simply layout. The large gateway was to his left, with a row of six heavy military trucks standing in line up to its right. Facing the gates in single file and closed up, front to rear, were four armored Creusot-Loire VAB, *transports de troupes,* as though in a readiness position. Few lights came from the barrack blocks which made up three sides of the yard. But Bond had few doubts that the *transport de troupe* crews would be in duty rooms nearby.

Keeping to the shadow of the walls, he moved quickly around two sides of the square, to bring himself close to the final dividing wall which backed on to the main palace. He found the archway, with its passage and, stepping into it, he was able to see up the wide tunnel, the darkness giving way to a picture of color and activity.

If his memory was correct, a small doorway lay to the right of the tunnel. This would take him up a short flight of steps and out on to the gallery in front of the Royal Chapel. He was amazed at the lack of security so far, and could only suppose that Murik had his men posted around the main courtyard or still in the town searching for him. Suddenly, from the shadows, stepped a gendarme, holding up a white-gloved hand and murmuring, *"Monsieur, c'est privé. Avez-vous un billet?"*

"Ah, le billet. Oui." Bond's hand went to his pocket, then swung upward, catching the policeman nearly on the side of the jaw. The man reeled against the wall, a look of surprise in his already glazing eyes, before collapsing in a small heap.

It took a further minute for Bond to remove the officer's pistol, throwing it into the darkness of the tunnel, then to find, and use, the handcuffs, and, finally, gag the man with his own tie. As he left, Bond patted the gendarme's head. *"Bon soir,"* he whispered, *"Dormez bien."*

Within seconds he found the doorway and the short flight of steps leading to the gallery. It was not until he reached the elegantly arched passage that the full realization of his mission's urgency penetrated Bond's consciousness. So far, he had pushed himself on, thinking only of speed and access. Now the lethal nature of matters hit him hard. He was there to save a life and deal with the shadowy Franco—terrorist organizer and unscrupulous killer.

The gallery was lined with people who had obviously paid well for the privilege of viewing the fashion show from this vantage point—even though it allowed standing room only. People stood at the high arched windows of the Throne Hall to his left and at those of the former royal apartments on the right of the courtyard. Across the yard, the King's Gallery was also crowded, and below, in the great yard itself, the show was in full swing. The main entrance, below the King's Gallery, led to a scaffold of carpeted steps, arranged to accommodate a small orchestra. A similarly carpeted catwalk stretched out from directly below where Bond stood, probably starting at the edge of the cloister in front of the Queen's chapel. It ran the length of the courtyard, to end only a short distance from the orchestra, and was flanked by tiered scaffolding rising in wide steps on either side, to give the best-paying customers a good close view—each step being arranged with those small gilt chairs so beloved by the organizers of major fashion shows the world over.

Murik's organization had certainly drawn a full house, all well-heeled and immaculately dressed. Bond caught sight of Murik himself on the first step to the left of the catwalk, sitting, resplendent in a white dinner jacket and maroon bow tie. Next to him was Mary Jane Mashkin, swathed in white silk, a necklace sparkling at her throat.

The setting for the Roussillon show was undoubtedly magnificent. It was brilliantly lit by huge arc lights, and the ancient arches and cobbles glowed soft and warm in tones of gray and red, sandstone and terracotta. The place was almost tangibly steeped in the history of eight hundred years.

The fashion show which Bond was now watching had an ambience that did not match others he had attended. It was a minute or so before he realized that the difference lay in the music. Looking closer, he saw that the musicians comprised a consort, a kind of chamber ensemble, using copies of early, probably fifteenth- or sixteenth-century instruments. James Bond knew little about old instruments, having been a devotee of popular music during his schooldays; yet, as he looked, the shapes and sounds began to take on names, slipping into his mind from long-forgotten lessons. He recognized instruments such as the lute, the viol, the cittern, an early flute, pipes and the tambour. The noise they produced was pleasing enough: simple, dancelike, romantic, with strong texture and melody.

Bond did not have to look further than the catwalk to understand the choice of music for this show. There were six models: three gorgeous black girls and a trio of equally delicious white ones, following each other on to and off the catwalk with amazing speed and precision. As he looked down, Bond saw Lavender just prancing off as another girl reached the far end of the catwalk, and yet another was stepping on, to take Lavender's place. The music was provided to match the dress designs. This year's Roussillon collection had undoubtedly been created to reflect medieval costume and patterns.

The materials were silks, brocades, chiffons and cords, the designs ranging from long-waisted dresses, with wide drooping sleeves, to elaborate costumes incorporating trains and surcoats. There was also a monastic look, with heavy circular collars, wimples and cowls; and off-beat little suits, made up of tunic and tight hose, with long decorated pallia which fell to the ground from the neck or trailed behind the wearer. The colors were dazzling, the varied cuts and shapes enchanting, as they flared, rustled and floated around the models. Bond reflected that these clothes were, like so many collections of *haute couture,* the stuff that dreams were made of, rather than the clothing of everyday life.

Lavender reappeared, whirling to a slow dance, clad in a loose gold creation of multi-layered chiffon, with a short embroidered surcoat dropping ecclesiastically in front and behind. Bond had to use a surge of willpower to drag himself from his reverie before the sights and sounds below took control and plunged him into a kind of hypnotic trance. It must be well after eleven-thirty by now. Somewhere, above or below him, Franco was waiting with a pellet of death, which he intended to use before the fashion show had ended.

Bond's eyes moved carefully over the crowds, up to the roofs, and any other possible vantage point for a marksman. There seemed to be no place for a man to hide. Unless . . . the answer came to him, and he glanced upward, toward the gallery ceiling. Directly behind him lay the Royal Chapel. Above that, the keep rose, topped with the small belltower. Above the keep, he knew, there was a loft that had once served as the ringing chamber and storeroom. The ringing chamber had at least three unglazed windows, or openings. All these looked straight down into the courtyard.

The door to the keep was set into the wall, to the right of the Royal Chapel door, not more than a dozen paces from where he stood. Behind that, a tight stone staircase coiled upward to various landings in the keep, and finally to the ringing chamber itself.

Bond whirled around, toward the Norman arched door, with its long iron hinge-plates and great ring latch. He tried the ring and it moved smoothly, soundless and well oiled. Gently he pulled the door open and stepped through. He was aware of a smell in the darkness—not mustiness, but the scent of oil mixed with an aftershave lotion, possibly Yves Saint Laurent. The stone spiral stairs was narrow and slippery from hundreds of years' usage. Bond started to climb as quietly and quickly as he dared in the darkness. His thigh muscles felt weak now after the exertions of the last half hour or so, but he plodded on silently, cheered by occasional shafts of light at the wider turns in the spiral and on the landings.

Three times he stopped to control his breathing. The last thing he could afford was to reveal his presence by any noise. Even through the thick walls, the sounds from the courtyard floated upward. If the ringing chamber were indeed Franco's hideout, the killer would have to be invested with an extra sense to detect him, unless Bond made some unnecessary sound.

As he neared the top of the climb, Bond felt the sweat trickling from his hairline and down the insides of his arms. Slowly he took out the Browning and slipped off the safety catch.

Holding his breath, he reached the topmost steps, his head just below the aged wooden-planked floor of the chamber. There were five more steps to negotiate to bring his feet level with the floor. Putting all his weight on the right foot, Bond slowly lifted his body so that his eyes came just above floor level.

Franco was at right angles to him, lying in the classic prone position of a marksman. The killer's concentration seemed to be centered completely on the scene below, his eyes close to a sniperscope fitted on top of the powerful Anschütz .22 air rifle. The butt was tucked against his cheek and pressed hard into his shoulder. Franco's finger was on the trigger, ready to fire. Bond could not afford to miss if he fired the Browning. And anyway the rifle could still go off on a reflex action. If Bond jumped the man, he might only precipitate the marksman's deadly shot.

There was no time for further appraisal of the situation. Bond leaped up the remaining steps, calling out softly but sharply, "Franco! Don't shoot!"

The marksman's head swiveled around as Bond heard the dull plop from the air rifle, a sound inaudible to anyone but Franco and Bond, high in the keep. In the same second, on an impulse, Bond flung himself onto the prone figure of Franco, landing with a bone-shattering crash across the marksman's shoulders. In a flash, lying spreadeagled across the terrorist's shoulders, James Bond took in the scene below, looking from Franco's viewpoint down through the rough square opening.

Lavender Peacock was alone in the center of the catwalk, pirouetting in magnificent scarlet which drooped in long folds, like a crimson waterfall, around her body. Her arms were outstretched, her feet moving to a haunting jig played by the consort. Slightly to her left and behind her, Anton Murik sat partly turned in his chair, frozen for a moment, looking towards Mary Jane Mashkin, who had half-risen, one hand at her throat, the other like a claw to her chest. Almost exactly in line with Lavender, she was doubling forward, and, in what seemed like slow motion, she teetered, hovered, and then pitched headlong among the chairs.

Underneath Bond, Franco was cursing and struggling to free himself from 007's grip on the back of his neck. *"Mierda!* I hit the wrong one. You'll . . ."* His voice evaporated in a hiss of air as he let his muscles relax, then arched his back and jerked his legs to dislodge his assailant. Bond was taken by surprise and thrown off, his shoulder thudding against the wall on the far side of the chamber. Franco was on his feet in a second, his hand dropping to his hip and coming away with a small revolver. Bond, winded from the throw, levered himself from the wall and kicked wildly at the terrorist's hand, loosening his hold on the gun. It was enough to send Franco weaving and ducking down the narrow spiral stairs.

The staircase would be a deathtrap for either of them, and no place for a shooting match. Taking air in through his mouth, Bond regained his lost balance and started after the terrorist, glancing quickly down into the courtyard as he went. The music had stopped, and a small huddle of people were gathered around where he had seen Mary Jane fall. He could see Lavender, who had come off the catwalk, and one of Murik's guards, who stood very close to her. Caber was also there, with Murik apparently shouting orders to him. From the main entrance, two white-clad figures came running with a stretcher.

Bond waited at the top of the stairs until he was certain Franco had passed the first landing. Then he began the difficult descent, the Browning held in front of him, ready to fire back, even if one of Franco's bullets caught him in the confined space.

But Franco was being just as careful. He had a head start. Bond could hear him, cautiously going down, pausing at each landing, then quickly negotiating the next spiral.

At last Bond heard the door close below, and took the last section of stairs in a dangerous rush, grabbing at the door, pushing the Browning out of sight and stepping out into the gallery, where a great many people were craning over, or leaving to get down into the courtyard. Franco was just ahead, making for the small flight of steps that would bring him into the archway through which Bond had made his entrance into the Palace. Taking little notice of people around him, Bond went after his quarry. By the time he reached the archway, there was no one to be seen, except the huddled figure of the gendarme, still out cold.

At the far side of the archway, the noise came only from behind. Nothing in front. From the rear courtyard just silence and the shapes of the heavy trucks lined up along the wall near the gate to his far right.

Franco was there though. Bond could almost smell him, lurking in the shadows or behind the line of *transports de troupes,* maybe taking aim at this very moment. The thought quickly sent Bond into the shadow of the wall to his right. Now he must outthink Franco. This man was clever, a survivor, a terrorist who, in his career, had passed through whole dragnets. Did he know of the narrow gap between the buildings on the far side, through which Bond had come? Or did he have another way? Would he wait among the shadows or by the vehicles, sweating it out, knowing that only Murik and his present assailant were aware of his presence?

Slowly Bond began to crab his way along the wall, edging to the right, deciding that Franco would most likely have made for the cover of the vehicles. Eventually the man would have to run a long way, for his contract had gone awry in the most deadly manner. A gelatin capsule, Bond thought. That had been the missile, which reached a low velocity as it hit, and had some thin coating which burst on impact, leaving little or no mark but injecting something—probably untraceable—into the victim's bloodstream. It would have to be very fast-acting, for Mary Jane had collapsed within seconds.

It had been meant for Lavender. Bond had no doubt about that. Now Franco would know that the full might of Murik's private forces would be out to hunt him down, just as they were already in full cry after Bond.

He was getting close to the first truck. If Franco was hidden there he would certainly keep his nerve, holding back a natural desire to be rid of his pursuer by chancing a shot which could only call attention to his position.

But Bond had misread the hunted man. Maybe Franco had been rattled by what had occurred in the ringing chamber. The shot came directly from beside the rearmost *transport de troupes,* a single round, passing like an angry hornet, almost clipping Bond's ear.

Dropping to the ground, Bond rolled toward the trucks parked against the wall, bunching himself up to present only the smallest target and coming to a stop beside the great, heavy rear right wheel of the first truck. He had the Browning up, held in the two-handed grip, pointing toward the flash from the shot.

Once more Bond set himself the task of outthinking his enemy.

Franco would have moved after firing, just as Bond rolled toward the truck, which was only a few yards from the rear-armored *transport de troupes*.

What would he—Bond—do in that situation? The trucks were at right angles to the little line of armored troop carriers facing the gate. Bond thought he would have moved down to the second *transport*, protected by its armor, and then skipped across the gap between the line of *transports de troupes* and the truck behind which Bond was sheltering. If he was right Franco should at this moment be coming around this very truck and trying to take Bond from the rear.

Moving on tiptoe, crouched low, Bond silently crossed the few yards' gap between his truck and the rear *transport de troupes*. Whirling around, he dropped to one knee and waited for Franco's figure to emerge from the cover which he had just relinquished.

This time his thinking was right. Bond heard nothing but saw the shape of the hunted man pressed hard against the hood of the big truck as he carefully felt his way around it, hoping to come up on his opponent from behind.

Bond remained like a statue, the Browning an extension of his arms, held in a vise with both hands and pointing directly toward the shadow that was Franco.

Still Franco's reputation held up. Bond was staking his life on his own stillness, yet the terrorist detected something. With a sudden move, the man dived to the ground, firing twice as he did so, the bullets screeching off the armor plating of the *transport de troupes*.

Bond held his ground. Franco's shots had gone wide, and the target remained in line with the Browning's barrel. Bond fired with steady care: two pairs of shots in quick succession, a count of three between the pairs.

There was no cry or moan. Franco simply reared up like an animal, the head and trunk of his body arching into a bow from the ground, then bending right back as the force of all four shots slewed him in a complete circle, then pushed him back along the ground as though wrenched by an invisible wire: arms, legs and what was left of his head flailing and flopping as a child's doll will bounce when dragged along the floor.

Bond could smell the death—in his head rather than nostrils. Then he became aware of lights coming on, running feet, shouts and activity. He moved, faster and even more silently than before, sprinting toward the minute gap between the far buildings, and so down the sandy track to the Caserne Maréchal Joffre. When he reached the Caserne, Bond slowed down. He was breathing hard. Never run away from an incident, they taught you—just as you should never run after lighting an explosive fuse. Always walk with purpose, as though it were your right to be where you were.

He saw nobody on the way back to the private entrance shown him by the French captain. He stepped with a smile into the Rue Waldeck Rousseau. He was home and dry. The street was empty.

Bond had walked four paces when the piercing whistle came from nearby. For a second he thought it was a police whistle. Then he recognized the human sound—the whistle of a man who has been brought up in the country, the kind of noise one makes to call in hounds, or dogs, or other beasts. Now it brought in the Mercedes, bearing down on him, lights blazing. A pair of steel-like bands took him from the rear, pinioning his arms to his sides and pressing so that pain shot down to his hands and fingers. The Browning dropped to the pavement.

"I suppose ye got Franco, then. But it'll do ye nae bluddy guid for yersel, Bond," Caber whispered in his ear. "The Laird's mor'n a mite upset—and wi' good reason. Ocht man, he's longing tae set his eyes on ye. Just longing for it. I doubt he has some grand plans for ye."

The car came alongside and Caber propelled Bond into the back seat as soon as the door was opened.

18

A WATCHED PLOT

M SAT GRAY-FACED, listening to the tape for the sixth time. "It's him all right." He looked up and Bill Tanner nodded in agreement. M turned to the Duty Officer. "And the number?" he asked.

The telephone equipment at the Regent's Park building was the most sophisticated in the country. Not only were all incoming calls monitored and taped, but a selective printout was immediately available. The printout included both the words spoken and the number from which the call had been dialed.

The Duty Officer shifted in his chair. "It's French. We're sure of that because of the code." He was a young man, in his first year of duty following the four-year training period. He sighed. "As to its origin . . . well . . ."

"Well?" M's eyes flashed angrily.

"You know what it's like, sir. They're cooperating, of course, but at this time of night . . ."

"I know," Bill Tanner cut in. "It *is* tricky, sir. But I'll go off, with your permission, and try to ginger them up."

"You do that, Tanner." M's gray eyes showed no emotion. "At least we're certain it was France?"

The Duty Officer nodded.

"Right." M picked up his red telephone. "Then it's time Duggan's people did something positive. Time for them to go into that damned castle—on suspicion of dirty work or however they want to put it. It's safe enough now."

"I shoulda finished yon man off long ago, Laird." Caber spoke softly. Everyone around the Laird of Murcaldy had become quiet, almost reverent. A death in the family, Bond thought grimly. Would it have been like this if the real target had been hit?

Anton Murik looked shaken—if anything a shade shrunken in height—as he waved Caber away. "I think not." He looked hard at the huge Scot.

"You did as you were bidden—brought him back alive. A quick breaking of the neck or an accurate bullet's really too good for him now, Caber. When the time comes . . ." He gave a thin smile.

They were in a comfortable room, fitted simply with what Bond considered to be Scandinavian furniture—stripped pine desk, table and chairs. There was only one padded and comfortable swivel chair, which was Murik's own preserve.

This time they had taken no chances. In the car, Bond had been immediately handcuffed. Now he sat shackled by wrists and ankles. He knew they were inside the Aldan Aerospace offices at the airport, but there were no windows to this room, which Murik had described as "Spartan, but suitable for our needs." He added that they had at least one very secure room in the place "from which the great Houdini himself could not escape."

The Laird dismissed Caber and sat looking at Bond for a long time. Then he passed a hand over his forehead wearily. "You must forgive me, Mr. Bond. I have been at the hospital, and with the police for some time. Everybody has been most kind."

"The Franco business?" Bond asked.

"In a way." Murik gave a bitter little laugh and repeated, "In a way. You did it then, Bond. Finished off Franco."

"There was no option. Even though you had canceled my contract."

"Yes." The Laird gave a small sigh, almost of regret. "Unhappily you have not only interfered a little early, but caused me great grief. Franco's death is, I gather, being treated simply as some gangland vendetta. They have yet to identify him." He sighed again. "The common flatworm," he muttered. *"Leptoplana tremellaris.* It seems strange that my dear Mary Jane has perished at the hands of the common flatworm. We've spent many years together, Mr. Bond. Now you have been the cause of her death."

Bond asked coolly if Murik would have mourned greatly had the death been that of his intended victim.

"Not in the least," Murik flared. "She is a useless little strumpet. Unnecessary. Mary Jane was a brilliant scientist . . ." He lapsed into silence, as though the death of his mistress and its repercussions had only just made themselves felt. Then he repeated, "The common flatworm."

Bond pressed home on the man's emotional disadvantage, asking what he meant by the common flatworm.

"Killed her." The Laird became matter-of-fact now. "There's no getting away from it, Franco was a clever devil—an organizer of ingenuity and a killer of even great skill. He explained it to me, Bond, after I had arranged things."

Franco, it appeared, had access to scientific work on untraceable poisions. In great detail, as if talking to himself, Murik explained. "For years we've known that a poison produced by the epidermal skin glands of the flatworm brings about cardiac arrest in animals. Very quick. A heart attack. It is only in the last year that an extract removed from the flatworm's skin has been made strong enough to bring about the same reaction in humans. A very small amount will bring on a perfectly natural heart attack in a matter of minutes, or seconds."

Franco had arranged with his tame scientists to prepare a delivery system for the poison: a gelatin capsule of just the right thickness, fired over a specific distance, through a specific weapon, in this case the powerful Anschütz .22 air rifle. The passage of the projectile, both through the barrel and at its maximum velocity during its trajectory, would strip some of the gelatin away, leaving only a very thin layer. "In fact it overshot the calculated distance." For the first time Murik smiled. "Yet still worked. A tiny sting—hardly felt by the recipient—but strong enough to just break the skin and inject the poison into the wound. Enough to produce a heart attack—and death."

Bond asked if the authorities suspected anything. No, not a thing, Murik told him. As far as everyone was concerned, Mary Jane Mashkin had suffered cardiac arrest. "I have the certificate." He patted his pocket. "We shall bury her when Meltdown is complete." As he said it, the Laird's mood changed, as though he had become his old self again. "She was a soldier, killed in action for my cause. It would be wrong to mourn. Now, there are more important things to be done. Really, Mr. Bond, it is a pity we cannot work together. I have to admit some admiration for you. The playacting after our arrival at Perpignan airport was worthy of a professional. But, then, it appears that you *are* a professional of some kind, aren't you?"

"If you say so." Bond was tight-lipped. It must now be well after one in the morning. Already two attempts to beat Anton Murik had failed. Third time lucky—if there was to be a third time, for the sands were trickling out fast. Less than twelve hours to go before the sinister Laird's Meltdown project went into action, with Warlock leading the way.

Murik leaned forward with one of his little pecking movements. Strange, Bond thought, how the man could look so distinguished, with that mane of white hair, yet give the impression of being a bulldog and a bird at one and the same time.

"The man whose face you smashed up in the telephone booth, Mr. Bond." Murik smiled again. "He heard the words you used. I can only presume that you are 007—a code of some kind. Who is M?"

Bond shook his head. "Haven't the foggiest."

"Well, I have." The Laird of Murcaldy leaned further across the desk. "In my time as a nuclear physicist, I too have signed the Official Secrets Act. I have been privy to what the novelists call the secret world. M, if I am correct, is the designation used for the person romantics like to call the head of the British Secret Service."

"Really?" Bond raised his eyebrows. Put your mind into overdrive, he told himself, knowing that, at the very least, the London headquarters would be able to identify the general locality of his telephone call. If they had already done so, Murik and his crew would have been flushed out by now—a depressing thought. He consoled himself with the fact that M would eventually put his finger on Aldan Aerospace. Yet there was no use pretending. It was going to be a damned close-run thing.

Murik was speaking again, and Bond had to pull his attention back to the little man's words. ". . . not much of a message to M, was it? I don't think we can expect too much trouble from that source." He gave a little cough, clearing his throat. "In any case, I am anxious to get Meltdown under way; there's no chance of stopping that chain of events now. Our late, unlamented Franco has seen to that. And my demands will go out the moment I receive information that certain nuclear power stations are in the hands of the departed Franco's fanatical, so-called terrorists."

"Six nuclear reactors, I believe," Bond said smoothly. He must do everything possible to ruffle the calm surface of Murik's confidence.

The bulldog face broke into a radiant smile. "Yes. Six." He sounded pleased, as though he had pulled off a clever trick.

Push him, thought Bond. "Six: one in England, one here in France, one in the Federal Republic of Germany, one in East Germany and two in the United States."

Murik spread his hands. "Clever, James Bond. So you know the locations—just as I know you cannot have passed them on to anyone who matters."

The wretched little man refused to be rattled. But Bond would not give up that easily. Quickly he recited the names of the nuclear plants: "Heysham One; Saint-Laurent-des-Eaux Two; Nord Two-Two; Esenshamm; Indian Point Three, and San Onofre One."

"Excellent. Yes, by the time we leave here, just before one o'clock local time, tomorrow afternoon—noon in England—Franco's hardboiled suicide squads will be preparing their individual assaults . . ."

"Which could go wrong." Bond wanted to say something about Murik's statement that they were leaving, but held his tongue. Maybe the Laird would spill everything without being pressed. Leaving for where? And how would they leave?

"I very much doubt that," Murik chuckled. "Meltdown has been a long time in the making."

"Good preparation or not, the security on those places just about precludes any serious terrorist activity." The conversation had become bizarre. Like a pair of wargamers discussing moves. It had about it a distinct air of unreality.

"From within?" Murik asked with mock surprise. "My dear Bond, you don't think something as important as this has been left to chance. Originally I provided poor Franco with a long list of possible targets. The ones we're going for were chosen because they were the easiest to infiltrate." He slapped the pine desk with the flat of his hand. "They were infiltrated about a year ago. We've had to be very patient. A year can seem a long time, but patience pays off. There are four of Franco's contacts working at each of the targets, four trusted people, there now, at each reactor. They all have skills, and they've proved their loyalty, worked hard, done their jobs. Over the year, each person has managed to reach a position where he or she is beyond reproach, his face is known to the security men—and each one has been most successful in smuggling in the equipment necessary for the task."

"Weapons can sometimes backfire." Bond tried hard not to crease his brow with the worry now nagging at him, opening an empty pit of horror within his mind.

"The weapons are only small things." Murik's eyes again stirred into that unpleasant deep movement—the deadly molten lava which seemed to betray a hint of madness. That he was wholly mad, in his genius, Bond did not doubt. Only a maniac would take the kind of risks this small monster was about to embark upon. "The weapons are needed for one moment only. The men and women, all twenty-four of them, will be on duty in their various plants at the required moment. All have access to the control rooms. Weapons will be used as a last resort only—possibly as a threat. The takeover of the control rooms in all six plants should be quite bloodless. And the staff inside will be freed immediately."

"How well do you know people like that?" Bond kept any hint of feeling out of his voice. Murik now began to look more like a slug than a bulldog, but one could not but have some awe for what was obviously such careful planning.

"I?" Murik looked up with surprise. "I do not know them at all. Only Franco, and he acted on my instructions. Franco, as I've said, was a highly intelligent man. I taught him all the necessary things. In turn he instructed the teams. I do assure you, James Bond, that we even went through each phase with plans—plans of the plants concerned. Nothing has been left to chance. You see, the initial moves in the control rooms will be elementary precautions only. First, the remote switches will be cut. This means that no master control can scram the plants in question."

"Scram?"

"It is a word we use. Scram means the sudden shutdown of a fission reactor. Remote control insertion of the control rods. In all but one of our target reactors there is a central master control covering several reactors. So each squad will first isolate its reactor so that it cannot be rendered safe from the master control."

His smile was as unpleasant and nerve-twitching as the lava look in his eyes. "It would defeat our purpose if the squads did not have complete control over their destinies."

Bond's muscles had gone as rigid as his tightened lips. Tension built steadily through his body. He had gone over the dozen or so possibilities which might defeat the terrorist assaults before they even had a chance to get off the ground. The facts concerning infiltration and the immediate isolation of the target reactors removed a whole range of opportunities.

"And the other thing?"

"Oh." Murik pecked his head forward. "The most obvious one, of course. As they separate themselves from the master control, they will also cut all communication lines to the outside world."

"No contact at all?"

"They won't need contact. That can lead only to a dangerous lack of concentration. We cannot possibly allow any dialogue between the squads and the authorities. They have their orders; the times and details." He gave his humorless smile once more. "They have one, and only one, method of communication. That lies with me. It will be used most sparingly.

"Each group is equipped with a small but immensely high-powered transceiver, developed by one of my own companies. This company. It is the most important item that the teams have smuggled in. And each one is set to a particular frequency. Once they're in and completely isolated, each team will signal one code word, together with an identification. Only one person in the entire world will be able to receive those messages." Smugly he tapped his chest. "Myself. In turn, the groups will be the only people able to receive my message—another code word of course—to inform them to abort their mission. That instruction will be given only when my demands are met in full. And it has to be received by them within twenty-four hours of their messages that the various takeovers have been successful. If they do not receive my abort signal . . ." He gave a sad little gesture with his hands. "If they do not receive it, they'll go ahead—on the dot—with the action. They will cut off the cooling systems to each of their reactors."

Bond's face was set like stone, his eyes locking with those of Anton Murik. "And if they do that, millions of lives will be lost, large parts of the world will be rendered uninhabitable for a long time, there will be huge damage and pollution . . ."

Murik nodded like a Buddha. "It is possible that the *whole* world will suffer despoilment, yes. Yes, Mr. Bond, that is why the governments concerned—and, almost certainly, other governments too—will not allow it to happen. My demands will be met—of that I am one hundred percent sure."

"And how will the world know of your demands?"

"You will see, Bond; you will see. You'll have a ringside seat." He chuckled. "You'll be able to observe everything, from start to finish."

"But . . ."

"And after it is all over." He spread his hands in a gesture meant to convey an inevitability. "Well, Franco had to go at some point. You have done that for me. You see, I could never have let Franco pass any of the ransom money on to his various terrorist organizations, because I need to keep it myself. It is essential that I retain every penny made from this operation in order to bring safety to the world. This is truly a case of the end justifying the means." Murik shifted uncomfortably in his chair, adopting a slightly sad tone as he went on. "Of course, I do feel it a little dishonorable withholding *your* small fee. After all, you did achieve success of a sort, even if not in the way I would have wished. And I have, as I say, rather taken to you, my friend. But then you have from the beginning betrayed my trust in you. And, under the circumstances, I cannot allow you to remain in possession of the facts. However, if you have any next of kin, I am prepared to make a token . . ." Murik's voice tailed away.

"So you'll kill me?"

"Something like that. I had a nice idea originally, but since Mary Jane's death, I think you deserve a longer agony. Surely you would like an exciting end, James Bond?"

"And Lavender?"

Murik hit the table hard, with a balled fist, "She should already be dead, instead of my Mary Jane. But don't worry, Bond, she'll be with you—right up to the very end." A throaty chuckle. "Or right down to the very end."

"You bastard." James Bond spoke quietly, in control of his emotions. "You've already tried to murder your ward, and you'll do it again. Your own ward . . ."

"Who has been a thorn in my side for many years." Murik also spoke with no trace of emotion. "Just as you have turned out to be a thorn over the past few days. My work will continue with no possible disruption, once Miss Lavender Peacock has disappeared."

"Why?" Bond stabbed in the dark. "Why? Because she is the rightful heir to your title, estate and money?"

Anton Murik raised his eyebrows. It was a movement which made the pugnacious face even more repellent. "Astute," he said sharply, uttering the word clearly, in two distinct syllables. "Most astute. There's no harm, I suppose, in your knowing, for there is very little to prove it. Yes, she is the rightful heir. I came to my own position by devious means, you see . . ."

"You mean the business with your grandfather? And then the doubts about your own mother being the rightful wife to your late lamented father?"

For the first time in the whole conversation, Murik looked bewildered, then angry. "How do you know this?" His voice began to rise.

Bond, feeling he was gaining a small ascendency, took his mind back to the moment M had explained the checkered and dubious history of the Muriks. "The business in Sicily? It's common knowledge, Laird. The graves at—where was it?—Caltanissetta? Those of your father and your mother's maid? The facts about that are well enough documented. I should've thought you'd've known. After all, the Lord Lyon King of Arms has been carrying out a very lengthy investigation . . ."

Murik's face twitched, then his voice returned to normal. Even the smile came back. "Ah, maybe. But nothing can be proved."

"Oh, I don't know. Your own mother was your father's maid, wasn't she, Anton?" It was the first time Bond had dared use the familiarity of his Christian name.

Murik nodded. "But I was *his* son."

Once more, Bond stabbed in the dark. "But you had a brother—a half-brother anyway. By your father and his true wife. A brother born at the time of the bandit episode in Sicily, when *your* mother, the maid, was already pregnant. What did he do? Come back to haunt you?"

"He came back with a wife, child, and every possible legal document," snapped Murik.

"And died, with his wife, in an air disaster."

Murik chuckled. "Oh, most certainly. He was what you might call intrepid—a man of many parts. Or at least he was when he died." A further chuckle. "The Sicilians have faults, but they love children. The bandits kept him, trained him, made him one of their own, and then told him the truth—after making sure he had been moderately well educated. Like myself, he was good at waiting. But not so good at judging character. Of course I told him I would relinquish Murcaldy and Murik Castle to him. He believed me. A mad flier. Such a pity. They said it was a fractured fuel line or something; I forget the details."

"But you made certain his wife was with him."

"How could I stop her?"

"Why didn't the child—Lavender—go along?"

Murik's eyes took on a distant look, as though he could see back into the past. "He wanted a new airplane. I encouraged him to buy it. After all, he was inheriting the money. He actually flew it into the glen—only a light thing. Wanted to give it a good test the next day, show it off to his wife and the child. I was not there, of course. I had to go to Edinburgh to see the lawyers about relinquishing my title. They had to peruse the documents. The child was taken ill; with a colic, as I remember it. They said it was terrible. You know, he avoided crashing into the castle by a matter of feet. Very brave. They both died instantly. At the time, everybody said the infant had a lucky escape."

Bond nodded. "You had to get back quickly, so the lawyers never saw the documents?"

Murik shook his head, in mock sadness. "No, they did not see them. Nobody's seen them. They lie safe in the castle, where nobody will find them. But they'll not be needed. Not after tomorrow. So now you know.

And if you've been doing a little work on behalf of the Lord Lyon King of Arms, he's out of luck. Just as you and Lavender have run out of luck—and time." His hand reached for a button by the telephone. "We all need a little rest. Tomorrow will be quite a day—or today, I should say, for it is very late, almost three in the morning. I'm afraid our facilities here are cramped. You'll have to share the one secure room with my ward. But you'll find she's not been harmed. As yet. There's always tomorrow."

Just before Caber came in to lead him away, Bond asked the final question. "You said we would be leaving here."

"Yes?"

"And that I'd have a ringside seat."

"Yes?"

"Where?"

Murik pecked forward. "Of course, you don't know. I mentioned the powerful transceivers we'll be using. Well, tomorrow my company here will be conducting tests with just such equipment—on another frequency, of course. Several influential people are interested. You see, not only are they incredibly powerful but, like my nuclear reactor design, they're ultra-safe. My clever associates here have developed high-frequency transceivers which have what we call a safety-screened beam. This means their signals *cannot* be monitored. Nobody, Mr. Bond, can listen in or even detect them. We have a large aircraft," he gave another little chuckle, "provided, incidentally, by the United States. It is our flying testbed, and not only can it carry all the equipment we need, but also stay aloft for a little more than twenty-four hours. Extra fuel tanks. All the time we need. That's where you'll get your ringside seat."

Caber and one of the other men arrived, took orders from the Laird and led Bond away down a series of passages. They handled him roughly, but Caber undid the shackles once they reached what he referred to as "the secure room."

"Ye'll no be gettin' oot o' here," Caber sneered. Bond could not fault Caber's confidence, for the place was simply a narrow cell with no windows and only a tiny ventilation grille set well back high in the wall. The door was of eight-inch steel, with no handles on the inside, and so hung that it became part of the wall when closed. It was like being pushed into a large safe—a use the room was almost certainly put to on occasions. There were two beds and one small light, which burned perpetually behind thick glass and a mesh cover, flush with the ceiling.

Lavender had been dozing on one of the beds, but woke with a start as soon as they shoved Bond into the cell. She leaped up, then, with a little squeal, grabbed at her blanket, embarrassed by the fact that she wore only her tiny lace underwear.

All modesty seemed to disappear when she realized it was Bond. "James!" She dropped the blanket and was in his arms. "Oh God, they caught you. I hoped that you, at least, had got away."

"No such luck. Not in the car—and not now . . ."

She looked up at him. "James, you do know I had nothing to do with how they caught you—with the car, I mean?"

He nodded, allowing her to go on.

"The first thing I knew about it was when the Laird told me you had been in a driving accident. I was forbidden to have any contact with you. They threatened, and Mary Jane . . . Did you know she was dead? She's had a heart attack."

This time Bond stopped her talking with a kiss that developed, just as it had done on the last occasion he had been with her, saying farewell on the night of his abortive escape in the Saab.

She began to move backward. On the bed she looked up at him. "Oh, James. I really thought you'd get away and bring some help. Terrible things are going on . . ."

"You can say that again." Bond smiled down at her. "Really terrible," he mused. "I don't know how long I can stand it."

The worried look on her face turned to one of delight. "It *is* terrible, isn't it? As far as I can see there's only one answer." She began to remove what little she was wearing.

An hour or so later, they lay together on the bed, side by side, their faces turned toward each other. "James," she whispered. "If we ever get out of this . . . ?"

He stopped her again with a kiss. She was a tough young girl, under that soft frilly exterior, and Bond felt it only right that she should know the truth. "Listen, Dilly," he began, and then with tact—missing out only the tiny details—told her the real facts of Mary Jane Mashkin's heart attack and how it had been meant for her. He also briefly outlined Murik's plans for the morning.

She lay silent for a time. Speaking at last with a voice that was calm and almost resigned, she said, "Then it looks as if we've had it. Darling James, thank you. You saved my life. But I wonder if it would have been better to go then. At the Palace. Suddenly, Anton's a reptile, and I should imagine he has something very very nasty planned for us."

Bond put a finger to her lips. "It hasn't happened yet." He tried to make light of things, saying that there was still time for help to arrive, that even he could find some way out. "Anyway, Dilly, I've never been thrown out of a plane before. Could be exciting. Like being here with you—at least we'll be together."

She bit her lip and nodded bravely, then pulled his head down to hers so that they were again united by passion. To Bond it felt as though they had both escaped from time and trouble and were floating with increasing joy toward a whirlpool of earthly delights.

Later, they fell asleep, entwined on the small bed.

It was almost six in the morning before Bill Tanner returned to M's office with the bad news that, because of it being the middle of the night, they had not yet received a positive trace on the number from which James Bond had dialed.

"They'll have it for you before nine o'clock," he said wearily.

M looked washed out, his skin like parchment and deep creases of worry around discolored eyes. "Nobody seems to know the meaning of urgency anymore," he growled. Deep inside, M had a nasty feeling that they were close to something terrible—even catastrophic. Logic told him that Anton Murik's disappearance, Bond's telephone call, and the fact of the FBI having no trace on Franco, were all linked. Maybe they now stood on the edge of a precipice, constructed during all those meetings between the international terrorist and the former nuclear physicist.

"Duggan's the same," he snorted. "Got huffy with me when I reversed my views about him going into Murik's Castle. But the issue's been forced now. They had to get some magistrate out of bed to sign the search warrant. Anyway, they've all buzzed off like a swarm of daft bees—Duggan, his men, and a load of Special Branch to lead the way." He gave a sign. "Even so, they won't be able to do anything much before nine either."

Bill Tanner, worried as he was, tried to make light of it. "Should've sent a gunboat in the first place, sir."

M grunted. "Send some coffee, that's more like it. Get some coffee up now, Chief-of-Staff. Black, hot, sweet and strong. I've got a feeling it's going to be a long hard day."

19

ULTIMATUM

THEY CAME ARMED, and in strength. Caber and three of the hoods; Caber carrying an automatic pistol, two of the hoods with trays.

"It's a special breakfast the Laird's been pleased to order for ye. He said ye'd understand." Caber motioned for the trays to be set down, and Bond vividly recalled his conversation with Murik just after their arrival at Perpignan the previous day: about the condemned man eating a hearty breakfast.

The hoods disappeared and Caber backed into the doorway. "And ye'll no try coming for us wi' them knives and forks when we collect the trays. All of us have got the wee shooters. Naebody's gonna get away this time."

One of the hoods brayed with laughter from behind him. "There's only the one way they'll be gettin' oot, eh, Caber?"

"Shut yer gob, cretin." Caber stepped back, swinging the door. Before he could close it, Bond called, "What about washing and things?"

"Och aye." Caber pressed something outside the door before slamming it. The great panel of metal thumped home and at the same time a small section of the wall slid back to reveal a little alcove containing the bare necessities—a washbasin, towels and lavatory. Bond examined it, but the alcove was as solid as the rest of the cell. "I can't shave," he said, trying to sound bright, "but at least we'll both be clean."

The trays contained steaming plates of bacon, eggs, sausages, two large silver pots of coffee, plenty of toast, butter and marmalade—laid out under ornate covers on the Laird of Murcaldy's personal china. Even the glass butter dishes were engraved. "Butter in a lordly dish," said Bond, realizing that the Biblical quote had sinister undertones—murder of some kind, he seemed to remember: an Old Testament character smiting someone with a tent peg after bringing in his butter. Caber came with guns, not tent pegs.

Lavender pushed her tray away. "It's no good, James. I can't eat it. I couldn't swallow."

Bond went over, catching her by the shoulders. "Dilly, where's your faith, girl? We'll find a way out—*I'll* find a way out: cling on to that. Murik'll be only too happy if you're frightened and show your fear. You have to fight with strength. Come on." He had no idea how they could possibly escape or even stop the events which were now, he knew, rolling inevitably toward what could be a holocaust of tragic and catastrophic proportions. Yet all Bond's experience told him Murik would only be beaten by some show of character.

Lavender swallowed and took in a deep gulp of air. "Okay," she nodded.

"At least have some coffee," Bond said, more kindly.

She gave a little shiver. "Of course, James. I've come a long way with Anton as well. Let's try and get the bastard."

Bond set an example, even though he too found it hard to eat. The bacon and eggs stuck in his throat, but he managed to wash it down by consuming cup after cup of coffee, taking in a lot of sugar. At least his body would be provided with something on which to feed—and extra energy was what he needed. Lavender did her best, nibbling on toast and sipping coffee. When they had finished, Bond stretched out on the bed, turning his face away while she completed her toilet and dressed.

He then got himself ready, stripping and washing from tip to toe. Pity about not being able to shave. If they were to die, he would rather go looking his best. Negative thinking. Bond cursed himself. From now on, it was his duty to be positive and alert; aware of everything going on; ready to take advantage of the smallest chink that showed in Murik's plan or actions.

There was no way of telling the time, but Bond guessed they had been allowed to sleep late. It must now be after midday, French time. The deadline here was one in the afternoon—noon in England. They would not have to wait much longer.

Five minutes later Caber and the other men reappeared. The trays were swiftly removed, and the two prisoners were ordered from the cell at gunpoint. They were taken through silent passages, narrow corridors and finally up steps which led to a metal fire door—Caber striding ahead, opening the door and waving them through.

Bond heard Lavender gasp behind him. They stood in the hangar he had seen on their arrival—a vast structure into which you could have easily fitted a block of houses: huge and echoing, smelling of oil and rubber, its temperature cool from the fans high up among the girders. The most impressive sight, though, was the aircraft standing in the center, its tail pointing toward the towering roller doors and a yellow tractor already hooked to the nose.

Bond recognized it at once. He also wondered at the sheer size of the aerial monster. It was the massive Lockheed-Georgia C-141 — the Starlifter: the great American strategic transport aircraft with a wingspan of over forty-eight meters and a length of over forty-four meters, towering to a height of nearly forty feet.

Even the hangar seemed dwarfed by this magnificent brute, decked out in standard United States camouflage, but with the added blue, white, red and yellow insignia of the French Armée de l'Air. Toward the rear of the wide fuselage the words "Aldan Aerospace" had been added. Below, Bond could see the outline of the huge rear ramp which could be hydraulically lowered, even in flight, for loading or dropping men and materials — tanks, vehicles of all kinds — even helicopters.

Murik could get everything he needed into this beast from technicians to all the electronic equipment he needed for his shielded radio beams. "Starlifter" was a good name for the plane, Bond thought, saying the word aloud.

"Yes, Mr. Bond, the Starlifter." Murik stood at his elbow, dressed casually in jacket and slacks. "A good name, I think. Specially modified, of course. You will be interested . . . It's time to go aboard."

From the front of the hangar came the sound of the roller doors starting to move. Caber prodded Bond with his pistol, and they began to climb the steps up to the forward doorway, low in the fuselage behind the flight deck.

Murik led the way, and Bond caught sight of the crew through the flight deck window, going through the pre-takeoff check. Two of Murik's men remained at the foot of the steps, while another couple who had been standing nearby followed behind Bond, Lavender and Caber.

Inside, the fuselage had obviously been altered to Murik's own specifications. The doorway took them into a brightly decorated canteen with a bar, small round tables and seating capacity for a dozen people. A deep pile carpet lay under their feet and Bond, looking forward, could see two men already at work in a galley.

"I'm afraid you'll not be eating here with the rest of us," said Murik, looking from Bond to Lavender. "That is one pleasure I shall reluctantly have to forgo. What will happen in the next hours needs great concentration and timing, so we cannot have you roaming around the aircraft. However, I shall see you do not go hungry or thirsty." He pointed toward the sliding hatchway leading to the rear of the fuselage. "I should be grateful if you would take care when passing through the next section. It contains the intestines of my electronic labors, and is, perhaps, the most important part of the whole project."

On the far side of this hatchway, the fuselage seemed to narrow and the carpet disappeared. The section ran back down the fuselage for about forty feet, its sides crammed from deck to the upper bulkheads with banks of electronic equipment housed in metal units and high cabinets. Toward the center there was a recess on either side, with two men in clean white coveralls sitting in each, at complex control consoles. As Murik's party passed, Bond asked loudly if they could get Beethoven's Fifth. He was rewarded with a jab from Caber and a filthy look shot at him by Murik.

At the end of this electronic cave there was another sliding hatchway, which was, to Bond's experienced eye, bullet proof and fireproof. He judged they had covered just over half the length of the aircraft. Murik paused, his hand on the sliding latch. "My personal preserve," he announced, tugging the door to one side. They stepped into a circular area lit by shaded lights, giving off a restful greenish glow. "The nerve center of my operation." Murik gave a smug look around him as the door closed with an automatic hiss. "This is where I shall control Meltdown."

Two small oval windows, one on each side, had their blinds down to keep out any extraneous light. On either side of the door, facing forward, was a pair of wide curved desks, each backed by another complicated array of electronic wizardry.

Three body-molded swivel seats were bolted to the deck in front of each of the desk consoles and behind them four seats were ranged, as though for spectators. Leading aft, toward the tail of the Starlifter, another hatchway was outlined in scarlet. In large letters on this door a legend had been stenciled: DO NOT ENTER IF RED LIGHT IS ON. Near this exit yet another, smaller passage was visible to the right. Murik gestured toward it. "The usual offices, as the real-estate agents say," he said, smiling. "We have everything on board for a pleasant day trip over the sea. Now, if you'll just take your seats . . ."

Bond felt Caber's arms gripping him, and at the same time he saw the two other men close in on Lavender.

"You will sit next to me," said Murik, turning to Bond. "On my left, I think."

Caber manhandled Bond into one of the chairs in front of the console on the right of the door—facing forward—and fastened a normal seat belt around his stomach.

"We have made certain modifications to the safety harnesses for you and my ward." Murik slid into the seat to Bond's right, and as he did so his jacket rode back slightly, revealing a holster behind his hip and the curved butt of a small deadly Colt Python—the four-inch model. Bond could have identified that weapon anywhere. Well, it was something— within reach, anyway.

Seconds later, Bond's hopes of the weapon being within reach were dashed.

"Put yer arms behind yer back, Bond," Caber hissed. He saw a short webbing strap in Caber's paw, then felt his hands being pressed together and the strap encircling his wrists tightly as the big Scot pulled it secure. Then, holding him firmly in the seat, Caber began to fit what Murik called the modified safety harness. Two further webbing belts, anchored to the underside of the seat, were now crossed over Bond's chest and shoulders and pulled hard. He felt them being adjusted and locked some-where at the back and underneath the seat, holding him immobile.

Murik had clipped on a seat belt and was already adjusting the console in front of them, his hands moving with professional precision as pin lights and visual units started to glow. Rising like a snake's head from the center of the desk was an adjustable microphone, a large "Speak" button set into a protective box directly in front of it.

Bond studied the row of digital clocks, each marked with a time zone, covering all six locations of the targets. British time showed at ten minutes to noon.

He glanced over to the other console, where Lavender had been fastened in exactly the same way as himself between two of Murik's men, who were now concentrating on the equipment facing them. These, Bond realized, were not just heavies, but trained technicians. At that moment he felt the deck beneath his feet tremble. The yellow tractor was moving, giving the aircraft a push-back from the hangar.

Murik looked up. "I promised you a ringside seat, Bond," he said, grinning, "and here it is. Everything."

Bond turned to see Caber disappearing through the red-outlined hatchway to their rear. He asked where it led, and Murik gave a loud, mocking laugh. "The exit," he almost shouted. "There's a ramp, you know. Everybody's seen pictures of vehicles being driven up that ramp, in the more conventional Starlifter, or parachute troops hurling themselves down it. I had thought of hurling you down it, Bond. Then a better idea came to mind."

"You didn't say what . . . ?" Bond began, then the first of the four powerful Pratt & Whitney turbofans began to throb. The Starlifter was coming alive. The second started; then the third and fourth.

"No, I didn't say." Murik glanced at the instruments in front of him. "But all in good time."

Caber returned and nodded to Murik, as though passing a message. "Good," said Murik in acknowledgment. Then, pointing to the seat on his right, he commented that Mary Jane should have been sitting in it. "She's here in spirit, though." He did not smile. "Sorry about the restraint, Bond, but I felt it necessary. My people were working on those harnesses all night, putting in the locks and releases, well out of anybody's reach under the seats."

The engines surged, one after another, then synchronized and the aircraft swayed along the taxiway. A metallic click from somewhere in the roof near the main entrance signaled contact being made from the flight deck. "Captain to all crew and passengers of Aldan Five-Six." The voice was English, with a drawl. One is usually wrong about putting invisible figures to voices, but it immediately made Bond think of a rather slim, tall *louche*-looking man with long hair, starting to thin and bald. "Please fasten your seat belts and extinguish cigarettes. We shall be taking off shortly."

"And it's going to be a bumpy ride," muttered Bond.

The British-time digital clock clicked toward 11:54 as the engines settled and then rose into a blasting roar as their combined 84,000 pounds' static thrust pushed the crew and two captives back into their seats.

As the aircraft ceased bumping along the runway, tipping itself smoothly into its natural element, Murik leaned over, placing a pair of foam-padded headphones over Bond's head. "You will hear everything, and I shall also be able to speak to you through these." He raised his voice. "A running commentary, like the Boat Race." He glanced toward the time displays. British time showed two minutes before noon. "The witching hour." Murik's chuckle had begun to irritate Bond. "Very soon you'll hear the terrorist squads making their reports."

Less than five minutes before the Starlifter rose from the runway at Perpignan, events were taking their course the world over. M, having now received information regarding the location of Bond's call, had checked on all possible connections with Anton Murik. His investigation led naturally to Aldan Aerospace (France), Inc., and their headquarters at Perpignan airport.

There had been rapid telephone calls to Paris and through the various police and security networks, to Perpignan itrself. It had, however, been slow work, and a van carrying members of the SDECE—the French Secret Service—together with a squad of armed police was only now tearing toward the airport.

They had received further encouraging news at the Regent's Park headquarters. A Mary Jane Mashkin, close friend of Dr. Anton Murik, had died of a heart attack in the middle of a fashion show in Perpignan, while the body of a man—originally thought to be the victim of a gangland shoot-out near the fashion show—had been identified as the much-wanted terrorist known as Franco.

"007's work, sir?" Bill Tanner was not really asking.

"Could be. Two of 'em out of it, anyway."

"Then there's a very good chance . . ." Tanner began.

"Don't count your chickens, Chief-of-Staff. Never do that. We could still be too late, fiddling around half the night waiting for information. Time's not with us."

On M's orders, several of his own officers were now on their way, by military aircraft from Northolt.

All too late. Just as M had predicted.

A little over sixty miles from Paris, not far from the city of Orleans, deep under the vast complex which makes up the nuclear power stations known as Saint-Laurent-des-Eaux One, Two and Three, certain people were quietly going through a well-rehearsed routine.

Two men tending the large turbine of Plant Two left their normal posts at just before twelve-thirty. A maintenance man, whose job was to keep the air conditioning system in good repair, excused himself from the duty room where he had been playing cards with three of his colleagues. The security man at the entrance leading down to the main control room some fifty feet below ground waited anxiously while the other three made their way along the pipe-lined, stark passages, picking up pieces of cached equipment as they went. At two minutes before one, French time, they met at the head of the emergency stairs near the elevator shaft and went down one flight to the gallery immediately outside the plant's control room, where they joined their companion, the security guard. It was one minute to one.

Inside the control room, the half a dozen men who watched the dials and controlled the flow of power, keeping an eye open for any unexpected fluctuation or change in the system, went about their work normally. One of them turned, shouting irritably at the security man as he opened the large main door. "Claude, what are you doing? You know you're not allowed . . ." He stopped, seeing the automatic pistol pointing at him and a second man with a folding-stock Heckler & Koch submachine gun, its barrel sweeping the room.

The security man called Claude was the only one to speak: "Hands on your heads. Stand away from all equipment. Now. Move or you will be killed. We mean it."

The tone of his voice convinced the six men. Flustered, they dropped clipboards and pens, clamped their hands to their heads and stepped clear of any piece of monitoring equipment. So hypnotized were they by the weapons that it is doubtful if they even saw the other two men slip past their comrades, and move quickly and unerringly to two points in the room. In a matter of seconds these two were giving the thumbs-up sign to their armed colleagues. They had cut off all links with the outside world by severing the communications cables and pulling the external control override switches. The reactor operating at Saint-Laurent-des-Eaux Two could be handled only from this room, which now had no contact with the outside world.

The man who had severed the communications link was completing the job by tearing the three telephone leads from their sockets as the gunmen ordered the six technicians to line up, facing the door.

A series of images flashed through the minds of these half dozen unfortunates—pictures of their wives and families crossing bleakly with incidents they had seen on television newsreels: hostages held in terrible conditions for long periods; hostages shot and killed as a warning to others; the drawn and haggard faces of men and women who had lived through ordeals like this. It was therefore with a sense of both great surprise and relief that they heard the gunmen tell them to leave quietly through the main door and get up the stairs.

"It would not be advisable for anyone to take panic action," the gunman called Claude told them. "Just report to the authorities and say that a message with certain demands will be coming through from outside within a few minutes. Any sudden move before that and we shut down the cooling system. We cause a China Syndrome. Tell them that, okay?"

The six men nodded, shakily leaving their place of work. The heavy door to the control room slammed behind them and the two gunmen clamped on the interior safety locks, watching through the reinforced glass which ran the length of the gallery as the released operators slowly filed away.

The other two men had been busy removing their most essential piece of equipment, the transceiver, from a canvas haversack. One of the men now ran out a cable and plugged it into a wall socket. The security guard, Claude, who was the squad leader, switched on the small, boxlike transceiver and watched as the red light glowed, then turned green. Pressing the transmit button, he said loudly and distinctly, "Number Three. War."

Similar scenes to these were being enacted in five other nuclear power stations in Europe and the United States.

James Bond heard the words clearly through the headphones: "Number Three. War."

"That's the French one," Murik said, his voice interrupted by another quick message: "Number One. War."

"England." Murik was ticking off the names of the plants on a clipboard lying in front of the console.

"Number Four. War."

"Number Five. War."

"Number Two. War."

They came in quickly, tumbling into the earphones, as though someone was speaking within Bond's head. Then a long pause. Bond saw Murik's hand clench and unclench. He looked hard at the man who was embarked on an operation from which there could be no turning back. The wait had Murik worried, drumming his fingers on the edge of the console. Then, after what seemed an eternity. "Number Six. War."

"All in." Murik grabbed Bond's arm, nodding his head excitedly.

"Now," he said, his voice strange, almost out of control, "now for *my* message. In a moment I shall activate the ultimatum. You see, everything is ordered, outside human control—except for the reaction of the governments concerned. Throughout Europe and the United States we have a series of hidden powerful microtransmitters controlled by a signal from the aircraft. The transmitters will relay a translated message to every European country and a number of Asian and Eastern countries too. The transmission is locked into the normal broadcasting frequencies of the countries concerned and will cut in on any program already going out." He adjusted a dial and watched a pair of needles center themselves on a VU below it. "You will hear the ultimatum in your own language, Mr.

Bond. You'll realize the seriousness of the situation and how it is impossible for me to lose."

Murik leaned forward, threw two switches and prepared to press a red button on the console. He added, "By the way, you will not recognize my voice. But it *is* me, even though I sound like a woman. There is an ingenious device called in the trade, the electronic handkerchief. By using it, you can alter your own voice beyond recognition. I have chosen the voice of a rather seductive lady. Now, listen."

Without warning, Bond heard the voice in his headphones; sharp and commanding at first, then calmer as it dictated a message. Slowly the full impact, and Murik's sheer ingenuity, came home to Bond. His eyes widened and he felt a sickening lurch in his stomach.

Almost an hour later M sat with members of the government, security services, and chiefs-of-staff who make up the secret crisis committee known as Cobra—in the Cabinet Office Briefing Room deep under Whitehall. They were listening again to a recording of that sudden, audacious and terrifying ultimatum. It was the seventh hearing for M, but the message still had its impact—an impact it had made on people all over Europe, the United States and many other parts of the world.

The only action M had taken was to call the French police back from Perpignan airport. But by the time he had made contact M discovered that they had been recalled anyway. They too had heard the message, on the radio in their van.

The voice relaying that message was a woman's. M thought of clandestine propaganda broadcasts during the Second World War, like those of Lord Haw-Haw and Tokyo Rose.

"Stop whatever you are doing. Stop now. Stop and listen. This is an emergency broadcast of extreme urgency to every man, woman and child. Stop. Stand still and listen," the voice clipped out, sharp and commanding. Then it continued, calm and deliberate. "This is a message of great urgency. It concerns everyone, but it is mainly directed at the governments of Britain, France, the Federal Republic of Germany, the German Democratic Republic and the United States. This message is being broadcast in all necessary languages throughout Europe and the United States, as well as to some countries not immediately affected. It will be the only message, the only set of instructions to the governments concerned.

"At exactly twelve noon British Summer Time, that is, GMT plus one, today, six nuclear reactor power plants were seized by terrorist groups.

These groups now occupy and hold the main control rooms of the following nuclear plants." The voice went on to list the full names of the plants and their precise locations. The tone rising, it continued, "I must make two things clear. The men who hold these nuclear power plants are dedicated to a point that some would call fanaticism. They will die if necessary. Second, all lines of communication have been cut between these groups and the outside world. They can make contact with one person only— myself. They are under orders to do the following: if an attempt is made to assault any one of the six power plants my men will immediately turn off the cooling system to the core of the nuclear reactor. This will cause immense heat to build up. Within a very short time there will be an explosion similar to a mild earthquake and a very large area surrounding the plant will be contaminated by radioactive material. The core of the reactor will proceed to burn its way through the earth. Eventually the core will find an exit point where further, possibly more devastating, radioactive material will be expelled. That is known, to those who have not heard of it, as the China Syndrome.

"These men are under instructions to carry out this same operation exactly twenty-four hours after I stop speaking unless certain demands are met. Let me repeat that the men who have taken over these nuclear plants will not hesitate to follow their orders to the death. If in twenty-four hours this becomes necessary the results will be catastrophic for the whole world. It will mean an end to all life in large areas; certainly an end to the growth of food, the keeping of livestock and fish, in even larger tracts of land. It is no exaggeration to say that it could well mean the end of the world as we know it. There will be no way to stop such a disaster if my demands are not met.

"These are my instructions: I require a ransom payable only in cut gem diamonds to a value of not less than fifty billion dollars, that is, five zero billion, B for Bertie, dollars to be paid in cut gem diamonds at their current rate—today's rate. These diamonds—easily obtained through the markets in London, Holland, Belgium and America—are to be placed, packed neatly in one large-sized yellow naval flotation bag. The bag is to be equipped with a normal naval or army recovery hoop. This consignment is to be dropped by aircraft at the following point." The voice calmly went on to give the latitude and longitude, repeating it three times so that there could be no error.

"Before the diamonds are delivered, an area of fifty square miles around the dropping point is to be cleared of all shipping, and once its mission is completed the aircraft employed is to fly well out of the zone. I shall not give the order for the nuclear plants to be released until the diamonds have been dropped. Until I have picked them up in safety and have been assured of the amount, and its lack of contamination. I have experts to hand, and this operation will take me approximately two hours from the moment of dropping. Thus the governments concerned have in reality around twenty-two hours to comply with my demands. If the ransom is *not* dropped; if I do *not* pick it up, and get it away in time, without any action being taken against me, no word of command will go out, and those who control the six nuclear power stations will carry out their threat.

"I stress that this is no hoax. This broadcast is my ultimatum. There will be absolutely no other contact. I repeat that any attempt to communicate with those holding the plants can only result in tragedy. You have exactly twenty-two hours. Message ends."

The Prime Minister, who had been brought back to London from an engagement in Hampshire—the car being driven at breakneck speed with a police escort—was chairing the meeting.

"I have been in touch with the President of the United States and the heads of all other governments concerned." The Prime Minister looked worried, but the natural poise was still there. "We are all agreed that, no matter how difficult, this is one terrorist action in which we have no choice. We are being asked for a very large sum of money, but at this moment all the threatened countries are gathering diamonds of good quality. We have experts working on it in London, and diamonds are being flown by the fastest possible methods to Paris, where a French military aircraft is standing by. A coordination unit is being set up there to ensure that there are no hitches and to check the quality of the stones. As you know, the dropping zone is in the Mediterranean and at the moment we are scheduling a drop to be made at nine o'clock our time tomorrow. The most difficult thing, apparently, is to clear the area of all shipping. There are specialists working on this now. I am, personally, depressed by this action. It is the first time this country has given way to blackmail by terrorist groups, but our combined advisers seem to think there are no options open. Has anybody got any further points to contribute?"

M cleared his throat. "Yes, on behalf of my Service, Prime Minister: we think we know who is behind this ingenious and horrific act. We also think we know where this person is—in an aircraft over the Med now.

With permission of the Chiefs-of-Staff, I am going to ask for this aircraft to be shadowed by the Armée de l'Air, by fighter-borne radar, of course. I know we can take no action until the terrorists have left the nuclear power plants, but it is a lead, and we might just be able to retrieve the diamonds after the event."

The Prime Minister nodded. "I read your confidential report on my way here. You mention something about one of your agents?"

"I can't be sure"—M looked solemn—"but there is a possibility that one of my people is on board the aircraft. However, I'm certain he would be the last person to ask for any special consideration."

"That's not the point." The Prime Minister looked down at the documents on the table. "Do you think he might be able to do something about the situation?"

"If he can't halt this ungodly mess, Prime Minister, nobody can."

20

WARLOCK

Bond sat in front of the console, the facts fighting each other in his mind, as though trying to drag him into despair. He recognized the symptoms: as when, caught in the sea, a man decides he can swim no farther; or feels the onset of fatigue in snow, making him lie down exhausted, to be encompassed by that strange euphoria that comes before death by freezing.

Murik had planned, using his great knowledge and privileged information. He had mustered his forces through the most elusive international terrorist in the world and set up a complicated and admirable tactical operation. There was little to stop him at this stage. For his own safety, Murik would have to get rid of both Bond and Lavender. Why Murik had not already killed them was almost beyond Bond's comprehension. After all, the Laird was ruthless enough to set an almost impossible deadline to his ultimatum. Bond could only presume they were still alive because

Murik's vanity needed to feed on the applause of doomed witnesses.

Don't let yourself go, Bond told himself. Keep alert. Do anything; try to combat the inevitable. He began by trying to feel the flight pattern being followed by the Starlifter. It appeared to him that the aircraft, having reached its cruising height, was locking into a wide, oval holding pattern, each circuit covering around fifty miles or so. That made sense—maximum altitude, with the aircraft using the minimum fuel and the Aldan Aerospace technicians in the forward compartment going about their prescribed tests with the equipment.

He glanced toward Lavender and smiled. She returned the look with a twist of her lips, bravely struggling with the horrors that must have been going through her head.

Anton Murik rarely stopped talking. "You see," he said, "we'll descend to the pickup point some ninety minutes before the deadline runs out. By then we'll know, by our radar, when their aircraft has made its dropping run. I want to keep them on the edge of their seats until the last moment. If the flotation bag is there—as I'm certain it will be—it's a simple matter: my air crew has been well-trained in the art of picking up from the sea. All we need is a couple of low-level passes while we trail a cable with grappling hooks from the rear of the aircraft. Once we've hooked on, we just winch up the bag. A rise in the price of diamonds, eh?" He cackled at his weak joke.

"A rise'll be right," Bond replied. "You'll get a glut. Could mess up the market."

"Oh, my dear Bond, why do you always underestimate me? I'm a patient man—waited too long for this. You don't think I'm going to send out a troop of Boy Scouts with the diamonds, and flood the market next week." He gave an irritated little sigh. "This has taken too long to set up. I don't mind waiting a little longer—a year or two. Softly softly. The diamonds'll trickle on to various markets. I've enough money to start work on my own reactor now. I simply wish to recoup from this little hoard." Looking straight at Bond, he gave a broad smile. "All for free. They'll fall over themselves to pay up."

"And if they stand fast? If they *don't* come up with your precious fifty billion?" Bond realized this was unlikely.

Murik held his gaze coldly. "Then the world will not be the world anymore. Not as we know it."

"You're really going to let the terrorist teams close down the cooling systems?"

Murik gave a dismissive wave of the hand. "There'll be no need. The governments will pay up and look happy. They have no option."

"But . . ." Bond was about to repeat his constant worry—that either one of the terrorist squads would lose control or some idiot security force would try an assault. There was a further possibility—that the governments would give in to the ultimatum, yet would lack time to fulfill Warlock's requirements. But what was the use? There was no point in arguing or even trying to reason with Anton Murik.

If argument would do no good, Bond had to think of some other way. Strapped into his seat, with Lavender in the same situation, he knew chances of survival were slim. He must go on searching for further chinks in the armor. Bond might play on Murik's vanity for a time, yet in the end that could not affect the outcome. To do anything concrete he had to be free and mobile. After that, there was the problem of taking out Murik, Caber and the two heavies who were sitting with Lavender at the other console.

Bond gazed blankly at the vast array of electronic units before him, particularly those directly in front of Murik. Think logically, he told himself. What would he do if free and unhindered? The earphones had been plugged into a unit bright with pin lights, VUs, a digital frequency display and half a dozen tuning dials. He had no doubt that this was the most important piece of equipment in Murik's impressive array—in particular the microphone with its transmit button. Press that button, speak, and you would be through to the squads holding the control rooms in the nuclear power plants. This was all too obvious. It was what Murik would do once he was away and safe with the diamonds, plucked from the sea. But what would he say? How would Murik defuse the situation?

Vanity. Use it. Play on the vanity. "What happens to the terrorist squads?" Bond asked casually.

Murik gave him a sly look. "What d'you mean, what happens to them?"

"Well, nobody can fault you on anything, Anton." Bond again chanced the familiarity. "This is probably the most brilliantly organized terrorist strategy of the century. But, when you've picked up the diamonds and got safe home—presumably not Perpignan . . ."

Murik laughed. "Unfortunately you won't be around to see."

Bond nodded, as though the point were academic. "I realize that. But I suppose you call off the dogs—radio on your shielded beam and give them the word. They give up. So what happens to them?"

Murik shrugged: the sly look again. "Franco's department." He lowered his voice. "And Franco isn't with us anymore. Those people have dealt entirely with him. They expect to die in action. A nuclear death from radiation. As far as I can gather, if they're ordered to abort, they simply come out with their hands up. Custody. Interrogation. Trial. A trip to the bridewell."

"They're willing to die for their various causes, so they're equally willing to serve a term in jail?"

"And, if any of them breaks, he can only point the finger at Franco, who is missing, believed killed in action." He paused, glancing up at the dials in front of him. "I imagine they won't be in jail for long. There will be hostages, deaths, demands."

Bond nodded slowly. "And you have to call up all six groups? Or does a blanket code cover it?"

For a second, Murik was caught off his guard. "Same code, but each group enumerated in case I want to leave one active until the others get clear. That was the arrangement. But, naturally, none are going to get clear."

"You don't think any of them'll be stupid enough to fight their way out?"

Murik shook his head very slowly.

It was enough for Bond. He needed the defusing code word, and, having already heard each of the groups come in with their "Number One . . . War; Number Four . . . War" and the rest, it required only common sense to work out the way in which the occupying groups could be made to abort. At least that was a logical step in the right direction. He had a reasonable idea of what to do *if* he managed to get free. But how to accomplish that part of the trick?

If only he could release his arms. Every time Murik moved, Bond glimpsed the butt of the Python revolver under the jacket. If his arms were free and the right moment could be found . . . Go on thinking. Work it out. There had to be a way, and there was still time. If he managed anything it would have to be late in Murik's scheme of things. Sometime tomorrow. A message to the terrorist squads now would only alert their suspicions. From what he knew of terrorist operations, Bond was clear about the psychological factors. For the first hours, hijackers or hostage-takers were suspicious of anyone and everything. Better to wait.

As he began to wrestle with the most difficult problem of all, the earphones suddenly came to life. He recognized the pilot's voice: "Captain to the Laird of Murcaldy, sir. Could you send someone up here for a moment?"

Murik gave a quizzical tilt of the head and beckoned Caber. "Up to the flight deck with you. See what it's all about." Caber left with a nod. Murik glanced at his watch. "Hope it's nothing too drastic. Time for some food, I think."

Caber was gone for around ten minutes, returning with a puzzled look. He bent low and muttered in Murik's ear. The Laird's face underwent no change as his hand gently eased Caber away and he swiveled his chair toward the console opposite. "The captain says they're picking up an intermittent trace on the flight deck radarscope, just on the periphery, to the north. They've tracked other aircraft—commercial stuff—but they appear to have two blips coming up every now and then, as though they were holding station with us. See what you can do."

The men bent over viewers, through which they were probably looking at radar screens. "What's your range?" Bond asked Murik coolly, knowing that if aircraft were shadowing the Starlifter, M had probably succeeded, late in the day, in getting the right answers to some difficult problems.

"On the flight deck? Around a hundred miles." There was no smile on Murik's face now. "In here a little more—nearer a hundred and fifty."

"There it is!" one of Caber's men exclaimed. "Two of them. In and out of this screen very quickly."

Nobody spoke. Then, about five minutes later, the same man said they were there again. "Could be shadow aircraft. Just keeping out of range. Coming in for an occasional look."

"Well, it won't do them any good," snapped Murik. "They can't take action."

"Not until you've collected your diamonds and given the abort order." Give him the facts now, Bond thought. Murik would come to it soon enough.

"And then?" asked the Laird with a lopsided smirk.

Bond sighed. "Blow you out of the sky. Force you down. Anything. Even shadow you to your lair."

Murik looked at him gravely for a full minute, then burst out laughing, his white hair ruffling as he threw his head back. "You think I've not taken precautions against that possibility? After all the planning, you think I've left *that* to chance?"

"A man of your capabilities? I shouldn't think so." Bond's stomach churned. The bastard. No, of course a man like Anton Murik would not take risks. Of course he had already eliminated any possible gamble from the Meltdown operation.

"Let them have their fun." Murik was still laughing. "Just keep an eye on them until the time comes." He spoke to the men at Lavender's console, then turned back to Bond. "You think I would undertake this without having some radar-jamming gear on board? If they really are shadow aircraft, then we'll fuzz their pictures as soon as we turn in to pick up the loot."

"And if they are? They'll already know where you're going—for the diamonds, I mean."

"I'll be away and out of it long before they'll dare come near. I'll hold off on the terrorist squads until literally the last moment." He gnawed his lip, something Bond had not seen him do before. "Anyway, they may have nothing to do with us. Routine. Coincidence. Could be."

"Could be. But somehow I don't . . ." Bond left the sentence unfinished.

Far away to the north of the Starlifter, the two Armée de l'Air Super Mirage fighters from the Fourth Fighter Wing turned in unison. Below, the pilots could see another pair of Mirages coming up fast. The leader of the pair which had been keeping station clicked on his transmitter and spoke. "Watchdog Five," he said.

Through his headphones came a voice from the approaching aircraft. "Watchdog Five, this is Watchdog Six on routine patrol. We take over now. Instructions you return to base and refuel. Over."

"Watchdog Five," the pilot of the first Super Mirage replied. "Instructions understood. All quiet. Headings as before. Good luck."

Watchdog Six acknowledged the message, the pilot turning his head in the shining cockpit to follow the first two Mirages as they peeled away. Then he called up his wingman and the two new aircraft swung into a long, looping pattern high over the sea. It was good exercise, he thought. But there must be more to it than a routine shadowing. It wouldn't be a Russian they were following; and he had not believed his squadron commandant, who had told them this was a spur-of-the-moment defense exercise. For one thing they were armed to the gills—everything from cannon to rockets.

The pilot bent his head to look at his small radar screen. The blip came up at the expected place. The two aircraft turned away, to begin another long circuit. If the blip vanished, they had orders to close until they made contact again.

Away to the south at Perpignan airport, Sepcat Jaguars sat, off the main runways, as though waiting to leap into the air for a kill. In the airport's operations room, senior Armée de l'Air officers were going over the flight plan filed by the Aldan Aerospace for their Starlifter. So far it had not deviated. The aircraft had made a long climb out to sea and then maintained a holding pattern while testing Aldan's specialized equipment. The holding pattern would continue, at almost 30,000 feet, for the best part of twenty-one hours. After that Aldan planned to descend almost to sea level before turning in to make their return approach to Perpignan at just before one o'clock the following afternoon.

In the building overlooking Regent's Park in London, M examined the latest reports radioed to him from France. Anton Murik's Starlifter was maintaining its filed flight plan. Yes, he thought, it probably will. Right up until the last moment, when he's got the ransom aboard. Unless—M hoped—unless James Bond was on board, and could do something about it.

It was a long and tiring evening—prelude to an even longer night of intense fatigue. Murik had drilled his staff to perfection, so that they followed a prescribed routine. Quite early on he told Bond that he did not expect the ransom aircraft to arrive anywhere near its drop zone until around nine or ten the following morning. "They can manage it by then—or so the computers tell me. That's why I set a minimum deadline. Twenty-four hours is just enough time." He grinned—a clever pupil showing off. "And it makes them jump—doesn't give them time to think hard."

Rest and eating periods were staggered, and either Murik or Caber was always left with Bond, just as one of the other two men remained next to Lavender. Caber, in fact, was there most of the time.

As for Bond and Lavender, they were fed—mainly on coffee and sandwiches—where they sat, their wrists being freed only for eating or when they were taken to the washroom by an armed man, who locked them into the simple closet and stood outside the door, letting them out at a knock from the inside. On returning, they were carefully strapped into their chairs again, always under the wicked eye of at least one pistol. On no occasion during the night would there have been any opportunity to reverse the situation, but Bond had far from given up hope. Already, in the washroom, he had begun to act.

On his last visit, Bond had quickly taken a large wad of tissue from the cardboard packet. This he had rolled into an elongated ball, around three inches in length and a good three inches thick. On being released and led back to his seat, Bond placed both hands behind his back, ready for his wrists to be strapped. At the same time he manipulated the wedge of tissue from the palm of his hand, up and between the wrists, which he held tightly together.

It was an old trick, favored by escapologists. When the wrist strap went on, Bond started to work with his fingers, pulling the tissue down from between his wrists. It was a lengthy business, but when the entire ball of tissue was removed and once more in his palm, the strap was looser around his wrists. There was freedom of an inch or so for him to work the strap around with his fingers and pick away at the fastening. The entire job took over an hour, but at last Bond knew that if he placed his wrists tightly together, then elongated his fingers in an attitude of prayer, the strap would slide away, leaving his hands and arms free.

Near dawn, he decided. Near dawn, when they were all tired and at their lowest ebb. It would be then, if the opportunity came, that he would act, whatever the consequences.

At around five-thirty in the morning, just after Murik had been to the forward part of the aircraft for coffee, Caber asked if he could go to the canteen.

"As long as it's only for coffee, Caber," Murik said, laughing, while his eyes scanned the equipment in front of him.

The big man saw nothing funny about the remark, gruffly saying that of course it would be coffee. He slid the door open and let it slam back into place as he disappeared.

Bond knew his movements would have to be both very fast and accurate. Murik seemed preoccupied with the appartatus in front of him, and Bond feigned sleep. The other two men were still at Lavender's console. One had his eyes closed but did not seem to be fully asleep, merely relaxed and resting. The other was intent on watching his screen through the viewer.

Gently James Bond flexed his hands, allowing the wrist strap to come free. He clenched his fists a few times to get the circulation going, making up his mind for the last time as to his plan of action.

Then he dropped the strap and moved. His right hand came up, arrowing toward the gun inside Murik's jacket, while the left swept round, with all the force he could muster, in a vicious chop at the Laird's unsuspecting throat. The blow from the heel of his left hand was slightly inaccurate, catching the side of his victim's neck instead of the windpipe. Nevertheless it had all Bond's strength behind it, and as it landed so the fingers of his right hand grabbed at the butt of the Colt Python, which came out of the holster easily as Murik crumpled onto the deck. Bond, still strapped in, swiveled his chair around with his feet, holding the Colt up firmly in a two-handed grip.

He fired almost before Murik's unconscious body hit the ground, yelling to Lavender, "Stay quite still!" Of the two men at the console, the heavy technician at the radar screen moved first, snapping his head up and going for his own gun a split second before his partner. As Bond squeezed the trigger it crossed his mind that this was one of the most foolhardy exploits he had ever attempted. Each bullet had to find its mark. One through the metal of the fuselage and bang would go the pressurization. The long hours on various firing ranges paid off in full. In all, he fired twice: two bursts of two—the "Double Tap" as the SAS call it—the .357 ammunition exploding like a cannon in the confines of the cabin. Four bullets reached their individual targets. He could not blame Lavender for screaming as the first of her captors spun to one side, a bullet lodged in his shoulder. The second caught him on the side of the head, hurling him into eternity with a great spatter of blood leaping from the wound. Yet while the blood was still airborne, Bond had fired his second two shots. The man who had been resting with his eyes closed caught both rounds in the neck, toppling backward, the sound of his gargling fall emerging from the after-echo of the shots.

Then there was silence except for a small whimper of fright from Lavender. "It's okay, Dilly. The only way. Sorry it was so close."

She looked in horror at the bodies, then took in a breath and nodded. Her guards lay dead and her clothes dripped with their blood. She shivered and nodded again. "It's okay, James. Sorry. It was unexpected, that's all. How . . . ?"

"No time now. Got to do something about those bloody terrorist squads before anything else." Transferring the revolver to his left hand, 007 grasped the microphone on its snakelike, jointed stand. Now he would see how far logic went. Having heard the squads report in with their "Number One . . War; Number Two . . . War," there was, for Bond, only one way to stop the nuclear operation from proceeding. He pressed the transmit button and began to speak, slowly and distinctly:

"Number One . . . Lock; Number Two . . . Lock; Number Three . . . Lock" right through all six of the squads—completing the word Anton Murik had used as his personal cryptonym for Meltdown—Warlock.

"Now we pray." He looked toward Lavender, still strapped helplessly in her seat. Bond's hands went to the buckle on his belt in order to reassemble the small knife concealed in its various components—the knife he had used to strip off the section of the money belt in Perpignan. He worked calmly, though it was a frustrating business. As he glanced toward Lavender, smiling and giving her a few words of confidence, he saw the means to his quick escape were very near the girl, if only she were free.

The technician who had been watching the radar screen when Bond's bullets had swept him from existence lay slumped in his seat, turned slightly toward Lavender. The man's trouser leg had ridden up on the right side, revealing a long woollen stocking into which was tucked a Highland dirk, safe in its scabbard. Bond had fleetingly feared, when among the festive crowds in Perpignan, that death would come silently by means of a dirk like this. It was the obvious weapon for these people to carry. Now, just when he needed the weapon, it was out of reach. As he completed fitting his own small knife together, he drew Lavender's attention to the dirk.

"Just get on with that handy little gadget you've produced from Lord knows where, James." Her face betrayed her frantic state of mind. "Caber's already been gone for nearly fifteen minutes. If you're not free by the time . . ."

"Okay, Dilly. *Nix panicus,* as my old Latin master used to say." He was already attacking the webbing straps binding him to the seat. The small blade was sharp, but its size did not make for speed—one slip and he could slash himself badly.

As he worked there were no sounds about them except for his own breathing counterpointed with that of the unconscious Laird of Murcaldy. Bond wondered how badly he had damaged Murik. If his aim had been really accurate the man would now be dead from a shattered trachea.

The first crossstrap came clear, but he was still not free. Bond sawed away at the second belt—an easier task, for with the first strap gone, he had more room in which to move. It still seemed an age before the tiny blade ripped its way through the tough webbing. It only remained for Bond to unclip the seat belt and he was completely out of the harness, springing up and flexing his muscles to get the blood flowing again.

In a second he was with Lavender, on his knees, feeling under the anchored chair, to find the release mechanism, which he unclipped, so that her restraining harness fell away. Another couple of seconds to undo the wrist strip and she too was free.

"Hadn't you better stand by with that gun?" She nodded toward the other console, where Bond had left the Python.

"Don't worry, Caber's not going to cause us much . . ." He stopped, seeing her eyes turn toward the sliding door, widening with a hint of fear.

Bond whirled around. Caber had returned and now stood in the doorway, one huge hand still holding the partition open, while his eyes darted around the control room, taking in the carnage. Both Caber and Bond were frozen for a second, looking at each other. Bond's eyes flicked toward Murik's console and the Python, and, in that second, Caber also saw the weapon.

As Bond came up from his crouched position, so Caber let out a great roar—a mixture of fury and grief for his master—and launched himself at Bond. For the first time, Lavender expressed her pent-up fear in a long, terrified shriek.

21

AIRSTRIKE

THE PREVIOUS DAY M had set up his own operations room, next to his suite of offices on the ninth floor of the headquarters building overlooking Regent's Park. He dozed fitfully, half dreaming of some odd childhood incident—running along a beach with water lapping at his feet. Then the familiar sound, which began in his dream as his long-dead mother ringing the bell for tea, broke into M's consciousness. It was the red telephone by the camp bed. M noted it was nearly five o'clock in the morning as he picked up the receiver and answered with a throaty "Yes?"

Bill Tanner was on the line, asking if M would come through to the main operations room. "They've surrendered." The Chief-of-Staff made no attempt to disguise his excitement.

"Who've surrendered?" M snapped.

"The terrorists. The people holding the nuclear reactors. All of them—those here in England, the French groups, the two in the United States and the Germans. Just walked out with their hands up. Said it was over."

M frowned. "Any explanations?"

"It only happened a short while ago." Tanner's voice now resumed its normal, calm tone. "Reports are still coming in, sir. Apparently they said they'd received the code message to abort the mission. Our people up at Heysham One say the terrorists seem to think their operation's been successful. I've spoken to one of the interrogators. He believes they've been given the call-off by mistake."

M grinned to himself. "I wonder," he grunted. "I wonder if it was an engineered mistake?"

"007?" the Chief-of-Staff asked.

"Who else? What about the Starlifter?" M was out of the camp bed now, trying to hang on to the phone and wrestle with his trousers at the same time.

"Still keeping station. The French are going in now. Two sections of fighters are on their way. They held off just long enough to get the okay from the technicians at the nuclear reactors, which all appear to be safe and operating normally, by the way."

M paused. "The French fighters? They're briefed to force the Starlifter down?" His grip on the receiver tightened.

Tanner's voice now became very calm—almost grave. "They're briefed to buzz it into surrendering, then to lead it back to Perpignan."

"And . . . ?"

"If that doesn't work, the orders are to blast it out of the sky."

"I see." M's voice dropped almost to a whisper.

"I know, sir." The Chief-of-Staff was fully aware of what must have been going through M's mind. "We just have to hope."

Slowly, M cradled the receiver.

Bond did not stand a chance of getting to the revolver, which was still lying on the console. Murik's chief lieutenant was enraged and dangerous as a wounded bull elephant. His roar had changed into the bloodcurdling cry of a fighting man who could only be stopped by a fusillade of bullets, as he seemed to take off through the air and catch Bond, halfway across the cabin. Bond felt his breath go from his lungs as the weight of the brute landed on him with full force. Caber was yelling obscenities and calling on the gods for vengeance. Now he had Bond straddled on the floor, his legs across Bond's thighs and the enormous hands at his victim's throat. Bond tried to cry out for Lavender's help as the red mist clouded his brain, but Caber's pressing fingers prevented him. Only a croak emerged. Then, with the same swiftness of Caber's attack, the whole situation changed.

The Starlifter's engines, which until now had been only a steady hum in the background, changed their note, rising and straining in a roar, while the deck under the struggling men lurched to one side. Bond was conscious of the aircraft's attitude altering dramatically as he rolled, still locked with Caber across the cabin floor. He caught a glimpse of Lavender, all arms and legs, being flung forward, as a great buffeting of the airframe ensued. Then the Starlifter lurched again, wallowing like a great liner plunging in a heavy sea. This action, followed by yet another sudden and violent change of attitude, as though they were making a steep downward turn, threw Caber free.

Bond swallowed, his throat almost closed by the pressure of Caber's hands, then heard Lavender calling that there were aircraft attacking. "Fighters!" she yelled. "They're coming in very close."

Bond's ears started to pop and he swallowed painfully again, trying to get to his feet and stay upright on the unstable deck, which was now angled downward, shuddering and bucking as though on a rollercoaster ride. He finally managed to prop himself against the forward door and began to make for the revolver. Out of the corner of his eye he saw that Lavender appeared to have been thrown some distance and was lying huddled near her console. There was no time to do anything for her now. Caber, on his hands and knees near Murik's console, was bracing himself for another attack, an arm stretched out toward the revolver.

The giant leaped forward, landing unsteadily on the rolling floor, his mask of fury giving way to a smile of triumph. "I'd rather do it another way—" he shouted. "Not by the bullet. I ken a bullet's too guid for ye." His hand almost hid the Python revolver, which pointed directly at Bond's chest, motioning his victim to the other side of the cabin, toward the large hatchway marked out in red and bearing the legend: DO NOT ENTER IF RED LIGHT IS ON.

"Ye'll get over there," Caber growled, keeping his balance even though the aircraft was undoubtedly in a nose-down attitude, descending rapidly.

There was no way to avoid the order without ending up with his chest torn away by the Python's bullets. Bond crabbed across the cabin toward the hatchway.

"Now"—Caber had managed to get close behind him, but not near enough for Bond to try a tackle—"now ye'll slide that thing open and hold it until ma own hand's on it."

Bond did as he was bidden; felt the revolver barrel jab at his back and saw Caber's hand take over the weight of the sliding hatchway as, together, they stepped through into the high sparred and girdered rear of the Starlifter. The aircraft made another fast and unexpected turn, throwing them apart, so that Bond banged his right arm against a rising, curved spar.

"I'm still behind ye, Bond, with the wee shooter, so dinna do anything daft. There's a wee bit of lever I have to pull over here."

The rear loading bay was cold—a bleak airborne hangar of metal, smelling of oil and that odd plastic scent of air that you get inside aircraft. The buffeting was worse here, almost below the high tail of the Starlifter. Bond had to grip hard on the spar to keep his balance, for the big plane seemed to be turning alternately left and right, still going down, with occasional terrifying bucketing and noise—which Bond now clearly recognized as other aircraft passing close and buzzing them.

"There we go," Caber called, and Bond heard the solid sound of a large switch going down. It was followed by the whine of hydraulics and an increased reverberation. Bond twisted around to see Caber leaning against a bulkhead just inside the hatchway, the revolver still accurately aimed, while his left hand was raised to an open metal box inside which a two-foot double knife-switch had just been pulled down and was locked into the "on" position. There was another great wallowing as the huge plane dropped a couple of hundred feet, and both men clung hard to their precious holds. Caber laughed. "The Laird had some daft idea of pushing ye out and trailing ye along with the pickup line when we went for the ransom. I'm gawn tae make sure o' ye, Bond."

There was a distinct decrease in temperature. Bond could feel air blowing around him. Looking back toward the tail end of the hold, he saw the rear sides of the fuselage moving away, long curved sections, slowly pivoting outward, while an oblong section of the deck gently dropped away to the increased whine of the hydraulic system. The ramp was going down. Already he could see a section of sky.

"It'll take aboot twa minutes," Caber shouted. "Then ye'll have a nice ski slope there. Ye'll be goin' doon that, Bond. Goin' doon it tae hell."

Bond's mind raced. If he was to die, then Caber would have to kill him with the gun. It was not likely that he could even get within grappling distance of the man. They were a good twenty feet from each other, and the Starlifter, still with its nose down, was yawing and performing what he recognized as evasive action of the most extreme kind. Perhaps it was his imagination, but Bond thought he could hear the metal plates singing and stretching with near human cries of pain as the aircraft was flung about the sky.

There is a dread, deep within most people, of falling to their death from a great height. James Bond was no exception. He clung on to his spar, transfixed by the quickly widening gap between metal and sky. Sudden death had never bothered him—in many ways he had lived with it for so long that it ceased to bring nightmares. One minute you would be alive, the next in irreversible darkness. But this would be different. He felt the clammy hand of death on his neck, and the cold sweat of genuine fear closed over him.

With a heavy rumble and thump, the ramp locked down, sloping away and leaving a huge open hole the size of a house in the rear of the aircraft. The sky tilted behind the opening, then swerved as the Starlifter went through yet another maneuver.

"This is where we say fare ye weel—For auld lang syne, Bond. Now git ye doon that ramp and practice flying wi'out wings."

"You'll have to shoot me down it," Bond shouted. He was not going without some show of a fight. Letting go of the spar, he aimed himself at Caber just as the Starlifter dipped lower, the tail coming up at a precarious angle. Bond lurched forward, almost losing his balance, going down out of control toward Caber. In this heart-stopping moment Bond saw the smile broaden on the man's face, his gun hand coming up to point the python straight at 007's chest.

Again the deck jerked under them and Bond staggered to one side as the aircraft dipped and the door to the hatchway slid open. For a second, Bond thought it was the movement of the aircraft. Then, still pushed forward by the angle of descent, he saw Lavender, the dirk from the dead guard's stocking firmly in her hand, raised to strike.

Caber tried to turn and bring the revolver to bear, but the instability of the deck combined with the unexpected assault gave him no chance. Almost with a sense of dread, Bond saw the dirk flash down—Lavender's left hand joining her right over the hilt as she plunged it with all her strength into Caber's throat. Even with the noise of rushing air, the buffeting and roar of engines, Caber's gurgling rasp of terror echoed around the vast hold. The revolver fell to the deck as he scrabbled at his throat, from which the blood pumped out and down his jersey. Then Caber spun around, still clamping hands to his neck, fell, and began to roll like a piece of freight broken loose in a ship's hold.

Bond reached the door, making a grab for the man as the aircraft once more changed its attitude, the nose coming up and the engines changing pitch in a surge of power as it started to gain altitude. Bond grasped Caber, but he could not hold the heavy man, who slipped away, rolling toward the point where the deck dipped into the long-angled ramp. Lavender turned her head away, hanging on to Bond, as Caber tumbled like a stuffed effigy, trailing blood, toward the ramp, hesitating fractionally as he began to fall. He must be dead already, Bond thought. But the horrible gargle of blood from the dirk-slit throat turned into a bubbling scream of terror as Caber slid down the ramp—a chilling and hideous sustained note.

As he reached the far end of the ramp, the big man's body seemed to correct itself, the gore-streaked face looking up toward Bond, arms outstretched, fingers clawing at the metal. For a second their eyes locked, and even though Caber's already held the glaze of death, they also contained a deep, dark hatred reaching out from what would soon be his grave. Then Murik's giant lieutenant slid over the edge, out of sight, into the air beneath the Starlifter.

"I killed him." Lavender was near to a state of shock.

"An obvious statement, Dilly darling." Bond still had to shout through the noise. "What matters to me is that you saved my life." He reached up to the big knife-switch, grasping the wooden handle and pulling it up, into the "off" position.

The hydraulic whine began again and the ramp started to move. Then, as Bond turned, he saw Lavender looking toward the closing gap, her eyes widening and lips parted. In the space still visible, a pair of Dassault Super Mirages could be seen hurtling in toward the Starlifter. As they watched, Bond and Lavender saw the bright flashes at the nose of each aircraft. The Mirage jets had passed, in a clap of air, with the crack and thunder of engines, before the Starlifter felt any effect from the short bursts of fire.

There followed a series of massive thuds, small explosions and the rip of metal. The deck under their feet began a long, wavelike dance and the Starlifter appeared to be poised, hanging in the air. Then the engines roared again and the deck steadied.

Bond's nose twitched at the acrid smell of smoke. Pushing Lavender to one side, he slid open the hatchway to be met by a billow of smoke. Two or three of the small-caliber shells from the Mirages had passed through the roof, slamming into the main console, from which the flames flicked upward, while smoke belched out in a deadly choking cloud.

Bond yelled at Lavender to keep out of the way. Already, during the tension in the rear hold, his subconscious had taken in the fact of two large fire extinguishers clipped into racks on either side of the sliding hatchway. He grabbed one of the heavy red cylinders, smashed the activating plunger against the nearest metal spar, slid back the door and pointed the jet of foam into the control room.

Coughing and spluttering from the fumes, Bond returned for the second cylinder. It took both the extinguishers at full pressure before the fire was out, leaving only eye-watering, throat-cloying fumes and smoke to eddy around the cabin.

Keeping Lavender close on the hold side of the door, Bond waited for the smoke to clear. He was now conscious of the Starlifter settling into a more natural flying pattern. Then came the heavy grind and thump as its landing gear locked into place. The one short burst of fire from the French fighters had done the trick, he thought. The international symbol for an aircraft's surrender was the lowering of its landing gear.

Inside the control cabin, the air was less foul, leaving only a sting in the nostrils. Lavender went straight toward one of the oval windows, and, sliding up the blind, reported that they seemed to be losing height. "There're a pair of fighter aircraft on this side," she called.

Bond made for the other window. Below, the coastline was coming up, and they were in a long wide turn. On his side as well two Mirages kept station. He peered down, looking for landmarks until he saw the familiar shape of the Canigou. The fighters remained in place, lowering their undercarriages and flaps. They were making an escorted final approach to Perpignan.

Bond looked around. The bodies of the two technicians had been thrown across the cabin, but of Anton Murik there was no sign. Lavender said that perhaps when he came to, the Laird of Murcaldy had gone forward to give instructions to his crew. But when they landed at Perpignan, and the police, together with M's envoys, came aboard, Murik had disappeared.

In the briefing that followed, one of the Mirage pilots reported seeing a man fall from the rear ramp—undoubtedly Caber. Another thought that a crew member might have bailed out, but in the general melée he could not be certain.

The jets had come in fast, and to start with, the Starlifter had only taken evasive action, refusing to comply with their orders. It was only as a last resort that two of the fighters had fired one short burst each. It was after this show of strength that the Starlifter had surrendered. It was also after the firing that the jet pilot thought there might have been a parachute descent into the sea, but, he maintained, it was difficult to be sure. A lot of smoke was coming from the rear of the transport for a while, and there was light, scattered cloud.

"If he did jump," one of M's officers said, "there wouldn't be much chance of survival in the sea."

In the aircraft back to London, Lavender voiced the view that she would never be convinced of her guardian's death until she had actually seen his body.

It was, then, with a certain number of unanswered questions, that Bond reported to M that evening at the Regent's Park headquarters.

22

WARLOCK'S CASTLE

"Y OU RAN IT a bit too close for comfort, 007." M sat at his desk, facing Bond.

"For whose comfort, sir?" James Bond was weary after the long debriefing, which had begun almost as soon as he had arrived back in London during the late afternoon. Since then Bond had gone over the story from the very beginning a number of times, and suffered the constant interruptions and cross-questioning that were par for the course. The lengthy conversation had been taken down on tape, and Bill Tanner joined Bond and M, while one of the senior female officers looked after Lavender— and, no doubt, grilled her as well, thought Bond.

"Even then you let him get away." M sounded irritated.

"Too close for whose comfort, sir?" Bond repeated.

M waved the question to one side. "Everybody's. What concerns me now is the whereabouts of Anton Murik, so-called Laird of Murcaldy."

The white phone bleeped on M's desk. Following a brief exchange, M turned to his Chief-of-Staff. "There's a signal in from Perpignan. Bring it up, will you?"

Tanner left, returning a few seconds later. The news at least solved part of the mystery. M read it over twice before passing it to Bond. The French authorities had now been over the Starlifter from stem to stern. Among the extra fixtures aboard, they had discovered a small hold, accessible from under one of the tables in the canteen section. It was large enough to conceal one man and was kitted out with sufficient rations and other necessities for a few days. There were signs that it had been used; and the exit, through movable plates on the underside of the fuselage, had been opened.

"That settles it," M snapped, picking up his phone. "Better get this report typed up and signed, Bond. I'll have to alert Duggan and Ross. The fellow's still at large."

Bond held up a hand as though appealing for M to put down the phone. "With respect, sir, can I ask some questions? Then maybe make a couple of requests?"

Slowly M put down the telephone. "Ask away. I can promise nothing, but be quick about it."

"The requests will be determined by the answers to the questions . . ."

"Get on with it then, 007. We haven't got all night."

"Are Duggan's and Ross's men still prowling around Murik Castle?"

"Moved out this afternoon. They've been over the castle and Murcaldy Village with the proverbial tooth-comb." M began to fiddle with his pipe.

"Did they find anything?"

"Made a number of arrests, from what I gather. A baker called MacKenzie; some of the brawnier lads in the village. Took away a number of small arms and a few automatic weapons. Gather they've left the Laird's collection of antique weapons intact. All the modern stuff's been brought back to London."

"Did they find papers? Legal documents, mainly concerning Miss Peacock? Possibly some convertible stocks, shares, that kind of thing? Well-hidden?"

"Haven't a clue, 007. Hidden documents? Melodramatic stuff, that."

"Can you find out, sir? Find out without mentioning when my report'll be going to Sir Richard Duggan and Special Branch?"

M raised his eyebrows. "This had better be good, 007." He stabbed at the telephone. Within minutes, Bond and Bill Tanner were listening to one side of a conversation, punctuated by long pauses, between M and

Sir Richard. At last M put down the phone, shaking his head. "They took away all stray papers. But no legal documents concerning Miss Peacock. There were a couple of safes. Duggan says they'll be going over the castle again in a day or so."

"And in the meantime it's unguarded?"

M nodded. "Now the requests, eh, Bond?"

Bond swallowed. "Sir, can you hold my report for about forty-eight hours? Particularly the facts about the Aldan Aerospace Flying Club—the place we took off from en route for Perpignan."

"Why?"

"Because I don't want Special Branch thumping around there. If Anton Murik's escaped by hiding in the Starlifter, I believe he'll be on his way to that flying club now. He has a lot of contacts, and his helicopter's there."

"Then we should have Special Branch waiting for him . . ."

"No, sir. There are legal documents hidden at the castle, and—as I've said—probably some mad money as a backup. Anton Murik will be heading for the castle. He'll know the time's come to destroy the evidence of Miss Peacock's claim to the title and estates of Murcaldy. I want him caught in the act, alive if possible."

"Then we should send in Duggan's men with Special Branch."

"Sir, he should be mine." Bond's voice was like the cutting edge of a saber.

"You're asking me to bend the rules, 007. That's Duggan's territory, and I've no right . . ." He trailed into silent thought. "What exactly were you thinking of?"

"That the Chief-of-Staff comes with me, sir. That you give us forty-eight hours and the use of a helicopter."

"Helicopter?"

"To get us there quickly. Oh yes, and just before we go in, I'd like some kind of overflight."

"Overflight," M came near to shouting. *"Overflight?* Who do you think I am, 007? President of the United States? What do you mean, overflight?"

Bond tried to look sheepish. Bill Tanner was grinning. "Well, sir, haven't we got a couple of old Chipmunks, fitted with infrared, and the odd Gazelle helicopter? Aren't they under your command?"

M gave a heavy cough, as though clearing his throat.

"If the Chief-of-Staff and I went up in the helicopter, we'd need an overflight about five minutes before landing. Just to make certain the coast is clear, that Murik hasn't arrived first."

M fiddled with his pipe.

"Just for safety, sir."

"You sure you wouldn't like a squadron of fighter-bombers to strafe the place?"

Bond grinned. "I don't think that'll be necessary, sir."

There was an even longer pause before M spoke. "On one condition, Bond—providing the Chief-of-Staff agrees to this foolhardiness." He looked toward Bill Tanner, who nodded. "You do *not* go armed. In all conscience I cannot, at this stage, allow you to move into Duggan's area of operations carrying arms."

"You did say the Laird's collection of antique weapons had been left intact, sir?"

M nodded, with a sly smile. "I know nothing about any of this, James. But good luck." Then, sarcastically, he added, "Nothing else?"

"Well . . ." Bond looked away. "I wonder if Sir Richard's people could be persuaded to let us have the keys to the castle for a while? PDQ, sir. Just so that I can recover clothes there, or some such excuse."

M sighed, made a grumbling noise, and reached for the telephone again.

It was almost four o'clock in the morning when the Gazelle helicopter carrying James Bond and Bill Tanner reached Glen Murcaldy.

Bond had already been through the landing pattern with the young pilot. He wanted to be put down on the track near to the point where the Saab had gone into the large ditch. Most of all, he was concerned that the Gazelle should be kept well out of sight, though he had armed himself with two sets of hand-held flares—a red and a green—to call up the chopper if there was trouble.

Exactly five minutes before reaching touchdown, they heard the code word "Excelsior" through their headphones. The Chipmunk had overflown the glen and castle, giving them the all clear. There was no sign of any vehicle or other helicopter in the vicinity.

The rotor blades of the Gazelle had not stopped turning by the time Bond and Tanner were making their way through the gorse and bracken toward the grim mass of Murik Castle below. The early-morning air was chill and clear, while the scents brought vivid memories back into Bond's head—of his first sight of the castle and of its deceptive interior, of the attempted escape, Murik's control room with its array of weapons, the East Guest Room and its luxurious décor, and the more unpleasant dankness of the twin torture chambers.

They carried no weapons, as instructed, though Bill Tanner had, rightly, managed to get hold of a pair of powerful flashlights. M had experienced difficulty with the keys, managing only to obtain those to the rear trades-men's entrance, which, Duggan told him, was the only door left for access, the rest having been left with the electronic locks on.

It took over half an hour for the pair to get as far as the Great Lawn. Bond, silently making signals, took Tanner alongside the rear of the castle, the old keep rising above them like a dark brooding warning against the skyline. If Bond was right it would be from the helicopter pad behind the keep that Anton Murik would make his final visit to the castle—War-lock's Castle, as Bond now thought of it.

In spite of the place only having been empty for a short time, the air smelled musty and damp once they got inside the small tradesmen's door. Again, recent memories stirred. It was only a few days ago that Bond had been led through this very door and into MacKenzie's van, at the start of the long journey which had ended with a deadly rendezvous over the Mediterranean.

Now he had to find his way down to the Laird's control room and collection of weapons—for Bond was certainly not going to face Anton Murik without some kind of defense. For a while they blundered around by the glow of their flashlights, until Bond finally led the way down to the long, weapon-adorned room in the cellars. Even Bill Tanner gasped as they swung the flashlights around the walls replete with swords, thrusting weapons, pistols, muskets and rifles.

"Must be worth a fortune by itself," whispered Tanner.

Bond nodded. They had, for some unaccountable reason, whispered throughout the journey down from the tradesmen's entrance, as though Murik and his henchmen might come upon them unawares at any moment. Outside, dawn would just be breaking, streaking the sky. If Murik was going to make his dash for freedom he would either arrive soon or they would still be waiting for him to come under the cover of nightfall. Bond was running his flashlight over the weapons when Tanner suddenly clutched at his arm. They stood, motionless, ears straining for a moment, then relaxed.

"Nothing," said Tanner. Then, just as suddenly, he silenced Bond once more.

This time they could both hear the noise—from a long way off, up through the brick, stone and earth, the faint buzz of an engine.

"He's arrived." Bond grabbed at the first thing he could lay hands on—a sporting crossbow, heavily decorated, but refurbished, with a thick taut cord bound securely to a metal bow, the well-oiled mechanism including a *crane-quin* to pull back and latch the cord into place. Taking this and three sharp bolts which were arranged next to it, Bond motioned Tanner out of the room.

"Up to the hall," he whispered. "The light's not in his favor. He'll want to get hold of the stuff and be away fast. Pray God he'll take it all with him and we can catch the bastard outside."

There would be more chance in the open. Bond was sure of that. As they reached the hall, the noise of the descending helicopter became louder. It would be the little Bell Ranger, hovering and fluttering down behind the keep. Standing in the shadows, Bond strained his ears. If the pilot kept his engines running, 007 knew his theory would be right—that Murik planned to remain in the castle for only a short time, leaving quickly with whatever documents he had cached there. But if the engine was stopped, they would have to take him inside the building.

Somewhere toward the back of the house, there was the scratch and squeak of a door. Murik was entering the same way that Bond and the Chief-of-Staff had come, by the tradesmen's entrance. Thank heaven for Tanner, whose wisdom had cautioned the locking of the door behind them. There was a click and then the sound of footsteps moving surely, as a man will move in complete darkness when he knows his house with the deep intimacy of years. The steps were short and quick—unmistakable to Bond. Murik—Warlock—was home again.

From far away outside came the gentle buzz of the Bell Ranger's engine, which meant the pilot was almost certainly waiting, seated in his cockpit. Bond signaled with the crossbow and they set off silently in the direction of the door through which the Laird had returned. Outside it was almost fully light now, with only faint traces of cloud, pink from the reflected rising sun. The noise of the helicopter engine was loud, coming from behind the keep, to which Bond now pointed. Side by side, Tanner and Bond sought the edge of the old stone tower, black and bruised with age, to shelter behind one angled corner, from which they had a view of the castle's rear.

Bond bent to the task of turning the heavy *cranequin*, panting at each twist of the wheel as the steel bow drew back and its thick cord finally clicked into place. Raising the weapon skyward for safety, Bond slid one of the bolts into place. He had no idea of its accuracy, though there was no doubt of it being a lethal weapon.

The seven or eight minutes' wait seemed like a couple of hours. Then, with surprising suddenness, they heard footsteps, fast, on the gravel. Bond stepped from the cover, lifting the crossbow to his shoulder. Anton Murik was running hard, to their right, heading for the far side of the keep. In the left hand he held a thick and bulky oilskin package, while in his right he clutched at something Bond could not quite see. Squinting down the primitive crossbow sights, Bond shouted, "Far enough, Murik. It's over now."

The Laird of Murcaldy hardly paused, seeming to turn slightly toward Bond's voice, his right hand rising. There was a sharp crack followed by a high-pitched screaming hiss. A long spurt of fire streaked from Murik's hand, leaving a comet trail behind it, passing so close between Bond and Tanner that they felt the heat from the projectile, which hit the side of the keep with the thud of a sledgehammer. A whole block of the old stone cracked and splattered away, sending great shards flying. Tanner gave a little cry, clutching his cheek, where a section of sharp stone sliced through.

Bond knew immediately what Murik was using a collector's item now, from the early 1950s, the MBA Gyrojet Rocket Pistol. This hand-held launcher fired high-velocity minirockets, propelling payloads of heat-resistant steel like bright polished chrome. The 13mm. bullets, with their rocket propellant, were capable of penetrating thick steel plates. Bond had handled one, and recalled wondering what they would do to a man. He did not think twice about their efficiency. The Gyrojet pistol contained a magazine holding five rockets. He had a one-shot crossbow and no margin for error.

Bond did not hesitate. Before Murik—still running—could hurl another rocket from his Gyrojet, he squeezed the trigger of the crossbow. The mechanism slammed forward, its power taking Bond by surprise. The solid noise of the mechanism drowned any hiss the bolt might have made through the air and was, in its turn, blotted out by Murik's cry as the heavy bolt speared the upper part of his chest.

Murik continued to run, as both Bond and Tanner started after him. Then he staggered and the Gyrojet pistol dropped onto the gravel. Swaying and weaving, Murik doggedly ran on, whimpering with pain, still clutching at the oilskin package. He had by now almost reached the rising ground behind the keep, above the helicopter pad.

Bond ran hard, pausing only to sweep up the Gyrojet and check that there was a rocket in place. Grunting with pain and anguish, Anton Murik was gasping his way up the bank as Bond shouted to him for the second time. "Stop. Stop, Anton! I don't want to kill you, but I'll fire if you don't stop now."

Murik continued, as though he could hear nothing, and, as he reached the top of the mound, Bond and Tanner heard the noise of the helicopter engine rise as lift power was applied. The target was outlined against the now red morning sky—Murik teetering on top of the mound, ready to make a last dash down the other side to the Bell Ranger lying just out of sight.

Bond shouted "Stop!" once more. But for Murik there was no turning back. Carefully Bond leveled the Gyrojet pistol and squeezed the trigger. There was a crack from the primer, then he felt the butt push back into his hand as the rocket left the barrel, gathering speed with a shower of flame—a long trace of fire getting faster and faster until it struck Murik's back, with over a thousand foot-pounds of energy behind it.

Only then did Bond know what such a projectile did to a man. It was as though someone had taken a blowtorch to the rear of a cardboard cut-out target, for the center of Murik's back disintegrated. For a second, Bond could have sworn that he was able to see right through the gaping hole in the man, as he was lifted from his feet, rising into the air before falling forward out of sight.

Tanner was beside Bond, his face streaked scarlet with blood, as they paced each other up the bank. Below, the helicopter pilot was revving his motor for takeoff. One glance toward Bond and the leveled Gyrojet pistol changed his mind. The pilot shut down the engine and slowly climbed from the cockpit, placing his hands over his head.

Bond handed the weapon to Bill Tanner and descended towards the mangled remains of Anton Murik, lying just inside the pad. He hardly looked at the body. What he wanted lay a short way off—a heavy, thick oilskin package, which he picked up with care, tucking it under his arm before turning to walk slowly up the rise toward the old keep. There Bond stood for a good two minutes, taking a final long look at the castle. Warlock's Castle.

23

QUITE A LADY

JAMES BOND STOOD on the station platform, looking up into Lavender Peacock's bright eyes. It had been one of the best summers in a life which held memories of many long and eventful holiday months. Though he felt a tinge of sadness, Bond knew that all good things must end sometime. Now, the moment had come.

The oilskin packet, recovered at Murik's death, contained a whole folio of interesting items, many of which would take months to unravel. Most important of all was the irrefutable documentation concerning Murik's real parenthood and Lavender Peacock's claim to the estates and title. These also proved her real name to be Lavender Murik, Peacock being a name assumed, quite illegally, by her father before he returned to make the claim which had ended in death.

Bond had been allowed to extract these documents, and M saw to it that they were placed in the hands of the best possible solicitors in Scotland. He was optimistic that there would be a quick ruling on the matter. In a few months Lavender would gain her inheritance.

In the meantime, Bond had been given a long leave to recuperate, though Bill Tanner had stayed on duty, his cheek decorated with sticking plaster for over a month.

A few days after his return from Murcaldy, Bond had left with Lavender by car for the French Riviera. To begin with, things had gone according to plan. Thinking it would be a great treat, Bond had taken the girl to the best hotels, but she was unsettled and did not like the fuss.

On one occasion, while staying at the Negresco in Nice, Lavender wakened Bond in the night, crying out and screaming in the clutches of a nightmare. Later she told him she had dreamed of them trapped in the Starlifter, which was on fire. James Bond gently cradled her in his arms, soothed her as one comforts a child, and held her close until the sun came up. Then they sat and breakfasted on the balcony, watching the early strollers along the Promenade des Anglais and the white triangles of yacht sails against the Mediterranean.

After a few days of this, they decided on more simple pleasures—motoring into the mountains, staying in small villages far away from the crowded resorts; or at little-known seaside places, basking in the sun, lazing, eating, talking and loving.

Bond explained the new responsibilities that would soon be thrust upon her, and Lavender slowly became more serious and withdrawn. She was still fun to be with, but, as the weeks passed Bond noticed she was spending more time writing letters, making telephone calls, sending and receiving cables. Then one morning, out of the blue, she announced that they must return to England.

So it turned out that, a week after their return to London, Lavender visited a solicitor in Gray's Inn—acting for a firm in Edinburgh—to be told that the Scottish courts had upheld her claim to the Murik estates and title. There was even an imposing document from the Lord Lyon King of Arms, stating that she had inherited the title Lady Murik of Murcaldy.

Two days later, Lavender visited Bond with the news that she had managed to obtain a place at one of the major agricultural colleges, where she was going to study estate management. In fact, she would be leaving on the sleeper that night, to tie up matters in Edinburgh.

"I want to get the place running properly again," she told him. "It needs a new broom and a blast of cold air blowing through it. I think that's what my father would have wanted—for me to give the estate, and the title, its good name again."

Bond, due back from leave the following day, would not have tried to stop her. She was right, and he felt proud of having had some part in what looked like a glowing future. He took her out to dinner, then drove to collect her things and get her to the station.

"You'll come and stay, James, won't you? When I've got it all going again, I mean." She leaned down out of the train window, the last-minute bustle going on around them.

"You try and stop me," he said with a smile. "Just try. But you might have to hold my hand at night—to lay the ghosts."

"The ghosts? Really? It'll be a pleasure, James." Lady Murik leaned forward and kissed him hard on the mouth, just as the whistle blew and the train started to move. "Goodbye, James. See you again soon. Goodbye, my dear James."

"Yes, Dilly, you'll see me again soon." He stepped back, raising a hand.

Quite a Lady, thought James Bond, as the train snaked from the platform. Quite a Lady.

FOR SPECIAL SERVICES

ACKNOWLEDGMENTS
AND AUTHOR'S NOTE

As with the first continuation James Bond novel, *License Renewed*, I must acknowledge grateful thanks to the literary copyright holders—Glidrose Productions—for inviting me to follow in Ian Fleming's footsteps, and attempt to bring Mr. Bond into the 1980's. In particular, my personal thanks to Dennis Joss, Peter Janson-Smith, and John Parkinson for their patience and trust.

Great acknowledgment must also go to Peter Israel, of the Putnam Publishing Group, and my personal manager, Desmond Elliott, both of whom have given me valuable assistance and support. I would also like to express my personal gratitude to all members of Saab (GB) Ltd., and Saab-Scania in Sweden, for the amount of time, trouble, patience and enthusiasm they have put into proving that the James Bond Saab really does exist. In particular, I must mention—among a host of others—John Smerdon, Steve Andresia, Phil Hall, John Edwards, Ian Adcock, Peter Seltzer, and Hans Thornquist.

When going through the acknowledgments for *License Renewed*, I realized I had omitted a most important name—the knowledgeable man who privately researched a short list of motorcars, which eventually led to my putting Mr. Bond into a Saab: Tony Snare.

Ian Fleming, being the great craftsman he was, always attempted—with some license, granted to all writers of fiction—to get the nuts and bolts correct. I have tried to do the same thing, with one exception. While the NORAD Command Headquarters exists—in the Cheyenne Mountains, Colorado—I found it impossible to get any accurate description of the way into this incredible defense base. It has, therefore, been necessary for some invention here. All the space satellites mentioned do exist, and it is my understanding that the race for a Particle Beam Weapon is going on at this moment.

The only exception, among the satellites, is the important one which I have designated the Space Wolf. However, I am firmly assured that the capability of these weapons does exist and that they are real, even though, at the time of writing, no country will admit to any being in orbit.

JOHN GARDNER

CONTENTS

for

DESMOND ELLIOTT

1

THREE ZEROS

Euro Air Traffic Control Center, at Maastricht on the Belgian-Dutch border, passed British Airways Flight 12 over to London Control, at West Drayton, just as the aircraft cleared the coast a few miles from Ostend.

Frank Kennen has been on duty for less than ten minutes when he accepted the flight, instructing the Boeing 747 Jumbo to descend from 29,000 feet to 20,000. It was only one of many aircraft showing on his radarscope—a green speck of light, with its corresponding number, 12, together with the aircraft's altitude and heading.

All appeared normal. The flight was entering the final phase of its long haul from Singapore via Bahrain. Kennen automatically began to advise Heathrow approach control that Speedbird 12 was inbound.

His eyes remained on the huge radarscope. Specdbird 12 began its descent, the altitude numbers reducing steadily on the screen. "Speedbird One-Two cleared to two-o; vector . . ." He stopped in mid-sentence, only vaguely aware of Heathrow approach querying his information. What he now saw on the scope made his stomach turn over. With dramatic suddenness, the indicator number 12—"squawked" by the Boeing's transponder—flicked off and changed.

Now, instead of the steady green 12 beside the blip, there were three red zeros blinking on and off rapidly.

Three red zeros are the international"squawk" signal for hijack.

His voice calm, Frank Kennen called up the aircraft. "Speedbird One-Two you are cleared to two-o. Did you squawk affirmative?"

If there was trouble on board, the wording would sound like a routine exchange. But there was no response.

Thirty seconds passed, and Kennen repeated his question.

Still no response.

Sixty seconds.

Still no response.

Then, at ninety-five seconds after the first "squawk," the three red zeros disappeared from the screen, replaced by the familar 12. In his headset, Kennen heard the captain's voice, and breathed a sigh of relief. "Speedbird One-Two affirmative squawk. Emergency now over. Please alert Heathrow. We need ambulances and doctor. Several dead and at least one seriously injured on board. Repeat emergency over. May we proceed as instructed? Speedbird One-Two."

The captain could well have added, "Emergency over, thanks to Commander Bond."

2

NINETY SECONDS

A LITTLE EARLIER, James Bond had been reclining, apparently relaxed and at ease, in an aisle seat on the starboard side of the executive-class area of Flight BA 12.

In fact, Bond was far from relaxed. Behind the drowsy eyes and slumped position, his mind was in top gear, while his body poised—wound, tight as a spring.

Anyone looking closely would also have seen the strain behind the blue eyes. From the moment James Bond had boarded the flight in Singapore, he was ready for trouble—and even more so following the takeoff at Bahrain. After all, he knew the bullion had come aboard at Bahrain. So did the four undercover Special Air Service men, also on the flight, spread tactically through the first, executive, and tourist classes.

It was not simply the tension of this particular flight that was getting to Bond, but the fact the Flight BA 12 from Singapore was his third long-haul journey, made as an antihijack guard, in as many weeks. The duty shared with members of the SAS, had come following the recent appalling spate of hijackings that had taken place on aircraft from a dozen countries.

No single terrorist organization had claimed responsibility, but the major airlines were already suffering from a shrinkage in passengers. Panic was rapidly spreading, even though many companies—and, indeed, governments—had poured soothing words into the ears of the general traveling public.

In each recent case, hijackers had been ruthless. Deaths among both passengers and crew were the norm. Some of the hijacked aircraft had been ordered to fly to remote airfields hidden in dangerous, often mountainous European areas. There had been one case of a 747, instructed to make a descent near the Swiss Bernese Alps onto a makeshift runway hidden away in a high valley. The result was catastrophic, ending with no recognizable bodies—not even those of the hijackers.

In some cases, after safe landings the booty had been off-loaded and taken away in small aircraft, while the original target was burned or destroyed by explosives. In every case, the slightest interference, or hesitation, had brought sudden death   crew members, passengers, and even children.

The worst incident, to date, was the theft of easily movable jewels, worth two million sterling. Having got their hands on the metal cases containing the gems, the hijackers ordered a descent and then parachuted from the aircraft. Even as the passengers must have been breathing sighs of relief, the airplane had been blown from the sky by a remote-control device.

Major United States carriers and British Airways had borne the brunt of the attacks; so, following this last harrowing incident—some six weeks before—both governments had arranged for secret protection on all possible targets.

The last two trips in which Bond had participated had proven uneventful. This time he had experienced that sixth sense that danger was at hand.

First, on boarding at Singapore, he had spotted four possible suspects. These four men, expensively dressed and carrying the trappings of commuting businessmen, were seated in the executive area: two on the port side of the center section, to Bond's left; the other two forward—about five rows in front of him. All had that distinctive military bearing, yet stayed quiet, as though at pains not to draw attention to themselves.

Then, at Bahrain, the worry had come aboard—almost two billion dollars' worth of gold, currency, and diamonds—and three young men and a girl embarked. They smelled of violence—the girl, dark-haired, goodlooking, but hard as a rock; the three men, swarthy, fit, with the compact movements of trained soldiers.

On one of his seemingly casual walkabouts, Bond had marked their seat positions. Like the supect businessmen, they sat in pairs, but behind him, in the tourist section.

Bond and the SAS men were of course armed, Bond with a new pair of throwing knives, balanced perfectly and well-honed, developed from the Sykes-Fairbairn commando dagger. One was in his favorite position, strapped to the inside of the left forearm, the other sheathed, horizontally, across the small of his back. He also carried the highly restricted revolver developed by an internationally reliable firm for use during inflight emergencies.

This weapon is a small smooth-bore .38 with cartridges containing a minimal charge. The projectile is a fragmentation bullet—lethal at a few feet only, for its velocity is spent quickly, so that the bullet disintegrates in order to avoid penetration of an airframe, or the metal skin of an aircraft.

The SAS men were similarly armed and had undergone extensive training, but Bond remained unhappy about any kind of revolver on board. A shot too close to the sides, or a window, could still possibly cause a serious depressurization problem. He would always stick with knives, using the revolver only if really close up to his target, and by "close" he meant two feet.

The giant 747 banked slightly, and Bond registered the slight change in pitch from the engines, signaling the start of their descent. Probably somewhere just off the Belgian coast, he considered, his eyes roaming around the cabin, watching and waiting.

A statuesque blond stewardess, who had been much in evidence during the flight, was passing a pair of soft-drink cans to two of the businessmen a few rows in front of Bond. He saw her face and in a flash sensed something wrong. Her fixed smile had gone, and she was bending unusually low, whispering to the men.

Automatically Bond glanced to his left, toward the other pair of neatly-dressed men. In the seconds that his mind had focused on the stewardess, the two other men had disappeared.

Turning his head, Bond saw one of the them, carrying what looked to be a can of beer, standing behind him in the aisle near the small galley at the rear of the executive-class section.

By this time the stewardess had gone into the forward galley.

As Bond began to move, all hell broke loose.

The man behind him pulled the ring on his beer can, tossing it down the aisle. As it rolled, dense smoke started to fill the cabin.

The two men forward were now out of their seats, and Bond caught sight of the stewardess back in the aisle, this time with something in her hand. On the far side, he glimpsed the fourth businessman, also hurling a smoke of canister as he began to run forward toward the nose of the aircraft.

Bond was on his feet and turning. His nearest target—the man in the aisle behind him—hesitated for a vital second. The knife appeared in Bond's right hand as though by some practiced legerdemain, held down, thumb forward, in the classic fighting pose. The hijacker did not know what hit him, only a sudden rip of pain and surprise as Bond's dagger slid home just below the heart.

The whole cabin was now full of smoke and panic. Bond shouted for passengers to remain seated. He heard similar cries from the SAS boys in the tourist class, and forward, in the first and so-called "penthouse suite." Then there were two small explosions, recognizable as airguard revolver shots, followed by the more sinister heavy bang of a normal weapon.

Holding his breath in the choking fog of smoke, Bond headed for the executive-class galley. From there he knew it would be possible to cross to the port side and negotiate the spiral stairway to the "penthouse" and flight deck. There were still at least three hijackers left—possibly four.

On reaching the galley, he knew there were only a probable three. The stewardess, still clutching a Model 11 Ingram submachine gun, in the swirl of smoke, lay sprawled on her back, her chest ripped away by a close-range shot from one of the airguard revolvers.

Still holding his breath, knife at his side, Bond sidestepped the body, oblivious of the screams and coughing of terrified passengers throughout the aircraft. Above the noise came a loud, barked order from overhead— "Orange One . . . Orange One"—the signal, from an SAS man, that the main assault was taking place on, or near, the flight deck.

At the foot of the spiral staircase, Bond dodged another body, one of the SAS team, unconscious and with a nasty shoulder wound. Then, from the short turn in the spiral, he spotted the crouched figure of one of the businessmen raising an Ingram, shoulder stock extended.

Bond's arm curved back, and the knife flickered through the air, so razor sharp that it slid into the man's throat from the rear like an oversized hypodermic. The hijacker did not even cry out as blood spurted in a hoselike jet from his severed carotid artery.

Crouching low, Bond clambered, cat-silent, to the body, using it as a shield to peer into the upper area of the aircraft.

The door to the flight deck was open. Just inside, one of the "businessmen," a submachine gun in his hands, was giving instructions to the crew, while his backup man faced outward from the doorway, the now familar Ingram—capable of doing a great deal of damage at a fire rate of 1,200 rounds per minute—swinging in a lethal arc of readiness. Behind the upper galley bulkhead, some six feet from where the hijackers stood, one of the SAS men crouched, airguard revolver clutched close to his body.

Bond looked across at the SAS man, and they exchanged signals: the teams had all worked together over a hard and concentrated week at Bradbury Lines, 22 SAS Regiment's base near Hereford. In very short order, both men understood what they had to do.

Bond edged to one side of the slumped man on the narrow stairway, his hand reaching for the knife sheathed to his back. One deep breath, then the nod to the SAS man, who leaped forward, firing as he went.

The hijacker guard, alerted by Bond's movement, swung his Ingram toward the stairwell as two bullets from the SAS airguard revolver caught him in the throat.

He was neither lifted nor spun by the impact. He simply topped forward, dead before he hit the ground.

As he fell, the hijacker on the flight deck whirled around. Bond's arm moved back. The throwing knife spun, twinkling and straight as a kingfisher, to carve into the hijacker's chest.

The Ingram fell to the deck. Then Bond and the SAS man, moving as one, were on the hijacker, frisking and feeling for hidden weapons or grenades. The wounded man gasped for air, his hands scrabbling for the knife, eyes rolling, and a horrific croaking rattle coming from the bloodstained lips.

"All over," Bond shouted at the aircraft's captain, hoping that it was, indeed, all over. Almost ninety seconds had passed since the first smoke bomb exploded.

"I'll check below," he called to the SAS man who knelt over the wounded hijacker.

Down in the main section of the aircraft, the smoke had almost cleared, and Bond grinned cheerfully at a white-faced senior stewardess. "Get them calmed down," he told her. "It's okay." He patted her arm, then told her not to go near the executive-class forward galley.

He went himself, pushing people away, firmly ordering passengers back to their seats. He covered the dead stewardess's body with a coat.

The two remaining SAS men had, rightly, remained in the rear of the aircraft, covering any backup action which might have been laid on by the terrorists. Walking the length of the Boeing, James Bond had to smile to himself. The three tough-looking young men and the girl who had become his suspects when boarding at Bahrain looked even more pale and shaken than their fellow passengers.

As he mounted the spiral staircase again, the quiet tones of the purser came through the interphone system, advising the passengers that they would shortly be landing at London Heathrow and apologizing for what he called "the unscheduled unpleasantness."

The SAS officer shook his head as Bond emerged into the "penthouse suite." The hijacker who had been the target for Bond's second knife was now laid out over two spare seats, his body covered with plastic sheeting.

"No way," the SAS officer said. "Lasted only a few minutes."

Bond asked if the man had regained consciousness.

"Just at the end. Tried to speak."

"Oh?"

"Couldn't make head nor tail of it myself."

Bond prodded him to remember.

"Well . . . well, he seemed to be trying to say something. It was very indistinct, though. Sounded like 'inspector.' He was rattling and coughing up blood, but the last part certainly sounded like that."

James Bond became silent. He took a nearby seat for the landing. As the 747 came whining in, flaps fully extended and the spoilers lifting as the airplane rolled out, touching down gently on runway 28R, he pondered the hijacker's last words. No, he thought, it was too farfetched, an obsession out of his past. *Inspector. In . . . spector.* Forget about the "In."

Was it possible after all this time?

No, he thought again, closing his eyes briefly. The long flight and the sudden bloody action at the end must have scrambled his brains. The founder, Ernst Stavro Blofeld, was dead beyond a doubt. SPECTRE as an organized unit had expired with Blofeld.

But who could tell? The original organization spanned the world and at one time had its fingers into practically every major crime syndicate, as well as most of the police forces, security, and secret intelligence services, in the so-called civilized world.

Inspector. In . . . spector. SPECTRE, his old enemy, the Special Executive for Counterintelligence, Terrorism, Revenge, and Extortion. Was it possible that a new SPECTRE had risen, like some terrible mutated phoenix, to haunt them in the 1980's?

The 747's engines cut off. The bell-like signal told the passengers to disembark.

Yes. James Bond decided it was highly possible.

3

THE HOUSE ON THE BAYOU

IT STOOD, DECAYING and corrupt, on the only firm piece of ground in the midst of swampland. The bayou channeled around it, then split to join brothers and disappeared in steamy green marshes.

The nearest town was six miles away, and the few people who lived near the edge of that great watery marsh, on the lower reaches of the Mississippi River, kept away from the soggy bank across from the house.

Very old people said some mad Englishman had built it, in the 1820's, as a grand palace from which he would tame the swamp. But he did not get far. There was trouble with a woman—and there had certainly been death, from fever and disease, also from violence. The house was surely haunted. There were unexplained noises. It was also protected by its own evil: guarded by snakes, great snakes, the likes of which were not seen in other parts of the swamp. These great snakes—up to thirty and forty feet in length, some reported—kept close to the house, but, as the nearest store owner, Askon Delville, said, "They don't seem to bother Criton none."

Criton was a deaf-mute. Children ran from his path, and adults did not like him. But, as with Criton and the great snakes, Criton did not bother Askon Delville none.

The deaf-mute would cross on a marsh hopper, about once a week, and walk the five miles to Askon's store with a list of necessities. He would collect the goods, then walk back the five miles, get into the marsh hopper, and disappear over the bayou.

There was a woman at the house also. People caught sight of her from time to time, and it was certain she wrote out the order that Criton carried to Askon Delville's store. She was, of course, some kind of witch, otherwise she would not be able to live in such a haunted place.

People took special care to stay away when the gatherings happened. They always knew when there was going to be one; Askon told them. He knew because of Criton's list. The day of a gathering, Criton usually made two trips because there was so much extra stuff needed at the house. Then, around dusk, you really kept clear. There would be noises— automobiles, extra marsh hoppers—and the house, they said, got all lit up. Sometimes there was music; and one day, about a year ago, young Freddie Nolan—who wasn't scared of anything—took his own marsh hopper out, about two miles upstream, planning to sneak up and take some pictures.

Nobody saw young Freddie Nolan again, but his marsh hopper turned up, all smashed to pieces, like some great animal—or snake—had got to it.

There was a gathering this week.

Nobody except Criton and the woman—who answered to the name Tic—and the monthly visitors knew that the inside of the house was as solid as the piece of rock on which it was built. The old rotting exterior clapboard was only a shell to the real thing: stone, brick, glass, and steel, not to mention a fair portion of opulence.

Eleven people had come this month: two from London, England; two from New York; one German; a Swede; a pair of Frenchman; one from L.A.; a big man who came every month all the way from Cairo, Egypt; and the Leader. The Leader was called Blofeld, though in the outside world the name was very different.

They dined magnificently. Later, after the liqueurs and coffee, the whole party went into the conference room at the back of the house.

The long room was decorated in a soft lime. Heavy matching drapes covered the huge French windows which looked out onto the far side of the bayou. The drapes were closed by the time the company assembled, wall lights glowing, with brass-shaded strips above the four paintings which formed the only decoration—two Jackson Pollocks, a Miró and a Kline. The Kline had been one of the pieces of art stolen in a recent hijack. Blofeld liked it so much that they had moved it to the house and not put it on sale.

A polished oak table occupied most of the center of the room. It was set for eleven people, complete with blotters, drinks, pens, paper, ashtrays, and agendas.

Blofeld took the place at the head of the table, while the others filed to their seats, all marked with name cards. They did not sit until the Leader had taken the chair.

"This month's agenda is short," Blofeld began. "Three items only: the budget; the recent debacle on Flight BA 12; and the operation we call HOUND. Now, Mr. El Ahadi, the budget, please."

The gentleman from Cairo, Egypt, rose to his feet. He was a tall, dark man with immensely handsome features and a honeyed voice that had charmed many a young woman in its time. "I am pleased to announce," he said, "that even without the hoped-for proceeds from Flight BA 12, our bank accounts in Switzerland, London, and New York contain, respectively, four hundred million dollars; fifty million pounds sterling; and nine hundred million dollars. The total, according to our calculations, will suffice for our present purposes, and if operations succeed according to budget—as our Leader predicts—we can expect to double the amount in one year. As agreed, all profits, over and above our initial investment, will be shared equally." He gave his most charming smile, and the assembled company sat back, relaxed.

Blofeld's hand came down hard on the table. "Very good." The voice had taken on a rasping edge. "But the failure of our assault on Flight 12 is inexcusable. Particularly after so much preparation on your part, Herr Treiben." Blofeld shot a look of disgust at the German delegate. "As you know, Herr Treiben, under similar circumstances, others on the executive committee of SPECTRE have paid the ultimate price."

Treiben, plump and pink, a warlord of the West German underworld in his own right, felt the color drain from his face.

"However," Blofeld continued, "we have another scapegoat. You may not know it, Treiben, but we finally caught up with your Mr. de Luntz."

"Ah?" Treiben rubbed his hands and said that he also had been looking for a Mr. de Luntz. All his best men had searched for de Luntz without success.

"Yes, we have found him." Blofeld beamed, the hands coming together in a clap which sounded like a pistol shot. "Having found him, I believe he should now join his friends." The drapes over the large windows slid back silently. As they did so, the room lights dimmed. Outside the window, the close environment appeared bright as day. "An infrared device," Blofeld explained, "so that the guardians of this house will not be frightened by light. Ah, here comes your Mr. de Luntz now."

A bald, frightened-looking man in a dirty, crumpled suit was led onto the patch of ground immediately in front of the window. His hands were tied behind his back and his feet shackled, so that he shuffled under Criton's grasp. His eyes rolled wildly, as though he was desperately searching the dark for a way of escape from something not defined, but obviously terrible.

Criton led the man to a metal stake, secured only a few feet from the thick glass of the window. Inside, the observers could now see that a short length of rope hung from the restraints around de Luntz's wrists. Criton attached the rope to the stake, turned, smiled toward the window, then stepped back and out of sight.

The moment Criton was clear, there came a thud from the far side of the window, and the captive, de Luntz, was hemmed in by a metal grille of Cyclone fencing attached to a heavy framework. This grille was three-sided, with a top like a small square ice-hockey goal. The open front ended almost at the edge of the water, which lapped some nine feet from the window.

"What's he done?" one of the Americans asked. It was Mascro, the white-haired avuncular man from Los Angeles.

"He was the backup man on BA 12. He did not go to the assistance of his comrades." Treiben sneered.

"Mr. Mascro"—Blofeld raised a hand—"de Luntz has told us exactly what happened. How the others died, and who did it. Ah, one of the guardians has spotted Mr. de Luntz. I've always wanted to see if a giant python really can eat a man whole."

Standing behind the French windows, the executive committee of SPECTRE watched with a fascinated horror. The infrared gave them a clear, daylight picture. They could also hear the unfortunate victim start to scream as he spotted the reptile squirming in from the tall reeds near the marshy water's edge.

The python was huge, at least thirty feet in length, with a fat solid body and a massive triangular head. De Luntz, tethered to the stake, began to pull and twist, trying to drag himself clear, but the python suddenly launched forward, entwining itself around the man.

The creature now moved with extraordinary speed, circling de Luntz's body like some great clining vine. It seemed only a matter of seconds before the python's head was in line with that of its victim—the two, interlocked, swaying as if in an obscene dance of death. De Luntz's screams grew more agonized as the python brought its head level with his face, the fanged jaws snapping in excited anger. Reptile and prey looked into each other's eyes for a few seconds, and the watchers could plainly see the python's crushing grip tighten on the man's body.

Then de Luntz went limp, and the pair fell to the ground. One of the observers, safe behind the window, gasped loudly. The giant snake had unwound itself with three fast flicks of its body, and was now examining its meal. The snapping jaws first made for the securing rope, tugging it clear, then moved toward the body's feet.

"That's quite amazing." Blofeld stood very close to the window. "See, the snake's pushing his shoes off."

Now the python squirmed around so that its head was exactly aligned with the body's feet, which the reptile pushed together, before opening its jaws to an almost unbelievable width and clamping down on the corpse's ankles.

The entire process took almost an hour, yet the group inside remained fascinated, hypnotized. The python swallowed in a series of jerks, resting, immobile, after each effort, until the last vestiges of de Luntz were gone. Then the snake lay quietly, exhausted by its exertions, its long body bloated from normal shape so that the watchers could clearly discern the outlines of the squeezed human frame halfway down the snake's body.

"An interesting lesson for us all." Blofeld's hands came together again, and the drapes slid back into place, the lights came up. Reflectively the group returned to the table, some white and visibly shaken at what they had witnessed.

The German, Treiben—who had known de Luntz well in life—was the most affected. "You said . . ." he began, his voice quavering a shade. "You said de Luntz spoke before . . . before . . ."

"Yes." Blofeld nodded. "He spoke. He sang whole arias. Pavarotti could not have done better. He even sang his own death warrant. Apparently there were people expecting us on Flight BA 12. We have yet to discover if someone talked, or whether all high-risk cargoes are now being protected.

"The plan went with clockwork precision. The girl did a magnificent job in getting herself scheduled on that flight and smuggling the smoke canisters and weapons on board. The attack took place on time to the second, there's no doubt about that. De Luntz, however, excused himself from taking part. He claimed to be boxed in at the rear of the plane. It seems there were five guards traveling on BA 12. From de Luntz's description, they were members of the British Special Air Service." Blofeld paused, looking at each man in turn. Then: "All except one."

The men around the table waited, on air of expectancy permeating the room.

"The reorganization of this great society, of which we are all members," the Leader continued, "has taken a long time. We have been in hibernation. Now the world will soon see that we are awake. In particular we will have to deal with one old enemy who was a constant thorn in the side of my illustrious predecessor. Mr. de Luntz—God rest his soul—identified four of the guards on that airplane as possible undercover SAS men. He also made a positive identification of the fifth man—the one, I might add, who caused the most damage. I personally questioned de Luntz. Gentlemen, our old enemy James Bond was on that aircraft."

The faces around the table hardened; all turned toward Blofeld.

At last it was Mascro who spoke: "You want me to put out a contract on him? In the old days, when your—"

The Leader cut him short. "It has been tried before. No. No contracts; no specialists sent to London. I have personal scores to settle with Mr. Bond. Gentlemen, I have devised a method to deal with him—call it a lure if you like. If it has worked, and I see no reason for it to fail, soon we shall have the pleasure of Mr. Bond's company on this side of the Atlantic. I intend to deal with him just as that reptile dealt with the wayward de Luntz."

Blofeld paused, looking around the table to make certain all concentration was on the subject at hand.

"Soon," Blofeld continued, "we shall be fully launched into the planning of what, by mutual decision, has—for security reasons—at this stage, been called HOUND."

The Leader chuckled. "Ironic, yes? A nice touch to talk of HOUND. Hound, taken from the Christian poem *The Hound of Heaven.*" The chuckle had turned into a smile. "The Hound of Heaven, or the Hounds of Heaven, eh? Hounds; Wolves. It is good, our target being America's great threat, the Wolves of Space, already circling the globe in their packs, waiting to pounce and tear their victims apart—and, in the midst of it, Mr. Bond. This time SPECTRE will wipe Mr. James Bond from the face of this planet."

There were murmurs of grim agreement from around the table before Blofeld, glancing at a small gold wristwatch, spoke again. "In fact, my bait should have been taken by now. Soon, gentlemen, soon we shall see James Bond face to face. And the beauty of it is that he will not know whom he is meeting or what is really in store for him."

4

PILLOW THOUGHTS

JAMES BOND GLANCED affectionately at Ann Reilly's face, quiet and beautiful in sleep, on the pillow next to him. The sleek and shining straw-colored hair was tousled around her oval face. For a fleeting second, she reminded Bond of Tracy—his wife of less than a few hours before Ernst Stavro Blofeld so viciously gunned her down on the Autobahn from Munich to Kufstein, as they were heading for their honeymoon.

Ann Reilly—a member of Bond's own Service, assistant to the Armorer, and second-in-command of Q Branch—was known by all and sundry within the big headquarters building overlooking Regent's Park as Q'ute. An apt nickname for the elegant, tall, and very efficient and liberated young lady.

After a slightly shaky start, Bond and Q'ute had become friends and what she liked to call "occasional lovers." This evening had been divided into two sections. First, duty—the checking and firing of Bond's new personal handgun, the Heckler & Koch VP70, the weapon which both M and the Armorer had now decided would be carried by *all* officers of the Service.

Bond had objected. After all, he had usually been allowed to choose his own handgun, and was more than put out when his trusted Walther PPK had been withdrawn from service in 1974. On his last mission he had been severely criticized for using an old, yet highly efficient Browning. In his own stubborn way, 007 had fought for his personal rights—an action applauded by Q'ute, a champion of feminism, which, by definition, meant she also championed certain male causes.

But if M's word was law, then the Armorer would see the ruling was carried out, and Bond had—in due course—been issued with VP70.

While the VP70 was much larger than the Walther, Bond had to admit that the weapon posed no problem as far as concealment was concerned. It felt good, with its longer butt and good balance. It was also both accurate and lethal—9mm, with an eighteen-round magazine and the ability to fire semiautomatic three-shots bursts when fitted with the light shoulder stock.

There was no doubt that it was also a man-stopper of considerable power, and—in recent days—between lengthy sessions with his old friend Bill Tanner, M's chief of staff, concerning the hijack and identity of the terrorists, James Bond had spent a lot of time getting to know his new pistol.

So, that evening, from five o'clock to seven-thirty, 007 was on the underground range going through a fast-draw and firing session with the expert Q'ute.

Almost from the moment he had first found himself working with Q'ute, Bond developed a respect for her immense professionalism. She certainly knew her job—from weaponry to the complex mysteries of electronics. But she could also hold her own as the most feminine of women.

When they finished on the range that night, Ann Reilly made it clear that if Bond was free, she was available until the following morning.

After dining at a small Italian restaurant—the Campana, in Marylebone High Street—the couple had gone back to Q'ute's apartment, where they made love with a disturbing wildness, as though time was running out for both of them.

The draining of their bodies left the agile Q'ute exhausted. She fell asleep almost immediately after their last long and tender kiss. Bond, however, stayed wide-awake, his alert state of mind brought about by the mounting anxiety of the past few days, and by what he had discovered with Bill Tanner.

The BA 12 terrorists had all been traced back to a German underworld figure who also dabbled in political and economic espionage, one Kurt Walter Treiben. Even the stewardess, it was now proven, had pulled strings to be assigned to that particular flight, and though she had been with British Airways for almost three years, her background also linked her to Treiben.

The most disturbing points were the dying terrorist's words and the fact that Treiben had once been an associate of the infamous Ernst Stavro

Blofeld, founder and leader of the original, multinational SPECTRE.

Further investigation led them to increasing worries. From all the hijacks, there was now positive ID on six men. Two were known hoodlums on the payroll of Michael Mascro, Los Angeles' ranking criminal; one could be linked to Kranko Stewart and Dover Richardson, New York "fixers" and gangsters; two worked exclusively for Bjorn Junten, the Swedish-born freelance intelligence expert whose private espionage service was always open to the highest bidder; while the sixth identified man was tied in to the Banquette brothers from Marseilles—a pair of villains upon whom both the French police and the Service de Documentation Extérieure et de Contre-Espionage—the French intelligence service—had been trying to pin evidence for the past twenty years.

Like the German Treiben, the principals in these identifications—Mascro, Stewart, Richardson, Junten, and the Banquette brothers—had their own personal connections to Ernst Stavro Blofeld and SPECTRE.

There could be but one conclusion: SPECTRE was alive and operating again.

Bond quietly lit one of his special low-tar cigarettes, originally made for him by Moreland's of Grosvenor Street and now produced—after much discussion and bending of rules—by H. Simmons of Burlington Arcade: the earliest-known cigarette manufacturers in London. This firm even agreed to retain the distinctive three gold rings—together with their own silhouette trademark—on each of the specially produced cigarettes, and Bond felt not a little honored that he was the only customer who could coax personalized cigarettes from Simmons.

Blowing smoke at the ceiling, conscious of Q'ute in deep and satisfied sleep beside him, Bond thought of the other women who had played such a decisive role in his Service career: Vesper Lynd, who, in death, had seemed molded like a stone effigy; Gala Brand, now Mrs. Vivian, with three kids and a nice house in Richmond—they exchanged Christmas cards but he had never seen her again after the Drax business; Honey Rider; Tiffany Case; Domino Vitale; Solitaire; Pussy Galore; the exquisite Kissy Suzuki; his last great conquest, Lavender Peacock, now managing her Scottish estate with great success. In spite of the warmth and genuine affection which flowed, even in sleep, from Ann Reilly, Bond's mind ran riot. Again and again his thoughts turned to Tracy di Vicenzo—Tracy Bond.

There had been a time when Bond's memory had been lost for a considerable period; but experts had brought him back from the darkness of unknowing, and the final moments of Ernst Stavro Blofeld now lived clearly and vividly in his mind—Blofeld in his grotesque Japanese Castle of Death, with the poisoned garden: the last battle, when Bond was ill-equipped to deal with the big man wielding his deadly samurai sword. Yet he had done it, with the greatest lust for another man's blood he had ever experienced. Even now, when he thought long of Blofeld, Bond felt an ache in his thumbs: he had choked the man to death with his bare hands.

Yes, Blofeld was dead; but SPECTRE lived on.

Bond stubbed out the cigarette, turned on his side, and tried to sleep. When at last, blessed darkness swallowed his consciousness, James Bond still did not rest. He dreamed; and his dreams were of his beloved lost Tracy.

He woke with a start. Light showed in a glimmer through the curtains. Turning to look at the Rolex on the night table, Bond saw it was almost five-forty-five.

"Late to bed, early to rise." Q'ute giggled, her hand moving under the bedclothes to add point to her humor.

Bond gazed down at her, breaking into a winning smile. She reached up, kissed him, and they began just where they had left off the night before, until the *beep-beep-beep* of Bond's pocket pager interrupted them.

"Damn," breathed Q'ute. "Can't they ever leave you alone?"

Reaching for the telephone, Bond caustically reminded her that she had personally paged him, on matters of business, three times in the past week. "No time's the right time," he said, smiling wearily as he dialed the headquarters number.

"Transworld Export," said the voice of the duty switchboard operator.

Bond identified himself. There was a pause, then Bill Tanner's voice: "You're needed. He's been here half the night and wants to see you soonest. Something very big's afoot."

Bond glanced back toward Q'ute. "On my way," he said into the instrument. Then, cradling the phone, he told her that Bill Tanner had just said something big was afoot.

She pushed him out of the bed, telling him to stop boasting.

Grumbling, mainly because he would get no proper breakfast, James Bond shaved and dressed, while Ann Reilly made coffee.

The Saab, gleaming silver, stood outside the block of flats. It had only recently been returned to him, completely refurbished by both Saab and the security firm which provided Bond, privately, with the special technology built into the turbo-charged vehicle. In seconds the car was picking up speed effortlessly.

There was little traffic, and it took only ten minutes of relaxed driving—

the car answering Bond's feet and hands like the thoroughbred it was—to get to the tall building overlooking Regent's Park. There Bond took the elevator up to the ninth floor and walked straight to M's anteroom where Miss Moneypenny sat dejectedly at her desk.

"Morning, Penny." Bond, though feeling jaded, put on a show for his old flirting partner's benefit.

"Maybe good for you, James. But I've been up half the night."

"Who hasn't?" A smile of sublime innocence.

Moneypenny gave a wan smirk. "According to the powder vine, James, it would be with a cute little girl from Q Branch. I suppose I can just eat my heart out."

"Penny"—Bond walked toward M's door—"I have but one heart. It's always been yours. Nibble away at mine whenever you desire."

"In a pig's eye," Moneypenny retorted with more than a hint of acid. "You'd better get in there, James. He told me to fire you through the door—his words—as soon as you arrived."

Bond winked, straightened his RN tie, and knocking at M's door, walked in.

M looked tired. It was the first thing Bond noticed. The second was the girl—short, well-proportioned, athletic, but with an undoubtedly feminine smile and dark hair cut into a mass of tight curls.

Her large brown eyes did not waver as they met Bond's gaze. There was something familiar about the eyes; as though he had seen, or met, the girl before.

"Come in, 007," M was saying, his voice edgy. "I don't think you've ever met this lady, but she's the daughter of an old friend of yours. Commander James Bond . . . Miss Cedar Leiter."

5

CEDAR

Later Bond felt that he must have looked like a ninny, standing there in M's office, jaw dropped, staring at the girl. She was something to stare at, even dressed in the casual denim skirt and shirt. Her face, like her brown eyes, showed a tranquillity which, Bond sensed, belied a fast-working mind—accurate and deadly as the body. The girl was an expert. Indeed she should be, when one considered her father.

"Well," was all Bond could muster.

Cedar's face blossomed into a smile that reminded him, almost painfully, of his old friend Felix. It was a devil-may-care look, one eyebrow raised as if to say: Get it right or go to hell.

M grunted. "You've not met Miss Leiter before, then, 007?" M still spoke of Bond as 007, even though the famous Double-O Section with its license to kill had long been disbanded.

Bond had known Felix was married, but when they had worked together, his old CIA friend—later turned private investigator—had never spoken of his wife or children.

"No," Bond replied somewhat tersely, for the full impact had just hit him. "How is Felix?"

Cedar's eyes clouded slightly, as though she had suffered a quick physical pain. When she spoke, the voice was low, husky, and without a hint of what the British think of as an American accent. Mid-Atlantic, they could call it.

"Daddy's fine. They've fixed him up with the latest thing in artificial limbs." Her momentary sadness disappeared, the smile returned. "He's got an incredible new hand, says it can do anything. Spends a lot of time shooting and practicing quick-draw techniques. I'm sure he'd want me to say hello."

In a split-second, Bond relived that time in his life he would rather banish into oblivion—the time when Felix had lost an arm and a leg, as well as suffering other damage which called for years of work by plastic surgeons. James Bond often blamed himself for Felix Leiter's predicament, though they had both been after a black gangster whose sadistic madness was an almost unique danger. Buonaparte Ignace Gallia: Mr. Big. In any case, as Felix would have been the first to admit, he was lucky to be alive at all after the shark attack engineered by Mr. Big; while Bond took consolation in the fact that, in the end, he had put the gangster away for good—and in the most unpleasant way possible, letting the punishment fit the crime.

Quickly Bond came out of his reverie, catching up on Cedar Leiter's last sentence: "He'd want you to say hello?"

She cocked her head, "If he knew I was here."

M grunted once more. "I think we'd better get down to business, 007. Miss Leiter is a sleeper, just brought to life. She arrived in the early hours." He hesitated, with a slight frown of displeasure. "On *my* doorstep. I've listened to what she had to tell me. Chief of Staff's just checking her out now, with a cipher through the U.S. embassy."

Bond asked if he could sit, and receiving the terse nod from M, asked what the business was.

"I've already been through it. Miss Leiter will pull you in the picture."

"Oh, please call me Cedar, sir. . . ." She broke off at M's withering look, realizing that she had made the gaffe of all time. M strongly disapproved of easy familiarity, particularly in Service matters.

"Start, Miss Leiter," M snapped.

Cedar's career had begun, when she was eighteen, as a secretary in the State Department. Within a year she was approached by the Central Intelligence Agency. "I suppose it was because of my father." She did not smile this time. "But I was warned that he was never to know." She kept her job at State, but went through a comprehensive course during vacations, weekends, and on certain evenings.

"They didn't want me active. That was made clear from the start. I was to be trained and to take regular refresher courses, but to keep my job at State. They specifically told me that I'd be called eventually.

"Well, the call came last week. I suppose they keep tabs on you. I was planning a short trip to Europe. As it's turned out, it's an official trip, and I've been used because I'm not what you call a 'face.'" Cedar meant that she was unknown to any of the world's intelligence communities. "There's one key word that M has to relay to Langley, and a key word in response, to show I'm on the level—I guess that's what we're waiting to clear now."

M nodded, adding that he had no doubt Miss Leiter was "on the level," as she had put it. Certainly the documents and the request she had brought made sense.

"I'm putting you onto this, 007, as it is a question of working in harmony with Miss Leiter in the United States. . . ."

"But SPE—?" Bond began.

"That matter will make itself clear in a moment. I'm putting you on Special Duty. Special Services to the U.S. government." M picked up several sheets of paper from his desk, and Bond could not help seeing that the first was a short typewritten note bearing the Presidential Seal. There was no further point in arguing with his chief. "What's the story then, sir?" Bond asked.

"Briefly," M began, "it concerns a gentleman by the name of Markus Bismaquer."

M glanced at the papers in his hand and rattled off the details of Bismaquer's life and background: Born 1919, New York City. Only son of mixed parentage—German and English. Both American citizens. Made his first million before the age of twenty, multimillionaire within three years. Avoided military service during World War Two by nature of being classified "undesirable"—he was, apparently, a firm and convinced member of the American Nazi party. Something he has since tried to keep quiet, but with little success." M made a noise which could only be interpreted as a sign of disgust. "Sold out all his business interests, at a great profit, in the early 1950's and has lived like a Renaissance prince ever since. Rarely seen away from his own principality, as it were . . ."

"His own what?" Bond frowned.

"Figure of speech, 007. Miss Leiter will explain."

Cedar Leiter took a deep breath. "Bismaquer owns one hundred and fifty square miles of what was once desert, about eighty miles southwest of Amarillo, Texas; and M is right to call it his principality. He's irrigated the area, built on it, and virtually sealed it off. No roads run into Rancho Bismaquer. You get in by one of two ways: there's a small airstrip, and he has his own private monorail system. There's a closed station fifteen miles out of town—Amarillo, that is—and you have to be very well connected with Mr. Bismaquer to take a ride on the monorail. If you're really desirable you can take your own car—they have car transports on the rail system, and there are roads out at the ranch, but within the compound. It's a hell of a place—huge house; auxiliary buildings; automobile race track; horses; fishing; everything your heart desires."

"You've been there?"

"No, but I've seen all the pictures—from the satellites and the high-fly reconnaissance. Langley has a three-D mock-up. They showed it to me as part of my briefing. I have smaller photographs with me. The whole area—all hundred and fifty square miles—is heavily fenced off, and Bismaquer has his own security outfit."

"So, what's he done wrong?" Bond took out his gunmetal cigarette case, looking at M for approval. M just nodded and began to load his pipe. Cedar refused a cigarette. "What's he done wrong? Apart from making a mint of money."

"That's the problem." Cedar looked uncertainly at M.

"Oh, you can go ahead, Miss Leiter—007's got to know it all before we finish."

"Until a few months ago it was all very vague," Cedar continued, folding her legs under her on the leather buttoned chair. M looked toward the ceiling as though appealing to the Deity for good manners, and posture, in the girl. "Politically, Bismaquer's always been suspect, but nobody's apparently worried too much, because he stays so far from the action. There is very firm evidence that he's—how do you put it?—run with the hare and hunted with the hounds."

Bond nodded.

"That's how Bismaquer's operated over the years—looking for an 'in'— a way to be accepted for political office. Nobody's ever taken him up." She laughed, and Bond was reminded again of Felix. "They've taken his money, but not him. In the Watergate backlash, it came out that money from Bismaquer went into the famous slush fund. Not peanuts, either. But successive administrations have kept him at bay."

"Reasons?"

She gave a little shrug, as though to say it was obvious. "There is also evidence that Bismaquer's been searching for a way into *any* administration, with a view to a takeover bid."

It was Bond's turn to laugh. "Take over what? The United States government?"

"I know it must sound farfetched, but that's exactly what the feeling has been." Cedar looked at him coolly. "You think some of those Arabs, and their retinues, are wealthy? Well, there are families in Texas who *do* live like royalty. There are a few—like in any country—who live with dangerous fantasy. When you combine the fantasy with immense wealth . . ."

Both Bond and M nodded, taking her point.

"The Nazi ideology still in him?" Bond blew a stream of smoke toward the ceiling.

"That's what the Agency thinks."

"But a nut like that can't really be dangerous unless . . ."

"Unless he's *doing* something. Yes?" Cedar locked eyes with Bond. "Yes, I agree, but there has been trouble—or a hint of it. Bismaquer's received a large number of very odd visitors at the ranch over the last year. He's also increased security and enlarged his staff."

Bond sighed, looking at M for help. "This is crazy. A fellow living in his own fantasies—"

"Hear her out, 007," M said quietly.

"He's up to something, all right. The FBI were monitoring him, checking on the visitors and the equipment that went to the ranch. They decided to pass some of their findings on to the Internal Revenue Service. They in turn came up with some possible tax dodges. That gave the IRS, and the FBI, something to work on. Last January, four agents two from each Branch—went in to try to talk with Bismaquer. They disappeared. The FBI sent in two more. They did not come back. So the cops in Amarillo called him and carried out an investigation. Friend Bismaquer knew nothing, could tell them nothing. No evidence. So the cops came out, and the Agency sent a girl in. They did not hear from her again.

"Then, a week or so back, a body turned up in some marshland near Baton Rouge, Louisiana. It was kept quiet—not a whisper from the media. Apparently the corpse was in a bad state, but they ID'd it as the Company girl. Since then, all the bodies have turned up—near the same place. Two can't be identified, but the others have been—by their teeth, mostly. Every officer who set out to nail something on Markus Bismaquer in Texas has turned up dead in Louisiana."

"And that's our business?" Bond did not like the sound of it. Bismaquer sounded like a psychopathic maniac, with money to burn, a private army, and a king-sized case of *folie de grandeur*.

"Very much so." Cedar Leiter looked at M. "Will you show him, sir?"

M delved among the papers neatly stacked in front of him, extracted one, and passed it over to Bond.

It was a clear photostat of a torn fragment of paper, the typewritten words plainly visible. Bond's face darkened as he read:

> ans should, of course, be destroyed. But we wished
> make certain you had full knowledge of our substan-

l backing, worldwide. The initial thrust will
most telling in Europe, and the Mid-East. But,
ntually, it will leave the United States wide
pen. With careful manipulation we can successfu
ivide and rule—or at least
I look forward to our next meeting.

Then the scrawled but plainly decipherable signature: *Blofeld*.
Bond felt a hand claw at his intestines.

"Where . . . ?" he began.

"In the rotting lining of our CIA girl's clothes. Taken from the body," Cedar answered, her voice level. "The analysts at Langley think Bismaquer's working in conjunction with a terrorist organization known as SPECTRE. I was told you are an expert, Mr. Bond."

"Blofeld's dead." Bond was equally cool.

"Unless, 007 . . ." M removed the pipe from his mouth. "Unless there was progeny? Or a brother? Or someone else? You've spent considerable time convincing me that SPECTRE's active again, and behind these wretched hijackings. Now there comes evidence that a Blofeld of some kind is still around and consorting with a very rich, mad Texan. That piece of paper"—he gestured toward the photostat—"suggests that Bismaquer, and SPECTRE, are embarking on some kind of venture that may set the world ablaze. God knows there's enough danger of that with the governments, unrest, political ineptitude, recession, and the draining of resources—on an official level. Some big free-lance operation could be catastrophic; and we already know, from past experience, that SPECTRE *can* cause international problems."

As he finished, there was a tap at the door and Bill Tanner entered to M's firm "Come."

Tanner nodded. "Checks out, sir. Just had the embassy signal back. They don't know what it means but said it had to be something special because it returned with considerable priority and the presidential cipher. Their people got a little nosy, I'm afraid."

"Well, I hope you put their noses out of joint, Chief of Staff."

Tanner smiled, giving Bond a welcome nod.

M took a draw on his pipe, tapping his teeth with the stem before continuing. "One of the other documents, 007, is a personal letter to me from the President of the United States. In it, he says the information is, in his opinion, so sensitive that he does not want to go through normal channels: hence the use of Miss Leiter. He asks for special help. In other words, he wants someone from this Service to accompany Miss Leiter to the United States and infiltrate the Bismaquer setup. Do you suggest anyone, 007? Anyone with a good working knowledge of that pustule SPECTRE?"

"Yes." Bond already felt the adrenaline stirring. "Yes, of course I'll go. But I've a couple of questions for Miss Leiter. What's Bismaquer's marital status?"

"Married three times," she answered. "First two died. Natural causes— an automobile accident and a brain tumor. His present wife's considerably younger than he. Stunning, elegant: Nene Bismaquer, formerly Nene Clavert. French birth. Lived in Paris, where she first met Bismaquer."

"Can we check if that's absolutely snow white?"

M nodded, giving Tanner a quick glance—an order without words.

"And the second question?" Cedar unwound her legs.

"How did Bismaquer make his first million? I presume the rest followed by careful investment."

"Ice cream." Cedar grinned. "He was the first great ice-cream king— came up with things you'd never believe. One of the big chains finally bought him out. But it's still a passion with him. He even has a lab out at the ranch. Apparently he's determined to find a completely new, untried method of making the stuff—always coming up with elaborate recipes and flavors."

M cleared his throat. "Getting close is going to be the problem, that's obvious."

"Apart from his wife and ice cream, Bismaquer has one other weak point," Cedar offered.

They looked at her expectantly.

"Prints. Rare prints. He has a terrific collection—or so the information goes. And it really is a weakness. I understand the top brass at Langley interrogated one of the few clean people ever to get into, and out of, Rancho Bismaquer in recent years. He was a well-known dealer in rare prints."

"Know anything about rare prints, 007?" M looked cheerful for the first time since Bond had entered the office.

"Not at the moment, sir." Bond lit another cigarette. "But I've a feeling I'm going to learn quite quickly."

"So is Miss Leiter." M allowed himself a rare smile, reaching for the telephone.

6

RARE PRINTS FOR SALE

JJames Bond was always amazed by New York. Other people said it was getting worse, going downhill fast. They talked about how dirty and dangerous it was. Yet, every time Bond was sent there on assignment, he found New York changed little from when he first knew it. Certainly, there were more buildings, and—like every city—more places you kept away from at night. But there was no denying that, as a city, it gave him more of an emotional charge than his beloved London.

This time, though, he was not in New York City as James Bond. His passport was in the name of Professor Joseph Penbrunner, whose occupation was listed as art dealer. Cedar Leiter had also changed her name—Mrs. Joseph Penbrunner—and the couple had received attention from the media: M and his chief of staff had already seen to that.

The evening of Cedar Leiter's arrival in London, Bond had taken her from the headquarters building to a safe house in a Kensington mews, one easily observed by the team of nursemaids assigned to them. Bill Tanner had arrived within the hour to give the pair a quick rundown on the cover chosen for them. Cedar, being unknown in the trade, needed no disguise; but Bond would have to undergo some changes in appearance, and Tanner had brought along a few ideas.

Disguise, as Bond knew well enough, was best when kept to the minimum—a change of hairstyle, some new mannerism in a walk, contact lenses, maybe the fattening of cheeks with rubber pads (a device not often used, as it causes difficulty in eating and drinking), spectacles, or a different mode of dress. These were the easiest things, and on that first night, Bond learned that he would be equipped with a graying mustache, heavy glasses—with clear lenses—together with a careful thinning and complete graying of the hair. It was also suggested that he develop a scholarly stoop and slow walk, as well as a rather pompous style of speech.

For the next few days, Bond traveled straight to the Kensington safe house each morning to work with Cedar.

M brought in a small, humorless cipher of a man, an expert in prints, especially rare English work. His name was never mentioned, but the crash course he gave to Bond and Cedar made them at least superficially knowledgeable in the subject.

Within the week they learned that from the early, simple woodcuts of Caxton until the middle of the seventeenth century, there were no English printmakers of any stature. Real brilliance came from the Continent, with masters like Dürer, Lucas van Leyden, and the like. They covered Holbein the Younger, the first English copper plates of John Shute, and on into Hollar, Hogarth and his contemporaries, through the so-called Romantic tradition, up to the revival and high standards of etching and printmaking in the nineteenth century.

On the third day, M came to Kensington asking that their instructor concentrate on Hogarth. The reason was revealed that night, when M turned up again, with Bill Tanner and a pair of his personal watchdogs in tow.

"Well, I think we've done it," M announced, seating himself in the most comfortable chair in the living room and wrinkling his nose in a gesture of distaste at the wallpaper. Like all Service safe houses, the place had the bare amenities of a low-rated hotel.

"Two things," M went on. "Nena Bismaquer née Clavert appears clean. Second, you, Professor Penbrunner, are not in good odor with certain people in the art world. Tomorrow the press could well go mad. They are, in fact, searching for you right now."

And what am I supposed to have done?" Bond felt distinctly wary.

"Not much." M resumed his most professional voice. "You've come across a set of hitherto unknown signed Hogarth prints, not unlike *The Rake's Progress*—or *The Harlot's Progress,* come to that. Six in all, beautifully executed and titled *The Lady's Progress*—causing a stir, I can tell you. They've been fully authenticated; you've been trying to keep it quiet, but the cat's out of the bag now. The story goes that you're not even putting them on offer in England, but are taking them to the United States. Oh, there will be questions in the House, no doubt."

Bond chewed his lips. "And the prints?"

"Beautiful forgeries." M beamed. "Very hard to prove otherwise, and they've cost the Service a mint. They'll be brought in tomorrow, and I'll see the press are tipped off just before you leave for New York next week."

"Talking about leaving . . ." Bond steered M from his chair to the privacy of another room. The job was going to be taxing enough, for they could not expect assistance from either the American or British intelligence services until the last possible moment—simply because so few would know of their presence or of their assignment.

"There's no backup," Bond began.

"You've done jobs without backup before, James." M softened, using Bond's Christian name in private.

"True. Arrangements have been made for my personal armament, I presume?"

M nodded. The VP70, ammunition, and his favorite knives were to be delivered in a briefcase—which also contained the six forged Hogarth prints—at their New York hotel. "Q Branch've set up one or two other useful things for you. There'll be a technology session with Miss Reilly before you go."

"Then I've got one more favor to ask."

"Ask, and it just might be given."

"The Silver Beast." Bond looked straight into M's eyes, noting the flicker of doubt. "Silver Beast" was the nickname members of the Service had given to Bond's personal car—the Saab 900 Turbo—his own property, with the special technology built into it at his own expense. Jibes about its being Bond's "toy" received only a polite smile from 007; and he knew that Major Boothroyd, the Armorer, had constantly sniffed around the machine in an attempt to discover all its secrets: the hidden compartments, tear-gas ducts, and new refinements recently built into the bullet-proofed vehicle. Even Q'ute, doubtless put up to it by Boothroyd, had tried a Mata Hari on Bond to wheedle out the secrets. At the time, 007 had merely slapped her playfully on her delicious bottom and said she should not meddle. Now he was about to place what could be his salvation in M's hands.

"What about the Silver Beast?"

"I need it in America. I don't want to be at the mercy of public transportation."

M gave a fleeting smile. "I can arrange for you to hire one—with the proper left-hand drive as well."

"That's not the same, and you know it, sir."

"And *you* know it's not a Service vehicle. Heaven knows what you've got hidden in that thing. . . ."

"Sir," Bond retorted, "I'm sorry, but I need *that* car and the documentation."

M thought, his brow creased. "Have to sleep on it. Let you know tomorrow." Sucking on his pipe, M left, grumbling under his breath.

In fact, Bond did not fancy his chances regarding the car, even though he was going to the United States on special orders. But on the following evening, after a long and testy lecture from M on the state of the Service finances, permission was granted. The Service would, reluctantly, have the Saab taken over to the United States. "Be there, waiting and ready for you on arrival," M told him grumpily.

Their arrival—Professor and Mrs. Joseph Penbrunner, and their Saab—had, in fact, been quite something. With his voice changed to a donnish, pompous, and rather plummy timbre, Bond neatly parried the media's questions at New York's JFK airport. The media had "assumed" he was selling the newly discovered Hogarth prints in America? Well, he was saying nothing yet. No, he did not have a particular buyer in mind; this was a personal visit to America. No, he did not have the prints with him, but, yes, they were already, he could reveal, in New York.

Privately the disguised Bond was pleased with the vocal change which he had based, from long memory, on his old housemaster during those two unfortunate "halves" at Eton. The man had been a pain—in all senses—to Bond, and now he took delight in mocking him. At the same time, he made certain they would hit the evening news as well as the headlines by turning crusty and rude. The media were not really interested in art, he said, only the trouble they could stir up. "When it all comes down to it," he added, pulling Cedar through the throng, "you fellows'll only be concerned with the price. Dollars, dollars, and more dollars. All you're after—the price."

"That means you *are* here to make a sale, Professor?" one of the contingent asked sharply.

"That's my business."

At the Loew's Drake Hotel on Fifty-sixth and Park, the briefcase awaited them. Bond unpacked carefully, quickly separating the prints from the weaponry. The prints would go to the hotel safe. As for the hardware? Well, he would carry the VP70, while the knives went into the specially sprung compartments—made years ago by Q Branch—in his own briefcase. He was so engrossed with sorting out these matters that he failed to notice the coolness which had started to build, like a weather front, around Cedar.

During the days in the Kensington safe house, she had insisted on calling him plain "Bond." When he had politely, and with his usual charm, asked her to address him as James, Cedar flatly refused. "I know you and my father were buddies," she had said, not looking at him. "But we're into a professional relationship now. I call you Bond—except in public when we're playing husband and wife. You call me Leiter."

James Bond had laughed. "Okay, you can keep it like that. But I'm afraid I shall go on calling you Cedar."

Now, on returning from the front desk after depositing the prints, Bond found her standing in the middle of the room, arms folded and foot tapping—a most attractive posture, whether she intended it to be or not.

"What's up?" he asked breezily.

"What d'you think's up?"

Bond shrugged. A creature of habit, he had started to unpack in the usual way, even dumping his terry-cloth robe on the large double bed. "Haven't a clue."

"That, for one," pointing at the robe. "We haven't even settled who's going to use the bed and who's sleeping on the couch. As far as I'm concerned, Mr. James Bond, the marriage is over once we're in private."

"Well, of course. I take the couch." Then, heading for the bathroom, Bond flung over his shoulder, "Don't worry, Cedar, you'll be safe as a nun with me; and you can take the bed every time. I've always preferred to live rough anyway."

He could sense her petulance behind him, but when he came out, Cedar still stood by the bed, looking almost contrite. "I'm sorry, James. I'm really sorry to have thought that of you. My dad was right. You're a gentleman, in the real sense of the word."

Bond did not blush, even though "gentleman" was scarcely a word ladies used to describe him. "Come on, then, Cedar. Let's go out and have a good time—or at least have dinner. I know a place not too far from here."

They walked to the elegant Le Perigord, on East Fifty-second. The meal could not have been bettered, Cedar admitted to herself, even though Bond chose for both of them: *asperges de Sologne à la blésoise*—plump and tender asparagus in a sauce of cream, lemon, and orange rind, with a dash of Grand Marnier, mixed into a hollandaise base; poached fillets of sole *au champagne;* and a mouth-melting *tarte de Cambrai,* made with pears.

As they shared a bottle of Dom Perignon '69—which Bond pronounced "safe"—Cedar relaxed and began to enjoy herself, experiencing as she did a strange sensation. For though Bond did not slip out of character as Joseph Penbrunner, she thought she could see the man behind the disguise, the man her father had spoken of so often: the blue, unforgettable eyes;

the dark, clean-cut face which had always reminded her father of Hoagy Carmichael in his younger days; the hard, almost cruel mouth which could soften so unexpectedly. A magnetic attraction—that was the only phrase for what she felt; and she couldn't but wonder how many others had felt it before her.

The meal over, they walked back to the Drake, collected the room key, and rode the elevator up to the third floor.

The three heavily built men in sharp, neatly cut suits converged on the couple as the elevator doors closed behind them. Before Bond could even reach inside his jacket to snatch at the butt of the VP70, a hand closed around his wrist, while another removed the pistol.

"We'll just go quietly to the room, honh, Professor?" one of them said. "No problems. We're just delivering an invitation from somebody who wants to see you, okay?"

7

INVITATION BY FORCE

THE WORK CEDAR and Bond had done together, at the Kensington safe house, included devising a series of signals and moves to be used in such a situation as this. Bond nodded toward the heavy who had spoken, scratched his right temple, and coughed. To Cedar this meant: Go along with them, but watch for my lead.

"No problems, honh?" The spokesman was the largest of the three men, a few inches taller than Bond, with the muscular frame of a weight lifter and a barrel chest. The others looked equally hard and fit. Professional hoods, Bond thought. Professional and experienced.

The big man had taken the room key from Bond. Now he calmly opened their door and ushered the couple inside. A quick hard shove propelled Bond into a chair, and hands which felt like twin monkey wrenches held his shoulders from behind. Cedar was treated in similar fashion.

It was a moment before Bond noticed the fourth man, standing by the window, occasionally glancing down into the street. He must have been in the room already as they entered. Bond recognized him at once as the slim athletic man with a neat military mustache, looking altogether over-dressed in a maroon tuxedo, who had approached him earlier in the hotel lobby and pressed a gold-edged card into his hand. The man had introduced himself as Mike Mazzard, had said something about being at the press reception at the airport and wanted a private talk about the prints. Bond had been rather brusque and brushed aside the suggestion of a quiet drink at some casino or other, taking the man for a journalist after an exclusive interview—though he hadn't mentioned a paper. Bond hadn't even looked at the card properly but simply pushed it into his pocket saying that he wouldn't be seeing anyone until they had had a night's rest.

"So, Professor," said the big man, who had taken a position in the center of the room and was idly tossing the big VP70 from hand to hand like a gorilla playing with a stone. "You're carrying a piece, honh? D'ya know how to use it?"

Bond, still in character, let out a pompous splutter, meant to convey outrage. "Of course I know how to use it," he blustered. "Let me tell you that in the War—"

"What war would that be, friend?" croaked the man holding him. "The American Revolution?"

The three heavies brayed with laughter.

"I was an officer in the Second World War," Bond said with dignity. "I've seen more action than . . ."

"The Second World War was a long time ago, friend," the big man interrupted, weighing the VP70 in his hand directly in front of Bond. "This is a pretty lethal piece you got here. Why're you carrying it, anyway?"

"Protection," snapped Bond in his best Penbrunner manner.

"Yeah, I figured that. But protection from what?"

"Muggers. Thieves. Ruffians like you. People intending to steal from us."

"When're you going to learn some manners, Joe Bellini?" said the cool, measured voice from the window. "We're here with an invitation, not to put Professor Penbrunner through a third degree in his own room. Remember?"

"Steal from you! We're not here to steal from you," the heavy man called Bellini went on with feigned politeness, his face displaying affronted inno-cence. "You got some pictures, right?"

"Pictures?"

"Yeah, some kinda special pictures."

"Prints, Joe." The man by the window spoke in a more commanding manner.

"Yeah, prints. Thanks, Mr. Mazzard. You got some prints by a guy called Ho-something."

"Ho-garth, Joe," prompted Mazzard, without taking his eyes off the street below.

"I own some Hogarth prints," Bond said firmly. "Owning them and having them aren't quite the same thing."

"You got them here, we happen to know," Joe Bellini said with mock patience. "In the hotel safe." Mike Mazzard, at the window, turned to face Bond, who now realized that he was by far the most dangerous of the four. He carried himself with a certain sleekness and authority.

"Let's get it straight," he said. "No one's going to hurt either of you. We're here to represent Mr. Bismaquer, who wants to see those Hogarth prints. Call it an invitation. But he doesn't figure on waiting till tomorrow for an answer. You got his card—the one I gave you in the lobby. I guess he wants to make you an offer . . ." Joe Bellini chuckled. "An offer he can't refuse, honh?"

Mazzard was not amused. "Be quiet, Joe. It's a straight offer. All you have to do is call the front desk and get them to send up the prints, and then we can get it moving."

Bond shook his head. "Can't be done," he said with a smile. "I have one key. They have the other. As in a bank. The prints are in a safety deposit box," he lied. "No one but the duty officer and myself can get at them. Not even my wife . . ."

With relief, Bond congratulated himself on his last-minute change of mind, when he had decided that the prints would be even safer in the Saab's secret compartment, especially if they needed to leave in a hurry.

"Like Mr. Mazzard says," Joe Bellini went on, all politeness now gone, "we don't want to hurt nobody. But if you don't cooperate, then Louis and the Kid here"—indicating the man holding Bond—"can get very unpleasant with your little lady."

Mazzard left the window, walked around Joe, who still toyed with the VP70, and halted in front of Bond.

"Professor Penbrunner. May I suggest you and Joe here take a little walk downstairs and collect the prints. Then we can all get to Kennedy. Mr. Bismaquer has sent his own private jet to pick you up. He *had* hoped you'd join him for dinner. It's a little late for that now. But we can make up for lost time, and you and Mrs. Penbrunner can still get a good night's rest at the ranch. You'd be more comfortable there than at this dump, I can assure you. Now, what d'you say?"

"Look here, Mazzard," Bond spluttered. "This is an outrage! I already told you earlier, we are not making any engagements before tomorrow. If you really represent the man—Bismaquer, did you say his name was . . . ?"

"Save it for posterity," interrupted Bellini, "and let's split. And don't try anything stupid." He moved across to Cedar, and, with a casual flick of his hand, tore her dress from neck to waist, revealing the fact that she wore no brassiere.

"Nice," breathed Louis, looking down over the shoulder he still held in a firm grip. "Very nice."

"Cut it out," commanded Mazzard. "There's no call for that sort of thing. I am sorry, Professor, but you see, Mr. Bismaquer isn't used to having no for an answer. Now I'll get your things together while you and Joe get the prints. We can be at Kennedy and away sharp if we get moving now."

Bond nodded. "All right," he said quietly, disconcerted because, for a second or so, he too found it impossible to take his eyes from Cedar's partially revealed breasts. "But my wife will need to change. We can collect the prints on the way out . . ."

"We'll get the prints *now,*" Mazzard said flatly, brooking no further argument. "Stop waving the Professor's gun about, Joe. Put it away in the closet. You've got your own."

Joe Bellini produced a small revolver from his coat. Having shown Bond that he was armed, he pocketed his own gun again and placed the VP70 on the bedside table.

Mazzard nodded to the Kid and the twin wrenches relaxed on Bond's shoulders. Bond moved his arms gingerly, trying to restore the circulation as quickly as possible. At the same time, he gave a small cough and flicked an imaginary thread from his lapel—the body language for Cedar to be ready. Aloud he said he would need his briefcase. "My key's in it." He gestured to where the case stood beside the collapsible steel and canvas luggage rack.

Mazzard picked up the briefcase, weighed it, and gave it a couple of quick upward jerks of the hand. Satisfied, he handed the briefcase over to Bond. "Just the key, and go along with Joe."

The case was a version of his original elaborate Swaine & Adeney bag, modified by Q'ute for 007's use on this present operation. It's main features—a more effective device based on one of the hidden compartments in the Bond original—were two spring-loaded slim compartments sewn into the inner lining on the right-hand side. At a setting of triple three on the left tumblers, and triple two on the right, the springs would operate at five-second intervals, delivering the handles of Bond's Sykes-Fairbairn knives through the bottom of the case.

As he took the briefcase onto his lap, Bond assessed the situation. They were certainly in a tight spot, for it now dawned on Bond that not only was there no option to complying over the night safety deposit box, but neither could he allow these hoods to discover the secrets of the Saab. For a fleeting moment, he considered the possibility of getting rid of Joe before they reached the car. Dealing with one in the open would be much easier than trying to tackle four in the confined room. But what then would happen to Cedar? If he raised an alarm, who could tell what they would do to her? He couldn't risk it. The alternative—turning the tables here and now on all four—seemed against all the odds. Could he rely on swift action from Cedar? A glance in her direction, a fractional meeting of the eyes, told him she was ready.

Mazzard was nearest to him and would have to go first, Bond decided, carefully turning the left-hand tumblers to triple three, then twisting the briefcase sideways so that two slim concealed knife apertures lay directly over his right thigh. Once Mazzard was taken out, he must tackle Joe Bellini and trust to luck and surprise for the other two. It all depended on three things: his own accuracy, Cedar's readiness, and how quickly the Kid moved.

He shifted the case slightly, then turned the right-hand tumblers to triple two. There was no sound as Bond moved the case again, sliding his hand to the underside ready to receive the first knife after the initial five-second delay. He felt the handle slip down into his right hand, and, with the knowledge that he only had five seconds before the next knife would be ready, made his move.

Throwing knives are so finely balanced that even an expert has difficulty making the weapon behave as intended. An agile throw, correctly performed, should always bring the point of the blade into a forward, horizontal position as it reaches its target.

Bond wanted nobody injured unless it proved unavoidable. To do this, both his throws had to be exceptionally accurate and at least one beat off so that the heavy pommel, above the grip, would reach the point aimed at before the razored edge.

Hardly moving in his chair, Bond flexed his wrist, putting maximum force behind the first throw, then reached down just in time for the second knife to be delivered from the case.

The first knife was aimed faultlessly, the pommel catching Mazzard with a thud-snap between the eyes. He could have known nothing as his head jerked back soundlessly, the knife falling to the floor and the body following it. Cedar moved at the same moment as Bond, pushing down with her feet and, with all her weight, toppling her chair back against Louis, who was caught off guard, diverted by Mazzard's sudden fall. Bond was only aware of the grunt and the crash as he went over, propelled by Cedar and the heavy furniture.

By this time, the other knife was in Bond's hand, his body turning minutely to position himself for Joe, whose reactions were considerably faster than 007 had anticipated. Luckily the big man only managed to move a few inches to his left, so that the pommel of the seecond knife landed heavily beside his right ear.

As though frozen in time, Joe Bellini stopped in his tracks, one hand halfway to the pocket containing the revolver. The knife fell away awkwardly, slicing at his ear and almost severing it. He let out a strangled cry, staggered forward and toppled across Cedar and Louis as they struggled on the floor.

The Kid moved indecisively behind Bond, who dropped the case and, putting full weight on the balls of his feet, sprang from the chair and leaped for the VP70 lying on the bedside table.

He went for the weapon with a wild karate shriek, expelling the air from his lungs, covering the three paces in less than two seconds. Even as his hand grasped the pistol butt, thumb flicking at the safety catch, Bond swiveled, arms outstretched, ready to fire at the first target to spell danger.

The Kid's right hand was halfway inside his jacket when Bond shouted, "Hold it. Stop!" The Kid showed a fortunate sense of survival. He stopped, hand wavering for a second, then—eyes meeting Bond's—obeyed.

Just then Cedar broke free, leaped to her feet with startling speed and brought both hands down, in a vicious double-chop, to the sides of Louis's neck. The man grunted and slumped to the floor. Bond walked up to the Kid, smiling, reached into his jacket, removed the weapon he had been preparing to use and then administered a sharp tap behind the ear, whereupon the Kid joined his friends in oblivion.

"Change your dress, Cedar," Bond said quietly, then, on second thought, "no, give me a hand with this lot first."

Together they stripped the four hoods of their weapons, Cedar apparently unaware that her breasts were on full display. Bond fished into the special compartment of his briefcase and brought out a small, sealed plastic box which he forced open. He drew out the chloroform pad and administered it to the four men who lay spreadeagled about the floor.

"Crude and not very effective, but it's easier than trying to get tablets down them," Bond said. "It's only meant for emergencies such as these. Old and tried methods are often best. At least we'll be sure of half an hour."

They secured the hands and feet of the four men with their own belts, ties and handkerchiefs. It was then that Cedar saw what Bond's knife had done to Joe Bellini's ear. The top half-inch had been sliced through, leaving a bloody flap dangling and joined by only a thin strip of tissue on the outer edge. Bond fetched from the all-providing case some ointment to help staunch the blood flow. Deftly Cedar fitted the flap back in place and bound it up as best she could with adhesive tape from the bathroom medicine cabinet.

At last she realized that she was half naked and, with no embarrassment, stripped to her tight white briefs and plunged her legs into a pair of jeans, pulling on a shirt as Bond threw their things into their bags. Suddenly he remembered the gold-edged card that he had thrust into his pocket at that first meeting with Mike Mazzard in the hotel lobby. He pulled it out and examined it.

On one side was a sort of crest, incorporating an elaborate letter B, with the words "Markus Bismaquer" underneath, embellished with curving flourishes. Below that, in tiny black capitals, were the words: ENTRE-PRENEUR—AMARILLO, TEXAS. Scrawled on the back of the card in a sloping hand was a brief message:

Prof. & Mrs. Penbrunner—

Honor me by being my guests for a few days. Bring the Hogarths. It will be worth your while. My Security Manager, Mike Mazzard, will see you to my private jet at Kennedy.

M.B.

Squashed in at the bottom, written as if an afterthought, was an insistence they should make it for dinner that night and a telephone number to call should there be any problems. Bond handed the card to Cedar.

"To Amarillo, then. By car, I think," he said curtly. "They won't expect that. Have you got all your things?"

Bond saw a furrow of worry cross Cedar's face. "Your reputation will go before you, James." There was a small twinkling smile as she used his first name.

"You mean an old man like Penbrunner doing a knife-throwing act and a few bits of karate?" Bond said, replacing the knives into their spring clips in the briefcase.

"Quite."

He thought for a moment. "Bismaquer's after us. He will know shortly that we're no pushovers. It'll be interesting to see how he reacts. Now, let's get a move on."

"What about them? Will you call the police?"

"We don't want to start a hue and cry now. I'll leave some money and the key in an envelope in the laundry room. I noticed they leave it open. Lucky we have an old-fashioned mortice lock on this door—the sort you can't undo from the inside without a key. They won't be in a hurry to ring down to the desk to be let out and it'll take them time to pick their way out."

Bond bent down to see if he could find another key in Mazzard's pocket and produced a skeleton that he must have got by bribing one of the chambermaids.

"Time to go," he snapped. "We'll take the back stairs."

8

INTIMATIONS OF MORTALITY

THEY DID NOT stop to look back across the river at that magnificent skyline twinkling with lights from the sharp outlines of skyscrapers, the vast twin towers of the World Trade Center dwarfing everything else. They needed to put distance between themselves and Bismaquer's hoods. Bond also had to have time to think. If, as they suspected, Bismaquer was part of SPECTRE and, possibly, the new Blofeld himself, their adversary could already be one step ahead of them.

Bond had learned never to underestimate SPECTRE. This was particularly important now that it had re-emerged into a world in which the major terrorist organizations often worked hand in glove with Moscow. M and other senior officers of both the Secret Intelligence Service and MI 5 were constantly underlining the fact that terrorist action could almost inevitably be equated with Soviet action.

In the old blood-and-thunder novels of his adolescence, Bond had read time and again of mad professors, or masterminds, whose aim was to dominate the world. At the time, the young Bond had wondered what the mad, or bad, villains would do with the world once it was in their power. Now he knew. SPECTRE, and other organizations like it—with close links to Russia and the Communist ideology—were dedicated to placing all mankind slowly under the heel of a society dominated by the state: a state which controlled the individual's every action and thought, down to what kind of music could be heard and what books read.

In crushing SPECTRE, James Bond would be striking a blow for true democracy—not the wishy-washy, half-hearted ideals that, of late, seemed to permeate the West.

Now his duty was to outthink the enemy.

His first reaction was to head for Texas and face Bismaquer—playing it dangerously by ear. On reflection, as he slid the Saab neatly through the traffic, Bond decided it would be best to hide somewhere for a couple of days. "If we watch each other's backs," he told Cedar, "and keep very low profiles, we'll soon find out if Bismaquer's really out for blood. Anyone with SPECTRE connections would have an army of underworld informers out searching for us by now."

It was Cedar who suggested Washington—"Not the metropolitan area or Georgetown. Somewhere nearby, though. There are plenty of big motels we can use, just off the main highway."

The idea made sense. Once on the turnpike, Bond put his foot down, winding the turbo up to a safe and legal maximum, then flicking in the cruise control. They reached the District of Columbia around three in the morning, both watching for any possible tail. Bond took them around part of the Capital Beltway, then finally located the Anacostia Freeway, where they spotted an exit with a motel sign.

The place they had chosen was large enough to get lost in for days— some thirty stories high, with an underground car park where the Saab could be tucked away. They registered separately, as Ms. Carol Lukas and Mr. John Bergin, and were assigned adjoining rooms on the twentieth floor, with balconies giving a view across the green belt of Anacostia Park and the river. In the distance, Cedar pointed out, they could just glimpse the Anacostia and the Eleventh Street bridges, with the Washington Navy Yard a smudge against the landscape.

Two days, Bond calculated. Two days lying low and keeping their eyes open. Then they could head west, and, to use his own words, drive like hell. "With luck we should get to Amarillo within forty-eight hours. One night's stop somewhere, to conserve energy, and by that time we should know if Bismaquer's put a tail on us. If not . . ."

"Straight into the lion's den," Cedar finished for him. She seemed cool enough about the prospect, though neither of them could fail to remember the fate of their colleagues—dragged dead and putrefied from the Luisiana marshes.

On Bond's balcony, as the dawn came up over distant Washington, they made plans.

"Time for a reverse in disguises," Bond announced. The management had them registered in new names, but had seen Bond in what he liked to call his "Penbrunner hat." Now he washed the gray from his hair, removed the mustache and spectacles, and—apart from the thinner hair, which would grow again quickly enough—looked almost his old self.

Cedar would be easily recognized by Bismaquer's lieutenants, so she worked for an hour or so on her own appearance—a restyling of the hair, darkening her eyebrows, severe pebble-lens spectacles. Using these simple devices, she changed her looks completely.

The main problem, as Bond saw it, was keeping a careful watch for Bismaquer's men. "Six hours on and six hours off. In the main lobby," he decided. It was the only way. "We find suitable vantage points, and just mark faces. If one, or all, of that unholy quartet turns up, then we take the necessary action. Two days, and I reckon we'll have thrown them." They then made the final decision—to leave the motel late the following evening. Bond was to stay out of his disguise, and Cedar would change back to her normal appearance before beginning the journey.

The routine began straightaway. They tossed for the first watch, and Cedar lost, heading down to the lobby to keep her six-hour vigil.

Before taking a rest, Bond quickly checked his luggage, the most important piece being the briefcase. The knives were back in their slots, but he removed one, strapping it on his left forearm before going through the other items in the case. Q Branch's personal survival kit.

The upper section contained papers, a diary, and the normal accoutrements of any businessman—calculator, pens, and the like. In the lower section, which was accessible by both hinged and sliding panels, Q'ute had assembled what she called backup material: a small snub-nosed S&W "Highway Patrolman" with the four-inch barrel and spare ammunition; a series of toughened steel picklocks, gathered together on a ring, which also held a slim three-inch jimmy and other miniature tools, all built to Q'ute's specifications; a pair of padded leather gloves; half a dozen detonators, kept in a compartment well-removed from a small lump of plastic explosive; and a length of fuse.

Originally they had planned to add in an electronic device for detonation purposes, but at the last moment it was decided that thirty-five feet of nylon half-inch rope, together with a couple of miniaturized grappling hooks, would be more likely needs. Even though the rope was slim and easily concealed, it took up space, leaving no room for any more sophisticated climbing gear. If put to it, Bond would be using the bare minimum. Everything in the hidden compartment was protected by shaped and cut-out foam rubber.

After checking the VP70 and spare magazines, 007 stretched out on the bed, quickly dropping off into a deep, refreshing sleep from which he was awakened, five hours later, by the alarm call he had ordered. "This is your eight o'clock alarm call, the temperature is sixty-seven degrees, and it is a pleasant afternoon. Have a nice day. . . ." Bond replied, "Thank you," and the voice chattered on, "This is your eight-o-one alarm call, the temperature is sixty-seven degrees, and it is a pleasant afternoon. Have a nice day. . . ."

"And you," Bond mouthed at the computerized voice.

Bond showered, shaved, and changed into dark slacks and one of his favorite Sea Island cotton shirts, then slipped his feet into a pair of heavy rope-soled sandals. A short, battle-dress-style navy jacket hid his holster and VP70 automatic. Right on time, James Bond took over from Cedar in the motel lobby.

They did not speak; merely a glance and nod effected the changeover. Bond soon discovered that you could view the lobby from a seat at the coffeeshop counter, as well as from the bar.

On that first spell of duty—during which 007 ate a large portion of ham, two eggs sunny-side-up with pan-fried potatoes, and visited the bar for a disciplined single-vodka martini—there was no sign of anyone showing photographs to the reception staff for identification purposes; nor did any of the four heavies from New York make an appearance.

So the forty-eight hours passed without a hint of any tail. Between shifts, both Bond and Cedar monitored the TV newscasts. There was no story about men being found bound and gagged at the Drake Hotel in New York; or of Professor and Mrs. Penbrunner and their prints being missing.

Bismaquer was either playing a waiting game or his henchmen were carrying out a fruitless search.

Neither Bond nor Cedar realized that a sharp-eyed bellboy had noted their punctual comings and goings in the hotel lobby. The bellboy waited for twenty-four hours, and instead of reporting the fact to the management, made a telephone call to New York.

During the call, he was closely questioned about the appearance of the man and woman. At the other end of the line, the man to whom he had reported sat back and thought for a while. He was one of the many agents on the payroll of a large consortium, the criminal nature of which remained unknown to him. What the private eye did know was that the consortium was on the lookout for a man and woman. The descriptions were different from those he had been given, but with a few simple changes this pair might well be those for whom a handsome bonus was being offered.

It took him some ten minutes to make up his mind. At last he picked up the telephone and dialed. When a voice came on the line, the private eye asked, "Hello, is Mike there?"

"We've either thrown them," Bond said at the motel on the second evening, "or they'll all be waiting for us somewhere along the route to Amarillo." He took a bite out of a large tunafish sandwich, washing it down with a draft of Perrier water. Cedar had brought food up from the coffee shop after her last watch. Tunafish sandwiches were hardly Bond's style, but they seemed to be Cedar's favorites. She was very silent, coming out her hair, returning to her normal appearance.

"Something worrying you?" Bond asked, noticing the look of concern on the girl's face, reflected in the mirror.

She took a long time to answer. Then: "How dangerous is it going to be, James?"

So far, Cedar Leiter had shown no sign of anything but utter professionalism. "Not losing your nerve, Cedar?" he asked.

Again a pause. "No, not really. But I'd like to know the odds." She turned from the mirror, crossing the room to where he sat. "You see, James, this is all kind of unreal for me. Sure, I've been trained, well-trained, but the training always seemed . . . well, kind of fantastic to me. Maybe I've been behind a desk too long—and not the right desk at that."

Bond laughed, nevertheless feeling the twitch in his own stomach, for he was not without anxiety when facing a threat from SPECTRE. "Believe me, Cedar, it's often far more dangerous to stalk the corridors of power. I'm never really at my best—sitting in at those endless meetings, sharing secrets with the Whitehall mandarins—in your case the people from State—or the military. Back in London, my Firm all look like gray faceless men. You never know where you stand. But in the field, it's still the old story: you have to be blessed with nerve, cheek, and a lot of luck."

He took another pull at the Perrier water. "This one *is* trouble, for two reasons. First, we have no proper backup team, nobody we can turn to at the last minute."

"And second?" the girl asked.

"That's the worst of it. If it really *is* SPECTRE we're up against, they're a hard and ruthless enemy. Also, they hate me personally. I killed their original leader, so they'll be out for blood; and when SPECTRE has a blood lust, nothing is done by halves. You can't expect it to be quick and painless with them. If they get the upper hand, SPECTRE will make sure we suffer either stark terror or what the books used to call a painful and lingering death. Cedar, if you want to get out, tell me here and now. You're a great partner and I'd like you with me. But if you can't make it . . . well, better we should split up now."

Cedar's large brown eyes melted into a look which Bond recognized as both appealing and dangerous. "No, I'm with you all the way, James. Sure I'm nervous, but I won't let you down. You've kept your part of the bargain." It was her turn to laugh. "I was worried to start with, I admit it. My dad painted a pretty lurid picture of you—a swashbuckling lothario, he called you once. I guess you're still a bit of a swashbuckler. As for being a lothario, I haven't had time . . ." She moved closer, looping an arm around his neck.

Bond took hold of her hand and gently removed the arm. His smile was touched with sadness. "No, Cedar. And don't think I'm not both flattered and tempted. It would be tremendous. But you're the daughter of one of my best friends—and one of the bravest men I know."

Still, in a different place and time, James Bond knew he would have taken Cedar Leiter to the bed across the room and slowly, languorously, made love to her.

"Come on, let's get going," he said, hearing the huskiness of his own voice. "When we get downstairs, I want you to pay the bill while I bring the car around to the front."

Cedar nodded, picking up the phone and alerting reception: they would be leaving in about fifteen minutes. "Can you have our bills ready, please? And send someone up for the luggage in ten minutes."

Bond was already completing his packing. "You can do the map-reading, too." He grinned. "And what do we want a bellboy for? To take the luggage down? That's usually my partner's job."

He ducked, just in time, as Cedar tossed a hair-brush at his head.

While Bond and Cedar were thus engaged, a black limousine pulled up at the main entrance, twenty floors below. Bond could have described the occupants precisely. A dark, tanned, and agile man, with a slightly hooked nose, was at the wheel. Next to him sat a large, tall, barrel-chested figure dressed in a dark suit and a somewhat old-fashioned broad-brimmed fedora. In the rear lounged a man with rodentlike features, the thinness of his face out of balance with the broad shoulders and large hands. A fourth man, with a military mustache, whom Bond might have expected in ostentatiously expensive clothes, was not in the car. This was strictly Joe's business, and Mazzard could go to hell if he didn't like it. No creep could make a mug of Joe Bellini and get away with it.

"Just do your jobs," Joe Bellini ordered. "Louis and me'll go through the routine cop act. Okay?"

Joe and Louis got out of the car, walked into the lobby, and, eyes taking in anything that moved, went up to the reception clerks, to whom they flashed leather walleted police badges. The badges were followed by a few terse questions and the handing over of photographs for identification.

Two of the clerks immediately identified Professor and Mrs. Penbrunner, adding their room numbers and the fact that they had checked in under different names.

"Is there something wrong?" one of the girls asked, looking concerned.

Bellini gave her a dazzling smile. "Nothing serious, honey. Nobody has anything to worry about. We're just supposed to be looking after them. The Professor's an important man. We'll stay out of their way and be discreet." He went on to say that he had another man in the car outside and would deeply appreciate it if his boys could have the run of the place—just to check it out.

That would be perfectly okay. The receptionists would report it to the duty manager. Was there anything else they could do to be of help? Yes, there was. Joe Bellini fired a dozen questions at them, and in less than five minutes had the answers he wanted.

Back in the car, Bellini went through the plan once more. "We only just made it," he told the Kid at the wheel. "They're leaving in the next few minutes. You got the walkie-talkies?"

His ear throbbed under the neat, fresh plaster. They had done their best with it at the hospital, but were fearful it would not heal, as Joe had left it too long before getting proper attention for it. His hand kept going up to the wound as he detailed the Kid to watch the elevators, which luckily were grouped and could be seen easily from a hidden vantage point on the twentieth floor. There were no back stairs, so it would be that way out or else by the fire escape.

"Louis and me'll be in the maintenance complex under the building. Don't get seen and don't miss 'em. Just use the walkie-talkie. Got it?"

Joe Bellini, with Louis in attendance, clutching a high-powered walkie-talkie, again left the limo and entered the building. The Kid parked the car and followed the other two.

Having been given precise directions by a staff anxious to cooperate with the police, Joe and Louis descended the four sections of concrete steps into the basement complex from which all the utilities—electricity, heating, air conditioning and the elevators—were monitored.

The engineer on duty was a smart, fresh-faced young man who looked puzzled when the two strangers entered, and even more puzzled as he crumpled into unconsciousness following a chop from Louis's right hand.

Bellini worked quickly, checking off the various banks of instruments and switches controlling the smooth running of the hotel's utilities, rather like the engine room of an oceangoing liner. It took him two minutes to find the section which controlled the elevators. Producing a small oblong box from his pocket, he located the sections he needed to work on, then opened the box, revealing a set of electrician's screwdrivers.

Each of the four elevators was operated by a separate bank of controls, the elevators themselves being standard, electrically propelled cars with a supplementary system for each unit: generator; motor; final limit switches; counterweights; drum; and secondary sheaves; plus the usual safety devices, designed to cut off power and apply clawlike brakes. Each electrical component was triple-fused, so the likelihood of all the fuses failing on one elevator was minimal.

Carefully Joe Bellini began to unscrew the fuse boxes for each elevator car. As he did so, Louis took a pair of heavy wire-cutters to the thick metal seals on the four levers marked "Drum Release. Danger!" at the top of the banks of instruments and fuses. The drum releases unlocked the governors controlling the drums that wound and unwound the elevators' main cables. Unlocking a drum would immediately allow it to spin freely. Only maintenance engineers would need to release the drums in this fashion, and then only when the car in question had been isolated and placed at the foot of the shaft against the special buffer.

To release the drum when a car was in motion would mean certain death for any occupant if it were not for the safety devices, with their backups.

Within six minutes, all four elevators were at grave risk. The fuse boxes were unscrewed, the fuses themselves plainly visible and accessible to Bellini, while the drum releases could be pulled at any time.

Standing back to look at their handiwork, they suddenly heard a familiar voice, clear on the walkie-talkie. "Christ," the Kid was whispering urgently into his unit. "We're just in time. They've left the room. Some luggage just went down. They're coming now. It's her, all right. He looks kinda different, but it's him too. It's them, Joe."

On the twentieth floor, Cedar and Bond, briefcase in hand, sauntered toward the elevators. Large leafy plants decorated the elevator alcove. Bond, his back now to the plants, pressed the Down button.

In the basement, facing the uncovered fuses, Joe Bellini waited, screwdriver in hand, while Louis's right arm hovered over the four drum-release levers. The third car stopped at the twentieth floor. With a smile, Bond ushered Cedar in, then followed. The doors closed noiselessly, and James Bond pressed the button for the lobby.

As he did so, the Kid's voice echoed around the maintenance room, far below. "Car three! They got into car three!"

Joe Bellini quickly flicked every fuse out of the banks controlling car three. As he did so, Louis hauled down on the drum-release lever for the same car.

Bond smiled at Cedar. "Here we go, then. Heading west."

"Wagons roll—" Cedar's words were cut short as the lights went out, and they were both thrown to one side. The elevator car lurched, then began to drop down the shaft at a sickening, gathering speed.

9

WHEN THE FUN REALLY STARTS

C EDAR OPENED HER mouth in a scream but there was no noise, only her face contorting in terror. Bond, seeing her dimly in the gloom, did not know if the sound was blotted out by the terrible crash and banging as the elevator plummeted, swaying and smashing against the sides of the shaft.

In those seconds, though, Bond seemed to hear her—a horrible diminishing shriek of terror, as if he stood apart, still at the top of the elevator shaft. It was a strange experience, in which half of his mind remained detached. "Hold on!" Bond's yell was drowned by the cacophonic crash of metal and wood, combined with a rushing windlike noise and pressure on his ears. When the car had started its fall he had his palm loosely on one of the hand rails which ran along three sides of the car. Pure reflex tightened his grip at the first jolt, before the long drop began.

A picture of the car, splintered and shattered out of all recognition at the bottom of the shaft, flashed in and out of Bond's mind.

From the twentieth floor, with increasing speed, they went past the fifteenth . . . fourteenth . . . thirteenth . . . twelfth . . . eleventh . . . unaware of their position in the shaft, only knowing the final horror would soon be on them.

Then, with a series of shaking bangs, as the sides rattled against the metal runners, it happened.

Down in the maintenance complex, Bellini and Louis had already taken to their heels. Their getaway would be simple in the panic which would follow—at any moment—when the car disintegrated against the huge buffer at the bottom of its shaft. But Joe Bellini had no way of knowing that the motel elevators were built with one old-fashioned extra safety device which did not depend upon complicated electronics.

Two metal cables ran down the length of the shaft, their use unaffected by the loss of power. These thick hawserlike ropes were threaded loosely through the claw safety brakes under the car itself. The very action of the car overspeeding on a downward path caused the hawsers to tighten, exerting pressure inward, with the result that two of the claws were activated, one on either side at the front of the elevator car.

In the first few seconds of the downward plunge, one of these "last-chance" automatic devices, on the right of the car, had been sheared off by the buffeting of metal against metal. The left-hand cable held, slowly pressing inward. At last, as they streaked past the eleventh floor, the safety brake clicked, and the claw automatically shot outward. Like a human hand desperately grasping for a last hold, the metal brake hit one of the rachets in the guide rail, broke loose, hit a second, then a third.

Inside the car, there was a series of reverberating, jarring bumps. The whole platform tilted to the right, and each jolt seemed to slow the downward rush. Then, to the sound of tearing wood and metal, the car tipped completely to the right. Bond and Cedar, both trying to keep a grip on the handrail, were conscious of part of the roof being torn away, of the ripping as they slowed, then of the final bone-shuddering stop which broke the forward section of the floor loose.

Cedar lost her grip.

This time Bond heard the scream, and even in the dimness, alleviated by light coming in through the splintered roof, saw Cedar sliding forward, her legs disappearing through the forward part of the floor.

Still gripping hard to the handrail, he lunged outward, just managing to grasp her insecurely by the wrist.

"Hang on. Try to get some kind of a hold." Bond thought he was speaking calmly, until he heard the echo of his distraught voice. He leaned forward at full stretch, allowing his hand to loose its grip for a second, then tightened on Cedar's wrist.

The whole car creaked under them, its floor sagging downward like a piece of cardboard, so that almost the entire length of the shaft below became visible. Slowly, giving her encouragement, goading her into trying to get her other hand onto his arm, Bond began to pull Cedar back into the car.

Though she was not heavily built, Cedar Leiter felt like a ton weight. Inch by inch, he hauled her back into the car. Together they balanced precariously, almost on tiptoe, clinging to the handrail.

How long the car could stay as it was, precariously jammed in the shaft, was impossible to tell. Bond was sure of only one thing: unless some of their weight was removed, their chances diminished with every minute that passed.

"How are they going to . . . ?" Cedar began, in a small voice.

"I don't know if *they* can." Bond looked down. Miraculously, he saw that his briefcase was still with them, trapped behind his feet. Moving gently, pausing after each shift in position, he reached down for the case.

Even this simple action proved the urgency of their situation, for every change of attitude caused the car to groan, rock, and creak.

Quietly he explained what he was going to do. Balancing the briefcase at an angle against the handrail, Bond sprang the tumbler locks. Carefully he delved into the hidden compartments for the nylon rope, gloves, the set of picklocks and tools and one of the small grappling hooks.

The hooks would take immense weight. In the packed closed position, each of them was about seven inches long, roughly three inches wide, and a slim couple of inches in thickness. It was necessary to go through a three-part unlocking sequence to unspring one of them, which then shot out to form a circle of some eight claws, all running from a steel securing base.

With the gloves on, tools and picklocks hanging from a large thong and clip on his belt, and the rope coiled over one arm, Bond closed the case. He passed it to Cedar, telling her to hang on to it at all costs, then secured the nylon rope to the grappling hook.

He leaned forward, one hand still on the handrail, to peer down through the ripped and broken floor. The sides of the shaft were plainly visible, together with the crisscross of metal girders.

Taking the bulk of slack on the rope and coiling it into his left hand, Bond dropped the grappling hook through the gaping mouth which formed the forward end of the floor. It took three or four swings on the rope before the claw clamped into place around one of the strengthening girders, some five feet below the car. Gently Bond paid the rope out, trying to gauge the exact length that would take him clear of the car and past the grappling hook.

It would have to be a straight drop, so that the hook would not become dislodged; but if it worked, he would then be able to use the elevator slide rails, and their cross girders, to climb back toward the car.

Bond went through the scheme for Cedar, trying to give her as many tips as possible. Then, with a grin and a wink, he took hold of the rope, wound it around himself in the simple old abseil position—the rope merely passing under the right arm, down his back and through the legs, being taken up again in the left hand, coming in under the arm. There was no time for improvised safety carabiners or double rope techniques.

Slowly he allowed himself to slide forward, feeling the car move, shuddering, as his weight shifted. It was now or never. Then, as he neared the final gap, the whole car began to vibrate. There followed a rasping noise, as though the metal holding it in place would give way at any moment. Suddenly he was clear and falling, trying to control the drop, keeping his body straight and as near to the side of the shaft as he dared. Metallic vibrations from the car seemed to surround him, and the fall went on forever, until the sudden jerk on the rope cut into his back, arms, and legs.

As Bond had feared, the weight of his fall pulled the nylon tight; then the tension released, and he felt himself rising again like a yo-yo. It only needed too much of a backward spring on the rope for the grapple to become unhooked.

Winded, and not quite believing it, Bond found himself hanging, swinging hard against the concrete and girdered wall. The rope cut deeper. Bond felt his muscles howling in protest, while his wrists and hands struggled to hang on.

The small, enclosed world gradually swung into focus: dirty concrete; girders, with traces of rust; oil; and, below, the dark cavern that seemed to descend into hell itself.

His feet were firmly against the wall now, and Bond was able to look upward. The car was jammed across the shaft, but for how long was anyone's guess. Already the upper section of woodwork had developed a long crack. It was only a matter of time before the crack would widen, then split and give way. The car would then drop heavily on its side.

It would be a hideous way for them to go if that happened. But it was SPECTRE's way, Bond was certain of that.

He took a deep breath and called up to Cedar, "Be up for you in a minute." Kicking out from the wall, he allowed his hands to slide on the rope, bringing his feet within touching distance of the nearest girder. As the bottoms of his rope-soled shoes slammed into the metal, Bond hauled on the rope, grabbing for support from the big oily guide rail.

The latticework of girders was reasonably easy to negotiate, and Bond climbed it with speed, keeping the rope firmly around himself, until he reached the grappling hook. There he paused for breath, the car rattling in the breeze that came up the shaft's tunnel. Vaguely, among the creaking metallic noises, he thought he could hear sounds—shouting and steady hammering.

The sagging floor of the car was some five feet from his head. Unhooking the grapple, he climbed higher, finally finding a suitable place among the girders to refix the hook: this time less than a foot below the car.

Turning his body so that he could lean back against the wall, Bond once more shouted to Cedar, giving orders in a voice designed to command immediate obedience.

"I'm going to throw the rope in. Tie the briefcase on, then let it down slowly. But don't lose the rope. Keep hold of it until I tell you."

By this time he had pulled in all the slack of the rope, which had snaked down the shaft almost out of sight. Hanging on to the girders with one hand, Bond coiled several feet of rope around the other. Then, with a cry of "Ready?"—and an answering affirmative from Cedar—he aimed the balled rope at the flapping mouth which was the open floor of the car.

The ball of rope went straight as an arrow. For a second or two he saw that the length now protruding from the opening in the car was sliding back. Then it stopped, and Cedar's voice came filtering down with a "Got it." About a minute later the briefcase, tied now to the end of the rope, descended slowly toward him.

Cedar paid out the rope until Bond shouted for her to stop. Precariously he reached forward, took the case, and balancing it on the girder, untied the knot. He attached one of the metal fastenings on the briefcase to the large clip on his belt. Then he shouted to Cedar to haul in the rope and get a tight hold on it. "Wrap it around your wrists and shoulders if you want," he called to her. "Then just slide out. It's around thirty feet down to the next floor and set of doors. If we can make that, we'll have a secure ledge, and I'll try to open the damned things. Come on when you're ready."

She came quickly. Too quickly. Bond saw her legs emerge, and the rope dropped past him. Then he felt the blow as the side of her shoulder hit him.

He was conscious of the grapple taking the strain and of the car shifting just above his head. But by that time his balance had gone, and he was suddenly scrabbling for the swinging rope in front of him.

His hands wrapped around the nylon, and they were both swinging gently, one above the other, bouncing off the walls of the shaft.

"We're going down one at a time," he called, short of breath. "Just straight rope-climbing stuff to the ledge of the next floor. The rope'll just about make it."

Cedar's voice came back, breathless and excited. "I only hope it'll hold our weight."

"It'll do that, all right. Just remember not to let go!"

You really think I'd forget?" she shouted back, starting to move, hand over hand, the rope wrapped around her ankles as she went.

Bond followed Cedar's lead, trying to imitate her rhythm on the rope in order to reduce the swing. He had been bruised and battered enough from bumping against the girders. Finally he saw below him that Cedar had made it, saw her standing on the narrow ledge, both hands still tight on the rope, her feet spread out and body leaning forward.

She was calling something up to him.

"There's someone on the other side of the doors," he heard her shout. "I've told them we're here."

Nodding, Bond continued his climb down until he felt his feet touch the ledge. Even as they did so, there was a hiss and the outer doors opened. A fire chief and three other uniformed, helmeted men stood aside, mouths agape, as Cedar and Bond stepped into the corridor.

"Ah, the visiting firemen," Bond said. Then he staggered, feeling the strain hit him. Cedar grabbed his arm, and he took a deep breath.

The firemen and hotel staff gathered around them. Bond waved away a doctor and asked that they should be taken straight downstairs. "We've got a plane to catch," he added.

As they went, he whispered instructions to Cedar. "Pay the bill, get what information you can. Then slip away and meet me at the Saab. We don't want too many questions, and certainly no cameras."

She nodded silently, and when they reached the crowded and noisy lobby, Bond melted away. Even Cedar did not see him go. "One of my disappearing tricks," he told her later. "Easy when you know how."

In fact it *was* relatively easy. Bond always worked on the principle that, in a crowd that was confused and uncertain, all you had to do was be positive: a determined move, in a definite direction, assuming the look of a man who knew precisely where he was going and why. It worked nine times out of ten.

In the underground parking lot, Bond did not go straight to the Saab, but waited out of sight behind another car directly opposite. It was over half an hour before Cedar appeared, running from the service elevator.

Bond emerged as soon as he saw she was alone. "I told them I had to go to the john," she said. "They want you as well. Questions, and more questions. We'll have to move fast."

In a matter of seconds they were in the Saab, and a few minutes later they were out and away, roaring down the Anacostia Freeway.

"You're the navigator," Bond told her. "We want Amarillo, Texas."

As she directed him, Cedar gave him what information she had gleaned. "Definitely our friends from New York," she told him. "I got their descriptions." She went on to explain how they had come in posing as detectives, asked for directions to the maintenance complex, and how the duty man had been found unconscious. "Apparently they'd stripped the controls for all the elevators," she added. "Whichever one we used, they had us."

Bond smiled grimly. "I told you. When SPECTRE wants you dead, they don't like doing it clean. Well, at least we know what we need to know. First Bismaquer wanted us as his house guests, then he tried to have us killed. I guess he'll have to settle for the first."

As he said it, the delayed shock took hold. He slowed slightly, and after a minute or two, the reaction passed. Taking a deep breath, he glanced at Cedar.

"We'll have to stop and buy some new luggage on the way. But at least we've got the essentials, including the prints." The prints had remained hidden in one of the many secret compartments in the Saab.

"So, my dear Cedar," he was grinning again; then he relaxed, and his mouth reformed into its hard, cruel line. "So now is when the fun really starts."

10

THE ROAD TO AMARILLO

THEY DROVE STEADILY through the night, skirting Pittsburgh around dawn, heading west again. The Saab, set on its cruise control, gobbled up the ribbon of road, and during that first long day they stopped only for snacks and gasoline. The car, tuned to perfection before being flown to America, took to the broad four-lane highways like an unleashed jet.

Just before nightfall, they had already come to within throwing distance of Springfield, Missouri. Bond pulled off the highway and drove into a small motel, where they registered in separate cabins, Cedar as Mrs. Penbrunner and Bond under his own name.

Already, before the incident with the elevator, he had explained their tactics to Cedar. "Even if Bismaquer doesn't know my true identity, I have to go in as myself."

Cedar was concerned. "Isn't that pushing our luck, James? You've already told me SPECTRE has a private and personal grudge against you. Why not keep the Penbrunner role going as long as possible?"

Bond shook his head. "It's not going to fool them for long—even if it's done so already, which I doubt. Now, *you* are really not known. 'Mrs. Penbrunner' will probably pass, and we may just get some advantage by making them believe I'm here to look after you."

She was still concerned about this when they reached the motel. "You're setting yourself up as a target: doesn't that worry you?"

"Of course, but I've done it before. Anyway, Cedar, do you really believe that the great Markus Bismaquer would go to all the trouble of having us removed, by way of an elevator shaft, if he didn't know it was me? Think about it: First the fearsome foursome turn up with an invitation: Bismaquer requests the pleasure of seeing the Hogarth prints before anyone else. Then we manage to disappear. True to form— SPECTRE's old form, that is—they winkle us out near Washington, and without the aid of any law-enforcement agencies. Think about it, Cedar, and you'll see how good they are. They always were in the past. So they find us and try to give us the fast elevator trip. No niceties about the

Hogarth prints. Just death, sudden, a very nasty way to go."

She nodded agreement. "I suppose you're right. But it still sounds crazy—the idea of just turning up at Bismaquer's Rancho Notorious. . . ."

"Tethered goats have been known to catch tigers."

"And goats often end up sacrificial," Cedar countered. "With their throats cut."

"Tough on us goats." Bond gave a sardonic smile. "Remember, Cedar, we go with knives as well. The fact is, I have no option. Our job is to find out if Markus Bismaquer's running the show; if it really is a reconstituted SPECTRE; and, most important, what they're up to. We're snoops, like the others. They got chopped. Why?"

The conversation went on, in rooms and again in the car, when they rode into Springfield to reoutfit themselves, and again over a meal in a small restaurant, where Bond declared the chicken pie as one of the best he had ever tasted and Cedar insisted that he try the apple Jonathan—that delicious baked concoction of green apples, cream, maple syrup, and eggs.

Back at the motel, they unwrapped their packages, filled the newly purchased suitcases, and arranged a series of signals in the event of trouble during the night.

Bond then quietly checked out the motel and its surroundings, paying special attention to the parked cars. Satisfied, he returned to his cabin, laid out a new pair of jeans, shirt, boots, and a windbreaker. He then luxuriated under a shower—scalding hot, followed by a fine spray of ice-cold water. Thus refreshed, he slid the VP70 under his pillow, placed a chair against the door, and secured the windows before getting into bed.

Almost as his head touched the pillow, he was asleep. He had long learned the art of resting, allowing the problems and anxieties to be swept from his mind, yet never dropping into really deep oblivion while he was on an assignment. Sleep he certainly had; but his subconscious remained alive, ready to prod him into instant awareness.

The night passed without incident, except for a momentary dream, just before waking, in which the elevator car was transformed into some kind of space satellite. The dream was to stay in Bond's mind, and later he wondered if it had been some kind of strange precognition.

By noon the next day they had circumvented Oklahoma City. The Saab, cool with its interior air conditioning, whined at high turbo power along the flat endless terrain of prairie and desert, leading to the edge of the Great Plains and the panhandle of Texas.

Once more they stopped as little as possible, and around nine in the

evening negotiated Amarillo, circling the city so as to enter from the
west, on the assumption that any watchers would be looking out for the
Saab along the eastern access roads.

As before, they chose a small, obscure motel. They climbed from the
car, and the heat hit them like a blast furnace. It was already dusk, lights
were among the trees and dry grass. Both men and women wore jeans,
boots, and large-brimmed Stetsons. With a shock, Bond realized they had
really hit the West.

The manager drawled them into an adjoining set of rooms, said there
was a saloon and diner across the street—if they did not want to use the
motel's coffee shop—then left them to their own devices.

"Well, Cedar," Bond asked, "how about food?"

The food turned out to be the best bowl of chili either of them had
tasted in a long time. But Cedar looked nervous as they said good night
at her door, and Bond, sensing her anxiety, told her not to worry.

"Just remember all they taught you," he said, "and all we've worked
out together. It'll only need one of us to get out if we strike gold. One
alert—to your contacts or mine, or both. We're equal partners in this,
Cedar. Our job is to pin them down, get proof, and if they've got some
nasty work on hand, stop them. Now, remember, six o'clock in the morning."

She bit her lip, nodding.

"Nothing wrong, is there?" Bond searched for clues in her eyes.

She gave a heavy sigh. "Of course there is, and you know it." She
smiled, reaching up to kiss his cheek. "And you're right. Dead right. So
if it can't be, then I wish my dad was here. He'd love to be working with
you again."

"Stop getting sentimental, Cedar. You're as good as your father ever
was, and I suspect you'll prove it in the next day or so. Now, let's get
some sleep."

Bond stretched out on his bed, fully clothed, the automatic near at
hand. He dozed, slept, and woke with an alert start as the alarm call
came through at five-thirty.

Showered, shaved, dressed, Bond was just in time to greet Cedar, who
arrived at the door bearing a flask of coffee and hot waffles with syrup
on a tray. The coffee shop did a twenty-four-hour service, she explained.
At six o'clock promptly, perched on the bed, sipping the coffee, Bond
dialed the number they'd pried from Mike Mazzard back in New York.

The telephone rang for almost thirty seconds. Then a male voice answered, although it took Bond a moment to realize a man was speaking, for the voice was thin, reedy, pitched very high, and inclined to squeak in the upper register.

"Rancho Bismaquer."

"Put me on to Markus Bismaquer." No "please" or any of the other niceties.

"I guess he'll still be asleep. He doesn't get up until six-thirty."

"Then get him up. This is very important."

A long pause. Then: "Who wants him?"

"Just say that I represent Professor Penbrunner. I have Mrs. Penbrunner with me, and I'm anxious to speak with Bismaquer."

Another silence.

"The name was . . .?"

"I didn't say. I'm only acting for the professor, but if you want to tell Bismaquer—and we've a lot to talk about—you can say my name's Bond. James Bond."

007 was not certain, but he thought he detected a slight intake of breath at the other end. Certainly the reply came back fast as a bullet. "I'll wake him right away, Mr. Bond. If you're acting for Professor Penbrunner, I'm sure he'll want to know."

There was a long wait; then another voice came on the line: soft, gently drawling and friendly, with a deep, pleasing chuckle.

"Markus Bismaquer."

Bond nodded at Cedar. "My name's Bond, Mr. Bismaquer. Mrs. Penbrunner's here with me. I have power of attorney for Professor Penbrunner, whom, I understand, you wished to meet."

"I did, that's right. Mr. . . . er . . . Bond did you say? Yes, yes, I invited Professor and Mrs. Penbrunner to fly out here in my private jet. I guess it wasn't convenient for them. Let me ask the big question: do you have the Hogarths with you?"

"Mrs. Penbrunner *and* the prints. Both."

"Ah. And power of attorney? Which means we could make a deal?"

"If that's what you really want, Mr. Bismaquer."

Bismaquer chuckled. "If the prints are all they're cracked up to be, that's the *only* thing I want. Where are you?"

"Amarillo," Bond clipped.

"At a hotel? Let me send Walter—Walter Luxor, he's my partner—out to pick you up. . . ."

"Just give me directions. I have wheels, and a good sense of location."

"I see. Yes, yes. Okay, Mr. Bond . . ." The deep voice gave simple instructions for leaving Amarillo, and slightly more complicated ones for the point at which they had to leave the main highway, following secondary roads to the monorail station.

"If you can be there at ten, I'll see the train is waiting for you. There's a section for automobiles. You should bring yours with you to the ranch." Once more the chuckle. "You'll need it to get around the place."

"We'll be there at ten o'clock, sharp." Bond hung up and turned to Cedar. "Well, Mrs. Penbrunner, he sounds very relaxed. We take the monorail at ten. So he's putting the ball neatly back in his own court. Sounds a very smooth gentleman." He added that they were to be met by Bismaquer's partner, one Walter Luxor. "Know anything about him?"

Cedar said there was a file. He appeared to be an innocent stooge, not more than a boy when Bismaquer took him into the old ice-cream business. "Been with him ever since. We don't know much more about him. Something of a glorified secretary, really, though Bismaquer always calls him his partner."

By nine-fifteen they were on the road once more. Cedar followed the instructions Bond had scribbled down during the conversation with Bismaquer. Five miles out of town, they reached the turnoff. They had also collected a tail.

In the golden haze which came with the sun, both Bond and Cedar could clearly make out the black BMW 528i riding at a comfortable distance behind them, two unidentifiable men in the front seat.

"Guard of honor?" Bond questioned aloud. Silently he thought: Guard of honor? Or a hit team? Quietly he leaned across Cedar to press one of the square black buttons on the dashboard. Silently a compartment slid open to reveal the large Ruger Super Blackhawk .44 Magnum he always carried in the car, part of the private, and most secret, "gee-whiz" technology built into the vehicle without even the Armorer's knowledge.

The .44 Magnum was not just a man-stopper. Bond liked to think of it as a car-stopper if necessary. One properly placed bullet from this magnificent single-action revolver could wreck an engine.

"Hey, that's . . . big," breathed Cedar.

"Yes, it is. A little extra protection if we need it."

As it turned out, however, they had no use for the Blackhawk. The monorail station became visible at a good ten miles' distance—a low building set behind high wire fencing.

The fencing, when they reached it, was some twenty feet high—double-

banked Cyclone, with large red notices attached: DANGER. THIS FENCE
AND THE FENCES AHEAD ARE DANGEROUS. TOUCHING OR TAMPERING
WITH THEM WILL CAUSE INSTANT DEATH BY ELECTROCUTION. Under
this unfriendly warning there was a red skull and the international double-
lightning-flash sign for electricity.

The fence could be breached only through a pair of firmly bolted heavy
steel gates. On the far side of the gates was a small blockhouse and a
large concrete area leading to, as they now saw, an oblong station building.

Two men uniformed in fawn slacks and blue shirts bearing the insignia
"Bismaquer Security" appeared from the blockhouse. They carried handguns holstered on their hips, and pump-action shotguns under their arms.

Bond let down one of the electric windows. "We're expected. Mrs.
Penbrunner and Mr. Bond."

"Ten o'clock the mono's expected." The men looked like identical
twins, spawned by a pair of Epstein's larger human sculptures. Both were
close to seven feet in height: big, tanned, and mean around the eyes.

Through his driving mirror Bond could see the BMW, still standing
well back. The BMW's lights winked twice, and one of the guards spat.
"Guess it's okay," he said in a Texas twang, then looked at his companion.
"Turn the juice off," nodding toward the blockhouse.

"Is that for real?" Bond pointed at the sign.

"Bet your ass."

"Ever kill anyone?"

"Plenty. They got permission for it up on the ranch. Nothin' any law
can do if someone gits hisself kilt. Place's lit up at night. Only take the
power off when people're comin' in or out. If you want privacy here, ole
buddy, you git it—if y'can pay fer it."

The other man came out of the blockhouse, unlocked the heavy bolts
on the gates, and the pair of guards swung them open. "Quick as y'can,"
shouted the one to whom Bond had been talking. "They don't like us
leavin' the juice off longer'n need be."

With care, Bond rolled the Saab into the yard, watching as the guards
closed the gates. One of them went back to the blockhouse. Through his
mirror, Bond saw that the BMW had disappeared. All part of the service,
he thought. Once the Saab was inside Bismaquer's domain, the nursemaids
could be quickly withdrawn. He pressed the button on the dash again.
There was a hiss, and the Blackhawk compartment slid back into place,
just as the first guard came up to the driver's side.

"You got the steerin' on the wrong side, buddy, y'know that?"

Bond gave a polite nod. "English car," he explained. "Well, not the car, but the steering."

"Yep. I heared they drive on the wrong side over there." The giant Texan thought for a moment. "Just point the nose at those doors and sit. Okay? Don't git out, or you end up dead as a frozen ox. Right?"

"Right," agreed Bond.

Large metal doors were built into the facing end wall of the oblong building. Bond shrugged, raised his eyebrows at Cedar. "Guess y'don't argue none," he muttered, breaking the tension and causing Cedar to giggle.

Cedar's briefing had reflected the tight security on Rancho Bismaquer, and Bond already had some idea of what to expect, if SPECTRE was involved. But the scale of this operation could only bring a sneaking admiration. No roads led into Bismaquer's large ranch, only the monorail protected by deadly electric fences, high as prison walls, together with automaton guards. Bond also wondered about the chase car, the BMW. Had they, in fact, been under discreet surveillance from the time they left Washington, after the elevator incident?

Wrapped in these thoughts, Bond took out his gunmetal cigarette case, offered one to Cedar, who refused, and lit a Simmons for himself. He felt an itch of concern. It had not been there when they had begun the long trek from England; and since then, life had been full of incident: the attempted kidnap in New York; the falling elevator; and then the long, fast drive to Texas. Now, poised on the brink of entering Bismaquer's world, Bond knew he should not dwell on the more morbid possibilities. As M would say, "Worry *at* it, 007, don't worry *about* it."

They did not have long to wait.

Just at ten o'clock, Bond felt the car vibrate slightly. He slid his window down and heard the heavy whine of a turbine. Bismaquer's system would, of course, be a split-rail suspension: one huge rail with the train suspended above it, so that it appeared the train was impaled, hanging on the rail. Yes, naturally, Bond repeated to himself: nothing but the best for Mr. Bismaquer.

The turbine whine grew louder. They could not see the vehicle arrive, but one of the guards walked slowly over to the doors facing them, unlocked a metal box in the wall, and pressed a button. Silently the doors slid back.

A long ramp climbed upward. The guard waved them on, and Bond started the engine, taking the ramp in first.

They climbed a good twenty feet before the ramp flattened to become a gently curving tunnel, like a very large version of the jetties used for boarding aircraft. In turn, this tunnel took them into the train itself.

Men in similar uniforms to the guards—but with the symbol "Bismaquer Services" in gold on their blue shirts—waved Bond into position. When the car was correctly parked, one of them approached and opened the door. He addressed them politely without accent: "Mrs. Penbrunner. Mr. Bond. Welcome aboard. Please leave your car here, with the hand brake on."

Another of Bismaquer's men opend the passenger door for Cedar. As it closed again, Bond—who had already put on the automatic device for securing the engine—clicked down the passenger-door lock. Then he climbed out, briefcase in hand, and locked his own door.

"The keys'll be safe with me, sir." The man stood waiting.

Bond did not smile. "Safer with me, always," he said. "If you want it moved, come and get me."

The man's face remained impassive. "Mr. Luxor's waiting for you, sir."

Standing at the end of the vehicle compartment was a man whose main features were the rake-thinness of his body and a face which looked like a skull over which thin, almost transparent skin had been tightly stretched. Even the eyes were sunk back deep into their sockets. In personal appearance, Walter Luxor looked like the walking dead.

"Mrs. Penbrunner. Mr. Bond." The voice was the same high-pitched squeak Bond had heard on the telephone that morning. "Welcome." Bond saw Cedar wince as she shook the hand. A second later, Bond knew why: it was indeed like clasping the palm of a corpse—cold, limp, and clammy. Press too hard, he thought, and you would end up with a handful of powdered bone.

Luxor ushered them into a beautifully designed coach, with upholstered leather swivel chairs, tables anchored to the floors, and an attractive hostess ready to serve drinks.

No sooner were they seated than the turbine whined, dropping in volume as they slid from the station and smoothly gathered speed.

Even at this height, Bond could see the protective electrified Cyclone fences on either side of the track. Above and beyond them the desert and plain stretched to the horizon.

The hostess came over, asking what they would like to drink. Bond asked for a very large vodka martini—shaken, not stirred—giving her the precise instructions. Cedar took sherry, as did Luxor. "An excellent choice," Luxor said. "A very civilized drink, sherry." He smiled, but there could be no humor in a face like his, only the grim joke of death.

As though to put them at ease, Walter Luxor continued talking. "Markus only had the vehicle transporter and club coaches on the rail today. Perhaps, when you leave, he'll let you make a choice."

"A choice of what?" Bond asked.

"Monorail cars." Luxor spread out the crab-bone hands. "Markus has had several famous replicas made to fit the system—one of his little idiosyncrasies. He even has a replica of your own Queen Victoria's special railroad car, one of the presidential car, a perfect one of the state railroad car used by Tzar Nicholas, and a copy of the coach in which the World War One armistice was signed. That one doesn't exist at all now. Hitler made the French sign their separate peace in it, but it was later destroyed."

"I know," Bond said abruptly. The face was bad enough, but the strangulated, high-pitched voice was almost unbearable.

"Why replicas?" Bond asked shortly.

"That's a good question," Walter Luxor went on. "Markus is a great collector, you know. He prefers the real thing. He tried to buy Queen Victoria's railroad coach to have it converted, but they weren't selling at the time. He did the same with the others. No sale. If a good one comes on the market, well, he'll probably be the top bidder. He usually is. You wouldn't be here if he didn't want the Hogarth prints."

"We nearly weren't here," Bond observed, but Luxor chose either not to hear or to ignore the remark.

The hostess arrived with the drinks. Bond approved: it was one of the best martinis he'd had, excepting those he made for himself. Luxor talked on to Cedar, while Bond stared out of the huge window. The monorail must have reached a speed of well over a hundred and fifty miles an hour, yet they appeared to glide effortlessly over the plain. It was not unlike low flying but without any buffeting or turbulence.

The journey took just over fifteen minutes. Then, gently, the speed reduced. Bond saw three or four long sections of Cyclone fence reaching away into the distance, then a high thick wall, wired at the top and reaching to at least twenty feet.

As they passed the wall, the monorail car slowed to a stop. Most startling of all, the scenery changed dramatically—a fleeting glimpse of green, with trees—before they were enveloped by the curved white walls of a station.

"Would there be room in your car for me?" Luxor looked at Bond, who was repelled to find that, even when you stared hard into the sunken eyes, there was little hint of life there.

"Plenty of room," Bond replied.

"Good. I will direct you from the station. The Bismaquer ranch is quite large, though of course you can't miss the big house. It's right near the station."

Once down the disembarking ramp, they could have been outside any small American railroad stop. Doubtless this was another of Bismaquer's collections: a small turn-of-the-century station, probably removed from a ghost town.

Bond glanced around. Only minutes before he had been looking at dry rock and brown, sunbaked desert grass. Now, with the great wall sweeping away to left and right, they could have been in a different country. There were grass and trees, macadam roads leading off from the station, tree-lined avenues, and even a small bridge crossing a creek.

"Turn right," Luxor said, "and straight down the main drive," and Bond heard Cedar give a startled intake of breath. Facing them, set amid lush lawns, was a huge white house. Wide steps led to a portico, where square columns rose to a flat roof. The roof then pitched back over the rest of the house, its red tiles a splash of color against the overall white.

There were dogwood trees forward of the house, flanking the drive, and Bond thought, vaguely, that he had seen it before.

"Tara," whispered Cedar. "It's Tara."

"Tara?" Bond was lost.

"*Gone With the Wind*. The movie—Margaret Mitchell's book. It's the house from the movie. You know, James, Vivien Leigh, Clark Gable . . ."

"Ah," said Bond.

"How very clever of you." The squeak rose excitedly from Walter Luxor. "It usually takes people longer. They think they've seen pictures of it. Markus fell in love with it when he saw the movie, so he bought the designs from M-G-M and built it here. Ah, here's Markus now."

Bond had pulled the Saab up in front of the broad steps, down which a great bearlike man was coming, trotting, his face wreathed in smiles. The voice, in direct contrast to Luxor's, was deep, gruff, and embracing. "Mrs. Penbrunner! Why couldn't your husband come too? Ah, this must be Mr. Bond. Come on, let's go onto the veranda and have a drink. There's plenty of time before luncheon."

The face was pink and chubby: the face of a well-scrubbed baby or an elderly cherub. Or, Bond speculated, a devil? Slowly he climbed out of the Saab. This bulky American, clad in a crumpled white suit, must have been in his late sixties—with wispy, soft silver hair—yet was full of energy, laughing with childlike enthusiasm in a manner clearly designed to make people like him at first meeting. Could this be the new Blofeld? The head of the resurrected SPECTRE?

"Come on, Mrs. Penbrunner," he heard Bismaquer say. "Come on, Mr. Bond. I know we're in Texas, but I make the best mint juleps in the world. How about that? Mint juleps, Texan style!" Once more the infectious, growling laugh. "You just fill the glass up with crushed ice, load in the gin, and add a sprig of mint on top." Bismaquer roared at his own recipe, then turned to watch Bond coming up the flat steps from the car.

Yes, Bond thought, seeing the happy gleaming eyes of this pink-white-and-silver billionaire. Yes, the new Blofeld could easily be just this sort of man.

Then he saw the sliver of Walter Luxor, the skull face ghastly in the shadow pattern on the portico. Or Luxor? Living in the shade of all this wealth, with easy access to power?

Bond's real work was only just starting—with a vengeance.

11

RANCHO BISMAQUER

JAMES BOND POLITELY declined Markus Bismaquer's lethal mint julep, choosing instead another vodka martini.

"Of course, of course!" Bismaquer exclaimed. "Anything you like. I never force a man to eat or drink what he doesn't want. As for women. . . . ? Well, that's different."

"Meaning?" Bond cut in tersely.

A white-coated servant had appeared from the main doors and stood waiting behind a large trolley-bar. But Bismaquer was content to serve his guests himself. He looked up over the bottles, hands poised, his cherubic face a mask of surprise. "I'm sorry, Mr. Bond. Did I offend you?"

Bond gave a shrug. "You said one should never force a man to eat or drink something he does not want; then you implied it was different for women."

Bismaquer relaxed. "A joke, Mr. Bond. Just a joke, among men of the world. Or maybe you're not a man of the world?"

"I've been accused of it." Bond did not let his mask slip. "I still don't see why women should be treated differently."

"I only meant that they have to be coaxed sometimes." He turned to Cedar. "Don't you sometimes like to be coaxed, Mrs. Penbrunner?"

Cedar laughed. "That depends on the coaxing."

The high-pitched voice of Walter Luxor joined in. "I think Markus was trying to make a joke based on the old saying that when a woman says 'no' she means 'maybe. . . .' "

"And when she says 'maybe,' she means 'yes,' " Bismaquer chimed in.

"I see." Bond took the proffered martini, flattening his voice to give the impression that he was a man without humor. When playing someone like Bismaquer, he calculated—all growl and laughs—it was better to take on an opposite role.

"Well, here's to us." Bismaquer raised his glass. "Then, perhaps, Mr. Bond, we can look at the Hogarths. There's time before luncheon."

Bond nodded silently, then observed, "Time is money, Mr. Bismaquer."

"Oh, the hell with time." Bismaquer smiled. "I've got the money, you've got the time. And if you don't, I'll buy it. When guests come all this way, we like to entertain them." He paused, as though appealing to Cedar. "You'll stay for a few days, won't you? I've even arranged for the guest cabins to be opened up."

"A day or two won't matter, will it, James?" Cedar looked at him in a pleading manner, giving just the right emphasis.

Bond sighed, turning down the corners of his mouth. "Well, I suppose . . ."

"Come on, James, I can always call Joseph if you want me to."

"It's up to you," Bond said, feigning surliness.

"Done." Bismaquer rubbed his hands together. "Now, could we . . . er . . . would it be possible to see the prints?"

Bond looked at Cedar. "If that's all right with you, Mrs. Penbrunner?"

Cedar smiled sweetly. "You have the last word on that, James. My husband put it into your hands."

Bond hesitated. "Well, I see no harm. I think you should examine them inside the house, though, Mr. Bismaquer."

"Please . . ." Bismaquer appeared to hop, his large body moving from foot to foot. "Please call me Markus. You're in Texas now."

Bond again nodded. He took out his car keys and went down the steps to the Saab.

The prints were in a special heatproof folder, neatly secured in a slim false compartment under the movable shelf in the Saab's large trunk. Without giving the men on the portico a chance to see the hiding place, Bond removed the folder, then locked the trunk.

"Nice little car," Bismaquer said from the portico, giving the Saab a condescending look which seemed somehow out of character.

"It'd show a clean pair of heels to most commercial cars in its class."

"Ah," Bismaquer gave a broad smile. An almost tangible ripple of happiness passed through the large frame. "Well, we'll have to see about that. I've got a few cars myself, and a track. Maybe we could organize something. A local Grand Prix."

"Why not?" Bond gestured with the folder, looking toward the house.

"Oh, yes. Yes!" Bismaquer all but trembled with excitement. "Let's leave Mrs. Penbrunner in Walter's safe hands. After luncheon, I'll see you're taken over to the guest cabins. Then we'll arrange a guided tour of Rancho Bismaquer—of which, Jim, I'm pretty proud."

He gestured toward the tall doors, allowing Bond to pass into the huge, cool, parquet-floored hallway, with its imposing gallery staircase. Whatever else, Markus Bismaquer had a certain style.

"The print room, I think." Bismaquer led the way down a wide, airy corridor, opening a pair of double doors at the end.

Bond almost gasped with surprise. It was not a large room, but the walls were high and screens jutted from them at intervals. Almost all the wall space was covered, and even from the limited education he'd had in the Kensington safe house, Bond could identify some of the prints which hung there.

There were at least four very rare Holbeins; some priceless though rather crudely colored playing cards; a signed Baxter color print which Bond's instructor had pointed out as almost unobtainable; and a set of what appeared to be original Bewicks, from the famous *General History of Quadrupeds*. As well as the walls, the prints covered the jutting screens. Somewhere, from hidden speakers, baroque music filtered into the room, giving it a pleasant, peaceful atmosphere. The floor was of highly polished wood, the only furniture high-backed chairs, set at intervals, and a large table in the bow of the room's one tall window at the far end. These too, Bond supposed, must have been priceless antiques.

"You'd have to call this a pretty handsome collection, wouldn't you, Jim?" Bismaquer waited patiently at the end of the room, visibly proud of his showplace.

"People call me James," Bond corrected, remaining somber. "But, yes, I'd say these are considered, and sensible, acquisitions. Joseph Penbrunner told me you had two passions in life . . ."

"Only two?" Bismaquer raised an eyebrow, the quizzical cherubic expression looking somehow incongruous on such a large body.

"Prints and ice cream." Bond reached the table as Bismaquer gave a bellow of laughter.

"Your Professor Penbrunner has had bad information. I have many more passions than prints and ice cream. But I'm lucky enough to have made my pile while I was young. Walter Luxor is an experienced investment counselor as well as a friend and colleague. The original fortune has doubled, trebled, quadrupled." Bismaquer's pudgy hands getured in the air, as though imitating the accumulation of wealth. "In fact, the man's a genius. The more I indulge my tastes, the more my holdings multiply!" He held out a hand, reaching for the prints. For a second, Bond wondered if the man was knowledgeable enough to spot them immediately as forgeries. But it was too late to worry about that in any case. Then, quite suddenly, Bismaquer changed the subject. "You must, by the way, forgive Walter's strange appearance. He looks like a dry stick, I know, like you could break him in two. But looks are deceiving. I don't suggest you try it. Really, he's strong as a horse.

"A car accident. I spent a fortune getting him rebuilt, from top to bottom," Bismaquer went on. "His body was severely damaged, and the burns were god-awful. We got the best surgeons money can buy. They had to regraft the face almost completely. One of Walter's passions is speed. He is a *very* good driver. In fact, when we organize that little Grand Prix I mentioned, we're going to put you up against Walter."

Skin grafts and an entirely new body? Bond wondered. True, Blofeld had been choked to death, but he did not know what might have happened after that. Could it possibly be that. . . ? No, better to let things take their course and get the fantasies out of his head.

"The Hogarths, please, James."

With great care, Bond opened up the folder, taking each print with its covering tissue, placing them in order on the table before removing the tissues.

The Lady's Progress was a typical Hogarthian subject. The first two prints depicted the Lady living in idle, rich luxury. The third was her downfall, when her husband—now dead—was revealed to have a multitude of creditors, so that she was left penniless. The final three prints showed the various stages of the Lady's disintegration, drink turning her into a common whore, so that she finally ends as a horrible image of her former self: raddled, craven and foul, among the seventeenth-century sinks and sewers of London's lower orders.

Bismaquer leaned over the prints in an attitude of reverence.

"Remarkable," he breathed. "Quite remarkable. See that detail, James, those faces. And the urchins, there, peeping out from that window. Oh, you could spend a lifetime just looking at these! You'd find something new every day! Tell me, what's your asking price?"

But Bond would not commit himself. Professor Penbrunner was still uncertain about selling. "You'd be the first to admit, Markus," he said, though he cared not at all for the easy familiarity of first names, "that it's tricky to value items such as these. They're unique. No other set seems to have survived. But they're genuine. I have the authentication documents in my car."

"I *must* have them," Bismaquer said, enthralled. "I simply *must*. . . ."

"What *must* you have, Markus?"

The voice—low, clear, and with a tantalizing trace of accent—came from the door, which neither Bismaquer nor Bond had heard open.

They both turned from the table, Bond almost doing a double-take, as Bismaquer gave a delighted growl. "Ah! Come and meet James Bond, darling. He's here representing Professor Penbrunner. James, this is my wife, Nena."

Bond was already prepared for Nena Bismaquer to be younger than her husband, but not this much younger. The girl—for she could at most have been in her mid-twenties—paused in the doorway, the sunlight from the great window pouring toward her like a floodlight. It was the entrance of an actress.

Dressed in exceptionally well-cut jeans and a royal-blue silk shirt with a bandanna knotted at her neck, Nena Bismaquer gave Bond a smile calculated to make even the most misogynistic male buckle at the knees.

She was tall—almost matching Bond's height—with long legs and a firm, striding walk. As she crossed the room, Bond saw in an instant that Nena Bismaquer would be at home and comfortable anywhere. She had that special poise which combined all the attributes he most admired in a woman: style, grace, and the obvious ability to take on the athletic pursuits of what is known, in some circles, as the great outdoors.

As she came closer, he felt a charge, an unmistakable chemistry, passing between them. It said she would also be more than athletic in the great indoors as well.

If such a thing as black fire could exist, it was there in her eyes, an ebony matching the long hair which fell to her shoulders and was pushed casually back on the left side, as though by the brush of her hand. The dark fire blazed with knowledge reaching beyond her obvious youth. Her face appeared perfectly balanced with her body—a long, slender nose and rather solemn mouth, the lower lip a fraction thicker than the upper, giving a hint of sensuality which Bond found more than engaging. Her grip, as they shook hands, was firm—a hand which could caress, or hold hard to the reins of a horse at full gallop.

"Yes, I know who Mr. Bond is. I've just met Mrs. Penbrunner, and it's a pleasure to meet you . . . may I call you James too?"

"Of course."

"Well, I'm Nena; and to what extravagances are you tempting my husband, James? The Hogarth prints he's been talking about?"

Bismaquer allowed a rumble of laughter to come from the back of his throat and break, like a waterfall. He gave his wife a bear hug, lifting her off the ground and swinging her around like a child's doll. "Oh, and who's talking about extravagance?" He shook with happy laughter—a summertime Santa Claus without the beard.

Bond could not help seeing the shadow cross Nena Bismaquer's face as her husband set her down, arms still around her, pulling toward the table. She almost seemed to flinch at his touch.

"Just look at these, my darling! The real thing. No others like them in the world. Look at that detail—the face of that woman. Look at the men there, drunk as skunks. . . ."

Bond watched as she examined the prints one by one, the trace of a smile starting at the eyes and dropping to her lips, as a long, beautifully manicured finger pointed to the last picture. "That one could have been drawn from life, chéri." A glissando laugh, harplike, and without malice. "He looks just like you."

Bismaquer gave a playful bellow of simulated rage, lifting his hands high. "Bitch!" he crowed.

"So, how much are you asking?" Nena Bismaquer turned to Bond.

"There's no price tag." He gave her a steady smile, staring unflinchingly into her eyes. For a second, he thought he detected mockery in them. "I cannot even promise they're for sale."

"Then why. . . ?" Her face remained calm.

"Markus invited the professor and his wife here. He wanted to be first to look at the prints."

"Come on, James. First to make an offer, you mean." Bismaquer did not seem to have changed, yet there was something between husband and wife: intangible, but something.

Nena hesitated, then said lunch would be ready shortly. "We'll take you over to the guest cabins later."

"And a grand tour, how about that, my little darling?"

She paused at the door. "Marvelous, Markus. Why not? You can charm Mrs. Penbrunner, and I'll show James around. How about that?"

Bismaquer chuckled again. "I'll have to watch you, James, if I leave you alone with my wife." He gave his cherubic beam.

Nena, though, had disappeared. Get the knife in quickly, Bond thought, and before giving Bismaquer a chance to continue talking, he asked bluntly: "Markus, what about your invitation to Professor Penbrunner?"

The pink-and-white face turned toward him, a mixture of puzzlement and innocence. "What about it?"

"Penbrunner asked me to take it up with you. To be honest, he didn't want Cedar—Mrs. Penbrunner—to come at all. It was she who insisted."

"But why? I don't . . ."

"The story, as I have it from both the Penbrunners, is that your invitation was delivered by force."

"Force?"

"Threats. Guns."

Bismaquer shook his head, puzzled. "Threats? Guns? All I did was send the jet to New York. And I asked Walter to organize it with a firm we sometimes use—a private-investigation and bodyguard service. Just a plain, simple invitation; and a guard to see that the prints and the Penbrunners got safely to the plane."

"And the name of the firm?"

"The name? It's Mazzard Security. Mike Mazzard's—"

"A hood, Markus."

"A hood? I wouldn't say that. He's taken care of lots of little things for us."

"You've got your own security people, Markus. Why use a New York agency?"

"I don't think . . ." Bismaquer began. "But . . . God! Guns, threats? My own people? But they're local boys, I'd never use them except here. You mean, Mazzard's men actually *threatened* the Penbrunners?"

"According to Mrs. Penbrunner and the Professor, Mazzard did the talking himself and the three armed heavies backed him up."

"Oh, God!" His mouth dropped. "I'll have to talk to Walter. He arranged everything. Is that *really* why the Professor wouldn't come?"

"That *and* an attempt on his life. And Mrs. Penbrunner's."

"Attempt? Jesus Christ, James! You're damned right I'll find out what happened! Maybe Mazzard misunderstood? Maybe Walter said something. . . ? God, I'm sorry. I had no idea! If we have to, we'll get Mazzard down here. You bet your ass we'll have him here before the day's over!"

A gong sounded discreetly from somewhere in the house. "Lunch," Bismaquer announced, visibly shaken.

It was quite a performance; Bond gave him that. Friend Bismaquer was an actor of no mean talent. He could also afford to make little mistakes about invitations, afford to deny responsibility. Bond would have to brief Cedar to drop in the full facts concerning the attempt in the elevator.

Before they went into the cool, pleasant dining room, with its shaded windows, silently moving servants, and colonial American furnishings, Bond slipped out to the Saab, returning the prints to safety. The meal turned out to be animated, if wearing. Bismaquer, Bond discovered, liked holding center stage all the time, so that his *éminence grise*—Walter Luxor—and Nena Bismaquer became merely part of his court.

Their host was inordinately proud of the ranch, and they learned a great deal about the Rancho Bismaquer before actually viewing it. He had purchased the large tract of land soon after making his first big killing—the sale of the ice-cream business. "The first thing we did was build the airstrip," he told them. The airstrip had since been much enlarged. "Had to be. Most of the water, for domestic use anyway, is flown in every two days. We have one pipeline underground, right out of Amarillo, but there've been problems with that, and we use it mainly for irrigation."

Once work began, Bismaquer had had to put his priorities in the right order. A third of the land was for grazing purposes—"Landscaped and everything. We've got a fine herd out there. Unusual, but actually it pays for a lot of the fun." The fun, as he liked to call it, was contained in the remaining hundred square miles, which had also been irrigated and land-scaped, with massive loads of fertile soil and fully grown trees, either flown in or brought overland by tractor. "You said, James, that you'd heard I had only two passions—collecting prints and ice cream. Well, there's more to it than that. I guess I'm a collector of just about everything. We've got a fine stable of cars, from antiques to modern, and some good horses too. Yes, ice cream is something I still tinker with. . . ."

"There's a laboratory and small factory right here on the ranch." This was about the only time Luxor managed to get a word in.

"Oh, that. " Bismaquer smiled. "Well, I suppose we make a little money from that, too. I still act as consultant to several companies. I like creating new flavors, new tastes for the palate. I tinker. Make the odd bulk load, then ship it off. Sometimes the companies turn it down. Too good, I guess. Don't you find people's palates are getting blander?" He did not wait for an answer, but went on to tell them about the special quarters built for the staff—"We keep over two hundred men and women here"—and the luxury conference center, which took up a couple of square miles. It was sheltered from the main tracts by a thick swatch of well-tended plants and trees—"a jungle really, but a jungle kept in check."

The conference center was yet another source of revenue. Large companies used it, but only as often as Bismaquer let them, which was four or five times a year. "In fact, there's some conference due in a couple of days, I think. Right, Walter?"

Luxor nodded in agreement.

"And there's this, of course. Tara, my very proud possession. Quite something, eh, James?"

"Fascinating." Bond wondered what was really going on in Bismaquer's mind. How long would it take him to offer on the prints—if he really wanted them? After that, what plans had he for his guests? Though Bismaquer had acted in the most natural way possible, he must, by now, know who Bond was—the name itself would mean a great deal to Blofeld's successor. And what was this conference in a couple of days' time? A meeting of SPECTRE's leading lights? The Rancho Bismaquer was just right for the new leader of SPECTRE—a flamboyant world, in which fantasy could mingle neatly with the hard realities of extortion and ter-rorism.

When something particularly unpleasant happened, Bismaquer could, like all good paranoids, forget about it: tinkering with new ice-cream flavors, motoring around his private racetrack, or just basking in the true Hollywood fantasy of the great screen house, Tara. Gone with the wind.

"Well, you folks'll want to freshen up," Bismaquer said, abruptly ending the meal. "I have something to discuss with Walter—you know what I mean, James. I'll get a guide to take you over to the cabins, then we'll pick you up for the grand tour around four. Say four-thirty. Is that okay?"

Both Bond and Cedar said it would be fine, and Nena spoke for the first time: "Don't forget, Markus, I've got a prior claim on James."

The now-familiar guffaw. "Sure you do, darling! D'you think I'd miss the chance of spending some time alone with our delightful Cedar? It's the two cabins you've arranged, dear, isn't it?"

Nena Bismaquer told him yes, and as they left the dining room, she brushed against Bond. "I look forward to showing you around the place, James." A look which was more than a simple pleasantry. "And talking to you, too."

There was no mistake to it! Nena was giving him some kind of message.

Outside, a pickup truck waited in front of the Saab, a scarlet flag flying from a rear antenna. "The boys'll lead you to the cabins." Bismaquer beamed. "Meanwhile, don't you worry, James, I'm going to get to the bottom of what you told me. Oh, and tonight I want to talk business with you. Seriously. An offer for the prints. Don't think I didn't notice, by the way, how neatly you took them out of the house again."

"My job, Markus." Bond thanked them for the delicious meal, and as they set off in the Saab, Cedar started to giggle. "Wow, what a setup!" she exclaimed.

" 'Setup' is the word," Bond answered.

"You mean the invitation to stay for a couple of days?"

"That, among other things."

"Everything to make you feel at home and put you at ease."

"Just fine," said Bond. "Markus is quite the king. He was innocent as a newborn about the goons in New York."

"You tackled him about that?" Cedar frowned as Bond ran through his conversation with their host.

They had gone about a mile from the house now, trailing the pickup which moved steadily ahead of them.

"Whatever the quarters are like," Bond cautioned, "we have to presume they're wired. The telephones too. If we want to talk, we should do it in the open." When they were given the tour, Bond said, they should single out places to reconnoiter. "The conference center sounds like a natural. But there'll be others. Time could be shorter than we think, Cedar, and we'd better begin straightaway."

"Like tonight?"

"Just like tonight."

Cedar laughed again. "I think you may find yourself otherwise occupied."

"Meaning?"

"Meaning Nena Bismaquer. She's ready to drop her expensive shoes under your bed anytime you feel like it, James."

"Really?" Bond tried to sound innocent, but he vividly remembered Nena's look and the way she spoke to him. Being married to Markus Bismaquer would obviously have its compensations; but maybe there were things that the fantasy of the ranch and Tara could not supply. "If you're right," he mused aloud, "if there's any truth in that, Cedar, I'll see we're not disturbed tonight. Heaven can wait."

Ceder Leiter gave him a hard look. "Maybe," she said. "But can hell?"

The landscape had gone through a couple of changes already. "Think of everything that man had ferried into this place," said Cedar, shaking her head in amazement. They had covered about ten miles and now were climbing to a ridge crested by a thick copse of fir trees. The truck signaled a left, taking them along a path directly through a thicket of evergreens, then, with dramatic suddenness, into a broad clearing.

The two log cabins stood facing one another, about thirty feet apart, beautifully built, with small porches and neat white paintwork.

"They're making sure," Bond muttered aloud.

"Sure of what?"

"That we're neutralized here. Only one entrance through the trees. Surrounded and easy to watch. It's going to be difficult, Cedar: difficult to get out of. I'd put my last dollar on TV monitors and electronic alarms; plus a few live bodies in the trees. I'll take a look later. You armed, by the way?"

Cedar shook her head, dismally, knowing Bond was right: the pair of cabins were places where guests could be easily monitored.

"Okay, I've got a Smith and Wesson in the briefcase. I'll let you have it later."

The driver of the pickup was leaning out of his cab. "Take your pick, folks," he called. "Have a nice stay."

"It makes a change from the motels," Bond said happily, "but I'd feel safer at Tara."

Cedar grinned at him. "Frankly, dear James," she replied, "I don't give a damn."

Some twenty miles away, in a small study with lime-green walls and the bare necessities—a desk, filing cabinets, and chairs—Blofeld dialed a New York number.

"Mazzard Securities," the New York number answered.

"I want Mike. Tell him it's Leader."

A few seconds later, Mike Mazzard was on the line.

"You'd better get down here fast," Blofeld's voice commanded. "We have problems."

Mazzard chuckled. "I'm already on my way. But there's other things to deal with, for the conference. I'll be there in a couple of days. Sooner if I get through."

"As quickly as possible." There was no doubt about the anger in Blofeld's voice. "You've bungled enough already; and we've got Bond here like a sitting duck."

"As soon as I can. You want everything right, don't you?"

"Just remember, Mazzard, the house on the bayou has very hungry guardians."

Blofeld cradled the telephone and sat back, thinking about the next move in SPECTRE's game. So much time and planning, and then that cretin Mazzard had almost wrecked it. No orders had been given for Bond to die, and Mazzard was always far too trigger-happy. Eventually, Blofeld thought, something would have to be done about Mr. Mike Mazzard.

HOUND. Blofeld smiled at the word. High above the earth, at this very moment, the Americans had their hounds out in force, with more in reserve. They claimed none of these weapons was in space, but this was merely a subterfuge. Within days now, SPECTRE would lay it hands on every piece of data concerning these Hounds of Heaven—the Space Wolves—and what a plan, what ingenuity, what profits! The Soviets alone would pay a fortune for the information.

From the conception of HOUND there had been the need for one major scapegoat, and in the back of Blofeld's mind, Bond had always fitted the part. Now James Bond was in Texas—trapped, lured, snared. Ripe for the allotted role and the disgraceful death Blofeld had planned for him.

The business in Washington—though unscheduled and contrary to instructions—must have shaken the Britisher; but Blofeld had other items in mind, other activites to keep Bond off balance. Only in the end would death come to Mr. James Bond.

Blofeld began to laugh, alone.

_12_

GUIDED TOUR

THE CABINS WERE identical except for their names—Sand Creek and Fetterman. If Bond remembered correctly, these were the names of two bloody massacres during the Indian wars of the 1860's. Sand Creek, he seemed to recall, was an act of revolting treachery, leading to the butchery of old men, women, and children. Pleasantly chosen names for guest cabins.

True Blofeld fashion, as was the whole ranch. Nor was Bond surprised to find the interiors of the cabins as spacious and well-appointed as everything else. Each had a large sitting room with TV, stereo, and VTR; bedrooms which would put even the most grandiose hotels to shame; and large bathrooms, each furnished with shower and sunken Jacuzzi. The only difference lay in the paintings. Sand Creek sported a large reproduction of Robert Lindneux's canvas depicting the massacre, while the other cabin contained a blowup reproduction of the *Harper's Weekly* engraving of the Fetterman battle.

There were telephones which, they soon discovered, connected with the main house and nowhere else. It would be impossible to call each other, and Bond was also disturbed to find out that neither of the cabins was provided with locks or keys. No privacy for these guests.

They tossed a coin for cabins, Bond getting Fetterman and helping Cedar move her luggage into Sand Creek.

"They're not picking us up until four-thirty," he told Cedar, "so I'll give you ten minutes, then we can do a short reconnaissance." It was essential, Bond thought while unpacking, to discover the secrets of

Rancho Bismaquer as soon as possible. At least there was the Saab. Their equipment could stay in the locked car and remain safe. A normal Saab was difficult enough for any would-be thief. Bond's personalized model—with its heavy bullet-proofing and other extras—was fitted with sensors which activated alarms, should anyone even attempt to tamper. For the time being, though, he was more concerned for their personal safety, having no illusions about the manner in which they had been isolated on this high, wooded knoll.

Cedar, taking her cue from Bond, was ready—in fresh jeans, shirt, and a fringed western jacket—within the allotted time. Bond had also changed, emerging in a lightweight cream suit bought in Springfield. He was, like Cedar, wearing leather boots, and he had also altered the holster position for the VP70—attaching it to his belt, slewing it around to the rear of his right hip.

Alone in his cabin, he had unlocked the briefcase. Now he gave the small revolver, with ammunition, to Cedar.

"Ready for anything," Cedar said, batting her eyelids at him.

"Let's play at being emotionally entangled," Bond said in a low voice, taking her hand as they walked toward the dirt track between the trees.

"I don't have to play, James." She glanced at him, gripping his hand tightly and moving closer.

Bond once more sensed the unthinkable temptation. Cedar, with those great saucer brown eyes, could have seduced a saint. "Don't, sweetheart," he murmured. "It's hard enough already. Your father's my oldest American friend, and you are the apple of his eye, I've no doubt. Please don't make it more of a problem."

She sighed. "Oh, James, you can be a fussy devil. Nobody thinks twice about things like that anymore." She stayed silent until they were well into the trees, then added through gritted teeth, "And you watch it with the Bismaquer woman. She'd eat you alive, make no mistake."

For the sake of any real, or electronic, watchers, they made it seem like a casual stroll, but both of them stayed alert, their eyes searching everywhere. Still, they spotted no surveillance gear.

"Perhaps they keep a watch with radar or some other system—straight from Tara," Bond said thinking aloud as they broke cover from the trees. The knoll gave them a superb view across the ranch. About eight miles below and ahead stood a veritable small town with brick and adobe buildings—the living quarters, Bond supposed, for Bismaquer's retainers, while off to the right, the stark blazing white of a T-shaped building glared in the sun. They could see that this large structure lay close to the protecting boundary wall and that it was circled by a thick layer of greenery. "The controlled jungle," Bond said, nodding toward the complex. "That's got to be the conference center. We have to get a look at that."

"Through the jungle?" Cedar raised her eyebrows. "I wonder what they've got hidden in all that stuff. See? There's some kind of pit on the outer edge, and fencing near the buildings."

Bond thought of the possibilities of wild animals, reptiles, even poisonous flowers. The previous head of SPECTRE had known all about poison gardens—there had been one at the Castle of Death in Japan. People could be kept out of, or imprisoned within, the conference center's compounds in hundreds of different ways, not to mention the more mundane devices such as high-voltage fences similar to those used to protect the monorail.

The view itself was certainly breathtaking, but Bond willed himself to keep things in perspective and his mind in high gear. Getting into the conference center remained a most necessary objective.

There was also Bismaquer's laboratory, which, they suspected, was the long building set near the ranch's main highway running below them. The laboratory looked like an easy target, though Cedar pointed out that there was a second building, like a warehouse, built to the back of the laboratory and partially camouflaged by trees. A wide exit road led from its rear, twisting and finally curving back to meet the main highway.

In the very far distance, covered by a bluish haze, lay grazing land; and even from their vantage point they could make out the tiny dots of cattle. It was also apparent that the knoll was not the highest ground. To the left of the conference center, Bismaquer's land sloped gently upward to a broad plateau upon which the airstrip had been built, a plateau long enough, they both judged, to accommodate very large aircraft.

Almost as though for their benefit, there was a sudden blast of engine noise, drifting across the thirty or forty miles, and, as they watched, a Boeing 747 hurtled into the air.

"If they can take jumbos, they'll be able to fly almost anything in and out." Bond's eyes narrowed against the harsh, hot light. "There's another target. Let's tick them off, Cedar: we need a good look at the conference building; Bismaquer's laboratory; the airfield . . ."

"And the monorail station at this end." Cedar's grasp tightened on his hand. "Just in case we have to get out that way. At least we know what we'd be up against at the other end."

"The Dracula brothers, and a quick burn-up on the fence." Bond's mouth tightened into a cruel smile. "All full of joy and money, Bismaquer may well be; but the whole place stinks like a dung hill. He's got a small army on the spot, and a nice fun palace, plus the racetrack, wherever that may be, plus the cattle. Bismaquerland, Texas' answer to Disneyland. But do you know, Cedar? Behind all the fun and frolics I can almost smell SPECTRE. It has all the outrageous splendors that would have appealed to its late and unlamented founder, Ernst Stavro Blofeld."

Bond, like a general planning the tactics of battle, wished he had some field glasses with him, or materials with which to make a map. After a while, Cedar asked if he thought they could get out.

"We only try that after we've made certain of two things, and you know it."

She nodded, her face set hard. "What SPECTRE's up to, if this is their base . . ."

"It's their base, all right."

". . . and who the real culprit is."

"Right." Bond's face remained impassive. "Who do you reckon? Bismaquer or Walter Luxor?"

"Or Lady Bismaquer, James."

"Okay, or Nena Bismaquer, why not? But my money's on Markus himself. He has all the paranoid symptoms: a Kris Kringle cover, an obsession with wealth and possessions, always wanting more. I vote for him, with Walter Luxor as his chief eunuch."

"Don't be so sure about the eunuch bit." Cedar swallowed. "I sat next to him at lunch. Those hands tend to wander." She shivered at the thought. "And I can't lock my door."

Bond moved her away from the edge of the knoll to inspect the woods once more. "They must have *some* kind of monitoring system," he said after half an hour's further search had produced no clues. "I think we try and shake any watchdogs they give us tonight, then go on a little tour of our own. Hallo . . ." He stopped still as the sound of a motor engine drifted up from the road below the knoll, and took Cedar's arm. "That'll be the grand-tour party. Don't forget, they'll split us up now, but after dinner at Tara we stick together. Right?"

"You're on, Mr. Bond." Cedar raised herself up to give him a quick peck on the cheek. "And don't forget what I said about the Dragon Lady."

"No promises." Bond's serious mask broke for a moment. "My old nanny used to say that promises are like piecrust — made to be broken."

"Oh, James . . ."

They broke cover, walking into the clearing just as Bismaquer, huge behind the wheel of an open racy-looking red Mustang GT, drove in with a flourish of dust. The Mustang screeched to a halt behind the Saab. Circa 1966, Bond thought, recognizing the car. Probably with a 289 V-8 engine.

Nena sat next to her husband, hair windblown and face radiant, flushed by what had probably been a fast drive. She vaulted out of the Mustang in a single graceful movement, her long legs clearing the door with agile ease.

"Nice little motor." Bond grinned. "I wouldn't mind taking it on, if you've still got the Grand Prix in mind."

"I can offer you competition livelier than this, James," Bismaquer answered. "But, it's on, okay. Everything's fixed. I'll fill you in on all the details later. Are you folks all organized? Who's in which cabin? Or are you sharing?" He chuckled wickedly but without the trace of a leer.

"Cedar's in Fetterman, and I've got Sand Creek," Bond said quickly, reversing the cabins before Cedar could blurt out the truth. If Luxor was a lecher, it might be better for him to come groping after Bond in the night.

"You all set, James?" Nena Bismaquer's eyes, dancing a moment ago, suddenly turned serious as she looked into Bond's eyes.

"You want to risk the Saab?" he replied.

"She'll risk anything." Bismaquer bubbled with laughter. "Come on, Cedar. I'll show you some real driving — and quite a bit of prime Bismaquer land."

Bond unlocked the Saab, handing Nena into the passenger seat. According to Bismaquer, the whole "grand tour" took around three hours, but they would cut it short this time. Dinner was at seven-thirty. "I want a half an hour with you and those prints, James. Let's rendezvous at the track about quarter of seven. Nena will show you. Be good, and if you can't be good . . ."

Bond lost Bismaquer's last words in the deep roar of the Saab's ignition. Then, with a wave he shut the door, and the noise went down to a soft rumble.

Nena Bismaquer turned toward him in her seat. "Okay, James, I'll show you the best of Markus' pride and joy."

"I can see it from here." Bond smiled. Certainly she looked fantastic, the healthy, sun-browned complexion vying with her incredible black eyes.

She laughed, the same musical sound sliding down the scale. "Don't you believe it. The Rancho Bismaquer's his one—and only—pride and joy. Come on, let me give you the tour, via the scenic route."

They drove out, taking the road toward the small town which housed the ranch staff. There were neat lawns, a small park where children played, and Bond could see men and women going about the usual chores of any town—shopping at the large store, working in their yards, hanging out washing. The air of normality was almost sinister. There was even a small church with a wooden bell tower. Like everything else around the ranch, the town looked like a movie set.

Nena waved to people as they drove through, and Bond noticed a patrol car with the "Bismaquer Security" flashes on the side.

"Highway Police?" he asked.

"Certainly. Markus believes in law and order. He thinks it makes people forget they're living in an enclosed area. These people very rarely leave here, you know, James."

Bond made no comment but just drove on, following her directions. They went out to the edge of the grazing land, then turned back, taking the airport road. It was clear Cedar and he had been right: this was no simple landing strip in the converted desert, but a full-scale operational airport.

"It's called Bismaquer International, would you believe that?" Nena's tone sounded like blatant mockery.

"I'd believe it. Where next?"

She gave instructions, and soon they were coasting close to the junglelike thicket surrounding the conference center. Bond asked if this was intended to keep people out, knowing very well, from the observations made on the knoll, that it was just that.

"Oh, keep-out; or keep-in. Keep-in, really. We get the strangest people here for conferences, and they tend to get nosy. Markus enjoys his privacy. You'll see. Once he's done a deal with you, and shown off all his toys, he'll have you out and away before you know it."

Bond slowed the car, glancing constantly at the high, impenetrable greenery. "Looks nasty. You've got a pit around it as well. Are there dragons in there to discourage the inmates?"

"Nothing as bad as that; but you can't get through without a machete and some skill. There's half a mile of thicket—some of it quite dangerous. And a high fence. *We* can get in, though."

"Well, somebody has to. Presumably you provide the staff. Unless you lift them in and out by chopper?"

"Conference delegates are in fact taken in by helicopter, but here, I'll show you. You follow the green belt for about two miles more."

". . . a lovely French girl doing in a dream world like this," Bond said, as though to himself.

There was a moment's pause, during which 007 cursed himself, thinking he had moved too soon.

Then: "I wonder about that myself." Nena's voice dropped, the sparkle gone. "All the time." Another silence before she said, "Oh, it's a long, involved, and not very edifying story, James. I come out of it something of a gold digger. Did you know that gold diggers always get their just desserts?"

"I thought they got diamonds, mink coats, smart cars, luxury flats, and—most evenings—zabaglione, crepes suzettes, or profiteroles for their just desserts."

"Oh, they get that too. But they pay a price. Here, straight ahead. Start slowing down." The road had circled almost to the high fencing and walls, on the other side of which, Bond knew, there was nothing but arid land, dry grass and rock, stretching almost as far as Amarillo.

"Pull up here," Nena ordered.

Bond brought the Saab to a halt, then, following Nena's lead, got out of the car.

She crossed to the side of the road and knelt down, as though afraid of being seen. "I shouldn't really be giving away the family secrets." Her smile, as she lifted her head, seemed to go like a lance to Bond's heart. This was madness, he told himself, sheer and utter. Nena Bismaquer had been unknown to him until, literally, a few hours ago; yet already he felt envy for the bearlike Markus Bismaquer. He had a surge of desire to know everything about her: her past, childhood, parents, friends, likes and dislikes, thoughts and ideas.

Warning signals rang in his head, pulling his mind back stubbornly to the reality of the moment.

Nena Bismaquer knelt beside what appeared to be a small, circular metal cover—about a foot in diameter—that looked as though it had something to do with drainage. A metal ring was recessed flush with the center of the cover, and Nena pried it open with ease, lifting out the thick round plate as though it were light as plastic.

"See?" She showed him a U-shaped handle, lying in the revealed recess. "Now, watch." As she pulled at the handle, a block of stone at the edge of the roadway slowly descended, as though on a hydraulic lift. The block was about five feet square. When it lowered to around a foot below the surface, there came the distant hiss of the suspected hydraulics. The slab slid to one side, revealing a wide, tiled chamber beneath. Metal hand- and footholds ran down the wall nearest the road.

"I don't think we should go down." A hint of nervousness came into her usually calm voice. "But the chamber leads to steps and a tunnel which comes out in a janitor's closet over in the main building. There's an opening and closing device down there, and another one when you get to the far end. Just one of Markus' little devices. Few people know about it. The staff we use in the conference center, of course, always go in this way, about a day before a delegation arrives. Food's ferried in by helicopter, and this is always here as an emergency escape route in case of trouble."

Her choice of words seemed odd to Bond. "What kind of trouble?" he asked.

"I told you: we get some very strange characters among conference delegates. Markus has this thing about security. He's quite right, of course. Oh, maybe I shouldn't have shown it to you. Come on, let's get out of here." She reached down and pulled the lever back. The slab of stone, on its hydraulic jacks, went through the reverse procedure. When it was settled in place, Nena returned the small circular cover to its place, brushing dust over it with her foot.

Back in the car, she seemed edgy.

"Where now?" Bond asked, giving the impression that the show with the hidden entrance was an interesting but unimportant event.

She looked at her watch. They had a good three-quarters of an hour before meeting Bismaquer. "Take the road toward the cabins." She spoke impulsively. "I'll show you where to turn off."

Bond pointed the Saab in the direction of the wooded knoll. Instead of taking the track up through the trees, though, she told him to skirt the knoll to the left. Ahead, Bond saw there was another track leading up the other side of the rising ground, wide enough for cars and trucks.

Halfway up the far side, Nena pointed to an exit among the trees, on the right, and in a few moments they were in a small clearing: dark and surrounded by trees, with just enough room to turn the car around.

"Have you got a cigarette?" she asked after he switched off the ignition.

Bond produced his gunmetal case, lighting cigarettes for both of them. He noticed that her fingers were trembling. Nena drew hard on the cigarette, exhaling the smoke in a long stream. "Look, James. I've been foolish. I'm sorry; I don't know why I did it, but please don't tell Markus I showed you that entrance to the center." She shook her head, repeating, "I don't know why I did it. You see, he's . . . well, he gets into a state about these things. I was carried away—a new face, someone nice, you know what I mean?" Her hands seemed to drift toward his, fingers interlocking his fingers.

"Yes, I think I know." The touch of her hand was like a tiny electric shock.

Quite suddenly she laughed. "Oh, dear. I'm not really very bright, am I? I could always have blackmailed you, Mr. James Bond."

"Blackmailed?" Concern, razor-sharp, sliced through Bond's nerves.

She raised her hand, lifting Bond's arm with hers, fingers tightening. "Don't worry. Please. You don't tell Markus I gave away a state secret, and I won't mention the fact that you're a . . . oh, what do they call it? A con merchant? A confidence artist? There's another slang name over here . . ."

"A flimflam man?" Bond offered.

"That's good." Again the glissando laugh. "A good description— flimflam." She pronounced it deliciously as "fleemflem."

"Nena, I don't know—"

"James." She shook a finger at him with her free hand. "You're in my power, my dear, and heaven knows, I need a good man in my power."

"I still don't know what you're—"

She shushed him. "Look, Markus is always the big expert. He knows about cars and horses, he certainly knows about ice cream. In fact, ice cream is really the one thing he does know about. But prints? He has books, he knows what he likes, but he's no expert. On the other hand, I am an expert. Until a few years ago when I became Mrs. Bismaquer, I studied art. In Paris, I studied from the time I was twelve, and my specialty was prints. You have a set of unknown Hogarths. Unique,

Markus keeps telling me. Worth a fortune."

"Yes. And authenticated. And I haven't said they're for sale yet, Nena."

She gave her brilliant smile. "No, and don't think I'm unaware of that being one of the oldest tricks in the book, James. Dangle them, yes? Be uncertain about a sale? Look." Still talking, she took his hand, locked with her own, and thrust it between her thighs. The gesture was so natural, as if she scarcely realized what she had done, but Bond felt a sudden difficulty in breathing naturally. "Look, James. *You* know there are no new, undiscovered sets of Hogarth prints. *You* know it. *I* know it. Just as I know the ones you have are a set of very, very good fakes. They are so good that I've no doubt future generations will believe they're Hogarth originals. They'll become real Hogarths. I know how the market works. A fake work of art, if handled properly, actually becomes the real thing. Somehow you've managed to convince some people that they're real; you have authentication, provided that's not forged."

"It's not." Bond knew he should admit to nothing illegal. "But what makes you so certain those are forgeries? You had only a quick look at them."

She moved closer so that their shoulders touched, her head leaning so near that he could smell her hair—not a distilled scent, made in some expensive factory, but the real thing, human hair, cared for, and containing its own elusive fragrance. "I know they're forgeries, because I know the man who did them. In fact I've seen them before. He's an Englishman called—variously—Miller, or Millhouse, or maybe it's Malting?" Nena then proceeded to give Bond an accurate and detailed description of the little expert who had so diligently put Cedar and himself through their paces at the Kensington safe house.

Blast, Bond thought to himself. M had been uncharacteristically careless. On the other hand, his chief was a sly old fox, quite capable of preparing a trail for SPECTRE to follow, regardless of the danger to Bond.

"Well, Nena, it's all news to me," he bluffed, hoping that no sign of shock showed in his face or eyes.

When she spoke next, Nena's voice gave the impression that she too was short of breath. "James. I'm not going to say anything. Just, please, don't tell him about the tunnel. I really should not have shown that to you, and . . . oh, James, sometimes he terrifies me . . ."

Her hand untwined from his, her arms reaching up as she pulled his lips down onto her own.

There was a moment, just after their lips touched, that Bond thought he heard the distant voice of Cedar telling him: "She'd eat you alive, make no mistake."

James Bond, however, had reached the stage when he would gladly have been eaten alive by the amazing Nena Bismaquer. In all his not inconsiderable experience, he could not remember ever having been kissed like this. It began as a caressing touch, as their lips met, then a tingling sensation as they both opened as one, the tips of their tongues touching, then retreating, then touching again. At last, both mouths capitulated willingly, and the kiss became almost a microcosm of the whole sexual act. Their lips, mouths, and tongues ceased to have separate identities but became one, reaching out, exploring, extending into passion.

Bond unconsciously reached for her body, but Nena's hand caught his wrist, holding him away until, breathless, they slowly gave each other up.

"James . . ." She spoke almost in a whisper. "I thought the art of kissing was dead."

"Well, it seems to be alive, well, and living in a Saab motorcar in the middle of Texas." He didn't mean it to be flippant, and the way he spoke, it did not come out that way.

She glanced at her watch. "We'll have to go soon." Her eyes shifted from him briefly. "I have to ask one thing." She looked away from him, staring out through the windshield. "You and Mrs. Penbrunner— Cedar . . . ?"

"Yes?"

"Are you . . . ? Well, is there . . . ?"

"Are we lovers?"

"Yes."

"No. Very definitely no. Cedar's husband happens to be one of my best and closest friends. But, Nena, this is crazy. Markus—"

"Would kill you." She sounded very calm about it. "Or have you killed. Maybe he'll kill you anyway, James. I was going to warn you, whatever. Now I'm doing it against my will, because I'd like nothing better than for you to stay here forever. But I'd rather have you here alive. Darling James. Let me give you advice: go. Go as soon as you can. Take Markus for what you can get, but do it tonight, and then leave as quickly as possible. There's evil here. More evil than you could dream of."

"Evil?"

"I can't tell you about it. To be honest, I don't know that much myself, but what I do know terrifies me. Markus may seem a nice buffoon—a rich, boisterous, amusing, and generous teddy bear. But the bear has claws, James, terrible claws, and powers that reach out far beyond this ranch. Far beyond America, in fact."

"You mean he's some kind of criminal—"

"It's not that simple." She shook her head. "I can't explain. Can I, perhaps, come to you—tonight? No, I can't tonight. There's no way. If you're still here tomorrow—and if you take my advice, you'll be gone—but if you're here, can I come to you?"

"Please." Bond could find no eloquent words. Nena seemed at the edge of some precipice lying hidden within her.

"We must go. He'll be all smiles even if we're late, but I'll go through hell later."

Silently Bond wiped his mouth, while Nena made use of the vanity mirror to brush off her lips and run a comb through her hair. As they drove off, Bond asked if she could explain her part in things. "Just the bare facts."

She spoke quickly, between giving him directions. Nena Clavert, as she had been, was an orphan living in Paris, with a passion for art. An uncle had helped with her education, but by the time she reached the age of twenty, he was a sick man. She worked as a part-time waitress and continued her studies, living off a pittance. In the end, she began to think there was only one way. "I seriously considered becoming a whore. It's melodramatic and laughable now. Yet then it seemed to be the only reasonable answer. Jobs were scarce, and I needed money: enough to be comfortable, to learn, and to paint."

Then the rich American, Bismaquer, had turned up. "He courted me like you read about in books—generous presents, clothes, the best places to eat. And he didn't touch me, didn't lay a finger on me: the perfect gentleman."

Finally Bismaquer had asked her to be his wife. She was worried because of the great difference in their ages; but he'd said it mattered not at all to him. If he got too old and useless, she could lead her own life.

"It wasn't until he brought me here that I found the real man behind that generous nature. Yes, there's a criminal—a terrible . . . connection. But there are other things too: his violent temper, which only those close to him see. And his predilections, of course . . ."

"Sexual?"

"He's amazing for a man of his age. I have to admit it. But he's sexually . . . what do you say, James? . . . ambivalent. Why do you think he has that terrible death's head, Walter Luxor, here all the time? It's not just the cleverness with money. He's . . . well . . . he and Luxor . . ."

Her voice trailed off, then regained its habitual calm.

"Sometimes he doesn't come near me for months. Then it all changes. Oh, he can plow a long furrow when he wishes. . . . You turn right here," she ordered. "I must stop talking, or he'll see I'm in a state. Don't give him a hint, James. Not a hint."

They followed a minor road, taking them around the back of the smooth lawns surrounding Tara, then through a belt of trees, high and thick, which explained why Cedar and Bond could not see the racing circuit from their vantage point on the knoll.

The trees screened everything—a device Bismaquer had been fond of using throughout the ranch's entire layout. This time they hid a huge oval circuit, wide enough to take three or four cars. The bends at the end nearest the house were gentle curves, but halfway down the far side there was a nasty chicane, followed by a crucifying right-angle turn, while the next bend—at the distant end of the rough oval—was almost a Z in shape.

The track must have been all of eight miles in full circuit, and Bond picked out its hazards, the very real danger points, with a practiced eye.

On the far side stood a banked wooden grandstand; below, there were pits and garages. The reed Mustang was just arriving under the grandstand, the skeleton figure of Luxor standing ready to greet Bismaquer and Cedar.

Bond took the Saab right around the access road which ran parallel to the circuit. As they approached, Bismaquer and Cedar became plainly visible, standing next to a car that was silver in color, like Bond's Saab, with Walter Luxor at the wheel.

"Be terribly careful, James." Nena seemed to have regained her self-control. "Once behind the wheel, Walter's a dangerous man to play around with. He's an expert, he knows this track like his own hand, and he can clock up incredible speeds. What's worse, since his own accident he's felt no fear—neither for himself nor for any opponent."

"I'm not bad myself," Bond said, hearing the anger he felt toward Bismaquer and Luxor etched deeply into his voice. "If they're set on this race, I think I can teach Walter Luxor a thing or two, especially if they match me properly. I'll only drive against my own class"—he stopped as they came up to the group and identified the other silver car—"and it looks as though they're giving me a reasonable chance, with room to spare." He braked the Saab to a halt, opened the door, and went around to help Nena Bismaquer from her seat as Markus came over, slapping him on the back, emitting another of the now-infuriating guffaws.

"Did you enjoy it? Isn't it great? You see why I'm so proud of Rancho Bismaquer?"

"It's quite a place. Makes any one of England's home counties seem like a small farm." Bond smiled, looking across to Cedar. "Eh, Cedar? Isn't it tremendous?"

"Something else," she answered. Nobody but Bond could have understood the tinge of irony, and only Bond noticed the dagger looks aimed directly at Nena Bismaquer.

"Tomorrow," Bismaquer said loudly, with a flourish toward the parked silver car. "Do you think you're well-matched, James? Walter'll drive against you. Tomorrow morning, I think. How about it?"

Bond looked toward Luxor, who sat at the wheel of the Mustang variant—the Shelby American GT 350. This had been a most popular high-performance competition car in the late 1960's: with a lightened body, free-flow exhaust, and the 289 V-8 engine.

"It's souped-up a little, of course." Bismaquer chuckled. "And it's all of thirteen years old. But I guess it'll give you a run on the track, even with that turbo of yours. You on, James?"

Bond reached out a hand. "Of course I'm on. Should be fun."

Bismaquer turned his head, calling back to Luxor, "Tomorrow, Walter. About ten in the morning, before it gets too hot. Eight laps. Okay, James?"

"Ten, if you like." If it was bravado they wanted, then he was game.

"Good. We'll invite some of the boys. Nothing they like better'n a good road race." Then, with a quick change, Bismaquer turned to Nena. "Let's get back, then. I have one or two things to do tonight, and I've got to talk with young James, here, before dinner. I expect the ladies'll want to freshen up a little as well."

Nena gave Bond an unperturbed smile. "Thank you for putting up with my lecture on the wonders of Rancho Bismaquer, James. I enjoyed showing you around."

"My pleasure." Bond opened the door for Cedar, who called her thanks in turn to Bismaquer. Engines fired, and Bismaquer led the way back to Tara, his wife at his side.

"Thank you very much for putting up with my lecture, James," Cedar mimicked. "Oh, my pleasure, Nena; my pleasure. You're a creep, James Bond."

"Possibly." Bond spoke sharply. "But I've learned a great deal. For instance, Nena Bismaquer may be the only friend we have here. Also, we can take our time over the conference center. There's a way in, directly off the road. No problem. I think tonight's activities have to be confined to that laboratory and the building behind it. Did you enjoy Bismaquer's company?"

Cedar, momentarily silenced by Bond's news, appeared to be counting to herself. "One hundred . . ." she finished. "To be honest with you, Bond, I wouldn't trust any of them; and if it wasn't for that predatory Nena woman, I'd put Bismaquer down as a faggot."

"Right the first time," Bond said.

"Lawks-a-mercy." Cedar gave a satisfied smirk as they turned into Tara's main drive. "I'ze sick, Mizz Scarlett, I'ze sick."

James Bond sat, a large vodka martini in his hand, facing Markus Bismaquer on the veranda. Walter Luxor hovered in the background.

"Now, come on, James." Bismaquer had—for the moment—put his hearty personality aside. "The prints are either for sale or they're not. I want a straight yes or no. We've fenced around, and now I'm ready to make you a proposition."

Bond took a sip of his drink, placed the glass on a side table, and lit another cigarette. "All right, Markus. As you say, the fencing's over. I have very precise instructions. The prints *are* for sale. . ."

Bismaquer let out a sigh of relief.

"They're for sale by auction, in New York, in one week's time."

"I'm not going in for any auction—" Bismaquer began, stopping as Bond held up a hand.

"They're for sale at public auction in New York, in one week's time, unless I'm offered a certain price before that. Further, my intructions are that there is a very firm reserve on the whole set; and I am not to disclose that reserve to any prospective buyer."

"Well . . ." Bismaquer began again. "I'll offer you—"

"Wait," Bond cut in. "I have to warn you further that the first bid for the prints, outside the auction, will be the only one taken. Which means, Markus, that if you come in below the secret reserve, you lose for all time. My principal will instruct the auctioneer to accept no bids from a person or persons connected with anyone who has already made a private bid. In other words, you have to be very careful."

For the first time that day, Bond thought he could detect a trace of malevolence in Bismaquer's face. "James," he began finally, "can I ask you two questions?"

"You can ask. I shall answer at my discretion."

"Okay. Okay." Bismaquer appeared to be rattled. "The first one's easy. Every man, in my experience, has a price. I presume you're corruptible?"

Bond shook his head. "No, in this matter, nobody can bribe me. Mrs. Penbrunner's on the premises. In any case, I'm under legal obligation. What's the second question?"

"Is the reserve based on a true value?"

"There is no true value. The prints are unique. But, to give you hope, the reserve is based on a price calculated to be the mean between a minimum and a maximum that would be achieved at an open auction. I don't understand computers myself, but that's how they arrived at the figure."

The cicadas had opened up their chirping music all around. Dusk was starting to close in, and far away, the moon began to show, big and yellow, against a clear darkening sky. In the silence, Bond heard Bismaquer cough.

Then: "Okay, James, I'll take a shot at it. One million dollars."

Bond had in fact been playing it by ear, with no figure in mind. Now he smiled inwardly as he spoke: "Right on target, Markus. They're yours. What do you propose? Do I call the professor? Do we shake on it, or what?"

"Oh, you've sure given me a hard time, James my friend. I think we have to take it a step further. Tell me, could you scrape together a milion bucks? I mean now, this minute?"

"Who, me personally?"

"It's you I'm asking."

"Not now, this minute. But in a day or so, yes. Yes, I could."

"Are you a gambling man?"

"It has been known to happen." Bond thought of the many chemmy tables, poker games, casinos, and private clubs in which he had played.

"Okay. I'm going to give you the biggest chance you've ever had. Tomorrow you're going out there to race against Walter. A late-1960's car against your fast turbo. I've offered one million dollars for those prints. If you beat Walter on the track, I'll gladly pay the million and add another million for your pains."

"That's very generous—"

But Bond stopped as Bismaquer held up his hand.

"Whoa, there, boy. I haven't finished. I've offered a million. If Walter beats you out there, you get nothing for your pains; I get the prints, and you do my paying for me."

It was a subtle scene—a gamble based on the knowledge Markus Bismaquer had of Luxor, the Shelby American GT, and the track, but a gamble nonetheless. Except, Bond knew, if Bismaquer was the new Blofeld—or even if it was Luxor—nobody was going to get anything for the prints. Bismaquer was playing with him, counting on Bond going for the bait and, in all probability, killing himself out on the hot circuit with its dangerous bends.

Whereas if he refused . . . ?

Giving Bismaquer his most charming smile, Bond nodded. He reached out in the gathering darkness to grasp the big man's hand.

"Done," said James Bond, knowing the word might well be his own death warrant.

13

TOUR DE FORCE

"WHAT THE HELL can we do now?" Cedar said, cheerfully waving farewell to the Bismaquers and Walter Luxor from the Saab.

"Sit still, fasten your seat belt, and prepare for some turbulence." Bond hardly moved his lips. Loudly he shouted to Bismaquer, who stood on the portico, "See you in the morning. At the circuit. Ten o'clock, sharp."

Bismaquer nodded and waved them on. The pickup, in front, slowly started to guide them down the drive.

After coffee and brandy, Bismaquer and Luxor had made their apologies. "When you own a spread like this," Markus Bismaquer had said, "there is paperwork which just has to get done, and tonight's the night. Anyhow, you two must be ready for bed. Get a good night's sleep, James. You've got the race tomorrow."

Bond had agreed, saying they could easily get back to the cabins without a guide. But the pickup was there, ready and waiting, and nothing by way of persuasion would change Bismaquer's mind.

So a guide they had, a fact which greatly reduced their chances of playing at being lost and carrying out a full-scale reconnaissance of the ranch.

Bond brought the Saab close to the tail of the pickup, crowding the driver as they turned onto the main arterial highway which crossed the ranch. They could, of course, follow him, go back to the cabins, and then take their chances on the open roads in the Saab. But there was little doubt in Bond's mind that the guide with the pickup would stay for stakeout duty.

"He'll probably drop us off and then get lost somewhere in the trees, where he can keep an eye on us. After what we saw, or didn't see, this afternoon, my impression is that Bismaquer prefers human surveillance to electronics. He's got a lot of people working for him, even his own highway patrol."

Cedar made a movement in the darkness. "So we're boxed in?"

"Up to a point. Time's short, though. We need a look at that laboratory, and I wouldn't mind showing you exactly how to get into the conference center. Correction—how *I* get into the center. Is your seat belt fastened tightly?"

She grunted a "Yes."

"Okay. What I've heard today clears my conscience." Bond smiled to himself. "I don't mind hurting a few people."

They turned off the highway, heading toward the knoll—about four miles to go. Get him in the trees, thought Bond, reaching down to press another of the buttons on the dash, which released the Nitefinder glasses he always carried.

The glasses consisted of an oblong control box, one end padded and shaped to the head. The brightness and focus controls were on the right side, while from the front there protruded two lenses, like a pair of small binoculars.

Using one hand, he strapped the system to his head, switching on as he did so.

Bond had done many hours' training, driving in pitch darkness, using only the Nitefinders, which he had also worn once operationally. They gave an almost clear picture in darkness, enough to let the viewer see clearly up to a hundred yards.

The adjustments made, Bond brought the Saab very close to the pickup's tail. They were now about a mile from the knoll.

Flatly he told Cedar what he was going to do. "It's going to get very dark in a minute. Then some action; then a lot of light. With luck, he'll go off the road without doing too much damage to the truck. We need that for ourselves."

They had almost reached the trees now. "Okay. Hold on." Bond flicked the Saab's lights off and saw, through the Nitefinders, the pickup wobble slightly on the road. For a second, the driver might well see the Saab's shape, but he would be puzzled, and the darkness behind him would have thrown him off balance.

Bond did not stay behind for long. Pulling out, he smoothly depressed the accelerator. The rev-counter needle rose fast, crossing the 3,000 limit, bringing the turbo charger into play.

The Saab shot forward, turbo building into the satisfying whine as they overtook the pickup. Bond crowded the driver so that, in the darkness, he was forced to pull over. He must have seen the shape pass him, then caught the Saab full in his headlights before it disappeared into the black zone, leaving no taillights in its wake.

"He'll be putting on speed now, trying to catch us," Bond said. "Hold tight." Without slowing noticeably, he stood on the brakes, changing down and wrenching at the wheel. The Saab went into a neatly controlled skid, and Bond, changing down for a second time, turned the car right around so that it now faced back along the road.

"Should be on us any minute." He sounded cool, like an experienced fighter pilot leading a section into attack. One hand dropped to the small button, set just behind the gearshift. The pickup's lights were coming now, closing fast. In a second the Saab would be clearly visible to the driver.

Still in the zone of darkness, Bond pressed the button. Another of his personalized pieces of equipment came into play. The Saab's front license plate flipped up, and at the same time, an aircraft light, fitted behind the license plate and below the bumper, blazed out—a great cone of white, dazzling light.

The pickup was caught full in the beam, and Bond could imagine the driver wrestling with the wheel, throwing up one hand to cover his eyes, feet fighting the brake and clutch.

The truck slewed to one side, bounced against a tree, then, out of control, turned sideways. The driver was free of the light's blinding glare, but too late. The pickup slid across the road, swinging violently as the skidding wheels pushed the vehicle into a spin. The rear wheels hit the track side, and with a sudden wrench the small pickup seemed to hurl itself against the trees before coming to a grinding stop.

"Hell!" Bond started ripping the Nitefinder set from his head. "Stay where you are," he yelled at Cedar, as he grabbed his flashlight, slid the VP70 automatic from its holster, and went out of the Saab, running fast.

The pickup lay at an angle against the trees, one side severely dented. There was no sign of broken glass. The driver was another matter, lying back in the small cab, his head lolling in a manner Bond knew only too well. The force of impact had whiplashed the man's head, breaking his neck.

Dragging the door open, Bond felt for the driver's pulse. He must have died instantly, without knowing what had happened. For a brief second James Bond felt a twinge of reget. He had not wished to kill the man: a few cuts and bruises would have easily sufficed.

The dead driver was in Bismaquer Security livery, and as Bond heaved the body from the truck, his mental reservations were tempered by the fact that a large Smith & Wesson .44 Magnum—the Model 29, Bond thought—hung, holstered, on his hip. In all probability he had been right: the security man was a watchdog as well as a guide.

He pushed the body off the track into the grass, among the trees, tracing the area with his flashlight, making sure he could find it again. Once the corpse was well-hidden, Bond removed the Smith & Wesson, returned to the pickup, and tried the engine. It started immediately, and with a little scraping as he backed away from the trees, seemed to be in reasonable running order. The tank was three-quarters full, and the other gauges showed normal. Bond drove the pickup alongside the Saab, keeping his eyes averted from the explosion of bright light, which burned like a magnesium burst from the front of the silver turbo.

"Think you can manage the pickup?" he asked Cedar, who was out of the Saab almost before Bond switched off.

She did not even bother to reply, simply climbed in, ready to take over. Bond said he would follow her up the hill and instructed her to stop at the cabins.

Once back in the Saab, he lowered the number plate extinguishing the aircraft light, switched on the headlights, and started the engine. Cedar began to move the pickup slowly up the track. With a swift, neatly executed three-point turn, the Saab followed in her wake, and without further incident they arrived back at the cabins.

There Bond explained exactly what he intended to do and what routes they would take. The Saab was to be left in its usual place, locked and with the alarm sensors set. The reconnaissance would be carried out in the pickup.

"People're less likely to stop us with Bismaquer's livery blazed on it."

They planned to move quckly down toward the conference-center area so Cedar could learn to operate the tunnel mechanism, then drive around the monorail station, and last, back to the laboratory area. "We should leave the pickup out of sight somewhere nearby and go in on foot," Bond cautioned. "Then, when we get back here, I think our poor friend down the road'll have to be involved in another accident—going downhill." He set the sensors on the Saab alarm system, locked the car, and was just about to get behind the wheel of the pickup—the guard's Smith & Wesson in hand—when another thought struck him.

"Cedar, to make absolutely certain, it may be a good idea to dummy up our beds a little. Who knows what Bismaquer or Luxor has in mind for us? You know how to do it?"

Cedar acidly replied that she had been dummying up beds since she was a teenager, turned on her heel, and strode off to Sand Creek. Bond lit a cigarette and sauntered unhurried into Fetterman. It took very little time to stuff pillows into shape under the thin sheets. In the darkness, the lump in the bed could certainly be that of a sleeping figure.

Cedar was already standing by the pickup, waiting, when Bond returned. He carried his Heckler & Koch VP70 on the back of his hip and placed the security man's Smith & Wesson on the floor of the pickup. Cedar still had the spare revolver, and Bond had not forgotten to equip himself with Q Branch's ring of picklocks and tools, as well as the flashlight from the Saab.

They coasted down the hill, side lights on and engine just turning over—an eerie sensation. Only the faint sound of the wheels against the track, the rustle of the airstream around them, and the light breeze through the silent archway of fir trees.

Bond slowly put in the clutch as they reached the subsidiary road. By now the moon had fully risen. They could easily have driven by its light, but that would only have caused suspicion, so Bond put the headlights on, turning right for the fifteen miles or so which took them to the edge of the main wall and the jungle surrounding the conference center.

It required only a few minutes to locate and demonstrate the hydraulically operated entrance to the tunnel, and they were soon on the road back, staying near to the outer perimeter of the ranch on what would, in the normal world, be secondary roads.

"I'm intrigued by the conference," Bond said, driving with more than usual care. "When the delegates begin to arrive, I want to take a quick look-see for myself. If SPECTRE has any large-scale operation planned, this would be an ideal place for the briefing."

"They start arriving tommorow night," Cedar told him, unable to disguise a certain amount of amusement.

"Oh?"

"Your friend Nena told me. In the powder room, as she so politely calls it, before dinner. The first batch arrive by air tomorrow evening—I mean *this* evening," it having already passed midnight.

"Well, if we're all still in one piece, I think I'll sit in on one of their discussions."

The monorail station was deserted, though the actual train, with the vehicle ramp in place, appeared to be permanently at the ready. No guards or Bismaquer patrol cars were in evidence. Bond turned the pickup onto the road taking them well past the fence surrounding the lawns of Tara.

Lights still blazed from the big house, and by the time they had covered the couple of miles to the trees which screened the long building behind the laboratory, it was clear that people were at work inside.

The rear section appeared to be deserted, but the smaller building was lit up like a Christmas tree.

They left the pickup among the trees some forty feet from the larger building, which, on closer examination, seemed to be a warehouse, as they had guessed. The gable end was made up of high sliding doors. Windows, securely barred, ran along the side of the warehouse, in the darkness, but, even at close quarters, it was impossible to see inside.

They moved forward, keeping low. Bond's eyes strained through the moonlit night, alert to the possibility of security guards, while Cedar watched their rear, the snub-nosed revolver in her hand.

There was a gap between the smaller, laboratory building and the warehouse. Glancing between them, Bond saw the two were connected, probably by a narrow passage. Then they arrived at the first windows of the laboratory. The light, very bright, cast a block beam onto the grass, reaching almost as far as the trees.

Straightening up, one on either side of the window, Cedar and Bond peered in.

Several women tended machinery, each of them dressed in white coveralls, their hair completely swathed in turbans, hands in tight rubber gloves. On their feet they wore the kind of short boots usually seen in hospital operating rooms.

The women worked with quiet, practiced expertise, hardly exchanging a word. "An ice-cream plant," Cedar whispered. "I got taken to one as a kid. See the pasteurizer at the far end? That's where the mixings go: the milk, cream, sugar, and flavoring."

Using dumb show and essential words, Cedar pointed out the standard parts of factory-made ice cream. Bond frowned, a little bewildered at her knowledge of how the mix was heated in the pasteurizer to kill bacteria, before being filtered on to the homogenizing vat. From there, he could clearly see the array of cold pipes for mushing and chilling the mix, and the vast stainless-steel holding tank, which controlled the flow into the freezer. Then the units which blocked the ice cream, before an endless belt took the finished blocks into a metal-doored hardening room. From the window it looked exceptionally efficient.

Bond tipped his head, motioning Cedar forward. Crouching near the wall, he whispered, "You seem to know it all. How professional is that system?"

"Very. They're even using real cream and milk, by the look of it. No chemicals."

"All this from a school trip to a factory?"

Cedar grinned. "I like ice cream," she hissed. "It's interesting. But that's a professional setup in there. Small, but professional."

"Could they turn out enough to market the stuff?"

She nodded, adding, "In a small way, yes. But it's probably for their local consumption."

Bond caught hold of Cedar's hand, tugging her in the direction of the next section. The windows were smaller, and this time they found themselves looking into a large laboratory. Glass tubing, vats, and intricate electronics were laid out on almost a grand scale.

The laboratory was empty, except for a Bismaquer security guard standing in front of a door on the far side.

"Hell!" Bond put his lips near to Cedar's ear. "If anything's happening, it's through there. We'll have to cut back and go around to the other side."

"Let's have the picklocks." Cedar touched his hand. "I'll see if I can look into the warehouse, while you try the windows around the corner."

They retraced their steps back along the wall. Bond handed over the picklock kit as they reached the sliding doors at the gable end. He left Cedar to wrestle with them while he crept forward, trying to gauge the exact position of the windows to the room of the main laboratory. After two errors, he discovered the right one. Peering in from the left-hand corner, he saw Bismaquer and Walter Luxor pacing a small, bare, cell-like chamber. On closer inspection he could clearly see that the room was in fact a cell—a padded cell. There were two soft chairs anchored to the center of the floor, both occupied by Bismaquer employees in uniform. An animated conversation was taking place between these two seated men and Bismaquer and Luxor.

Bond, still crouching low, put his ear hard against the window and could just make out what was being said. Bismaquer had ceased to punctuate his conversation with the jolly laughter. Now he seemed serious indeed, his body tense, his gestures economical.

"So, Tommy," he was saying to one of the seated men. "So you'll give me the keys to your house, let me drive over and take your wife by force, right?"

The man called Tommy chuckled. "Anything you say, chief. You just go right ahead." His speech was distinct, unslurred, and he appeared to be absolutely in command of himself.

The other man joined in: "Anything to make anybody happy. Take my keys too. No problem. Take the car. I just like seeing people enjoy themselves. Me? I do what I'm told." This one also gave a perfectly natural impression, someone meaning what he said, under no stress or influence.

"Do you want to continue working here?" It was Luxor asking.

"Why not?" came the reply from the second man.

"I'd sure hate to leave. It's great here," the one called Tommy added.

"Listen to me, Tommy." Bismaquer had walked across the room and stood near the window. But for the protective screening and glass, Bond could have touched him. "Would you worry a lot if, after I've raped your wife, I kill her too?"

"Be my guest, Mr. Bismaquer. Anything you want. Here, I'll give you the keys. I told you."

Luxor had joined his chief. Even though he spoke quietly, Bond heard every word. "Ten hours, Markus. Ten hours, and they're both affected."

"Amazing. Better than we ever expected." Bismaquer raised his voice. "Tommy, you love your wife. I attended your wedding. You're a nice couple. Why would you allow me to do such a terrible thing?"

"Because you outrank me, Mr. Bismaquer. You give the orders, I obey. That's the way it works."

"Would you question Mr. Bismaquer's orders?" Luxor asked, the squeaky voice rising.

"Why shoud I? Like I just said, that's the way it works. Like in the army. You take orders from the senior man, and you obey them."

"Without question?"

"Sure."

"Sure." The other man nodded. "That's how it works."

By the window, Bismaquer muttered something Bond couldn't make out, and shook his head as though in disbelief.

Luxor turned, and for a second Bond thought the walking death's-head would see him through the glass. "Uncanny maybe, Markus. But a real breakthrough. We've done it, my friend. Think of the results."

Bismaquer frowned, and Bond caught his tone. The voice was cold, bleak as a blizzard. "I *am* thinking of the results. . . ." The rest was lost to Bond, who ducked down and—having heard enough—started to go back, padding softly along the wall. Then he stopped, stock-still, pressed hard against the wall. Someone was moving in his direction, and out of reflex habit, Bond found the large VP70 in his hand.

Seconds later he relaxed. The figure, coming with exceptional speed, was Cedar. "Let's go. Fast." She was almost out of breath. "I nearly got spotted by a security guard. That warehouse—they've enough ice cream in freezing units to supply the whole state of Texas for a month."

By the time they got back to the pickup, Bond's mind was working overtime. He started the engine, waited for a few moments before letting out the clutch, and pulled away slowly.

The roads were empty.

"So they're stockpiling ice cream," he said as they reached the turnoff from the highway.

"I'll say." Cedar had recovered her breath. "The warehouse is divided up into huge refrigerators. I'd looked into three of them; then this guard came in. Thank God I hadn't gotten one of the doors open—they're heavy as sin—and I'd mostly closed the main doors, leaving just enough space for a quick getaway."

Bond asked if she was absolutely sure she had not been seen.

"Absolutely. He'd have been after me like a bullet. I just stayed flat against one of these damned great cold stores. He came partway into the warehouse, then went back . . . back toward the laboratory section."

"Good. You want to hear the bad news now?" As they reached the knoll, beginning to climb the sloping track to the cabins, Bond finished telling her what he had seen and heard at the window of the padded cell.

"So they've got a couple of very normal-seeming guys in there, willing to obey even the most unlikely orders—like getting their wives raped and murdered?" Cedar shivered.

It was not strange, Bond thought, for her to sound incredulous. "That's about it. *Very* normal guys. There was no way of telling, from what I could see, but Bismaquer and Luxor must've been feeding them something. They said the effect had lasted for ten hours, and when you take the padded cell into account, there's little doubt those two men are human guinea pigs."

"Hopped up to the eyeballs."

"Yes. The worrying thing is that they didn't look or sound like it. They were taking orders, and complying, that's all. But orders that went against all reason or conscience. Why, Cedar? Making people into unknowing hit men or something like that? Why?"

"How?" she volleyed back. "Why're you stopping?"

Bond said she was to stay in the cab. "We have to take the driver up the hill, I'm afraid. I'll put him in the back. No need for you to do any of this."

Cedar said it was most gallant of him, but corpses did not worry her. Nevertheless, she stayed in the pickup while Bond dragged the dead driver to the truck and dumped the body in the back, then returned to cover up any marks among the trees.

"If they've developed a drug that shows no outward effects . . ." Cedar began when Bond returned.

"Yes." He continued to drive up the hill. "No side effects. No staggering or slurring. People functioning normally . . ."

"Except in one sense." Cedar took up a mutual train of thought. "They'll obey orders which, in usual circumstances, would either be questioned or acted against."

"It's a weapon in a thousand," Bond said. Then, as they reached the cabins, he asked, "The ice cream? You think that could be the delivery system?"

"They've got enough of the lousy stuff."

"I thought you liked ice cream."

"I'm going off it very quickly."

They climbed out, and this time Cedar helped with the grisly job of putting the dead driver in the cab behind the wheel. Bond checked that they had left nothing of their own in the pickup, then returned the revolver to the driver's holster. Cedar even insisted on squeezing in next to Bond as he started the engine and, leaning over the body, drove the pickup slowly back down the hill.

When they reached the top of the steepest slope, he stopped, applied the handbrake, and helped Cedar out.

The engine was running smoothly, and the wheels turned slightly off-center. With a nod to Cedar, indicating that she should get out of the way, Bond leaned through the driver's side window and released the hand brake.

He was carried for a few yards before jumping clear. Then, picking himself up, Bond watched the truck gathering speed, slewing from one side of the road to the other.

Fascinated by the outcome, he hardly noticed Cedar alongside him, linking an arm through his.

The pickup's lights showed its progress, wild and careering, as it hurtled down the slope. Then they heard the first crunch as the truck hit the trees. Its lights seemed to dance their beams into the air, then down, in a rolling, catherine-wheel effect—the motion of the lights accompanied by an attendant clattering and grating as the vehicle began to fall apart.

It took about twenty seconds. Then the whoosh, followed by a crump as the truck finally piled up, its tank catching fire in the impact.

"The trees look like they're alive," murmured Cedar.

"Ancient peoples held them to be very much alive and sacred," Bond said. He also felt something old and terrifying about the strange shadows and odd movements created by the fire. "Modern people also—some of them. Trees are living things. I know what you mean."

"We'd better go." Cedar slipped her arm free and turned abruptly on her heel, as though not able to watch the wreck any longer. "The whole place'll see that fire. We'll have visitors before you know it."

Bond caught up with her, striding toward the clearing and the cabins.

"We've got a lot to think about," she said as they reached the door of Sand Creek.

"A great deal, Cedar. Makes me wonder if we shouldn't turn and run for it now, give the authorities what we have, and see if they'll come in force." As he said it, Bond knew this was not the way.

"It wouldn't worry me if we got out here and now." Cedar gave him a kiss on the cheek, then tried to move in closer, but Bond gently held her off. She gave a long sigh. "I know. I know, James. Just like I know you won't really leave this place until we have concrete evidence, with all the ends tied up."

Bond said yes, that was really how it was. "Okay," Cedar shrugged. "As long as you have the Dragon Lady tied into it as well. That would make me really happy. Good night, James. Sleep well."

Bond started to walk past the Saab, back toward Fetterman. His hand was on the doorknob when Cedar began screaming from the other cabin.

14

REPELLENT INSECTS

THE VP70 AUTOMATIC was in Bond's hand as he reached the door of Cedar's cabin, seconds after the first scream.

His right leg came up in a vicious kick, smashing the handle and almost ripping the door back from its hinges. Bond jumped into the doorway, then to one side, the VP70 in the double-hand grip and the word "Freeze" already on his lips.

But there was only Cedar, standing in the bedroom doorway, shrinking back in revulsion, her body shaking with fear.

Bond crossed the room. He grasped her shoulder, ready to fire at anything—animal, reptile, or man—inside the bedroom.

Then he also took an involuntary step back. The room was alive with them—large, dark, creeping, and malevolent ants. They covered the floor, walls, ceiling. The bed itself had turned black in a constantly moving sea of the creatures.

There were hundreds of them, the smallest a good inch in length, squirming together, fighting to get to the bed, where the dummy was now a dark seething lump.

Bond slammed the door behind them, then looked to see how much space remained between it and the floor. "Harvesters, I think, Cedar. Harvester ants. Out of their environment and looking for food." If they were harvesters, Bond thought, they had not come in by accident. Harvesters live in arid areas and store seeds for food. They would never have drifted in from the desert—at least not in such large numbers.

The other fact he hesitated to mention was that one sting from a harvester ant could be painful; it could even, in the right circumstances, be lethal. But hundreds—maybe a few thousand—of the large insects, out of their natural environment, excited, possibly frustrated for food, was another matter. Several stings from enraged harvester ants would be deadly.

"There's only one way to deal with them." Bond bundled Cedar out of the cabin, swiftly looking behind him to make certain none of the ants had advanced into the living room. He closed the door behind him.

Bond hurried the girl across to his own cabin, one arm around her. Once inside, he told her to stay in the main room. "And keep down. Right?" Then he dashed to the bedroom for the briefcase.

Flicking the tumbler locks, Bond opened up the case, sliding and lifting the false bottom until he found what he needed: a small detonator and a couple of inches of fast-burning fuse. Quickly he inserted the fuse into the little metal core of the detonator, and breaking all the rules, crimped the detonator to the fuse with his teeth. His old instructors would have winced. "You can lose your teeth and kissing equipment that way, Mr. Bond," they used to tell him.

Reaching deeper into the briefcase, Bond retrieved one of the bags which contained plastic explosive. He tore off a small section and rolled the plasticine material until he had something roughly the size and shape of a golf ball.

Keeping fuse and detonator well away from the plastic, Bond was out of the room again, and—with a further caution for Cedar to stay where she was—ran full-tilt out of the cabin toward the Saab. Working with speed, he unlocked the alarm sensors, then the trunk, lifting the rear of the car and searching with his hand.

He found the spare container immediately. For years now Bond had rarely traveled without at least a could of spare gallons of gasoline in a plastic container, held in place by restraining webbing in the large trunk.

At the door of Sand Creek, Bond unscrewed the container's cap, molding the plastic ball around the lip. Still keeping detonator and fuse well clear, he paused at the bedroom door before pushing the detonator hard into the plastic. The only problem now was to light the fuse without ingniting the gasoline fumes.

Gently Bond opened the bedroom door, his flesh creeping at the sight of an entire room moving, in obscene waves, with the fat crawling insects. Placing the container just inside the door, he took out his Dunhill lighter. He held it low, well clear of the vaporizing gasoline, and thumbed the wheel. The flame appeared. Quickly Bond applied it to the fuse, which spluttered immediately.

Closing the door softly to prevent the homemade bomb from being knocked over, Bond walked slowly away and outside. Walk, never run, they taught you: running increased the possibility of falling near a planted charge.

He had just reached the door of Fetterman when the crude device blew with a hollow roar. The explosive shot the gasoline up in a fireball, straight through the cabin roof, a hand of brilliant flame clawing at the air, then fanning out inside so that the interior of Sand Creek became an inferno within seconds.

The door of Fetterman was wrenched open. For a moment Bond thought it was the blast effect, as the knob was pulled from his hand. But he saw Cedar standing there, her mouth agape. Bond pushed her inside, sent her sprawling, and landed on top of her. Outside, flaming and smoking debris arched and showered across the clearing.

"Just stay down, Cedar." Bond realized he was pinning the girl, lying almost astride her.

"If you stay like this, James, I'd be glad to." Even in the aftermath of shock—first the ants and then the sudden blast from the bomb—Cedar managed to laugh.

Quickly Bond rolled away. "Just stay down," he ordered, then headed for the door again.

Bits of burning debris littered the area. With admirable thought for priorities, Bond quickly checked that no heavy pieces of wood or burning material had slammed into the Saab. Next he turned to the cabin called Fetterman, circling it, making absolutely certain that no secondary fire had started there.

It was only then that two vital facts came into sharp focus. The first, Bond had already realized: such a large colony of harvester ants could not possibly have gotten into the cabin by accident. But the second was even more revealing: the ants were, of course, meant to sting and kill, and the target was Bond himself. Had he not told Bismaquer that he was staying in Sand Creek, and precisely to protect Cedar, whom he had considered the more vulnerable?

Already he could hear the sound of motors: vehicles were approaching below them. Bismaquer—or Luxor—had meant to get Bond.

When help—if you could call it that—arrived, one of two things would happen: Bismaquer and his henchmen, finding both Bond and Cedar unharmed, would either try to dispense some fast, rough justice, or they would take advantage of the situation and split them up, moving either Bond or Cedar from the cabins to Tara.

Whatever happened, it was unlikely they would be given the opportunity to be alone together during the next day or so. Some quick planning had to be done, and now, before anyone came near.

Swiftly Bond made his way to the cabin where Cedar sat with a stiff drink in her hand. "My clothes," she said mournfully, before Bond had a chance to speak. "Everything we bought. Up in smoke. James, I haven't even got a pair of panties left."

Bond could not resist the obvious: "Don't worry, my dear, I'm sure Nena Bismaquer will outfit you."

Cedar started to retort, but Bond then silenced her with a quick word. If they were separated, he said, there would have to be some means of communication. Handing over the one spare key to the Saab, he told her where the car would be hidden, if he suddenly went to ground. She would have to devise some way of getting away from wherever they lodged her.

"If you're right, and the delegates for this conference start arriving tonight, I shall try to get into the conference center in the early hours of tomorrow morning." Bond hesitated, suddenly recalling the assignation he had made with Nena Bismaquer for what was now tonight. "Midnight," he said. "Midnight *tomorrow*. If I'm not there, make it the following night. If the car's gone, you'll know I had to leave you in the lurch; but, Cedar, that'll be a last resort, and I'll be back—probably with a horde of FBI, CIA, and state troopers. So just stay put."

Bond was still making Cedar repeat the car's hiding place and their meeting arrangements when two pickup trucks and a car hurtled into the clearing.

"Hey! . . . Hey there! James, Cedar, are you okay?" Bismaquer's voice boomed from outside, to an undercurrent of shouts and orders.

Bond went to the door. "We're taking cover in here, Markus. This is no way to treat your guests, you know."

"What?" Bismaquer appeared in all his bulk, a few feet from the door. Behind him, Bond caught sight of Nena's face and thought he detected a look of relief when she saw he was safe.

"What in hell happened here?" Bismaquer waved toward the smoldering skeleton that had once been Sand Creek cabin. People milled around the ruins, and Bond noticed that Bismaquer's men had come prepared, for one of the pickups was fitted with a large tank of pressurized foam. Already a group in Bismaquer livery had started to smother the embers.

"There were—" Cedar began.

"There were a few bugs around," Bond said casually, leaning against the doorjamb, "so I came out to the car where I always carry a small first-aid kit. I wanted some insect repellent. Cedar heard me and thought I was an intruder." He laughed. "Funny, really. I must explain—when we told you earlier that I was in Sand Creek and Cedar in Fetterman, we'd got them muddled. In fact, it was the other way around. But when we got back tonight, Cedar decided she preferred Fetterman after all. She didn't like the picture in Sand Creek. We were tired and, apparently, both sleep in the raw, so we didn't bother to move our things. Thought we'd change over properly in the morning. All Cedar's stuff was in there"—he nodded toward the ruins—"while my stuff's intact. But Cedar's only got the clothes she's standing—"

"The prints?" Bismaquer interrupted. "Are they okay? You didn't have—?"

"The prints are fine, I promise you."

"Thank the good Lord for that."

"Markus," Bond snapped, sharply, "you sound like an alcoholic in a shipwreck—'Is the brandy safe?' instead of 'How many have we saved?'"

"Yes." Nena moved close to the group by the door. "You really are callous, Markus. James could've been killed."

"Very nearly was. What do you use for cooking in these cabins? Bottled gas?"

"As a matter of fact—" Bismaquer began.

"Well, some idiot must have left a faulty cylinder. I lit a cigarette, left it on an ashtray in the bedroom. I only got as far as the car, then, whoomp, up it went."

"Oh, James, I wouldn't have had this happen. . . . It's terrible!" Nena was looking at him in a way that brought back the smell of her hair and the shared kiss among the dense trees. Bond found it genuinely difficult to tear his eyes away. Then he realized that another car was coming up the slope.

Bond took a step toward Bismaquer. "While we're at it, Markus," he resumed his aggressive tone, "what about those damned bugs?"

"The bugs?" Bismaquer looked around him, as though about to be attacked by a plague of hornets.

"Yes, the bugs. Big, black, nasty creatures—like huge ants."

"Oh, my God." Bismaquer took a pace back. "Not harvesters?"

"I think so." Bond started to pour on the anger. "You get a lot of those around here, Markus? If so, why didn't you warn us? Can't harvesters—?"

"They can kill, yes." For a second, as he said it, Bismaquer seemed to have shed any fear.

"Well, do you often get them?"

Bismaquer did not meet Bond's eyes. "Sometimes. Not many, though."

"There were hundreds. We could've both been stung to death. I think you're taking it a shade casually, Markus."

Whatever Bismaquer might have replied, though, was cut off by the brusque arrival of the other car. Luxor was at the wheel, with two security men in attendance. They had hardly stopped—in a braking cloud of dust—when Luxor shouted for Bismaquer.

Bismaquer went over a shade too fast for Bond's peace of mind. Was Luxor in command? he wondered. The two were in close conversation, the gap in Luxor's skull-head moving in rapid monologue.

"Will you be okay here, tonight, James?" Nena had come into the cabin.

"We can both stay here," Cedar chimed in. "We'll toss for the sofa."

"I wouldn't hear of it, my dear." Nena smiled sweetly. "You'll have the guest room at Tara. And we'll do something about clothes for you first thing. If I get your sizes, one of my more intelligent girls can make a trip into town. I'd lend you some of mine, but I fear they'd be too long, and maybe a little tight for you."

"You're so kind," mouthed Cedar so that they could hardly hear her.

"Cedar's coming back to the house for the night, Markus." Nena turned as Bismaquer approached them.

"Good." He spoke almost as an aside. "James, something else has happened. Unpleasant as hell. The guy who brought you up here, the one you followed. The one in the pickup . . ."

"Yes?"

"What happened when he left you?"

Bond shrugged, frowning. "What do you mean? He waved us good night and off he went."

"Did you hear anything after?"

Bond thought for a minute. "No. We went into my cabin, put on some music, and had a drink. That was when we decided to change cabins. Cedar said she liked this one better than Sand Creek. I think it was the picture that did it. I know what she means—a lot of white men riding around killing off boys, women, and children. But why the questions, Markus?"

Bismaquer scowled. "Your guide was a hell of a good man . . ."

"Fisher?" asked Nena with a trace of anxiety.

Bismaquer nodded. "Yep. One of the best we had."

"What's happened?" Nena Bismaquer was now definitely alarmed and could not hide it.

Markus took a deep breath. "It seems like he blew it tonight. Trouble with Fisher was that he . . . well, he liked the juice from time to time."

"Partial to a few glasses when the mood took him. I know the syndrome." Bond sounded unconcerned.

"I may as well tell you. Fisher's job was to—how do I put it?—well, to look after you. His instructions were to stay in the trees, make sure there were no problems like animals. There are a few around."

"Like harvester ants?" Bond asked.

"Animals," Bismaquer repeated.

"And he went for a drink instead?" Cedar prompted.

Bismaquer shook his head. "Not the first drink anyway. He'd probably already had a few. Maybe he was going for more."

"Was?" from Nena.

"The pickup went off the road. It's burned out in the trees at the bottom of the hill. We were in such a hurry getting up here, we didn't spot it. Walter did."

"And Fisher?" Nena's mouth was half-open.

"Sorry, honey. I know you liked him around the place. Fisher got burned."

"Oh, my God. You mean. . . ?"

"As a doornail. Most unpleasant." Bismaquer looked from Bond to Cedar, and back again. "You sure you heard nothing?"

"Not a thing."

"Nothing at all."

"Poor Fisher." Nena turned away, her face creased. "His wife . . ."

"It would be best if you broke it to her, my dear," Bismaquer said peremptorily, turning away.

"Of course, Markus. First, we'll settle Cedar at Tara." Nena moved toward her husband. "Then"—a small sigh—"then I'll go and break the news to Lottie Fisher."

"Good. Yes." Bismaquer's mind was clearly elsewhere. "You'll be okay, then, James?"

Bond said he would be fine, then, smiling, asked if the Grand Prix was still on. "I mean, after all this?"

In the light from the cabin and the headlights, he may have imagined a cloud cross Markus Bismaquer's face before the bear of a man spoke. "Oh, yes, James. This has been unfortunate, sure, but the Grand Prix's definitely on. Ten in the morning. Walter's looking forward to it. I am too."

"I'll see you there, then. At the track. 'Night, Cedar. Sleep well, and don't worry about any of this."

"Oh, this is the last thing I'll worry about." Cedar flashed him a false smile. "Good night, James."

"And *I'll* see you tomorrow as well, James." Nena looked him full in the face. This time it was no trick of light among the trees: the fire lay buried deep in the dark pools of her eyes, and the smile spoke of wonders to be unfolded the following night.

When they had all left the clearing, James Bond checked that the Saab was secure, then went back into the cabin. He blocked the door with a chair and scoured the window crevices for possible entrance points. A second dose of harvester ants, while he slept, would be a little hard to take.

It took a further ten minutes to repack the briefcase, after which he stretched out on the bed, fully clothed, but with the Heckler & Koch automatic within easy reach.

Nena had spoken of evil. Bond could feel it now, as though Rancho Bismaquer was alive with malevolence. Earlier, he had caught a trace of SPECTRE in this place; now the scent was very strong. He had tangled with them before, and his instincts were finely tuned to them and their first leader, Ernst Stavro Blofeld. Even now, alone in the cabin on a wooded knoll, set, paradoxically, in the middle of desert, the distinct smell of Blofeld came wafting back from the hell to which Bond had sent him during that final encounter in Japan.

One of these men was somehow connected with his old enemy. Which one? Luxor or Bismaquer? He could not tell, but he knew he would discover the truth soon enough.

He thought of the delegation, arriving in just over twelve hours, of the sinister play he had watched being enacted in the padded cell off the laboratory next to the ice-cream plant. A kind of hypnotic drug, he presumed—a "happy pill" that removed all moral scruples, leaving the victim outwardly normal but pliable beyond belief.

He looked at his watch. It was almost five in the morning and would soon be getting light. Within twenty-four hours he had to go to ground—literally into the tunnel to the conference center. In the darkness Bond smiled, thinking of the irony if it turned out to be just another mundane and boring business conference, all aboveboard. Yet experience told him this would not be so. His training, his logic, and the times he had warred with SPECTRE on previous occasions, all shouted at him, setting his mind and senses on a collision course with their joint destiny.

Before then, he would clash with Walter Luxor on the racetrack, allegedly for a million dollars but with much more clearly at stake. Confident as he was of his car and himself, Bond was nonetheless well aware of the danger. After that—before going off on his lone mission—

there would be Nena, with her luscious body and those strangely blazing black eyes.

Bond's mind spun in circles. Blofeld? Bismaquer? Luxor? The conference? SPECTRE? The ice cream? The Grand Prix? . . . Nena . . . Nena Bismaquer, unhappy, keyed-up against the evil of this place. Cedar crossed his thoughts for a moment, and again he smiled into the darkness, knowing that if he did not hold her father, Felix Leiter, in such respect, Cedar would have also become yet another diversion. But, as though hypnotized, Bond's thoughts curved back to Nena, and he dropped into sleep with her picture in this head, and the smell of her hair close to him—as it would be, soon enough.

15

GRAND PRIX

THE SUN CLIMBED into a diamond-clear sky, and you could already feel the dormant heat of the day. Within an hour or so it would become scorching: a day for staying in the cool and sipping iced drinks, for lazing and passing the time with a good conversationalist—preferably female, Bond thought.

He had not slept for long, having learned, many years ago, to take advantages of short periods of rest. An hour had been spent going over the Saab. These people had tricks up their sleeves, but so did 007's Saab turbo, though he could leave nothing to luck. The Saab had to be perfect. Even allowing for a highly souped-up engine, Bond was confident that the Shelby-American, driven by Walter Luxor, would stand little real chance.

With the turbo-charger in full operation, a normal Saab 900 can reach a cruising speed of 125 mph with ease. Restrictions, moreover, forbid commercial models to exceed this kind of maximum, and the turbo-charger itself normally limits performance to within the 125-mph range. But increase the fuel-line pressure to wind up the boost, add in the special rally conversion kit, and you get really high performance.

Bond, in fact, knew of police forces in the world who used Saab turbos with these very variations. "What's the use of a turbo to us if we can't catch a commercial turbo?" one senior police officer had said.

Bond had himself already clocked over 180 mph on an open track, after his car was fitted with the new water-injection system, and there was no reason why he should not do it today. He did not fear the possibility of blowouts—or even of a well-placed bullet in a tire—for his personalized car ran on Michelin Autoporteur tires, look-alikes of the TRX tires, which are standard. The Autoporteurs are possessed of properties spoken about only in hushed tones within the motor industry.

No problems, Bond thought, as, with air conditioning at full blast, he eased the silver beast along the side road which ran along the outside of the circuit.

Markus Bismaquer, with Nena and Cedar, was plainly visible in front of the grandstand, which already seemed to be three-quarters full. Bismaquer's staff had obviously turned out—or been dragooned—as spectators for this special occasion.

He pulled the Saab into the slip road leading to the pits, coming to a stop beside Bismaquer's group. Of Walter Luxor and the Shelby-American there was no sign.

"James, you look quite the part." Nena Bismaquer's smile was so natural and all-embracing that Bond could not resist kissing her on the cheek, something which he normally deplored. Then he realized that Cedar Leiter was giving him a hard and tough look.

"Morning, Cedar," he said cheerfully, kissing her on both cheeks. "Twice, for luck." He smiled.

For comfort, Bond wore a light blue-and-red track suit—bought with the other items in Springfield—and little else. Even with the air conditioning, he knew it would get hot out there behind the wheel, especially if Walter Luxor pressed him.

"James, I hope you slept the sleep of the just." Bismaquer roared with his accustomed mirth, slapping Bond on the back just hard enough to make the skin tingle.

"Oh, yes. Like the proverbial log." Bond looked straight into Bismaquer's face. Gone was any sign of the previous night's strain.

"Do you want a few practice runs, James, before we start? It looks easy from here, but I can promise you that the chicane and the zigzag on the far side are real bitches. I know, I built it."

Bond nodded toward the gas pumps. "Okay, I'll take her around a couple of times to get the feel. Then can I fill up, deal with my oil and all that?"

"We've got a whole crew for you, James." Bismaquer pointed to five of his men, dressed in coveralls. "The real thing. You want to get your spare wheel out, in case you need a change? We've got everything at your disposal."

"I'll manage. Ten laps, wasn't it?"

"Yes. And don't forget, the crew's there if you need help. We have track marshals standing by, in case anything big goes wrong."

Did Bond detect something in Bismaquer's voice? A hint? Some sense that he expected something to go wrong? Well, they'd just have to wait and see. In the end, it could be that the best driver, and not the best car, would be first across the finish line.

Bond nodded at the group, winked at Cedar, and climbed back into the Saab. He pulled on his gloves and adjusted the Polaroid sunglasses.

Easing onto the grid, Bond took a final swift look at the instruments. Twice around for luck, he thought. A slowish first run—around seventy where possible—and a faster second, taking the Saab near to a hundred but not going higher. Keep the trumps up your sleeve. He smiled, slipping the stick into first, releasing the hand brake, and pulling away. He gathered speed, going through the gears, taking her to fourth as the speedometer hit fifty and giving the car a fraction more power to knock the revs over the 3,000 mark, then bringing in the turbo—a comforting whine—hitting seventy miles an hour right on the button.

On the first run, Bond did not go right through the gears into fifth. He kept the engine in check, getting the feel of the track at the relatively low speed.

From the grid to the chicane there was a good two and a half miles of straight track; but once you hit the chicane, both car and driver knew it. The track—from a distance—looked as though it merely narrowed, then went through a graceful though tight elongated-S shape. It was not until the Saab came out into the last curve of the S that Bond realized the chicane ended with a nasty, sudden, sharp lump—like a small hump-backed bridge.

The bends proved to be no problem, even at 60 mph, calling for only a quick movement of the wheel—left, right . . . left, right. The Saab's curved spoiler and its weight held the machine to the track like glue. It was only when he hit the hump that Bond realized the danger.

At sixty, the car lifted off the ground for a second, as it crested during the final easy curve. For a moment, all four wheels were in the air, and it needed considerable concentration not to go off-line as the spinning tires touched down, screeching against the metaled surface.

Bond exhaled, releasing all the breath from his lungs, realizing the dangers the hump might create at real speed. He held the car out of the turn and onto another mile of straight track before the more obvious, vicious, right-angle bend.

He held the car at seventy, leaving the shift down until almost the last moment, going into the right-hander in third, but keeping the power on to make certain there was no tendency to slide outward. Again, the Saab did her stuff. Bond always likened cornering at speed, in this machine, to being held to the road by some invisible hand. When the pressure was really on, you could feel the rear being pushed down by the speed of airflow caught in the curved spoiler.

He came out of the bend with the clock still smack on seventy miles an hour. Half a mile of straight—in which, when flat-out, he could again build up speed. Resisting temptation, Bond kept her to the seventy, going up to fourth and hitting the nasty Z-bend with a shift down to second, the speed dropped drastically to fifty.

The Z was, indeed, nasty. By rights, it crossed Bond's mind, he should have allowed himself more time to practice. You really had to haul the wheel around, and even at this speed, it was not possible to get her up again into fourth, and a steady acceleration to the seventy mark, until the last sharp point in the Z was behind you. That would need watching.

The rest was easy. Three miles or so of straight track, followed by a very gentle right-hander. Another mile and a half, then the second right-hand bend, and so into the final mile, back to the grid.

The last bend, Bond quickly discovered, was a shade deceptive, the curve suddenly sharpening as you went in. But all in all, he could cope with that. On the first run, he shifted down to third as the angle steepened, piling on the revs, going up again as soon as the track straightened, to show a long ribbon in front of him, past the stands, and with three flat miles to run before the chicane.

A mile from the stands, Bond slid up into fifth gear and began to pile on some speed. He touched one hundred as he saw the grandstand blur past and held it until half a mile from the chicane.

He went into the gentle turns at ninety, slowing to seventy on the final curve and hitting the hump—for which he was not ready—with the needle still hovering just below the seventy mark. The Saab took off from the top of the hump, arrow-straight, with Bond waiting for the thump as all four wheels hit the track. They landed as one, Bond easing the wheel to correct any slewing.

Gently, building up to a hundred, Bond moved to his right to give himself plenty of room on the turn. It would be make-or-break, he decided. Hit the nasty, hard right-angle at around eighty and stay there, trusting the weight, tires, and spoiler to keep him under control.

The figures on his head-up display—and the needle—did not drop a fraction: dead on eighty for the whole turn, though Bond found himself leaning his body to the right, as if to compensate, and the wheels started to drift fractionally to the left.

He could do it. The right-angle could be negotiated—if positioned correctly to the right—at eighty miles an hour and, possibly, even a hundred.

This was not as easy on the Z-bend. Here, you had to shift down: brake; accelerator; brake; accelerator; and again, then out the other side, and pile on the horses.

The Saab took the first of the final two bends at ninety, with no trouble, dropping, with a change down, at the steeping curve on the second.

He came into the last straight still at ninety, allowing the speed to drop away steadily until the stand and pits seemed to drift toward him. Forty; thirty; twenty . . . slowing to a stop.

Through he windshield he saw Bismaquer's face, a small crease of concern between his eyes. Walter Luxor, who had now appeared, fully dressed in racing overalls decorated with the Bismaquer insignia, took no notice. He busied himself with the silver Shelby-American, which was getting a final going-over from his crew.

Bond stayed in his seat for a moment, watching the vehicle that had been matched against his own, trying to recall all he knew about the car.

The original competition Ford Mustang had been exceptionally successful in its day: first and second in the 1964 Tour de Force touring-car class, where its many variations showed fine performances. The GT 350, as Shelby-American's derivation of the Mustang was designated, had sleek body lines of the old fast-back variety, the most obvious outward alterations being a large air scoop on top of the hood and rear-wheel air scoops. The earlier versions usually had fiberglass construction around the hood—or bonnet—and there was a multitude of possible combinations of engine and transmission, together with the necessary special-handling package to stop the alarming roll experienced on cornering with the stock Mustang suspension.

From what he could recall, Bond thought the car lighter than its parent Mustangs but capable of speeds well in excess of the 130 mark. The one he looked at now, through the Saab's windshield, seemed at first sight to be an original, but the closer he viewed the car, the more uncertain Bond became. The bodywork had a very solid look to it—an indefinable depth. Steel, he thought. Like a Shelby-American, but only in its lines. The tires, he could see, were heavy-duty, and if the original design had to be a stress factor at very high speeds, Bonds would still have liked to look under that hood. Bismaquer, being the man he was, would be unlikely to match a standard souped-up car like this against a Saab turbo. Whatever engine they had hidden away, it would almost certainly be, like Bond's, turbo-charged.

Sliding from the driving seat, Bond walked quickly toward the car, calling out within a couple of paces of the machine to attract Luxor's attention.

Bismaquer moved with unexpected agility in an attempt to cut Bond off from getting too close—a move which finally succeeded, but not before Bond managed to get a hand on the hood. It was stressed steel, all right. The feel was there under his palm. Also, the suspension, from the one quick downward push Bond managed—seemed very firm.

"Good luck, Walter—" Bond began as Bismaquer cut him away from the Shelby-American. "I only wanted to wish Walter good luck." Bond scowled, as though offended, feeling Bismaquer's large hand around his arm, literally pulling him away.

"Walter doesn't like to be distracted before a race, James," Bismaquer growled. "He's an old professional, remember."

"And this is a friendly race, with an important side bet between us, Markus." Bond sounded cool, though concern had already begun to itch at the back of his mind.

Bismaquer probably had a car capable of high performance, but he could not know about the water injection or the increased boost on the Saab. Bond was in no doubt, though, about Luxor. He was up against a man who really knew racing, and—what was even more of an advantage—a man who knew the Bismaquer track backward.

"Okay, Markus. You tell your professional, from me, that I hope the best man wins. That's all. Now, can I juice up the Saab?"

Bismaquer looked at him blankly. There was something dreadfully sinister about the gaze, for the eyes were blank and the mouth sullenly slack—no hint, no trace, of the expansive buffoon. With a certain coldness in the pit of his stomach, Bond recognized the look.

It was an expression he had seen many times, the dead expression of a professional hit man. A contract killer about to do his job.

As suddenly as the look came, it vanished, and Bismaquer smiled, his whole face lighting up. "My boys'll do it all for you, James."

"No, thank you." Bond preferred to see to everything himself—gas, oil, hydraulics, coolant.

The final check took around twenty minutes, after which Bond walked over to Bismaquer, who was chatting amiably with Nena and Cedar.

"I'm ready," Bond announced, allowing his gaze to take in all three of them.

There was a pause; then Bismaquer nodded. "If you'd like to come draw for positions on the grid . . ."

"Oh . . ." Bond laughed. "Let's keep it friendly. Surely we can just toss for it here. I'm sure Walter won't mind, you—"

"James," Bismaquer said softly. Did Bond detect menace? Or was he merely edgy, jumping at verbal shadows? "James. You must understand about Walter. He takes this very seriously. I'll see if he's ready."

Left alone with the women, Bond did not even attempt small talk. "I'll say farewell now, ladies," he said, allowing his lips to break into a winning smile. "See you after the race."

"For God's sake, Bond, be careful." Cedar walked with him for a moment, speaking low. "The bastards are out to get you. Don't take any risks. It's not worth it. Please."

"Don't worry." Bond waved cheerfully, turning to see Bismaquer approaching with Walter Luxor.

Luxor was most correct. They shook hands, said "May the best man win," and tossed for the starting position on the grid. Bond lost. Luxor took the inside, right-hand lane.

Solemnly Bismaquer intoned, "This will be a race of a full ten laps of the circuit. Your lap numbers will be held up in the pits as you pass. Walter's in red; James, yours in blue. I am acting as chief marshal, and you will obey my instructions. You will drive down to your positions on the grid, then shut down your engines. I will place myself on the starter's rostrum—over there—and raise the flag. You will both indicate that you have an unrestricted view of me by giving a thumbs-up sign. I will then wave the flag in a circular motion, and you will start engines. When you are both ready, you will again signify. After that I will raise the flag, count down from ten to zero, and drop the flag. You may then drive. The flag will not come down again until the winning car passes the rostrum at the end of the tenth lap. Is that clear?"

Bond slowly steered the Saab to his place on the grid. There had been little time to think of tactics, and his mind now raced ahead. He had no real idea of the standard he faced, so his first job would be to gauge the performance of both his rival driver and the car.

He hoped the impression given during the two-lap trial run was that he had pushed the Saab to a point near its limit. Tactics had to be right now, or he would stand no chance.

As he placed the Saab on its mark, Bond made the final decision. He would let Luxor have his head for at least the first five laps. This would give him valuable experience of the circuit at various speeds and let him see whether Luxor was capable, as he suspected, of blocking any attempt to overtake by using really dangerous maneuvers.

At the beginning of the sixth lap, provided Bond could match Luxor's skill and the Saab was powerful enough to compete by staying close, he would begin to make his bid. Then, once ahead, Bond could unleash the reserve power and make a run for home. If he drove with a little dash, but within the safety limits of both car and circuit, there was the distinct possibility that he could outdistance Luxor by at least half a lap. That should be his place no later than lap eight.

Bismaquer was looking at him. Bond raised his thumb, and the flag twirled. Luxor's engine fired with a roar, denoting more power than would usually be under the hood of a Shelby-American.

The Saab grumbled quietly, and Bond glanced around, noting the distance between the two cars and at the same moment, catching Luxor's sunken eyes. They seemed to bore into him with an expression of intense hatred.

Bond faced forward and signaled to Bismaquer.

The flag went up. Bond slid into first, released the hand brake, and hovered his right foot over the accelerator.

The flag came down.

The so-called Shelby-American shook its tail as it streaked away from the grid. With such a fast start, Luxor was out to thrash him completely. As Bond started to build up power, he realized that Bismaquer's driver intended to put a lot of distance between them in the shortest possible time. He kicked down hard on the accelerator, bringing the turbo in quickly, watching the speed rise.

Already, Luxor must have been averaging a hundred on the straight before the chicane. Bond kept piling on the pressure, hearing the turbo whine like a jet engine as he thrust the gears into fifth, passing the 120 mark, bringing him close up behind the sloping fast-back of Luxor's car.

It was a matter of feet now, and Bond was forced to decelerate, changing down, to hold a hundred, riding directly behind Luxor. He saw the brake lights flicker as they came up to the chicane. Bond shifted down rather than use his brakes, easing the car through the sashay of the chicane, the speedometer showing around seventy as Luxor appeared to become airborne over the hump at the end.

Bond hit the hump at just under seventy miles an hour, leaving his hands loose on the wheel, until he felt the solid jar of the Saab come into contact with the track again. Then he shifted up, his foot toeing the accelerator.

Around a full hundred appeared to be Luxor's safe limit, and Bond followed him through the right-angle turn without letting up on speed. He allowed the Saab to drift in the Shelby-American's wake—to the right, then hard right, feeling the rear tires protest as they kept their grip. Ten of those and the rubber would start to really burn off, Bond thought. By the time the knowledge had been assimilated, they were at the Z-bend.

Here Luxor had his own technique—using the brakes constantly on the hairpins of the zigs and zags of the bend, but putting on power, even during the short runs between.

Through, and into the next straight, Bond realized they must have taken the Z at a minimum of seventy, rising to eighty. Luxor was undoubtedly not only a confident, technical expert but also a man with steel nerves. Yet, on this long straight, he hardly took the little silver car above a hundred.

Before they reached the first of the two final bends, Bond decided that Luxor cruised at around one hundred miles an hour, with a possible forty, maybe fifty in reserve for the straights when he needed it.

It was a good technique. The circuit called for accuracy at speed, and hard work as well as concentration. Outthink him, Bond whispered to himself. If he read it correctly, Luxor was going to keep up the pace until the last three, possibly four laps, and then—sure that Bond was both tired and running the Saab flatout—he would push down and surge ahead, using his maximum speed.

They flashed past the stands. Bond, at a glance, saw that the head-up display speedometer was showing a fraction above a hundred. Luxor had drawn slightly ahead.

Maybe it was time to change tactics, not to wait until later in the race. Stick with him for this one anyway; then decide when to make his first pass.

By the time they had negotiated the second lap and were screaming past the stands, Bond was sweating, working hard, still loath to use brakes, keeping a check on speed with gears and accelerator.

This would be the ideal place, he decided, as they whined on toward the chicane. As they ended the third lap, he would have a go.

The Saab was less than six feet behind the square tail of Luxor's car as they came out of the final turn on lap three. Now, he thought, watching Luxor drift slightly to the left. Not really enough room, but if he obeyed the rules, Luxor would have to let Bond through.

A fraction of pressure on the wheel and the Saab slid to the right, coming very close to the Shelby-American. Farther to the right, Bond saw the edge of the track too close to his front inside wheel, but he pressed on, up into fifth gear and a hard kick down. The turbo reacted, and he felt the push of power, like a jet engine. The Saab's nose was reaching out, halfway down Luxor's chassis, unmistakably clearing to overtake.

Then, with a jarring horror, Bond saw Luxor veer over at an angle, cutting across to stop him, increasing speed, so that Bond almost had to stand on the brakes to avoid slamming into the other car's side. In a fraction of a second, the Saab was behind again, losing ground. Bastard, Bond snarled to himself. He shifted down, dropping speed to negotiate the chicane. Once through, he put his foot down again, closing so that they went onto the right-angle bend almost locked together.

This time, Bond felt considerable drift, the Saab sliding over to the left during the final moments of the turn. Not surprising, as he glanced at the head-up digital figures of the speedometer. They registered 105, and by the time he was aware of the speed building to 125, the zigzag of the Z-bend was on them.

Try him on the far right, Bond thought. Force the bastard off the road if need be; the Saab had the weight to do it.

They came out of the Z-bend, Luxor still accelerating, and Bond, determined not to lose an inch, trying to position for a breakthrough.

Then it happened.

Later he knew he could prove nothing. The blame would be put firmly on an overheated turbo or some other excuse. At the time, however, he saw both the maneuver and the action quite plainly.

Luxor accelerated slightly, moving ahead by a few feet—three or four at the most. As Bond curled his own toes on the Saab's accelerator, he distinctly saw the small object drop away from Luxor's rear bumper. For a fraction of a second he thought Luxor was in trouble, that stress was causing a breakup of some rear component. But the whooshing noise under the Saab made the truth plain enough.

Luxor had jettisoned some form of incendiary device, set to ignite as it hit the track.

All Bond knew after that was a sheet of flame surrounding the car, engulfing him, and then rapidly dying away.

They were about midway to the penultimate bend, and James Bond at first thought the bid had failed. The enveloping flame could have been there only for a second, and he had probably outrun it at this speed. Then, with the same sense of shock, the fire warning buzzed and the red light began to blink on the dash.

One of the last things Bond had had fitted to the Saab was the relatively new DEUGRA on-board fire-detection-and-extinguisher system, marketed in Britain by Graviner. Fixed-temperature detectors—set high, and at a very fine pitch for the Saab—monitored the engine and underside of the car, especially those areas adjacent to the fuel tank. The guts of the system were situated deep within the Saab's large trunk. In a protected bed sat a seamless chrome-and-steel container, filled, under pressure, with the most efficient of extinguishants, Halon 1211. From the container, spray pipes ran to the engine compartment and around the car, particularly along the underside.

The extinguisher automatically fired when the detectors signaled a definite fire warning, while the whole system could be activated manually from a thump button on the dash. The light and buzzer warnings were also automatically operated the moment heat set off the sensors.

In the present case, fire had engulfed the car, catching the underside, thereby activating the system without further help from Bond.

Literally within seconds, ten kilograms of Halon 1211 loosed in the Saab, sweeping from underside to engine compartment, extinguishing the fire immediately and leaving no damage in its wake, for the properties of Halon are nondamaging to engine components, electrical wiring, or humans. Halon is also noncorrosive and, once the fire had been extinguished, the evaporation rate was so fast that no residue remained.

Bond, very much aware of what was going on, shifted down, braked, and took the last two bends at a moderate sixty-five. It was only when he was into the long straight—past the stand—with the knowledge that he was entering the fifth lap, that Bond opened up the car again, relieved to feel no change in engine response.

Luxor, however, was well away—a good two miles ahead, just entering the chicane. Deep within his head where anger boiled, Bond willed coolness. Luxor had deliberately attempted to burn him to death on the track—expecting the incendiary device to blow the Saab's gas tank and probably the turbo-charger at the same time.

Settling himself firmly, Bond did not waver his eyes from the road ahead. His hands ran through the gears as he increased power, roaring along the straight toward the chicane. His speed rose to over a hundred, until the little green digital figures on the head-up display steadied at 130.

Bond shifted down, but still took the chicane at his highest speed yet. The Saab rose like an aircraft rotating on takeoff, then bounced on its rear end first, almost out of control. Bond wrestled with the wheel. The screen of trees off the edge of the track slewed into vision. He heard the tires protest until he brought the car back on line, pouring on a little more speed, then slowing as the Z-bend approached.

From then onward, it was a question of using speed on the straights, without even trying to push the Saab to its full stretch, in order to gain on Luxor, who was going all-out now, clinging to his lead.

It took another two laps before the Saab came within striking distance of its adversary. Then, nose to bumper, they crossed the line once more into the eighth lap. Bond searched for his chance, jinking and pushing hard, while Luxor piled on more and more power.

Walter Luxor was rattled, Bond decided. The more he pushed, the more Luxor began taking chances. His driving was still immaculate, countering every move Bond made, but speed appeared to be his blind spot. He risked going through the chicane, the right-angle and Z-bends, with the narrowest of safety limits.

Lap nine. Only one to follow; then it would be all over. For the penultimate time, the stands blurred past them. Bond realized he was involuntarily gritting his teeth. Whatever the consequences, there had to be some way of overtaking Luxor if he was to win.

The idea germinated fast. One hope in a thousand; a risk which could end in disaster. They slid through the chicane, Luxor slowing this time as he hit the hump. Perhaps the driver's nerves were, at last, getting ragged. Now the killing, dangerous, right-angle bend.

Luxor lined himself up, keeping far to the right—his wheels almost touching the grass at the track's edge—in order to take the punishing bend at one hundred. Bond, three feet or so behind him, was himself pushing almost a hundred.

Luxor went into the turn, holding to the right, fighting the strain, to stay close to the verge for as long as possible, before pressure and speed forced the car over to the left. He reached the maximum point of turn, and the car, under the stress of angle, speed, and torque, started to slide outward. A touch on the brakes slowed him fractionally.

It was the moment Bond had been waiting for: that second before Luxor was dragged to the left and forced to slow. Bond took his final opportunity.

Instead of following directly in Luxor's slipstream, the Saab suddenly went out of line, flicking to the left. Bond checked the turn of the wheel, feeling the stress hauling the Saab even further to the left than he intended, correcting with the wheel, steering right, and knowing that if the wheels locked, he would be in a spin and off the road.

The Saab was drifting. Then, for a second, a space appeared—clear road on the bend to Luxor's left. In a moment, Luxor's car would itself be dragged into that clear area—just as it had been each time they took the right-angle bend. But in that fraction of time, Bond felt the Saab steady. He kicked on the accelerator, sensing the Saab's spoiler push the rear down onto the road. His own body was forced back into the driving seat as full power took hold.

Almost aloud, Bond prayed that the turbo's constantly increasing forward speed would overcome any further slide to the left and that he could still hold the Saab into the turn without touching the verge. The turbocharger whined, rising to a pitch of noise which should, by rights, have ended in some kind of explosion.

Then, quite suddenly, it was over. The Saab shot through on the outside of the sliding Shelby-American, the numbers on the head-up display just below the 140 line. Bond straightened the wheels and poured power through the engine.

The front of Luxor's car must have just missed grazing the Saab's rear as Bond overtook. For a moment the low body and windshield of the other car appeared to fill the Saab's rearview mirror. Then it dropped back a few feet. As they slowed to go into the Z-bend Luxor managed to stay close, as though attached by cable. But as Bond cleared the final hairpin, he slammed through the gears, up to the fifth, his right foot smoothly depressing the accelerator.

The Saab—with a clear road ahead at last—leaped forward. He touched 150 on the far straight, slowed for the two corners, and at the start of the last lap took the car right through its paces. At one point—before the chicane—the numbers hit the magic figure of 175, then a little higher on the final far straight. Luxor was now well behind by three or four miles.

It was only when Bond brought the car toward the last two bends that he began to gear down, allowing the speed to drop away. Then he took an extra lap at a relatively gentle pace, allowing the engine to settle and himself to readjust. He had seen Bismaquer's face, dark and angry, as he brought down the checkered flag, proclaiming Bond the winner.

Yet when the Saab finally coasted into the pits—with the grandstand crowd applauding even though their man had lost—Bismaquer seemed to have regained his temper. "A fair race, James. A fair and exciting race. That car of yours sure knows how to move."

Bond, dripping with sweat, did not answer immediately, but turned to watch Walter Luxor the skull face more menacing than usual—coast in behind him.

"I don't know how fair, Markus," Bond said at last. "If that's really a converted Shelby-American, I'll eat my track suit. As for the fireworks display . . ."

"Yes, what happened there?" Bismaquer's pink scrubbed face was a mask of innocence.

"I think Walter must've been having a quick cigarette and dropped a match. Look forward to my bonus, Markus. A great race. Now, if you'll excuse me . . ." He turned, walking back toward the Saab, which would certainly need his attention.

But Bismaquer was at his heels. "We'll settle all debts tonight, James—the money, I mean. And I'll take the prints. But then, I'm afraid my hospitality has got to end. Dinner tonight—at seven-thirty. Come at seven, then we can clear up the business before we eat. Okay?"

"Fine."

"I'm sorry, but I have to ask you to leave in the morning. You see, we have this conference . . . the first people are arriving tonight. . . ."

"I thought you kept clear of conferences." Bond was already halfway into the Saab, pulling on the hood release.

Bismaquer hesitated, then laughed—not the booming guffaw, but a deep nervous rumble. "Yes, yes, that's true. I can't stand conferences. Can't really stand crowds anymore. I guess that was what finally convinced me to throw in the towel in politics. Did you know I had political ambitions at one time?"

"No, but it figures," Bond lied.

"I usually keep well clear of the conferences here." Bismaquer appeared to be searching for words. "You see," he went on, "well, these people coming tonight are all automotive engineers. Walter is an expert." His face shaped into a slow, rather sly grin. "I guess you know that by now. You realize he built that Shelby replica with his own hands?"

"Extras and all?" Bond's eyebrows tilted.

Bismaquer boomed out a laugh, as if it was all a good joke. Either of us could have died out there because of that car, Bond reflected, yet Bismaquer thinks it's funny.

The bearlike man hardly paused for breath. "Well, these people being engineers and . . . Well, Walter's addressing them tomorrow morning: some very advanced talk on mechanics, I don't know what. Like a fool— and to make him happy—I promised to be there too. So there won't be much time for me to play host to Cedar and you."

Bond nodded. "Okay. We'll be away in the morning, Markus." Then he turned back to the car.

"Help yourself from the barbecue," Bismaquer called back over his shoulder.

Bond wondered when the action would start, as he watched the big man walk away, flat-footed and heavy. Either Bismaquer was going to let them off the ranch and then have them picked up outside, or he would see to it here, on the premises. If the latter, then everything could be blown. He needed to talk to Nena, among other things, and then go to ground in the conference center, his last hope to gain hard information. If Bismaquer pounced first, the whole mission would be lost.

From the start, Bond had been certain the spectacular, and lethal, hijacks were part of the resurrected SPECTRE's plan: a money-raising operation for something much bigger. All he had felt and seen since arriving in the United States—and particularly at Rancho Bismaquer—pointed toward a SPECTRE-directed coup of very large proportions. The hub lay here, as did Ernst Stavro Blofeld's successor.

Now, after Bismaquer's words, he knew that it would be necessary to drop out of sight at any moment, even if it meant leaving Cedar to face the music. Luxor or Bismaquer? he wondered. Which was the new Blofeld? Which of them held the key?

Bond's concern mounted as he worked on the Saab, then backed it toward the gas pumps. He would at least have a full tank, with an oil and coolant if warranted.

Luxor had not even bothered to come over and shake hands or congratulate him on the win. Worse, Cedar had disappeared without exchanging a word, hustled away, with Nena, by the security staff.

After the adrenaline-pumping danger of the race, James Bond now felt a reaction which came near to depression. Bismaquer could not be seen anywhere, and only a couple of chefs tended the deserted barbecue. Bond went over and helped himself to a massive steak, bread, and coffee. At least he would not go hungry.

He dealt with the Saab quickly, glancing up to the stands, which were being cleared. The only thing possible was to watch his own back, return to the cabin, then leave quickly and hide and wait until the night. Then down to Tara for dinner, armed to the teeth, strong in the hope that Bismaquer would not give an order for him to be snatched—with Cedar—before he could go to ground and get some real answers.

As the Saab drew away from the pits, a man with a neat military mustache and dressed in a white silk jacket watched from high in the grandstand. The car purred out of sight, heading for the rising wooded ground.

Mike Mazzard smiled and left the stand.

16

NENA

Even at eleven-thirty, the night seemed to have lost little heat from the day.

Bond, clad now in dark slacks, black turtleneck, and short jacket—to hide the holstered VP70—lay among the trees, covered by branches and odd ferns already gathered during the afternoon.

Around him the noises of night animals, combined with the chirruping cicadas, had become a natural background. His hearing was acute enough to break through the series of calls and songs and would pick up any human sound, should it come near.

In some senses, the events of the day had been anticlimactic. Bond, on getting back to the cabin, had taken a quick shower, changed, made certain all was ready for a fast getaway. He had laid out clothes for dinner that night and packed everything else, even the reassembled briefcase, which he locked away in the Saab.

All he carried was the set of picklocks and tools, together with the Heckler & Koch, plus spare magazines. He went through the routine quickly, leaving himself in the clothes he now wore, except for a black shirt, during the day, instead of the turtleneck which, he considered, would be more suitable later that night.

His hiding place was constructed with equal haste among the trees in a corner of the clearing, affording good sightlines of the track, cabin, and Saab. There, Bond stayed until dusk, leaving soon after six to change into the lightweight suit, decent shoes, and tie before driving down to Tara.

Bismaquer was his usual jovial self, dispensing drinks on the veranda. Cedar looked cool in dark blue skirt and blouse, while Nena sparkled, her dark eyes twinkling and that glissando laugh like music to Bond's ears.

Almost as soon as he arrived, Nena asked what he was drinking, allowing their eyes to meet, and, in that meeting, signaling she had not forgotten about their tryst.

Cedar remained calm, but she also seemed to be flashing signals at Bond—as though they needed to talk.

The only off-key note came from Walter Luxor, who sat, sullen, hardly speaking to anyone. A bad loser, Bond thought, and a man with more important things on his mind than the small talk which seemed to roll naturally from Markus Bismaquer.

After one drink, Bismaquer suggested that if Bond had brought the prints, they conclude their business. "I'm a man of my word, James." He chuckled. "Even though, like any other man, I don't like having to part with money."

Bond went down the steps to the Saab, retrieved the prints, and followed Bismaquer into the house. They went straight to the print room, where, with no fuss, Bond handed over the prints in exchange for a small briefcase, which Bismaquer opened. "Count it if you want to," he growled pleasantly. "Only, you'll miss dinner if you do. The whole amount's in there. One million for Professor Penbrunner, and another for yourself."

"I believe you." Bond closed the case. "Nice to do business, Markus. If I have anything else . . ."

"I'm sure you'll be of use to me again, James." Bismaquer gave him a quick, almost suspicious look. "In fact, I'm positive of it. Now, if you don't mind returning to the others, I'll put these away. I have a horror of anybody else knowing where I keep my really rare treasures."

Bond hefted the briefcase. "And this needs locking up, safe and sound. Thank you, Markus."

On reaching the portico again, Bond found it empty but for Cedar.

"Nena Bismaquer's talking to the cook, and the death's-head just wandered off," Cedar told him quickly.

Bond was already halfway down the steps. He called back quietly: "Come, help me put this away."

She joined him at the back of the car, and immediately Bond detected the vibrations of fear emanating from her, like an animal.

"They've got something really heavy going on, James. Christ, you had me worried in that race."

"I wasn't exactly happy myself, Cedar. But listen to me." He told her, in a few words, that—provided they were both alone when dinner was over—he would be returning to the cabin. "I'm going to do exactly as we planned, only Bismaquer's given us marching orders for tomorrow morning. I suspect they plan to let us get clear and then really nail us, but I could be quite wrong. There's a chance they'll snatch both of us here, tonight, on the ranch. Do you still have that weapon?"

She gave a little nod, whispering that it was strapped to the inside of her thigh and that it was damned uncomfortable too.

"Right." Bond, having put the briefcase in the trunk, slammed it shut and twisted the key. "As soon as you can, after dinner, I want you to get out. Don't come anywhere near the knoll or the cabin, but around dawn try to make your way to the place I told you about, where I'm going to stash the Saab. Steal a car, walk, do it any way you can. But get out. Don't get too near, just hide and watch. Meeting and pickup times as we arranged."

"Okay. There're things to tell you, though, James."

"Quickly, then."

"They know exactly who and what we are," she began. "And Mike Mazzard arrived last night."

"And the other three hoods?"

"I don't know, but Mazzard got hell from Luxor for not being able to control his men. Apparently they were acting without orders in Washington. No harm was to come to you, James. I'm not so sure about myself—they called me Cedar Leiter, by the way—but they want you alive."

"The car race . . . ?"

"Was to keep you off-balance. And the harvester ants as well. They *knew* you weren't going to be in that cabin. The ants were definitely meant for me. Apparently you're fireproof. You should have heard Luxor, he really let Mike Mazzard have it. That's all for sure, James. I heard everything. Orders are that you're to be kept on tap but not killed."

"Well . . ."

"That's not all. Something's happened over at the warehouse."

Bond made questioning noises.

"I saw by accident. A refrigerated truck came out of the trees at the back of the warehouse late this afternoon, and there are at least two more down there. The first truck was heading toward the airfield. They're moving that ice cream."

Bond's brow was lined in thought. "I wish we knew more," he murmured. "Perhaps I will by tomorrow night. Be very careful, though; if it's some criminal or terrorist activity and we've vanished, they'll be digging the place up to find us. I—" He stopped, conscious that somebody had come onto the portico.

A second later, Nena Bismaquer spoke. "James? Cedar? Didn't anyone call you? Dinner's served."

They went back up the steps, and Cedar entered the house first, leaving Bond to shepherd Nena through the great high doors. She let Cedar get well ahead, then turned, saying softly to Bond, "James. I'll be with you as soon as I can after dinner. Please be careful. It's very dangerous. We have to talk."

Bond merely bowed his head to signal he understood. The black eyes gave his a pleading look, quite out of character with the sophisticated, very beautiful Frenchwoman who now walked past him, striding with poise toward the dining room.

So now Bond waited in his hiding place in the trees. For Nena? Almost certainly, he thought. Though it could well be something else. During dinner there had been some tension, and Bismaquer had undergone a sudden change of character on two occasions, once in the way he spoke to the servants, and once to Nena. Perhaps the strain was starting to tell. From what he and Cedar had observed, something was about to happen. If Bismaquer was, indeed, the new Blofeld, the mask could be about to crack.

Was it significant, he wondered, lying in the dark, that Walter Luxor had not stayed to dine with them? According to Bismaquer, the skeleton of a man had gone off to prepare his speech for the next day.

Luxor or Bismaquer? Bond still wondered, his eyes—now accustomed to the darkness—watching for the slightest movement.

He shifted to glance at his watch. The dial glowed clearly. Eleven-thirty-five, and at that moment he heard the distant sound of a motor.

Bond turned his head, trying to gauge direction. The sound was approaching from below. A small car, he judged, as he distinctly heard the gear change and the engine alter as it began its climb up the long track, through the trees.

About five minutes later the headlights shafted into the clearing, followed by the little car itself, a small black sports model which Bond could not immediately identify.

The car pulled up directly behind the Saab. Shutting it in, Bond thought to himself. If he wanted out quickly, he would have to clear the open space in a fast turn.

The driver killed the engine and lights. Through the night air, Bond heard the rustle of silk. He could just make out Nena Bismaquer, standing beside the car, then her voice calling quietly, "James? James, are you there?"

Softly Bond surfaced. He crossed the clearing, one hand ready near the holstered VP70. She did not hear him until he was almost behind her.

"Oh, my God. Oh, James, don't *do* things like that." Nena, quivering, clung to him.

"You told me to take care." Bond smiled down at her.

Nena Bismaquer was still dressed as she had been at dinner—a pleated silk dress patterned in white and black, very simple but revealing her particular style and personality. Simple, maybe, Bond thought, his hand touching the smooth and provocative material, but he would bet a month's salary on this little creature costing a fortune.

"Can we go inside, James? Please." Her lips close to his. Once more Bond smelled her particular scent, the clean fresh hair, though now it was mingled with something very expensive: the touch of a distillation, probably unique, and made especially for Markus Bismaquer's wife. For a moment Bond felt a tiny pang of jealousy. Then she urged him again. "Please, James. Inside, please."

Bond took a step forward, letting Nena enter the cabin first, then switching on the light. Almost as the cabin door closed behind them, she was in his arms, trembling, then pulling away. "I should not have come." Her voice took on the same breathless quality he had heard in the Saab when they first kissed.

"Why, then?" Bond wrapped his arms around her, feeling her turn inward toward him, pressing her limbs close to his.

"Why do you think?" She lifted her face and kissed him on the lips, pulling back again quickly. "No. Not yet, anyway. I don't know what's going on, James. All I can tell you is that Markus and Walter are both out for blood. They're doing something really dangerous, James. That's all I know, all I can tell you. Both of them, they hide everything from me. Men came last night, men from the East, from New York. I heard some of the conversation. Walter said that if he didn't win on the racetrack today . . ."

"You looked relaxed enough at the track."

"There was no way to warn you, James. You could see. I was surrounded by Markus' men. You have to get away, James."

"Markus has asked us to go in the morning."

"Yes. Yes, I know . . . but . . ." She clung closer. "But they'll be waiting, I know that. There are a lot of new people around, and I think they have the ranch surrounded—dogs, half-tracks. Is that right, half-tracks?"

"They'd be useful in desert conditions, yes." Bond did not say that he thought as much. Bismaquer was verbally acting as a sheep dog, moving them out and into the arms of waiting killers.

"Listen, Nena." He held her away by the shoulders, roused by her presence, the smooth skin against his hands, and the feel of the silk. "Listen hard. Cedar is going. *I* am going. We're both vanishing. Not tomorrow, as Markus wants, but tonight—or in the early hours. I know something's up, so we're going to earth here, on the ranch, until one of us can get clear."

"If it's you, James, don't take chances. From what I've heard, they really have got the place surrounded. Is it the money, perhaps? I don't know."

In the short silence that followed, there came the roar of a heavy aircraft flying over the ranch.

Nena looked toward the cabin's rafters. "That'll be part of the delegation coming in. Two separate flights tonight. Either that, or one of Markus' freighters—"

"Freighters?"

She gave a small, nervous laugh. "Oh, his damned ice cream. He's in the middle of something criminal, horrible—I know that—but he can't leave the ice cream alone. He's got yet another new flavor, and he's sold it to some distributor somewhere. Tons of it. They're shipping it out tonight."

Ice cream going to some distributor, Bond thought. Would it be straight, or spiked with whatever dreadful drug Luxor and Bismaquer had concocted? The stuff he'd seen in action, turning men into pliable pleasant monsters who would obey, even to the selling of their wives and loved ones.

"Where are you going to hide?" she asked.

"No!" Bond was sharp. "Better you should not know anything, then they can't get at you as well. We'll just disappear. Hang on, Nena. Just hang on and wait. Someone will come, I'll see to that. Then the whole thing'll be over."

"Will I see you again?"

"Of course."

He felt her hand drop to his thigh. "I haven't long." She moved very close now, whispering in his ear. "James, just in case something happens . . ." She did not need to finish the sentence.

Gently Bond led her in the direction of the bedroom, crossing to the bed and turning on the night-table lamp.

"No, my darling James. No lights. In the dark."

"That's a little old-fashioned. . . ."

"For my sake. No lights."

He nodded, switched off the lamp, and climbed out of his clothes, hearing the noise of her dress sliding over her head.

Naked and lying on the bed, Bond was about to place the automatic within reach when a sudden instinct took his hand up to the lamp again. "Sorry, Nena. I've got to have some light."

She gave a little cry as the lamp came on, revealing her slim and lithe sun-brown figure, with those magnificent long legs. She was dressed only in silk bra and panties. She was in the act of unclipping her bra.

"James. I asked you . . ." She stopped, realizing that her voice had turned harsh, like a whiplash.

Bond apologized. "I'm sorry. Jittery, Nena, that's all. I don't think we should be in the dark. You look so lovely, so why the modesty?"

Her face crumpled as she came slowly toward the bed. "You would have found out. Just as Markus found out. Everybody. It can't be helped.

James, I'm not a whole woman. I didn't want you to see me. It's always been like this. I . . . I . . . I feel deformed, and I don't like people . . ."

He pulled her down onto the bed, a hand searching for her. Nena's mouth opened, locking against his, and they were off again into a whirlpool of emotions, their mouths acting out the desires of their bodies.

Presently she pulled away. "The light, James. Can we have it . . . ?"

"Show me." Bond was determined. "Whatever it is, there can't be any harm in seeing . . ."

She slid sideways onto him, her hands going to the clasp on her bra. Bond noticed that she could not look him in the eyes. "I was born like this, James. I'm sorry. Some people—like Markus—find it revolting."

Sliding her bra away, she revealed the truth. The left side of her chest was smooth and flat as that of a young boy, perfectly formed but with no female beast. On the right side, the firm, beautiful curve of one glorious breast—full and golden.

Strangely, perhaps because her one breast was so wonderful, an exact half-globe with a proportioned brown-and-pink nipple erect, the oddity appeared more erotic to Bond.

He pulled her close, one hand cupping her. "Dear, lovely Nena. You *are* unique. You're beautiful. There's nothing revolting about you. Certainly you're *not* a half-woman. Let me show you that."

Slowly, punctuating his actions with kisses, Bond completed undressing her, and she wrapped herself around him, so that, for an hour or so, the evil which surrounded them in this strange, manmade desert island melted away—taking them into other worlds and to higher peaks, shrinking, eventually, to two human beings turned by the magic of the love act into one.

Nena left around four in the morning, with constant kisses and worried admonitions for Bond to be on his guard. "I *shall* see you again, James? Tell me I shall see you again."

Bond kissed her hard on the mouth and told her they would certainly be together again.

"If . . ." she told him finally, as they got to her car, "if anything does go wrong, James, rely on me. If it happens here, I'll do my best to help. I love—"

Bond stopped her with a last kiss. "It's too easy to say." He smiled in the darkness. "Just think of what we've had, and hope for more."

He stood near the Saab, in the clearing, watching the little car's lights disappear into the trees. Then, refreshed and cleansed by the loving contact of another person, Bond gathered his things together, climbed into the Saab, and drove away, using only parking lights. He took the route down the track, then the road bordering the knoll, climbing up the far side to the hidden cutoff where he had sat with Nena, hearing her story of poverty in Paris and the dream of wealth turned sour with Bismaquer.

Having concealed the car as well as possible, he set out for the last long walk that would take him to the conference center.

There was not much time left before dawn—less than two hours, he supposed—so Bond, still lightly dressed, carrying only the Heckler & Koch automatic, spare ammunition, and the ring with its picklocks and tools, adopted the old commando speed-marching technique of alternate fast walking and running.

The trek was farther than even he had gauged, and the darkness of night had already given way to that gray half-light before dawn by the time he reached the manhole cover on the edge of the jungle. The metal cover came away easily, and Bond threw the big handle underneath, watching, and willing, the large slab of stone to move faster on its hydraulic jacks.

Once the entrance was clear, he replaced the metal cover and climbed down inside the tiled chamber, looking around the mechanism which Nena had assured him was there to seal the stone from the inside. He was a good twelve feet underground and could see the entrance to the tunnel itself, lit by small blue bulbs which glowed into the distance.

The mechanism was there—near the final rung of metal holds. Pulling the lever below ground brought the hydraulic sound even closer, so that the whole tunnel seemed to reverberate as the stone slab lifted itself back into place. The faint light which had filtered in through the opening was now obliterated, and Bond was bathed in the low, eerie blue light which did not even reflect off the white tiles.

The tunnel was curved at the top, to the height of around eight feet, and wide enough for a man of Bond's size to stretch out his arms and just touch the walls with his fingertips.

From the initial chamber, one could walk straight through the tunnel archway, and Bond had not gone far when he noticed the ground angle to a slightly downward slope. There was no sound, and no dank chill, as he had expected. The rope-soled moccasins, which he had chosen to wear for comfort, made little noise; yet he still took the precaution of stopping every minute or so to stand listening for any sounds coming from either ahead or behind. If the complex was already in use, there was always the possibility of Bismaquer's people using this entrance to move freely between the ranch and the center.

He encountered nobody, though the walk was long—about a mile, Bond judged. The ground first sloped down, then seemed to flatten for a few hundred yards before it rose again. On the far side, the rise was steeper. After the speed march from the knoll, Bond could now feel his thigh muscles protesting with a dull ache.

He plodded on, as silently as before. Soon the path he followed began to rise even more steeply and to turn in a slow curve. Then, with hardly any warning, the whole tunnel widened and the end was in sight: another arched entrance to a chamber, this one larger than the entrance from the road.

Facing Bond was a smooth, tiled wall. He turned to examine the entire chamber, remembering Nena had told him there was a mechanism at this end too, which led to a janitor's closet. She had given him no details, however, of the device. All Bond could see in the bath of blue light were the smooth, tiled walls. No boxes, metal covers, or switches.

Logic told him that the wall facing him as he came into the chamber was the most likely exit point. Further, it seemed that if the door was at the rear of a closet, the handle, or whatever was used, would be situated in line with a man's hand.

Starting with the center of the wall, Bond began to examine the individual tiles one by one, working along the rows methodically. He pushed and probed each tile in turn, until, after fifteen minutes or so, he found the right spot. The tile slid back on a small metal runner, operating like a model of a push-up garage door. Behind it was a perfectly normal doorknob.

Gently he tried the knob. Part of the tiling moved, and as Bond pulled back, a whole section was revealed as a hinged door. The door moved noiselessly, with great ease. On the far side was a plaster wall, complete with shelves—the shelving angled to the left, so that the door could carry parts of the shelves back with it.

Bond stepped out, holding the door back until he had checked out the handle on the far side, which was, in fact, hidden out of sight, directly under one of the shelves. Only then did he allow the door behind him to close.

The closet afforded little room—enough for a man of reasonable build to hide behind its normal door, about a pace and a half from the rows of shelves.

Once the secret door was closed, Bond had to wait for a moment so that his eyes could adjust to the now complete darkness before edging toward the main closet.

Again he found himself turning the handle gently and, this time, pushing the door outward.

After the blue light and silence of the tunnel, it was startling to hear noise. Men's and women's voices echoed from above and to the side. The passageway in which Bond stood—by the closet door—was flooded with light. A window, almost adjacent, showed him that dawn had well and truly broken, and sunlight poured in.

The whole journey down from the knoll and the long walk through the tunnel had taken him much longer than he imagined. Glancing at his watch, Bond saw it was almost seven-thirty. At least that would reduce the waiting time. But where to wait? How could he infiltrate the conference without being immediately noticed?

Leaving the closet door open for a quick getaway, Bond took a few steps into the passageway. The voices were very loud and seemed close at hand, possibly just around the angle at the end of the passageway some twenty feet away. The sounds reminded him of something, and it took a moment to sort out the various combinations in his head—the lively chatter, the clink of china. He was somewhere near to a communal dining room.

From the window, Bond could see out across a wide lawn, in the center of which a large white stone H had been inlaid among the grass. In the far distance was a tall wire fence, then a wall above which the greenery of jungle showed clearly. He was looking out directly onto a helipad.

Turning back toward the closet, Bond spotted a pair of double doors, each with a panel of thick clear glass in the upper half. In neat gold script a legend told him that the doors led to the conference hall. He crossed the passageway to peer through the glass panel, immediately moving to one side, out of sight.

The quick look had revealed a plush hall, like a modern and most exclusive theater. Row upon row of tip-back, well-padded chairs ran in a wide crescent, aisles cutting through them like a sunburst. At the front of the seats was a wide stage, already prepared with a long table, behind which stood a dozen chairs. In front of the table—downstage center—a microphone appeared to be guarding a large lectern, while behind, like a backdrop, hung a movie screen.

The conference hall was not empty. At least a dozen of Bismaquer's security men were passing through the hall, a couple of them with dogs and some armed with explosive-detection devices and antibugging sniffers.

They were—it was obvious—screening the hall before use. Before Walter Luxor's paper to the automotive engineers? Bond wondered. Or was it really Markus Bismaquer who was going to address the meeting?

Alert now, Bond realized that some of the Bismaquer security people were quite near the far side of the conference-hall doors. Silently he moved back inside the janitor's closet, the Heckler & Koch automatic steady in his hand with the safety off. The security men could well pass this way; on the other hand, other Bismaquer aides might even now be using the tunnel.

No sooner was he inside the closet, the door not quite closed, than there came the sound of the security men emerging into the passage. Voices were quite clear, only a foot or so away.

"Okay?" a man said.

"They all say it's clear, Mack," from a second voice.

Then a third. "You went right under that damned stage, didn't you, Joe?"

"Right under, right through the access flap down there on the left. Took my flashlight, too. It's clean as a new bar of soap down there. 'Cept for the dirt and spiders and all."

There was a chorus of laughter, and Bond guessed the inspection was now finished.

"What time they coming over?" someone asked.

"The ladies and gentlemen have to be in their seats, ready and waiting, by eight-forty-five. That's the order. Eight-forty-five, sharp."

"Well, we all got plenty of time, then. Let's get some chow ourselves."

"Is Blofeld coming over?" It was the man called Joe who asked, and Bond felt the hair on his neck bristling with anticipation.

"Guess so. Won't do the talking, though. Never does."

"No. Too bad. Okay, fellas, let's tell the folks where they've got to be, and when . . ."

The voices receded, the clarity blurring, then vanished altogether. Bond heard boots clicking down the passage. The cleaning squad had gone.

Bond did not have to think about his next move. He stepped from the closet, gun still in hand, glancing up and down the passage. It was clear. A few seconds later he was inside the conference hall and running down one of the aisles, making for what the voice had described as "the access flap" on the left of the stage.

Within another five seconds he had found it, an ordinary hinged flap with a recessed brass ring to lift it up. Bond had the flap up and had crawled under the stage within sixty-five seconds of leaving the janitor's closet.

All he had to do now was wait. At eight-forty-five the delegates would start coming in. Then, soon after that, Blofeld would arrive. Not the Blofeld he had killed, but the new Blofeld. The name was in the open now, and soon, James Bond knew, he would be able to identify the man from his two suspects. Would it be Luxor or Bismaquer himself? He knew which one his money would ride on.

17

HEAVENLY WOLF

LYING SILENT IN the dark under the conference-hall stage, Bond pondered again the question of Blofeld—the original man, the first leader of SPECTRE. Was his successor—the here-and-now leader—a relative? In organizations like this, a chain of command would not necessarily demand kinship. Yet, having known and fought Ernst Stavro Blofeld, Bond knew there had been a streak of dynastic ambition about him. The king is dead; long live the king.

When Blofeld had died at his hands, some provision must have been made for a future leader, even if that person did not immediately appear— and there had certainly been a lengthy period before SPECTRE rose again.

Bond considered the arrogance, cunning, and madness of the original Blofeld—the shadowy figure he had first glimpsed, through reports, who worked behind the cover of the Fraternité Internationale de la Résistance Contre l'Oppression, in Paris, on the boulevard Haussmann.

A man of many faces, yes. Disguise, with Blofeld, had been a way of life, and with those various faces came the same utter sense of purpose: the complete ruthlessness and determination.

Bond thought of the known lineage—half Polish, half Greek—born in

Gydnia, and a wizard with money. If the new Blofeld was related, then Bond still had scores to settle. The death of his beloved wife of but a few hours was already revenged. Ernst Stavro Blofeld had paid the ultimate penalty for that; but now Bond again made a silent vow: anyone remotely connected with the original Blofeld would also pay. The light of his own happiness had been extinguished without compassion. Why, then, should he show compassion now?

He felt his own fatigue begin to swamp him and thought of Nena. If anyone commanded compassion, it was this gorgeous lady—undeniably mistreated by her husband and put psychologically off-balance by a deformity which made her feel only part woman. This was nonsense, of course, as Bond had proved to her. Poor wretched woman. When this was over, he thought, Nena would need some very special care. A picture of her, naked on his bed, came vividly into his mind, and it was still with this image in his mind that Bond drifted into sleep.

He woke with a start. Noise around him—the babble of conversation. Shaking sleep from him like a dog, Bond stretched his limbs and settled down to listen. Out there a large audience—male and female—was already gathered. He looked at his Rolex, gleaming in the darkness. It was almost nine o'clock.

A minute or so later, the murmur of the audience subsided. Applause took its place, rising to a thunder as Bond heard feet, heavy, on the stage itself, above him.

Slowly the applause diminished. There were some coughs, a clearing of throats, and then a voice—not Bismaquer's, as he had expected, but the thin reed of Walter Luxor. There was a difference, though. As Luxor spoke, so the odd high notes altered. The dreadfully disfigured man appeared to find a new confidence, testing his vocal cords until he caught the acoustics of the hall, at which the voice dropped down the scale.

"Ladies and gentlemen. Fellow members of the executive council of SPECTRE. World section heads of our organization. Welcome." Luxor paused. "As you see, our Leader—Blofeld—is among us, but he has asked me to speak to you. It is I who have been at the center of planning for the operation which, until now, we have spoken of simply as HOUND.

"Let us dispense with the preliminaries as quickly as possible. Time is short. We have known from the outset that when the moment came, it would come quickly—leaving little time for maneuver. That moment is at hand.

"To set your minds at rest, you should first know two things. The very large sums of money earned from those daring, and, I must say, imaginative series of airplane operations, have proved to be ample for our purposes.

"Secondly, we have had a client for the major objective of our present operation for some time now. If all goes well, the profit from HOUND will not only fill SPECTRE's coffers but also give each and every member of our organization a handsome return on investment."

Bond heard an outbreak of applause, which then died as quickly as it began. Then Luxor seemed to be shuffling and rearranging his papers. Bond heard him clear his throat and begin again. "I do not wish to make this into a marathon briefing. However, there are certain strategic and tactical points which must first be made clear to you. This is necessary so that a full understanding of the military and political situations can be grasped.

"The world, as we all know, appears to be on a permanent brink of chaos. There are the usual wars, terrorism, skirmishes, and rumors of war. The people are afraid. It should be quite plain to us all that many of their fears are fomented and manipulated by the military men and politicians of the so-called superpowers.

"We see marches, demonstrations, and pressure groups building, particularly within the Western powers. These action groups are motivated by fear: fear of a nuclear holocaust. So, as we hear and see, people take to the streets in an attempt to halt what they see as a nuclear arms race.

"We, of course—like the great military strategists—know that the whole business of a conventional nuclear arms race is a piece of neat misdirection. Agitators, foolish and ill-informed people, see only a nuclear threat." He gave a tiny dismissive cackle of laughter. "What they do not see is that the bogeymen—the neutron bombs, cruise missiles, intercontinental ballistic missiles—are merely makeshift weapons, temporary means of attack and defense. The same applies to the coast-to-coast tracking systems and the idiocies that are proclaimed about the airborn early-warning systems, such as the AWACS Sentry aircraft. All these things are like slingshots, to be used as stopgaps until the real armament is unleashed.

"The problem is fear—fear that homes, countries, lives, are at stake. Those who take to the streets and demonstrate can think only in terms of war here on this planet. They do not see that in a matter of a very few years now, the ICBM's and the cruise missiles will be negated, outdated, useless. The so-called arms race is purposely being allowed to dominate the public mind, while the superpowers pursue the real arms race: the race to provide the true weapons of attack and defense—most of which will not be used here on this planet, earth, at all.''

There was a shuffling among the audience before Luxor continued.

"What I am about to tell you is already common knowledge among the world's leading scientists and military experts. The arms race is now *not* directed toward the stockpiling and tactical deployment of nuclear or neutron weapons, though that is exactly what both Soviet and American propaganda would like people to believe.

"No." Luxor thumped his lectern, sending vibrations through the joists and boards above Bond's head. "No. The arms race is really concerned with one thing—the perfection of an ultimate weapon which will render all existing nuclear weapons utterly impotent." Luxor gave his reedy laugh again. "Yes, ladies and gentlemen, this is the mad scientist's dream, the plots of science fiction for years past. But now the fiction has become *fact.*"

Bond held his breath, already knowing what was to come. Luxor would, he was certain, talk about the ultrasecret Particle Beam Weapon.

"Until recently," Luxor went on, "the Soviet Union was undoubtedly ahead in its program for the development of what is known as a Particle Beam Weapon, a charged-particle device, very similar to a laser, combined with microwave propagators. Such a weapon is indeed well on the way to finalization, and this weapon can, and will, act as a shield—an invisible barrier—to ward off any possibility of nuclear attack.

"As I have said, the Particle Beam Weapon was thought to be more advanced in the Soviet Union than in the United Staes. We now know that *both* superpowers have reached roughly the same point in development. Within a few years—a very few years—the balance of power could either swing dramatically in one direction or become absolute on both sides. For the Particle Beam is designed to effectively neutralize any of the existing nuclear delivery systems.

"The superpowers can escalate millions of cruise missiles, ICBM's, or rocket-delivered neutron bombs. Much good will it do them. Therefore they are *not* stockpiling these arms. The Particle Beam—once operational—will prevent any country from launching a conventional nuclear attack. Particle Beam means absolute neutralization. Stalemate. Billions of dollars' worth of scrap metal sitting in silos all over the globe. If one superpower wins the Particle Beam race, then that power holds the entire world in thrall.

"The arms race hinges on this superweapon of defense; time is at stake, and any nuclear actions must be held off until the race is won. In turn, this means we must fully understand what nuclear action really means; and, to see this, we have to look, not at those dreaded missiles and bombs, but at the strategic devices which make their use possible."

Bond shifted uneasily. He knew that all Luxor was saying made complete sense, even though, for a nonscientist, it did sound like high-flown fiction. Bond had the advantage of having already been briefed, along with other Service officers. He had spent hours poring over pages of technical data, and reading long, if simplified, reports on the Particle Beam Weapon. As Luxor said, it *was* a fact, and both the United States and the Soviet Union were now neck and neck in this, the most important arms race in history.

Luxor now started to talk about the current highly advanced satellites actually in space, orbiting or stationary, operational and fully active: that whole series of hardware which made an immediate nuclear confrontation and conflagration possible.

"It is really a question of old military strategy," Luxor continued, "History can always teach mankind The problem is that to learn from history—particularly in military matters—man must adapt. For instance, World War Two began as a failure for the greater part of Europe because the military thinking of the so-called Allies was based on the strategy of former wars. But the world had changed, and with those changes came a new strategy.

"Now, at this crucial point in history, we have to think, strategically, in a very different environment. An American senator once said, 'He who controls space controls the world.' There is also an old military maxim which says you must always control the higher ground. Both these statements are true. Now, the high ground is space, and space controls the nuclear potential of nations until the Particle Beam race is won or lost.

"So, member of SPECTRE, it is our task to provide our present clients with the means to control space until that race is won."

Luxor continued, giving a great deal of information about the present satellites in use—the reconnaissance satellites: Reconsats and electronic ferrets, Big Bird and Key Hole II; the radar satellites, such as the White Cloud system; the Block 5D-2 military weather satellites which carry banks of solar cells, giving each satellite a greater longevity, plus a broad and very accurate coverage of world weather conditions.

Bond's anxiety increased. The facts—simple and incomplete—concerning these satellites were easily obtainable. But Walter Luxor showed a knowledge far and above any published data. The information he now passed on to the SPECTRE audience was of the most highly classified variety.

The same turned out to be true when he came to talk about the military communications satellites—the DSCS-2's; DSCS-3's; and the Flastcom systems for naval communications. There was also highly confidential material on the SDS—the Satellite Data Systems—which tracked and monitored all the hardware of space. The man, Bond could hear, knew exactly what he was talking about; and the bulk of it was considered highly secret, and sensitive, on both sides of the Atlantic.

After about an hour and a half of the session, Luxor announced that they would break for some light refreshment. Bond again heard the footsteps move above him and listened, with ears straining, as the audience left the hall.

For a while, he had thought SPECTRE's plan centered on the United States' progress with the Particle Beam Weapon, but this, he now guessed, was wrong. They were after the satellite systems already in operation. The primary targets in any conventional nuclear war—which would all be changed on the advent of the Particle Beam Weapon—had to be the communications and reconnaissance satellites, for they were the heart of military strength in an age of long-range warfare.

But where would SPECTRE wish to strike? How, and what, would be their target? Slowly James Bond realized the full implications of HOUND. Of course. HOUND. Why had he not thought of it before? Hound? Wolf? The Space Wolves, as they were called. The United States was well ahead there. SPECTRE's target was the Space Wolves; but before Bond could follow through along this line of thought, there were sounds from the auditorium, as already people filed back. Then, within minutes, the complete target and action was revealed.

Luxor quickly called the audience to order and launched into the second part of his briefing in a brisk, concise manner.

"The long preamble during our first session," he began, "was necessary for us to come to the heart of our project.

"The control of space, ladies and gentlemen, means the ability to neutralize the enemy's eyes and ears in space. It has been considered, for a long time now, that the Soviets had a fair, if limited, capability for space control. They were able, in theory, to neutralize United States satellites within a twenty-four-hour time scale. It was also thought that the United States had no such capability. In the past eighteen months, however, this has proved to be incorrect. The killersats, as they have been called, have now emerged as the current essential weapons. Powerful weapons. That power, my good colleagues, lies totally with the United States."

"It has, of course, been denied that any such satellites are in orbit. But there is no doubt that the United States has at least twenty laser-equipped killersats already in space, disguised as weather satellites. They also have the capability of launching over two hundred of these weapons in a matter of minutes."

Luxor again paused. Bond felt the anxiety in his throat and a twanging, like a plectrum, at his nerve ends. Once more, he had seen the documentation and knew the truth.

"Our problem," Luxor continued, "or, I should say, our client's problem, is that these satellite craft are hidden under one of the most successful security schemes ever mounted by the United States. We know the satellites are laser-armed; that they have a superlative chase ability; and that these facts are held on computer tapes and microfilm — their numbers, place, present orbital patterns, position of silos, order of battle. All this information exists, and is, naturally, required by our clients.

"The full intelligence concerning these killersats is held in the Pentagon. But the Americans have been so careful to isolate each section of information that our two sources inside the Pentagon reported, some months ago, that theft was virtually impossible. In fact, we have lost a great deal of time attempting to procure microfilm and other documentation in this manner. Each attempt has led to failure.

"However, there is another way. By the year 1985, these weapons — known, in military jargon, as Space Wolves — will be controlled and operated through See-Sok, an abbreviation for the lengthy title North American Air Defense Command's Consolidation Space Operations Center."

There was polite laughter, which seemed to ease the tension in the hall. Luxor went on to say that See-Sok was already under construction. Vast modifications were being carried out at Peterson Air Force Base, not far from the existing NORAD — North American Defense Command — headquarters, deep within Cheyenne Mountain in Colorado.

"And until See-Sok becomes operational" — Luxor's voice rose to its high pitch again — "until Peterson field is converted, the Space Wolves are controlled from NORAD headquarters in Cheyenne Mountain. That, fellow members of SPECTRE, is the weak link.

"Because NORAD HQ controls the Space Wolves, all information must be available to the headquarters. And so it is. Where it has been hidden away, in segments, at the Pentagon, it lies open and together, on the computer tapes in Cheyenne Mountain."

It was all true enough; Bond could vouch for that. But the really big question still had to be answered. How did you walk into the well-screened NORAD HQ and lift computer tapes giving every detail of the Space Wolves? Bond had a feeling that under Blofeld's instructions, Luxor was about to answer the question. At least, Bond thought, he now knew that Blofeld equaled Bismaquer. Luxor was the specialist in many fields, but the final planning would go to SPECTRE's leader: Markus Bismaquer, ice-cream maker and squire of Rancho Bismaquer.

"Operation Heavenly Wolf," Luxor intoned. "That is the true name for project HOUND. Object: to penetrate NORAD headquarters and bring out all the computer tapes carrying information on the U.S. Space Wolves.

"Method? We have considered two possibilities and rejected one, the obvious one: an assault using all SPECTRE's forces. However, our Leader, Blofeld, has come up with a positively brilliant alternative."

As Luxor began to explain Operation Heavenly Wolf, many of the dark pieces of the jigsaw fell into place. "Simplicity," Luxor maintained, "is often the answer to all things. Here, at this very ranch, we have been doing two things which have now provided the key to Cheyenne Mountain. First, as you know, we have an ice-cream-manufacturing plant on the premises. We have also made many contacts, including supplying the distributors of foodstuffs to military bases. One such is the sole distributor to NORAD headquarters."

Luxor paused. Bond could also see him smiling that ghastly gaping grin.

"Ladies and gentlemen, we have just sent that distributor four days' supply of ice cream. Apparently they consume a great deal of ice cream at NORAD—it must be the atmosphere within the mountain, and those long hours spent underground. We are told that over ninety percent of the staff and technicians eat ice cream regularly.

"The very large consignment which we have just shipped is not, moreover, a normal brand. We have also developed the ultimate in happiness—a mild narcotic, harmless and with no side effects. It produces a state of euphoric well-being, an ability to operate normally but with a suspended sense of moral right or wrong. Anyone taking even a minimum dosage will obey, without question, the orders of a superior. He or she would even kill his best friend or most loved wife or husband."

Bond nodded to himself, thinking of the two men he had seen in the padded cell off the laboratory.

"What is more"—Luxor sounded highly pleased with himself—"our most recent tests have proved that the effects of our happy cream last up to twelve hours. Tomorrow at around noon, the shipment will go into

Cheyenne Mountain. We are reliably informed that distribution will start tomorrow night. This means that Operation Heavenly Wolf begins after lunch on the day after tomorrow. We simply go in, ask for the Space Wolves computer tapes, and they will give them to us. They will also smile happily while they commit this gross act of treason."

"Is it really as simple as that?" a voice called from the audience.

"Not quite." Luxor's voice generated confidence. "Naturally, there will be some officers, technicians, and enlisted men who will spurn our dessert. Ten percent, according to our latest information. We may well, therefore, encounter some slight unpleasantness. Also, you must remember, the drug works only if commands are given by somebody with authority and seniority. Therefore, we plan to give NORAD HQ a surprise inspection by a four-star general. In fact, it will be the new inspector general of Air/Space Defense. I've arranged for the officer commanding NORAD HQ to be warned of his arrival roughly an hour before he makes an entrance—together with, say twenty or thirty aides and military personnel. All will be armed, of course, and ready to handle the unlucky few who reject our ice cream. A sad prospect, I admit, to die for not liking such a delicious dessert."

There were chuckles around the room, and one voice asked who was to wear the lucky four stars.

There followed a terrible silence. It was as though the questioner, in his jesting way, suddenly realized he had put his foot in it—making a most ghastly error by even asking.

Bismaquer, Bond thought—Blofeld himself—would be the four-star general. Nobody else would do. Then came Luxor's voice, chilling, like a sharp piece of ice forced into his gullet.

"We have someone very special in mind for that job," he rasped. "Someone *very* special indeed. Poor fellow. I'm afraid he will not survive the ordeal. Now, we must decide on schedules, times, weapons, and escape routes. May I have the map, please?"

It was almost noon. In twelve hours, Bond thought, Cedar would be at the roadside tunnel entrance with the Saab. If her luck held. Meanwhile Bond had twelve hours to remain hidden, listening under the stage, sorting out facts in his mind. Then, once the hall emptied, to find somewhere to wait until he could safely negotiate the trek back down the tunnel. After that, assuming Cedar was on time, they would either have to fight their way out or find some way for Bond to draw the fire, priming Cedar with the bare information so that she could get help.

In any case, one of them had to make it. Until the real arms race for the Particle Beam Weapon was won or lost, the United States—possibly all of the Western powers—needed the Space Wolf satellites, for they were the one big edge over any aggressor.

In the middle of his personal tension, 007 recognized a chilling prospect: the one person in all the West who might yet be able to avert disaster was . . . James Bond.

18

SHOCK TACTICS

BOND HAD LOOKED forward to emerging from the tunnel into a deep velvet-blue night, with stars like diamonds. In fact he came out through the roadside opening into a steambath of hot air, with the sky at war. Far away, great sheets of lightning sizzled and cracked, while distant thunder rolled—as though heaven had taken a preemptive strike into its own hands.

He drew a deep breath, hoping for fresh air, and inhaled only the cloying damp scents of the jungle area. Muttering belligerently, Bond operated the lever, returning the slab of stone to its proper place.

Hidden for so long under the conference-hall stage, Bond had been forced to remain still and silent, breathing stale air, for the better part of nine hours. Now he felt in need of a shower and, not least, a change of clothes.

The day's work had finally come to an end late in the afternoon, and when the coast appeared to be clear, Bond had crept out—his head now crammed with details of Operation Heavenly Wolf: locations, methods of transport, weapons, rendezvous points, contingency plans. Now he had everything there was to know about the great, and dangerous, confidence trick to be played out at NORAD HQ in Cheyenne Mountain—everything except the vital role: who was to play the four-star general, the inspector general of U.S. Air/Space Defense.

The hall was empty, and the urgency of Bond's mission preyed on his mind. The Space Wolves were, certainly, the most important link in the current Western defense system. Alone, they could hold off the threat of any nuclear conflagration. Any crucial emergency would bring the Space Wolves into play, as they roamed high above the world—a cover for all continents. Every NATO power was secretly alert to the situation, as well as to the capability of other Space Wolves, ready to be hurled into orbit, with their chase tracks controlled and monitored from the operations rooms deep within Cheyenne Mountain, Colorado.

Bond had known of the plan to change the operational control center, but it made sense. Nobody had any doubts—within the secret corridors of power—that the next few years before the perfection of the Particle Beam Weapon were as crucial to the world as those which had passed when the early cannon took over from the siege catapult and ballista.

Standing by the roadside, eyes straining for any sign of the Saab and Cedar, Bond thought of the moves now being made: of the refrigerated trucks ready to take the deadly cargo of innocent-seeming ice cream into NORAD HQ and of the Space Wolves themselves, circling the earth.

It was almost midnight, and still no sign of Cedar. Bond's agitation grew as he crouched close to the jungle edge. Then, at around ten minutes after midnight, he heard the growl of the Saab: the side lights coming fast from the direction of the wooded knoll.

Cedar's face showed the kind of strain which Bond felt. Her eyes were red-rimmed, her reactions fast, nervous, and jumpy. Like Bond, she was dressed in dark jeans and a sweater. As he leaped for the Saab's door, Bond saw she had the revolver ready near the gearshift, easily within reach.

"They're looking for us. Everywhere," she gasped. "Do I go on driving?"

Bond told her to carry on and head for the monorail depot.

"It's no good saying that." Her voice cracked. "They've got most of the roads blocked, and there are guards at the station."

Bond unholstered the big automatic pistol. "Then we'll just have to blast our way out. If you spot roadblocks, turn away. They can't cover everything. If we have to shoot our way onto that monorail and then at the other end deal with the terrible twins who opened the gates into this place, so be it. I've got the hottest information since the warnings about Pearl Harbor—only, they'll listen this time. Look, I've got to share it with you, Cedar, in case only one of us gets out."

He began to talk, giving her the bare but most important facts. When he was done Cedar repeated what Bond had told her, adding, "Let's both try to make it, though, James. I don't feature doing it alone."

She kept to side roads, sometimes slewing off tracks and roads, punishing the Saab on grass and rutted ground. Soon they were in sight of Tara. Great banks of floodlights were turned on all around the area, while the distant flashes of sheet lightning seemed to be slowly coming nearer. Even in the car they could hear the heavy, approaching thunder of the storm.

It was, in the end, the storm which helped them. Like most desert weather, the change was both extreme and spectacular. As they kept close to the boundary walls with their screens of trees, the thunder and lightning swept in on a raging wind—a massive thunderhead, like an anvil, hanging directly over Rancho Bismaquer. In its wake came torrential rain.

They could hardly see through the windshield, even with the wipers going full speed, and the storm appeared to have driven the watchful guards to cover. Sitting it out—about half a mile from the monorail depot—Bond waited for the first break as rain lashed against them, buffeting the car like rifle fire on the armor plating.

Cedar said that as far as she knew, the monorail was in place. "They had some plan to take cars out early in the morning," she told him, explaining that her own escape had been made more difficult by the advent of more men and guards at the house.

"In the end I screwed up my courage and went for a walk. Markus saw me and asked what I was doing. I just told him I needed some air. I took off like a jackrabbit after that, haven't run so fast since I was a sophomore in college and the captain of the football team took me out."

"Did he catch you?" Bond asked.

"Of course, James. I slowed down after a while, Why not? He was cute."

At this point in the conversation, the rain appeared to ease slightly.

"This is it." Bond spoke quickly, giving her instructions. "Drive like the devil. Don't worry about shooting, we can't be hurt in here. As long as you can see through the rain, go straight for the monorail ramp and take us into the vehicle-transport compartment."

"Do you know how to run a monorail?" Cedar shouted as they took off.

Bond said there was always a first time for everything.

They got within a couple of hundred yards of the rail depot without being spotted. Then some security guard must have glimpsed them through the rain.

Bond saw the car pull out behind them, then lost it again as a squall drove a great wet shower between the two cars. Then another appeared, from the right, just as they were racing alongside the depot. Cedar's head pushed forward, almost on the windshield, as she searched for the ramp.

The two sets of headlights—behind, and to the right—appeared and disappeared through the rain. Then the Saab rocked as a bullet struck the armor on Bond's side. Another two squashed into the thick, impenetrable toughened glass of the driver's window.

But the weather saved them. The rain, which had eased for a moment, suddenly turned on a last downpour, as though giant buckets were being emptied from the skies.

"There," Cedar shouted, realizing they were practically alongside the ramp and overshooting it. Grimly peering through the windshield, she backed up, shifted into first, and smoothly set the Saab's wheels on the covered way leading to the monorail.

Bond wondered if the chase cars would find their way through the shield of rain or if they even realized where the Saab was heading. Cedar had the headlights on now in the dark tunnel, and there appeared to be no one behind them.

A minute later, the Saab's lights picked up the big metal sliding doors, and they bounced into the transporter van, coming to a standstill right in place on the restraining rails.

Bond shouted for Cedar to get the doors closed as he sprang from the Saab, praying that the entrance to the driver's cabin was not locked. As he passed through into the cab he heard the satisfying thud of the doors closing. Now it was a matter of using common sense and sorting out the controls.

The rain still lashed down, driving against the big windows of the cabin. A small fixed seat perched in front of a flat bank of levers and instruments. To Bond's relief, they all appeared to be marked. A red button, with two switches below it, was designated as "Turbine: On/Off." His hand tripped the switches and pressed the button as his eyes scanned the other controls. The throttle was a metal arm which swept in a half-circle across spaced terminals; the braking mechanism was near his feet, with a secondary device to the right of the throttle. He found the speed indicator, the windshield wipers, the lights, and a series of buttons marked "Doors: Automatic. Close/Open."

Pressing the red button brought a comforting throbbing whine as the turbine turned over. Bond slammed down all the automatic-door buttons on the "Close" circuit, switched on the wipers and lights, released the brakes, and tentatively moved the throttle arm.

He did not expect such a sudden reaction. The train jerked, took the strain, then moved with oiled smoothness from the depot. Cedar was at his elbow now, peering out of the big forward windows, trying to see the track through the rain as the big headlight cut into the downpour.

Bond increased the power, then up another notch, watching the speed gauge rise to seventy miles an hour. At eighty, they seemed to be clearing the storm. It was dying away as fast as it had come, for the rain was now only a slight drizzle, and the long single track became visible in the bright cutting cone of light which arrowed from the train's nose.

On either side, the protective, electrified fencing rose intimidatingly, prompting Cedar to ask what they would do at the far end. "They'll be ready and waiting. Shotguns, and electrified fences, everything."

"Worry when we get there." Bond increased the power and then wondered aloud if the train could stand the shock of going right through the far station. "If we were in the car, there'd be protection."

"Not if the whole thing capsized," Cedar said. "You'd telescope us all, James. There're bound to be bumpers at the other end."

"And they'll be waiting," Bond reflected.

The monorail sliced on, speed rising, as though floating on a soft cushion of air. No vibration, and now that the rain had cleared, they had perfect forward vision.

Bond thought for a few moments. They had been traveling for roughly ten minutes. Gently he eased back on the throttle, then told Cedar to get her revolver and the Nitefinder glasses from the Saab.

While she was gone, he eased back even more on the throttle, feeling the train slowing in a gentle vibration.

"I'm going to switch the main lights off in a minute," he told Cedar when she got back. "There's only one way to do this. Use the Nitefinders, and stop well short. You'll hold the fort here, while I go in: up the track."

It was pitch black outside beyond the beam of the great spotlight. In the far distance, the storm raged on and an occasional great sheet of lightning flared and faded.

Bond strapped on the glasses, took out the VP70, placed it on the instrument shelf, and continued to slow the turbine. Then he switched off the lights.

Now they slid along, slowly, in complete darkness. Cedar stood by Bond, one hand resting on his arm as he looked out through the Nitefinders. The track curved slightly, and he would have to judge how far they were from the desert depot. About a mile, he thought, bringing down the throttle another notch, then cutting it altogether and gently applying the brakes.

The driver's cabin had its own sliding door, which would, presumably, unlock when the other doors were set to "Automatic/Open." There should also be rungs from the cab that would take him down for part of the way at least. After that, it would be a long drop.

With his usual economy, Bond told Cedar exactly what he proposed. "I have night eyes with these things," touching the Nitefinders. "After I've unlocked the doors, the turbine has to be switched off and you'll be left alone here while I go quietly up the track."

"James, be careful of those protective fences." A slight quaver in Ceder's voice betrayed her state of mind.

"Don't worry about that. Nothing'll concentrate my mind so well as that damned fence." In the darkness, Bond watched through the glasses for any movement in front of the train. "If they're waiting—and I've no doubt they will be—I should imagine the brothers Grimm will be intrigued by the fact that we've stopped short, and with no lights. If I'm lucky, at least one of them'll come looking, which is all I need. Once I've dealt with them, switched off the current, and opened the gates, I'll be back fast. Your job is to stay here and kill—I mean kill—anyone who attempts to board. I'm the only one that you let back into this contraption, okay?"

She agreed, with a very firm "Yes."

Bond activated the automatic-door buttons and turned off the turbine. As he had hoped, the cabin door slid open easily. "Okay, Cedar. Be as quick as possible." He peered down, spotting the runs leading to the underside of the cabin.

Adjusting the Nitefinders to their maximum brightness and range, Bond swung himself from the cabin and started to descend.

At the bottom of the train itself, he paused, craning his neck to see along the track. He estimated the drop to be around fifteen feet. There was a good twelve feet between the great concrete pillars that held the track and the electrified fence.

Grasping the bottom rung, Bond allowed his body to fall free. He dangled in midair, swinging slightly, until he had controlled the oscillation of his body, then glanced down into the blur below, positioned himself, and let go. The ground was flat and firm. Bond landed neatly, knees bent, not even staggering or rolling.

As his feet touched the earth, so the automatic came out, and he froze, still and silent, peering through the goggles, ears straining.

The night seemed unnaturally quiet, and there was that particular, clear, sweet smell of the desert after rain. No movement ahead. Holding the pistol against his thigh, Bond started forward, keeping close to the high, pillared, concrete track supports, and noting with some relief that there were rungs—for maintenance, he supposed—on each third pillar.

Every now and then Bond stopped to listen and take a longer look. For a big man, he could walk with that silent, stalking manner of a cat. Within ten minutes the desert depot was clearly visible ahead.

They had turned the lights off, to make the train's approach difficult, and there was definitely movement now ahead of him. One tall figure slowly walked toward him, staying close to the pillars.

The man carried a shotgun, not under his arm but at the ready, held professionally away from the body, the butt a few inches from the shoulder and the barrel pointing downward.

Bond sidestepped, flattening behind a pillar. Soon the approaching man was clearly audible—an expert, Bond judged, for the sound came only from the man's low, controlled breathing.

The hunter must have instinctively sensed danger. About a foot from Bond's pillar, he stopped, listening and turning. Then Bond saw the barrel of the shotgun come into view.

He waited until the man cleared the pillar before making a move—quick as a cobra, and just as deadly. Bond's heavy automatic was balanced firmly in the right hand. His arm came back, then shot forward with all the force that 007 could muster. As the punch came out of the darkness, the hunter sensed activity. Not soon enough. Bond's wrist turned so that the full force of the punch lay behind the barrel of the VP70—the arm fully extended at the point of impact, which landed on target, just below the man's right ear.

There was a sudden hiss as the victim expelled air from his lungs, then a ghost of a groan before he fell backward. Bond grabbed out at the unconscious man, but it was too late. The tightly meshed protective fence danced with a flash of blue fire which, in turn, played around the man's body as he fell against the heavy wires, jerking and kicking when a massive voltage poured through him.

The smell of burning and singed flesh floated into Bond's nostrils, almost making him retch. But in a moment it was over, and the depot guard lay still, thrown away from the fencing, his gun—a Winchester pump—almost between Bond's feet.

Even through the Nitefinder glasses, the flash from the electrified fence left traces of light floating in Bond's vision. All thought of surprise had gone. Blinking to clear his eyes, Bond dropped to one knee, picked up the Winchester, and returned his automatic to its holster.

The pump-action Winchester was loaded and ready. As his hands touched the weapon, Bond heard a cry less than fifty yards up the track: "Brother? You okay, brother? You git him?"

The other guard, twin giant to the dead man, was thumping along the little path between pillars and fence, flushed out by the flash and noise. Bond lifted the Winchester, holding the oncoming figure in the center of the barrel, and called out, "Stay where you are. Drop the gun. Your brother's had it. Stop now."

The man did stop, but only to aim his Winchester in the general direction of Bond's voice. Before the first shots came, Bond ducked behind the pillar, coming out at the other side and lining up the shotgun again.

The man charged on, firing at random, hoping, in rage, for a lucky shot. Bond fired once, low and accurate. The target's legs seemed to be yanked back from under him, the force of the shot dragged the whole body facedown. A long shriek of pain, followed by a whimper; then silence.

Gently Bond searched the body of the electrocuted guard. No sign of keys there, so gingerly he walked forward, not knowing what reinforcements Bismaquer might have ordered to man the desert depot.

The other guard was unconscious but would live. His legs, peppered with shot, bled badly, but there was no jetting from severed arteries. Bond went over him thoroughly. No keys either. The guards, he decided, must have been caught offbalance and had left the keys in their little blockhouse, which also controlled the electric protective fencing. It was either that or there were others waiting, ready to trap Bond and Cedar.

He took his time approaching the end of the line, repumping the Winchester, crabbing sideways on toward the low buildings.

Silence. Not a movement as Bond reached the platforms, where the big motor ramp extended, ready to meet the monorail.

He stayed close to the buildings, well in the darkness, watching.

Nothing.

At last Bond broke cover, walking quickly to the blockhouse, where the lights still burned. It was deserted. There seemed to be no sign of life anywhere inside the fence or out on the desert track.

The keys lay on a table near the big fuse boxes and main switching gear that controlled the fences. In less than a minute Bond had thrown the master switch, picked up the keys, and after hurling the Winchester at the fence to make certain it was no longer live with electricity, unlocked the main gates, pulling them back to full extension so that they could drive the Saab straight off the train and through.

If luck held, they would be in Amarillo and telephoning people who mattered within an hour.

He ran, fast, all the way back. The injured guard was still unconscious but had begun to groan. His brother lay silent, reeking of burned clothing and flesh.

At last Bond saw the train, ahead and above him. Its great curved sides hung over the edge of the platform, supported by the pillars. Without pausing, Bond swarmed up the nearest metal rungs. There was a space on the platform, about three or four feet of stressed steel—with concrete overlay—between the edge of the pillar and the big rail.

Standing upright, Bond crabbed his way along this catwalk until the front of the train towered over him. With just room to kneel, he could see around the long drooping side of the monorail. The cab door was still open, its rungs leading down to the point below him where he had swung and dropped before.

Now the cab's rungs were just out of reach. Straightening up, Bond shuffled back a couple of steps, then leaned forward with his hands close together, as far to the left of the train's metal front as he could get without slipping.

The angle of his body was obviously too steep, so he gently edged his feet forward, flexing the knees, his eyes not leaving the line of rings—elongated D shapes—coming down from the cabin. If he let his hands slide now, Bond would simply fall headlong from the platform holding rail and train.

He needed a little more agility this time. Once his hands released their grip on the smooth metal, he would have to spring, trying to leap toward the cabin rungs, grabbing as he went in the hope of maintaining a firm hold.

A deep breath, flexed knees again, then a hard push away from the platform, using all his skill to place the weight of his body forward, near to the train's side. One hand touched a rung, one palm—but not quite firmly enough. He was falling, arms flailing and hands snatching at the rungs as they streaked by him. It took only a second, but the fall gave the impression of suspended time. Then his whole body jarred—an arm almost wrenched from its socket—as he left hand closed around the penultimate rung.

Bond remained swinging by one arm for a second or two, until at last he had a firm grip with both hands. Another second to catch his breath, and he began a steady ascent.

As his face came level with the cab door, Bond called out: "It's okay, Cedar, I'm back. We're on our way." He hoisted himself into the cabin, a trifle breathless.

Cedar was not in the cabin. Nor did she answer when he called to her again.

Bond leaped toward the control panel to activate the light switches. The whole train lit up, and as it did so, the cabin door slammed closed inexplicably. He reached across, hauling on the manual handle, but without success.

Turning, Bond once more called for Cedar. He had the pistol out again as he made his way back into the vehicle compartment. The Saab stood as they had left it, but still no trace of Cedar. Then, as he stood there, the door to the cabin—and the one at the far end—slammed shut simultaneously.

"Cedar?" Bond yelled. "Where are you? Those bastards got you?"

A disembodied voice answered, making his flesh crawl: "Oh yes, Mr. Bond. Mrs. Penbrunner will not get away, any more than you will. Why not relax, Mr. Bond. Relax and have a rest."

It was the voice of Walter Luxor, thin and strangled, from a loudspeaker system.

Startled, Bond took a few seconds to realize the other phenomenon—an odor of the air, oddly pleasant, but stinging to the nostrils. Then he saw the faint cloud, like thin smoke, rising from tiny grilles on the floor. Gas; some form of gas. He understood.

In an almost detached way, Bond became aware that he was functioning more slowly. His brain took longer to make decisions. Oxygen. Yes, that was it. He had oxygen. In the car: the oxygen kit which slid out from under the passenger seat.

Now he was moving in slow motion, his brain repeating, "Oxygen . . . oxygen . . ." over and over again.

Bond's hand reached out for the Saab's door, wrenching it open, his body swerving, turning toward the interior. Then he felt himself sliding—going down a long gentle slope—a chute, which descended into grayness, growing darker and darker, until he seemed to hurtle into space and the world turned black, while all knowledge was blotted out.

19

FOUR-STAR GENERAL

THERE WAS ONE tiny moment, on regaining consciousness, when James Bond knew who he was: James Bond, a field agent for the SIS, holding the special double-0 prefix. Number 007.

The knowledge lasted for a second or two and was accompanied by the sensation of floating in warm, pleasant water; as though suspended. He also heard a voice saying something about Haloperidol. He recognized the name—a drug, a tranquilizer, hypnotic in action. Then came the tiny prick, as the needle slid home. James Bond ceased to exist.

Lord, what time was it? He had been dreaming. Vivid dreams, nightmares almost, about his time at the academy. There were voices in the dream. Mum and Dad, God rest their souls. Friends, training, then his first appointment after he was commissioned.

General James A. Banker fumbled on the night table for the digital watch. Three in the morning. Shouldn't have had that last whiskey. Must give it up. Since the new promotion, there had been too many nights like this.

He flopped back onto the pillows, sweating, and immediately fell asleep again.

Watching through the infrared glass, Walter Luxor turned to Blofeld. "Going well," he squeaked. "There's plenty of time. I'll give him some war experience now." He pulled the microphone toward him and began to speak quietly, soothingly.

Below them was a bedroom, very military in décor: an on-base senior officer's room, functional, with only a few personal photographs and momentos to break its austerity.

In the deep hypnotic sleep, General James A. Banker was not really aware of the whispering voice coming close to his ears, from the pillow.

"Now, General," the voice said, "you know exactly who you are. You know, and remember, things about your childhood, your training, and your rise through the service. I shall tell you more about that rise through the service now. More about your active service; and a lot more about your present job." The voice launched into a long, vivid description of the general's work up to the time of Vietnam, then of his special duties during that war. There were acts of bravery and passage of fear. There were desperate times and the deaths of friends. Some of the incidents were almost completely relived, complete with sound effects: the sounds of weapons and of other people speaking.

General James A. Banker muttered in his sleep, turned, then woke again. Lord, he felt terrible; and he had a job to do in the morning. Pretty important. He'd had more dreams. He could recall them as clearly as he knew his wife Adelle. Nam: he'd been dreaming about all the guts and blood and hell in Nam.

He desperately wanted to call Adelle, but she was off into dreamland as soon as her head touched the pillow. Adelle got kind of huffy with him if he called in the middle of the night.

The general wondered how long it would be before he found the right house for her. Was it this weekend she was coming down to have another look? He hoped he felt better than this by morning, otherwise he'd walk through that inspection like a zombie. Sleep. Must get more sleep. Another look at his watch. It was only four o'clock. Too early to get up. He'd try to grab a little more shut-eye.

Gently the general slid back into his jumbled dreams, and just as gently Walter Luxor, in the window overlooking the bedroom, started to talk again.

He had done this only once before, and even with that one he had had more time. Putting a hand over the microphone, he said to Bismaquer, "Not bad, you know. He really believes, deep down inside, that he is a four-star general. Very good for twenty-four hours' work. I'll reinforce it now." As Luxor spoke, the door to the bedroom below opened and the large figure of Mike Mazzard appeared. Looking up at the unseen hiding place and making a twirling motion, Mazzard tiptoed toward the bed, picked up the clock, and altered it, as he had been instructed.

Luxor began to talk again. He also felt tired. Usually, he knew, the technique took a lot longer than twenty-four hours, but as the subject had to alter personality for only a relatively short time, he was convinced it could be done with complete success.

They had started almost as soon as Bond had been brought back to the ranch. Injections of Haloperidol and other hypnotics, followed by short in-and-out sessions of audiohypnotic implant, first to give the subject complete disorientation, then to put him back together—with new memories and a new identity.

The technique entailed small, frequent doses—implanting ideas and memories which would, they knew, be rejected within a day after the subject was brought around. But a day was long enough.

Bond had been a thorn from the start. Someone who had to be isolated and destroyed as quickly—and, if possibly, naturally—as convenient. So Blofeld had first instructed. But Blofeld's mind could change, and with that flexibility, that mercurial brilliance, came great ideas.

After Luxor had failed out on the racetrack, it had become necessary to get Bond alive. Blofeld had suddenly become adamant about that.

Originally they had planned for another candidate to play the general. Indeed Luxor had practiced this very technique on the man in question, right to the breaking point. He had died as a result.

Then Blofeld, having lured SPECTRE's old enemy to Texas, had picked on Bond, keeping him off balance, and now, with the minutes ticking away and a very definite need for the new general to have at least three hours' peaceful sleep, Luxor realized the wonderful irony of the whole scheme. Bond, as the general, could perish in Cheyenne Mountain, and many people would be highly embarassed.

Luxor talked on for another fifteen minutes, then switched off the microphones. "That's as far as I dare go. He'll be a little disoriented, but that'll be put down to a hard night's drinking. I've implanted that most firmly. At least you've got your four-star general. I would suggest, Blofeld, that you brief Mazzard personally. That man down there must die in the mountain, preferably while he still believes he is General James A. Banker."

Blofeld smiled. "The irony is complete. I'll see to it. Close down now, and let him sleep."

General Banker at last got some good rest. The dreams had gone, and he slept the sleep of the just. It was only as he became fully awarke that he had another kind of dream, oddly erotic, about a woman with only one breast. He even thought she was leaning over him. At some point there was a voice, too, though he could not make out if it was male or female. "James," the voice said. "My dear James. Take these pills.

Here . . ." A hand cradled his head, lifting, and he felt something in his mouth, then a glass to his lips. He was very thirsty and drank what was offered, without resistance. "They'll take a few hours to work," the voice said. "But when they do, you'll be your proper self again. God help you; and God help me for doing this."

When he was dragged fully out of sleep by a sergeant serving his usual steaming black, sweet coffee, it was the only dream the general could remember. He was conscious that he had not slept well, but that was the wretched party last night.

His mouth felt terrible, his stomach queasy; but at least he was well enough to do his job.

The general shaved, showered, and began to dress. Sometimes, James, he thought, I don't recognize you in this outfit. It was always amazing, for the general, to think he had come so far in the service. But here he was, a four-star general, with plenty of combat experience, a beautiful wife, and an exacting job. To be inspector general, U.S. Air/Space Defense, was quite something.

The tap at his door heralded the usual appearance of his adjutant, Major Mike Mazzard, who entered quietly to the general's call, saluting as he always did.

"Good morning, General. How're things today?"

"Terrible, Mike. I feel like I've been dragged through several swamps, infected with swine fever, and swallowed something out of the latrine."

Mazzard laughed. "With respect, General, you've only yourself to blame. That party was really too much."

The general nodded. "I know, I know. Don't tell me—and for heaven's sake don't tell my wife. I'm going to have to cut down, Mike."

"You want breakfast, sir? We can—"

"Perish the thought, Mike. Perish the thought. Another good slug of coffee would help."

"I'll fix it, sir. In here?"

"Why not? Then we can go through today's arrangements without interruption. I'm afraid you're going to have to carry me through most of it."

"Tut-tut, General. A good Bostonian like you." Mazzard paused by the door. "You know something funny, sir?"

"You think I should hear it?"

"Well, it's the Boston thing again. I heard one of the other officers talking. He said you were true-blue Boston, and anyone could tell by the way you spoke . . ."

"Yes?"

"The funny thing, sir, was that he said, 'Put General Banker in one of those bowler hats and a pinstripe, then give him an umbrella, and you'd think he's walked straight out of a British bank.' "

The general nodded. "I get it all the time, Mike. Had a British journalist in Nam take me for one of their own. I'm not ashamed of it, though." He put on a sly smirk. "You want I should take lessons? Learn to say 'boid,' and 'absoid,' like in Brooklyn?"

Mazzard grinned back and went out for more coffee.

Outside the room, Luxor waited. "Well?"

"Amazing." Mazzard shook his head. "I wouldn't have believed it. Will it last?"

"Long enough, *Major* Mazzard. Long enough. You have your orders from Blofeld?"

"I'll do it personally, and with pleasure. Don't worry. Now what about the general's coffee?"

About two hours earlier, a young captain who worked in the Pentagon's Space Intelligence Department had come on duty early. The skeleton night staff were still around, but nobody took much notice of the captain. He was known as an eager beaver.

At this time in the morning, however, the main communications teletype machine—personal to his superior officer, the general in charge of Air and Space Defense Administration—was not in use. The young captain held a set of keys, not only to his general's office but also to the teletype machine.

The little suite of offices was empty when the captain let himself in, quietly locking the door behind him. He then unlocked the teletype and began to transmit.

The first message was to the officer commanding movements, U.S. Air Force Base, Peterson Field, Colorado. The text read:

> BE PREPARED ONE SMALL ARMED CONTINGENT CONSISTING
> APPROX TWO OFFICERS FOUR SERGEANTS AND THIRTY EN-
> LISTED MEN OF AIR SPACE ADMIN STAFF ARRIVE BY ROAD THIS
> MORNING STOP TWO GENERAL JAMES A BANKER INSPECTOR
> AIR SPACE DEFENSE ARRIVE BY HELICOPTER FLIGHT CLEAR-
> ANCE FOUR-ONE-TWO TO RV WITH THIS GROUP AND PROCEED
> NORAD HQ STOP REQUEST YOU AFFORD ALL COURTESIES AND
> ASSISTANCE STOP ACKNOWLEDGE AND DESTROY STOP

He signed the communication in the name and rank of his superior.
Within ten minutes the acknowledge-and-wilco signal came back.

The second message was addressed to the officer commanding NORAD
HQ, Cheyenne Mountain, Colorado. It read:

> AS FAVOR I ADVISE YOU MY INSPECTOR GENERAL—GENERAL
> JAMES A BANKER—WILL VISIT YOU TODAY FOR NONSCHED-
> ULED INSPECTION STOP PLEASE GIVE HIM EVERY COURTESY
> STOP DO NOT REPEAT OR INFORM HIM OF THIS PREVIOUS
> WARNING STOP ACKNOWLEDGE AND DESTROY STOP

This was also signed with the captain's superior's name and rank. The
acknowledged-and-wilco signal came back with one rider:

> REGRET OFFICER COMMANDING ON LEAVE FOR ONE DAY THIS
> DAY STOP I SHALL PERSONALLY SEE ALL IS IN ORDER STOP

It was signed by a colonel as acting commanding officer.

The captain smiled, shredded all his copies, then picked up the telephone
to dial a number with a Texas prefix.

When the number answered he asked if Captain Blake was there.

"I'm sorry, sir, I think you have a wrong number." The voice on the
line was thin, reedy, with a slight squeak.

"I'm sorry as well, but no harm's done, sir. I must have misdialed. I
hope I haven't disturbed you."

"Not at all," replied Walter Luxor. "Good-bye, sir."

General Banker and his adjutant, Major Mike Mazzard, walked out of
the officers' mess, receiving smart salutes from the two private soldiers
on guard duty. They had been greeted by a number of the officers as they
left. At least two of them had remarked to the general: "Quite a party last
night, sir."

"And I'm getting quite a reputation," the general grunted. "Nothing
tonight, Mike, see to it. Early night. All right?"

"As you say, sir."

The Kiowa helicopter was already sitting on the pad in front of the
officers' mess, its rotor turning idly.

"Oh, no," the general groaned. "We doing the whole trip in that, Mike?"

"I'm afraid so, sir."

"Well, I just hope the flying weather's good. I don't think I'm well enough to stand much bumping around today."

"Weather report's excellent, sir."

They had sat together over a large jug of coffee while the general's adjutant went over the day's schedule.

"Fly direct from here to Peterson Air Base, where there should be two trucks with around thirty enlisted men, some NCO's, and a couple of officers—Captain Luxor and another one. They'll be there for show. Unless you decide the main security of the NORAD Combat Operations Center needs testing. Your car and the driver'll be waiting as well, sir."

"Good. And we go straight to Cheyenne Mountain?"

"We go to the number-two entrance. That's the best way, takes us straight to the main command-post levels. You said in your memo that the object was to test readiness and examine the command-post structure. That was the priority."

"Yes, I seem to remember . . . "

". . . that we were going to pull a fast one?" Mazzard finished for him. "That's right. The Space Wolf question."

The general frowned. "The memory's going, Mike. Yes, wasn't I going to ask them point-blank to hand over the computer tapes to me for personal keeping?"

"That was the idea. There's a regulation regarding the S.W. tapes. They're closed, restricted, and on the Most Secret list. Nobody down there has the right to hand them over, or even let you see them. The idea was to test reaction to an order from a very senior officer."

"Okay, we'll see if it works." They were still talking about it as the general swung himself into the Kiowa helicopter, greeted the pilot, and strapped himself in. Mazzard climbed aboard, after the general, and took the seat next to him.

A few moments later, the rotor turned, and the small chopper lifted, nose down, circling, then climbing—heading northwest toward Colorado.

20

CHEYENNE MOUNTAIN

THE GENERAL DOZED a little during the flight and seemed less hungover by the time the pilot turned in his seat, pointing down. They were high in the clear, endless blue skies over Colorado. In the distance the mountain peaks reached up: serrated and sharp jags of rock.

A few minutes later they descended toward Peterson Field and the general's waiting convoy. Mazzard helped General Banker from the helicopter, asking if he wanted to inspect the men who were drawn up in front of their vehicles. The general took a perfunctory look, nodded, and walked over, to be greeted by a painfully thin captain whose face looked like a skull.

"Captain Luxor, sir." The officer saluted, leading the general along the ranks.

"Did I meet you before, Captain?" The general stared hard at Luxor.

"No, sir."

As they went toward the staff car, with Luxor just out of earshot, General Banker muttered to Mazzard, "That captain. I'm sure I've seen him before, Mike."

"You saw his picture, General." The major spoke in an equally low voice. "In all the papers. Some hotshot plastic surgeon did one hell of a job on him. Poor guy had his face burned off in Nam."

"Bastards," spat the general.

The convoy was impressive: two motorcycle outriders, followed by an M113 armored personnel carrier, fully loaded with its two-man crew and section of combat troops, the heavy 12.7mm Browning manned at its curved swivel mounting.

General Banker's staff car rode behind the 113, while another APC boxed the car in from the rear.

The staff-car driver was not known to the general, who thought the man had probably been built from the leftovers of the Mount Rushmore carvings. Certainly his sergeant's uniform appeared to be very tight on him, but he drove smoothly enough and showed all the correct courtesies. The general would have preferred his own regular driver, whose name eluded him at this moment.

Major Mazzard sat in the rear with the general, while the hideously scarred captain took his seat up front, next to the driver. The small convoy moved slowly away from the helipad toward the main gates of Peterson Field, the general's pennant bright and flying from the offside wing of the hood, matched, on the other side, by the Stars and Stripes.

The barriers were raised without question, the guard turning out to present arms as the staff car swept through, while other officers and enlisted men came to attention, saluting as befitted the exalted rank of a four-star general.

Within the hour they were traveling at a steady rate through the foothills, on restricted military roads. The area was well-policed by both Air Force and Army, but nobody made any attempt to stop them or ask for documentation. The small police detachments simply came to attention as the convoy passed by. The general was impressed—two men on motorcycles, two more crewing each of the APC's. He also counted twelve or thirteen combat troops to each APC, including one young officer. Thirty-two men—possibly more. With his driver, Mazzard, and the captain, the force was at least thirty-five strong. Very good, and all armed with M16's and handguns. Mike Mazzard, the captain, and his driver also carried sidearms. What general could have wanted for better protection?

"You've got it sewn up nicely, Mike." The general beamed. "Very good organization. Well done."

"I only pick up a telephone, General. You know that, sir."

They were climbing into the mountains now, passing a side road marked with a military arrow sign: NORAD HQ.

"That's the way up to the main entrance, sir," Mazzard told him. "We go some five miles up here and turn back to come in at the side. It's like a kind of service entrance for the control rooms. I figure someone from Peterson'll have tipped them off by now. They'll probably all be on edge around the main entrance buildings."

"They'll know at this end too," the general grunted. "Not fools, these people. They'll all know. Be expecting us exactly where we're going in."

Ten minutes or so passed before the convoy reached the next slip road, duly marked NORAD 2. "Here we go, then, sir. You really feeling better?" Mazzard craned forward to take a good look at the general, and the skull-faced captain turned in the front seat.

"Is the general not well?"

"Captain," General Banker growled, "when a man's just been given a new and highly responsible posting, is parted from his wife while the house gets fixed up, and is living on base, he sometimes makes a fool of himself. No, I am not ill; but I used up a lot of cleaning fluid last night."

The captain made a sound which the general took to be humorous.

Turning to Mazzard, the general continued, "I feel a shade like a puppet. You walk me through it, okay? I'll be fine if you simply guide me."

"Don't worry, sir, we've done it all before."

"Sure have." The general nodded. From above came the clatter of a helicopter, flying low, as though following the convoy.

They were in a gap now, hewn through solid rock, the great slanting sides closing them in. Then out of the gap into a left turn, the gray road widening, white dust falling around them like a fine lawn spray as they came onto a clean macadam stretch.

The mountain reached up above them, and there—a mile ahead—stood a solid pair of gates, with a great high circle of Cyclone fencing reaching out on each side. Large steel girders were set at intervals in the fencing, each topped by constantly moving cameras. Behind the fence, a cluster of buildings stretched back to the rock face of Cheyenne Mountain

There were two GI's out in front of the gates. As the convoy appeared, one of them turned to shout toward the blockhouse on the right of the gates. Before they came within a hundred yards of the barriers, an officer appeared through a smaller gateway by the blockhouse.

The convoy slowed, the motorcycle escort wheeling off, left and right, to come in close to the staff car. The first APC also turned, moving right, then circling on its own axis to point inward. Precise and very military. The general was, once more, most impressed. These people knew what they were doing. Turning toward Mazzard, he said, "You do the introductions, Mike, will you? As usual. No fuss. I'll stay slightly aloof."

Major Mazzard looked very pleased as the electric windows slid down and the NORAD officer—a young captain—approached the staff car.

Yes, thought the general, they were well prepared here too. Looking forward through the Cyclone fencing, he could see that an honor guard had already turned out, forming up on the flat area immediately inside the gates.

The young NORAD officer saluted as though his life depended upon it, and Mazzard spoke to him, clipped and humorless: "General Banker— inspector general, United States Air/Space Defense—to officially inspect your base, Captain." he handed over an impressive-looking document, at which the captain merely glanced. He knew top brass when he met it.

"Very good, sir." The NORAD captain smiled. He turned his head, ordering the gates to be opened. "We're delighted to see you, General, sir. The base is open to you. If there's anything we can do to make your trip more pleasant . . ."

"It's not meant to be pleasant, Captain," the general snapped. "I'm here to look at your operations rooms and ask a few questions. You follow me, Captain?"

The NORAD officer's smile did not fade. "Whatever you say, sir. Anything we can do for you, anything at all. Please drive right in."

"The general's anxious to go inside the mountain as soon as possible," Mazzard interpolated.

"Right, sir. Our acting C.O. is already waiting for you in Operations. It won't take you long to get there."

The gates had opened, and they drove through, followed by one of the APC's. The other stayed outside the perimeter, turning to point back down the road, its cargo of troops disembarking and taking up defensive positions. In minutes the general's team had NORAD's number-two HQ entrance neatly sealed off.

As the car came to a halt, the honor guard snapped to attention and presented arms. "That young officer seemed a hair casual, Mike," the general muttered, climbing from the car.

"Yes. I'll get his name. Probably hasn't had many dealings with inspectors general before, sir, and thought the friendly approach would be best."

"Get his name." The general had begun to sound crusty.

"You don't want to inspect that honor guard, do you, sir?" Mazzard asked. But the general, in spite of his hangover, appeared intent on doing everything correctly. Slowly he passed down the ranks of men, stopping to ask questions of every third soldier.

At the end of the last rank, the general dismissed the guard commander, returning his sharp salute, then looked at the young NORAD captain who had met them. "Right," he snapped. "I want you, Captain, to take me, with my adjutant and the captain here . . ."

"Luxor," the thin damaged officer prompted. "Captain Luxor."

"Yes." The general shot Luxor an unfriendly look. "Yes, you; Major Mazzard; and Captain Luxor. Nobody else, just the four of us, will go in; and I wish to meet your commanding officer."

Mazzard at the general's elbow, quickly asked, "Sir, don't you think half a dozen of the men should—?"

"No, Major." The general was very firm. "They don't need to see any of this. Don't really know why we bothered with an escort of this size. No, *we* go and have a look. Now, let's move. I don't want to hang around here all day. Just the four of us." Before he had even stopped speaking, the general began to walk with purpose, his back plumbline straight, toward the buildings huddled close to the rock face.

He was well ahead of Mazzard and Luxor, while the NORAD captain came up fast, trotting at the general's heels. "The commanding officer, sir . . ."

"Yes?"

"Well, sir. As I said, we have a full colonel on duty, waiting for you. The commanding officer's away on leave today, sir. I think you should've been informed."

The general nodded. "There's nothing to bother about. Your colonel'll do as well as anybody."

The buildings, set against the rock face, were purely a defensive camouflage for the entrance. Solidly built, reinforced with steel, and housing a few small administrative officers, their main purpose was to block the tunnel which led into the mountain.

The young captain was still speaking. "At the main entrance—around the other side—we have an underground park for vehicles and other facilities," he chattered. "This is really a kind of back door." They passed through a pair of steel doors, which swung open when the captain pressed his hand against a small screen.

Behind the steel doors, the world changed. The passage narrowed into a short metal-lined alley, wide enough to accommodate only one man at a time. This led to a small command post, occupied by four sturdy marines who stood guard over the next entrance of sliding steel panels.

The marines, for all their immaculate appearance, were cooperative and unquestioning. After a word from the NORAD captain, one of the marines spoke into a white intercom, then stood to one side as the blast-proof panels slid noiselessly back.

The general and his entourage did not really know what to expect within the mountain. The general himself supposed that his mental picture would be colored by other similar installations he had visited, though they all had seemed somewhat like movie sets. He expected large elevators, to take staff deep below the earth, or open railcars, like a modern coal mine.

There turned out to be no such devices. Once through the doors, they were already inside the mountain and standing in a great circular chamber—a reception area, fashioned from inside the bare rock. Air conditioning kept a pleasant, comfortable temperature, and there were carpets underfoot, though the place was, basically, a refurbished cavern.

Four large desks were manned by strangely disinterested staff, in charge of electronic sniffers for bugs, weapons, and explosives. The general insisted on checking each of these desks before turning to meet a tall, bronzed colonel who wore pilot's wings and a plethora of medal ribbons. The colonel was backed up by a team of some four officers, most of whom wore the rank of major. All seemed to be around the same age—late thirties or early forties.

The colonel saluted, introduced himself and his staff, apologized for the absence of his commanding officer, and offered the general what he called "every possible facility."

General Banker nodded, noting that the colonel and his men wore sidearms. He then introduced his own two staff members.

The colonel, who felt in strangely benign spirits that morning, had noticed immediately that General Banker was in dress uniform while his staff officers wore combat dress and carried sidearms. It struck him as unusual, but not sinister. Before coming up from the control room, he had also received a bizarre message—from the main gate—that the general's detachment of troops had sealed off the number-two HQ entrance, taking up positions both within and outside the perimeter fence.

Now the general was oddly uncommunicative, so the colonel explained that the four officers with him had volunteered to stay on duty. "By rights they should be just coming off shift." The colonel smiled proudly. "But they all offered to stay on so you could be well briefed, General." He continued to explain that, when on duty, these officers supervised the various command posts, the main control room, and the monitors. "When you're on duty here, it's a full-time six hours of concentration." He appeared to be exceptionally serious when talking about the work. "The officers on duty at this moment are not in a situation where they could be certain of answering all your questions, sir."

The general thanked the colonel for his officers' thoughtfulness, and deferred to him, asking what he should see first.

"Oh, whatever you like, General. We're at your service here. Look at anything, take over if you want to. Nobody will mind. We're serious people, doing a very special job; but we have to let you see everything, and give you any information you need."

For a serious officer, the general considered that the colonel had suddenly taken leave of his senses. A bit casual for a man in charge, he thought. Then Major Mazzard stepped in. "I think the general's particularly interested in seeing how you control the Space Wolves, sir."

The general held up a hand. "Now, don't let us rush into anything, Major. The colonel knows how this outfit works. After all, this is one of the most important bases in the entire country. . . ."

"Well." The colonel had a pleasant, slow drawl. "Well, we'd certainly be the first to know if anything went sour, if that's what you mean, sir. I'd recommend we look at the main operations control first."

"Whatever you say." General Banker nodded.

The colonel gestured toward another pair of antiblast doors, set in the center of the half-circle wall behind the security desks.

"After you, sir." The general followed the NORAD colonel across the soft carpet and through the doors, the other officers, including Mazzard and Luxor, at their heels.

On the other side of the doors, a wide passage led to a T-junction corridor. Looking to left and right, the general saw large swing doors set at intervals along the cross-stroke passage. Straight ahead were similar doors, marked in bold white lettering: GALLERY: MAIN OPERATIONS.

The colonel stepped to one side, allowing General Banker to be the first through, the other officers following respectfully.

They were on a wide viewing platform, fitted with chairs and a high, angled thick glass screen. The view from this gallery was both impressive and virtually unique.

Below them lay a vast amphitheater in which the audience consisted of about a hundred men and women, each seated behind a bank of computer and electronic instruments—keyboards, scanners, and other complex hardware. Each person on duty appeared to be completely wrapped up in his or her work, making occasional entries on keyboards or speaking into headsets.

Above them—on the far, huge, curved wall—were three massive electronic Mercator projections, each mapping the world. All three projections were topped by rows of digital clocks, showing the accurate time along the earth's varied zones. But most important, each of the projections was crisscrossed by slow-moving colored lines—blues and greens; brilliant whites; blacks; orange; even lines which broke up into different, segmented hues.

The general let out a slow whistle. He remembered seeing small versions of things like this, but never anything on such a grand scale. "I'd be grateful, Colonel, if you'd come over by me and tell us about this amazing display." He smiled.

The colonel started to speak, his voice a strange monotone as he explained the use, and purpose, of the main control.

The three projections showed the exact number of known satellites and other space hardware in orbit—the left-hand projection being all non-U.S.A. satellites; the one to the far right showing American equipment; while the center projection monitored all new indications.

At the same time, this center screen could be programmed, in an instant, to show everything—both American and non-American: even down to the juxtaposition of satellites.

"That is also the so-called early-warning projection," the colonel told them. "Any foreign power who throws something new into space will be spotted on the central screen."

All three of these great electronic maps were monitored and operated by the technicians seated in the amphitheater, while they, in turn, were passed information from a number of sources: "Anything new would come from one of our tracking stations: ground-based or satellite. Our own hardware is passed on through individual command posts within this complex." As the colonel said it, the whole display sounded very simple, yet nobody seeing it could fail to be awed.

The colonel was still speaking. "For instance, the Big Bird and Keyhole II reconnaissance satellites are shown on the right-hand projection, but their work is monitored by their own command post, which is just along the passage outside this gallery. Of course, all the information those particular satellites send back goes to other stations.

"Now, if we get something new from . . . let us say, the Soviet Union, this is immediately picked up on the trace. Within seconds, our SDS—Satellite Data System—relays details. We would take action before knowing exactly what the new object is; but it's all very fast when it happens, which it does quite often."

He went on to explain how each satellite system had its own headquarters, working independently. The weather satellites, for instance, passed their data directly to meteorological centers, and the same applied to the reconnaissance eyes in the sky.

"In a way, we're like police patrols." The colonel spoke directly to General Banker. "We can see what's up there, check it out, pass on information, and take action. But we're not responsible for the individual tasks."

"Except for the Space Wolves," Major Mazzard said, on the general's right.

The colonel nodded. That was a very special project, he said. "Would the general like to see the Space Wolf command post? It's possibly the largest we have."

Major Mazzard and Captain Luxor both answered for General Banker. Yes, the general would very much like to see the S.W. command post.

"Anything you want, sir." The colonel led them out of the main-operations gallery and along the corridor to their left until they came to one of the sets of swing doors, marked "KS Control." "Killersat," the Colonel explained, leading the way into a large chamber.

Inside there was semidarkness. Against the far wall, a small version of one of the electronic Mercator projections glowed with light—creeping red lines sweeping above the world—while three men, an officer and two master sergeants, tended the computer and controls.

"There it is." The colonel waved a hand. Then he spoke louder, for the benefit of the three men controlling the Space Wolf command post. "Gentlemen, General Banker, the inspector general of Air/Space Defense. Just taking a look."

Mazzard was close to the general now. "I think the general wants to take more than a look," he said loudly.

General Banker turned toward Mazzard, a question forming on his lips.

"You remember, sir," Mazzard prompted. "You're the senior officer here."

Banker's brow creased and he looked around. The colonel stood next to him, while the rest of the staff crowded in the doorway. Captain Luxor stood behind the colonel's staff, out in the corridor.

"Sir, the computer tapes and printouts," Mazzard prompted, close at his right elbow.

"Of course. Sorry, Mike." The general smiled, then raised his voice. "I don't wish to bother you, gentlemen, but who's in charge of this command post?"

The officer seated in front of the central bank of controls raised a hand. "Sir."

"Would you be good enough to unhook your computer tapes and box up all available prints, please? I need to take them away for study," the general said calmly.

The officer in command slowly stood up, muttered, "Very well, sir," and began to move around to the rear of the large console. Within a few minutes he had the big spools of tape in containers, on top of which he placed a number of flat metal boxes, containing the computer printouts. "Anything else the general requires?" the officer asked.

"No, that'll be all," Mazzard answered for his general. "Just bring them over here."

The Space Wolf command-post officer started coming toward them in the dim light.

Then, with speed and complete surprise, General Banker moved, his body pivoting in front of the colonel, one hand reaching out to wrench the colonel's pistol from its holster.

Even as he turned, the general let out a yell: "Stop! Don't hand those over! The rest of you, grab the two officers with me. They're not what they seem. Now! Get them *now!*"

It had all happened that morning during the helicopter ride to Peterson Field.

The general, feeling decidedly queasy from the previous night's party, had closed his eyes, intending to doze. But as soon as he relaxed, General Banker began to suffer a light-headedness, followed by strange mental experiences.

At first he thought it was something serious, like a heart attack. He felt faint, and images began to flash through his mind.

It was like a film running backward at great speed, intercut with odd things he could not properly identify. There were memories from recent days, just after his promotion; scenes from his time in Vietnam; and moments before that—as though the reel was taking him back to childhood.

The intercut images were very odd. A woman with one breast had come to give him pills. At least he thought it was her, for he smelled her hair. Nena. Tara. Cedar. Bond. James Bond. 007.

The general opened his eyes and realized that he was not General James A. Banker at all. Still feeling lightheaded, he was flooded by the truth, as though through an open window to his mind.

She had come and given him pills for this very purpose. Then and there, in the helicopter, Bond had not even attempted to work out how he had been drugged and hypnotized into another personality. All he could think of was how to keep in character until the best possible moment.

That moment was here, and now.

As he swung around, grasping the colonel's big Colt .45, Bond realized that Mazzard was reaching for his gun, yelling as he did so : "Don't listen to the general! Don't listen to him! The man's crazy! Take no orders from him!"

Mazzard's pistol came out of its holster a second too late. Bond's arm was up, and the roar from his two shots came as gigantic, echoing explosions in the chamber.

Mazzard was lifted off his feet. His body hung aloft for a second, blood beginning to spout from his chest, then slammed back against the wall. Immediately, Bond turned, looking for Luxor.

The skeleton man had vanished.

With every ounce of authority he could muster, Bond shouted for the computer tapes to be returned. "Colonel, get your men into action, and fast. Those troops who came with me mean business. See to your defenses."

The colonel hesitated for a moment. The command post reeked of cordite and death; two of the other officers had drawn their weapons but seemed uncertain about what to do. From the moment of his arrival, Bond had recognized the workings of Bismaquer's sinister drug. They had been within an ace of actually handing over the tapes. Now it was a question of making sure they were not taken by force.

Bond shouted orders again, this time demanding to know what had happened to Luxor.

"He went—After you shot at—He walked away," one of the NORAD officers stammered.

"Colonel, your defenses. Get onto the nearest base. You'll need help," Bond commanded, his voice sharp as a whip.

As though to underline the order, the entire chamber shook with the dull thud of an explosion from the direction of the main entrance.

A marine appeared in the doorway. "Antitank rockets being fired at the entrance block, sir!" he shouted at the colonel, who had already leaped to the nearest telephone.

Another *whoomp,* sending a tremor through the mountain complex.

Bond looked at the marine. "The officer who came in with me?"

"Sir?"

"The one with a face like a skull . . ."

"There were shots from here, and he ran past us, sir, saying he had to get help."

The complex shook again, to another rocket burst. "That's the help he was going for," said Bond. "Muster everyone you can. The colonel's getting word out. This base is under attack. It's not a drill. It's the real thing."

By this time, they had all realized the danger. Bond turned to the colonel. "They'll try for a quick breakin," he said, willing himself to remain calm. "Blast their way through with antitank rockets . . ."

"M72's, by the sound of them." The colonel looked quite ashen. "I don't understand this. We nearly handed over—"

"Don't worry, Colonel, that's not your fault. The point is that those bastards'll smash their way in, hacking with knives if they have to. If that skull-face is out there, they'll be even more determined. What've we got in the way of defense?"

The colonel gave a couple of quick orders to his officers, who hesitated until Bond—realizing the problem with Bismaquer's drug—told them to carry on. "The guard out front is fighting back." The colonel swallowed. "Doing quite well, I'd guess. We've got reinforcements coming in, but the problem is here. Within the mountain. They've blasted through the first doors, and the section into the reception area's now catching it. I gather they're close to the doors . . ."

"And when those doors are down, the force that's left'll come piling through the narrow entrance. What've we got?"

"A few grenades, the sidearms, and a pair of AR18's"

"Get the Armalites, then. Quickly!" The AR18, as Bond knew it, was the latest commercial Armalite weapon. It was fully automatic with a fire rate of 800 rpm, and magazines holding twenty rounds. He was at the colonel's heels as the two men made their way to the arms locker, set into the wall near the main-operations gallery doors.

The weapon felt good in Bond's hands, and he grabbed magazines from the colonel, stuffing them into his uniform jacket and slamming one into position on the gun.

As they turned away from the locker, a larger explosion ripped from the reception area, and several soldiers staggered back through the entrance to the main complex.

One was the marine Bond had spoken to earlier. "They've broken through, blown the doors into reception," the man gasped, and Bond saw he was clutching a jagged tear in his shoulder, the blood trickling through his fingers.

As he reached the doors to the big, circular reception area, Bond briefly took in the carnage. The neat desks were shattered and bodies lay everywhere, some dead, others crying with pain from the wounds. From the main entrance directly opposite him, smoke poured into the reception area.

The assault would come down the narrow passage, one man at a time, Bond thought. He braced himself against the wall, gripping the weapon against his hip.

From the corner of his eye he saw the colonel taking up a similar stance. One of the officers who had been with them in the Space Wolf command post was sprawled on his back within a few feet of them, a slashed cut where his throat had been. It crossed Bond's mind that Bismaquer already had a great deal to pay for.

Then, through the smoke, SPECTRE's men started to enter the reception area.

Both the colonel and Bond opened up at the same moment, sending a double spray of bullets into the hole which had once been a pair of sliding steel doors.

"Like shooting fish in a barrel, General," shouted the colonel, for SPECTRE's troops came pounding down the narrow passageway and into the reception area like sheep being penned into an abattoir.

Their AR18's rattling, the colonel and Bond scythed through the attackers as they appeared through the smoke. The bullets hurled them back, threw them aside, cut through them, until suddenly there was an unearthly silence.

Finally the smoke began to clear, and even Bond winced to see the damage they had done. Then he reloaded, bracing himself.

From outside there came yet another explosion, then a shout: "Colonel? Colonel, sir? Any NORAD officer in there? . . ."

"Yes," the colonel shouted back. "State your name and rank. What is it?"

"They're finished out here, sir. The other APC's pinned down on the road by forces from the main entrance. It's Sergeant Carter here."

The colonel nodded at Bond. "It's okay, General. I know Carter."

Bond thought it best he should remain a four-star general for the time being. At least that would stave off awkward questions. His main concern, now that Heavenly Wolf had been foiled, was Cedar Leiter. Then, once he knew what had happened to her, he would hunt down Bismaquer.

Outside, there was more carnage. Medical teams worked on the wounded and carried away the dead. The one APC was still burning, and there were great gaps in the Cyclone fencing.

From down the road, out of sight, came occasional bursts of rifle and automatic fire.

"How's it going?" the colonel shouted to a three-man team crouched over a field communications radio. A sergeant answered him. More aid was on the way, and the other APC was now almost finished, the troops on their last legs.

"Still can't understand why we nearly gave the stuff away," the colonel muttered almost to himself. "I don't feel good about any of this."

"You will—eventually. Not your doing. Colonel. They had me as a sitting duck as well . . ."

The sergeant with the radio called to the colonel that there was a civilian helicopter a mile away. "A woman. Keeps making calls, asking persmission to put down. Wants to know if we've got a Mr. Bond with us, sir."

"Let her down," Bond ordered, still pulling rank. "I know what that's all about. Bring her in here." It could easily be Bismaquer, holding a pistol to either Cedar's or Nena's head, but it was his only quick route out. Alternatively, it could be a fast lead to Bismaquer, and Bond could not resist that. He remembered there had been a helicopter following the convoy on the way in. —

"That okay, sir?" the radioman called to the colonel.

"If the general says so. Yes."

Bond went over to the radio sergeant. "You don't like ice cream, do you,

Sergeant?" he asked, having just witnessed the man clear a four-star general's order with his immediate known superior.

Reaching for the hand mike, the communications man shook his head. "Hate the shit, sir. I can't even look at it." He gave Bond a puzzled look as he started to call in the helicopter.

Bond quickly made his excuses to the colonel, saying he would get back to him as soon as possible. "Any problems, call the White House. Say you ran into a Mr. Bond. They'll clear it, I think."

The colonel was obviously dazed as he watched the little white metal insect dropping gently into the compound, neatly sliding to one side at the last moment in order to avoid the burned-out APC—a final memorial to Bismaquer's ruined attempt on the security of Cheyenne Mountain.

The small helicopter was a modern twin-seater version of the old Bell 47. Bond could see only one figure seated within its perspex bulb. It was certainly not Bismaquer. This figure was slim, in white overalls and helmet.

She already had the door open and was swinging herself down as Bond reached the machine.

"Oh, James. Thank God. Oh, thank God you're safe." Nena Bismaquer wrapped her arms around Bond's neck, clinging to him as though she could never bear to let him out of her sight again.

Tired as he was, and worried about Cedar's safety, and anxious to discover if Luxor had escaped, and where Bismaquer had hidden himself, James Bond still felt it might be a good thing never to let go of Nena.

21

BLOFELD

IT WAS ALREADY growing dark as the helicopter flew in low over the Louisiana swampland. Nena craned forward at the controls, trying to spot the landmark she said would be there.

They had stayed for only a few minutes in the compound of the NORAD base while Bond shot questions at her. What had happened? How did she manage to get there? Did she know what had become of Cedar?

Flushed and excited, Nena gave him the answers as quickly as he fired the questions. In the early days at the Rancho Bismaquer, her husband had given her lessons in the helicopter. She had taken her pilot's license a year ago. It had been her personal salvation.

Wakening in the night—a good forty-eight hours ago—she heard noises. Bismaquer did not seem to be in the house, so she crept down and saw Luxor with some other men. They had Cedar with them.

Then her husband arrived; orders were given. She had no idea what was going on but heard talk about Bond being taken away in the other helicopter. She also heard Bismaquer tell them where they were to rendezvous when it was all over. "I still don't know when *what* was all over. They talked about Cheyenne Mountain, that's all. Lord, you look so dashing in that uniform, James. Now, I need to know what's been going on."

He would tell her later. Now he needed the urgent facts. Where was Bismaquer? What happened to Cedar?

"He's taking her to Louisiana. I know exactly where—and Luxor'll head for the same place." Her face, glowing with pleasure until then, suddenly darkened. "It's horrible, James. I know what they'll do to her. Markus took me there once. I never thought I'd go again. The people know me there, and—if we hurry—we should make it well before Markus arrives with Cedar. They're going by road. It was always she they wanted dead, James. I know that. I heard Markus say it was she they tried to kill with harvester ants. Horrible. He wanted you alive, but Cedar was to die. I just hope to God we're in time, because I can guess what he'll do to her now."

A few minutes later they were airborne, and now, after a long steady flight, the swamps and bayous slid by in the dusk beneath them.

Bond was pleasantly surprised by Nena's standard as a pilot. She handled the helicopter with skill and great flair, as though she was used to flying it every day.

"Oh, I take it out when I can." She laughed. "It's always been a way of getting clear from Markus for a while. Funny, I always knew that when I finally left him, it would be in the chopper."

She had switched on the main landing lights, slowing almost to a hover, peering down, then suddenly exclaiming, "There! That's the place. On that spit of land right between the two bayous."

Bond thought that, even allowing for the light, the house seemed pretty run-down.

"Just wait." She laughed again. "Markus keeps a couple of people there to look after it. The outside's only a shell—like some conjurer's box that fits over the real thing. It's a palace inside."

She tilted the little Bell, to come in low, telling Bond that she thought there was a place on the far side of the bayou where she could put down. "Markus keeps a number of marsh hoppers around; only I don't want to take the one nearest the road. It'd be best if he doesn't know we're here."

Bond went along with that. The one thing he needed most was total surprise for the final confrontation with Bismaquer, the new Blofeld. He wondered, to himself, what would happen to SPECTRE now that the expensive and ingenious attempt on the Space Wolf secrets had collapsed on them.

"I haven't thanked you yet." He turned to look toward Nena, who was concentrating on the ground below.

"For pulling you out of Cheyenne Mountain?"

The helicopter faltered, then gently let down. Nena clicked off the switches. The engine died, and they sat there, the rotor cleaving the air, making its *whupping* noise as it slowed to a stop.

"No, Nena, for what you did after they'd gone over me with the drugs and hypnotism. How did you get in to give me the antidote?"

She paused. "Oh that? Well, I had to do something. It was clear they had you doped up to the eyeballs. I just had to pray I'd chosen the right stuff."

"Well, you did—and it worked. Very quickly, really. You saved the day, Nena. *You* really stopped it all from working, stopped Markus' and Luxor's plans."

The darkness closed in on them like a wall. Nena had to switch the lights on again. "You'll tell me what it was all about, James, won't you? Everything. I only heard parts of it. It seemed complicated to me—difficult and daring. Would they really have gotten a lot of money for whatever they were after?"

"Billions." Bond closed the subject. "Now let's find this marsh hopper. I'm ravenous, need a bath, and could do with a rest before I come face to face with your venomous husband."

"Yes," she said, unbuckling her straps. "Yes, he is pretty venomous, isn't he?"

They found the marsh hopper exactly where she said it would be. A small narrow-beam spotlight was fitted to the front, and Nena switched it on after the motor fired.

As they reached the water surrounding the old rotting house, a light flashed out from what appeared to be the porch. Bond went for the .45, but Nena put out a restraining hand. "It's okay, James. Only a deafmute Markus keeps on the place. Named Criton."

"Admirable," Bond muttered.

"Criton, or the woman, Tic—she's a first-rate cook. You won't have to worry about food, James. Yes, I can see him now. It's Criton guiding us."

The marsh hopper came alongside a small pier, the sullen-looking deaf-mute nimbly stepping down to help tie the craft to the pier. Criton gave Nena a little bow but took no notice of Bond, who kept the .45 at the ready, to be on the safe side.

She had been right about the house. Going up the crumbling and rotten wooden steps to the main door, Bond kept his reservations, but, once inside, it was a different matter. You immediately forgot the camouflage, for the interior was beautiful, immaculate, and drenched in style and taste.

Nena spoke to Criton, facing him and enunciating carefully, while Bond looked around at the heavy silk wall coverings, the antiques, and the fresh flowers which seemed to have been gathered only a few hours ago.

"Has Mr. Bismaquer been here?" Nena asked.

Criton shook his head. A negative.

"Understand me, now, Criton," she continued. "You take the marsh hopper, and you put it out of sight. Okay?"

He nodded.

"Then tell Tic we need food and drink. In the main bedroom."

Criton nodded vigorously, grinning broadly.

"Now, most important. You understand? *Most* important. Mr. Bismaquer is coming. As soon as he is on the way—in a marsh hopper—you come wake us up. Right away. You watch all night. You do that, and I give you a good present. Okay?"

The deaf-mute nodded as though trying to dislocate his neck.

"He'll do it." Nena locked eyes with Bond. "We're safe, James. We can relax. Criton'll warn us when Markus shows up; then we'll be ready for him."

"You sure?"

"Certain."

She took hold of his hand, tugging gently, leading him up the stairs.

The master bedroom was huge, with carpeting so thick you could roll up in it and go to sleep without recourse to sheets. The bed itself was typical of Bismaquer's style: a huge gilded four-poster, with a headboard carved and glinting with gold leaf—a large B displayed prominently among the scrollwork.

The bathroom sported bath, shower, and Jacuzzi. It was, Bond decided, only half the size of the bedroom.

Later, wrapped in toweling robes, they sat on the bed to eat a delicious crab-and-okra gumbo, which, Nena maintained, was reckoned among the locals to be a great aphrodisiac.

Bond, who had felt near exhaustion on arrival, did not know whether to thank the gumbo or Nena's natural feminine powers. But they made love several times—with concentrated power, and increasing mutual delight— before switching the lights off and cradling each other into sleep.

At first, Bond thought he was dreaming, that the shot was simply part of some immediately forgotten nightmare. His eyes snapped open, and he lay still for a second, listening in the dark.

The next moment, though, he knew it was the real thing. Two more heavy reports. He reached out for Nena, but she was not there.

He snapped the light on, grabbing for the toweling robe and the .45 as his feet touched the carpet.

The robe was there, but the big automatic—which he had so carefully left by the bed—had disappeared.

Once in the robe, he switched the light off again and felt his way to the door. The house still seemed to echo from the shots. Downstairs, he thought, knees bent, his bare feet silent on the carpet.

He stopped, to listen again, at the top of the staircase. He thought he heard sounds from behind a door adjacent to the big carved newel post at the stair foot. A thin sliver of light showed under the door. Nena, he thought, his heart thudding. Bismaquer had arrived, and the deaf-mute had given no warning. Either that or she had tried to go it alone.

He moved more quickly down the stairs, pausing for a moment just outside the door, listening to the muted sounds coming from the other side. Gradually the noises took form—a whimpering, pleading babble. Without waiting another second, Bond kicked the door open just in time to see the last act of Bismaquer's drama being played out.

It was a long room. Most of the space was taken up by a polished oak table, the chairs pushed neatly in around it. The far wall appeared to be made of glass. But it was the tableau close to this huge window that stopped Bond, like a kind of paralysis, in the doorway.

It was a grotesque scene. Slumped against the wall lay the big pink-faced Markus Bismaquer, one shoulder and both legs covered in blood where the three bullets had chewed their way into kneecaps and arm. The cherubic face was changed—a child in pain and terror.

Standing over him, stark naked, her one magnificent breast caught as though by a spotlight, was Nena. She held the Colt .45, pointing directly at Bismaquer's head, as he pleaded through his pain, begging her to stop. The bear, finally overcome and helpless.

She seemed not to see—or even notice—that Bond was there. In turn, he was momentarily so shaken by the sight that he stood rooted, mesmerized, for too long.

"I always knew your heart wasn't in it, Markus." The glissando laugh had changed to a harsh crow, while the endearing French accent was now guttural, rough, and coarse.

"No, Markus. I might just have spared you, but you didn't cover your tracks. The Britisher, Bond, gave it all away. When we had him set up—with the new personality well implanted in him—you crept in, from my bed no doubt, because he told me that he smelled my hair.

"You went to him and filled his mouth full of wakeup pills, didn't you? Another of your loves, Markus? Did you fall for him? Like you fell for the Leiter bitch? Anything that moves, eh? Luxor, me, Leiter, Bond. Well, there's no reason to keep you any longer . . . *husband.*"

Bond actually jumped as she pulled the trigger, and Bismaquer's head disintegrated like a burst bloodfilled bladder, the gore splattering Nena's naked body.

"My God. You bitch." For a single beat in time, Bond thought he had not said it aloud. But Nena Bismaquer turned quickly, the deadly eye of the Colt steady and pointing directly at Bond's chest.

Her face had changed, and in the clear light Bond could see that she appeared older. The hair was tousled, and the black fire now burned a hatred in her eyes. It was the eyes which brought the whole thing into perspective. No matter how he had tried to cover it, even with the use of contact lenses, Ernst Stavro Blofeld's eyes had been black: black as the Prince of Darkness himself.

Nena smiled, lopsided, and in the smile revealed her paranoia.

"Well, James Bond. At last. I'm sorry you had to watch this nasty business. I really *was* thinking of sparing him, until you thanked me for feeding you wakeup pills. Then I knew he had to die. It's a pity. He was quite brilliant in his way. My organization can always make room for chemists who have a streak of genius—like Markus Bismaquer. But his stomach wasn't up to it, I'm afraid."

She took a step toward Bond, then changed her mind. "In spite of everything—and I have to admit you have prowess in some areas—I don't think we've really met. My name is Nena Blofeld." She laughed. "I might say, your name is James Bond and I claim my reward."

"His daughter?" Bond's voice was barely audible.

"My reward," she continued. "I've had a price on your head, ready to be claimed for some time. Are you surprised? Surprised that I managed to fool your people and the Americans? We knew you would be called in—Mr. James Bond, the expert on SPECTRE. Yes, from a distance I enticed you, James. And you fell for it.

"Now I can claim my reward myself. You killed my father, I think. He warned me, even as a child, about you."

"And your mother?" Bond played for time.

She made a dismissive retchy sound from the back of her throat. "I'm illegitimate, though I know who she was. A French whore who lived with him for a couple of years. I did not, knowingly, meet her. I loved my father, Mr. James Bond. He taught me all I know. He also willed the organization to me—SPECTRE. That's all you really have to be told. Markus has gone. Now it's your turn."

She raised the Colt just as Bond dived toward the side of the table, and at the same moment the dusty, frail figure of Walter Luxor came hurtling through the door, shouting: "The place is surrounded, Blofeld. They're here—police, everywhere!"

She fired, and Bond saw part of the table splinter about a foot from his head. Twisting his body, he grabbed at the legs of the nearest heavy chair, hauling it out as Walter Luxor made a lunge for him, throwing himself directly into the path of Nena Blofeld's next shot.

The bullet gouged into the left side of Luxor's chest, spinning him like a top against the wall. He seemed to be pinned there for a second before sliding down, a collapsed skeleton, leaving a crimson trail behind him.

Bond heard Blofeld gasp, cursing, and in that moment when she was still off-balance, he summoned all his energy, heaving at the heavy chair, making a supreme effort to fling it, with every ounce of strength, at Nena Blofeld.

The chair appeared to hang, almost suspended in midair, as she tried to duck it. But the combination of need for survival, hatred for any member of the Blofeld family, and some hidden well of strength served Bond's purpose well.

The bottom of the chair's seat hit her full in the chest. The four legs neatly pinioned her arms, and the full force of the impact hurled her back against the window.

There was a sickening noise of cracking glass, then a terrible screaming. Nena Blofeld was thrown out onto the hard earth, which sloped down to the dense reeds and the water of the bayou.

The screaming continued, and Bond stood transfixed at what happened next. As Blofeld hit the ground, so a metal cage, protected by tight wire mesh, dropped from the darkness above. At the same time, the area immediately outside the broken window became alive. The cage, Bond could see, had a roof and three sides, being open at the front and reaching down to the reeds.

As the cage descended, so the lights dimmed in the room, but it was still bright enough to give a reasonable view of the reptiles which came squirming in. At least two of them—though Bond had the distinct impression there were others nearby—were huge, fat, lethal pythons, thirty feet of more in length.

As the creatures slid over the screaming and kicking body, Bond heard the chair crack like thin plywood. Then the screams stopped. He was conscious of other people coming into the room, of a back he recognized as his old friend Felix Leiter.

Leiter limped toward the window, black gloves on the hands of his artificial limbs. Bond saw the arms raised and Leiter's hands come together. He turned his eyes away after the third explosion, as Felix put a bullet into the brain of each python, and—in case she was crushed, but not yet dead—the *coup de grâce* to Nena Blofeld.

"Come on, James." It was Cedar, by his side, who guided him out of the body-strewn room.

A few minutes later, in the hall of the bayou house, she told him, simply, what had happened to her on the monorail. "I couldn't kill them all. You told me to kill anybody who tried to get in. There were at least a dozen. Maybe they were already on board when we left the ranch. I just got out fast. Sorry, James, I tried to catch up with you, give some kind of warning, but it was all over too quickly. I didn't dare shout—they seemed to be everywhere. I couldn't see. We must have missed each other by inches. The only thing I bumped into was a body."

"How—?" he began.

"I walked. Straight out through the gate and into the night. By the time I finally made Amarillo, it was too late to do anything. There *really* is nothing between that depot and the city.

"Then things opened up, and reports started to come in from Cheyenne Mountain. By that time, Daddy arrived, and a lot of other people. They finally got a trace on Madame Bismaquer's helicopter. That's how they tracked you down here. I always told you she was no good."

Bond merely shook his head. It had not yet quite sunk in.

Felix Leiter came into the hall. "Nice to see you again, James, old buddy." His grin still had that sense of fun and impetuosity that Bond had always warmed to, trusted, and admired. "You do realize that my daughter's in love with you, James." Another quick grin. "As her father, I hope you're going to make an honest woman of her—or a dishonest one. Either one will do, just to keep her quiet."

"Daddy!" said Cedar in a shocked voice that fooled nobody.

22

TO JAMES BOND: THE GIFT OF A DAUGHTER

CEDAR LEITER AND James Bond stood on the balcony of his room at the Maison de Ville, New Orleans, looking out at the view. Somewhere near at hand below them, a pianist was trying to re-create Art Tatum playing "Aunt Hagar's Blues." Cedar and James were arguing.

"But you've said it *would* be different if I wasn't your old friend's daughter, James. Can't you forget about that?"

"Difficult." Bond had turned monosyllabic, particularly since talking long distance to M, who had sounded exceptionally cheerful and told him to take a couple of weeks' leave. "No, 007, make that a month. You really deserve it this time. Very good show indeed."

"What do you mean difficult?" Cedar became petulant. "You have said it all, James. You'd take me to bed like a shot if—"

"If it wasn't for your father, yes. And there's an end to it."

"It's *not* incest!"

"But it wouldn't seem right." Bond knew very well that it *would* seem very right if it happened. But . . .

"Look. I've got time to kill. So have you. At least let's go off and have a vacation together." She held her hands up, palms facing outward. "No strings, James. I promise, no strings."

Cedar immediately put her hands behind her back, crossing her fingers in the old childhood ritual which allowed you to lie.

Bond sighed. "Okay. But just to keep you quiet. But I warn you, Cedar, you try anything, and heaven save me—I'm just about old enough to be your father anyway—I'll warm that pretty little backside for you."

"Oh. Promises." Cedar giggled.

They stood in silence for a while, and she groped for his hand. "Isn't it fantastic out there? That sky, all velvet, and the stars?

They were not to know it, but at that very moment, a rocket blasted off from Russia's Northern Cosmodrome, near Plesetsk, to the south of Archangel. A very few minutes later, a bleep showed on the center projection in the main control room of the NORAD center in Cheyenne Mountain.

Within seconds, the Space Wolf command post, just along the passageway from Main Control, was setting one of its laser-armed platforms into a similar orbit, to close on the unidentified new object.

The Space Wolf was held off, within range, for the next thirty minutes, until the Satellite Data System recognized the newly launched arrival on another Meteor weather satellite. Only then was the Space Wolf quietly withdrawn and placed back into its normal orbit.

But Cedar and James Bond knew nothing of this. They simply stood there looking out at the stars, with Bond's hand gradually gripping Cedar's palm. He gave it a little squeeze. "Okay, daughter," he asked, "where to you want to go?"

"Well—" Cedar's answer was cut short by the telephone.

"Hi, James." Felix Leiter's voice made Bond feel oddly guilty. "I'm in the bar, and there's a package for you, old friend," Felix told him.

"Down in a couple of minutes." Bond cradled the telephone. "Your father. With a horsewhip, I should think." He told Cedar to wait for him, then they would go out to dinner.

Felix was not in the bar, however, nor could he be found in any of the hotel's public rooms. But the barman told Bond that a man with a limp had been in. There was a package, and a note, for Mr. Bond at Reception.

Sure enough, a heavy package, beautifully wrapped, waited for him, together with a neatly typed envelope. Bond tore open the envelope, and a note. "Open the package first," it read. "It's from someone really important. Then try the envelope. Felix."

Bond took the package into the bar, ordered a vodka martini, lit one of his specially made H. Simmons cigarettes, and carefully unwrapped the parcel. Inside was a large box, similar to those made for expensive jewelry.

This one carried the Presidential seal embossed into the lid.

Slowly Bond undid the clasp and lifted the lid. Lying in a specially molded bed of silk was a silverplated Police Positive .38 revolver. Engraved along the barrel were the words "To James Bond. For Special Services." There followed the signature, and title, of the President of the United States of America.

Bond closed the box, tearing open the other envelope. A single card, handwritten with great care. It read: "To James Bond: The gift of a Daughter — or whatever you want her to be."

It was signed "Felix Leiter," and as Bond read it, he knew that the planned holiday with Cedar was going to be laughter, fun, and a purely platonic relationship right down the line.

Waiting for Bond upstairs, Cedar had other ideas, and they were both stubborn as mules.

In his cab heading for the airport, Felix Leiter chuckled to himself.

Afterword

IN 1941 [Ian] Fleming accompanied Admiral Godfrey to the United States for the purpose of establishing relations with the American secret-service organizations. In New York Fleming met Sir William Stephenson, "the quiet Canadian," who became a lifelong friend. Stephenson allowed Fleming to take part in a clandestine operation against a Japanese cipher expert who had an office in Rockefeller Center. Fleming later embellished this story and used it in his first James Bond novel, *Casino Royale* (1953). Stephenson also introduced Fleming to General William Donovan, who had just been appointed coordinator of information, a post which eventually evolved into the chairmanship of the Office of Strategic Services and then of the Central Intelligence Agency. At Donovan's request Fleming wrote a lengthy memorandum describing the structure and functions of a secret-service organization. This memorandum later became part of the charter of the OSS and, thus, of the CIA. In appreciation, Donovan presented Fleming with a .38 Police Positive Colt revolver inscribed "For Special Services."

—Joan DelFattore,
University of Delaware

ICEBREAKER

ACKNOWLEDGMENTS
AND AUTHOR'S NOTE

I would like to thank those who gave invaluable assistance in the preparation of this book. First, my good friends Erik Carlsson and Simo Lampinen, who put up with me in the Arctic Circle. To John Edwards, who suggested that I go to Finland, and made it possible. To Ian Adcock, who did not lose his temper, but remained placid, when, during a cross-country ride in northern Finland—in early February 1982—I took him, not once, but three times, into snowdrifts.

My thanks also to that diplomat among Finnish gentlemen, Bernhard Flander, who did the same thing to me in a slightly more embarrassing place—right on the Finnish-Russian border. We both thank the Finnish Army for pulling us out.

Acknowledgments would not be complete without reference to Philip Hall, who has given me so much support throughout.

JOHN GARDNER

for

PETER JANSON-SMITH

with thanks

CONTENTS

1

THE TRIPOLI INCIDENT

THE MILITARY TRADE Mission Complex of the Socialist People's Republic of Libya is situated some fifteen kilometers southeast of Tripoli.

Set close to the coast, the complex is well hidden from prying eyes, screened on all sides by sweet-smelling eucalyptus, mature cypresses, and tall pines.

From the air it might easily be taken for a prison. The kidney-shaped area is enclosed by a boundary of three separate six-meter-high cyclone fences, each topped by a further meter of barbed and electrified wire.

At night, dogs roam the runs between the fences, while regular patrols, in Cascavel armored cars, circle outside the perimeter.

The buildings within the compound are mainly functional. There is a low barracks, constructed in wood, for the security forces; two more comfortable structures act as "hotels"—one for any foreign military delegation, the other to house their Libyan counterparts.

Between the hotels stands an imposing, single-story block. Its walls are over a meter thick, their solidity disguised by the pink stucco finish and an arched cloistered facade. Steps lead to a main door, and the interior is cut down the center by a single corridor. Administrative offices and a radio room extend to left and right of this passage which ends, abruptly, at a pair of heavy, high doors, the entrance to a long, narrow room, bare but for its massive conference table and attendant chairs, together with facilities for showing films, VTR, and slides.

There are no windows in this, the most important room of the Complex. Air-conditioning keeps an even temperature, and a small metal door at the far end, used by cleaners and security personnel, is the only other entrance.

The Military Trade Mission Complex is in use about five or six times a year, and the activities within are constantly monitored—as best they can be—by the intelligence agencies of the Western democracies.

On the morning it happened, there were, perhaps, one hundred and forty people working within the compound.

Those in the capitals of the West, who keep a weather eye on Mideastern events, knew a deal had been struck. Although the likelihood of an official statement remained minimal, eventually Libya would receive more missiles, aircraft, and assorted military hardware to swell its already well-stocked arsenal.

The final session of the negotiations was to begin at nine-fifteen, and both parties stuck rigidly to protocol. The Libyan and Soviet delegations — each consisting of around twenty people — met cordially in front of the pink stucco building and, after the usual greetings, made their way inside, down the corridor to the high doors, which were opened on their well-oiled, noiseless hinges by two armed guards.

About half of the two delegations had already advanced into the room when the whole phalanx halted, rooted in shock from the sight that met their eyes.

Ten identically dressed figures were lined up in a wide crescent, at the far end of the room. They wore combat jackets, and gray denim trousers tucked into leather boots. Their appearance was made more sinister by the fine camouflage netting which covered their faces and was held in place by black berets, each of which carried a polished silver badge. The badge was that of a death's-head above the letters NSAA, the whole flanked by lightning runes.

Incredible fact: Libyan officers had swept the room less than ten minutes before the two delegations arrived outside the building.

The ten figures each assumed the classic firing posture — right legs forward, bent at the knee, with the butts of machine pistols, or automatic rifles, tucked hard into their hips. Ten muzzles pointed toward the delegates already in the room, and at the remainder in the corridor outside. For a couple of seconds the scene was frozen. Then, as a wave of chaos and panic broke, so the firing started.

The ten automatic weapons systematically hosed the doorway with fire. Bullets chewed through flesh and bone, in a din magnified by the enclosed surroundings.

The burst of fire lasted for less than a minute, but, when it stopped, all but six of the Soviet and Libyan delegates were either dead or fatally wounded. Only then did the Libyan troops and security officers go into action.

The assassination squad was exceptionally disciplined and well trained. The firefight — which lasted for some fifteen minutes — caught only three of the intruders while they remained in the room. The remainder escaped through the rear entrance, taking up defensive positions within the compound. The ensuing running battle claimed another twenty lives. At the end, the whole ten-man team lay dead with its victims, sprawled like pieces from some bizarre jigsaw puzzle.

At nine o'clock GMT the next morning, Reuters received a message by telephone. Within minutes the text was flashed to the media around the world.

The message read:

> In the early hours of yesterday morning, three light aircraft, flying low to escape radar detection, cut their engines and glided in over the well-guarded Military Trade Mission Complex just outside Tripoli, the capital of the Socialist People's Republic of Libya.
>
> An Active Service unit of the National Socialist Action Army landed undetected, by parachute, within the grounds of the complex.
>
> Later in the day, this unit struck a blow for International Fascism by executing a large number of people engaged in furthering the evil spread of the Communist ideology, which remains a threat to world peace and stability.
>
> It is with pride that we mourn the deaths of this Active Service unit while carrying out its noble task. The unit came from our elite First Division.
>
> Retribution—for fraternization or trade between Communist and non-Communist countries, or individuals—will be swift. We shall cut away the Communist bloc from the remainder of the free world.
>
> This is Communiqué Number One from the NSAA High Command.

At the time, it struck nobody as particularly sinister that the arms used by the NSAA group were all of Russian manufacture: six Kalashnikov RPK light machine guns and four of the RPK's little brothers—the light, and very effective, AKM assault rifle. Indeed, in a world well used to terrorism, the raid itself was one headline among many for the media, who put the NSAA down as a small group of Fascist fanatics.

A little under a month after what came to be known as "the Tripoli Incident," five members of the British Communist Party held a dinner to entertain three visiting Russian members of the party, who were on a goodwill mission to London.

The dinner was held in a house not far from Trafalgar Square, and coffee had just been served when the ringing of the front doorbell called their host from the table. A large amount of vodka, brought by the Russians, had been drunk by everybody present.

The four men standing outside the front door were dressed in paramilitary uniforms similar to those worn during the Tripoli Incident.

The host—a prominent and vociferous member of the British Communist Party—was shot dead on his own doorstep. The remaining four Britons and three Russians were dispatched in a matter of seconds.

The killers disappeared and were not apprehended.

During the postmortems on these eight victims, it became clear that all had died from shots fired through Russian-manufactured weapons— probably Makarov, or Stechkin, automatic pistols. The ammunition was also identified as made in the USSR.

Communiqué Number Two, from the NSAA High Command, was issued at nine o'clock GMT the next day. This time, the Active Service unit was named as having belonged to "the Adolf Hitler Kommando."

In the following twelve months, no fewer than thirty "incidents" involving multi-assassinations ordered by the NSAA High Command became headline news.

In West Berlin, Bonn, Paris, Washington, Rome, New York, London— for the second time—Madrid, Milan, and several Mideastern cities, known and prominent Communists were killed, together with people engaged in official, or merely friendly, association with them. Among those who died were three outspoken British and American trade unionists.

Members of the assassination squads also lost their lives, but no prisoners from the organization were taken. On four occasions, NSAA men committed suicide to escape capture.

Each of the assassinations was quick, carried out with careful planning and a high standard of military precision. After every incident, the inevitable High Command Coimmuniqué was issued, presented in the same stilted language common to all ideologies. Each communiqué gave details of the supposed Active Service unit involved.

Old names brought back ugly memories of the infamous Third Reich— the Heinrich Himmler SS Division; the Heydrich Battalion; the Hermann Goering Assault Squadron; the First Eichmann Kommando. To the world's police and security services, this was the only constant: the one clue. No evidence came from the bodies of dead NSAA men and women. It was as though they had suddenly appeared fully grown, born into the NSAA. Not a single corpse was identified. Forensic experts toiled over small hints; security agencies investigated their leads; missing-person bureaus followed similar traces. All ended at brick walls.

One newspaper, sounding like an advertising poster for some nineteen-forties' movie, editorialized melodramatically:

> They come out of nowhere, kill, or die, or disappear—returning to their lairs. Have these followers of the dark Nazi Age returned from their graves, to wreak vengeance on their former conquerors? Until now, the bulk of urban terrorism has been motivated by far left ideals. The self-styled and efficient NSAA brings with it a new and highly disturbing dimension.

Yet, in the shadows of that hidden and secret world of intelligence and security communities, people were beginning to stir uneasily as though awakening from bad dreams, only to find that the dreams were reality. It began with exchanges of views, then, cautiously, of information. Finally they groped their way toward a strange and unprecedented alliance.

2

A LIKING FOR BLONDES

LONG BEFORE HE joined the Service, James Bond used a particular system of mnemonics in order to keep telephone numbers in his head. Now he carried the numbers of a thousand people or so filed away, available for immediate recall, in the computer of his memory.

Most of the numbers came under the heading of work, so were best not committed to writing in any case.

Paula Vacker was not work. Paula was strictly play and pleasure.

In his room at the Inter-Continental Hotel at the north end of Helsinki's broad arterial Mannerheimintie, Bond tapped out the telephone number. It rang twice and a girl answered in Finnish.

Bond spoke in respectful English. "Paula Vacker, please."

The Finnish operator lapsed easily into Bond's native tongue: "Who shall I say is calling?"

"My name's Bond. James Bond."

"One moment, Mr. Bond. I'll see if Ms. Vacker's available."

Silence. Then a click and the voice he knew well. "James? James, where are you?" The accent was only lightly touched by that singsong lilt so common to the Scandinavian countries.

Bond said he was at the Inter-Continental.

"Here? Here in Helsinki?" She did not bother to disguise her pleasure.

"Yes," Bond confirmed, "here in Helsinki. Unless Finnair got it wrong."

"Finnair are like homing pigeons," she laughed. "They don't often get it wrong. But what a surprise. Why didn't you let me know you were coming?"

"Didn't know myself," Bond lied. "Sudden change in plan." That at least was partly true. "Just had to pass through Helsinki so I thought I'd stop over. A kind of whim."

"Whim?"

"A caprice. A sudden fancy. How could I possibly pass through Helsinki without seeing Paula Beautiful?"

She laughed; the real thing. Bond imagined her head thrown back, and mouth open, showing the lovely teeth and delicate pink tongue. Paula Vacker's name suggested she had Swedish connections. A direct translation from Swedish would make her Paula Beautiful. The name was well matched.

"Are you free tonight?" It would be a dull evening, he knew, if she was not available.

She gave her special laugh again, full of humor and without that stridency some career women develop. "For you, James, I'm always free. But never easy." It was an old joke, first made by Bond himself. At the time it had been more than apt.

They had known each other for some five years now, having first met in London.

It was spring when in happened, the kind of London spring that makes the office girls look as if they enjoy going to work, and when the parks dress themselves with yellow carpets of daffodils.

The days were just starting to lengthen, and there was a Foreign Office binge to oil the wheels of international commerce. Bond was there on business—to watch for faces. In fact there had been words about it, for internal security was a matter for MI 5, not for Bond's Service. However, the Foreign Office, under whose auspices the party was being held, had won the day. Grudgingly, "Five" compromised, on the understanding they would have a couple of men there as well.

From a professional viewpoint the party was a flop. Paula, however, was another matter.

There was no question of Bond seeing her across a crowded room, you just could not miss her. It was as though no other girls had been invited; and the other girls did not like it one bit—especially the older ones and the Foreign Service *femmes fatales* who always haunt such parties.

Paula wore white. She had a tan needing no help from a bottle, a complexion which, if catching, would put all the makeup firms out of business, and thick blond hair, so heavy that it seemed to fall straight back into place even in a force ten gale. If all this was not enough, she was slender, sexy, had large gray-flecked eyes, and lips built for one purpose.

Bond's first thoughts were wholly professional. What a flytrap she would make, he decided, knowing they had problems getting good flytraps in Finland. He stayed clear for a long time, making sure she had come unescorted. Then he moved in and introduced himself, saying that the Minister had asked him to look after her. Two years later, in Rome, Paula told him the Minister had himself tried it on quite early in the evening— before Mrs. Minister arrived.

She was in London for a week. On that first evening, Bond took her to a late supper at the Ritz, which she found "quaint." At her hotel, Paula gently but unmistakably gave him the elbow—king-size.

Bond laid siege. First he tried to impress, but she did not like the Connaught, The Inn on the Park, Tiberio, The Dorchester, Savoy, or the Royal Roof; while tea at Brown's she found merely "amusing." He was just about to take her on the Tramps and Annabelle's circuit when she found Au Savarin in Charlotte Street for herself. It was "her," and the *patron* came and sat at their table toward the end of meals, so that they could swap risqué stories. Bond was not so sure about that.

They became firm friends very quickly, discovering mutual interests—in sailing, jazz, and the works of Eric Ambler. There was also another sport which finally came to full fruition on the fourth evening. Bond, whose standards were known to be exacting, admitted she deserved the gold star with oak leaves. In turn, she awarded him the oak leaf cluster. He was not sure about that either.

Over the following years, they stayed very good friends and—to put it mildly—kissing cousins. They met, often by accident, in places as diverse as New York and the French port of Dieppe, where he had last seen her, the previous autumn. This night in Helsinki would be Bond's first chance of seeing Paula on her home ground.

"Dinner?" he asked.

"If I can choose the restaurant."

"Didn't you always?"

"You want to pick me up?"

"That, and other things."

"My place. Six-thirty? You've got the address?"

"Engraved on my heart, pretty Paula."

"You say that to all the girls."

"Mostly, but I'm honest about it; and you know I have a special liking for blondes."

"You're a traitor, staying at the Inter-Continental. Why aren't you staying Finnish—at the Hesperia?"

"Because you get electric shocks off the lift buttons."

"You get them at the Inter-Continental, too. It's to do with the cold and the central heating . . ."

". . . and the carpets, I know. But these are more expensive electric shocks, and I'm not paying. I can charge it, so I may as well have luxurious electric shocks."

"Be very careful what you touch. Any metals give shocks indoors here, at this time of the year. Be careful in the bathroom, James."

"I'll wear rubber shoes."

"It wasn't your feet I was thinking about. So glad you had a whim, James. See you at six-thirty," and she hung up before he could come up with a smooth reply.

Outside, the temperature hovered around twenty-five below centigrade. Bond stretched his muscles, then relaxed, taking his gunmetal case from the bedside table and lighting a cigarette—one of the "specials" made for him by arrangement with H. Simmons of Burlington Arcade.

The room was warm, well insulated, and there was a glow of immense satisfaction as he exhaled a stream of smoke towards the ceiling. The job certainly had its compensations. Only that morning, Bond had left temperatures of forty below, for his true reason for being in Helsinki was connected with a recent trip to the Arctic Circle.

January is not the most pleasant time of year to visit the Arctic. If, however, you have to do some survival training of a clandestine nature, in severe winter conditions, the Finnish area of the Arctic Circle is as good a place as any.

The Service believed in keeping its field officers in peak condition and trained in all modern techniques. Hence, Bond's disappearance, at least once a year, to work out with 22 Special Air Service Regiment, near Hereford; and his occasional trips to Poole, in Dorset, to be updated on equipment and tactics used by the Royal Marine Special Boat Squadron.

Even though the old elite Double-O section, with its attendant "license to kill in the course of duty," had now been phased out of the Service, Bond still found himself stuck with the role of 007. The gruff Chief of Service—known to all as M—had been most specific about it. "As far as I'm concerned, you will remain 007. I shall take full responsibility for you, and you will, as ever accept orders and assignments only from me. There are moments when this country needs a trouble-shooter—a blunt instrument—and by heaven it's going to have one."

In more official terms, Bond was what the American Service speaks of as a "singleton"—a roving case officer who is given free rein to carry out special tasks, such as the ingenious undercover work he had undertaken during the Falkland Islands conflict in 1982. Then he had even appeared, unidentifiable, on TV, but that had passed like all things.

In order to keep 007 at a high, proficient level, Bond usually found that M managed to set up at least one grueling field exercise each year. This time it had been more cold climate work, and the orders came quickly, leaving Bond little time to prepare for the ordeal.

During the winter, members of the SAS units trained regularly among the snows of Norway. This year, as an added hazard, M had arranged that Bond should embark on a training exercise within the Arctic Circle, under cover, and with no permission either sought or granted from the country in which he would operate—Finland.

The operation, which had no sinister, or even threatening, implications, entailed a week of survival exercises in the company of a pair of SAS men and two officers of the SBS.

These military and marine personnel would have a tougher time than Bond, for their part would demand two clandestine border crossings—from Norway into Sweden; then, still secretly, over the Finnish border to meet up with Bond in Lapland.

There, for several days, they would "live off the belt," as it was called:

surviving with only the bare necessities carried on their specially designed belts. Their mission was survival in difficult terrain, while remaining unseen and unidentified.

This week would be followed by a further four days with Bond as leader, making a photographic and sound-stealing run along Finland's border with the Soviet Union. After that they would separate, going their different ways—the SAS and SBS men to be picked up by helicopter in a remote area while Bond took another course.

There was no difficulty about cover in Finland, as far as Bond was concerned. He had yet to test drive his own Saab Turbo—"the Silver Beast" as he called it—in harsh winter conditions. Saab-Scania hold an exacting Winter Driving Course each year within the Arctic Circle, near the Finnish ski resort of Rovaniemi. These two facts were a window to his cover.

Arranging an invitation to take part in the course was easy, requiring only a couple of telephone calls. Within twenty-four hours Bond had his car—complete with all its secret "extras," built in at his own expense by Communications Control Systems—freighted to Finland. Bond then flew via Helsinki to Rovaniemi, to meet up with driving experts, like his old friend Erik Carlsson and the dapper Simo Lampinen.

The Driving Course took only a few days, and after a word to the massive Erik Carlsson, who promised to keep his eye on the Silver Beast, he left the hotel near Rovaniemi in the early hours of a bitterly cold morning.

The winter clothing, Bond thought, would do little for his image with the ladies back home. Damart thermal underwear is scarcely conducive to certain activities. Over the long johns he wore a track suit, heavy rollneck sweater, padded ski pants and jacket, while his feet were firmly laced into Mukluk boots. A thermal hood, scarf, woolen hat, and goggles protected his face; Damart gloves below leather gauntlets did the same for his hands. A small pack contained the necessities, including his own version of the SAS/SBS webbing belt.

Bond trudged through snow, which came up to his knees in the easier parts, taking care not to stray from the narrow track he had reconnoitered during the daylight hours. A wrong move to left or right could land him in snowdrifts deep enough to cover a small car.

The snow scooter was exactly where the briefing officers said it would be. Nobody was going to ask questions about how it got there. Snow scooters are difficult machines to manhandle with the engine off, and it took Bond a good ten minutes to heave and pull this one from its hiding place among unyielding and solid fir branches. He then hauled it to the top of the long slope which ran downwards for almost a kilometer. A push and the machine moved forward, giving Bond just enough time to leap onto the saddle and thrust his legs into the protective guards.

Silently, the scooter slid down the long slope, finally coming to a stop as the weight and momentum ran out. Though sound carried easily across the snow, he was now far enough from the hotel to safely start the engine — after taking a compass bearing, and checking his map with a shaded torch.

The little motor came to life. Bond opened the throttle, engaged the gear, and began to travel. It took twenty-four hours to meet up with his colleagues.

Rovaniemi had been an ideal choice. From the town one can move quickly north to the more desolate areas. It is also only a couple of fast hours on a snow scooter to the more accessible points along the Russo Finnish border; to places like Salla, the scene of great battles during the war between the Russians and Finns in 1939–40. Farther north, the frontier zone becomes more inhospitable.

During the summer, this part of the Arctic Circle is not unpleasant; but in winter, when blizzards, deep-freeze conditions, and heavy snow take over, the country can be treacherous, and wretched for the unwary.

When it was all over and the two exercises with the SAS and SBS completed, Bond expected to be exhausted, in need of rest, sleep, and relaxation of the kind he could only find in London. During the worst moments of the ordeal his thoughts were, in fact, of the comfort to be found in his Chelsea flat.

He was, then, quite unprepared to discover that, on returning to Rovaniemi a couple of weeks later, his body surged with an energy and sense of fitness he had not experienced for a considerable time.

Arriving back in the early hours, he slipped into the Ounasvaara Polar Hotel — where Saab had their Winter Driving Headquarters — left a message for Erik Carlsson saying he would send full instructions regarding the movement of the Silver Beast, then hitched a lift to the airport, boarding the next flight to Helsinki. At that point, his plan was to catch a connection straight on to London.

It was only as the DC9-50 was making its approach into Helsinki's Vantaa Airport, at around 12:30 P.M., that James Bond thought of Paula Vacker. The thought grew, assisted no doubt by his new-found sense of well-being and physical sharpness.

By the time the aircraft touched down, Bond's plans were changed completely. There was no set time for him to be back in London; he was owed leave anyway, even though M had instructed him to return as soon as he could get away from Finland. Nobody was really going to miss him for a couple of days.

From the airport, he took a cab directly to the Inter-Continental and checked in.

As soon as the porter brought his case to the room, Bond threw himself onto the bed and made his telephone call to Paula. Six-thirty at her place, he smiled with anticipation.

There was no way that Bond could know that the simple act of calling up an old girlfriend and asking her out to dinner was going to drastically change his life over the next few weeks.

3

KNIVES FOR DINNER

AFTER A WARM shower and shave, Bond dressed carefully. It was pleasant to get back into one of his well-cut gray gabardine suits, plain blue Coles shirt, with one of his favorite Jacques Fath knitted ties. Even in the depths of winter, the hotels and good restaurants of Helsinki prefer gentlemen to wear ties.

The Heckler & Koch P7—which now replaced the heavier VP70—lay comfortably in its spring-clip holster under the left armpit, and to stave off the raw cold, Bond reached the hotel foyer wearing his Crombie British Warm. It gave him a military air—especially with the fur headgear—but that always proved an advantage in the Scandinavian countries.

The taxi bowled steadily south, down the Mannerheimintie. Snow was neatly piled off the main pavements, and the trees bowed under its weight, some decorated—as though for Christmas—with long icicles festooning the branches. Near the National Museum, with its sharp tower fingering the sky, one particular tree seemed to crouch like a white cowled monk clutching a glittering dagger.

Over all, through the clear frost, Bond could glimpse the dominating floodlit domes of the Uspensky Cathedral—the Great Church—and knew immediately why movie makers used Helsinki when they wanted location shots of Moscow.

The two cities are really as unlike one another as desert and jungle, the modern buildings of the Finnish capital being designed and executed with flair and beauty, compared to the ugly cloned monsters of Moscow. It is in the older sections of both cities where the mirror image becomes uncanny—in the side streets and small squares where houses lean in on one another, and the ornate facades remind the eye of what Moscow once was in the good old, bad old days of tsars, princes, and inequality. Now, Bond thought, they simply had the Politburo, commissars, the KGB and , , , inequality

Paula lived in an apartment building overlooking the Esplanade Park, at the southeasterly end of the Mannerheimintie. It was a part of the city Bond had never visited before, so his arrival was one of surprise and delight.

The park itself is a long, landscaped strip running between the houses. There were signs that in summer, it would be an idyllic spot with trees, rock gardens, and paths. Now, in midwinter, the Esplanade Park took on a new original function. Artists of varied ages and ability had turned the place into an open-air gallery of snow sculpture.

From the fresh snow of recent days, there rose shapes and figures lovingly created earlier in winter: abstract masses; pieces so delicate you would imagine they could only be carved from wood, or worked at with patience in metal. Jagged aggression stood next to the contemplative curves of peace, while animals—naturalistic or only suggested in angular blocks—squared up to one another or bared empty winter mouths towards hurrying passers-by, huddled and furred against the cold.

The cab pulled up almost opposite a life-sized work in which a man and woman entwined in an embrace from which only the warmth of spring could rend them apart.

Around the park the buildings were mainly old, with occasional pieces of modernity looking like new buffer states bridging gaps in living history.

For no logical reason, Bond had imagined that Paula would live in a new and shining apartment house. Instead, he found her address to be a house four stories high, with shuttered windows and fresh green paint, decorated by blossoms of snow hanging like windowbox flowers and frosted along the scrollwork and gutters, as though December vandals had taken spray cans to the most available parts.

Two curved, half-timbered gables divided the house, which had a single entrance, glass-paneled and unlocked. Just inside the door, a row of metal mailboxes signified who lived where: the cards, slid into tiny frames, each telling a small tale about the occupants. The hallway and stairs were bare of carpet. Shining wood spoke back with the smell of good polish, mingled now with tantalizing cooking fragrances.

Paula lived on the third floor—3A—and Bond, slipping the buttons on his British Warm, began to make his way up the stairs.

At each landing he noted two doors, to left and right, solid and well-built, with bell-pushes, and the twins of the framed cards on the mailboxes set below them.

At the third turning of the stairs, Paula Vacker's name was elegantly engraved on a business card under the bell for 3A. Out of curiosity, Bond glanced at 3B. Its occupant was a Major A. Nyblin. He pictured a retired army man holed up with military paintings, books on strategy, and the war novels which are such a going concern in Finnish publishing; they kept people remembering those three Wars of Independence in which the nation fought against Russia: first against the revolution; then against invasion; and finally, cheek by jowl with the Wehrmacht.

Bond pressed Paula's bell hard and long, then stood square to the small spy-hole visible in the door's center panel.

From the inside came the rattle of a chain; then the door opened, and there she was, dressed in a long silk robe fastened loosely with a tie belt. The same Paula—as inviting and as attractive as ever.

Bond saw her lips move as though trying to get out words of welcome. In that fraction he realized that this was not the same Paula. Her cheeks were drained white, one hand trembled on the door. Deep in the gray-flecked eyes was the unmistakable flicker of fear.

Intuition, they taught in Service training, is something you learn through experience: you are not born with it like an extra sense.

Loudly Bond said, "It's only me from over the sea," at the same time sticking one foot forward, the side of his shoe against the door. "Glad I came?"

As he spoke, Bond grabbed Paula by the shoulder with his left hand, spinning her, pulling her onto the landing. The right hand had already gone for the automatic. In less than three seconds, Paula was against the wall near Major Nyblin's door, while Bond had sidestepped into the apartment, the Heckler & Koch out and ready.

There were two of them. A small runt with a thin, pockmarked face was to Bond's left, flat against the inside wall, where he had been covering Paula with a small revolver which looked like a Charter Arms Undercover .38 Special. At the far side of the room—there was no hallway—a large man with oversized hands and the face of a failed boxer stood poised beside a beautiful chrome and leather chair-and-sofa suite. His distinguishing marks included a nose which looked like a very advanced carbuncle. He carried no visible weapon.

The runt's gun came up to Bond's left, and the boxer began to move.

Bond went for the gun. The big Heckler & Koch seemed to move only fractionally in Bond's hand as it clipped down with force onto the runt's wrist.

The revolver spun away, and there was a yelp of pain above the sharp crack of bone.

Keeping the H & K pointing towards the larger man, Bond used his left arm to spin the runt in front of him like a shield. At the same time, Bond brought his knee up hard.

The little gunman crumpled, his good hand flailing ineffectually to protect his groin. He squeaked like a pig and squirmed at Bond's feet.

The larger of the two seemed undeterred by the gun, which indicated either great courage or mental deficiency. H & K could, at this range, blow away a high percentage of human being.

Bond stepped over the body of the runt, kicking back with his right heel. Raising the automatic, arms outstretched, Bond shouted at his advancing adversary: "Stop or you're a dead man."

It was more of a command than a warning; Bond's finger was already tightening on the trigger.

The one with the carbuncle nose did not do as he was told. Instead, he suggested in bad Russian that Bond should commit incest with his female parent.

Bond hardly saw him swerve. The man was better than he had estimated and very fast. As he swerved, Bond moved to follow him with the automatic. Only then did he feel the sharp, unnatural pain in his right shoulder.

For a second, the blossom of agony took Bond off balance. His arms dropped, and Carbuncle-nose's foot came up. Bond realized that you cannot be right about people all the time. This was a live one, the real thing—a killer, trained, accurate, and experienced.

Together with this knowledge, Bond was conscious of three things going on simultaneously: the pain in his shoulder; the gun being taken from his hand by the kick and the weapon flying away to hit the wall; and, from behind him, the whimpering of the runt, decreasing in volume as he made his escape down the stairs.

Carbuncle-nose was closing fast, one shoulder dropped, the body sideways.

Bond took a quick step back and to his right, against the wall. As he moved, he spotted what had caused the pain in his shoulder.

Embedded in the door's lintel was an eight-inch knife with a horn grip and a blade curving toward the point. It was a skinning knife, like those used to great effect by the Lapps when separating the carcass of a reindeer from its hide.

Grabbing upwards, Bond's fingers closed around the grip. His shoulder now felt numb with pain. He crabbed quickly to one side, the knife firmly in his right hand, blade upwards, thumb and forefinger to the front of the grip in the fighting hold. Always, they taught, use the thrust position, never hold a knife with the thumb on the back. Never defend with a knife; always attack.

Bond turned, square on, toward Carbuncle-nose, knees bending, one foot forward for balance in the classic knife-fighting posture.

"What was it you said about 'my mother?" Bond growled, in better Russian than his adversary's.

Carbuncle-nose grinned, showing stained teeth. "Now we see, Mr. Bond," he said in broken Russian.

They circled one another, Bond kicking away a small stand chair, giving the pair a wider fighting arena. Carbuncle-nose produced a second knife and began to toss it from hand to hand, light on his feet, moving all the time, tightening the circle. It was a well-known confusion tactic: keep your man guessing and lure him in close, then strike.

Come on, Bond thought, come on; in ; closer; come to me. Carbuncle-nose was doing just that, oblivious to the danger of winding the spiral too tightly. Bond kept his eyes locked with those of the big man, his senses tuned to the enemy knife as it glinted, arcing from hand to hand, the grip slapping the palm with a firm thump on each exchange.

The end came suddenly and fast.

Carbuncle-nose inched nearer to Bond, continuing to toss the knife between his hands.

Bond stepped in abruptly, his right leg lunging out in a fencing thrust, the foot midway between his antagonist's feet. At the same moment, Bond tossed his knife from right to left. Then he feinted, as though to return the knife to his right hand as the opponent would have expected.

The moment was there. Bond saw the big man's eyes move slightly in the direction the knife should be traveling. There was a split second when Carbuncle-nose was uncertain. Bond's left hand rose inches, then flashed out and down. There was the ringing clash of steel against steel.

Carbuncle-nose had been in the act of tossing his knife between hands. Bond's blade caught the weapon in mid-air, smashing it to the floor.

In an automatic reflex, the big man went down, his hand reaching after his knife.

Bond's knife drove upwards.

The big man straightened up very quickly, making a grunting noise. His hand went to his cheek, which Bond's knife had opened into an ugly red canyon from ear to jawline.

Another fact upward strike from Bond, and the knife slit the protective hand. This time, Carbuncle-nose gave a roar of mingled pain and anger.

Bond did not want to kill—not in Finland, not under these circumstances. But he could not leave it like this. The big man's eyes went wide with disbelief and fear as Bond again moved in. The knife flicked up again twice, leaving a jagged slash on the other cheek and removing an ear lobe.

Carbuncle-nose had obviously had enough. He stumbled to one side and made for the door, breath rasping. Bond considered the man had more intelligence than he had first thought.

The pain returned to Bond's shoulder, and with it a sensation of giddiness. Bond had no intention of following the would-be assailant, whose stumbling, falling footsteps could be heard on the wooden stairs.

"James?" Paula had come back into the room. "What shall I do? Call the police, or . . . ?"

She looked frightened. Her face was drained of color. Bond thought he probably didn't look so hot either.

"No. No, we don't want the police, Paula." He sank into the nearest chair. "Close the door, put the chain on, and take a look out the window."

Everything seemed to withdraw around him. Surprisingly, he thought vaguely, Paula did as he asked. Usually she argued. You did not normally give orders to girls like Paula.

"See anything?" Bond's own voice sounded far away.

"There's a car leaving. Cars parked. I can't see any people . . ."

The room tilted, then came back into normal focus.

"James, your shoulder."

He could smell her beside him.

"Just tell me what happened, Paula. It's important. How did they get in? What did they do?"

"Your shoulder, James."

He looked at it. The thick material of his British Warm had saved him from serious injury. Even so, the knife had razored through the epaulette, and blood seeped up through the cloth leaving a dark, wet stain.

"Tell me what happened," Bond repeated.

"You're wounded. I have to look at it."

They compromised. Bond stripped to the waist. A nasty gash ran diagonally across the shoulder. The knife had cut to the depth of around half an inch in the fleshy parts.

Paula, with disinfectant, tape, hot water, and gauze, cleaned and dressed the wound, telling her story at the same time. Outwardly she was calm, though Bond noticed how her hands shook slightly as she recounted what had happened.

The pair of killers had arrived only a couple of minutes before he himself rang the doorbell. "I was running a little late," she made a vague gesture, indicating the silky robe. "Stupid. I didn't have the chain on and just thought it was you. Didn't even look through the spy-hole."

The intruders had simply forced their way in, pushing her back into the room and telling her what to do. They also described in some detail what they would do to her, if she did not carry out instructions.

Under the circumstances, Bond considered she had done the only possible thing. As far as he was concerned, however, there were questions that could only be answered through Service channels, which meant that as much as he might like to stay on in Finland, he had to get back to London. For one thing: the very fact that the two men were inside Paula's apartment only a few minutes before he arrived led him to deduce they had probably been waiting for his cab to stop in Esplanade Park.

"Well, thanks for tipping me off at the door," Bond said, easing his now taped and dressed shoulder.

Paula gave a little pout. "I didn't mean to tip you off. I was just plain frightened."

"Ah, you only acted frightened." Bond smiled at her. "I can tell when people are really frightened."

She bent down, kissed him, then gave a little frown. "James, I'm *still* frightened. Scared stiff if you really want to know. What about that gun, and the way you operate? I thought you were just a senior civil servant."

"I am. Senior and very civil." He paused ready to begin the important questions, but Paula moved across the room to retrieve the automatic pistol, which she nervously handed back to him.

"Will they come back?" Paula asked. "Am I likely to be attacked again?"

"Look," Bond told her, spreading his hands. "For some reason a couple of hoodlums were after me. I really don't know why. Yes, sometimes I do slightly dangerous jobs—hence the weaponry. But there's no reason I can think of for those two having a go at me here, in Helsinki."

He went on to say that he might find out the real answer in London and felt that Paula would be quite safe once he was out of the way. It was too late to catch the British Airways flight home that night, which meant waiting for the regular Finnair service, just after nine the next morning.

"Bang goes our dinner." His smile was meant to look apologetic.

Paula said she had food in the house. They could eat there. Her voice had begun to quaver. Bond made a quick decision about his order of questioning, deciding it would be best to show some very positive side before he tackled the really big problem: how did the would-be assassins know he was in Helsinki and, particularly, how did they know he was visiting Paula?

"You got a car near here, Paula?" he began.

She had a car, and a parking space outside.

"I may well ask a favor of you—later."

"I hope so." She gave him a brave come-on smile.

"Okay. Before we get down to that, there are more important things." Bond fired the obvious questions at her—rapid shooting, pressing her for fast return answers, not giving her time to avoid anything or think about answers.

Had she ever talked about him to friends or colleagues in Finland since they had first met? Of course. Had she done the same in any other country? Yes. Could she remember the number of people she had talked to? She gave some names, obvious ones—close friends and people with whom she worked. Did she have any memory of other people being around when she had spoken about Bond? People she did not know? That was quite possible, but Paula could give no details.

Bond moved on to the most recent events. Had anyone been with her in the office when he telephoned from the Inter-Continental? No. Was there any way the call could have been overheard? Possibly, someone could have been listening in at the switchboard. Had she spoken to anyone after the call, told them that he was in Helsinki, and picking her up at six-thirty? Only one person. "I had a dinner date with a girl, a colleague from another department. We'd arranged to discuss some work over dinner."

This woman's name was Anni Tudeer, and Bond spent quite a long time getting facts about her. At last he lapsed into silence, stood up, crossing to the window and peering out, holding back the curtain.

Below it looked bleak and a little sinister, the white frozen sculptures throwing shadows onto the layer of frost on the ground. Two small fur bundles scuffed their way along the pavement opposite. There were several cars parked along the street. Two of them would have been ideal for surveillance: the angle at which they were parked gave good sightlines to the front door. Bond thought he could detect movement in one of them but decided to put it out of mind until the time came.

He returned to his chair.

"Is the interrogation over?" Paula said.

"That wasn't an interrogation." Bond took out the familiar gunmetal case, offering her one of his Simmons specials. "One day, maybe, I'll show you an interrogation. Remember I said I may have to ask a favor?"

"Ask, and it'll be given."

There was luggage at the hotel, Bond told her, and he had to get to the airport. Could he stay in her apartment until about four in the morning, then drive himself to the hotel in her car, pay the bill, and get out "clean" before going on to the airport? "I can arrange for your car to be brought back here."

"You're not driving anywhere, James." She sounded stubbornly serious. "You've got a nasty wound in your shoulder. It's going to need treatment, sooner or later. Yes, you stay here until four in the morning; then I'll drive you to the hotel and the airport. But why so early? The flight doesn't leave until after nine. You could make a booking from here."

Once more, Bond reiterated that she wouldn't really be safe until he was out of her company. "If I get to the airport in the early hours you'll be rid of me. Also I'll have the advantage. There are ways to position youself in a place like an airport concourse so that nobody can give you nasty surprises. And I'm not using your telephone for obvious reasons."

She agreed, but remained adamant that she would do the driving. Paula being Paula, Bond conceded.

"You're looking better." Paula gave him a peck on the cheek. "Drink?"

"You know my fancy."

She went off into the kitchen and mixed a jug of his favorite martinis. It was over three years ago, in London, that he had taught her the recipe — one which, because of certain publications, had become a standard with many people. After the first drink the throbbing in his shoulder seemed less intense. With the second, Bond felt he was almost back to normal. "I love that robe." His mind began saying things to his body, and wound or not, his body answered back in kind.

"Well," she gave a shy smile. "To tell you the truth, I've already got dinner organized here. I had no intention of going out. I was *ready* for you when those . . . when those brutes turned up. How's the shoulder?"

"Wouldn't stop me playing chess, or any other indoor sport you might name."

With a single movement she pulled the tie belt, and her robe fell open.

"You said I knew your fancy," she said lightly, then: "That is, if you feel up to it."

"Up to it is the way I feel," Bond replied.

It was almost midnight when they ate. Paula set a table with candles and a truly memorable repast: ptarmigan in aspic, glowfried salmon, and a delicious chocolate mousse. Then, at four in the morning, now dressed for the fierce cold of dawn, she allowed Bond to lead the way downstairs.

With the P7 unholstered, Bond used the shadows to creep into the street and made his way across the road now slick with ice, first to a Volvo, then an Audi.

There was a man asleep in the Volvo, his head back and mouth open, far away in whatever dreams bad surveillance men let spring up during the night.

The Audi was empty.

Bond signaled to Paula, who came very sure-footed across the pavement to her car, which started the first time, the exhaust sending out thick clouds in the freezing air.

She drove with the skill of one used to taking a car through snow and ice for long periods each year. At the hotel, the pick-up and check-out went without a hitch, nor was there a tail on them as Paula headed north towards Vantaa.

Officially, Vantaa Airport is not open until seven in the morning, but there are always people about. At five o'clock it had that look you associate with a sour taste of too many cigarettes, constant coffee, and the tiredness of waiting for night trains or planes anywhere in the world.

Bond would not let Paula linger. He assured her that he would ring from London as soon as possible, and they kissed goodby gently, not making a big thing of it.

There were people sweeping up the main departure concourse where Bond chose his spot, his shoulder starting to throb again. Several stranded passengers tried to sleep in the deep comfortable chairs, and quite a number of police walked around in pairs, looking for trouble that never materialized.

Promptly at seven the place became alive. Already Bond had taken up a stance at the Finnair desk, so as to be first in line. There was plenty of room on Finnair's 831, due out at 9:10.

The snow began to fall around eight o 'clock. It had become quite heavy by the time the big DC9-50 growled off the runway at 9:12. Helsinki quickly disappeared in a storm of white confetti, which soon gave way to a towering cloudscape below a brilliant blue sky.

At exactly 10:10 A.M. London time, the same aircraft flared out over the threshold of Heathrow's runway 28 Left. The spoilers came in as they dumped lift, the whining Pratt & Whitney turbofans wailed into reverse thrust, and the aircraft's speed was gradually killed off as the landing was completed.

An hour later, James Bond arrived at the tall building overlooking Regent's Park, which is the headquarters of the Service. By this time his shoulder throbbed like a misplaced toothache, sweat dripped from his forehead, and he felt sick.

4

MADEIRA CAKE

"THEY WERE DEFINITELY professionals?" M had already asked the question three times.

"No doubt on that score." James Bond answered, just as he had done before. "And I stress again, sir, that I was the target."

M grunted.

They were seated in M's office on the ninth floor of the building: M, Bond, and M's Chief of Staff, Bill Tanner.

Immediately on entering the building Bond had taken the lift straight up to the ninth floor, where he lurched into the outer office, the domain of M's neatly efficient PA, Miss Moneypenny.

She looked up and, at first, smiled with pleasure. "James . . ." she began, then saw Bond totter and ran from her desk to help him into a chair.

"That's wonderful, Penny," Bond said, dizzy from pain and fatigue. "You smell great. All woman."

"No, James, all Chanel; while you're a mixture of sweat, antiseptic and a hint of something, I think, by Patou."

M was out, at a Joint Intelligence Committee briefing; so within ten minutes, with Moneypenny's help, Bond was down in the sick bay being tended by the two permanent nurses. The duty doctor was already on the way.

Paula had been right: the wound needed attention, antibiotics as well as stitches. By three in the afternoon Bond was feeling a good deal better, well enough to be taken back to an interrogation by M and the Chief of Staff.

M never used strong language, but his look now was of a man ready to give way to the temptation.

"Tell me about the girl again. This Vacker woman." He leaned across the desk, loading his pipe by feel alone, the gray eyes hard, as though Bond was not to be trusted.

Bond painstakingly went through everything he knew about Paula.

"And the friend? The one she mentioned?"

"Anni Tudeer. Works for the same agency; similar grade to Paula. They're apparently cooperating on a special account at the moment, promoting a chemical research organization based up in Kemi. In the north, but this side of the Circle."

"I know where Kemi is," M almost snarled. "You have to land there en route to Rovaniemi and all places north." He inclined his head towards Tanner. "Chief of Staff, would you run the names through the computers for me? See if we have anything. You can even go hat in hand to 'Five': ask them if there's anything on their books."

Bill Tanner gave a deferential nod and left the office.

Once the door was closed, M leaned back in his chair. "So, what's your personal assessment, 007?" The gray eyes glittered, and Bond thought to himself that M probably had the truth already locked away in his head, together with a thousand other secrets.

Bond chose his words carefully. "I think I was marked—fingered—either during the exercise in the Arctic, or when I got back to Helsinki. Somehow they got a wire onto my hotel phone. It's either that, or Paula—which I would find hard to believe—or someone she spoke to. It was certainly an ad-lib operation, because even I didn't know I was going to stay until we landed in Helsinki. But they moved fast, and certainly they were out to put me away."

M took the pipe from his mouth, stabbing it toward Bond like a baton. "Who are *they?*"

Bond shrugged, his shoulder giving a twinge at the movement. "Paula said they spoke to her in good Finnish. They tried Russian on me—terrible accents. Paula thought they were Scandinavian, but not Finnish."

"Not the answer, Bond. I asked who are *they?*"

"People able to hire local non-Finnish talent—professional blackout merchants."

"Who did the hiring, then? And why?" M sat quite still, his voice calm.

"I don't make friends easily."

"Without the frivolity, 007."

"Well," Bond sighed. "I suppose it could have been a contract. Remnants of SPECTRE. Certainly not KGB, or unlikely. Could be one of a dozen half-baked groups."

"Would you call the National Socialist Action Army a half-baked group?"

"Not their style, sir. They go for Communist targets—the big bang, complete with publicity handouts."

M allowed a thin smile. "They could be using an agency, couldn't they, 007? An advertising agency, like the one your Ms. Vacker works for."

"Sir." Flat, as though M had become crazed.

"No, Bond. Not their style, unless they wanted a quick termination of someone they saw as a threat."

"But I'm not . . ."

"They weren't to know that. They weren't to know you had stopped off in Helsinki for some playboy nonsense—a role which becomes increasingly tiresome, 007. You were instructed to get straight back to London when the exercise in the Arctic was completed, were you not?"

"Nobody was pushy about it. I thought . . ."

"Don't care a jot what you thought, 007. We wanted you back here. Instead you go gadding around Helsinki. May have compromised the Service, and yourself."

"I . . ."

"You weren't to know." M appeared to have softened a little. "After all, I simply sent you off to do a cold weather exercise, an acclimatization. I take the responsibility. Should've been more explicit."

"Explicit?"

M remained silent for a full minute. Above him, Robert Taylor's original *Trafalgar* set the whole tone of M's determination and character. That painting had lasted two years. Before then there had been Cooper's *Cape St. Vincent,* on loan from the National Maritime Museum, and before that . . . Bond could not recall, but they were always paintings of Britain's naval victories. M was the possessor of that essential arrogance which put allegiance to country first, and a firm belief in the invincibility of Britain's fighting forces, no matter what the odds, or how long it took.

At last, M spoke. "We have an operation of some importance going on in the Arctic Circle at this moment, 007. The exercise was a warm-up—if I dare use that expression. A warm-up for *you*. To put it in a nutshell, you are to join that operation."

"Against?" Bond expected the obvious answer.

"The Nationalist Socialist Action Army."

"In Finland?"

"Close to the Russian border." M hunched himself even farther forward, like a man anxious not to be overheard. "We already have a man there—or I should say we *had* a man there. He's on his way back. No need to go into details just now. Personality clashes with our allies mainly. The whole team's coming out to regroup and meet you, put you in the picture. You get a briefing from me first, of course."

"The whole team being?"

"Being strange bedfellows, 007. Strange bedfellows. And now we may have lost some tactical surprise, I fear, by your dalliance in Helsinki. We had hoped you'd go in unnoticed. Join the team without tipping off these neo-Fascists."

"The team?" Bond repeated.

M coughed, playing for time. "A joint operation, 007; an unusual operation, set up at the request of the Soviet Union."

Bond frowned. "We're playing with Moscow Center?"

M gave a curt nod. "Yes," as though he also disapproved. "And not only the Center. We're also involved with Langley and Tel Aviv."

Bond gave a low whistle, which brought raised eyebrows and a tightening of M's lips. "I said strange bedfellows, Bond."

Bond muttered, as though repeating something unbelievable aloud, "Ourselves, the KGB, CIA, and Mossad—the Israelis."

"Precisely." Now that the cat was out of the bag, M warmed to his subject. "Operation Icebreaker—the Americans named it, of course. Soviets went along with it because they were the supplicants . . ."

"The KGB *asked* for cooperation?" Bond still sounded incredulous.

"Through secret channels, yes. When we first heard the news, the few of us in the know were dubious. Then I had an invitation to stop over to Grosvenor Square." The reference was to the United States Embassy in Grosvenor Square.

"And they'd been asked?"

"Yes, and naturally, being the Company, they knew Mossad had been asked, too. Within a day we had arranged a tripartite conference."

Bond gestured wordlessly, asking if he could smoke. M went on speaking, giving a tiny motion of his hand as permission, pausing only now and again to light and relight his pipe. "We looked at it from all sides. Searched for the traps—and there are some, of course—examined the options if it went sour, then decided to nominate field officers. We wanted at least three each. Soviets heel-tapped on three—too many, the need to contain, and all that kind of thing. Finally we met the KGB's negotiator, Anatoli Pavlovich Grinev . . ."

Bond nodded, knowingly. "Colonel of the First Directorate, Third Department. Covering as First Secretary, Trade, in KPG."

"Got him," M acknowledged. KPG meant Kensington Palace Gardens and, more specifically, number 13—the Russian Embassy. The Third Department of the KGB's First Directorate dealt entirely with intelligence operations concerning the United Kingdom, Australia, New Zealand and Scandinavia. "Got him. Little fellow, Toby Jug ears." That was a good description of the wily Colonel Ginev. Bond had dealt with the gentleman before and trusted him as he would trust a dud land mine.

"And he explained?" Bond was not really asking. "Explained why the KGB would want ourselves, the CIA, and Mossad, to combine in a covert op on Finnish territory? Surely, they're on good enough terms with SUPO to deal direct."

"Not quite," M replied. SUPO was Finnish Intelligence. "You've read everything we have on the NSAA, 007?"

Bond gave him an affirmative, adding, "What precious little there is—the detailed reports of their thirty-odd assassination successes. There's not much more than that . . ."

"There's the Joint Intelligence Analysis. You've studied those fifty pages, I trust?"

Bond said he had read them. "They elevate the National Socialist Action Army from a small fanatical terrorist organization to something more sinister. I'm not certain the conclusions are correct."

"Really," M sniffed. "Well *I* am certain, 007. The NSAA are still fanatics, but the leading intelligence communities and security arms are agreed. The NSAA is led and nurtured, on old Nazi principles. They mean what they say; and it seems as though they're pulling more people into the net every day. The indications suggest that their leaders see themselves as the architects of the Fourth Reich. The target, at present, is organized Communism; but two other elements have recently appeared."

"Such as?"

"Recent outbreaks of anti-Semitism throughout Europe and the United States . . ."

"There's no proved connection . . ."

M silenced him with a hand raised. "And, secondly, we have one of them in the bag."

"A member of the NSAA? Nobody's . . ."

"Announced it, or spoken, no. Under wraps tighter than a mummy's shroud."

Bond asked if M's statement that "we" have one literally meant the United Kingdom.

"Oh, yes. He's here, in this very building. In the guest wing." M made a single stabbing downward motion, to indicate the large interrogation center they kept in the basement. The whole place had been redesigned when government defense cuts had denied the Service its "place in the country," where interrogations used to take place.

M continued, saying they had taken the man concerned "after the last bit of business in London," which meant the slaughter, in broad daylight, of three British civil servants who had just left the Soviet Embassy after some trade discussions. That was six months ago, and one of the assassins had tried to shoot himself as members of the SPG closed in.

"His aim was off," M smiled without humor. "We saw to it that he lived. Most of what we know is built around what he's told us."

"He's talked?"

"Precious little," M shrugged. "But what he has said allows us to read between the lines. Very few people know about any of it, 007. I'm only telling you this much so that you won't doubt we're on the right track. We are eighty percent certain that the NSAA is global, growing and, if not stopped at this stage, will eventually lead to an open movement, one which might become tempting to the electorates of many democracies. The Soviets have a vested interest, of course."

"Why go along with them, then?"

"Because no intelligence service, from the *Bundesnachrichtendienst* to the SDECE, has come up with any other clues . . ."

"So . . . ?"

"Nobody, that is, except the KGB."

Bond did not move a muscle.

"They, naturally, don't know what we've got," M continued. "But they've provided a clue of some magnitude. The NSAA armorer."

Bond inclined his head. "They've always used Russian stuff, so I presume . . ."

"Presume nothing, 007, that's one of the first rules of strategy. The KGB have persuasive evidence that the NSAA's equipment is cleverly stolen within the Soviet Union and shipped out, probably by a Finnish national, to various pick-up points. That's the reason they wanted it clandestine: without knowledge of the Finnish government."

"And why us?" Bond was beginning to see light.

"They say," M began, "they say it's because there has to be a back-up from countries other than the Eastern bloc. The Israelis are obvious, because Israel would be the next target. Britain and America would present a formidable front to the world if they were seen to be involved. They also say that it is in our common interest to share."

"You believe them, sir?"

M gave a bland, unsmiling look. "No. Not altogether; but I don't think it's meant to be anything sinister, like some complicated entrapment of three intelligence services."

"And how long's Operation Icebreaker been running?"

"Six weeks. They particularly asked for you at the outset, but I wanted to test the ice, if you see what I mean."

"And it's firm?"

"It'll carry your weight, 007. Or I think it will. After what's happened in Helsinki, of course, there is a new danger."

There was silence for a full minute. Far away, behind the heavy door, a telephone rang.

"The man you put in . . . ?" Bond broke the silence.

"Two men really. Each organization has a resident director holed up in Helsinki. It's the field man we're pulling out. Dudley. Clifford Arthur Dudley. Resident in Stockholm for some time."

"Good man." Bond lit another cigarette. "I've worked with him." Indeed, they had done a complicated surveillance and character assassination on a Romanian diplomat in Paris a couple of years before. "Very nimble," Bond added. "Good all-rounder. You say there was a personality clash . . . ?"

M did not look at Bond directly. He rose, walking over to the window, hands clasped behind his back as he gazed down across Regent's Park. "Yes," he said slowly. "Yes. Punched our American ally in the mouth."

"Cliff Dudley?"

M turned. He wore his sly look. "Oh, he did it on my instructions. Playing for time, like I said, testing the ice—and waiting for you to get acclimatized, if you follow."

Again the silence, broken by Bond. "And I'm to join the team."

"Yes." M seemed to have gone a little absent-minded. "Yes, yes. They've all pulled out. You're to meet them as soon as possible. I've chosen the rendezvous, incidentally. How do you fancy Reid's Hotel in Funchal, Madeira?"

"Better than a Lapp *kota* in the Arctic Circle, sir."

"Good. Then we'll give you a full briefing here, and if you're up to it, we'll speed you on the way tomorrow night. I'm afraid the Arctic'll be your next stop after Madeira though. Now, there's a lot of work to be done, and you'll have to realize this thing's not going to be a piece of cake, as they used to say in World War Two."

"Not even Madeira cake?" Bond smiled.

M actually allowed himself a short laugh.

5

RENDEZVOUS AT REID'S

IN THE EVENT, James Bond did not get away from London as quickly as expected. There was too much to be done, and the doctors also insisted on a complete check up. Then, too, Bill Tanner appeared with the trace results on Paula Vacker and her friend, Anni Tudeer.

There were a couple of interesting, and troubling, pieces of information. As it turned out, Paula was of Swedish birth, though she had assumed Finnish citizenship. Apparently her father at one time had been with the Swedish Diplomatic Corps, though a note listed him as having "militant right-wing tendencies."

"Probably means the man's a Nazi," M grunted.

The thought worried Bond, but Bill Tanner's next words disturbed him even more.

"Maybe," the Chief of Staff said. "But her girlfriend's father certainly is, or was, a Nazi."

What Tanner had to say made Bond yearn for a quick opportunity to see Paula again and, more particularly meet her close friend, Anni Tudeer.

The computers had little on the girl, but they disgorged a great deal about her father, a formerly high-ranking officer in the Finnish Army. Colonel Aarne Tudeer was, in fact, a member of the great Finnish Marshal Mannerheim's staff in 1943, and in the same year—when the Finns fought side by side with the German Army against the Russians—Tudeer had accepted a post with the Waffen SS.

Though Tudeer was a soldier first, it remained clear that his admiration of Nazi Germany and, in particular, Adolf Hitler, knew no bounds. By the end of 1943 Aarne Tudeer had been promoted to the rank of SS-Ober-führer and moved to a post within the Nazi Fatherland.

When the war ended, Tudeer disappeared, but there were definite indications that he remained alive. The Nazi-catchers still had him on the wanted list; for among many of the operations in which he played a prominent part was the "execution" of fifty prisoners of war, recaptured after the famous "Great Escape" from Stalag Luft III at Sagan, in March

1944—an atrocity well chronicled in the annals of infamy.

Later, Tudeer fought bravely during the historic, bloody march of the 2nd SS Panzer Division ("Das Reich") from Montauban to Normandy. It is well-known that during those two weeks in June 1944, there were acts of unbridled horror which defied the normal rules of war. One was the burning of 642 men, women, and children in the village of Oradour-sur-Glañe. Aarne Tudeer had more than a hand in that particular episode.

"A soldier, first, yes," Tanner explained, "but the man is a war criminal and, as such—even though he's an old-age pensioner now—the Nazi-hunters are still after him. There were confirmed sightings in South America during the 1950s, but it's pretty certain he came back to Europe in the sixties after a successful identity transplant."

Bond filed the information in his head, asking for the chance to study any existing documents and photographs.

"There's no chance of me slipping back into Helsinki, seeing Paula and meeting the Tudeer woman, I suppose? Bond looked hard at M, who shook his head.

"Sorry, 007. Time is of the essence. The whole team's come out of its operational zone for two reasons: first, to meet and brief you; second, to plan what they reckon's going to be the final stage in their mission. You see, they think they know where the arms are coming from, how they're being passed on to the NSAA and, most important, who is directing all NSAA ops, and from where."

M refilled his pipe, settled back in his chair and began to talk. In many ways, what he revealed was enough to make Bond's hair stand on end.

They stayed until late that night, after which Bond was driven back to his Chelsea flat and the tender mercies of May, his redoubtable housekeeper, who took one look and ordered Bond straight to bed in the tones of an old-fashioned nanny. "You look washed out, Mr. James. To bed with you. I'll bring you a little eggy something on a tray. Now, away to your bed."

Bond did not feel like arguing. May appeared soon afterwards with a tray of smoked salmon and scrambled eggs, which Bond ate while he looked through the pile of mail that had been waiting for him. He had scarcly finished the meal before fatigue took over and, without a struggle, he dropped into a deep refreshing sleep.

When he woke, Bond knew that May had allowed him to sleep late. The numbers on his digital bedside clock showed that it was almost ten. Within seconds he was calling for May to get breakfast. A few minutes later the telephone rang.

M was shouting for him.

Extra time spent in London paid dividends. Not only was Bond given a thorough in-depth rundown on his partners for Operation Icebreaker, but also had an opportunity to talk at length with Cliff Dudley, the officer from whom he was taking over.

Dudley was a short, hard, pugnacious Scot, a man whom Bond both liked and respected. "If I'd had more time," Dudley told him, "likely I'd have sniffed out the whole truth. But it was really you they wanted. M made that clear to me before I went. Mind you, James, you'll have to keep your back to the wall. None of the others'll look out for you. Moscow Center're definitely on to something, but it all stinks of duplicity. Maybe I'm superstitious by nature, but their boy's holding something back. He's got a dozen aces up his sleeve, and all in the same suit, I'll be bound."

"Their boy," as Dudley called him, was not unknown to Bond, at least by reputation. Nicolai Mosolov had plenty of reputation, none of it particularly appetizing.

Known to his friends with the KGB as Kolya, Mosolov spoke fluent English, American English, German, Dutch, Swedish, Italian, Spanish, and Finnish. Now in his late thirties, the man had been a star pupil at the basic training school near Novosibirsk, and worked for some time with the expert Technical Support Group of his Service's Second Chief Directorate, which is, in effect, a professional burglary unit.

In the building overlooking Regent's Park they also knew Mosolov under a number of aliases. In the United States he was Nicholas S. Mosterlane, Sven Flanders in Sweden and other Scandinavian countries. They knew, but had never nailed him—not even as Nicholas Mortin-Smith in London.

"Invisible man type," M said. "Chameleon. Merges with his background and disppears just when you think he's bottled up."

Bond was no happier about his American counterpart on Icebreaker. Brad Tirpitz, known in intelligence circles as "Bad" Brad, was a veteran of the old-school CIA who had escaped a multitude of purges which had gone on within his organization's headquarters at Langley, Virginia. To some, Tirpitz was a kind of swashbuckling, do-or-die hero: a legend. There were others, however, who saw him in a different light—as the sort of field officer capable of using highly questionable methods, a man who considered that the end always justified the means. And the means could be, as one of his colleagues put it, "pretty mean. He has the instinct of a hungry wolf, and the heart of a scorpion."

So, Bond thought, his future lay with a Moscow Center heavy and a Langley sharpshooter who tended to shoot first and ask questions later.

The rest of the briefing, and medical, took the remainder of the day and some of the following morning. So it was not until the afternoon of this third day that Bond boarded the two o'clock TAP flight to Lisbon, connecting with one of the Boeing 727 shuttles to Funchal.

The sun was low, almost touching the water, throwing great warm red blotches of color against the rocks, when Bond's aircraft—now down to around 600 feet—crossed the Ponta de Saõ Lourenço headland to make that exhilarating low-level turn which is the only way to get into the precarious little runway, perched like an aircraft carrier's flight deck among the rocks at Funchal.

Within the hour a taxi deposited him at Reid's Hotel, and the following morning found him searching for either Mosolov, Tirpitz, or the third member of the Icebreaker group—the Mossad agent whom Dudley had described as "an absolutely deadly young lady, around five-six, clear skin. The figure's copied from the Venus de Milo, only this one's got both arms, and the head's different."

"How different?" Bond asked.

"Stunning. Late twenties, I'd say. Very, very good. I'd hate to be up against her . . ."

"In the professional sense, of course." Bond could not resist the quip.

As far as M was concerned, the Israeli agent was an unknown quantity. The name was Rivke Ingber. The file said "Nothing known."

So now James Bond looked out over the hotel's twin swimming pools, his eyes shaded by sunglasses as he searched faces and bodies.

For a moment, his gaze fell on a tall, elaborate blonde in a Cardin bikini whose body defied normal description. Well, Bond thought, as the girl plunged into the warm water, there was no law against looking.

He shifted his body on the sun lounger, wincing slightly at the ache in his now rapidly healing shoulder, and continued to watch the girl swimming, her lovely long legs opening and closing while her arms moved lazily in an act of almost conscious sensuality.

Bond smiled once more at M's choice for the rendezvous. Among the package tourist traps which run from Gran Canaria to Corfu, Reid's remains one of the few hotels which have maintained standards of cuisine, service, and stuffiness that date back to life in the 1930s.

The hotel shop sells reminders of the old days—photographs of Sir Winston and Lady Churchill taken in the lush gardens. Lath-straight elderly men with clipped mustaches sit reading in the airy public rooms; young couples, dressed by YSL and Kenzo, rub shoulders with elderly titled ladies on the famous tea terrace. He was, Bond considered, in "The-Butler-Did-It" territory; unquestionably M's cronies came to this idyllic time warp with the regularity of a Patek Philippe wristwatch.

As he lay there, Bond covered the pool and sunbathing area with carefully regulated sweeps of the eye. No sign of Mosolov. No sign of Tirpitz. He could recognize those two easily enough from the photographs studied in London.

There had been no photograph of Rivke Ingber, and Cliff Dudley had merely smiled knowingly, telling Bond he would find out what she looked like soon enough.

People were now drifting towards the pool restaurant, open on two sides and protected by pink stone arches. Tables were laid, waiters hovered, a bar beckoned; a long buffet had been set up to provide every conceivable kind of salad and cold meats, or—if the client so fancied—hot soup, quiche, lasagne or cannelloni.

Lunch. Bond's old habits followed him faithfully to Madeira. The warm air and sun throughout his morning watch had now produced that pleasant need for something light at lunchtime.

Putting on a terrycloth robe, Bond padded to the buffet, selected some thin slices of ham, and began to choose from the array of colorful salads.

"Don't you fancy a drink, Mr. Bond? To break the ice?" Her voice was soft and unaccented.

"Miss Ingber?" Bond did not turn to look at her.

"Yes, I've been watching you for some time—and I think you me. Shall we have lunch together? The others have also arrived."

Bond turned. It was the spectacular blonde he had seen in the pool. She had changed into a dry black bikini, and the visible flesh glowed bronze, the color of autumn beech leaves. The contrast of colors—skin, the thin black material, and the striking gold curls cut close—made Rivke Ingber look not only acutely desirable, but also an object lesson in health and body care. Her face shone with fitness, unblemished, classical, almost Nordic—with a strong mouth and dark eyes within which a spirit of humor seemed to dance almost seductively.

"Well," Bond acknowledged, "you've outflanked me, Ms. Ingber. Shalom."

"Shalom, Mr. Bond . . ." The pink mouth curved into a smile which appeared open, inviting, and completely genuine.

"Call me James." Bond made a small mental note of the smile.

She was already holding a plate carrying a small portion of chicken breast, some sliced tomatoes, and a salad of rice and apples. Bond gestured toward one of the nearby tables. She walked ahead of him, her body supple, the slight swing of her hips almost wanton. Carefully placing her plate on the table, Rivke Ingber automatically gave her bikini pants a tiny hitch, then ran her thumbs inside the rear of the legs, setting them over her high, neat buttocks. It was a gesture performed naturally and without thought countless times each day by women at beaches and swimming pools; but, as executed by Rivke Ingber, the movement became a tantalizing, overtly sexual invitation.

Now, sitting opposite Bond, she gave her smile again, running the tip of her tongue across her upper lip. "Welcome aboard, James. I've wanted to work with you for a long time"—a slight pause—"which is more than I can say about our colleagues."

Bond looked at her, trying to penetrate the dark eyes, an unusual feature in a woman of Rivke's coloring. His fork was poised between plate and mouth as he asked, "That bad?"

She laughed musically. "Worse than that," she said. "I suppose you were told why your predecessor left us?"

"No," Bond gazed at her innocently. "All I know is that I was suddenly whisked onto this with little time for briefings. They said the team—which seems a pretty odd mix to me—would give me the detailed story."

She laughed again. "There was what you might call a personality clash. Brad Tirpitz was being his usual boorish self, at my expense. Your man belted him in the mouth. I was a little put out. I mean, I could have dealt with Tirpitz myself."

Bond took the mouthful of food, chewed and swallowed, then asked about the operation.

Rivke gave him a little flirtatious look from under slightly lowered eyelids. "Oh," a finger mockingly to her lips, "that's a no-no. Bait—that's what I am. I'm to lure you in to the pair of experts. We *all* have to be present at your briefing. To tell you the truth, I don't think they take me very seriously."

Bond smiled grimly. "Then they've never heard the most important saying about your service . . ."

"We are good at our task because the alternative is too horrifying to contemplate." She spoke the words on a flat note, almost parrotlike.

"And are *you* good, Rivke Ingber?" Bond chewed another mouthful.

"Can a bird fly?"

"Our colleagues must be very stupid, then."

She sighed. "Not stupid, James. Chauvinists. They're not noted for their confidence in working with women, that's all."

"Never had that trouble myself." Bond's face remained blank.

"No. So I've heard." Rivke suddenly sounded prim. Maybe it was even a "keep off" warning note.

"So. We don't talk about Icebreaker?"

She shook her head. "Don't worry, you'll get enough of that when we go up to see the boys."

Bond felt a hint of warning, even in the way she looked at him. It was as though the possibility of friendship had been offered, then suddenly withdrawn. Just as quickly, Rivke became her old self, the dark eyes locking onto James Bond's equally startling blue irises.

They finished their light meal without Bond attempting to touch on the subject of Icebreaker again. He talked about her country—which he knew well—and of its many problems, but did not try to advance the conversation into her private life.

"Time to meet the big boys, James." She dabbed at her lips with a napkin, her eyes darting upward toward the hotel.

Mosolov and Tirpitz had probably been watching them from their balcony, Rivke said. They had rooms next to one another on the fourth floor, with both balconies giving good views of the gardens, and sightlines which allowed constant surveillance of the swimming pool area.

They went off to separate changing rooms and emerged in suitable clothes: Rivke in a dark pleated skirt and white shirt; Bond in his favorite navy slacks, a Sea Island cotton shirt, and moccasins. Together they entered the hotel and took the elevator to the fourth floor.

"Ah, Mr. James Bond."

Mosolov was as nondescript as the experts maintained. He could have been any age—from mid-twenties to late forties. His face appeared to change with moods and in different lights; and with the change came either an aging or shedding of years. His English seemed flawless, with the slight hint of a suburban London accent, and some colloquialisms thrown in from time to time.

"Kolya Mosolov," he introduced himself, taking Bond's hand. Even the handshake was neither one thing nor the other, and the eyes, a clouded gray, looked dull, not meeting Bond's gaze with any certainty.

"Glad to be working with you," Bond gave his most charming smile, while taking in what he could of the man: on the short side, blond hair cut with no style, but paradoxically neat. No character—or so it would seem—in either the man or his clothes: a short-sleeved brown check shirt, and slacks that looked as though they had been run up by an apprentice tailor on a particularly bad day.

Kolya indicated a chair, though Bond did not quite see how he did it without gestures, or moving his body. "Do you know Brad Tirpitz?"

The chair contained Tirpitz, a sprawled, large man with big rough hands and a face chiseled, it appeared, out of granite. His hair was gray and cut short, almost to the scalp, and Bond was pleased to note the traces of bruising and a slight cut around the left side of the man's unusually small mouth.

Tirpitz lazily lifted a hand in a kind of salutation. "Hi," he grunted, the voice harsh, as though he had spent a lot of time getting his accent from tough-guy movies. "Welcome to the club, Jim."

Bond could detect no glimmer of welcome or pleasure in the man.

"Good to meet you, *Mr.* Tirpitz." Bond paused on the *Mister.*

"Brad," Tirpitz growled back. This time there was the hint of a smile around the corners of his mouth. Bond nodded.

"You know what this is all about?" Kolya Mosolov seemed to assume an almost apologetic mood.

"Only a little . . ."

Rivke stepped in, smiling at Bond. "James tells me he was sent out here on short notice. No briefing from his people."

Mosolov shrugged, sat down, and indicated one of the other chairs. Rivke dropped onto the bed, curling her legs under her as though settling in.

Bond took the proffered chair, pushing it back against the wall into a position from which he could see the other three. It also gave him a good view of the window and balcony.

Mosolov took a deep breath. "We haven't much time," he began. "There's need for us to be out of here within forty-eight hours and back into the operational area."

Bond gestured with his hand. "Is it quite safe to talk in here?"

Tirpitz gave a gruff laugh. "Don't worry about it. We checked the place over. My room's next door; this one's on the corner of the building; and I sweep the place all the time."

Bond turned back to Mosolov who had waited patiently, almost subserviently, during the slight interruption. The Russian waited a second more before speaking: "Do you think this strange? The CIA, Mossad, my people, and your people all working together?"

"Initially." Bond appeared to relax. This was the moment M had warned him about. There was a possibility that Mosolov would hold certain matters back. If so, then he needed every ounce of extra caution. "Initially I thought it strange but, on reflection . . . well, we're all in the same business. Different outlooks, possibly, but no reason why we shouldn't work together for the common good."

"Correct," Mosolov said curtly. "Then I'll give you the information in outline." He paused, looked around him, giving a credible imitation of a nearsighted and somewhat vague academic. "Rivke. Brad. Please add in any points that you think I should stress."

Rivke nodded, and Tirpitz laughed unpleasantly.

"All right." The transmogrification trick again: Kolya transformed from the slow professor into the sharp executive, decisive, in control. He was a joy to watch, Bond thought.

"All right, I'll give it to you quickly and straight. This—as you probably *do* know, Mr. Bond—concerns the National Socialist Action Army: a terrorist organization of immense skill, dedicated against my own country, and a proven threat to your countries also. Fascists in the old mold."

Tirpitz gave his unpleasant laugh again, "Moldy old Fascists."

Mosolov ignored him. It appeared to be the only way to deal with Brad Tirpitz's wisecracks. "Governments all over the world who've been victims of the NSAA attacks have publicly claimed there are no clues." He glanced around, hesitating for a second at each of them, holding the eyes to be certain of his audience. "There *have* been clues, however. First, the bulk of those who make up the NSAA come from the neo-Nazi organizations. There is no doubt about that. All of our governments have pooled the information—they come from Britain, Sweden, Germany, and the South American republics which gave succor and shelter to some of the most obnoxious scum of the Third Reich after the Great Patriotic War . . . the Second World War . . ."

Bond smiled inwardly. Mosolov had used the Russian name for World War Two quite consciously, not as a slip of the tongue.

"I am not a fanatic," Kolya dropped his voice. "Nor am I obsessed by the NSAA. However, like your government, I believe this organization to be large and growing every day. It is a threat . . ."

"You can say that again." Brad Tirpitz took out a pack of Camels, thumped the end against his thumb, extracted a cigarette and lit it, using a book match. "Let's cut through it, Kolya. The National Socialist Action

Army's got you Soviets scared out of your skulls."

"A *threat*," Kolya continued, "to the world. Not just to Soviet Russia and the Eastern bloc."

"You're their main target," Tirpitz grunted.

"And we're implicated, Brad, as you know. That's why my government approached your people; and Rivke's Knesset; and Mr. Bond's government." He turned back to Bond. "As you may or may not know, all the arms used in operations carried out by the NSAA come from a Soviet source. The Central Committee were informed of this only after the fifth incident. Other governments and agencies suspected we were supplying arms to some organization—possibly Middle Eastern—which was in turn passing them on. This was not so. The information solved a problem for us."

"Someone had their fingers in the till," Brad Tirpitz interjected.

"True," Kolya Mosolov snapped. "Last spring, during a snap inspection of stores—the first for two years—a senior officer of the Red Army discovered a huge discrepancy: an inexplicable loss of armaments. All from one source." He rose, walked across the room to a briefcase from which he took a large map, which he spread on the carpet in front of James Bond.

"Here." His finger pointed at the paper. "Here, near Alakurtti, we have a large ordnance depot . . ."

Alakurtti lay some sixty kilometers east of the Finnish border, well into the Arctic Circle—about two hundred-plus kilometers northeast of Rovaniemi, where Bond had based himself before moving much farther north during his recent expedition. It would be barren and bleak country, well iced and snowed in at this time of the year, with some tree cover from firs.

Kolya continued. "During last winter that particular ordnance depot was raided. We were able to connect all the serial numbers of captured weapons used by the NSAA. They definitely come from Alakurtti.

Bond asked what was missing.

Kolya's face went deadpan as he rattled off a rough list: "Kalashnikovs; RPK's; AK's; AKM's; Makarov and Stechkin pistols; RDG-5 and RG-42 grenades . . . A large number, with ammunition."

"Nothing heavier than that?" Bond made it sound casual, an off-the-cuff response.

Mosolov shook his head. "It's enough. They disappeared in great quantities."

First black mark, Bond thought. He already knew from M—who had his own sources on the Soviet claims—that Kolya Mosolov omitted the most significant weapon: a large number of RGP-7V Anti-Tank launchers, complete with rockets that carried several different kinds of warheads—conventional, chemical, and tactical nuclear—and large enough to wreck a small town and devastate a fifty-mile radius from point of impact.

"This equipment disappeared during the winter, when we keep a small garrison at Base Blue Hare, as we call the depot. The colonel who made the discovery used his common sense. He told nobody at Blue Hare, but reported straight back to the GRU."

Bond nodded. That figured: the *Glavnoye Razvedyvatelnoye Upravleniye*—Soviet Military Intelligence, an organization linked umbilically with the KGB—would be the natural source to be informed.

"The GRU put in a pair of *monks*. That's what they like to call undercover men working in government offices, or army units."

"And they lived up to their holy orders?" Bond asked without a smile.

"More than that. They've located the ringleaders—greedy NCO's being paid off by some outside source."

"So," Bond interruped, "you know how the stuff was stolen . . ."

Kolya smiled. "How, and the direction in which it was moved. We're fairly certain that last winter the consignment was taken over the Finnish border. It's a difficult frontier to cover, though parts are mined, and we've cut away miles of trees. People still come in and go out every day. That's the way we believe the stuff went."

"You don't know the exact first destination, then?" It was Bond's second testing question.

Mosolov hesitated. "We're not certain. There's a possibility. Our satellites are trying to pinpoint a possible location, and our people have their eyes open for the prime suspect. But the facts are still unclear."

James Bond turned to the others. "And is it just as uncertain to you two?"

"We only know what Kolya's told us," Rivke said calmly. "This is a friendly operation of trust."

"Langley gave me a name nobody's mentioned yet, that's all." Brad Tirpitz was obviously not going to say more, so Bond asked Mosolov if he had a name to say aloud.

There was a long pause. Bond waited for the name which M had given him on the last night, in that office high on the ninth floor of the building overlooking Regent's Park.

"It's so uncertain . . ." Mosolov did not wish to be drawn.

Bond opened his mouth to speak again, but Kolya quickly added: "Next week. By this time next week we may well have it all sewn up. Our GRU monks report that another consignment is to be stolen and transported away. That's why we have little time. As a team, our job is to gain evidence of the theft, then survey the route by which the arms are removed—right up to their final destination. Obviously, this consignment will be for a new NSAA campaign."

"And you think the man who'll receive them will be Count Konrad von Glöda?" Bond gave a broad smile.

Kolya Mosolov did not show any signs of emotion or surprise.

Brad Tirpitz chuckled. "London has the same information as Langley, then."

"Who's von Glöda?" Rivke asked, not attempting to disguise her shock. "Nobody's mentioned any Count von Glöda to me."

Bond removed the gunmetal cigarette case from his hip pocket, placed a slim white H. Simmons cigarette between his lips, lit it, inhaled smoke, then let it out in a long thin stream. "My people—and the CIA also, it would appear—have information that the principal acting on behalf of the NSAA in Finland is a Count Konrad von Glöda. That true, Kolya?"

Mosolov's eyes still remained cloudy. "It's a code name. A cryptonym, that's all. There was no point giving you that information as yet."

"Why not? Are you hiding anything else, Kolya?" Bond did not smile this time.

"Only that I would hope to lead you to von Glöda's retreat in Finland next week when we carry out our surveillance on Blue Hare, Mr. Bond. I had hoped you would accompany me into Russia and see it all for yourself."

James Bond could hardly believe it. A KGB man was actually inviting him into the spider's web, under the pretext of witnessing the theft of a large quantity of arms. And there was no way, now, in which he could tell whether Kolya Mosolov meant it as a genuine part of Icebreaker, or whether Icebreaker was merely some carefully dreamed-up device to trap Bond on Soviet soil.

It was the latter possibility that M dreaded, and warned Bond about before 007 had left for Madeira.

6

SILVER VS. YELLOW

THE FOUR MEMBERS of the Icebreaker team had arranged to meet for dinner, but Bond had other ideas. M's warnings of possible—and dangerous—duplicity among the uneasy quartet had been made all too apparent at the short briefing in Kolya's room.

If it had not been the hinted nudge from Brad Tirpitz, the name of Count Konrad von Glöda would not have been mentioned; and according to M, this mystery man was a key figure to any combined security investigation. Nor had Kolya bothered to give full details of the more dangerous items missing from the Russian Blue Hare ordnance depot.

While Brad Tirpitz was obviously as well informed as Bond, it seemed that Rivke remained very much in the dark. The whole projected operation, including the business of surveying a second large theft from the Russian side of the border, did not bode well.

Even though the dinner meeting was agreed to, Kolya had been insistent that all four members of Icebreaker had to be off the island, heading back into the operational area in Finland over the next forty-eight hours. Even a rendezvous had been given, and accepted, by all.

Bond knew there were things he had to do before joining the others in the bitter climate of the Arctic Circle. They would not expect him to move quickly. There were several flights out of Madeira on the Sunday morning, so doubtless Kolya would make suggestions at dinner as to how they should split up and travel separately. James Bond was certainly not going to wait on Kolya Mosolov's instructions.

On leaving the room, he made his excuses to Rivke, who wanted him to have a drink with her in the bar, and made for his own quarters. Within fifteen minutes, James Bond was in a cab on his way to Funchal Airport.

There followed a long wait. It was Saturday, and he had missed the three o'clock flight. He didn't get away until the last aircraft of the night—the ten o'clock, which at that time of year runs only on Wednesdays, Fridays, and Saturdays.

During the flight, Bond reflected on his next move, knowing that his colleagues would almost certainly begin arriving in Lisbon after the first aircraft out on Sunday. Bond would prefer to be away, heading towards Helsinki, long before any of them reached the mainland.

His luck held. Technically there were no flights out of Lisbon after the final aircraft from Funchal. But the afternoon KLM service to Amsterdam had been badly delayed because of bad weather conditions in Holland, and there was a spare seat.

Bond finally made Schiphol Airport, Amsterdam, at four in the morning. He took a cab straight to the Hilton International, where even at that early hour, he was able to book a seat on the Finnair 846, leaving for Helsinki at five-thirty that evening.

In his room, Bond quickly checked his overnight bag and the customized briefcase, with its hidden compartments for the two Sykes Fairbairn commando knives and the Heckler & Koch P7 automatic, all screened so that they would not show up on airport X-ray machines or during security examinations—a device which the Armorer's assistant in Q Branch, Ann Reilly (known to all as Q'ute), had perfected to such a degree that she was loath to give even members of her own department the technical details.

After some argument, mainly from Bond, the Armorer had agreed on Heckler & Koch's P7, "squeeze cocking" 9mm automatic in preference to the rather cumbersome VP70, with its long "double-action" pull for each single shot. The weapon was lighter and more like his old beloved Walther PPK, now banned by the Security Services.

Before taking a shower and going to bed, Bond sent a fast-rate cable to Erik Carlsson in Rovaniemi, with instructions about his Saab; then he ordered a call for eleven-fifteen, with breakfast.

He slept peacefully even though, in the back of his mind, the concerns regarding Mosolov, Tirpitz, and Ingber—particularly Mosolov—nagged away. He woke refreshed, but with those thoughts uppermost.

Adhering to his usual scrambled eggs, bacon, toast, marmalade and coffee, Bond finished breakfast before dialing the London number where he knew M would be found on a Sunday morning.

There followed a conversation using a doubletalk which was standard so far as Bond and his chief were concerned, when it came to open telephone calls in the field.

Once contact had been established, Bond gave M the outline details: "I talked to the three customers, sir. They're interested, but I cannot altogether trust they'll buy."

"They tell you everything about their plans?" M sounded uncommonly young on the telephone.

"No. Mr. East was decidedly cagey about the Principal we spoke of. I must say Virginia seemed to know most of the details, but Abrahams appeared to be completely in the dark."

"Ah." M waited.

"East is keen for me to go and see the source of the last shipment. He says there's another due out any time."

"That's quite possible."

"But I have to tell you he did *not* give me the full details of that last consignment."

"I suggested he might hold back." You could almost see M smile with the satisfaction of having been right.

"Anyway, I'm moving north again late this afternoon."

"You have any figures?" M asked, giving Bond the opportunity to provide a map reference of the proposed meeting point.

He had already worked out the reference, so rattled off the figures, repeating them to give M the opportunity to jot down the numbers, which were purposely jumbled, each pair being reversed.

"Right," M answered. "Going by air?"

"Air and road. I've arranged for the car to be waiting." Bond hesitated. "There's one more thing, sir."

"Yes?"

"You remember the lady? The one we had the problem with—sharp as a knife?"

"Yes."

"Well, her girlfriend. The one with the funny father." His reference was to Anni Tudeer.

M grunted an affirmative.

"I need a photograph for recognition. It may be of use. "

"I don't know. Could be difficult. Difficult for you as well as us."

"I'd appreciate it, sir. I really think it's vital."

"See what I can do." M did not sound convinced.

"Just send it if you can. Please, sir."

"Well . . ."

"If you can. I'll be in touch when there's more." Bond hung up abruptly. There it was again—a reluctance in M: something he had not experienced before. It had been there when Rivke Ingber was mentioned during the London briefing. Now it was back at the first hint of positive ID on Anni

Tudeer who, to Bond, was simply a name mentioned by Paula Vacker.

The Finnair DC9-50 that was Flight 846 from Amsterdam to Helsinki began its final approach at 9:45 that evening. Looking down on the lights diffused by the cold and snow, Bond wondered if the other three had already reached Finland. In the short time since his last visit, more snow had fallen, and the aircraft put down on an ice-cleared runway which was in reality a cutting through snow banks rising on either side, higher than the DC9 itself.

From the moment Bond walked into the terminal building, his senses went into high gear. Not only did he watch for signs of his three partners, but also for any other possible tail. He had good reason to remember his last brush with the two killers in this beautiful city.

Bond now took a cab to the Hesperia Hotel—a calculated choice. He wanted to do the journey to their RV on his own, and it was quite possible that Mosolov, Tirpitz, and Rivke Ingber were separately already en route and in the Finnish capital. If any single member of the group was looking for Bond, that individual would almost certainly watch the Inter-Continental.

With these thoughts in mind, Bond took great care about the way in which he moved—pausing in the icy cold when paying off the cab to give himself time to look around; waiting, for a moment, outside the main doors of the hotel; checking the foyer the moment he stepped inside.

Even now, while asking the girl at Reception about the Saab Turbo, Bond managed to place himself at a vantage point.

"You have a car here, I believe. A Saab 900 Turbo. Silver. Delivered in the name of Bond. James Bond."

The girl at the long reception desk gave an irritated frown, as though she had better things to do than check on cars delivered to the hotel on behalf of foreign guests.

Bond registered for one night and paid in advance, but he had no intention of spending the night in Helsinki if the car had arrived. The journey from Rovaniemi to Helsinki at this time of the year took around twenty-four hours: that was providing there were no blizzards, and the roads did not become blocked. Erik Carlsson should make it easily, with his great skill and experience as a former rally driver.

He had made it, in staggering time. Bond had expected a wait but the girl at the desk was waving the keys, as if to prove the point.

In his room, Bond took a one-hour nap and then began to prepare for the work ahead. He changed into Arctic clothing—a track suit over Damart underwear, quilted ski pants, Mukluk boots, a heavy rollneck sweater and the blue padded cold-weather jacket, produced by Tol-ma Oy in Finland for Saab. Before slipping into the jacket, he strapped on the holster especially designed by Q Branch for the Heckler & Koch P7. This adjustable holster could be fitted in a variety of positions, from the hip to the shoulder. This time Bond tightened the straps so that the holster lay centrally across his chest.

He checked the P7, loaded the weapon, and slid several spare magazines—each with its ten rounds—into the pockets of his jacket.

The briefcase contained everything else he might need apart from the clothes in his overnight bag; any other necessary armaments, tools, flares, and various pyrotechnic devices were in the car.

While dressing, Bond dialed Paula Vacker's number. It rang twenty-four times without answer, so he tried the office number, knowing in his heart of hearts that there would be nobody there, not on a Sunday night at this late hour.

Cursing silently—for Paula's absence meant an extra chore before he left—Bond completed dressing: a Damart hood slid over his head and was topped by a comfortable woolly hat, while his hands were protected by thermal-lined driving gloves. He also slipped a woolen scarf around his neck and pocketed a pair of goggles, knowing that if he had to leave the car in sub-zero temperatures, it was essential to cover all areas of his face and hands.

Finally, Bond rang Reception to say he was checking out, then went straight to the parking area where the silver 900 Turbo gleamed under the lights.

The main case went into the hatchback trunk, where Bond checked that everything was loaded as he had asked: the spade; two boxes of field rations; extra flares; and a large Schermuly Pains-Wessex Speedline line-throwing pack, which would deliver 275 meters of cable over a distance of 230 meters with speed and accuracy.

Already Bond had opened the front of the car, in order to turn off the anti-intruder and tamper alarm switches. He now went forward again to go through the other equipment up front: the secret compartments which contained maps, more flares and the big new Ruger Super Redhawk .44 Magnum revolver which was now his added armament—a man-stopper and also, if handled correctly, a car-stopper.

Again, at a press of one of the innocent-looking buttons on the dash, a drawer slid back, revealing half a dozen egg-shaped, so-called "practice grenades," which are in reality stun grenades used by Special Air Services. At the rear of this "egg box" there lay four, more lethal hand-bombs—the L2A2's that are standard British Army equipment, derived from the American M26's.

Opening the glove compartment, Bond saw that his compass was in place, together with a little note from Erik—*Good Luck Whatever You're Doing,* to which he had added, *Remember what I've taught you about the left foot!!! Erik.*

Bond smiled, recalling the hours he had spent with Carlsson learning left-foot braking techniques, to spin and control the car on thick ice.

Lastly, he walked around the Saab to be certain all the tires were correctly studded. It was a long drive to Salla, something like a thousand kilometers: easy enough in good weather, but a slog in the ice and snow of winter.

Running through the control check like a pilot before take off, Bond switched on the head-up display unit, modified and fitted from the Saab Viggen fighter aircraft. The display illuminated immediately, reflecting digital references regarding speed and fuel, as well as the graded converging lines which would help a driver to maintain the car in his own road area—tiny radar sensors showing any snowdrifts or piles to left and right, thereby eliminating the possibility of plowing into any deep or irregular snow.

Before leaving for Salla, he had one personal call to make. He started the engine, reversed, then took the car up the ramp into the main street, turning down the Mannerheimintie, heading toward Esplanade Park.

The snow statues were still decorating the park; the man and woman remained clamped in their embrace; and as he locked the car, Bond thought he could hear, far away across the city, a cry like an animal in pain.

Paula's door was closed, but there was something odd. Bond was aware of it immediately: that extra sense which comes from long experience. He quickly unclipped two of the center studs on his jacket, giving access to the Heckler & Koch. Placing the ungainly rubber toe of his right Mukluk boot against the outer edge of the door, he applied pressure. The door swung back, loose on its hinges.

The automatic pistol was in Bond's hand in a reflex action the moment he saw that the lock and chain had been torn away. From a quick glance, it looked like brute force—certainly not a sophisticated entrance. Stepping to one side, he stood holding his breath, listening. Not a sound, either from inside Paula's apartment or from the rest of the building.

Slowly Bond moved forward. The apartment was a shambles: furniture and ornaments broken and strewn everywhere. Still walking softly, and with the P7 firmly in his grip, he went toward the bedroom. The same thing. Drawers and closets had been opened, and clothes were scattered everywhere; even the down comforter had been slashed to pieces with a knife. Going from room to room, Bond found the same wreckage, and there was no sign of Paula.

All Bond's senses told him to get out: leave it alone, maybe telephone the police once he was clear of Helsinki. It could be a straight robbery, or a kidnapping disguised to look like a burglary. A third possibility, though, was the most probable, for there was a paradoxical order among the chaos, the signs of a determined search. Somebody had been after a particular item.

Bond quickly went through the rooms a second time. Now there were two clues—three if you counted the fact that the lights were all on when he arrived.

On the dressing table, which had been swept clear of Paula's rows of unguents and makeup, lay one item. Carefully Bond picked it up, turning it over and weighing it in his hand. A valuable piece of World War Two memorabilia? No, this was something more personal, more significant: a German Knight's Cross, hanging on the distinctive black, white, and red ribbon, with an Oak Leaves and Swords clasp. A high honor indeed. As he turned it, the engraving was clearly visible on the reverse side of the medal: SS-OBERFÜHRER AARNE TUDEER. 1944.

Bond slipped the medal into one of the pockets of his jacket and, as he turned away, heard a tinkling noise, as though he had kicked something metallic on the floor. He scanned the carpet and spotted the dull glow near the chrome leg of a bedside table. Another decoration? No, this was a campaign shield, again German: a dark bronze, surmounted by an eagle, the shield stamped with a rough map of the far north of Finland and Russia. At the top, one word: LAPPLAND. The Wehrmacht shield for service in the far North, also engraved on the back but dated *1943*.

Bond added it to the Knight's Cross and headed for the main door. There were no bloodstains anywhere, and he could only hope that Paula was simply away on one of her many business, or pleasure, jaunts.

Back in the Saab, he turned up the heating and wheeled the car out of Esplanade Park, going back up the Mannerheimintie heading for Route 5, which would take him on the long trek north, skirting the cities of

Lahti, Mikkeli, Varkaus and on into Lapland, the Arctic Circle, Kuusamo and then, just short of Salla, to the Hotel Revontuli, the RV arranged with the other three members of Icebreaker.

It had been bitterly cold when he left Paula's apartment building. There was the smell of snow in the air, and frost almost visibly rising around the buildings of Helsinki.

Once clear of the city, Bond placed all his concentration on driving, pushing the car to its limits within the road and visibility conditions. The main Finnish roads are exceptional, even when you get far north; and there, in the depths of the winter, snow plows keep the main arteries open, though for most of the time as a solid surface of ice.

There was no moon, and for the next eight or nine hours, Bond was conscious only of the glaring white, thrown back as his headlights hit the snow, suddenly dulling as great acres of fir trees, sheltered from snow, loomed ahead.

The others would be traveling by air—of that he was sure—but Bond wanted his own mobility, even though he knew it would have to be abandoned at Salla. If he was to cross the border with Kolya, they would have to move with great stealth, through the forests, across the lakes, and over the hills and valleys of the winter wasteland of the Circle.

The Saab's head-up display was invaluable—almost a complete guidance system showing Bond the way the snow was banked on either side. The farther north he traveled, the more sparse the villages, and at this time of year, there were only a couple of hours that could be called daylight. The rest was either dusk, a seemingly perpetual dusk, or utter darkness.

He stopped twice for gas and a quick snack. By four in the afternoon—though it could well have been midnight—the Saab had taken him to within some forty kilometers of Suomussalmi. Now he was relatively close to the Russo-Finnish border, and within a few hours of the Arctic Circle. There was still a lot of driving to be done, though, and so far the weather conditions had not proved overly hostile.

Twice the Saab had run into patches of heavy snow, whipped into white and blinding whirlpools by strong winds. But each time, Bond had pressed on, outrunning the blizzards and praying they were isolated. They were; yet so strange was the weather that he had also encountered sudden rises in temperature which set up misty conditions, slowing him even more than the snow.

There were times when the Saab traveled on long, flat stretches of iced road, through small communities going about their daily round—lights bright in shops, muffled figures stomping along pavements, women pulling tiny plastic sledges behind them piled high with groceries purchased at small supermarkets. Then, once out of the town or village, there seemed to be nothing but the endless landscape of snow and trees, the occasional heavy lorry, or a car heading back towards the last town, or great monster logbearing trucks, lumbering in either direction.

Fatigue came in small waves. Bond occasionally pulled over, allowing the bitter cold to enter the car for a few moments, then resting for a very short period. Occasionally, he sucked a glucose tablet, blessing the comfort of the Saab's adjustable seating, which relieves the body of normal driving strain.

After some seventeen hours on the road, Bond found himself around thrity kilometers from the junction between Route 5 and the fork which would take him farther east, on the direct road running east-west between Rovaniemi and the border area of Salla. The fork itself is 150 kilometers east of Rovaniemi, and just over forty kilometers west of Salla.

The landscape picked up in his headlights remained unchanged: snow, blank to an unseen horizon; great forests frosted with ice, suddenly turning to brown and a mat green, as though camouflaged, in sections which had escaped the full force of blizzards or remained unaffected by the heavy frost. Occasionally, he glimpsed a clearing with the shape of a snow-covered *kota*—the Lapp wigwam made of poles and skin, very similar to that of some North American Indians—or the wreckage of a log cabin, collapsed by the weight of snow.

Bond relaxed, fighting the wheel, correcting, alert to any sudden shift in control as he sent the Saab screaming on at a safe rate across the ice and packed snow. He could already smell success—arrival at the hotel without having had to use air transport. He might just conceivably get to their RV first, which would be a bonus.

He was on a lonely stretch now, with nothing but the fork in the road about ten kilometers ahead, and little between this point and Salla except for the odd Lapp camp or deserted summer log cottages.

He slackened speed to take a long curve in the road and, as he rounded the bend, was conscious of a turning to his right and some lights ahead.

Bond flicked down the headlight beams, then up again for a second, to see what was ahead. In the dazzle he caught sight of a giant yellow snow plow approaching, its lights on full and the great bow of the plow like that of a warship.

This was not a modern snowblower, but the more sturdy kind of monster. The quick view from his lights, and now the silhouette, told Bond the worst. The snow plows they used mainly in this part of the world consisted of a great high body with a thick glass cabin on top, giving maximum view. The body was driven by wide caterpillar tracks, like those on self-propelled field artillery, whereas the actual plow was operated ahead of the vehicle, by a series of hydraulic pistons which could alter angle or height in a matter of seconds.

As for the plows on these massive machines, they were sharp, steel, V-shaped bows, some fifteen feet high, curving back from the cutting edge so that the snow and ice were forced to each side, then tossed away by the sheer momentum of the blade's attack.

Though they appeared cumbersome, the machines could reverse, traverse, and turn with the ability of a heavy tank. What was more, they were specifically designed to remain mobile in the worst possible winter conditions.

The Finns had long since conquered the problems of snow and ice on their main arterial roads, and these brutes were often followed by the big snowblowers to clean up after the first devastating assault on deep snow and ice.

Damn, Bond thought. Where there were snow plows there would almost certainly be the remnants of a blizzard. Silently he cursed, for it would be bad luck, having already outrun two blizzards, to be caught in the aftermath of a third.

Shifting down, Bond glanced into his mirror. Behind him, with its lights also full on, a second plow appeared, presumably from the turning he had just passed.

He allowed the car to coast, then picked up the engine again, edging gently forward. If there were bad falls of snow ahead, and even off to the east, he wanted to pull over as far as possible and allow the great juggernaut complete right of passage.

As he pulled over, Bond realized the plow ahead was holding the center of the road. Another glance in the mirror told him the plow behind was doing the same thing. In that instant, Bond felt the hair on the nape of his neck prickle with the sense of danger. He passed a crossroads and one glance to the right told him the road was relatively clear. These plows, therefore, were not out on their normal job: their purpose was more sinister.

Bond was only three seconds past the crossroads when he acted, turning the wheel hard right, slamming his left foot hard onto the brake, feeling the back begin to swing into the inevitable skid, then gunning the accelerator, spinning the Saab in a controlled turn. In that one instant, Bond had changed direction. Gently, he increased the revs, correcting the back swing which would send him into a second spin across the coating of ice below him.

The plow which had been behind was considerably closer than he had judged and, as he increased his own speed, concentrating on the feel of the car, ready to correct at the first hint of a developing swing, the solid metal hulk grew larger, bearing down on him as they closed.

He would be lucky to make the crossroads before the plow and, though there was no time to look, Bond knew the other snow plow had also increased speed. If he did not reach the crossroads in time, there would be no possible way out. Either he would hit the snow bank at the side of the road—burying the Saab's nose deep so that the car would be at anyone's mercy—or the pair of plows would catch him, front and rear, crushing even the tough sturdy Saab between their knifelike curved blades.

One hand left the wheel for a second to punch at two of the buttons of the dash. There was a quiet hiss as the hydraulic system opened two of the hidden compartments. Now the grenades and his Ruger Super Redhawk were within reach. So was the crossroads. Straight ahead.

The snow plow in front of him, burning yellow and steel in Bond's headlights, was about twelve yards from the intersection. Feinting like a boxer, Bond started to turn right. He saw the plow grind to its left, pounding out speed in an attempt to cut into the Saab as it took the right angled turn.

Then, at almost the last moment, when he had all but committed himself to the turn, Bond swung the wheel even harder right, left-footed onto the brake again, and once more increased the revs, tramping down on the accelerator.

The Saab spun like an aircraft, Bond's feet coming off both brake and accelerator at the same moment, just as the vehicle was halfway through the spin and starting to move, broadside on, lining up with the road opposite—the road that would have been his left turn.

Correcting the steering and slowly increasing the revs, Bond felt the Saab react like a perfectly controlled animal, the rear sliding slightly. Correct. Slide. Correct. Accelerator. Then he was on line, moving comfortably forward with the huge bulk of the two snow plows rising to his right and left.

As he cleared the blade of the more dangerous plow—now on his right—Bond snatched at the grenades, doing the unforgivable and ripping the pin from an L2A2 with his teeth as he part-opened the driving-side door to drop it clear, and in his wake.

The bitter air blasted into the car for a second as Bond struggled to slam the door shut. Then he felt a shudder as the Saab's rear grazed the steel blade of the plow on his right.

For a second, he thought the touch would throw him right off track and into the heavily piled snow on either side of the secondary road into which he was heading. But the car steadied and he regained control, hearing the snow at the edge of the drift spume upwards as his wheel guards touched. There was just enough room to take the car up the smaller road between the high white mounds. Then, from behind, came the crump of the grenade.

One quick glance into the mirror—for he hardly dared take his eyes from the road and the head-up display—showed a dark red flower of flame coming from directly under one of the high yellow plows.

With luck, the grenade, would be enough to bog down at least one plow for ten minutes or so, while the other pushed it out of the way.

In any case, Bond figured, even along this narrow, dangerous, snow-flanked gulley of a road, he could outrun any snow plow. That was, any snow plow behind him. He had not counted on yet another—dead ahead, spotlights splitting the darkness, dazzling him as it came seemingly from out of nowhere. This time there was no place to hide. Nowhere to go.

Behind, with good fortune, one plow would be out of action, but another ready to follow up as soon as the way was clear. Ahead, yet a third yellow monster came on, snow pluming from its bows. Presumably, Bond thought, there would be a fourth lying silent, with lights dowsed, along the road of the cross.

Like some classic military armored operation, someone had laid an ambush, strictly for Bond and his Saab. Just at the right place, and the right time.

But he did not stop to work out the logic, or the intelligence, which might have led someone to set the trap. The yellow plow had locked lights with the Saab, but even through the dazzle, Bond could see the curved blade move downward until it was just clipping the ice at the center of the road, its bows still distributing the gathered snowdrifts away and behind it with the ease of a motorboat throwing off water at speed.

Mind racing, Bond pulled over as far as he dared and stopped the car. Staying in the Saab now would be lunacy. Think of it as a military assault.

He was cornered, and there was only one thing to be done—stop the snow plow bearing down on him.

The Redhawk, with its .44 Magnum punch—and fast double-action—was the handgun needed now. Bond grabbed it, and also stuffed two L2A2's into his jacket pockets. Opening the door gently just before rolling, low out of the door, he snatched at one of the stun grenades—"flash-bangs" as the Special Air Service dubbed them.

The ground was hard, and the biting cold hit Bond like a great drench of iced water as he rolled to the rear of the Saab, seeking its cover before launching himself into the high snowdrift to the left.

The snow was powdery and soft. In a second he was waist deep and sinking. Bond kicked backwards, getting his legs into a kneeling position, still sinking until he was buried almost to the shoulders.

But this was a new and very different vantage point from which to fight. Gone was the dazzle of the snow plow's lights and the big spot above the cab. Through his goggles, Bond could see two men at the controls and the cumbersome vehicle shifting, aiming itself towards the Saab.

There was no doubt. They were going in for the kill, prepared to slice the Silver Beast in half. Silver versus yellow, Bond thought, and raised his right arm, the left hand still clutching the stun grenade, wrist under right wrist to steady his aim.

His first shot took out the spotlight; the second shattered the glass screen of the plow's cabin. Bond had aimed high. He wanted no killing if it could be avoided.

One of the doors opened and a figure began to climb out. It was at that moment Bond lowered the Redhawk, switched it to his left hand in exchange for the stun grenade, pulled the pin, and lobbed the hard green egg with all the force he could muster toward the shattered screen of the cab.

The grenade must have gone off right inside the cab. Bond heard the thunderclap *whoomph,* but averted his eyes from the flash. The flash and explosion would do no damage to the occupants, except possibly rupture their eardrums and certainly cause temporary blindness.

Holding the revolver high, Bond rolled himself out of the snowdrift, almost swimming his way through the thick, heavy powder until he could stand and move, with some caution, toward the plow.

One of the crew was lying unconscious beside the big machine: the man who had tried to jump clear, Bond reckoned. The other, in the driver's seat, had both arms over his face and was rocking to and fro, moaning in harmony with the wind which screamed down the funnel of the road.

Bond found a grip, pulled himself up onto the driver's side, and tugged the cab door open. Some instinct must have told the driver of danger nearby for he cringed away.

Bond soon put him out of his misery. He clipped him sharply on the back of the neck with the Ruger's barrel, and the driver went to sleep with no argument.

Oblivious to the cold, Bond hauled the man down, dragging him around the front of the plow and dumping him next to his partner before returning to the cab.

The snow plow's engine was running, and Bond felt as though he was sitting a mile high above the wicked hydraulics and the great blade. The array of levers was daunting, but the engine still chugged away. All that concerned Bond was getting the brute off the road, or at least past the Saab and into a position in which it would block the remaining plow at the crossroads.

In the end it was simple. The normal mechanism worked with a wheel, clutch and throttle. It took Bond about three minutes to edge the giant down past the Saab and then across the road. He turned off the engine, removed the key, and threw it out over the smooth dunes. The crew were both still unconscious and would probably suffer from frostbite as well as the damage to their ears. That was little enough to pay, Bond thought, for having tried to carve him into frozen steaks.

Back in the Saab, he turned the heating full up to dry out, returned the Redhawk—after reloading—and the grenades to their respective hiding places, reset the buttons and consulted the map.

If the snow plow had come down the entire track, it should be clear right up to the main Salla road. Two hours more driving and he would make it. In the end, it took almost three full hours, for the track twisted and doubled back on itself before reaching the direct road.

At ten past midnight, Bond finally spotted the big illuminated sign proclaiming the Hotel Revontuli. A few minutes later, there was the turn-off and the large crescent building with a great ski jump, chair lift and ski run, brightly lit, climbing up behind the structure.

Bond parked the car, surprised that within a few moments of turning off the engine, the screen and bonnet began to frost over. Even so, it was difficult to believe the cold in the open air. Bond slipped the goggles into place, made certain his scarf covered his face; then, taking the briefcase and his overnight bag from the car, set the sensors and alarms before operating the central locking device.

The hotel was all modern carved wood and marble. A large foyer with a bar leading off. People talked, laughed and drank at the bar. As Bond trudged towards Reception, a familiar voice greeted him.

"Hi, James," called Brad Tirpitz. "What kept you? You ski the whole way?"

Bond nodded, pushing up the goggles and unwinding his scarf. "Seemed a nice night for a walk," he replied, straightfaced.

They were expecting him at Reception, so check-in took only a couple of minutes. Tirpitz had returned to the bar where, Bond noted, he drank alone, and neither of the others was in view. Bond needed sleep, and the plan was to meet up at breakfast each day until the whole team arrived.

A porter took his case, and he was just turning towards the lifts when the girl on duty at Reception said there was an express airmail package for him. It was a slim manila envelope with a stiff card backing.

Once the porter had left his room, Bond locked the door and slit open the envelope. Inside were a small plain sheet of paper and a photograph.

M had written in his own hand: *This is the only available photograph of the subject. Please destroy.* Well, Bond thought, at least he would know what Anni Tudeer looked like.

He dropped onto the bed and held up the photograph.

Bond's stomach turned over, then his muscles tensed. The face that stared back at him from the mat print was that of Rivke Ingber, his Mossad colleague. Anni Tudeer, Paula's friend, daughter of the Finnish Nazi SS officer still wanted for war crimes, was Rivke Ingber.

With painful slowness, James Bond took a book of matches from the ashtray by the bed, struck one and set both photograph and note on fire.

7

RIVKE

For years Bond had nurtured the habit of taking cat naps and being able to control his sleep—even under stress. He had also acquired the knack of feeding problems into the computer of his mind, allowing the subconscious to work away while he slept. Usually he worked with a clear mind, sometimes with a new slant on difficulties, inevitably refreshed.

After the exceptionally long and hard drive from Helsinki, Bond felt natural fatigue, though his mind was active with a maze of conflicting puzzles.

There was nothing he could do immediately about the break-in and wrecking of Paula's Helsinki apartment. His main concern was for the girl's safety. In the morning, a couple of telephone calls should establish that.

Much more worrying was the obvious attack on him by the snow plows. Having left Madeira quickly, dog-legging his way to Helsinki via Amsterdam, this attempt on his life meant only one thing. Someone was watching all points of entry into Finland. They must have picked him up at the airport and, later, had knowledge of his departure in the Saab.

Someone obviously wanted him out of the game just as they had wanted him out before he had even been briefed: hence the knife assault in Paula's apartment, when Bond had still been innocent of, and quite oblivious to, any covert operation against the NSAA.

Dudley, who had filled in while M was waiting for Bond's return, had indicated his mistrust of Kolya Mosolov. Bond himself had other ideas, and the latest development—the fact that Mossad's agent Rivke Ingber appeared to be the daughter of a wanted Finnish Nazi SS officer—was much more alarming.

Bond allowed these problems to penetrate his mind as he showered and prepared for bed. Momentarily he considered food, then opted against it. Better fast until morning when he would breakfast with the others, providing they had all arrived at the hotel.

He seemed to have been asleep for only a few minutes when the tapping broke through to his consciousness. His eyes snapped open. The tapping continued—soft double raps at the door.

Noiselessly, Bond slipped the P7 from under his pillow and crossed the room. The tapping was insistent. The double rap, then a long pause followed by another double rap.

Keeping to the left of the door, his back against the wall, Bond whispered, "Who's there?"

"Rivke. It's Rivke Ingber, James. I have to talk with you. Please. Please let me in."

His mind cleared. There were several answers to the questions facing Bond when he went to sleep. One was so obvious that he had already taken it into account. If Rivke was, in fact, the daughter of Aarne Tudeer, there could easily be a natural link between her and the National Socialist Action Army. She must only be thirty years of age, maybe thirty-one at the most, which meant her formative years had probably been spent in some hiding place with her father. If this was so, then it was quite possible that Anni Tudeer was a neo-Fascist deep penetration agent, working inside Mossad.

Therefore, it followed, she may just have been tipped off that the British were wise to her true identity. It was also possible that she suspected Bond's colleagues would not be averse to withholding the information from the CIA and KGB. It had been done before, and Icebreaker was already proving to be an uneasy alliance.

Bond glanced at the illuminated dial of his Rolex Oyster Perpetual. It was four-thirty in the morning, that unsettling hour when the mind is far from its sharpest, when babies are more apt to start the last stages of their journey into the world, and when death often stalks most easily into the geriatric wards of hospitals. Psychologically, Rivke could not have chosen a better moment.

"Hang on," Bond whispered, recrossing the room to shrug himself into a terrycloth robe and return the Heckler & Koch automatic under his pillow.

When he opened the door, Bond quickly decided she had come unarmed. There were very few places she could manage to hide anything in the outfit she wore: an opalescent white negligee hanging loose over a sheer, clinging matching nightdress.

She would have been enough to make any man drop his guard, with her tanned body quite visible through the soft material, and the dazzling contrast of color underlined by the blond shimmer of hair, and the eyes pleading in a hint of fear.

Bond allowed her into the room, locked the door, and stood back. Well, he thought, his gaze quickly traveling down her body, she is either an ultra-professional or a very natural blonde.

"Didn't even know you'd got to the hotel," he said calmly. "You obviously have. Welcome."

"Thank you." she spoke quietly. "May I sit down, James? I'm terribly sorry to . . ."

"My pleasure. Please . . ." He indicated a chair. "Can I send for anything? Or do you want a drink from the fridge?"

Rivke shook her head. "This is so silly." She looked around as though disoriented. "So stupid."

"You want to talk about it?"

A quick nod. "Don't think me a complete fool, James, please. I'm really quite good with men, but Tirpitz . . . Well . . ."

"You told me you could handle him, that you could have dealt with him before, when my predecessor thumped him."

She was quiet for a moment, then, when she spoke it was a snap, a small explosion: "Well, I was wrong, wasn't I? That's all there is to it." She paused. "Oh, I'm sorry, James. I'm supposed to be highly trained and self-reliant. Yet . . ."

"Yet Brad Tirpitz you can't handle?"

She smiled at Bond's mocking timbre, replying in kind: "He knows nothing of women." Then her face tightened, the smile disappearing from the eyes. "He really has been most unpleasant. Tried to force his way into my room. Very drunk. Gave the impression he wasn't going to let up easily."

"So, you didn't even hit him with your handbag?"

"He was really scary, James."

Bond went over to the bedside table, picked up his cigarette case and lighter, offering the open case to Rivke who shook her head as Bond lit up, blowing a stream of smoke towards the ceiling.

"It's out of charcter, Rivke." He sat on the end of the bed facing her, searching the attractive face for some hint of truth.

"I know," she spoke very quickly. "I know. But I couldn't stay alone in my room. You've no idea what he was like . . ."

"You're not a wilting flower, Rivke. You don't normally come running to the nearest male for protection. That's back-to-the-cave-dwellers stuff— everything people like you hate and despise."

"I'm sorry." She made to get up, her anger almost tangible for a second. "I'll go and leave you in peace. I just needed company. The rest of this so-called team doesn't give anyone company."

Bond put out a hand, touching her shoulder, quietly pushing her back into the chair. "Stay, by all means, Rivke. But please don't take me for an idiot. You could handle Brad Tirpitz, drunk or sober, with a flick of your eyelashes . . ."

"That's not quite true."

The ploy, Bond thought, dated back to the Garden of Eden, the oldest in the book. But who was he to argue? If a beautiful girl comes to your room in the middle of the night asking for protection—even though she is quite capable of looking after herself—she does so for one reason. But that was in the real world, not this maze of secrets and duplicity in which both Bond and Rivke lived and worked.

Sex was still a vital factor in covert operations—not for blackmail anymore, as it had been in years past, but for more subtle pressures, like trust, entrapment, and misdirection. As long as he remembered that, Bond could turn the situation to his own advantage.

Taking another long pull on his cigarette, he made the vital decision. Rivke Ingber was alone in his room, and he knew who she *really* was. Before she made any other move it would, perhaps, be best for him to put the cards firmly on the table.

"A couple of weeks ago, Rivke, maybe even less—I seem to have lost all sense of time—did you do anything when Paula Vacker told you I was in Helsinki?"

"Paula?" She looked genuinely perplexed. "James, I don't know . . ."

"Look, Rivke," he leaned forward, taking her hands in his. "Our business breeds odd friends; and sometimes strange enemies. I don't want to become your enemy. But you need friends, my dear. You see, I know who you are."

Her brow creased, the eyes become wary. "Of course. I'm Rivke Ingber. I work for Mossad, and I'm an Israeli citizen."

"You don't know Paula Vacker?"

There was no hesitation. "I've met her. Yes, a long time ago I knew her quite well. But I haven't seen her for . . . oh, it must be three, four years."

"And you haven't been in touch with her lately?" Bond heard his own voice, slightly supercilious. "You don't work with her in Helsinki? You didn't have a dinner date—which Paula canceled—just before leaving for the Madeira meeting?"

"No." Plain; open; straightforward.

"Not even under your real name? Anni Tudeer?"

She took a deep breath, then exhaled, as though trying to expel every ounce of air from her body. "That's a name I like to forget."

"I'll bet."

She quickly pulled her hands away. "All right, James. I'll have that cigarette now." Bond gave her one of his cigarettes, lighting it for her. She drew in deeply, then allowed the smoke to gust from her mouth. "You seem to know so much; I should let you tell *me* the story," her voice cold, all the friendly, even seductive, undertone gone.

Bond shrugged. "I only know who you are. I also know Paula Vacker. She told me she'd confided in you that we were meeting in Helsinki. I went to Paula's apartment. There were a couple of knife experts keeping an eye on her and ready to treat me like a prime steak."

"I've told you, Paula hasn't spoken to me in years. Apart from knowing my old name and, presumably, the fact that I'm a former SS officer's daughter, what do you really know?"

Bond smiled. "Only that you're very beautiful. I know nothing about you, except what you call your old name."

She nodded, face set, masklike. "I thought so. All right, Mr. James Bond, let me tell you the full story, so that *you* can set the record straight. After that, I think we'd both better try to find out what's going on—I mean what happened at Paula's . . . I'd like to know too where Paula Vacker fits into all this."

"Paula's apartment was done over. I went there before leaving Helsinki yesterday. There was also a slight altercation with three—maybe four—snow plows on my way here. The snow plows indicated they wanted to remodel my Saab, with me inside it. Somebody does not want me here, Anni Tudeer, or Rivke Ingber, whichever is your real name."

Rivke frowned. "My father was—is—Aarne Tudeer; that's true. You know his history?"

"That he was on Mannerheim's staff, and took the Nazis up on an offer to become an SS officer. Brave; ruthless; a wanted war criminal."

She nodded. "I didn't know about that part until I was around twelve years old." She spoke very softly, but with a conviction Bond felt was genuine. "When my father left Finland he took several of his brother officers and some enlisted men with him. In those days, as you know, there was a fair assortment of camp followers. On the day he left Lapland, my father proposed to a young widow. Good birth, had large holdings of land—forest mainly—in Lapland. My mother was part Lapp. She accepted and volunteered to go with him, so becoming a kind of camp follower herself. She went through horrors you'd hardly believe." She shook her head, as though still not crediting her own mother's actions. Tudeer had married on the day after leaving Finland, and his wife stayed near him until the collapse of the Third Reich. Together they had escaped.

"My first home was in Paraguay," she told Bond. "I knew nothing, of course. It wasn't until later I realized that I spoke four languages almost from the beginning—Finnish, Spanish, German and English. We lived in a compound in the jungle. Quite comfortable, really, but the memories of my father are not pleasant."

"Tell me," Bond said. Little by little he coaxed it out of her. It was, in fact, an old tale. Tudeer had been autocractic, drunken, brutal, and sadistic.

"I was ten years old before we escaped—my mother and I. To me it was a kind of game: dressed up as an Indian child. We got away by canoe, and then with the help of some Guarani, made it to Ascunción. My mother was a very unhappy lady. I don't know how it was managed, but she got passports for both of us, Swedish passports; and some kind of grant. We were flown to Stockholm, where we stayed for six months. Every day my mother would go to the Finnish Embassy, and eventually we were granted our Finnish passports. Mother spent the first year in Helsinki getting a divorce and compensation for her lost land—up here, in the Circle. We lived in Helsinki and I got my first taste of schooling. That's where I met Paula. We became very good friends. That's about it."

"It?" Bond repeated, raising his eyebrows.

"Well, the rest was predictable enough."

It was while she was at school that Rivke began to learn the facts about her father. "By the age of fourteen I knew it all, and was horrified; disgusted that my own father had left his country to become part of the SS. I suppose it was an obsession—a complex. By the time I was fifteen, I knew what had to be done as far as my life went."

Bond had heard many confessions during interrogations. After years of experience you develop a sense about them. He would have put money on Rivke's being a true story, if only because it came out fast, with the minimum of detail. People operating under a deep cover often give you too much.

"Revenge?" he asked.

"A kind of revenge. No, that's the wrong word. My father had nothing to do with what Himmler called The Final Solution—the Jewish problem—but he was associated, he was a wanted criminal. I began to identify with the race that lost six million souls in the gas chambers and the camps. Many people have told me I overreacted. I wanted to do something concrete."

"You became a Jew?"

"I went to Israel on my twentieth birthday. My mother died two years later. The last time I saw her was the day I left Helsinki. Within six months I began the first steps of conversion. Now I'm as Jewish as any Gentile-born can be. In Israel they tried everything in the book to put me off—but I stuck it out—even military service. It was that which finally clinched it." Her smile was one of pride this time. "Zamir himself sent for me, interviewed me. I couldn't believe it when they told me who he was—Colonel Zwicka Zamir, the head of Mossad. He arranged everything. I was an Israeli citizen already. Now I went for special training, for Mossad. I had a new name . . ."

"And the revenge part, Rivke? You had atoned, but what about the revenge?"

"Revenge?" Her eyes opened wide. Then she frowned, anxiety crossing her face. "James, you *do* believe me, don't you?"

In the couple of seconds which passed before he replied, Bond's mind ran through the facts. Either Rivke was the best deception artist he had ever met or, as he had earlier considered, completely honest.

These feelings had to be put next to his long and intimate knowledge of Paula Vacker. From their first meeting, Bond had never suspected Paula of being anything else but a charming, intelligent, hard-working girl. Now, if Rivke was telling the truth, Paula became a liar and a possible accessory to attempted murder.

The knife artists had cornered him in Paula's apartment, yet she had taken care of him, had driven him to the airport. Someone obviously had fingered him on the road to Salla. That could ony have been done from Helsinki. Paula?

Bond switched back to the Paula connection. "There're reasons why I shouldn't believe you, Rivke," he began. "I've known Paula for a long time. When I last saw her, when she told me she'd confided in you, Anni Tudeer, she was very specific. She said Anni Tudeer worked with her in Helsinki."

Rivke slowly shook her head. "Unless someone else is using my name . . ."

"You've never worked in her world? In advertising?"

"You're joking. I've said no already. I've told you the story of my life. I knew Paula at school."

"And did she know who you were? Who your father was?"

"Yes," softly. "James, you can easily settle it. Call her office, check with them; ask if they have an Anni Tudeer working for them. If so, then there are two Anni Tudeers—or Paula's lying." She leaned closer, speaking very distinctly. "I'm telling you, James, there are *not* two Anni Tudeers. Paula's lying, and I for one would like to know why."

"Yes," Bond nodded. "Yes, so would I."

"Then you believe me?"

"There's no point in you lying to me, when all the facts can be proven in a very short space of time. I thought I knew Paula very well, but now . . . well, my instincts tell me to believe you. We can run traces, even from here, certainly from London. London already says that you're Anni Tudeer." He smiled at her, his mind sending signals to his body. She was, at close proximity, a very lovely young woman. "I believe you, Rivke Ingber. You're straight Mossad, and you've only left one thing out—the question of vengeance. I cannot believe you simply want to atone for your father's actions. You either want him in the bag or dead. Which is it?"

She gave a provocative little shrug. "It doesn't really matter, does it? Whichever way it goes, Aarne Tudeer'll die." The musical voice altered for a second, steel hard, then back once more to its softness and a small laugh. "I'm sorry, James Bond. I shouldn't have tried to play games with you. Brad Tirpitz *was* a pest tonight, but, yes, I could've taken care of him. Maybe I'm not the professional I thought. I was naive enough to imagine I could con you, James. Lure you."

"Lure? Into what web?" Bond, ninety-nine percent sure of Rivke's motives and claims, still kept that tiny single percent of wariness in reserve.

"Not a web, exactly." She put out a hand, fingers resting in Bond's palm. "To be honest, I don't feel safe with either Tirpitz or Kolya. I wanted to be sure you'd be on my side."

Bond let go of her hand, placing his own fingers lightly on her shoulders. "We're in the business of trust, Rivke; and we both need it from someone, because I'm not happy with this set-up any more than you are. First things first, though. I have to ask you this, simply because I suspect it. Do you know, for certain, that your father's mixed up with the NSAA?"

She did not pause to think. "Completely sure."

"How do you know?"

"That's why I'm here; it's why I was put on this job. Back in Israel the computers, and people on the ground, began analysis immediately after the first National Socialist Action Army incident. It was natural they should look at the old leaders—the former Party members, the SS, and those who'd escaped from Germany. There were several names. My father was high on the list. You'll have to take my word for the rest, but Mossad has evidence that he is tied in very closely. It's not coincidence that the arms are coming out of Russia through Finland. He's here, James—new name, almost a new face, the whole business of a new identity. There's a new mistress as well. He's spry and tough enough, even at his age. I know he's here."

"A game bird." Bond gave a wry smile.

"And game is in season, James. My dear father's well in season. Mother used to say that he saw himself as a new Führer, a Nazi Moses, there to lead his children back to their promised land. Well, the children are growing in strength, and the world's in such a mess that the young or the pliable will lap up any half-baked ideology. You only have to look at your country . . ."

Bond bridled. "Which has yet to elect, or allow, a madman into power. There's a stiff backbone there that will eventually—sometimes a little late, I admit—get matters straight."

She gave a friendly pout. "Okay, I'm sorry. All countries have their faults." Rivke bit her lip, her mind drifting off course for a few seconds. "Please, James. I *do* have an edge, privileged information if you like. I need you on my side."

Go along with it, Bond thought. Even though you are almost sure, take every bit of the bait, but hold back the one percent and remain alert. Aloud he said, "All right. But what about the others? Brad and Kolya?"

"Brad and Kolya're both playing death and glory games, and I'm not certain if they're doing it together or against each other. They're serious enough; yet not serious enough. Does that sound stupid? A paradox? But it's true. You only have to watch them." She looked straight into his eyes, as though trying to hypnotize him, her voice giving the impression that this was a very important matter. "Look, I get the feeling—and it's only intuition—that either the CIA or the KGB has something they want to bury. Something to do with the NSAA."

"I'd put my money on it being Kolya," Bond replied lightly. "The KGB asked us in, after all. The KGB came to *us*—to the USA, Israel and the

UK. I suppose it's possible they've found more than a simple arms leak to the National Socialist Action Army. That may be part of it, but what if there's more? Something hideous?"

Rivke shifted her chair closer to the end of the bed where Bond sat. "You mean if they've found themselves with an arms leak, and some other funny business that's going to look very bad? Something they can't contain?"

"It's a theory. Plausible enough." She was so close that Bond could smell her: the traces of her scent, plus the natural odor of an attractive woman. "Only a theory," he repeated. "But it's possible. This is all out of character for the KGB. They're usually so closed up. Now they come and ask for help. Could they be pulling us in? Having us for suckers? So that when the truth—whatever it is—comes spewing out, we'll be implicated? Israel, America, and Britain will all take the blame. It's devious enough for them."

"Fall guys," Rivke spoke softly again.

"Yes. Fall guys." Bond wondered what his old and ultra-conservative chief M would make of the expression. M hated slang in any form.

Rivke said if there was even a possibility of a KGB plot to discredit them, it would be wise to make a pact now to stick together. "We really do have to watch each other's backs, even if our theory doesn't hold."

Bond gave her his most charming smile, leaning close, his lips only inches from Rivke's mouth. "You're quite right, Rivke. Though I'd be much happier watching your front."

Her lips, in return, seemed to be examining his mouth. Then: "I don't frighten easily, James, but this has got me twitchy . . ." Her arms came up, winding around his neck, and their lips brushed, first in a light caress. Bond's conscience nagged at him to take care.

But the warnings were cauterized in the fires started by their lips, then fanned by the opening of their mouths and the conflagration as their tongues touched.

It seemed an eternity before their mouths unlocked, and Rivke, panting, clung to Bond, her breath warm near his ear as she murmured endearments.

Slowly, Bond drew her from the chair onto the bed where they lay close, body to body, then mouth to mouth once more, until together, as though at some inaudible signal, their hands groped for one another.

Within a few moments they were both naked, their flesh burning against flesh, mouths devouring as though each contained some untapped ambrosia upon which they needed to slake their thirst.

What began as a kind of lust or an act of need—two people alone and responding to a natural desire for comfort and trust—slowly became tender, gentle, even truly loving.

Bond, still vaguely aware of the tiny remaining doubt in the back of his head, was quickly lost in this lovely creature, whose limbs and body seemed to respond to his own in an almost telepathic kind of way. They were as two perfectly attuned dancers, able to predict each other's moves.

Only later, with Rivke curled up like a child in Bond's arms under the covers, did they speak again of work. For them, the brief hours they had spent together had been but a short retreat from the harsh reality of their profession. Now it was after eight in the morning. Another day, another scramble through the dangers of the secret world.

"For the sake of this operation, then, we work together." Bond's mouth was unusually dry. "That'll cover both of us . . ."

"Yes, and , "

"And I'll help you see SS-Oberführer Tudeer in hell."

"Oh please, James darling. Please." She looked up at him, her face puckered in a smile that spoke only of pleasure—no malice or horror, even though she was already pleading for the death of her hated father. Then the mood changed again: serenity, the laugh in her eyes and at the corners of her mouth. "You know, this is the last thing I thought would happen . . ."

"Come on, Rivke. You don't arrive in a man's room at four in the morning, dressed in practically nothing, without the thought crossing your mind."

"Oh," she laughed aloud, "the thought was there. It's just I didn't really believe it would happen. I imagined you were much too professional, and I thought I was also so determined and well trained that I could resist anything." Her voice went small. "I did go for you, the moment I saw you, but don't let it get to your head."

"It didn't." Bond laughed.

The laugh had hardly died when Bond reached over for the telephone. "Time to see if we can get something out of our so-called friend Paula." He began to dial the apartment in Helsinki, while casting an admiring eye over Rivke as she put on the film of silk which passed as a nightdress.

At the distant end of the line, the telephone rang. Nobody answered.

"What do you make of it, Rivke?" Bond put down the telephone. "She's not there."

Rivke shook her head. "You'll ring her office of course—but I don't understand any of it. I used to know her well enough, but why lie about me? It doesn't make sense; and you say she was a good friend . . ."

"For a long time. I certainly didn't spot anything sinister about her. None of it makes sense." Bond was on his feet now, walking towards the sliding louvered doors of the wardrobe. His quilted jacket hung inside, and he took the two medals from the pocket, tossing them across the room so that they jangled onto the bed. This would be his last testing of her. "What d'you make of those, darling?"

Rivke's hand went out and she held the medals for a moment, then let out a tiny cry, dropping them back onto the bed as though they were red-hot.

"Where?" The one word was enough: delivered fast, like a shot.

"In Paula Vacker's apartment. Lying on the dressing table."

All humor had gone from Rivke Ingber. "I haven't seen these since I was a child." Her hand went out to the Knight's Cross and she picked it up again, turning it over. "You see? His name's engraved on the back. My father's Knight's Cross with Oak Leaves and Swords. In Paula's apartment?" The last with complete bewilderment and disbelief.

"Right there on the dressing table, for anyone to see."

She dropped the medals back onto the bed and came toward him, throwing her arms around his neck. "I thought I knew it all, James; but what's it really about? Why Paula? Why the lies? Why my father's Knight's Cross and the Northern Campaign Shield?—he was particularly proud of that one, by the way—but why?"

Bond held her close. "We'll find out. Don't worry. I'm as concerned as you. Paula always seemed so . . . well, level. Straight."

After a minute or so, Rivke drew away. "I have to clear my head, James. Will you come down the ski run with me?"

Bond made a negative gesture. "I've got to see Brad and Kolya; and I thought we were going to watch out for each other . . ."

"I just have to get out there alone for a while." She hesitated before adding, "Darling James, I'll be okay. Back in time for breakfast. Make my apologies if I'm a little late."

"For heaven's sake be careful."

Rivke gave a little nod. Then shyly, "That was all quite something, Mr. Bond. It could become a habit."

"I hope so." Bond pulled her very close and they kissed by the door.

When she had gone, he turned back to the bed, bending over it to retrieve Aarne Tudeer's medals. The scent of her was everywhere, and she still seemed very close.

8

TIRPITZ

JAMES BOND WAS deeply disturbed. All but one tiny doubt told him that Rivke Ingber was absolutely trustworthy, just who she said she was: the daughter of Aarne Tudeer; the girl who had taken to the Jewish faith, and was now—even according to London—a Mossad agent.

There was a sense of shock, however, over the mystery of Paula Vacker. She had been close to Bond over the years, never giving him cause to think of her as anything but an intelligent, fun-loving, hard working girl who excelled in her job.

Set against Rivke and recent events, Paula appeared suddenly to have feet of melting wax.

Rather more slowly than usual, Bond showered and shaved. He dressed in heavy cavalry twill slacks, a cable-knit black rollneck, and short leather jacket to hide the P7, which he strapped in place, checking the mechanism and adding a pair of spare magazines, clipping them into the specially sewn-in pocket at the back of his slacks.

This gear, with soft leather moccasins on his feet, would be warm enough inside the hotel. As he left the room, Bond made a vow that from now on he would go nowhere without the weapon.

In the corridor Bond paused, glancing at his Rolex. Time had been whittled away since the early hours. It was already nearly nine-thirty. Paula's office would be open. He returned to the room to dial Helsinki, this time the office number. The same operator who had greeted him on that fateful day of impulse, which seemed so long ago now, answered in Finnish.

Bond switched to English and the operator complied, just as she had done previously. He asked to speak to Paula Vacker and the reply came back—sharp, final and not entirely unexpected.

"I'm sorry. Miss Vacker is on holiday."

"Oh?" Bond feigned disappointment. "I promised to get in touch with her. I suppose you've no idea where she's gone."

The operator asked him to wait a moment. "We're not sure of the exact location," she told him at last, "but she said something about going to get some skiing up north—too cold for me, it's bad enough here."

"Yes. Well, thank you. Has she been gone for long?"

"She left on Thursday, sir. Would you like me to take a message?"

"No. No, I'll catch her next time I'm in Finland." Bond started to hang up. Then: "By the way, does Anni Tudeer still work for you?"

"Anni who, sir?"

"Anni Tudeer. A friend of Miss Vacker, I believe."

"I'm sorry, sir. I think you're mistaken. We have no one here by that name."

"Thank you," said Bond, returning the receiver to its cradle.

So, he thought, Paula had moved north, just like the rest of them. He glanced out of the window. You could almost see the cold—as though you could cut it with a knife—in spite of the clear blue sky and bright sunshine. Blue as they were, those incredible skies held no promise of warmth; and the sun shone like dazzling light reflected from an iceberg. The signs, from the warmth and safety of a hotel room, could be treacherously deceptive in this part of the world, as Bond well knew. Within an hour or so the sun could be gone, replaced by slanting, stinging snow, or hard visible frost blotting out the light.

His room was at the rear of the building, and from it he had a clear view of the chair lift, with the ski run and the curve of the jump. Tiny figures, taking advantage of the short spell of daylight and the clear atmosphere, were boarding the endlessly moving lift, while high above, outlined like black speeding insects against the snow, others made the long descent, curving in speed-checking traverses, or racing straight on the fall line with bodies leaning forward and knees bent.

Rivke, Bond thought, could well be one of those dots schussing down over the pure, sparkling white landscape. He could almost feel the exhilaration of a straight downhill run, and for a second wished he had gone along. Then, with one last glance at the snowscape, relieved only by the skiers, the movement of the chair lift and the great banks of fir trees sweeping away on either side, green and brown, decorated like Christmas trees by the heavy frozen snow, James Bond rose, left the room and headed down to the main dining room.

Brad Tirpitz sat alone at a corner table near the windows, looking out on the same view Bond had just observed from higher in the building.

Tirpitz spotted his arrival, and nonchalantly raised an arm in a combination of greeting and identification.

"Hi, Bond." The rocklike face cracked slightly. "Kolya sends his apologies. Been delayed organizing some snow scooters." He leaned closer. "It's tonight apparently—or in the early hours of tomorrrow if you want to be accurate."

"What's tonight?" Bond responded stiffly, the perfect caricature of the reserved Englishman.

"What's tonight?" Tirpitz raised his eyes to heaven. "Tonight, friend Bond, Kolya says a load of arms is coming out of Blue Hare—you remember Blue Hare? Their ordnance depot near Alakurtti?"

"Oh that." Bond gave the impression Blue Hare and the theft of arms was the last thing to interest him. Picking up the menu, he immersed himself in the long list of dishes available.

When the waiter appeared, he merely rattled off his usual order, underlining his need of a very large cup for coffee.

"Mind if I smoke?" Tirpitz was laconic to the point of speaking like an Indian sign.

"As long as you don't mind me eating." Bond did not smile. Perhaps it was his background in the Royal Navy, and working all these years close to M, but he considered smoking while someone else ate to be only a fraction below smoking before the Loyal Toast.

"Look, Bond." Tirpitz moved his chair closer. "I'm glad Kolya's not here. Wanted a word with you alone."

"Yes?"

"Got a message for you. Felix Leiter sends his best. And Cedar sends her love."

Bond felt a slight twinge of surprise, but he showed no reaction. His best friend in the USA, Felix Leiter, had once been a top CIA man; while Felix's daughter Cedar was also Company-trained. In fact Cedar had worked gallantly with Bond on a recent assignment.

"I know you don't trust me," Tirpitz continued. "But you'd better think again, brother. Think again, because maybe I'm the only friend you have around here."

Bond nodded. "Maybe."

"Your chief gave you a good solid briefing. I was briefed at Langley. We probably had the same information, and Kolya wasn't letting it all out of the bag. What I'm saying is that we need to work together. Close as we can. That Russian bastard isn't coming up with all the goodies, and I figure he has some surprises ready for us."

"I thought we were all working together?" Bond made it sound bland, urbane.

"Don't trust anyone—except me." Tirpitz, though he had taken out a package of cigarettes, made no attempt to light up. There was a pause while the waiter brought Bond's scrambled eggs, bacon, toast, marmalade and coffee. When he had gone, Tirpitz continued. "Look, if I hadn't spoken up in Madeira the biggest threat wouldn't even have been mentioned—this phony Count. You've had the dope on him, same as me. Konrad von Glöda. Kolya wasn't going to give him to us. D'you know why?"

"Tell me."

"Because Kolya's working two sides of the street. Some elements of the KBG're mixed up in this business of arms thefts. Our people in Moscow gave us that weeks ago. It's only just been cleared for consumption by London. You'll probably get some kind of signal in due course."

"What's the story then?" It was Bond who played it laconically now, for Brad Tirpitz appeared to be firming up the theory already discussed with Rivke.

"Like a fairy tale," Tirpitz gave a growling laugh. "The word from Moscow is that a dissatisfied faction of senior KGB people—a very small cell—have got themselves mixed up with a similarly dissatisfied Red Army splinter group." In turn, Tirpitz maintained, these two bodies became contacts with the nucleus of what was later to emerge as the National Socialist Action Army.

"They're idealists, of course," Tirpitz chuckled. "Fanatics. Men working within the USSR to subvert the Communist ideal by Fascist terrorism. They were behind the first arms theft from Blue Hare, and they got caught—up to a point . . ."

"What point?"

"They got caught, but the full facts never came out. They're like the Mafia—or ourselves, come to that. Your people look after their own, don't they?"

"Only when they can get away with it." Bond forked some egg into his mouth, reaching for the toast.

"Well, the boys in Dzerzhinsky Square have, so far, managed to keep the Army man who caught them out at Blue Hare as sweet as a nut. What's more, they're conducting this combined clandestine operation with one of their own in the driving seat—Kolya Mosolov."

"What you're saying is that Kolya's going to fail?" Bond turned, looking Tirpitz full in the face.

"He's not only going to fail, he's going to make sure the next shipment gets out. After that, it'll look as though Comrad Mosolov got himself killed among all this snow and ice. Then guess who's going to be left holding the bucket?"

"Us?" Bond suggested.

"Technically us, yes. In fact the plan is for it to be you, friend Bond. Kolya's body'll never be found. I suspect yours will. Of course Kolya'll eventually rise from the grave. Another name, another face, another part of the forest."

Bond nodded energetically. "That's more or less what I thought. I didn't think Kolya was taking me into the Soviet Union to watch arms lifted just for the fun of it."

Tirpitz gave a humorless smile. "Like you, buddy, I really have seen it all—Berlin, the Cold War, Nam, Laos, Cambodia. This is the triple cross of all time. You *need* me, brother . . ."

"And I suspect you need me also . . . er, brother."

"Right. If you play it my way. Do it the way I ask—as the Company asks—while you're playing snowman on the other side of the border. If you do that, I'll watch your back and make sure we all end up in one piece."

"Before I ask what I'm supposed to do, there's one important question." Bond had ceased to be bemused by the conversation. First Rivke had craved him, now Tirpitz: it added a new dimension to Operation Icebreaker. Nobody trusted the next person. All wanted at least one ally whom—Bond suspected—would be ditched or stabbed in the back at the first hint of trouble.

"Yeah?" Tirpitz prodded, and Bond realized he had been distracted by some guests who had just arrived and were being treated like royalty by the waiters.

"What about Rivke? That's what I wanted to ask. Are we leaving her in the cold with Kolya?"

Brad Tirpitz looked astounded. "Bond," he said quietly, "Rivke Ingber may well be a Mossad agent, but you do, I presume, know *who* she is. I mean, your Service must have told you . . ."

"The estranged daughter of a Finnish officer who went along with the Nazis and is still on the wanted war criminals list? Yes."

"Yes and no," Brad Tirpitz's voice rose. "Sure, we all know about that bastard of a father. But nobody really has any idea about what side of the line the girl stands on—not even Mossad. The likes of us haven't been told that part, but I've seen her Mossad PF. I'm telling you, even they don't know."

Bond spoke calmly. "I'm afraid I believe she's genuine—completely loyal to Mossad."

Tirpitz made an irritated little noise. "Okay, believe away, Bond; but what about The Man?"

"The Man?"

"The so-called Count Konrad von Glöda. The guy who's behind the arms shipments and is probably running the whole NSAA operation—correction, almost certainly running the whole NSAA. Reichsführer-SS von Glöda."

"So?"

"You mean nobody at your end put you in the full picture?"

Bond shrugged. M had been precise and detailed in his briefing, but stressed that there were certain matters about the mysterious Count von Glöda which could not be proved. M, being the stickler he was, refused to take mere probability as fact.

"Brother, you're in trouble." Brad Tirpitz's eyes turned to broken glass. "Rivke Ingber's deranged and estranged Papa, SS-Oberführer Aarne Tudeer, is also the Ice King of this little saga. Aarne Tudeer *is* the Count von Glöda: an apt name."

Bond moistened his lips with coffee, his brain racing. If Tirpitz was giving correct information, London had not even suggested it. All M had provided was the name, the possibility that he was behind at least the arms running, and the fact that the Count almost certainly arranged staging posts between the Soviet border and the final jumping off point for the arms supplies. There had been no mention of von Glöda being Tudeer.

"You're certain of this?" Bond refused to show anything but nonchalant calm.

"As sure as night follows day—which is pretty fast around here . . ." Tirpitz stopped abruptly as he looked across the dining room, his gaze resting on the couple who had come in to such an enthusiastic welcome.

"Well, what do you know?" The corners of Tirpitz's mouth turned down even further. "Take a look, Bond. That's The Man himself. The Count Konrad von Glöda, and his lady, known simply as the Countess." He gulped some coffee. "I said it was an apt name. In Swedish, Glöda means *glow*. At Langley we cryptonymed him Glowworm. He glows with bread, from old Nazi pickings, and those he must be raking in now as Commander of the NSAA; and he's also a worm. I am personally going to bottle that specimen."

The couple certainly looked distinguished. Bond had seen the heavy and expensive fur coats borne away when they had arrived. Now they even sat as though they owned Lapland, looking almost like a Renaissance prince and his lady.

Konrad von Glöda was tall, well muscled, holding himself straight as a lath. He was also one of those men whom age does not weary. He could be an old-looking fifty, or a very young seventy, for it was impossible to calculate the age of a man whose bone structure and face were so fine and bronzed. He sported a full head of iron-gray hair, and as he talked to the Countess, he leaned back in his chair, using one hand for gestures while the other was draped over the chair arm. The brown face, glowing with health, had about it an animation which would not have been out of place in that of a thrusting young executive; and there was no doubt about his looks—from the glittering gray eyes to the aristocratic sharp chin and arrogant tilt of the head. This man was someone to be reckoned with. *Glow* was the word.

"Star quality?" Tirpitz asked.

Bond gave a small nod. You only had to see the man to know he possessed that sought-for quality: charisma.

The Countess also carried herself with the air of one who possessed the means, and ability, to buy or take anything she wanted. She was obviously—despite the impossibility of predicting the Count's age—much younger than her partner, though she too had the look of a person who valued her body and its physical condition. Even now, at the breakfast table, she gave the impression of one to whom all sport and exercise came as second nature. Bond reflected that this would certainly include the oldest of indoor sports, for the woman's smooth-skinned beauty, the svelte grooming of her dark hair drawn back to a pleat, and the classic features spoke poems of sex.

Bond was still covertly watching the couple when a waiter came hurrying over to the table. "Mr. Bond?" he asked.

Bond signified an affirmative.

"There's a telephone call for you, sir. In the box, by the reception desk. A Miss Paula Vacker wishes to speak to you."

Bond was on his feet quickly, catching the slightly quizzical look in Brad Tirpitz's eye.

"Problems, Bond?" Tirpitz's voice appeared to have softened, but Bond refused to react. "Bad" Brad, he decided, should be treated with a caution reserved for rattlesnakes.

"Just a call from Helsinki." He began to move, inwardly bewildered that Paula could have found him here.

As he passed the von Glödas' table, Bond allowed himself a straight, seemingly disinterested, glance at the couple. The Count himself raised his head, catching Bond's eye. The look was one of near tangible malice: a hatred which Bond could feel long after he had passed the table, as though the Count's glittering gray eyes were boring into the back of his head.

The receptionist indicated a small, half-open booth containing a tele- phone. Bond was there in two strides, lifting the receiver and speaking immediately.

"Paula?"

"One moment," from the operator. There was a click on the line, and the certain sense that someone was on the distant end.

"Paula?" he repeated

If questioned there and then, Bond could not possibly have sworn an oath that it was Paula's voice, though he would have claimed a ninety percent certainty. Unusually for the Finnish telephone system, the line was not good. The voice seemed hollow, as though from an echo chamber.

"James," the voice said. "Any minute now, I should imagine. Say goodbye to Anni." There followed a long and eerie laugh, which trailed away as though Paula was deliberately moving the receiver from her lips, then slowly returning it to its cradle.

Bond's brow creased, a concern building quickly inside him. "Paula? Is that you . . . ?" He stopped, knowing there was no point in talking into a dead instrument.

Say goodbye to Anni . . . What in hell? Then it struck him. Rivke was on the ski run. Or had she even reached it? Bond raced for the main doors to the hotel.

His hand was already outstretched when the voice behind him snapped, "Don't even think of it, Bond. Not dressed like that." Brad Tirpitz was at his shoulder. "You'd last less than five minutes out there— it's well below freezing."

"Get me some gear, and fast, Brad."

"Get your own: What in hell's the matter?" Tirpitz took a step towards the cloakroom near Reception.

"Explain later. Rivke's out on the ski run and I've a hunch she's in danger." It crossed his mind that Rivke Ingber might not, after all, be on the slopes. Paula had said, "Any minute now, I should imagine." Whatever was planned could have already happened.

Tirpitz was back, his own outdoor clothes grasped in his arms—boots, scarf, goggles, gloves and padded jacket. "Just tell me," the voice commanding, "and I'll do what I can. Go get your own stuff. I always play safe and keep the winter gear close at hand." Already he was kicking off his shoes and pulling on boots. There was obviously no arguing with Tirpitz.

Bond turned towards the bank of elevators. "If Rivke's on the slopes, just get her down fast, and in one piece," he shouted, banging at the button and disappearing into the cage.

On reaching his room, Bond took less than three minutes to get into winter gear. As he did the quick change, he took constant quick looks out of the window towards the chair lift and ski slopes. All appeared normal, as it did when he finally reached the bottom of the chair lift outside, having made the round trip in just over six minutes.

Most people had already made their way back into the hotel: the good period for skiing was over. Bond made out the figure of Brad Tirpitz standing near the hut at the bottom of the lift with a couple of other figures.

"Well?" Bond asked.

"I got them to telephone the top. Her name's on the list. She's on her way down now. She's wearing a crimson ski suit. Give me the full dope on this, Bond. Is it to do with the op?"

"Later." Bond craned, narrowing his eyes behind the goggles, searching the upward sheen of snow for sight of Rivke.

The main slope came down the shallow mountain ridge in a series of steps, covering some one and a half kilometers. The top was hidden from view, but the marked slope was wide and intricate: sliding between fir trees at points, some of it so gentle that it appeared almost flat, while there were sections, following easy downhill runs, that steepened to awesome angles.

The last half kilometer was a nursery slope, no more than a long, straight, gentle runout. Two young men in black ski suits with white striped woolen hats were expertly completing what had obviously been a fast run down from the top. They both executed showy finishes on the runout, laughing and making a lot of noise.

"Here she comes." Brad handed over his binoculars, with which he had been scanning the top of the final fall line. "Crimson suit."

Bond raised the glasses. Rivke was obviously very good, sideslipping and traversing the steep slope, coming out of it into a straight run, slowing as the snow flattened, then gathering a little speed as she breasted the rise and began to follow the fall line down the long final slope.

She had just touched the runout—less than a half kilometer away from them—when the snow seemed to boil on either side of her and a great white mist rose behind. In the center of the blossom of fine snow, a sudden fire—red, then white—flashed upwards.

The sound of the muffled crump reached them a second after Bond saw Rivke's body turning over in midair, thrown up with the exploding snow.

9

SPEEDLINE

BOND FELT THE gut twist of impotent horror as he watched, peering through the goggles into the rising haze of snow. The crimson figure, twirling like a rag doll, disappeared into the fine white spray, while the few people standing near Tirpitz and Bond flattened themselves onto the ground, as though under mortar fire.

Brad Tirpitz, like Bond, remained upright. Tirpitz's only action was to grab back the binoculars, lifting the rubber protective shields to his eyes.

"She's there. Unconscious, I think." Tirpitz spoke like a spotter on the battlefield, calling in an air strike or ranging artillery. "Yes, face up, half-buried in snow. About one hundred yards down from where it happened."

Bond took back the glasses to look for himself. The snow was settling, and he could make out the figure quite clearly, spreadeagled in a drift.

Another voice came from behind them. "The hotel's called the police and an ambulance. It's not far, but no rescue team's going to get up there quickly—snow's too soft. They'll have to bring in a helicopter."

Bond turned. Kolya Mosolov stood with them, also with raised binoculars.

In the few seconds following the explosion, Bond's mind had gone into overdrive. The signals came clearly, in a logical pattern of thought which led to certain obvious conclusions.

Paula's telephone call—if it was Paula—bore out most of what Rivke had said, hardening Bond's earlier conclusions. Paula Vacker was certainly not what she had seemed. She had set up Bond at the apartment during the first visit to Helsinki. Somehow she knew about the night games with Rivke—or Anni, whichever name applied—and had set her up as well. Even more, Paula—he could only think of her as Paula—had arranged this present ski slope incident with incredible timing. She *knew* what had been arranged. It could add up to one thing only: Paula had some kind of access to the four members of Icebreaker. It was either a direct link, known by the person concerned, or some clandestine method as though she was plugged into them with sophisticated electronics. That was certainly possible. But either way, Paula was undoubtedly here, in the hotel or its vicinity, near the small town of Salla—maybe even watching them at this moment.

Bond pulled himself from his thoughts, "What do you reckon?" He turned to Kolya for a second before looking back up the slope.

"I said. A helicopter. The center of the run out here is hard, but Rivke's bogged down in the soft snow. If we want action fast, it has to be a helicopter."

"That's not what I meant," Bond snapped. "What do you reckon happened?"

Kolya shrugged under the layers of winter clothing. "Land mine, I guess. They still get them around here. From the Russo-Finnish Winter War, or World War Two. Even after all this time. They move, too—in early winter with the first blizzards. Yes, I'd guess a land mine."

"What if I told you I was warned?"

"That's right," Brad said, his binoculars still glued to the flash of red that was Rivke. "Bond had some kind of phone call."

Kolya seemed uninterested. "Ah, we'll have to talk about it. But where the hell're the police and the helicopter?"

As if on cue, a police Saab Finlandia came skidding into the main hotel car park, pulling up a few paces short of where Kolya, Tirpitz, and Bond stood.

Two officers got out. Kolya was immediately beside them, speaking Finnish like a native born. There was some uncharacteristic gesticulating, then Kolya turned back to Bond, muttering an obscene Russian oath. "They can't get a copter here for another half-hour." He looked very angry. "And the rescue team'll take as long."

"Then we have . . ."

Bond was cut short by Brad Tirpitz. "She's moving. Conscious. Trying to get up. No, she's down again. Legs, I think."

Bond quickly asked Kolya if the police car carried such a thing as a loud-hailer. Then Kolya shouted back to Bond, "Yes, they've got one."

Bond was off, running as best he could over the frozen ground, his gloved hand unclipping a jacket pocket to reach for his car keys. "Get it ready," he shouted back. "I'll bring her down myself. Get the loud-hailer ready."

The locks on the Saab were well oiled and treated with antifreeze, so Bond had no difficulty in opening up. He switched off the alarm sensors, then went to the rear, pulling up the big hatchback and removing a pair of toggle ropes and the large drum that was the Schermuly Pains-Wessex Speedline.

He locked up again, resetting the alarms, and hurried back to the foot of the ski run where one of the policemen—looking a little self-conscious—held a Schermuly-Graviner loud-hailer.

"She's sitting up. Waved once, and indicated she couldn't move anymore." Tirpitz passed on the information as Bond approached.

"Right." Bond held out his hand, taking the loud-hailer from the policeman, flicking the switch and raising it towards the patch of red that was Rivke Ingber. He took care not to let the metal touch his lips.

"If you can hear me, Rivke, raise one arm. This is James." The voice, magnified through the amplifier to a volume ten times that of his normal speech, echoed around them.

Bond saw the movement, and Tirpitz, the binoculars up, reported it: "She's lifted an arm."

Bond checked that the loud-hailer was aimed directly toward Rivke. "I'm going to fire a line to you, Rivke. Don't be scared. It's propelled by a rocket that should pass quite close to you. Signify if you understand."

Again the arm raised.

"When the line reaches you, do you think you can secure it around your body, under the arms?"

Another affirmative.

"Do you consider we could then slowly pull you down?"

Affirmative.

"If this proves to be impossible, if you are in any pain as we drag you down, signify by raising both hands. Do you read me?"

Once more the affirmative sign.

"All right," Bond turned back to the others, giving them directions.

The Schermuly Pains-Wessex Speedline is a complete, self-contained, line-throwing unit which looks like a heavy cylinder with a carrying handle and trigger mechanism at the top. It is arguably the best line-throwing unit in the world. Bond removed the protective plastic covering at the front of the cylinder, exposing the rocket, well-shielded in the center, and the 275 meters of packed, ready-flaked line which took up the bulk of the space.

He removed the free end of the line, giving instructions for the others to make it safe around the Finlandia's rear bumper, placing himself almost directly below the crimson figure above them in the snow.

When the line was secure, Bond removed the safety pin at the rear of the carrying handle, shifting his hand to the molded grip behind the trigger guard. He dug the heels of his Mukluk boots into the snow and advanced four paces up the slope. The snow was soft and very deep to the right of the broad ski slope fall line, where it was rock hard and only negotiable upward with the aid of ice-climbing equipment.

Four steps and Bond was almost sinking to his waist, but the position was reasonable for a good shot with the line—the far end of which trailed out behind him to the bumper of the Finlandia.

Bracing himself, Bond held the cylinder away from his body, allowing it to find the correct point of balance. When he was certain the rocket would clear Rivke as she lay in the snow above, he pressed the trigger.

There was a dull thud as the firing pin struck the igniter. Then, with spectacular speed and a plume of smoke, the rocket leaped high into the clear air, its line threading out after it, seeming to gain speed as it went, a single-strand bow of rope curling high above the snow.

The rocket passed well clear of Rivke's body, but right on course, taking the line directly above her and landing with a dull plot. For a second, the line appeared to hang in its arc, quivering in the still air. Then, with an almost controlled neatness, it began to fall—a long brown snake running from a point high above where Rivke lay.

Bond fought his way through the thick snow back to the others, taking the loud-hailer from one of the policemen.

"Raise your arm if you can pull the rope above you down to your body." Bond's voice once more echoed off the slopes.

In spite of the freezing weather, several people had come out to watch. Others could be seen peering through the hotel windows. Far away the sound of an ambulance's Klaxon approached with increasing volume.

"Binoculars, please." Bond was commanding, not asking. Tirpitz handed over the glasses, and Bond adjusted the knurled wheel, bringing Rivke into sharp focus.

She appeared to be lying at an odd angle, waist deep in snow, though there were traces of cracked, hard snow and ice around the area in which she lay. From what little he could see of the girl's face, Bond had the impression that she was in pain. Laboriously she hauled back on the line, pulling the far end towards her from above.

The process seemed to take a very long time. Rivke—obviously in distress, and suffering from cold as well as injury—kept stopping to rest. The simple job of hauling the line down towards her had turned into a major battle. From his view through the binoculars, it seemed to Bond that she was pulling a heavy dead weight on the line.

From time to time, Bond urged her on when he could see she was flagging, his loud voice throwing great bouncing echoes around them.

Finally she pulled the whole line in and began the struggle of getting it around her body.

"Under the arms, Rivke," Bond instructed. "Knot it and slide the knot to your back. Then raise your hands when you're ready."

After an age, the hands lifted.

"All right. Now we're going to bring you down as gently as we can. We will be dragging you through the soft snow, but don't forget, if it becomes too painful, raise both arms. Stand by, Rivke."

Bond turned to the others, who had already unknotted the line from the Finlandia's bumper, and slowly pulled in the slack, taking up the strain from Rivke to the bottom of the slope.

Bond had been aware of the ambulance arriving but now registered its presence for the first time. There was a full medical team on board, complete with a young, bearded doctor. Bond asked where they would take her, and the doctor—whose name turned out to be Simonsson—said they were from the small hospital at Salla. "After that"—he raised his hands in an uncertain gesture—"it depends on her injuries."

It took the best part of three-quarters of an hour to pull Rivke to within reaching distance. She was only half-conscious when Bond, pushing through the snow, reached her. Gently he guided those who pulled on the line to bring her right down to the edge of the runout.

She moaned, opening her eyes as the doctor got to her. She immediately recognized Bond.

"James, what happened?" The voice was small and weak.

"Don't know, love. You had a fall." Under the goggles and scarf muffling his face, Bond felt the anxiety etched into his own features, just as the telltale white blotches of frostbite were visible on the exposed parts of Rivke's face.

After a few moments the doctor touched Bond's shoulder, pulling him away. Tirpitz and Kolya Mosolov knelt by the girl as the doctor muttered, "Both legs fractured, by the look of it." He spoke excellent English, as Bond had discovered during their earlier exchange. "Frostbite, as you can see, and advanced hypothermia. We have to get her in fast."

"As quick as you can." Bond caught hold of the doctor's sleeve. "Can I come to the hospital later?"

"By all means."

She was unconscious again, and Bond could do nothing but stand back and watch, his mind in confusion, as they gently strapped Rivke onto a stretcher and slid her into the ambulance.

Pictures seemed to overlap in his head: the present cold, the ice and snow, and the ambulance crunching off towards the main exit of the hotel flashed among the visions which came, unwanted, from his memory bank: another ambulance; a different road; heat; blood all over the car; and an Austrian policeman asking endless questions about Tracy's death. That nightmare—the death of his one and only wife—always lurked in the far reaches of Bond's mind.

As though the two pictures suddenly merged, he heard Kolya saying, "We have to talk, James Bond. I have to ask questions. We also must be ready for tonight. It's all fixed, but now we're one short. Arrangements will have to be made."

Bond nodded, slowly trudging back towards the hotel. In the foyer, they agreed to meet in Kolya's room at three.

In his own room, Bond unlocked his briefcase and operated the internal security devices which released the false bottom and sides—all covered by Q'ute's ingenious screening device.

From one of the side compartments he took out an oblong unit, red in color and no larger than a package of cigarettes—the VL34, so-called "Privacy Protector," possibly one of the smallest and most advanced electronic "bug" detecting devices. On his arrival the previous night, Bond had already swept the room and found it clean, but he was not going to take chances now.

Drawing out the retractable antennae, he switched on the small machine and began to use it to sweep the room. In a matter of seconds, a series of lights began to glow along the front panel. Then, as the antennae pointed towards the telephone, a yellow light came on, giving complete verification that there was a transmitter and microphone somewhere in the telephone area.

Having located one listening bug, Bond carefully went over the entire room. There were a couple of small alarms near the radio and television sets, but the failsafe yellow signal light did not lock on. Within a short time, he had established that the only bug in the room was the first one signaled—in the telephone. Examining the instrument, he soon discovered it contained an updated version of the old and familiar "infinity bug," which turns your telephone into a transmitter giving twenty-four-hour service wherever the operator is located. Even at the other end of the world, an operator can pick up not only telephone calls, but also anything said within the room in which the telephone is located.

Bond removed the bug, carried it to the bathroom and ground it under the heel of his Mukluk before flushing it down the lavatory. "So perish all enemies of the state," he muttered with a wry smile.

The others would almost certainly be covered by this, or similar, bugs. Two questions remained: how and when had the bug been planted, and how had they so neatly timed the attempt on Rivke's life? Paula would have had to move with great speed to act against Rivke—or any of them. Unless, Bond thought, the Hotel Revontuli was so well penetrated that dangerous traps and pitfalls had been set well in advance of their arrival.

But to do that, Paula—or whoever was organizing these counter-moves—would have had to be in on the Madeira briefing. Since Rivke had become a victim, she was already in the clear. But what of Brad Tirpitz and Kolya? He would soon discover the truth about those two. If the operation connected with the Russian ordnance depot Blue Hare was really "on" tonight, perhaps the whole deck of cards would be laid out.

He stripped, showered, and changed into comfortable clothes, then stretched out on the bed, lighting one of his Simmons cigarettes. After two or three puffs Bond crushed the butt into the ashtray and closed his eyes, drifting into a doze.

Waking with a start, Bond glanced at his watch. It was almost three o'clock. He crossed to the window and looked out. The snowscape appeared to change as he stood there: the sudden sharp white altering as the sun went down. Then came the magic of what they call "the Blue Moment," in the Arctic Circle, when the glaring white snow and ice on ground, rocks, buildings and trees turns a greenish-blue shade for a minute or two before the dusk sets in.

He would be late for the meeting with Kolya and Tirpitz, but that could not be helped. Bond quickly went to his now bug-free telephone, asking the operator for the hospital number at Salla. She came back quite quickly. Bond got the dial tone and picked out the number. His first thought on waking had been Rivke.

The hospital receptionist spoke an easy English. He enquired about Rivke and was asked to wait.

Finally the woman came back on the line. "We have no patient of that name, I'm afraid."

"She was admitted a short time ago," Bond said. "An accident at the Hotel Revontuli. On the ski slopes. Hypothermia, frostbite, and both legs fractured. You sent an ambulance and doctor . . ." he paused trying to remember the name, ". . . Doctor Simonsson."

"I'm sorry, sir. This is a small hospital and I know all the doctors. There are only five, and none is called Simonsson . . ."

"Bearded. Young. He told me I could call."

"I'm sorry, sir, but there must be some mistake. There have been no ambulance calls from the Revontuli today, I've just checked. No female admissions either; and we have no Doctor Simonsson. In fact we have no young, bearded doctors at all. I only wish we had. Three are middle-aged and married; the other two come up for retirement next year."

Bond asked if there were any other hospitals nearby. No. The nearest hospital was at Kemijärvi, and they would not operate an emergency service in this area any more than the hospital at Pelkosenniemi. Bond asked for the numbers of both those hospitals and the local police, then thanked the girl and began to dial again.

Within five minutes he knew the bad news. Neither of the other hospitals had attended an accident at the hotel.

What was more, the local police did not have a Saab Finlandia operating on the roads today. In fact, no police patrol had been sent to the hotel. It was not a mistake; the police knew the hotel very well. So well that they did their ski training there.

They were very sorry.

So was Bond. Sorry, and decidedly shaken.

10

KOLYA

JAMES BOND WAS furious. "You mean we aren't going to do anything about Rivke?" He did not shout, but his voice was cold, brittle as the ice decorating the trees outside Kolya's window.

"We'll inform her organization." Kolya appeared unconcerned. "But later, after this is over. She could've turned up by then anyway, Bond. We haven't got time to go snow-shoeing around the countryside after her now. If she doesn't surface, Mossad'll have to look for her. What does it say in the Bible? Let the dead bury the dead?"

Bond's temper was frayed. Already he had been within an ace of losing it a couple of times since joining the remnants of the Icebreaker team in Kolya's room. Kolya had opened up at his knock, and Bond had pushed past him, a finger to his lips, the other hand holding up the VL34 detector like a talisman.

Brad Tirpitz gave a sarcastic grin, which changed to a withering look of displeasure as Bond unearthed yet another infinity device from Kolya's phone, plus some additional electronics from under the carpet and in the bathroom toilet roll dispenser.

"Thought you dealt with the sweeping," Bond snapped, looking suspiciously at Tirpitz.

"I did all our rooms when we first got here. Checked yours out as well, buddy."

"You also claimed the rooms were clean in Madeira."

"So they were."

"Well, how come they—whoever *they* are—were able to pinpoint us here?"

Unruffled, Tirpitz repeated he had swept the rooms for electronics. "Everything was hygienic. In Madeira and here."

"Then we've got a leak. One of *us*—and I know it's not me." Bond dripped acid from each word.

"One of *us*? Of *us*?" Now Kolya's voice turned nasty.

As Yet Bond had not been able to give Kolya the full details of his telephone call from—he supposed—Paula, nor the warning she had duly delivered. He did so now, watching the Russian's face change. Mosolov's features were like the sea, Bond thought. This time the change was from anger to concern, as Bond outlined how the trick could have been managed. Whoever was operating against them knew a great deal about their private lives.

"That was no aging land mine out there," Bond stated bleakly. "Rivke is good on skis. I'm not bad myself, and I should imagine you're not exactly a novice, Kolya. Don't know about Tirpitz . . ."

"I can hold my own." Tirpitz had assumed the expression of a surly schoolboy.

The explosion on the slopes, Bond expanded, could have been operated by a remote control system. "They could also have used a sniper, in the hotel. It's been done before—a bullet activating an explosive charge. Personally, I go for the remote control because it ties with everything else; the fact that Rivke was on the slopes, that I got a telephone call which must have coincided with her leaving the top of the run." He spread his hands. "They have us bottled up here; they've taken one of us out already, which makes it easier for them to close in on the rest of us . . ."

"And the gallant Count von Glöda was here for breakfast with his woman." Tirpitz came out of his sullen mood. He pointed at Kolya Mosolov. "Do you know anything about that?"

Mosolov gave a half-nod. "I saw them. Before the business on the slopes. Saw them when I got back to the hotel."

Bond followed up what Tirpitz had started. "Don't you think it's time, Kolya? Time you came clean about von Glöda?"

Mosolov made a gesture meant to convey that he was at a loss about all the fuss. "The so-called Count von Glöda is an essential suspect . . ."

"He's the *only* suspect," Tirpitz snapped.

"The probable power behind the people we're all trying to nail," added Bond.

Kolya sighed. "He was not mentioned in previous meetings because I've been waiting for positive proof—identification of his command headquarters."

"And you have that proof now?" Bond moved close to Kolya, almost menacing him.

"Yes," clear and unshakable. "All we need. It's part of the briefing for tonight." Kolya paused, as though pondering the wisdom of going any further with information. "I suppose you both know who von Glöda really

is?" It was as though he intended to deliver some great *coup de grâce*.
  Bond nodded. "Yes."

"And the relationship with our missing colleague," added Tirpitz.

"Good," a slightly peeved tone. "Then we'll get on with the briefing."

"And leave Rivke to the wolves." The thought still stung Bond.

Very quietly Kolya turned his head, eyes clashing with Bond. "I suggest
that Rivke will be okay. That we leave her in—what's your expression?—
leave her in balk? I predict that Rivke Ingber will reappear when she's
ready. In the meantime, if we are to collect the evidence that will eventually
smash the National Socialist Action Army—which is our sole reason for
being here—we must go into tonight's operation with some care."

"So be it," Bond said, masking his anger.

The object of the exercise, as Kolya Mosolov had already put forward,
was that they should view, and possibly photograph, the theft of arms
from ordnance depot Blue Hare, located near Alakurtti. Kolya spread an
ordnance survey map on the floor. It was covered in marks—crosses in
red, various routings in black, blue and yellow.

Kolya's forefinger rested on a red cross just south of Alakurtti—around
sixty kilometers from where they now sat.

"I understand," Kolya continued, "that we're all fairly expert on snow
scooters." He looked first at Tirpitz, then at Bond. Both men nodded their
assent. "I'm glad to hear it, because we're all going to be under pressure.
The weather forecast for tonight is not good. Subzero temperatures, rising
a little after midnight when light snow is expected, then dropping to hard
freezing conditions again."

Kolya pointed out that they would be traveling through difficult country
by snow scooter during much of the night.

"As soon as I realized Rivke would be in the hospital . . ." he began
again.

"Where she is not," interruped Bond.

"I made other arrangements." Kolya disregarded Bond's interruption.
"We need at least four bodies on the ground for what we have to do. We
must cross the Russian border without help from my people, following
a route which I suspect will also be used by NSAA vehicles. The intention
was to leave two of us as markers along the route, while Bond and myself
went all the way to Alakurtti. My information is that the NSAA convoy
will be arriving by arrangement with the officer in command of the Blue
Hare and his subordinates, at about three in the morning."

The loading of whatever vehicles were to be used would take only an hour or so. Kolya guessed that they would employ amphibious tracked APC's, probably one of the many variants of the Russian BTR's. "They have everything ready, so my people tell me. Bond and myself will take VTR and still pictures, using infrared if necessary; though I presume there'll be a lot of light. Blue Hare is the back of beyond—that's the correct expression, yes?—and nobody's going to bother much during the loading. The care will be taken on the way in and, more especially, during the transportation out. At Blue Hare itself, I expect all the floodlights to be on."

"And where does von Glöda come into all this?" Bond had been examining the map and its penciled hieroglyphics. He was not happy with it. The way across the border looked more than difficult—through heavily wooded areas, over frozen lakes and long stretches of open, snow-covered country which, in summer, would be flat tundra. Mainly, though, it was the heavily forested patches that worried him. He knew what it was like to navigate and find a trail with a snow scooter through these great black blocks of fir and pine.

Kolya gave a kind of secret smile. "Von Glöda," he said very slowly, "will be here." His finger hovered over the map, then stabbed down at a section marked out in oblongs and squares. The map reference showed it to be just inside the Finnish border, a little to the north of where they would expect to cross and return.

Both Bond and Tirpitz craned forward, Bond quickly memorizing the coordinates on the map. Kolya continued talking.

"I am ninety-nine percent certain that the man your people, Brad, call Glowworm will be safely tucked away there tonight; just as I'm sure the convoy from Blue Hare will end up at that same point."

"Ninety-nine percent certain?" Bond raised an eyebrow quizzically, his hand lifting to brush the small comma of hair from his forehead. "Why? How?"

"My country . . ." Kolya Mosolov's tone contained no jingoism or especial pride. "My country has a slight advantage, from a geographical viewpoint." His finger circled the whole area around the red oblong marks on the map. "We've been able to mount considerable surveillance over the past weeks. It's also to our advantage that agents on the ground have made exhaustive enquiries." He went on to state what should have been obvious to all of them: there were still a large number of ruined old defensive points along this part of the frontier. "You can still see the remains of defenses in many European countries—in France, for instance, even in England. Most are intact but unusable, the bunker walls sound enough but the interiors crumbling. So you can imagine how many block-houses and fortifications were constructed all along here during the Winter War, and again after the Nazi invasion of Russia."

"I can vouch for that." Bond smiled, as though trying to let Kolya know he was not entirely a stranger to this part of the world.

"My people know about them, too." Tirpitz was not to be outdone.

"Ah." Kolya's face lit up in what might have passed for a benign smile.

Silence, for a good half minute.

Then Kolya nodded, his strange trick of sudden facial change turning him sagelike. "Once we were alerted to what was going on at Blue Hare, our Special Operations Departments were given precise orders. High-fly aircraft and satellites were set on new routes. Eventually they came up with these." He slid a small, clear plastic folder from under the map and began to pass out a series of photographs. There were a number of pictures obviously taken from reconnaissance aircraft—probably the Russian *Mandrake, Mangrove* or *Brewer-D,* all ideal for the purpose. Even in their black and white format, the photographs clearly showed large areas of disturbed ground. They had been taken during the late summer months, or in early autumn before the snows, and on most of them some kind of large concrete bunker entrance was unmistakably evident.

The other photographs were also of a type with which both Bond and Brad Tirpitz were familiar: military reconnaissance satellite pictures, taken from miles above the earth with varied cameras and lenses. The most interesting were those which showed, in graphic color, changes in geological structure.

"We put one of our Cosmos military intelligence birds on the job. Good, eh?"

Bond's eyes flicked from the satellite pictures to the small drawings on the map. The pictures, mostly magnified and blown up, showed considerable work had taken place under the earth's surface. The textures and colors made it plain that the building was well executed, with a great deal of steel and concrete in use. There was also the symmetry—all the signs of a complete and active underground complex.

"You see," Kolya continued, "I have more than just the photographs." He produced yet another folder, containing both plan and elevation drawings of what could only be a very large bunker. "We were alerted by the satellite findings. Then our field agents moved in. There were also one or two interesting maps of the area, used at the time of the Winter War, and later. Finnish military engineers built a large, underground arms dump on exactly this spot during the late 1930s. It was big enough to contain at least ten tracked tanks as well as ammunition and facilities for repair. The main bunker entrance was large—here." He pointed directly to the photographs and the plan view drawing. "From our people on the ground, and existing records, we know the bunker was, in fact, never used. However, about two years ago, during the summer, much activity was reported in the general area—builders, bulldozers, the usual paraphernalia. It is without much doubt, von Glöda's lair." His finger started to trace along the drawings. "There, you see, the original entrance has been rebuilt and sealed off—large enough to take vehicles, with plenty of room below for storage."

It was a very clear and convincing batch of evidence. The complex seemed large. It divided into two areas: one for vehicles and stores; the other a vast honeycomb of living quarters. At least three hundred people could live underground in this place, year in and year out.

The bigger entrance lay parallel to a smaller access and both sloped down a similar gradient, leading to a depth of some three hundred meters— just over a quarter of a mile which, as Tirpitz said, was "deep enough to bury a lot of bodies."

"We consider it is where *all* the bodies are buried." Kolya showed no sign of humor. "I personally think it constitutes the headquarters and planning control command post of the National Socialist Action Army. The place has also been built as a major staging point for the arms and munitions stolen from Red Army bases. The refurbished bunker, in my opinion, is the heart of the NSAA."

"So all we have to do"—Tirpitz glanced at Kolya, the cynicism practically tangible—"is take some pretty pictures of your army people betraying their country; then follow the vehicles back to here," finger on the map, "to the bunker. Their cozy little Ice Palace."

"Exactly."

"Just like that. With three of us—me, I presume, acting as a backstop on the frontier, where any jerk could pick me off like a jackrabbit."

"Not if you're as good as they tell me," Kolya said, returning like for like. "For my part I've taken the liberty of bringing another of my people— simply because there are *two* crossing points." He indicated another line, slightly further north than the initial route he and Bond would be taking, explaining that both border crossings should be covered. "Originally I wanted Rivke up there, just in case. We needed a spare, so I've arranged it."

Bond thought a minute. Then: "Kolya, I have a question."

"Go ahead." The face lifted towards him, open and frank.

"If this runs to plan—if we get the evidence, and we follow the convoy back to the bunker you say is here," Bond pointed at the map, "when we've done all that, what's the next move?"

Kolya did not even stop to think. "We make certain we have our proof. After that, we do one of two things. Either we report back to our respective agencies or, if it looks feasible, we finish the job ourselves."

Bond made no further comment. Kolya had signaled an interesting end game. If he was, in fact, involved in any KGB–Red Army conspiracy, the action of "finishing the job ourselves" was as good method as any to cover up and silence things forever. The more so, Bond calculated, if Kolya Mosolov saw to it that Bond and Tirpitz did not return. Meanwhile, if the conspiracy theory held any water, the NSAA Command HQ could already be set to move out; another hiding place; another bunker.

They talked on, going over the minutiae: where the snow scooters were hidden, the kind of camera they would be using, the exact point at which Tirpitz would take up his post and the position of Kolya's new agent, identified solely by the cryptonym *Mujik,* a little joke of Kolya's or so he maintained—a *mujik* being, in old Russia, a peasant, regarded by the law as a minor.

After an hour or so of this close briefing, Kolya handed out maps to both Tirpitz and Bond. They covered the entire area, were as near to Ordnance Survey standard of cartography as you could get, and had the routes over the frontier marked in thin pencil, together with the position of Blue Hare, and the same series of oblongs denoting the underground complex of what they had taken to calling the Ice Palace. Blue Hare and the Ice Palace, Kolya maintained, were drawn in to exact scale.

They synchronized their watches. They were to meet at midnight at the RV point, which meant leaving the hotel individually between 11:30 and 11:40.

Bond reentered his room silently, taking out the VL34 to recheck the entire suite. Gone were the days, he thought in passing, when you could keep a watch on your room by leaving tiny slivers of matchstick in the door or wedged into drawers. In the old days, a small piece of cotton would do wonders; but now, in the age of the micro-chip, life had become more sophisticated and considerably more difficult.

They had been at it again during the briefing. Not just the automatic infinity in the telephone this time, but a whole screen of listening devices as back-ups: one behind the mirror in the bathroom; another in the curtains, neatly sewn in place; a third disguised as a button in the small "housewife" pack of thread and needles, tucked into a pocket in the hotel stationery folder, and a final bug ingeniously fitted *within* a new lamp bulb by the bed.

Bond treble-swept the place. Whoever was doing the surveillance certainly knew the job. As he destroyed the various items, Bond even wondered if the new infinity bug in the telephone was merely a dummy, placed there in the hope he would not continue the search after finding it.

Assured now that the room was clean, Bond spread out his map. From the briefcase, he had already removed a military pocket compass which he intended to carry that night. Using a small pad of flimsies and a credit card as a ruler, Bond started to make calculations and retrace the routes on the map—noting the exact compass bearings they would have to follow to get across the border and locate Blue Hare, then the bearings out from Blue Hare, following the route in and its alternative.

He also took care to check angles and bearings that would lead them to the Ice Palace. The whole time he worked, James Bond felt uneasy—a sense he had experienced more than once since the Madeira meeting. He was aware of the basic cause: from time to time he had worked in conjunction with another member of either his own, or a sister, Service. But Icebreaker was different. Now he had been forced to act with a team, and Bond was not a team man—especially a team that blatantly contained grave elements of mistrust.

His eyes searched the map as though looking for a clue, and quite suddenly—without really trying to find it—an answer stared back at him.

Ripping off one of the flimsies from his small pad, Bond carefully placed it over the Ice Palace markings. With equal care he traced in the pencil lines drawn to show the extent of the underground bunker. Then he added in the local topography. When this tracing was completed, Bond slid the flimsy in a northeasterly direction on the map, covering the equivalent of around fifteen kilometers.

The diagonal move carried the Ice Palace across the frontier zone into Russia. What was more, the local topography fitted exactly, down to the surrounding ground levels, wooded areas, and summer river lines. The topography in general was all very similar, but this was quite extraordinary. Either the maps had been specially printed, or there really were two locations—one on either side of the frontier—exact in every topographical detail.

With the same concentration, Bond copied the possible secondary position of the Ice Palace onto his map. He then made one or two further compass bearings. It was just possible that von Glöda's headquarters, and the first stage of the arms convoy, lay not in Finland, but still on the Russian side of the frontier. Even bearing in mind the similarity of the landscape at any point along this part of the border, it was a strange coincidence to find two exactly identical locations within fifteen kilometers of one another.

He also thought about the position of the main bunker entrances at the Ice Palace. Both entrances faced towards the Russian side. If it was on the Russian side of the border, he had to remember that this section of the Soviet Union had once belonged to Finland—before the great clash of the Winter War of 1929–40. But either way, for the entrances of the original fortifications to face Russia was odd; particularly if the bunkers had been built *before* the war of '39.

To Bond, it was a definite possibilty that the Ice Palace was of Russian origin. If it truly was the Headquarters of the Fascist National Socialist Action Army, then it proved two things: the leader of the NSAA was an even more cunning and daring terrorist leader than Bond had imagined; and the coercion, and betrayal, within the Red Army GRU might be more widespread than anyone had first imagined.

Bond's next job was to get some form of message out to M. Technically, he could merely dial London through his room telephone. Certainly it was now free of listening devices, but who knew if calls were also being monitored via the hotel exchange.

Quickly, Bond committed the compass bearings and coordinates to memory, using his well-tried form of mnemonics. He then tore up the flimsies from his pad—removing several of the backing sheets at the same time—and flushed them down the lavatory, waiting for a few moments to make certain they had all been carried away.

Bond climbed into his outdoor gear and left the room, went down to reception and thence to the car. Among the many pieces of secret equipment he now carried in the Saab, there was one only recently fitted by Q Branch.

Forward of the gear stick, there nestled what seemed to be a perfectly normal radio telephone, an instrument which was useless unless it had a base unit somewhere within a twenty-five-mile radius. But twenty-five miles would be no good to Bond, any more than a normal telephone was any good to him in the present circumstances.

The Saab car phone had a pair of great advantages. The first of these was a small black box, from which hung a pair of terminals. The box was not much larger than a pair of cassettes stacked one on top of the other, and Bond took it from its hiding place, in a panel behind the glove compartment.

Reactivating the sensor alarms, he now trudged through the hard, iced snow, back to the hotel and his room.

Taking no chances, Bond did a quick sweep with the VL34—relieved to find the room still clean after his short absence. Quickly he unscrewed the underside plate on the telephone. He then connected the terminals of the small box and removed the receiver from its rests, placing it close at hand. The advanced electronics contained in that small box now ensured that Bond had an easily available base unit from which to operate the car telephone. Access to the outside world, illegally using the Finnish telephone service, was assured.

There was, moreover, the car phone's second advantage. On returning to the Saab, Bond operated yet another of his unmarked square black buttons on the dashboard. A panel slid down behind the telephone housing, revealing a small computer keyboard and a minute screen—a telephone scrambler of infinite complexity, which could be used to shield the voice or send messages that would be printed out on a compatible screen in the building overlooking Regent's Park. Once there, with some expert manipulation, the printed message would read out in clear computer language.

Bond pressed the requisite keys, linking the car phone with his base unit, attached to the telephone in his hotel room. Tapping the get-out code from Finland, followed by the dial-in code for London, he followed on with the London code and the number for the Headquarters of his Service.

He then fed in the required cipher of the day and began to tap out his message in clear language. It came up on his screen—as it would at the Headquarters building—in a jumble of grouped letters.

The whole transmission took around fifteen minutes, Bond bent within the dark car, lit only by the glow from the tiny screen, very conscious of the ice build-up on the windows. Outside there was a light wind and the temperature still continued to drop.

When the whole message had been sent, Bond closed up, reactivated the sensors, and returned to the hotel. Once more, playing it safe, he quickly swept the room, then removed the base unit from the telephone provided by the management.

He had only just packed away the base unit in his briefcase—intending to return it to the Saab before the real business of the night began—when there was a knock at the door.

Now playing everything by the book, Bond picked up the P7 and went to the door, slipping the chain on before asking who was there.

"Brad," the answer came back. "Brad Tirpitz."

"Bad" Brad Tirpitz looked a shade shaken as he came into the room. Bond noticed a distinct pallor, and a wariness around the big American's eyes.

"Bastard Kolya," Tirpitz spat.

Bond gestured towards the armchair. "Sit down, get it off your chest. The room's clean now. I had to delouse again after we had the meeting with Kolya."

"Me too." A slow smile spread over Tirpitz's face, stopping short, as always, at the eyes. It was as though a sculptor had worked slowly at the rocky features and suddenly given up. "I caught Kolya in the act, though. Did you figure out who's working for who yet?"

"Not exactly. Why?"

"I left a small momento in Kolya's room after the briefing. Just stuffed it down behind the chair cushion. I've been listening in ever since."

"And heard no good of yourself, I'll warrant." Bond opened the fridge, asking if Tirpitz wanted a drink.

"Whatever you're having. Yeah, you're right. It's true what they say—you never hear good of yourself."

Bond quickly mixed a brace of martinis, and handed one to Tirpitz.

"Well." Tirpitz took a sip, then nodded his approval. "Well, old buddy, Kolya made several telephone calls. Switched languages a lot and I couldn't figure most of it—doubletalk on the whole. The last one I did understand, though. He talked to someone without beating about the bush. Straight Russian. Tonight's trip, friend, is taking us to the end of the line."

"Oh?"

"Yep. Me they're giving the Rivke treatment—right on the border, to make it look like a land mine. I even know the exact spot."

"The exact spot?" Bond queried.

"No dead ground—if you'll excuse the expression—but right in the open. I'll show you," Tirpitz held out his hand, silently asking to look at Bond's map.

"Just give me the coordinates." Nobody, trusted or not, was going to see Bond's map, particularly now that he had added in the possible true location of the Ice Palace.

"You're a suspicious bastard, Bond." Tirpitz's face changed back to the hard granite: chipped, sharp, and dangerous.

"Just give me the coordinates."

Tirpitz rattled off the figures, and in his head Bond worked out roughly where the point came in relation to the whole area of operations. It made sense—a remote-controlled land mine at a spot where they would be traveling a few meters away from real mine fields anyway.

"As for you," Tirpitz growled, "you ain't heard nothing yet. They've got a spectacular exit organized for our Mr. Bond."

"I wonder what's in store for Kolya Mosolov?" Bond said with an almost innocent look.

"Yeah, my own thoughts, too. We think alike, friend. This is a dead-men-tell-no-tales job."

Bond nodded, paused, took a sip of his martini and lit a cigarette. "Then you'd better tell me what's in store for me. It looks like a long cold night."

11

SNOW SAFARI

EVERY FEW MINUTES, James Bond had to reduce speed to wipe the rime of frost from his goggles. They could not have chosen a worse night. Even a blizzard, he thought, would have been preferable. "A snow safari," Kolya had laughingly called it.

The darkness seemed to cling to them, occasionally blowing free to give a glimmer of visibility, then descending again as though blindfolds had blown over their faces. It took every ounce of concentration to follow the man in front, and the only relief was that Kolya—leading the column of three—had his small spotlight on, dipped low. Bond and Tirpitz followed without lights, and the three big Yamaha snow scooters roared on through the night, making enough noise, Bond thought, to draw any patrols within a ten-mile radius.

After his lengthy talk with Brad Tirpitz, Bond had prepared himself with even greater care than usual. First there was the job of clearing up—packing away anything that would not be required and taking it out to the Saab, where other items had to be collected. Having gone out and locked the briefcase and overnight bag in the boot, Bond slipped into the driving seat. Once there he had reason to thank whatever saint watched over agents in the field.

He had just replaced the telephone base unit in its hiding place behind the glove compartment when the tiny pinprick of red light started to blink rapidly beside the car phone.

Bond immediately pressed the chunky button which gave access to the scrambler computer and its screen. The winking pinhead light indicated that a message from London was stored within the system.

He ran quickly through all the activating procedures, then tapped out the incoming cipher code. Within seconds the small screen—no larger than the jacket of a paperback novel—was filled with groups of letters. Another few deft movements of Bond's fingers on the keys brought the groups into a further jumble, then removed them completely. The instrument whirred, clicked, as its electronic brain started to solve the problem. A running line of clear print ribboned out on the screen. The message read:

> FROM HEAD OF SERVICE TO 007 MESSAGE RECEIVED MUST WARN YOU TO APPROACH SUBJECT VON GLÖDA WITH UTMOST CAUTION AS THERE IS NOW POSITIVE REPEAT POSITIVE ID VON GLÖDA IS CERTAINLY WANTED NAZI WAR CRIMINAL AARNE TUDEER STRONG POSSIBILITY THAT YOUR THEORY IS CORRECT SO IF CONTACT IS MADE ALERT ME IMMEDIATELY AND RETURN FROM FIELD THIS IS AN ORDER LUCK M

So, Bond considered, M was concerned enough to haul in the line if he went too close. The thought of "line" brought other expressions to his mind—"the end of the line"; "line of fire"; being sold "down the line." All these could well be applicable now.

Having secured the car, Bond returned to the hotel where he rang down for food and a fresh supply of vodka. The agreement was that all three would stay in their rooms until it was time to RV at the snow scooters.

An elderly waiter brought in a small trolley-table with Bond's dinner order—a simple meal of thick pea soup laced with lean chunks of meat, and excellent reindeer sausages.

As he ate, Bond slowly realized that his edginess concerning Icebreaker was not entirely due to the mental excuses he had made about his operational habits. There was another element—one that had appeared with the name Aarne Tudeer, and the linking of that name with the Count von Glöda.

Bond pondered on other powerful individuals with whom he had fought dangerous, often lonely battles. Nearly all of them had been men, or women, with whom he could identify personal hatred. At random he thought of people like Sir Hugo Drax, a liar and cheat, whom he had beaten by exposing as a card sharp, before taking the man on in another kind of battle. Auric Goldfinger was of the same breed—a Midas man whom Bond had challenged on the field of sport as well as the deeper, dangerous zone of battle. Blofeld—well, there were many things about Blofeld which still chilled Bond's blood: thoughts about Blofeld, and his relative, with whom 007 had only recently come face to face.

But the Count Konrad von Glöda—Aarne Tudeer as he really was—seemed to have cast a long and depressing gloom over this whole business. A massive question mark. "Glöda equals Glow," Bond said aloud, between chewing on a mouthful of delicious sausage.

He wondered if the man had a strange sense of humor? If this pseudonym contained a message? A key to his personality? Glöda was a cipher, a ghost, glimpsed once in the dining room of the Hotel Revontuli—a fit, elderly, weatherbronzed, iron-haired, military-looking man. If Bond had met him in a London club he would not have given him a second thought—ex-Army written all over him. There was no aura of evil around the person, no way of telling.

For a flitting second, Bond experienced the strange sensation of a clammy hand running down his spine. Because he had not really met von Glöda face to face, or even read a full dossier on the man, the ex-SS officer—a long shadow emerging from the minor monsters of recent history—created an unease Bond rarely felt. In that fraction of time, he even wondered if at long last he might have met his match.

Bond inhaled sharply, mentally shaking himself. No, Konrad von Glöda was not going to beat him. What was more, if contact came with the phony Count, 007 would turn a blind eye to M's instructions. James Bond could certainly not leave the field and run from von Glöda, or Tudeer, if he really was responsible for the terrorist activities of the NSAA. If there was any chance of wiping out that organization, Bond would not let it slip through his fingers.

He felt confidence leap back into his system—a loner again, with no one to trust out here in the crushing cold of the Arctic. Rivke had vanished—and he cursed the fact that there had been no way or time to search for her. Kolya Mosolov was about as credible as a wounded tiger. Brad Tirpitz? Well, even though they were allies on paper, Bond could not bring himself to a state of complete faith in the American. Certainly in the emergency they had worked on a contingency plan to cover the attempt which, according to Tirpitz, was to be made on his life. But that was all. The chains of trust between them were not yet welded.

At that moment, before the night even got under way, James Bond made a small vow. He would play it alone, to his rules. He would bend his will to nobody.

So now they proceeded, at somewhere between sixty and seventy kph, swerving and bucketing along a rough track between the trees, about a kilometer from the Russian border and parallel to it.

Snow scooters—known by tourists as "Skidoos"—can rip across snow and ice at a terrifying speed. They are to be handled with care. Unique in design, with their wicked-looking blunt bonnets and long strutting skis protruding forward, the scooters are driven over their natural element by revolving tracks, studded with great pointed spikes which thrust the machine along, giving initial momentum which builds up very quickly as the skis glide over the surface.

There is little protection for the driver—or any passenger—apart from short deflector wind shields. At first ride, people tend to handle them like motorcycles—wrongly. A motorcycle can turn at acute angles, while a snow scooter has a much wider turning circle. There is also a tendency for a tyro rider to stick out a leg on the turn. He does it once only and probably ends up hospitalized with a fracture, for the leg merely buries itself in the snow, dragged back by the speed of the scooter.

Ecologists cursed the arrival of this particular machine, claiming that the spikes have already rutted and destroyed the texture of land under the snow; but they have certainly altered the pattern of life in the Arctic—particularly for the nomadic natives of Lapland.

Bond kept his head down, and was quick with his reactions. A turn meant considerable energy, especially in deep, hard snow, as you had to pull the skis around with the handlebars, then hold them, juddering, as they tried to reassume their normal forward angle. Following someone like Kolya presented other difficulties. You could easily get caught in the ruts made by the leader's scooter, which gave problems of maneuverability, for it was like being trapped on trolley lines. Then, if the leader made an error, you would almost certainly end up by screaming into him.

Bond tried to weave behind Kolya, slewing from side to side, glancing up continually, trying to glimpse the way ahead from the tiny glow of Kolya's light. Occasionally he pulled out too far, sending the scooter rearing up like some fairground ride, producing a roll first to the right, then left, slipping upward almost to the point of losing control, then sliding back again and up the other side until, wrestling with the handlebars, he recovered.

Even with face and head completely covered, the cold and wind sliced into Bond like razor cuts, and he was constantly flexing his fingers in the fear that they would go numb on him.

In fact, Bond had done everything within his power to come prepared. The P7 automatic was in its holster across his chest, inside the quilted jacket. There was no chance of getting at it quickly, but at least it was there — with plenty of spare ammunition. The compass hung from a lanyard around his neck, the instrument tucked safely inside the jacket where a jerk on the lanyard would free it. Some of the smaller pieces of electronics were scattered about his person, and the maps were accessible in a thigh pocket of his quilted ski pants. One of the long Sykes-Fairbairn commando daggers lay strapped inside his left boot, and a shorter Lapp reindeer knife hung, secured, from his belt.

On his back, Bond carried a small pack containing other items — a white coverall complete with hood, in case there was need for snow camouflage, three of the stun grenades, and two L2A2 fragmentation bombs. The rest lay with him alone — professionalism, experience, and the two vital attributes of his trade: intuition, and being able to think quickly on his feet.

The trees seemed to be getting thicker, but Kolya twisted in and out with ease, obviously knowing the exact route. Palm-of-his-hand stuff, Bond thought, keeping well up, holding position some six feet from the Russian's tail, aware of Brad Tirpitz somewhere behind him.

They were turning. Bond could sense it even though the move was not blatantly obvious. Kolya took them through gaps in the trees, twisting left and then right, but Bond could feel them pulling even further right — to the east. Soon now they would break cover. Then it would be a kilometer of open country, into the winds again, and the long dip into the valley, where there was a great swathe cut through the forests to make the frontier and deter people from attempting a crossing.

Quite suddenly they shot out of the trees and, even in the darkness, the transition was unnerving. Within the forest there had been a kind of safety. Now, the blackness lifted slightly as the open snow, showing gray around them, took over.

Their speed increased—straight run with no dodging or suddenly
swerving in a change of direction. Kolya seemed to have set his course,
opened the throttle, and given his machine its head. Bond followed,
straying slightly to the right, dropping back a little now that they were
in open country.

The cold became worse, whether from lack of shelter or the simple
fact that they were making more speed across open country. Maybe it
was also because they had been on the trail for the best part of an hour,
and the cold had begun to penetrate into their bones, even through the
layers of warm clothing.

Ahead, Bond caught sight of the next belt of trees. If Kolya took them
through that short line of forest at speed, they would be in the long open
dip in a matter of ten minutes.

The valley of death, Bond thought; for it was down in the open valley
floor, which made up the border protection zone, that the trap was to be
sprung on Brad Tirpitz. They had worked out the theory in Bond's hotel
room. Now the moment drew closer as the three scooters sent snow flying
around them. When it came, there could be no stopping or turning back
for Bond to see if their planned counter measures worked. He simply had
to trust Tirpitz's own timing, and ability to survive.

Into the trees again—like going from relative light into the instant
darkness of a nocturnal cathedral. Fir branches whipped around Bond's
body, stinging his face as he hauled on the handlebars—left, then right,
straight, left again. There was a moment when he almost misjudged the
wide turn, feeling the forward ski touch the base of a tree hidden by
snow; another when he thought he would be thrown off as the scooter
crunched over thick roots covered with ice, slewing the machine into the
start of a skid. But Bond held on, heaving at the controls, straightening
the machine.

This time, when they broke cover, the landscape ahead seemed more
clear and visible, even through the frost-grimed goggles. The white valley
stretched away on either side, the slope angling gently downwards to
flatten, then climbing up the far side into a regiment of trees lined up in
battle order.

In the open again, their speed increased. Bond felt his scooter nose
down as the strain came off the engine. Now the struggle was to prevent
the machine from skidding into a slide.

As they descended, so the feeling of vulnerability became more intense.

Kolya had told them this route was used constantly by border crossers, for there were no frontier units within ten miles on either side, and they rarely made any night patrols. Bond hoped he was right. Soon they would flatten out, curving into the bottom of the valley—half a kilometer of straight ice before climbing up the far side and into the trees of Mother Russia. Before then, Brad Tirpitz would be dead—at least that was what had been planned.

Bond's mind flitted back to a drive he had made in winter, a fair time ago now, through the Eastern Zone to West Berlin. The ice and snow were not as bad, raw, or killing as this; but he recalled going through the checkpoint from the West at Helmstedt, where they cautioned him to follow the wide freeway through the Eastern Zone without deviation. For the first few kilometers the road had been flanked by woods, and he clearly saw the high wooden towers with their spotlights and Red Army soldiers in white winter garb, crouching in the woods and by the side of the road. Was that what awaited them in the trees at the top of the slope?

They flattened out, beginning the straight run. If Brad had it right, the whole thing would happen in a matter of minutes—two, three minutes at the most.

Kolya increased his speed, as though racing ahead to get well up front. Bond followed, allowing himself to drop back slightly, praying that Tirpitz was ready. Moving himself in the tough saddle, Bond glanced behind. To his relief, Brad's scooter had dropped well back, just as they planned. He could not see if Tirpitz was still there: only the blur and black shape as the scooter slowed.

As Bond turned his head, it happened. It was as though he had been counting the seconds: working out the exact point. Maybe intuition?

The explosion came later. All he saw was the violent flash from where the dull black shape sped behind him—the crimson heart of flame and a great white phosphorescent outline, lighting the column of snow which soared into the night.

Then the noise, the heavy double crump, stunning the eardrums. The shock waves struck Bond's scooter, hammering him in the back propelling him off course.

12

BLUE HARE

A T THE MOMENT of explosion, Bond's reflexes came automatically into play. He hauled on the controls, throttling back so that his scooter slewed sideways into a long skid, then slowed towards its inevitable halt.

Almost before he knew it, Bond came alongside Kolya's scooter.

"Tirpitz!" Bond yelled, not really hearing his own voice, ears tingling from the cold and deadened by the passing shock waves.

Strangely he knew what Kolya was shouting back at him, though he was uncertain if he actually heard the words.

"For God's sake don't come alongside!" Kolya shrieked, his voice rising like the wind within a blizzard. "Tirpitz is finished. He must've strayed off course and hit a mine. We can't stop. Death to stop. Keep directly behind me, Bond. It's the only way." He repeated: *"Directly behind me!"* and this time Bond knew he had heard the words clearly.

It was over. A glance back showed a faint glow as pieces of Tirpitz's scooter burned out in the snow. Then the whine of Kolya's scooter, zipping away over the ice.

Bond gunned his motor and followed, keeping close now and well in line behind the Russian. If it had worked, Tirpitz would already be on the skis which he had smuggled out to the scooters a good hour before they were due to leave.

The plan had been to drop skis, sticks, and pack about three minutes from the point where he had overheard Kolya order the explosion to take him out. A minute later, Tirpitz was to set and lock his handlebars; then a slow roll-off, low into the snow, opening the throttle at the last moment. With good timing and luck, he could lie well clear of the explosion, then take to the skis almost at leisure. There was time enough for him to reach the point arranged with Bond.

Put him from your mind, Bond thought, in any event. Consider Tirpitz dead. It's yourself and nobody else.

The far slope was not easy, and Kolya maintained a cracking pace as though anxious to reach the relative cover of the trees. Half-way up the long open ground, the first flurries of fresh falling snow started to eddy around them.

At last they reached the trees and their blackness. Kolya pulled up, beckoning Bond alongside him, leaning over to speak. But for the gentle throb of the idling engines, it was very still among the tall firs and pines. Kolya did not appear to shout, and this time his words were perfectly clear.

"Sorry about Tirpitz," he said. "It could've been any of us. They may have rearranged the mine pattern. Now we're still one short."

Bond nodded, saying nothing.

"Follow me like a leech," Kolya went on. "The first two kilometers are not easy, but after that we're more or less on wide tracks. A road, in fact. Any sign of the convoy and I'll switch off my light, then stop. So pull up if my light goes out. When we get near to Blue Hare we'll hide the scooters and go in on foot with the cameras." He tapped the packs attached to the back of his machine. "It'll be a short walk through trees, about five hundred meters."

Around half a mile, Bond thought. That was going to be fun.

"If we take it steadily—roughly an hour and a half ride from here," Kolya continued. "You fit?"

Bond nodded again.

Kolya slowly took his machine forward and Bond, pretending to check his gear, yanked on the lanyard, pulling out the compass. He opened it, fumbling with his gloves, then lifted it flat on his palm and lowered his head to see the luminous dial.

He watched the needle settle and took a rough bearing. They were approximately where Kolya had said they should be. The real test then, would come later, if they managed to follow the convoy from Blue Hare to the Ice Palace.

Bond slid the compass back inside his jacket, straightened himself, and raised an arm to indicate his readiness to continue. Slowly they moved off, covering the difficult first two kilometers at almost a walking pace. It was obvious there had to be a wider path leading into this protective stretch of woods, if the convoy was coming in from Finland.

As Kolya had predicted, however, once past the first stage they found themselves on a wide, snow-covered track—the snow hard and packed, frozen solid, but deeply rutted in places. Perhaps Kolya was playing straight after all. The ruts bespoke a previous passage of tracked vehicles, though it was impossible to tell how recently they had been made. The cold was now so intense that anything heavy breaking the surface of the frozen snow would leave tracks frozen equally hard within minutes.

Kolya began to pile on the speed, and as Bond followed easily on the flat surface, his mind, numbed as it was by the chill and marrow-freezing temperature, started to ask questions. Kolya had shown almost incredible expertise on the way over the border—particularly going through the forests. It was impossible for him not to have followed the same route before: many times. For Bond it had been a time of unrelieved concentration, yet Tirpitz had stayed well to the rear for most of the trip. Now the impression came back to Bond that Brad Tirpitz had not even been close during the zigzagging journey through the trees.

Had both of them crossed the frontier by this route before? It was certainly a possibility. On reflection, Bond was even more puzzled, for Kolya had kept up a rapid pace even in the most difficult area, and had done so without reference to bearings by compass or map. It was as though he was being navigated through by external means. Radio? Perhaps. Nobody had seen him out of his gear, once they'd rendezvoused at the scooters. Had Kolya brought them through on some kind of beam? Earphones would be easy to hide under the thermal hood. He made a note to look for possible leads plugged into Kolya's scooter.

If not radio, was there a marked path? That was also a likelihood, for Bond had been so busy keeping his own machine on Kolya's tail that it was doubtful he would have noticed any pinpoint lights or reflectors along the way.

Another thought struck him. Cliff Dudley, his predecessor on Icebreaker, had not been forthcoming about what kind of work the team had been doing in the Arctic Circle, before the row with Tirpitz and the briefing in Madeira. Had not M suggested, or said outright, that they had wanted Bond on the team from the outset?

Indeed, what had those representatives of four different intelligence agencies been up to? Was it possible they had been into the Soviet Union already? Had they already reconnoitered Blue Hare? Yet, almost all the hard information had come from Kolya—from Russia; from the hi-fly photographs and the satellite pictures, not to mention the sniffing out of information on the ground.

There had been talk of the search for von Glöda, of identifying him as the Commander in chief of the NSAA, even as Aarne Tudeer. Yet, von Glöda was there, at breakfast, large as life—in the hotel—recognized by all. And nobody had appeared to be in the least concerned.

If Bond had started by trusting nobody, the feeling had now grown into deep suspicion toward anybody connected with Icebreaker. And that even included M, who had also been like a clam when it came to detail.

Was it just possible, James Bond wondered, that M had deliberately set him up in an untenable situation? As they racketed and slid through the snow, he saw the answer plainly enough. Yes: it was an old Service ploy. Send a very experienced officer into a situation almost blind, and let him discover the truth. The truth for 007, hammered home again, was that he was well and truly on his own. The conclusion to which he had privately come earlier was, in reality, the basis of M's own reasoning. There had never been a "team" in the strict sense of the word: merely representatives of four agencies, working together, yet apart. Four singletons.

The thought nagged away at Bond's mind as he heaved and hauled the scooter at speed, following Kolya over the never-ending snow and jagged ice. He lost all track of time, just the cold, and the motor growl, and the endless ribbon of white behind Kolya's machine.

Then, slowly, Bond became conscious of light somewhere to his left front—to the northwest—rising bright from among the trees.

A few moments later, Kolya flicked the small beam of his headlamp off. He was slowing down, pulling into the trees to the left of the road.

Bond brought his scooter to rest beside Kolya's machine.

"We'll haul them into the woods," Kolya whispered. "That's it over there—Blue Hare, with all the lights blazing like a May Day celebration."

They parked the scooters, camouflaging them as best they could. Kolya suggested they get into the white snowsuits. "We'll be in deep snow, overlooking the depot. I have night glasses, so don't bother with anything special."

Bond, however, was already bothering. Under cover of getting into the snow camouflage, his numbed fingers struggled with the clips of his quilted jacket. At least he could now get at the P7 automatic quickly. He also managed to transfer one stun grenade and one of the L2A2 fragmentation bombs from his pack to the copious pockets of the loose, hooded white garment that now covered him.

The Russian did not seem to have noticed. He carried a weapon of his own, quite openly on his hip. The large night glasses were slung around his neck and, in the gloom, Bond thought he could even detect a smile on that mobile face as Kolya handed over the automatic infrared camera. The Russian was carrying a VTR pack clipped to his belt, the camera hanging by straps below the binoculars.

Kolya gestured toward the point where the light now seemed to blast straight up between the trees, behind a slope above them. He led the way, with Bond close on his heels — a pair of silent white ghosts passing into dead ground, moving from tree to tree.

Within a few paces they had reached the bottom of the uphill climb. The top of the rise was illuminated by the lights, which cast their beams up from the far side. There was no sign of guards or sentries, and Bond found the going difficult at first, his limbs stiff with cold from the long scooter ride.

As they neared the crest, Kolya gave a "get down" signal with the palm of his hand. Close together the pair squirmed in among the deep snow which buried the roots and trunk bases of the trees. Below them, in a blaze of light, lay the ordnance depot known as Blue Hare. Having strained to see through darkness and snow for over three hours, Bond was forced to close his eyes against the sudden shock of arc lights and big spots. It was not surprising, he thought fleetingly as he peered down, that the men and NCO's of Blue Hare had been so easily suborned into a treasonable act of selling military weapons, ammunition, and equipment. To live the year round in this place — bleak and uninviting during the winter, mosquito-ridden through the short summer — would be enough to tempt any man, even just for the hell of it.

As his eyes adjusted, Bond thought about their dreary life. What was there to do in a camp like this? The nightly games of cards; drink? Yes, a perfect place to post alcoholics; crossing off the days to some short leave, which probably entailed a long journey; the occasional trip into Alakurtti which, by his reckoning, was six or seven kilometers away. And what would there be in Alakurtti? The odd cafe, the same food cooked by different hands, a bar where you could get drunk. Women? Possibly. Maybe some Russian-born Lapp girls, easy prey to disease and the brutal licentious soldiery.

Bond's eyes had cleared now. He studied Blue Hare without discomfort: a long, wide oblong cleared from among the trees, some of which had begun to grow again, encroaching on the tall wire fences with their barbed tops and angled lights. A pair of high gates had been hauled open immediately below them, and the road that snaked in through the trees had been cleared of snow and ice, either by burners or hard sweat.

Within the compound, the layout was neat and orderly. A guard room, wooden towers and searchlights on either side, stood near the gate, and the metaled roadway ran straight through the center of the base, around a quarter of a kilometer long. The storage dumps were placed on either side of this interior road: large Nissen Hut-like structures with corrugated curved roofs and high sides, each with a jutting loading ramp.

It all made sense. Vehicles could drive straight in, load or unload at the ramps, then follow the road to the far end of the camp at which there was a hard-standing turning circle. Any delivery or collection could be made at speed—the lorries or armored vehicles could come in, take off their cargo; then go on to the turn and drive back out the same way as they had come.

Behind the storage huts were long log cabins, certainly the troops' quarters, mess halls, and recreation centers. It was all very symmetrical. Take away the wire enclosure and the long lines of ramps, add a wooden church, and you had the makings of a village, built to support a small factory.

Bond's circulation had been restored slightly by the walk up to the ridge. Now the cold began to build in him again. He felt as though melting snow flowed through his veins and arteries, while his bones were made of the same ice that hung, sharp and glistening, Damoclean, from the branches above.

He glanced to his left. Kolya was already recording the scene for posterity, the VTR camera buzzing as he pressed the trigger, adjusted the lens, and pressed again. Bond held the small infrared camera, loaded and lensed, in front of him. Leaning on his elbows, he raised his goggles and pressed the rubber eyepiece to his right eye, bringing the lens into focus. In the next few minutes he was to shoot a full thirty-five still pictures of the armament transfer at Blue Hare.

Kolya's information was impeccable. The lights were on, heedless of any security. Drawn up beside the ramps were four big, tracked armored troop carriers. BTR-50's, just as Kolya had predicted. Give the man another crystal ball, Bond thought. Too good to be true.

The Russian BTR's came in various forms: the basic tracked amphibious troop carrier, for two crew and twenty men; the gun carrier; or the type now below them. These versions were strictly for transporting loads over difficult terrain. They had been stripped down to the bare essentials, with much of the support armor removed, and they sat on their well-chained tracks, each with a heavy dozer in front so that rubble, ice, deep snow, or fallen trees could be swept from their paths. The BTR's were each painted an identical gray, and their flat tops were unlocked, folded back down the sides to reveal deep metal oblong holds into which crates and boxes were being stored with efficient speed.

The crews of the BTR's stood to one side, as though above the manual labor of dragging and lifting the heavy cargo, though one man from each BTR occasionally spoke to the chief loading NCO on the ramp, who was checking off items on a clipboard.

The men doing the work were dressed in light gray fatigues, with rank badges and shoulder boards plainly visible. The fatigues were obviously worn over heavier winter gear, and their heads were encased in fur hats with enormous ear flaps which came almost to the chin. The caps were decorated in front with the familiar Red Army star.

The two-man crews, however, wore a different dress which brought a crease to Bond's brow and a sudden churning of the stomach. Under short leather coats, thick navy blue trousers could be seen, while their feet and calves were encased in heavy, serviceable jackboots. They wore earmuffs, but, above those, simple navy berets with glinting cap badges. The rig reminded Bond all too vividly of another era, a different world. These men looked like movie extras playing Waffen SS tank crews.

Kolya jogged his arm, handing over the night glasses, pointing to the foremost part of the first ramp. "The Commanding Officer," he whispered. Bond took the glasses, adjusted them, and saw a pair of men in conversation. One was from the BTR crews, the other a stocky, sallow-faced figure, muffled in a greatcoat which bore the shoulder boards of a warrant officer, the thick red stripe plainly visible through the glasses.

"Noncommissioned officers here," Kolya again whispered. "Mainly disgruntled NCO's or people other units want to get rid of. That's why they were such a pushover."

Bond nodded, handing back the glasses.

The depot at Blue Hare appeared very close—a trick of the brilliant light and the frost, which hung tendril-like in the air. Below, the working men seemed to be emitting steam from mouths and nostrils like overworked horses, while orders floated up, muffled by the atmosphere: sharp Russian growling urging the laborers. Bond even caught the sound of a voice saying, "Faster then, you dolts. Just think of the nice bonus at the end of this, and the girls coming over from Alakurtti tomorrow. Get the job done and then you'll rest."

One of the men turned towards him, shouting back clearly, "I'll need all the rest I can get if Fat Olga's coming over . . ." The sentence was lost on the air, but the raucous laughter meant that it ended with some lewd witticism.

Bond edged his compasss out on its lanyard, surreptitiously taking a bearing and doing some quick mental calculations. Then there was a roar below. The first BTR's motor had come to life. Men were swarming over the metal, folding up the thick flaps and locking them into place to form the flat top.

The other BTR's were almost fully loaded Men worked in their holds, making final adjustments to straps and ropes. Then number three's engine started.

"Time to be getting down," Kolya whispered, and they saw the first carrier advance slowly towards the turning circle. It would take the whole convoy around fifteen minutes to lock up, turn, and form their line.

Slowly the pair edged back. Once below the skyline they had to lie still for a few moments, allowing their eyes to readjust to darkness.

Then the slippery descent—much quicker than the climb up—and down among the trees, feeling their way through to where the snow scooters were hidden.

"We'll wait until they've passed." Kolya spoke like a commander. "Those BTR's have engines like angry lions. The crews won't hear a thing when we start up." He put out a hand to retrieve the camera from Bond and stowed it with the VTR pack.

The lights still cut into the sky from Blue Hare but now, in the stillness, the sound of the BTR's motors assumed a loud, raucous, aggressive tone. Bond did another quick calculation, hoping he was right. Then the noise rose towards them and began to echo from the trees.

"They're on the move," Kolya said, nudging him. Bond craned forward, trying to see the convoy up the road.

The motor reverberations grew louder and, even with the deceptive acoustics manipulated by the ice and trees, they could be pinpointed, advancing from Bond's and Kolya's left.

"Ready," muttered Kolya. He appeared suddenly nervous, half-standing in the saddle of his scooter, head turned, as though wound by a key.

The grumble of engines reduced to a low growl. They've reached the road junction, Bond thought. Then, quite plainly, he heard one BTR's motor rise to the grind of gears. The sounds all took on new patterns, and Kolya raised himself even higher.

The engine noise settled. All four BTR's were now on the same track, moving at a similar speed, in a convoy. Yet something was wrong. It took Bond a second or two to realize that the echoes, from the engines, were decreasing.

Kolya swore in Russian. "They're going north," he said, spitting the words out. Then his voice appeared to mellow. "Ah, good. It means they're taking the alternative route back. My other agent'll be covering them. Ready?"

Bond nodded, and they started up the scooters. Kolya wheeled out onto the snow, picking up speed immediately.

The rumble from the BTR's was audible even above the snow scooters' engines, and they were able to keep well back—with the last vehicle just visible—for a matter of ten or eleven kilometers. The small convoy stayed on the same main road until Bond thought they were getting dangerously near to Alakurtti. Then he saw Kolya signal him for a turn—a left angle into the woods again, though this time the track was of reasonable width, the snow deep and hard, newly rutted by the heavy armored and chained tracks of the BTR's.

It seemed uphill all the way. Constant weaving, to stay clear of the BTR's now dangerous tracks. The engine of Bond's scooter constantly protested at the strain while Bond himself tried to get a fix on their direction.

If they really were heading back to the border, this was a cross-country run which should take them almost to the same point at which they had entered the trees on the Russian side. For a long time that was where they seemed headed: southwest. Then, after an hour or so, the track forked. The BTR's moved right, taking them northwest.

There was a moment when Kolya considered they had got too close and motioned a halt. Bond just had time to haul out the compass and take a fix from the luminous dial. If the BTR's continued on their present course, they would, without doubt, end up very near to the pinpointed position of the Ice Palace *if it was on the Russian side*—in the location that Bond had thought possible.

Another few kilometers and Kolya stopped again, motioning Bond up to him. "We'll be crossing in a few minutes," he spoke loudly. The wind was in their faces now, cutting through the protective clothing and dragging the heavy noise of the BTR convoy back towards them. "My replacement agent should be up ahead, so don't be surprised if another scooter joins us."

"Shouldn't we cross an open patch this way?" Bond asked with as much innocence as he could muster in the teeth of the biting wind.

"Not this way. Remember the map?"

Bond remembered the map vividly. He also saw his own marks, and the way the Ice Palace could, in reality, lie well to this, the Russian, side of the border. For a second he contemplated shooting Kolya out of hand, dodging his other agent, making certain that the loaded BTR's went into the bunker, and then hightailing it out of the Soviet Union as fast as the scooter would carry him.

The thought lasted only for a moment. See it through, a voice said from deep inside him. Follow on, and maybe you'll reach your crock of gold.

It was a good fifteen minutes later before they saw the other scooter. A tall, slim figure, heavily muffled against the cold, sat upright in his seat, waiting to move forward.

Kolya raised a hand and the new scooter pulled out, taking the lead. Ahead, the BTR's grumbled and cracked on the forest road which, at this point, was only just wide enough to take them through.

Half an hour and no change of direction. A faint light spreading over the sky. Then, almost with no warning, Bond felt the hairs rise on the back of his neck. Up to now they had been able to hear the BTR's quite clearly, even above the three scooter engines. Now only their own noise came to his ears. Automatically he slowed, swerving to avoid a rut and, as he swerved, caught a clear silhouette of Kolya's new agent in the saddle ahead. Even in the winter gear, Bond thought he recognized the shape of the head and shoulders.

The thought jarred for an instant, and in that fraction of time everything happened.

Ahead of them a sudden blaze of light cut through the trees. Bond caught sight of the last BTR and what looked like a vast cliff of snow rising above them. Then the lights grew brighter, shining from all sides, even, it seemed, from above. Great arc lights and spots made Bond feel naked, caught, out in the open.

He slewed his scooter, trying for a tight turn in the available space, ready to make a run for it, one hand plunging inside his jacket for the pistol. But the trenches cut in the snow by the BTR's made the turn impossible.

Then they came from the trees—in front, from behind, and both sides: figures in uniform of a field gray with coalscuttle helmets and long, sheepskin-lined jackets, converging on the trio, rifles and machine pistols glinting in the searing lights.

Bond had the automatic out but allowed it to dangle from his hand. This was no time for a death duel. Even 007 knew when the odds were stacked against him.

He stared forward. Kolya sat, straight-backed, on his scooter, but his other agent had dismounted and was walking back past Kolya toward Bond. He knew the walk, just as he had thought he recognized the head and shoulders.

Lowering his head against the glare from a spotlight turned full on him, Bond saw the boots of the men now surrounding him. The crunch in the icy snow came nearer, as the boots of Kolya's agent approached. A gloved hand moved out and took the P7 from his hand. Squinting, Bond looked up.

The figure pulled off the scarf, lifted the goggles, then dragged away the knitted hat, allowing the blond hair to tumble down to her shoulders. Laughing pleasantly, and speaking with a mock stage-German accent, Paula Vacker looked Bond straight in the eyes.

"Herr James Bond," she said, "vor you der var iss over."

13

THE ICE PALACE

THE UNIFORMED MEN closed in. Hands frisked Bond, removed his grenades and the pack. As yet they had not gotten the commando knife in his Mukluk boot: a small bonus.

Paula still laughed as the men pulled Bond from his scooter and began to urge him forward through the snow.

He was cold and tired. Why not? A feigned collapse might bring advantages. James Bond went limp, allowing two of the uniformed men to take his weight. He let his head loll, but followed their progress through half-closed lids.

They had come straight out of the trees into a semicircular clearing which ended in a large, backward-raked flat slope, like a mini ski run. It was, of course, the bunker—the Ice Palace—for huge, white-camouflaged doors had opened in the side of the slope. Warmth seemed to pour out from the brightly lit interior.

Vaguely, Bond was also aware of a small entrance to the left. This fitted completely with the original drawings Kolya had provided of the place. Two areas: one for storage of arms and maintenance; the other for living quarters.

He heard a motor start up and saw one of the BTR's—the last one—crawl through the opening, then dip to disappear down the long internal ramp, which Bond knew took them deep into the earth.

Paula laughed again nearby, and a scooter engine revved. Bond's own scooter went past, driven by a uniformed man. Then Kolya said something in Russian, and Paula replied in the same language.

"You feel better soon," one of the men dragging him said in heavily accented English. "We give you drink inside."

They propped him against the wall, just inside the massive doors, and one of them produced a flask which he held to Bond's lips. Flame seemed to hit his mouth, searing a line down to the stomach. Gagging, Bond gasped, "What . . . ? What was . . . ?"

"Reindeer milk and vodka. Good? Yes?"

"Good. Yes." Bond blurted out. He fought for breath. There was no way he could feign unconsciousness after swallowing that particular firewater. He shook his head and looked around. The smell of diesel fumes floated upward from the rear of the cavern, and the sloping, wide-ramped entrance disappeared at a steady angle into the bowels of the earth.

Outside, the uniformed men were being lined up in columns of threes. All of them, Bond recognized now, wore the distinctive field gray of the Waffen SS: the short winter boots and baggy field trousers, the loose, fur-lined coats with their slanting pockets, insignia just showing through on the collars of their jackets underneath. The officers wore jackboots and, presumably, breeches under their heavy greatcoats.

Kolya stood by his scooter, still talking to Paula. Both looked intense, and Paula had donned her scarf and hat against the cold. At one point, Kolya called out to an officer, his form of address commanding, as though he could, at will, lord it over anyone and everyone.

The officer to whom Kolya had spoken nodded and gave a sharp order. Two men detached themselves from the group and began to remove the snow scooters. There appeared to be a small concrete pillbox, large enough to take several scooters, to the right of the main entrance.

The uniformed men were now marched into the bunker past Bond and the two who guarded him with Russian AKM's: the only note of discord, Bond noted, in this weird Teutonic scene. The troop of men disappeared down the ramp, their boots clipping in unison at the reinforced concrete.

Kolya and Paula strolled towards the great opening as though they had all the time in the world. Behind them, in the trees, Bond saw a couple of wigwamlike Lapp *kotas*. Smoke came from a fire between them while a figure bent over a cooking pot, a woman in Lapp costume: heavily decorated black skirt over thick, legginglike trousers, feet wrapped in fur boots, head covered with knitted hat and shawl, mittens on the hands. Before Paula and Kolya reached the entrance, she was joined by a man who also wore the colorful dress, the patterned jacket, and a vividly embroidered black cloak slung over his shoulders. Somewhere behind the *kotas* a reindeer snorted.

From somewhere else, high up in the curved roof, came a metallic click followed by a high-pitched series of warning whistles. Paula and Kolya began to move faster, and there was the hiss of hydraulics. The great metal doors slowly began to roll down: a safety curtain against the world.

"Well, James, surprise," said Paula, pulling off the woolen cap again.

He could now see that she was dressed in a leather jacket over some kind of uniform. Behind her, Kolya shifted, moving like a boxer. Kolya certainly knew how to adapt, Bond thought. A face for all seasons.

"Not really a surprise." Bond managed to smile. Bluff seemed the only way now. "My people know. They even have the location of this bunker." His eyes switched to Kolya. "Should've been more careful, Kolya. The maps were not really well done. It isn't likely that you'd find two identical areas with exactly the same topography within fifteen to twenty kilometers of each other. You're all blown."

For a split second he thought Kolya's face showed concern.

"Bluff, James, will get you nowhere," said Paula.

"Does he want to see us?" Kolya asked.

Paula nodded. "In due course. I think we can afford to take James via the scenic route. Show him the extent of the Führerbunker . . ."

"Oh my God," Bond laughed. "Have they really got you at it, Paula? Come to that, why didn't you let the goons finish me off at your place?"

She gave an acid little smile. "Because you were too good for them. Anyway, the deal is to get you alive, not dead."

"Deal?"

"Shut up," Kolya snapped at Paula.

She waved an elegant, dismissive hand. "He'll know soon enough. There's not all that much time, Kolya. The Chief has got what you wanted as promised. The current stocks have to be moved out in a day or two. No harm done."

Kolya Mosolov made an impatient noise. "Everyone's here, I presume?"

She smiled, nodding, stressing the word: "Everyone."

"Good."

Paula turned her attention back to Bond. "You'd like to look over the place? Lot of walking. Are you up to it?"

Bond sighed. "I think so, Paula. What a pity though, what a waste of such a pleasant girl."

"Chauvinist." She did not say it unpleasantly. "Okay, we'll go for a walk. But first," her eyes moving to the guards, "search him. Thoroughly. This one has more hiding places than a Greek smuggler. Look everywhere—and I mean *everywhere*. I'll go down the ramp with our Russian comrade."

They looked everywhere and found everything, and not very gently.

Paula and Kolya then took station on either side of Bond. The pair of soldiers—AKM's at the ready—followed. After a few meters, the ramp started to plunge, angling sharply, and they all headed to the left side, where a walkway had been built incorporating a handrail and steps.

The bunker had clearly been built with great skill. Warm air surrounded them and, high up on the walls above them, Bond was aware of the water and fuel pipes, air-conditioning channels, and other underground life-support systems. There were also small metal boxes set into the concrete at intervals, indicating some kind of internal communications system. The whole place was well lit with large strip lights set into the walls and the arched roof. As they descended, so the passage widened. Below, Bond saw that it opened up into a giant hangar.

Even Bond was shaken by the size of the place. The four BTR's they had seen picking up arms at Blue Hare were lined up with another four— eight altogether—but the whole unit of vehicles was dwarfed like toys by the height and area of the vault.

Crews of uniformed men unloaded the cargo recently brought in. Neat stacks of crates and boxes were being trundled away on fork-lift trucks, then restacked in carefully separated chambers equipped with fireproof doors and large wheel locks. Aarne Tudeer, alias Count von Glöda, was certainly taking no chances. The men worked in soft rubber shoes so there would be no possibility of sparks igniting ammunition. There must— Bond considered—be enough arms in this place to set off a sizable war, certainly enough to sustain a carefully planned terrorist operation, or even guerrilla action, for a year or more.

"You see, we have efficiency. We will show the world we mean business." Paula smiled as she spoke, evidently with great pride.

"No nukes, or neutrons?" said Bond.

Paula laughed again—a dismissive chuckle.

"They'll get nukes, chemicals, neutrons if they ever need them," from Kolya.

Bond kept his eyes well open, observing arms and munition shelters, also counting off the exit doors. In the far corner of his mind he thought, too, of Brad Tirpitz. If Tirpitz had escaped the blast, there was still a chance of his making some vantage point on skis; still a possibility that he would not be far behind; still a hope that he would raise some kind of alarm.

"You've seen enough?" The question—from Kolya—was sharp, sarcastic.

"Martini time, is it?" Bond relaxed—there was no other way. At least he might soon find out the whole truth about Aarne Tudeer—von Glöda as he liked to call himself—and the operations of the National Socialist Action Army.

Already he knew the bare minimum about Paula: that she was part of von Glöda's quasi-military machine, and that Kolya had somehow become mixed up in the act. There was also the odd reference to a deal.

Bond thought he had spotted the main control booth, behind a catwalk looking down over the great underground store area. The large doors to the bunker would certainly be operated from there, maybe the heating and ventilation systems also. He had to remind himself, though, that this was only a relativly small part of the entire bunker. The living quarters, which he already knew lay next to this section, would be even more complex.

"Martini time?" Kolya answered. "Maybe. The Count is very big on hospitality. I should imagine there'll be some kind of meal ready."

Paula said she understood food would be served. "He's really most understanding. Particularly with the doomed, James. Like the Roman emperors feeding up their gladiators."

"I had a feeling it was going to be something like that."

She smiled prettily, gave him a tiny nod, and led the way across the expanse of concrete, the click of her boots sounding clearly. She took them to one of the metal doors set in the left-hand wall. There she waited until Kolya, Bond, and the two guards joined her. There was a small ansaphone system beside the door. Paula spoke into it. With a click the door slid back. She turned, smiling again.

"There's good security between the various sections of the bunker. The interconnecting doors only open to predetermined voice patterns." The pretty smile once more, then they passed through, the metal door sliding shut behind them.

On this side, the passages seemed as bleak and unadorned as their larger companions. The walls were of the same rough concrete—doubtless strengthened with steel, Bond thought. Pipes for the various systems ran uncovered along the walls.

From Bond's observation, the second, living bunker appeared to be, in area, around the same size as the storage, ordnance, and vehicle one. It was also laid out in a symmetrical fashion, with a crisscrossing of passages and tunnels.

The rough entrance corridor led to a larger central passage, which it crossed at right angles. Glancing to his left, Bond saw metal fire doors, one of which stood open, giving a view back down the passage. From the general layout, he presumed other passages led from the arterial tunnel. On the left there appeared to be barrack quarters for the men. Here be dragons, Bond thought, for to the left would lie the way in—and out—of the living bunker. To get out, you would have to pass through the barracks section and, most probably, some kind of exit control by the main door.

Kolya and Paula nudged him to the right. They passed through two more sets of fire doors, between which other corridors dissected the main route, and doors studded each side. Voices could be heard, and the occasional clatter of typewriters. The security appeared tight to Bond. He spotted armed guards blatantly dressed in the old Waffen SS uniform—they were everywhere: some in doorways, others at points where the tributary passages joined the main walkway.

Once through the third pair of fire doors, however, the whole ambience changed. The walls were no longer cold, rough stone, but lined with hessian in pastel shades. The impedimenta of heating, water, air and electricity systems also disappeared behind curved, decorative cornices, and the doors on both sides became double-swing accesses with inset windows. Through the windows men and women were plainly visible working at desks and surrounded by electronic or radio equipment. All wore uniforms of one kind or another.

Most sinister of all, Bond thought, were the occasional photographs and framed posters which now broke up the line of the walls. The photographs were well known to Bond and would have been to any student of the 1930s and '40s: Heinrich Himmler, overlord of the Nazi SS; Reinhard Heydrich, Himmler's *éminence grise,* architect of SS power and Hitler's Security Service, the great Nazi martyr, assassinated in Prague; Paul Joseph Goebbels; Hermann Goering; Kaltenbrunner; Mengele; Martin Bormann; "Gestapo" Müller.

The posters also spoke for themselves. A young German soldier held a Nazi banner above the inscription SIEG UM JEDEN PREIS: "Victory at any price." Three young uniformed Aryans, in descending age, were backed by a Wagnerian lightburst through which a tank hovered in the air, while a clean-cut profile before a lightning-runed flag urged the youth to join the Waffen SS after the age of seventeen.

Bond felt he had somehow walked into a time warp. Certainly, no matter how hard people tried to wipe the slate clean and erase the excesses of Adolf Hitler's Nazi Party from history, its ideals, mysteries, ceremonies and political dogmas lingered on in small pockets of the world, just as a few of the old diehards remained alive and at liberty. But this place was like a museum—a shrine. More than a shrine, for there was action here, and was not that what it was all about? The National Socialist Action Army? A serious threat, M had said. A growing army. Terrorists today, Bond thought, a political and military might for the world to reckon with tomorrow.

Perhaps tomorrow was already here.

In front of them another set of doors—metal like the others, but once through they trod on deep pile-carpet. Paula put up a hand. The little party stopped.

They stood now in a kind of anteroom. Again, Bond considered, it was the kind of place you saw only in movies: a tall pair of polished heavy pine doors were set at the far end, flanked by Doric pillars and two men in the dark blue uniforms, peaked caps, and skull badges of the Gestapo. Their boots gleamed; their red, black and white armbands displayed the swastika. A smooth gloss shone on their Sam Browne belts and holsters, and the Death's Head silver skull prominent on their caps.

Paula spoke quickly in German, and one of the "Gestapo" men nodded, tapped on the high doors, then disappeared into the room beyond. The other man eyed Bond with a tilted smile, his hand moving constantly to the hoster on his belt.

The minutes ticked by, then the doors opened and the first man reappeared, giving Paula a nod. Both "Gestapo" men grasped the handles of the doors and swung them back. Paula touched Bond's arm. They moved forward into the room, leaving their original guards behind them.

The first, and only, thing Bond saw on entering was Fritz Erler's huge portrait of Adolf Hitler, towering over everything else in the room. It took up almost the entire rear wall. Its impact was so forcefully shattering that Bond simply stood, staring for the best part of a minute.

He was conscious of other people present, and that Paula had straightened herself to attention, raising an arm in the Fascist salute.

"You like it, Mr. Bond?"

The voice came from the far side of a large desk, neatly laid out with papers on a blotter, a bank of different-colored telephones, and a small bust of Hitler.

Bond tore his eyes from the painting to look at the man behind the desk. The same weather-beaten countenance, ramrod military bearing— even when seated—and well-groomed, iron-gray hair. The face was not that of an old man, for the bone structure would last a long time yet. Count von Glöda was, as Bond had already noted at the hotel, a man blessed with ageless features—classic, still good-looking, but with eyes which held no twinkle of pleasure. At the moment they were turned on Bond as though their owner was merely measuring the man for his coffin.

"I've only seen photographs of it," Bond said calmly in return. "I didn't like them. It follows that, if this is the real thing, I don't really care much for it either."

"I see."

"You should address the Count as Führer." The advice came from Brad Tirpitz, who sprawled comfortably in an easy chair near the desk.

Bond had ceased to be surprised by anything. The fact that Tirpitz was also part of the conspiracy caused him merely to smile and give a little nod, as though suggesting he should have known the truth in the first place.

"You managed to avoid the land mine after all, then?" Bond tried, successfully, to make it sound matter-of-fact.

Tirpitz's granite head made a slow negative movement. "You've got the wrong boy, I fear, James old buddy."

A humorless laugh came from von Glöda, as Tirpitz continued. "I doubt you've ever seen a photograph of Brad Tirpitz. 'Bad' Brad was always careful—like Kolya here—of photographs. I'm told, though, that in the dark, with the light behind me, we were the same build. I fear Brad did not make it. Not ever. He got taken out, quietly, before Operation Icebreaker even got under way."

"Out, downwards," Kolya said. "Through a nasty hole in the ice."

There was a movement from the desk, a slapping of the hand, as though von Glöda decided he was being neglected.

"I'm sorry, mein Führer." Tirpitz was genuinely deferential. "It was easier to explain directly to Bond."

"I shall do the explaining—if there is need for any."

"Führer." Paula spoke, her voice hardly recognizable to Bond. "The last consignment of arms is here. The whole batch will be ready for onward movement within forty-eight hours."

The Count inclined his head, eyes resting on Bond for a second, then flicking over Kolya Mosolov. "So. I have the means to keep my part of the bargain then, Comrade Mosolov. I have your price here at hand: Mr. James Bond. All as I promised."

"Yes." Kolya sounded neither pleased nor disgruntled. The single word expressed simply that some bargain had been fulfilled.

"Führer, perhaps . . ." Paula began, but Bond cut across her.

"Führer?" he exploded. "You call this man Führer?—Leader? You're crazy, the lot of you. Particularly you." His finger stabbed out towards the man behind the desk. "Aarne Tudeer, wanted for crimes committed during World War Two. A small-time SS officer, granted that dubious honor by Nazis fighting with Finnish troops against the Russians—against Kolya's people. Now you've managed to gather a tiny group of fanatics around you, dressed them up like Hollywood extras, put in all the trappings, and you expect to be called Führer? Aarne, what's the game? Where's it going to get you? A few terrorist operations, a relatively small number of Communists dead in the streets—a minuscule success. Aarne Tudeer, in the kingdom of the blind the one-eyed man is king. You're one-eyed and cock-eyed . . ."

His outburst, calculated to produce the maximum fury, was cut short. Brad Tirpitz, or whoever he was, sprang from his chair, arm rising to deliver a stinging backhander across Bond's mouth.

"Silence!" The command came from von Glöda. "Silence! Sit down, Hans." He turned his attention to Bond, who could taste the salty blood on his tongue. Given half a chance, he thought, Hans, or Tirpitz, or whoever, was going to get the slap returned in kind before long.

"James Bond." Von Glöda's eyes were more glassy than ever. "You are here for one purpose only. I shall explain to you in due course. However," he took a moment, lingering over the last word, then repeating it, "however, there are things I wish to share with you. There are also things I trust you will share with me."

"Who's the cretin disguished as Brad Tirpitz?" Bond wanted to throw as many curves as possible, but von Glöda appeared to be unshakable, used to immediate obedience, and with a mind which obviously reveled in military power.

"Hans Buchtmann is my SS-Reichsführer."

"Your Himmler?" Bond laughed.

"Oh, Mr. Bond, it is no laughing matter." He moved his head slightly. "Stay within call, Hans—outside."

Tirpitz, or Buchtmann, clicked his heels, gave the old, well-known Nazi salute, and left the room. Von Glöda addressed himself to Kolya. "My dear Kolya, I'm sorry but our business will have to be delayed for a few hours—a day perhaps. Can you accommodate me in that respect?"

Kolya nodded, "I suppose so. We made a deal, and I led your part of the arrangement right into your hands. What have I to lose?"

"Indeed. What, Kolya, have you to lose? Paula, look after him. Stay with Hans."

She acknowledged with "Führer," took Kolya's arm, and led him from the room.

Bond studied the man carefully. If this really was Aarne Tudeer, he had kept his looks and physique exceptionally well. Could it be that . . . ? No, Bond knew he should not speculate anymore. Already so many things had become distorted: Rivke disappearing; Tirpitz not being Tirpitz; Paula involved in a fantasy Nazi nightmare; Icebreaker shot through; and 007 himself now held in a Führerbunker, just inside the Russian border on the Arctic Circle.

"Good, I can now talk." Von Glöda stood, hands clasped behind his back, a tall straight figure, every inch a soldier. Well, Bond reflected, at least he was that—not a pipsqueak military amateur Hitler had proved himself to be. This man was tall, tough, and looked as shrewd as any seasoned army commander.

Bond sank into a chair. He was not going to wait to be asked. Von Glöda towered over him, looking down. "To set the record straight, and get any hopes out of your mind," the self-styled Führer began, "your Service resident in Helsinki—through whom you are supposed to work . . ."

"Yes?" Bond smiled.

A telephone number—that was all he had as a contact with the resident in Helsinki. Though the London briefing was precise about using their man in Finland, Bond had never even thought of it, experience having taught him years ago that one should avoid resident case officers like the plague.

"Your resident was—to use the term in vogue—'taken out' as soon as you left for the Arctic."

"Ah." Bond sounded enigmatic.

"A precaution." Von Glöda waved his hand. "Sad but necessary. There was a substitute for Brad Tirpitz, and I had to be very careful about my errant daughter. Kolya Mosolov acted under my orders. Your Service, the CIA, and Mossad, all had their controllers removed and the contact phones—or radio in Mossad's case—manned by my own people. So, friend Bond, do not expect the cavalry to come to your aid."

"I never expect the cavalry. Don't trust horses. Temperamental beasts at the best of times, and since that business at Balaclava—the Valley of Death—I've not had much time for the cavalry."

"You're quite a humorist, Bond. Particularly for a man in your present situation."

Bond shrugged. "I'm only one of many, Aarne Tudeer. Behind me there are a hundred, and behind them another thousand. The same applies to Tirpitz and Rivke. I can't speak for Kolya Mosolov because I don't understand his motives." He paused for a second before continuing. "Your own delusions, Aarne Tudeer, could be explained by a junior psychiatrist. What do they amount to? A neo-Nazi terrorist group, with access to weapons and people. Worldwide organization. In time the terrorism will become an ideal, something worth fighting for. The movement will grow; you will become a force to be really reckoned with in the councils of the world. Then, bingo, you've managed what Hitler failed to do—a world-wide Fourth Reich. Easy." He gave a dry laugh. "Easy, but it won't work. Not anymore. How do you get someone like Mosolov—a dedicated Party member, a senior officer of the KGB—to go along with you even for some of the way?"

Von Glöda looked at Bond placidly. "You know Kolya's department in the First Directorate of the KGB, Mr. Bond?"

"Not offhand. No."

The thin smile, eyes hard as diamonds, the facial muscles hardly moving. "He belongs to Department V. The department that used, many years ago, to be called SMERSH."

Bond saw a glimmer of light.

"SMERSH has what I understand is called, in criminal parlance, a hit list. That list includes a number of names—people who are wanted, not dead but alive. Can you imagine whose name is number one on the chart, James Bond?"

Bond did not have to guess. SMERSH had undergone many changes, but as a department of the Russian Service, SMERSH had a very long memory.

"Mmmm." Von Glöda nodded. "Wanted for subversion and crimes against the state. Death to spies, Mr. Bond. A little information before death. James Bond is top of SMERSH's list and, as you well know, has been for a long time. I needed help of a particular kind. Something to get me . . . how would you say it? . . . off the hook, with certain gentlemen of the KGB. Even the KGB—like all men—have a price. Their price was you, James Bond. You, delivered in good condition, unharmed. You've bought me time, arms, a way to the future. When I've finished with you, Kolya takes you to Moscow and that charming little place they have off Dzerzhinsky Square." What passed for a smile vanished completely. "They've waited a long time. But come to that, so have we. Since

1945 we have waited." He dropped his long body into the chair opposite Bond. "Let me tell you the whole story. Then possibly you'll understand that I will have purchased the Fourth Reich, and the political future of the world, by fooling the Soviet Union and selling them an English spy: James Bond, for whom they lust. Foolish, foolish men, to stake the future of their ideology on one Englishman."

The man was unhinged. Bond knew that, but possibly so did many others. Listen, he thought. Listen to all von Glöda has to say. Listen to the music, and the words, then, perhaps, you will find the real answer, and the way out.

14

A WORLD FOR HEROES

"WHEN THE WAR was over and the Führer had died, gallantly, in Berlin," von Glöda began.

"He took poison *and* shot himself," interpolated Bond. "*Not* a gallant death."

Von Glöda did not seem to hear him. "I thought of returning to Finland, perhaps even hiding there. The Allies had my name on their lists but I would, possibly, have been safe. Safe, but a coward."

As the story came out: the hiding in Germany, then contact with the organized escape groups, *Spinne* and *Kameradenwerk,* so Bond saw clearly that he was not just dealing with some old Nazi living with dreams of a past glory which had died in the Berlin Bunker.

"The novelists call it ODESSA," von Glöda almost mused to himself, "but that was really a rather romantic notion—a loose organization for getting people out. The real work was done by dedicated members of the SS who had the wit to see what could go wrong."

Like many others, he had shifted from place to place. "You know, of course, that Mengele—Auschwitz's Angel of Death—stayed in his home-town for almost five years undetected. In time though, we all left."

First, von Glöda and his camp-following wife had gone to Argentina. Later, he had been among the vanguard of those to hide in the well-protected camp, deep and difficult to get at, in Paraguay.

"They were all there—the wanted ones. Müller, Mengele, even Bormann. Oh yes, Bormann lived. He's dead now, but he did escape from the bunker, and lived for a long time. There was even a deathbed visit from an American writer who got laughed off the bookshelves for publishing the truth."

But Aarne Tudeer—as he still was then—became dissatisfied with the company he kept. "They all play-acted," he snarled. "When Perón was still in control, and later, they openly showed themselves. Even rallies and meetings: beauty contests—Miss Nazi 1959. The Führer's dream would come true." He gave an outraged, disgusted snort. "But it was all talk; idle. They lived on dreams and allowed the dreams to become their substance. They lost guts; threw away their heroism; became blind to the truth of the ideology Hitler had laid out for them.

"You see, Bond, I am convinced that Adolf Hitler was the only one who held the key: the only one who possessed the will and conviction to give the world true peace under a National Socialist regime. The others? Dross—just as those since have been dross. Hitler stood head and shoulders above any leader of his time: you only have to look at his contemporaries in Fascism. Of course, Franco was a survivor, but cursed with a town clerk mentality; lacking in vision and ambition. After his Civil War it was all too easy for him."

"And Mussolini?" Bond asked.

This time, von Glöda guffawed, "That street trader? Lazy, vain—a whoremaster. Don't talk to me about Benito Mussolini; nor those who have followed in recent years. No, only one true Leader existed, Bond. Hitler. Hitler was right. If National Socialism was reduced to ashes, a phoenix had to rise from those ashes. Otherwise, before the end of the century, Communism would overthrow Europe, and eventually the world."

Von Glöda had urged the few who still held onto the dream: the time to strike was at the moment of transition, when the world appeared to lose its bearings and direction, when everyone cried out for somebody to lead them. "That would be the time. Inevitably," he claimed, "the Communist regime would hesitate just before throwing all its might into the domination of the world."

"It hasn't quite happened like that." Bond knew his only hope was to establish some kind of common ground with this man—as a hostage must woo his captors.

"No?" There was even a laugh now. "No, it's better than we ever imagined it could be. See what's happening in the world. The Soviets have penetrated trade unions and governments, from Britain to America—and much good will it do them. The Eastern bloc is, you'll agree, slowly collapsing in on itself."

Bond, in fact, did agree to a point, and mad as he might be, von Glöda had hit on a truth. If the old Nazi ideology was to reappear, it should start as yet another so-called terrorist group. In that way it would be attacked, dismissed as a fanatical mushroom which would eventually die. Only von Glöda was making sure it would not die.

"Last year, we showed the world by a few well-planned operations—starting with the Tripoli Incident. This year it will be different. This year we are better armed and equipped. We have more followers. We will gain access to governments. Next year the Party will emerge, into the open. Within two more years, we shall be a true political force again. Hitler *will* be vindicated. Order *will* be restored, and Communism—the common enemy—*will* be swept from the map of history. People are crying out for order—a new order; a world of heroes, not peasants and victims of a regime."

"No victims?" Bond queried.

"You know what I mean, Bond. Of course the dross must go. But once gone, there will be a master race—not just a German master race, but a European master race."

Somehow the man had managed to convince some of the older Nazis in Paraguay that all this was possible. "Six years ago," he said proudly, "they allotted me a large sum of cash. Most of what had been left in the Swiss accounts. I had assumed a new name in the late sixties, or at least reassumed it. There are true links between my old family and the now defunct von Glödas. I returned from time to time, then began work in earnest four years ago. I traveled the world, Bond, organized, plotted, sorted out the wheat from the chaff.

"I planned to begin the supposed terrorist acts last year." Von Glöda had truly hit his stride now. "The problem, as always, was arms. Men I could train—there are plenty of troops, many experienced instructors. Arms are another matter. It would have been difficult for me to pose as PLO, Red Brigade, IRA even."

By this time, he moved back to Finland. His basic organization was taking shape. Arms and a secret headquarters were his only problems.

Then he'd had an idea . . ."I came up here. I knew the area well. I remembered it even better."

Particularly, he remembered the bunker, built initially by the Russians and improved by German troops. For six months von Glöda had lived in Salla and used the recognized "smuggling" routes in and out of Russia. Amazed, he found a great deal of the bunker was intact, and he had openly gone to the Soviet authorities with permission from the Finnish Board of Trade. "There was some haggling, but finally they allowed me to work here: mining for possible mineral deposits. I was not over-specific, but it was a good investment. It cost the Soviets nothing."

Another six months—with teams brought in from South America, Africa, even England—and the new bunker was built. And in that time von Glöda had made contact with two ordnance depots nearby. "One was closed down last year. I got the vehicles from them. *I* got the BTR's," he punched himself in the chest, "just as *I* did all the deals with those treacherous imbeciles at Blue Hare. Sold themselves for nothing . . ."

"Themselves and a lot of hardware—rocketry you haven't used yet, I gather," Bond slipped the fact in, receiving a cutting stare in return.

"Soon," von Glöda nodded. "The second year will see us using the heavy weapons—and more."

Silence.

Was von Glöda expecting congratulations? Possibly.

"You seem to have pulled off a coup of some magnitude," Bond said. He meant it to sound like a comic book bubble, but von Glöda took him seriously.

"Yes. Yes, I think so. To go out and buy from Russian NCO's, who have no sense of their own ideology—let alone that of the NSAA. Dolts. Cretins."

Silence once more.

"Then the world catches up with them?" Bond suggested.

"The world? Yes. The authorities catch up with them, and they come running to me for cover. I don't know why I'm telling you all this, Bond. Probably because you're the one person to whom I *can* boast—yes, really boast of our successes so far. One thousand men and women here, in this bunker. Five thousand men out in the field—in the world. An army growing daily; attacks on main government centers all over Europe and the United States, all planned down to the last detail; and the armaments ready for shipment. After the next assault, our diplomacy. If that does not work, then more action, and more diplomacy. In the end we will have the largest army, and the largest following, in the Western world."

"The world fit for heroes?" Bond coughed. "No, sir. You're under-manned and outgunned."

"Outgunned? I doubt it, Mr. Bond. Already during this winter we've shipped very large quantities of munitions out of here—BTR's, Snow-cats, piled high. Straight across Finland, over rough country. Now waiting for onward shipment as machine tools and farming implements. My methods of getting supplies to my troops are now highly sophisti-cated."

"We knew you were bringing them out through Finland."

Von Glöda actually laughed. "Partly because I wanted you to know. There are other things, however, you should not know. Once this consign-ment is on its way, I am ready to move my forces nearer to the European bases. We have bunkers already prepared. That, as you may realize, is one of my problems which concerns you." Bond frowned, not understand-ing, but the proposed leader of the new Reich was now caught up in the story of how he had dealt with the people at Blue Hare.

A healthy trade with the NCO's at Blue Hare was established and worked well for some time. Then suddenly their CO—"A man of little imagination"—came in a panic to the Ice Palace. A spot inspection had been called, and two Red Army colonels were spinning around like Catherine wheels, accusing anyone and everyone—including the warrant officer CO. Von Glöda suggested that the warrant officer should stand on his dignity and ask the colonels for an investigation by the KGB.

"I knew they'd go for it, Bond. If there's one thing I like about the Russians it is their ability to pass the buck. The warrant officer and his men at Blue Hare were caught; the colonels were aghast at the amount of matériel missing. They were all caught in a kind of crossfire. Everyone wanted to drop the problem into someone else's lap. Who better than the KGB, I suggested?"

Count von Glöda, Bond admitted, had shown ideal common sense. An incident like this would be shunned by the Armed Forces (Third) Directo-rate. The disappearance of vast quantities of weapons and ammunition, in the wastes of the Arctic, would not appeal to the Third Directorate. Whatever else he was, the new-styled Führer knew strategy, and the Russian mind. After the GRU the job would end up with Department V, and the thinking behind such a move was obvious. If Department V moved in, there would be no traces of anything when they were finished—no missing arms and nobody to question. A clean sweep: probably an ordnance depot with a terrible accident, such as an explosion claiming the lives of all personnel.

"I told the idiot warrant officer to alert whoever came from the KGB. Tell him to talk to me. First some GRU people came to Blue Hare. They only stayed for a couple of days. Then Kolya came. We had a few drinks. He put no questions. I asked him what he needed most, in all the world, to enhance his career. We did the deal here, in this office. Blue Hare will cease to exist in a week or so. Nobody will make waves. No money changes hands. Kolya wanted one thing only. You, Mr. James Bond. You, on a plate. I simply acted as puppet master, and told him how to get you; deliver you to me; give me a few hours with you. After that, Department V—who you have so often dealt with as SMERSH—has you. For life. Or death, of course."

"And you go on to form the Fourth Reich?" James Bond said. "And the world lives happily ever after?"

"Something like that. But I have delayed matters. My people are waiting now, to talk with you . . ."

Bond raised a hand. "I have no right to ask, but did you set up the joint operation too? CIA, KGB, Mossad and my people?"

He nodded. "I told Kolya how to do it, and how to substitute people. I did not bargain for Mossad sending my own errant daughter after me."

"Rivke." Bond remembered the night at the hotel.

"Yes, that's what she calls herself nowadays, or so I understand. Rivke. Behave yourself, Mr. Bond, and I may be tender-hearted and allow you to see her before you leave for Moscow."

She was alive then; here in the Ice Palace. Bond willed himself to show no emotion. Instead he shrugged. "You said people wanted to talk with me?"

Von Glöda returned to his desk. "Doubtless the authorities in Moscow want you badly, but my own intelligence people also wish to speak with you about certain matters."

"Really?"

"Yes, really, Mr. Bond. We know your Service has one of our men—a soldier who failed in his duty."

Bond shrugged, his face blank with feigned incomprehension.

"My troops are loyal, and know the Cause comes before anything else. That is why we have been successful so far. No prisoners. All members of the NSAA take an oath pledging death before dishonor. In all operations last year, none of my men was taken prisoner—except . . ." He let it hang in the air. "Well, would you like to tell me, James Bond?"

"Nothing to tell," bland and flat.

"I think there is. The operation against three British civil servants, just as they left the Soviet Embassy. Think hard, Bond."

Bond had been way ahead of him. He remembered M's briefing and the grave look on his chief's face when he referred to the interrogation of the one NSAA man they had in custody at the Headquarters building — the one who had tried to shoot himself. What was it M had said? "His aim was off." No details, though.

"It is my guess," von Glöda's voice dropped to almost a whisper, "*my* guess, that any information prized from that prisoner would have been given to you at your briefing, before you joined Kolya. I need to know — *must* know — how much the traitor has given away. You will tell me, Mr. Bond."

Bond managed to draw a laugh from the back of his dry throat. "I'm sorry, von Glöda . . ."

"Führer!" von Glöda shrieked. "You will be as everybody else, and call me Führer."

"A Finnish officer who defected to the Nazis? A Finnish-German who has delusions of grandeur? I cannot call you Führer." Bond spoke quietly, not expecting the tirade that was to come.

"I have renounced any nationality. I am not Finnish, nor am I German! Wasn't it Goebbels who proclaimed Hitler's feelings? The German people had no right to survive because they had been found wanting; they could not live up to the ideals of the great Nazi movement. They would be wiped out so that a new Party could eventually rise and carry on the work . . ."

"But they weren't wiped out."

"It makes no difference. My allegiance is to the Party, and to Europe. To the world. Now is the dawn of the Fourth Reich. Even this small piece of information is necessary to me; and you will give it to me."

"I have no knowledge of any NSAA prisoner. No information about an interrogation."

The man who stood erect before Bond suddenly appeared to be convulsed with rage. His eyes blazed. "You *will* tell all you know. Everything British Intelligence knows about the NSAA."

"I have nothing to tell you," Bond repeated. "You cannot force me to say things I know nothing about. In any case, what can you do? To carry on your own struggle you have to hand me over to Kolya — that's your deal for silence."

"Oh, Mr. Bond, don't be naive. I can get my men and military matérials out within twenty-four hours. Kolya has also sold his soul to ambition. He sees a power of his own if he walks into Dzerzhinsky Square with you—the man SMERSH has wanted for so long. Do you think his superiors know what he is doing? Of course not. Kolya has a sense of the dramatic—like all good agents and soldiers. As far as Department V of the First Directorate is concerned, Kolya Mosolov is on a mission to sniff out missing armaments in this area. Nobody's going to come looking for a while if they don't hear from him. Understand, James Bond? You have bought me time, that's all. A chance to finish my little arms deal, and an opportunity to get out. Kolya Mosolov is expendable. *You* are expendable."

Bond's mind raced through the logic. Von Glöda's neo-Nazi terrorist army had, indeed, carried out most successful work in the past year. Moreover, M himself was adamant that the National Socialist Action Army was being taken very seriously by all the Western governments. M's gravity, and warning, had followed his remarks about the one NSAA man taken alive and now incarcerated in the building overlooking Regent's Park. Logically, this meant the man had said enough to provide the Service with high-grade intelligence on von Glöda's strength and hiding places. QED, Bond thought, the real answer was that his own Service, if not others, knew exactly where von Glöda's HQ lay hidden at this moment and, possibly, through interrogation analysts, any future command post.

"So, I'm expendable because of one prisoner," Bond began. "*One* man who may or may not be held by my people. That's rich when you consider the millions your former Führer held in captivity, murdered in the gas chamber, killed off with slave labor. Now, one man holds the balance."

"Oh, a good try, Bond," von Glöda replied dryly. "Would that it were as simple. But this is a serious matter, and I must ask you to treat it as such. I can take no chances."

He paused for a second, as though considering how best to convey the situation to Bond. Then: "You see, there is nobody here, not even on my General Staff, who knows the exact location of my next headquarters. Not Kolya, whose path to great power was handed to him by me, engineered by me. Nor Paula, or Buchtman—Tirpitz to you. None of them knows.

"Unhappily, however, there are a few people who, however unwittingly, hold this information in their heads. The men and women who await me at the new headquarters, at this moment, of course they are well aware.

But there are others. For instance, the unit which carried out the operation in Kensington Palace Gardens, outside the Soviet Embassy, went from here to be briefed—en route for London—at the new command post.

"From that new and highly secret headquarters they went out to do their work. All are accounted for but one. My information is that he failed to commit suicide when he fell into the hands of your Service. He is a well-trained man, but even the most clever officers can fall into traps. You know how two and two can be put together, Mr. Bond. I need two things from you. First, if he gave you the location of my new headquarters, where I intend to be established shortly; second, where is he being held prisoner."

"I know nothing about any NSAA prisoner."

Von Glöda gave Bond a blank, completely unemotional look. "Possibly you are telling the truth. I doubt it, but it is possible. All I want is the truth. My personal feelings are that you do know where he is and that you are aware of everything he has said. Only a fool would send you into the field without the full facts."

Clever von Glöda might well be, Bond thought. He certainly had an eye for detail, and a sharp brain; but his last remark left no doubts about his complete ignorance concerning security matters. For obvious reasons, Bond also took extreme offense at the inference that M was a fool.

"Do you think I would be given access to *all* the facts?" Bond allowed himself an indulgent smile.

"I am certain of it."

"Then you are the fool, sir. Not my superiors."

Von Glöda gave a hard, short one-syllable laugh. "Have it your own way, but I dare not take risks. I *will* know the truth. We have ways of taking a man to the limit here. If you have nothing to say, you will say nothing, and I shall know there is little danger. If you only know where my man is being held, that information can be flashed to London. He can be held in the most inaccessible place, but my team in London will still get him—with time to spare."

Could one of von Glöda's teams penetrate the Service's HQ? As much as Bond doubted it, he was disinclined to put it to the test.

"And what if I break down and lie to you? What if I say, yes, there is such a prisoner—though I do assure you I know of none—and he has given us all the information we need?"

"Then you also will know the location of the new command post, Mr. Bond. You see, there is no way you can win."

Not in your book, Bond thought. The man could see nothing unless it was in clear black and white.

"One other thing," von Glöda rose to his feet. "Here, Mr. Bond, we rely on the older techniques of interrogation. Painful, but very successful. I have yet to trust what friend Kolya would call a chemical interrogation. So know what you face, Mr. Bond. Exceptional discomfort, to put it mildly. I plan to take you to the threshold of pain; and doctors tell me that no man has yet been born who will not crack under the method we shall use."

"But I know nothing."

"Then you will not crack, and I shall know. Now, why not avoid the worst? Tell me about the prisoner, where he is held; what he has revealed."

Seconds ticked away, almost audible in Bond's head. Far off he even imagined the sound of singing—voices from the past—the old Nazi rally call:

> *For the last time the rifle is loaded . . .*
> *Soon Hitler banners will wave over the barricades.*

The Horst Wessel Song—the anthem which had helped knit together the original Nazi Party. The Horst Wessel; the Fascist salute; the uniforms; and the "Heil Hitler" greetings, which flowed into the massive, hysterical chanting of "Sieg Heil . . . Sieg Heil . . . "

The outer door opened and the man Bond had known as Brad Tirpitz entered, followed by the two dark-uniformed guards who had been in the anteroom.

They raised their arms in salute, and Bond realized that he actually could hear the singing, coming from within the bunker.

"You know, Hans, what information I require from this man," von Glöda commanded. "Use all your powers of persuasion. Now."

"Jawohl, mein Führer." The arms raised in unison, heels clicking. Then the two men converged on Bond, seizing his arms. He felt handcuffs encircle his wrists, the grip of strong fingers as they caught hold, bundling him from the room.

They took him no further than the anteroom. Tirpitz/Buchtman went to the hessian-covered wall and pushed it with his fingers, revealing a section which swung back with a click.

Buchtman disappeared through the door, followed by one of the officers, his hand grasping Bond's jacket. The other man kept a tight hold on

007's handcuffed wrists. One in front and the other behind. Bond soon found out the reason: Once inside the door, they were crammed into a narrow passage, just wide and high enough to take a man.

After half a dozen paces, it was clear they were descending, then, quite quickly, they came to a bare stone staircase lit by dim blue lights set into the walls at intervals, a rope running through metal eyes down one side as a guide rail.

Their progress was very slow, for the staircase went a long way down. Bond tried to work out the depth but gave up quickly. The steps appeared to steepen. At one point there was a small platform, leading to an open chamber. Here Buchtman and the two guards put on heavy greatcoats and gloves. None were offered to Bond who, even in the outdoor winter gear he still wore, began to feel the dreadful uprush of intense cold from the depths below them.

The steps became slippery as they went. Bond sensed ice growths on the sides of the walls. Their progress continued—down, down, until at last they emerged into a brightly lit circular cave—the walls of natural rock, the flooring beneath them seemingly pure, thick ice.

Heavy wooden crossbeams spanned the cave, passing over its center. Attached to the beams was a block and tackle mechanism, with a long, solid metal chain dangling down and ending in what looked like an anchor hook.

One of the dark-uniformed SS men took out his pistol, staying close to Bond. The other opened a large, ice-encrusted metal box, from which he took a small, motordriven chainsaw.

The breath of all four men in this freezing dungeon thickened the air in clouds. Bond smelled the gasoline from the chainsaw motor as it fired. "We keep it well protected!" Buchtman had not lost his American, Tirpitz's, accent. "Okay," he nodded to the SS man with the gun. "Strip the bastard."

As Bond felt hands starting to undo his clothing, he saw the chainsaw biting into the floor of the cell, sending chips of ice flying. Even with his clothes on, the cold had become painfully crippling. Now, as the layers were roughly removed, his body seemed to be enveloped in an invisible coat of sharp needles.

Buchtman nodded toward the man with the chainsaw. "He's cutting a nice bathtub for you, James, old buddy." He laughed. "We're well below the main line of the bunker here. In summer the water rises quite high. Small natural lake. You're gonna get to know that lake very well indeed, James Bond."

As he spoke, the chainsaw broke through the ice, showing it to be at least a foot thick. Then the operator began to chew out a rough circle, the center of which lay directly under the chain and hook dangling from the block and tackle.

15

DEAD COLD

THEY UNLOCKED THE handcuffs. By that time, James Bond was too cold to resist. The removal of the top half of his clothing, which followed, did not seem to make any appreciable difference. He could hardly move, and it seemed that even his desire to shiver was denied him.

One of the SS men pulled Bond's arms in front of his stark-naked body, then clasped the handcuffs into place again. The metal on his wrists felt as though it burned.

Bond began to concentrate. Try to remember something . . . Forget the cold . . . Close your eyes . . . See just one spot in the universe, let the spot swell . . .

The rattle of chains, and Bond heard rather than felt that his handcuffed wrists were being clipped over the hook. Then, disorientation for a moment, as they hoisted the block and tackle. Rrrrrrrch . . . Rrrrrrrch . . . Rrrrrrrrchchch . . . His feet left the ground and he spun and swung as the chain lifted. Acute pain, now, as the handcuffed wrists took the strain. Arms stretched, pulled from their sockets. Then numbness again. It did not matter about the weight on his arms, shoulders, and wrists, for the freezing temperature almost acted as an anesthetic.

Strangely, the thing that did matter was the swinging and spinning. Bond did not normally react to disorientation while flying, doing high-speed aerobatics, or the many other stress tests included in his yearly check-out. Now, however, he felt the bile rise in his throat as the swinging became more regular—pendulumlike—and the spinning slowed, first one way, then the next.

Opening his eyes was as painful as anything else. A struggle against light frost forming on the lids. Necessary though, for he desperately needed some fixed point on which to focus.

The ice-streaked sides of the cave turned in front of him, the hard light from above throwing off color—yellows, reds and blues. It was impossible to keep his head up with arms stretched above him taking all the body weight.

Bond's head slumped forward. Below him a wide dark eye, figures moving on the periphery, the eye turning lazily, squinting, slanting. It was a moment before the numbness of his body and brain took in the fact that the eye was not moving. The illusion came from his own swinging motion, at the end of the chain.

The needles continued to assault his body. They seemed to be everywhere at once, then localized—clawing at his scalp, moving to a thigh, or rasping against his genitals.

Concentrate: he fought to get a proper perspective, but the freezing numbness was like a barrier, a chill wall preventing his brain from working. Harder; concentrate harder.

Finally Bond took in the eye, as the swaying and spinning motion settled. The eye was a circle cut in the ice. Its darkness was the frozen water below. Slowly they were letting out the chain, so that his feet seemed poised directly over the water.

Now a voice. Tirpitz–Buchtman: "James, buddy, this is going to be dirty. You should tell us now before we go on. You know what we want? Just answer yes or no."

What did they want? Why was this happening? Bond's very brain felt as though it was freezing. *What?* "No," he heard his voice croak.

"Your people have one of our men. Two questions: where is he being held in London? What has he told your interrogators?"

A man? Held in London? Who? When? What had he told? For a few seconds Bond's mind cleared. The NSAA soldier, being held at the Regent's Park HQ. What had he told? No idea, but hadn't he worked it out? Yes, the man must have said a great deal. Tell nothing.

Aloud he said, "I know nothing about anyone being held prisoner. Nothing about any interrogations." His voice was unrecognizable, echoing against the walls of the cavern.

The other voice floated up to him, each word a struggle for Bond to recognize or comprehend.

"Okay, James, have it your way. I'll ask you again in a minute."

From above, the rattle of something. The chain. His body moving down toward the black eye. For no reason, Bond suddenly thought he had lost all sense of smell. Odd, why no sense of smell? Concentrate on something else. He struggled, setting his mind on a new course. A summer day. The countryside. Trees in full leaf. A bee hovered above his face, and he could smell—the sense of smell was back—a mixture of grass and hay. Far in the distance the sound of some farm machinery peacefully purring.

Don't say anything. You know nothing except this—the hay and grass. Nothing. You know nothing.

Bond heard the final rattle of the chain just as he hit the middle of the black eye. His brain even registered that a scum of ice had already reformed over the water. Then the slack of the chain dropped him into the center.

He must have cried out, for his mouth filled with water. Sunlight. The oak tree. Arms being dragged down by the chain. He could not breathe.

The sensation was not one of biting cold, simply an extreme change. It could have been boiling water just as easily as freezing. Bond's only conscious moments, after the first shock, were of his body enveloped by a blinding pain, as though his eyes had been scorched by white light.

He still lived, though he was only aware of it because of the pain. His heart pumped in his chest and head like timpani.

There was no way of telling how long they had held him under the ice. He gulped and spluttered for air, the whole of his body jerking in spasms like a puppet controlled by a convulsive master.

Opening his eyes, Bond saw that he was, once more, suspended over the eye cut in the ice. Then the real cold set in—the shaking as he swung to and fro, while the needlepoints turned into barbs, excoriating his skin.

No. His brain broke through the pain of cold. No, this was not happening. The grass; smells of summer; sounds of summer: the tractor drawing near, and the soughing of a breeze in the oak tree's branches.

"Okay, Bond. That was just a taste. You hear me?"

He was breathing normally, but his vocal cords did not seem to be working properly. At last—"Yes, I hear you."

"We know just how far to go, but don't kid yourself, we'll go further. The full limit. Where is our man being held in England?"

Bond heard his own voice, again as though it did not belong to him: "I don't know of any man being held."

"What has he told your people? How much?"

"I know of no man being held."

"Have it your own way." The chain sounded its death rattle.

They let him stay under, weighted down by the chain, for a long time. He fought for breath, the red mist mingling with a white light which seemed to fuse every muscle, every vein and organ. Then the blessed relief of darkness, soon to be blasted apart by the pain as his naked body swung gently, pulled clear again of the ice pool.

The cold air of the dungeon made the second time worse. Not just needles, but tiny animals gnawing and biting into the numbed flesh. The more sensitive organs alive with agony, so that Bond wrestled with the handcuffs and hook, wanting to get his hands down to cover his loins.

"There is a National Socialist Action Army man being held prisoner in England. Where is he?"

The summer. Try . . . Try for the summer. But this was not summer, only the terrible teeth, small and sharp, biting through the skin into the muscle and flesh. The NSAA man was at the Regent's Park HQ. Was there harm in telling them? Summer. The green leaves of summer.

"You hear me, Bond? Tell us and things will get easier."

Sumer is icumen in, . . .
Sing, cuccu! . . .

"Don't know. Don't know about prisoner . . . Nobody . . ." This time the voice came from right inside his head, the sentence cut short as the chain clattered down, plunging him into the gelid mass.

He struggled, not reasoning what he would, or could, do if the handcuffs became unhooked. This was pure reflex: the body automatically fighting for life, trapped by an element in which it could not possibly survive for long. He was conscious of the muscles not responding, the brain ceasing to operate rationally. Streaking pain. Darkness.

Alive and swinging once more. Bond wondered how near he hovered between life and the unknowing, for the white pain was now centered in his head—a blinding, searing, flashing explosion within the skull.

The voice was shouting, as if trying to get through to him from a distance. "The prisoner, Bond. Where are they keeping him? Don't be a fool; we know he's somewhere in England. Just give us the place. The name. Where is he?"

My Service Headquarters. Building near Regent's Park. Transworld

Export. Had he said it? No, there had been nothing, even though the words were clearly formed in his brain, waiting to leap out.

The green leaves of summer; Sumer is icumen in; The living is easy; the last rose of summer; Indian summer . . .

Vipers lashed at his brain. Then the words: Bond's voice aloud—"No prisoner. I don't know about a prison—"

The crash of ice around him, the red hot, blinding liquid, then agony, as the body became aware again. Out, swinging and dripping, gasping, every minute centimeter of him torn to shreds. The brain had finally hit on the real source of pain. Cold. Dead cold. A death by slow freezing.

The sun was dazzling. So hot that the perspiration dripped from Bond's forehead and into his eyes. He could not even open his eyes, and he knew he'd had too much to drink. Drunk as a lord. Why drunk as a lord? Drunk for a penny, dead drunk for twopence.

Balance gone. Laughter: Bond's laughter. He did not usually get drunk, but this was something else. High as a . . . high as something . . . When? On the fourth of July? At least it made you feel good. Let the world go by. Lightheaded . . . lighthearted . . . darkness. Lord, he was going to pass out. Be sick. No, he felt too good for that. Happiness . . . very happy . . . the darkness coming in, closing around him. Just a hint of what it really was as the night swallowed him. Dead cold.

"James . . . James." The voice familiar. Far, far away from another planet. "James . . ." A woman. A woman's voice.

Then he recognized it.

Warmth. He was lying down and warm. A bed? Was it a bed?

Bond tried to move, and the voice repeated his name. Yes, he was wrapped in blankets, lying on a bed, and the room was warm.

"James."

With care, Bond opened his eyes—a stinging of the lids. Then he stirred, slowly because each movement was painful. Finally he turned his head towards the voice. His eyes took a few seconds to focus.

"Oh, James, you're all right. They gave you artificial respiration. I've pressed the bell. They said to get someone in quickly when you came to." The room was like any other hospital room, but there were no windows. In the other bed, her legs raised in traction and encased in plaster, lay Rivke Ingber, her face alive and happy.

Then the nightmare returned and Bond realized what he had come through. He closed his eyes but saw only the dark, cold, circular eye of freezing water. He moved his wrists, and the pain returned where the steel handcuffs had bitten into his flesh.

"Rivke," was all he could manage, for his mind was assaulted by other demons. *Had* he told them? *What* had he told them? He could remember the questions, but not his answers. A summer scene flitted through his mind—grass, hay, an oak tree, a buzzing in the distance.

"Drink this, Mr. Bond." He had not seen the girl before, but she was correctly dressed in a nurse's uniform and held a cup of steaming hot liquid to his lips. "Beef tea. Hot, but you've got to have hot drinks. You're going to be fine. Don't worry about anything now."

Bond, propped on pillows, had neither the strength nor inclination to resist. The first sip of the beef tea rolled back the years. The taste reminded him of a far distant past—just as a piece of music will recall a long-forgotten memory.

Bond, recalled a long-lost childhood: the hygienic smell of school sanatoriums, the bouts of winter flu at home.

He swallowed more, feeling the warmth creeping into his belly. With the inner heat, the horrors also returned: the ice dungeon and the terrible cold as he was dunked into the freezing water.

Had he talked? As hard as Bond cudgeled his brains, he could not tell. In the midst of the sharp, satanic pictures of torture, there was no memory of what else had passed between him and his interrogators.

Depressed, he looked at Rivke. She was staring at him, her eyes soft and gentle, just as they had been in the early morning before the explosion on the ski slopes.

Her lips moved, soundlessly, but Bond could easily read what she was mouthing: "James, I love you."

He smiled and gave her a little nod as the nurse tipped the cup of beef tea so that he could swallow more.

He was alive. Rivke was there. While he lived there was still a chance that the National Socialist Action Army could be stopped and their Führer and his "new world" wiped from the map.

16

PARTNERS IN CRIME

AFTER THE BEEF tea, an injection, and the nurse said something about frostbite. "Nothing to worry about," she said. "You'll be right in a few hours."

Bond looked across at Rivke and started to say something, but he drifted off into a cloud of sleep. Later he did not know if it was a dream or not, but there seemed to be a waking period during which von Glöda stood at the foot of the bed. The tall man was smiling, unctuous and evil. "There, Mr. Bond. I told you we would get all we needed from you. Better than drugs and chemicals. I trust we haven't ruined your sex life. I think not. Anyway, thank you for the information. A great help to us."

On finally waking, Bond was more or less convinced that this had been no dream, so vivid was the picture of von Glöda. There were dreams, however, dreams about the same man: dreams in which von Glöda stood decked out in Nazi uniform, surrounded by the trappings of power at a kind of Nuremberg Rally. His voice had that same charismatic quality which Hitler himself was able to produce, leading to near hysterical trust from his audience.

In sleep, Bond thought he could hear the stamp of jackboots and the martial music, combined with ritual chanting and the swell of voices. He finally awoke, sweating, and with complete knowledge that M had been right. Von Glöda really meant what he said; there was nothing idle about his threats, nor any emptiness in his theory. He really *could* gather together an army—many from the streets of the great European and, maybe, American cities, organizing them, as Hitler had done, into the new Party. This, in turn, could lead in one country after another to a wave of National Socialism.

Bond breathed deeply and stared at the ceiling. He worried over whether von Glöda's little speech had been a dream or not. Then a wave of terror washed through him as the memory of the ordeal under the ice water returned, then passed quickly. He felt better now, if disoriented, and anxious to get going. Indeed, he had little choice. Either find a way out of von Glöda's labyrinth, or take the inevitable trip to Moscow, with its final showdown between himself and the heirs of SMERSH.

"You awake, James?"

In the few seconds of returning to the world, Bond had forgotten Rivke's presence in the room. He turned his head, smiling. "Mixed sanatoriums. What will they think of next?"

She laughed, inclining her head towards the two great lumps of plaster— strung up on pulleys—that were her legs. "Not much we can do about it though. More's the pity. My stinking father was in here a little while ago."

That clinched it. Von Glöda's speech had not been a dream. Bond swore silently. How much had he given away to them, under the pain and disorientation of the ice dunking? There was no way to tell. Quickly he calculated the chances of a determined team getting into the Regent's Park building. The odds would be about eighty to one against. But they would only need to penetrate one man. That would shorten the odds and, if he had told them, it was a certainty that the NSAA would already have their team briefed. Too late for him to even warn M.

"You look worried. What terrible things did they do to you, James?"

"They took me for a swim in a winter wonderland, my darling. Nothing that dreadful. But what about you? I saw the accident. We thought you were taken away by a regular ambulance and police. Obviously we were wrong."

"I was just coming down the final slope, looking forward to seeing you again. Then, poof—nothing. I woke up with a lot of pain in my legs and my father standing over me. He had that woman with him. I don't think she's here though. But they did have some kind of hospital organized. Both legs broken, and a couple of ribs. They plastered me up, took me for a long ride, and I finally woke up here. The Count calls it his Command Post, but I've no idea where we are. The nurses're friendly enough but won't tell me anything."

"If my calculations're correct . . ." Bond eased himself onto his side so that he could more easily talk to Rivke and look at her simultaneously. There were signs of strain around her eyes, and obvious discomfort caused by the casts on her legs, and the traction. "If I'm right, we're in a large bunker, situated around ten to twelve kilometers east of the Finnish border. On the Russian side."

"Russian?" Rivke opened her mouth, eyes wide with amazement.

Bond nodded. "Your beloved Papa has pulled a very fast one." He made a grimace, conveying a certain admiration. "You have to admit he's been exceptionally clever. We have searched everywhere for clues, and he's been operating right out of the most unlikely place—within Soviet territory."

Rivke laughed quietly, the sound tinged with bitterness. "He always was clever. Who'd have looked in Russia for the headquarters of a Fascist group?"

"Quite." Bond stayed silent for a moment. "How bad are the legs?"

She lifted a hand, made a helpless gesture. "You can see for yourself."

"They haven't given you any therapy yet? Let you try and walk—even with crutches or a Zimmer?"

"You're joking. I can't feel much pain. It's just very uncomfortable. Why?"

"There's got to be a way out of this place, and I'm not going alone or leaving you behind." He paused, as if making up his mind. "Not now that I've found you, Rivke."

When he next looked, Bond thought he could detect a moistness in the large eyes. "James, that's wonderful of you, but if there is a way out, you'll have to try it yourself, *by* yourself."

Bond's brow creased. If there was a way, could he get back in time? Bring help? He put the answers into words. "I don't think the clock's on our side, Rivke. Not if I've told them what I think . . ."

"Told them . . . ?"

"Being ducked in almost frozen water without your clothes on is slightly disorientating. I passed out a couple of times. They wanted the answers to two questions." He went on to say that he knew one answer, but could only guess the other.

"What kind of questions?"

In a few words Bond told her about the NSAA man captured in London before he could commit suicide. "Your father's got a new command post. This fellow has enough information to tip off our people. The devil of it is that the London prisoner probably doesn't realize he knows. Your maniac father had a group sent to his new command post for briefing, before leaving for London. Our interrogators, like yours with Mossad, are not fools. The right questions'll yield the answers. Two and two make four."

"So you think your Service already knows where this new place—this second command post—is located?"

"I wouldn't put money on it. But if I've told von Glöda's inquisitors we have the man, and that he's been interrogated, they can add up the answers as well as our people. I should think your father's moving everyone out of here pretty damned fast."

"You said there were two questions?"

"Oh, they wanted to know where our people were keeping him. That's no problem really. There's a chance one man could get at him; but any full-scale assault's out of the question."

"Why, James?"

"We keep a special interrogation center in the basement of our Headquarters' building in London. He's holed up there."

Rivke bit her lip. "And you really think you told them?"

"There's a possibility. You said your father was in here earlier. I can vaguely remember that. He gave the impression they knew about it. You were awake . . ."

"Yes." She looked away for a second, not meeting his eyes.

Agents of Mossad, Bond considered, tended to opt for a suicide pill rather than face an interrogation which might compromise them. "Do you think I've failed my own Service," he asked Rivke, "and this unholy alliance we were supposed to be involved in?"

For a second, Rivke was silent. Then: "No, James. No. You had no alternatives, obviously. No, I was thinking about what my father said—God knows why I call him a father. He's really no father of mine. When he came in, he said something about you having provided information. I was dozing, but he sounded sarcastic. He thanked you for the information."

Bond felt the lead of despair deep in his guts. M had sent him blind into a compromising situation, though he could not blame his chief for that. M's reasoning would have been the least knowledge the better, as far as Bond was concerned. Like himself, M was almost certainly duped by what had transpired: the real Brad Tirpitz's elimination, Kolya Mosolov's double-dealing with von Glöda. And then there was the duplicity of Paula Vacker.

The despair came from the knowledge that he had let his country down, and failed his Service. In Bond's book these were the cardinal sins.

By now von Glöda would almost certainly be going through all the standard routines of moving shop: packing, organizing transport, loading up the BTR's with all the arms and munitions they could carry, shredding documents. Bond wondered if von Glöda had some temporary base—apart from the major new command post—from which he could operate. Now he would want to get out as quickly as possible, but it might take up to twenty-four hours.

Bond looked around to see if any of his clothes had been left with him. There was a locker opposite the bed, though not large enough to contain clothing. The rest of the room was bare, just the formal trappings of a small private hospital ward: another small locker opposite Rivke's bed; a table with glasses, a bottle, and medical equipment standing in the corner. Nothing useful that he could see.

There were curtain-bearing rails around each bed, two lamps above the bed heads and a strip light set in the ceiling. The usual small ventilation grilles.

The idea came to him that he might overpower the nurse, strip her, and try to get out disguised as a woman. But the notion was self-evidently ludicrous, for Bond scarcely had a build which lent itself to female impersonation. In addition, just thinking it made him feel dopey again. He wondered what drugs they'd shot him with after the torture.

Providing von Glöda was going to keep his bargain with Kolya—which seemed highly unlikely—Bond's only chance would be an escape from Kolya Mosolov's custody.

There was a sound in the passage outside. The door opened and the nurse came in, bright, starched and hygienic. "Well," she started briskly. "I have news. You'll both be leaving here soon. The Führer has decided to take you out with him. I'm here to warn you that you'll be moving in a few hours." She spoke perfect English, with only the slightest trace of an accent.

"Hostage time," Bond sighed.

The nurse smiled brightly, saying she expected that was it.

"And how do we go?" Bond had some notion it might help to keep her talking, if only to gain a little information. "Snowcat? BTR? What?"

The nurse's smile did not leave her mouth. "I shall be traveling with you. You're perfectly fit, Mr. Bond, but we're concerned about Miss Ingber's legs. She prefers being called Miss Ingber, I gather. I must be with her. We'll all be going in the Führer's personal aircraft."

"Aircraft?" Bond did not even realize they had flying facilities.

"Oh, yes, there's a runway among the trees. It's kept clear even in the worst weather. We have a couple of light aircraft here—ski-fitted in winter, of course—and the Führer's executive jet, a converted Mystère-Falcon. Very fast but lands on anything . . ."

"Can it take off on anything?" Bond thought of the bleak ice and snow among the trees.

"When the runways's clear." The nurse seemed unconcerned. "Don't worry about a thing. We have ice burners out along the metal runway just before he leaves." She paused in the doorway. "Now, is there anything you need?"

"Parachutes?" Bond suggested.

For the first time, the nurse lost her brightness. "You will both be given a meal before we leave. Until then, I have other work to do." The door shut, and they heard the click of a key turning in the lock from the outside.

"That's it, then," said Rivke. "If you'd ever thought about it, dear James, there'll be no cottage for us, with roses around the door."

"I had thought about it, Rivke. I never give up hope."

"Knowing my father, he'll like as not drop us off at twenty thousand feet."

Bond grunted. "Hence the nurse's reaction when I mentioned parachutes."

"Shhh," Rivke made a sharp noise. "There's someone in the passage. Outside the door."

Bond looked towards her. He had heard nothing, but Rivke suddenly appeared alert, if not edgy. Bond moved—surprised that his limbs worked witt such ease and speed. Indeed the action seemed to produce a new and sudden alertness in him. The dopey feeling had left him and there was a sudden new clarity of mind in its place. Bond cursed himself again, for he realized he'd broken another elementary rule: by blabbing his head off to Rivke without making a rudimentary surveillance check.

Bond sprinted, unembarrassed by his nudity, to the medical table in the corner, grabbed a glass and returned as quickly to the bed. Whispering, he told Rivke, "I can always smash it. Surprising how effective a broken glass can be on flesh."

She nodded, her head cocked, listening. Still Bond heard nothing. Then, with a speed and suddenness that even took Bond unawares, the door shot open and Paula Vacker was in the room.

Silently, she moved—as Bond's housekeeper May would have said—"like greased lightning." Before either Rivke or Bond could react, Paula had snaked between the two beds. Bond caught a glimpse of his own P7 automatic raised twice and heard the tinkle of glass as Paula put the two bed head lights out of action with a pair of quick butt strokes from the gun.

"What . . . ?" Bond began, realizing that the reduction of light made little difference, as most of the illumination came from the ceiling strip light.

"Just keep quiet," Paula cautioned, the P7 circling the two beds as she moved back towards the door, crouched, pulled a bundle into the room, then closed the door again, locking it behind her. "The electronics, James, were inside the bed head light bulbs. Every word—all your conversation with sweet little Rivke here—has now been relayed to the Count von Glöda."

"But . . . ?"

"Enough." The P7 was pointed at Rivke not Bond. With her foot, Paula pushed the bundle towards Bond's bed. "Get into those. You're going to become an officer in the Führer's army for a while."

Bond got up and undid the bundle. There were thermal underwear, stockings, heavy rollneck, and a field gray winter uniform smock and trousers; boots, gloves, and a uniform fur hat. Quickly he started to dress. "What's all this about, Paula?"

"I'll explain when there's time," she snapped back. "Just get on with what you're doing. We're going to cut it fine in any case. Kolya's taken a run for it, so there's only the two of us now. Partners in crime, James. At least we're going to get out."

Bond was already almost dressed. He moved to the door side of his bed. "What about Rivke?"

"What *about* her?" Paula asked in a voice stabbing like a stalactite.

"We can't get her out. Whose side are you on anyway?"

"Surprisingly enough, yours, James. More than can be said for the Führer's daughter."

As she said it, Rivke moved. Bond saw a kind of blur as, with alarming ease, Rivke slid her legs from the plaster casts, swiveled sideways, and swung off the bed, one hand clasped around the butt of a small pistol. There was not a single mark on her body, and the supposed broken legs worked like those of an athlete.

Paula swore, shouting at Rivke to drop the gun. Bond, still getting into the last pieces of clothing, saw the whole thing in a kind of slow motion.

Rivke, dressed only in a pair of briefs, with the gun arm rising as her feet hit the floor. Paula's arms extending into the full-lenth firing position. Rivke still moving forward, then the one loud echoing blast from the P7. A cloud of gunsmoke making swirling patterns. Rivke's face disintegrating in a fine mist of blood and bone, as her body, looped backwards by the blast, arced away from them over the bed.

Then the smell of the burned powder.

Paula swore again. "Last thing I wanted. The noise."

For one of the few times in his life, James Bond felt out of control. He had already recognized the beginning of emotional feelings towards Rivke. He knew of Paula's treachery. Now, balanced on the balls of his feet, Bond prepared to make a last, desperate attempt: a leap towards Paula's gun arm. But she merely tossed the P7 towards him, making a grab for Rivke's small pistol.

"You'd better take that, James. May need it. We could be lucky. I filched the nurse's key, and set her off on some fool's job. There's nobody in this wing, so the shot may not have been heard. But we're going to need wings on our heels."

"What're you talking about?" Bond said, suspecting, even as he spoke, the sickening truth.

"I'll tell you the whole thing later, but can't you understand? You didn't give them anything under torture, so they rigged you up with Rivke! You spilled it all to his daughter because you trusted her. She's Daddy's little helper, always has been. From what I understand she hoped to be the first woman Führer, in due course. Now, will you come on. I've got to try and get you out of here. Partners in crime—like I said."

17

A DEAL IS A DEAL

PAULA WORE A heavy, well-cut officer's greatcoat over the uniform Bond had last seen her in. The boots were visible under the coat, and to crown the effect she had added a military fur hat.

Bond glanced towards the bed that had lately contained Rivke. The plaster leg casts were obviously hollow frauds, bearing out Paula's accusations. He felt the bile rise at the sight of the wall behind, spattered like some surrealist painting with blood and tissue. You could still smell Rivke in the room.

He turned away, picking up his own officer's fur hat, which Paula had provided. Given the history of Icebreaker, where allegiances swerved back and forth like tennis balls, he still couldn't be sure of Paula's true intentions, but at least she seemed serious about getting him away from the bunker. In turn this meant putting distance between himself and von Glöda, which was a most appealing possibility.

"As far as guards and others are concerned, I'm acting on the Führer's orders," Paula said. "Here, there's a standard pass for each of us." She handed over a small square of white plastic, like a credit card. "We don't go anywhere near the main workshops or the arms stores. Just keep your head well down in case we run into anyone who's seen you before; and stay close to me. Let me do the talking as well, James. The exit is through the small bunker, and the chances are well above average. They're running around like proverbial scalded cats, because there's one hell of a flap on since von Glöda gave the movement orders—*after* you spilled the beans to Rivke . . ."

"About that, I . . ." Bond began.

"About nothing," Paula spoke sharply. "All in good time. Just trust me, for once. Like you, I'm not in this for fun." Her gloved hand rested on his arm for a second. "Believe me, James, they caught you by using that girl, and I had no way to warn you. The oldest trick in the book as well. Shove a prisoner in with someone he trusts, then listen to the conversation." She laughed again. "I was with von Glöda when they brought the tapes. He leaped about ten meters into the air. Idiot—he was so sure that, because you'd gone through the water torture without saying anything, there was nothing for him to worry about. Now, James. Stay close to me."

Paula unlocked the door and they stepped out into the passageway, pausing for a second while she relocked the door from the outside.

The passage was empty. It was lined with white tiles, highly sterile with a hint of disinfectant in the air. Other small hospital wards led off to the left and right, and the end of the passage, which lay to their left, was blocked by a metal door. If nothing else, von Glöda was well-organized.

Paula led the way forward towards the metal door. "Keep the gun out of sight, but ready for Custer's last stand," she cautioned. "If we get into a shootout, the chances are not all that brilliant." Her own hand was thrust deeply into her right pocket, where she had placed Rivke's pistol.

The corridor on the far side of the hospital wing was well decorated—the hessian covering, with some framed posters and pictures similar to those Bond had seen near von Glöda's personal suite. From this alone, he reasoned, they were deep within the bunker, probably parallel to the passages which ran down to the new Führer's offices.

Paula insisted on walking slightly ahead; and Bond, his gloved fingers around the pocketed P7, remained in place, about two steps to the rear and slightly to Paula's left, hugging the wall. Almost the standard position for a bodyguard.

After a couple of minutes, the passage divided. Paula turned right and climbed up carpeted steps. The stairs were angled at a steep gradient and took them to a very short stretch of passage at the end of which a pair of double doors, complete with small mesh-covered windows, swung them into what must have been an arterial tunnel.

Now they were back to the rough walls, with the utility pipes and channels visible. Paula glanced behind every few seconds to make sure Bond was with her. Then a left turn, and the simple act of walking told Bond they were on a slight upward slope.

As the slope became steeper, they came to a walkway on the right, complete with boards to give their feet traction, and a handrail — all similar to the one on which they had first entered the bunker. Here, as with the larger entrance, doors and passages led off on either side. For the first time since leaving the hospital section, Bond was aware of noise — voices, the click of boots, an occasional shout or the sound of running feet.

As he glanced into the tributary passages, Bond glimpsed all the signs of hurried, though controlled, activity. Men were carrying personal belongings, metal cabinets, boxes and document files; others appeared to be stripping offices; some even lugged weapons. Most appeared to be heading away towards the left, bearing out Bond's sense of direction. He was now certain they were in the main tunnel, which would take them to the smaller bunker entrance.

A section of half a dozen soldiers came down the slope at the double, well drilled, their faces to the front, the NCO in charge ordering a salute to Paula and Bond. Then another group went by, their faces set and almost fanatical, full of a pride Bond had seen only in the old films of the Third Reich during its early days.

Now, ahead, a small detachment stood guard at what seemed to be their final hurdle. The tunnel came to an abrupt end, closed off by a massive steel shutter. Towards the roof, Bond could see hydraulic equipment to lift the shutter upward, but there was also a small, heavily bolted door set low on the right-hand side.

"Now for it," Paula muttered. "Look the part. Don't hesitate, and for

God's sake let me do the talking. Once we're out, move left."

Bond's mind drifted back fractionally to advice given to him very early in his career by a young naval officer. "Always look as if you know exactly where you're going, and as if you're on urgent business."

The rules still stood.

As they came nearer to the entrance, he saw that the detachment consisted of an officer and four men, all armed. Near the door stood a small machine—like a ticket vending module for an underground rail network.

Four paces from the exit, Paula called out in German: "Prepare to let us out. We're on personal orders from the Führer himself."

One of the private soldiers moved to the door, and the officer took a step forward, standing by the machine. "Do you have your pass, Fräulein? And you, sir?"

They were close now.

"Of course," Paula said. She took out the piece of plastic in her left hand. Bond followed suit.

"Good." The officer had the sour and humorless face of an old army hand who did everything by numbers. "Do you know anything about this sudden movement order? We've only heard rumors."

"I know a great deal." Paula's voice hardened. "You'll all be told in time."

They were right up to the officer now. "They say we have to be out within twenty-four hours. Some sweat."

"We've all been through sweat before." There was no emotion in Paula's voice as she offered her card, to be checked by the machine.

The officer took both cards, fed them one at a time into a small slot near the top, then waited until a series of lights ran their course, sounding a soft buzzer for each pass.

"Good luck, whatever your mission." He returned their cards. Bond nodded. The private soldier by the door was already opening up the bolts.

Paula thanked the officer in charge, and Bond followed her lead, giving the Nazi salute. Heels clicked and orders barked as the door swung back. The sense of some incredible time warp returned inside Bond's head—all this was 1930s and 1940s stuff.

A few seconds later they were outside, and the biting cold hit them like a fine spray of raw ice. It was dark, and Bond—with no wristwatch— had lost all sense of time. There was no immediate way of telling whether they were in the late afternoon or near dawn. The complete blackness gave the impression that it was the middle of the long Arctic night.

They advanced to the left, following tiny blue guide lights which outlined the exterior of the bunker. Under the snow, Bond could feel the hard metal of the long strips of chain-link "roadway" that must have been laid down around the command post. There would be similar wide strips for runways on von Glöda's airfield.

The main doors of the bunker towered, white, above them, and as they passed them, Bond realized where Paula was taking him—to the small concrete shelter where he had seen the snow scooters being stored. He could just make out the circle of trees to his right—remembering how they had suddenly broken cover from those trees, to be bathed in light when Kolya first lured him to this outpost.

Paula seemed to have forgotten nothing. As soon as they reached the small, low structure built hard against the rock face, she produced a keyring, on a thin chain.

The shelter smelled of fuel and oil, while the switch by the door produced only a dim light. The scooters were neatly parked, looking like giant insects huddled together in hibernation.

Paula made for the first one that suited her purpose—a big, long, black Yamaha, much larger than the ones on which Kolya had led them over the border.

"You don't mind if I drive." Paula was already checking the fuel. In the poor light, Bond could only sense, not see, the cheeky smile on her lips.

"And where're we going, Paula?"

She glanced up, peering at Bond through the gloom. "My people have an observation post about ten kilometers away." Her hand waved, towards the south. "It's partly wooded, but on high ground. You can see the whole of the Ice Palace and the runway from there." She heaved at the scooter, pulling it into position so they could run it straight out of the door.

Bond's hand closed around the butt of his P7. "You'll forgive me, Paula. We've known each other a long time, but my impression was that you're somehow tied up with the Count von Glöda, or Kolya. This operation hasn't been straightforward from the word go. Hardly anybody has been what they seemed. I'd just like to know whose side you're on and who your 'people,' as you call them, really are."

"Oh come on, James. All our files on you say that 007 is one of Britain's best field men. Sorry, you're not officially 007 any more, are you?"

Bond slowly produced the P7. "Paula? My instincts tell me that you're KGB."

Her head tilted back and she laughed. "KGB? Wrong, James. Come on, we haven't much time as it is."

"I'll come once you've told me. I expect the proof afterwards—even if you are KGB."

"Idiot." A friendly laugh this time. "James, I'm SUPO, and have been since long before we first met. In fact, my dear James, our meeting wasn't a complete accident. Your own Service has now been informed."

SUPO? Maybe she was at that. SUPO was the abbreviation for *Suojelupoliisi*—the Protection Police Force. The Finnish Intelligence and Security Agency.

"But . . ."

"I'll prove it within the next couple of hours," she said. "Now, for God's sake, James, let's get going. There's a lot to be done."

Bond nodded. He climbed onto the back of the scooter behind Paula as she started the motor, put the machine in gear, and gently eased it from the shelter. Once outside, she stopped to go back and close the door behind them. Then, within seconds, they were away into the trees.

For a good minute, Paula did not even bother to turn on the large, broad-beamed headlight. After that, Bond simply clung on for dear life. She rode the Yamaha as though it was part of her body, zigzagging with an accuracy that took Bond's breath away. She had slipped goggles over her eyes and was well muffled, but Bond's only protection was Paula's body as the wind ripped around them.

His arms were wound tightly around her waist. Then at one point, with another of her wonderful laughs drifting back on the wind, Paula took her hands off the controls and lifted Bond's arms, so that his hands cupped her breasts through the heavy padding of the greatcoat.

Their route was far from easy. They skirted the bottom of a long rise through tightly packed trees, then made a lengthy run up the slope, swerving among the trees all the way. Yet Paula hardly slowed for anything. Holding the throttle open wide, she took the scooter side on through gaps in the trees, allowing it to ride dangerously at an almost forty-five-degree angle on some banks, yet retaining control all the time.

At last Paula slowed, slewing from left to right at the crest, following what was certainly a natural trail. Then, quite suddenly, two figures rose from the side of the track. His eyes now well adjusted to the night, Bond caught the shapes of machine pistols against the snow.

Paula slowed and stopped, then raised an arm. Bond found his hand searching for the P7.

There was a short, muttered conversation between Paula and the larger of the men. He was dressed in Lapp costume and wore a huge mustache which made him look even more like a brigand. The other was tall and thin, with one of the most evil faces Bond had ever seen—sharp and weasel-like, with small eyes that darted everywhere. For his own sake, Bond hoped Paula had, at last, told him the truth. He wouldn't have enjoyed finding himself at the mercy of either of these people.

"They've been keeping clear of the two *kotas* we've got up here," Paula said turning her head towards Bond. "I've got four men in all. The other two have gone in at regular intervals, to check the radio equipment and keep the fires going. It seems that all's safe. The other pair are in the camp now. I've said we'll go straight to the *kotas*—you'll want food, and I've got to get a message off to Helsinki on the shortwave. They'll relay it to London. Anything you want to tell your boss—M?"

"Only details of what's been going on, and where I am. Do we know where von Glöda'll head for?"

"Tell you after I've talked to Helsinki," she said, gunning the engine.

Bond nodded vigorously. "Okay." They advanced at a walking pace, the two Lapps taking station ahead and behind them. Bond leaned forward and whispered loudly, "Paula, I'll shoot you where you stand if you're taking me for a ride."

"Shut up and trust me. I'm the only one you *can* trust out here. Right?"

A few steps out of the woods, perched on the ridge, were two *kotas*. The reindeer skin which covered their wigwamlike structures loomed dark against the snow. Smoke drifted up from the apex crisscross of forked poles at the top. From below, Bond thought, they would be difficult to spot against the tall firs and pines.

Paula stopped the Yamaha, and they both dismounted.

"I'm going to use the radio straight away." Paula pointed to the right-hand *kota,* and Bond could just make out the aerials among the poles at the top. "My other two boys are in there. I've told Knut to stay on guard outside." She indicated the evil-looking Lapp. "Trifon'll go with you to the other *kota,* where there's food cooking."

The Lapp with the large mustache—Trifon—grinned, nodding encouragement. His machine pistol pointed towards the ground.

"Okay, Paula," Bond said. The smell of wood smoke reached him before they got to within six paces of the *kota,* and Trifon went forward, lifted the hide flap, and peered inside. When he was sure everything was safe, the Lapp waved Bond towards him. Together they entered the *kota,* and immediately Bond felt his eyes sting as the smoke hit him.

He coughed, wiped his eyes and looked around. The thin fog of smoke gradually made its way towards the outlet at the top of the tent. Mingled with it was a strong, pleasant cooking smell, and quickly Bond's eyes adjusted enough to make out mounds of sleeping bags, blankets, plates and other accessories carefully organized within the tent.

Trifon put down his weapon and motioned for Bond to sit. He pointed at the pot bubbling over the fire that was burning in a square trench cut into the earth. Trifon then touched his mouth. "Food." He gave a pleased nod. "Food. Good. Eat."

Bond nodded back.

Trifon took a plate and spoon, went to the fire, bent over it and began to fill the plate with what loked like some kind of stew.

The next moment the Lapp was sprawled, yelling, in the fire. His feet had been kicked from under him. One of the blankets seemed to take on human shape, but before Bond could retrieve his pistol, Kolya's voice came quietly from the other side of the fire.

"Don't even think of it, James. You'll be dead before your hand touches the butt." He then said something in Finnish to Trifon, who had rolled clear of the fire and now sat nursing his hand.

"I should've known." Bond spoke as quietly as Kolya. "It was all too easy. Paula's certainly led me a dance."

"Paula?" Kolya's face was clear for a moment in the glare from the fire. "I've just told this bandit here to pass me his machine pistol. I will kill him if he tries anything. Personally I'd like to be better armed when Paula comes in here. You see, James, I'm on my own. Outnumbered. But I have friends waiting, and I don't expect to go back to Moscow empty-handed."

Half of Bond's mind began to work on the immediate problem—should he try to warn Paula? How could he deal with Kolya Mosolov, here and now? His eyes moved carefully around the gloomy interior of the *kota* as Trifon—in a state of some agony—gently pushed the automatic weapon toward Kolya with his foot.

"From that, I presume you're taking me with you." Bond peered through the haze.

"That was the deal I had with that Fascist pig, von Glöda." Kolya's laugh was genuine enough. "He really thought he could get away with running a Nazi operation from inside the Soviet Union."

"Well, he *has* run it. All his terrorist operations have been successful. He's used Russian weapons; and now he's getting out."

Slowly Kolya shook his head. "There is no possible way that the so-called Count von Glöda will get out."

"He was taking me. By air. May even have left already."

"No. I've been watching and listening. His beloved little private jet hasn't left the runway, and will not even try to get off before dawn. We have a couple of hours left."

So, it was now only two hours before dawn. At least Bond had some reference point of time in his head. "How can you stop him?" he asked blandly.

"It's already in motion. Von Glöda has a military force on Soviet soil. They will be blasted at dawn. The Red Air Force will brew that bunker like a boiling kettle." Kolya's face changed in the fire glow. "Unhappily our base at Blue Hare will also be taken out. An unfortunate error, but it solves all problems."

Bond thought for a moment. "So, you're going to decimate von Glöda and his whole little army. Breaking your part of the deal but keeping his?"

"My dear James—a deal is a deal. Tough, sometimes it doesn't work out for one of the participants. How could I let you go, my friend? Especially as my department—which used to be SMERSH—has tried to catch you off balance for so long. No, my deal with von Glöda has always been slightly lopsided."

18

THE FENCERS

THERE WAS SILENCE for several seconds, then Mosolov spoke a few words to the groaning Trifon.

"No need to let good food go to waste," Kolya Mosolov said softly. "I've told him to straighten that pot and stir up the fire. I don't think he'll try anything stupid. You should know that I have some of my men here, and they'll already have taken Paula. So, I think the best thing . . ." He stopped in mid-sentence, with a sudden intake of breath indicating the shock of fear.

The smoke thickened for a second, then quickly cleared, as Trifon urged the fire into flame. Bond saw that Mosolov's head was being forced back. A hand grasped his hair, while another fist held a glinting reindeer knife across his throat.

The fire leaped into life again, and the evil face of Knut became plainly visible behind Kolya's shoulder.

"Sorry, James." Paula stood just inside the leather flap entrance to the *kota,* a heavy automatic pistol in her hand. "I didn't want to tell you, but my boys spotted Kolya digging his way in here a couple of hours ago. You were my bait."

"You could've told me." Bond sounded acid. "I'm quite used to being a tethered goat."

"Again, sorry." Paula came right into the *kota.* "We had other problems as well. Comrade Mosolov brought some playmates. Six of them. Knut and Trifon dealt with that little group once they saw Kolya safely tucked away in here. That's why I'm a free woman and not a KGB prisoner . . ."

"There's plenty more . . ." Mosolov began, then thought better of it.

"Do be careful, Kolya," Paula said brightly. "That knife Knut's holding to your throat's as sharp as a guillotine. He could sever your head with one well-placed stroke." She turned to Trifon and spoke a few rapid words.

A grin crossed the big Lapp's face in the flickering firelight. Holding his burned hand with great care, he moved over to Mosolov, took back his own machine pistol, removed the automatic, and began to search the Russian.

"They're like a couple of kids," Paula said. "I've told them to strip him, take him into the woods, and tie him to a tree."

"Shouldn't we keep him with us until the last minute?" Bond suggested. "You say he had men with him . . ."

"We've dealt with them . . ."

"There could be more. He has an air strike coming in at dawn. Having already experienced Kolya in action, I don't fancy letting him out of our sight."

Paula thought for a moment, then relented, giving new orders to the Lapps.

Kolya was silent, almost sullen, as they tied his hands and feet, pushed a gag into his mouth and shoved him into the corner of the *kota.*

Paula gave Bond a nod, directing him towards the exit. Outside, she lowered her voice. "You're right, of course, James. It's safer with him here; and more of his men could still be around. We'll only be really safe back in Finland. But . . ."

"But, like me, you want to see what happens to the Ice Palace." Bond smiled.

"Right," she accepted. "Once that's over I think we can turn him loose—unless you want to take his head back to London—and let his friends find him."

Bond said taking Kolya Mosolov all the way with them could prove to be an encumbrance. "Better to get rid of him just before we leave," was his final verdict. In the meantime they had work to do—Paula's message to Helsinki and Bond's to M.

In the radio *kota* Bond began to tap his pockets.

"These what you're looking for?" Paula came close to him, holding out the gunmetal cigarette case and his gold lighter.

"You think of everything."

"Maybe I'll get to prove it later on." In spite of the presence of the Lapps in the radio *kota,* Paula Vacker reached up and kissed Bond gently; then again, with some urgency.

The radio *kota* contained a powerful shortwave transmitter, with facilities for Morse and clear speech. There was also a fast-sending device, allowing a transmission to be taped and then run through in a fraction of a second, ready for slowing, and decoding, at the other end. These messages—as the general public knows nowadays—often appear as a bleep of static in the earphones of the many listeners who monitor signal traffic.

Bond watched for a few minuates while Paula organized her own message to Helsinki. There was no doubt in his mind that hers was a thoroughly professional setup. Paula definitely worked for SUPO—something he should really have known about years ago, considering how far back their relationship went.

Already he had asked for her field cryptonym and was delighted to learn that—for this operation against von Glöda—she was known as *Vuobma:* the old Lapp word for stockade, or corral, in which reindeer are trapped and herded for breeding.

With all his equipment, except for the Heckler & Koch P7, either gone or still in the Saab at the Hotel Revontuli, Bond was without any method of ciphering his signal. While Paula worked at the transmitter, one of the two Lapps who had been in the radio *kota* for most of the time stood close to her. The other was sent off to keep a watch on the bunker and its airstrip.

Finally, after a few dud tries, Bond composed a suitable clear language message, settling on:

VIA GCHQ CHELTENHAM TO M STOP ICEBREAKER BROKEN BUT OBJECTIVE SHOULD BE ACHIEVED BY DAWN TODAY STOP RETURNING SOONEST STOP MOST URGENT FLASH REPEAT MOST URGENT GET YOUR BEST BOTTLE OUT OF THE CELLAR STOP I WORK THROUGH VUOBMA ENDS 007.

The 007 would raise some eyebrows, but it could not be helped. His instructions to move the prisoner were fairly obvious. Not the best, but—if any NSAA listening post picked it up—they presumably already knew where M's prisoner was being held anyway. This message, if intercepted, would only alert them to the fact that he was being moved. At short notice, and without the facilities, it was the best Bond could do.

When Paula completed her signal she took Bond's piece of paper, added a coding of her own to make certain that it would go on to GCHQ, Cheltenham, via her own Service's Communication Department, and rattled it off onto tape, before zipping it through the fast-sending machine.

When all this was done, they held a conference. Bond suggested how best a continual watch could be kept on the bunker. The dawn air strike was uppermost in his mind; after that it would be necessary to get away as quickly as possible, dump Kolya Mosolov, and clear the frontier without undue hazard.

"Can you find our way back?" he asked Paula.

"Blindfolded. I'll give you all the information later, but there's no problem as far as that's concerned. Except we'll have to move from here, then wait to make the crossing as soon as it's dark enough."

Through Paula, Bond gave orders for the radio *kota* to be dismantled and packed away—the four Lapps had their large snow scooters hidden near at hand—and organized periods of rest, with one of the Lapps briefed to rouse them in plenty of time to strike the other *kota* before dawn.

"Mosolov's a liability," he declared. "But we'll have to hang onto him for as long as possible."

Paula shrugged. "Leave it to my Lapps and they'll take care of Kolya," she murmured. But Bond did not want the Russian's blood on his hands except as a last resort; so the arrangements were made, and the orders given.

While the radio *kota* was being dismantled, they trudged back to the remaining shelter. A blood-chilling howl was carried on the wind through the trees, long and drawn out, followed by another, similar sound.

"Wolves," Paula said. "On the Finnish side, our border patrols have had a bumper year: at least a couple of wolves a week for most of them, and three bears since Christmas. It's been a particularly hard winter and you mustn't believe all you hear about wolves not being dangerous. During a bad winter, when food's scarce, they'll attack anything: man, woman or child."

Trifon, his hand bandaged, had already fed Kolya, whom he'd propped in the corner of the *kota*. Previously, Bond had cautioned Paula that they should not under any circumstances discuss plans in front of him. Instead they did their best to ignore the Russian, though there was always one armed Lapp nearby making certain he was well guarded.

Trifon's reindeer stew proved to be delicious and they ate with enjoyment, the Lapp nodding and smiling at their pleasure. In the short time spent at Paula's observation post, Bond had acquired a great admiration for her tough, resilient Lapp assistants.

As they ate, Paula produced a bottle of vodka, and they drank a toast to final success, knocking the little paper cups together and chanting *"Kippis,"* the Finnish equivalent of "Cheers."

After the meal, Paula settled down with Bond in one of the larger sleeping bags. Mosolov seemed to have dozed off, and soon the couple, after several tender embraces, also slept. Eventually they were awakened by Knut urgently shaking Bond's shoulder. Paula was already awake and translated that there was some activity at the bunker. "And a good half-hour to go before dawn," she announced.

"Right." Bond then took charge. The *kota* would be dismantled here and now, after which one of the Lapps would stay in the cover of the trees to guard Mosolov, while the rest could gather at the observation point.

Within five minutes, Paula and Bond had joined Trifon, who lay among rocks and snow on the rise, scanning the view below through a pair of night glasses. Behind them, Paula's other Lapps went quietly about the business of striking camp, and Bond glimpsed Kolya being hustled away into the trees—Knut prodding him along with a submachine gun.

Bond was amazed at the sight, even in the gloom of half-light which now heralded a dawn that would not come for twenty minutes or so. From Paula's observation post, the view down to the small clearing among the trees, and the huge rocky area of the bunker's roof, was unimpeded.

It was plain now that the entrance to the Ice Palace itself was built into a rising wall of rock, like a giant stepping stone forming a rough crescent in the center of a thick forest. The trees had been expertly cleared to allow only minimal open space in front of the main entrances, while other paths were cut through trees, rock, and ice to form routes around the bunker to the higher, more open, ground above.

To the south, and above the huge spur of rock, the thick forest was broken by carefully prepared clear tracks, through which a wide runway pointed a long gray-white finger, from the rock to a threshold which appeared to end abruptly in the heart of the surrounding forest.

There was no sign of an aircraft. Bond presumed the Mystère-Falcon Executive Jet and the two light airplanes were tucked away in concrete pens, built into the rock which helped form the roof of the bunker itself.

In the present light, and at this distance, it was not possible to make an accurate calculation about the length of the runway. All Bond considered was that a take off among trees left little margin for error. Yet von Glöda had already proved his ability in most things, so it was unlikely that the true length of the runway would present much of a genuine hazard for landing or take-off.

Below them, von Glöda's private army was about to get under way. The floodlights were on under the trees, while the big doors leading to the vehicle ramp running deep inside the Ice Palace were open, sending a sharp-angled flood of light out over the trees.

Paula spoke a few words to Trifon, then turned to Bond. "Nothing's come out yet. No vehicles or aircraft sighted, though Trifon says there's a lot of troop activity among the trees."

"Let's hope Kolya was specific," Bond replied, "and the Russians are going to hit them on time."

"When they do get here, we'd better dig ourselves into the snow and pretend to be rocks," murmured Paula. "I think Kolya's instructions would be accurate enough, but we don't want to catch a stray rocket up here."

She had hardly said the words before the sound of a jet whine became audible a fair distance away—like a distant wail carried on the wind. Just then the sun glowed blood red in the east.

They looked at each other. Bond lifted his hands, showing gloved fingers crossed for good luck. Shifting slightly, all three of the watchers tried to dig themselves deeper into the snow. For a second, Bond realized how cold he was—the elements forgotten as he concentrated on the bunker far below, and about a kilometer away. Then even that brief moment of discomfort was gone as a great double crump seemed to blast the air around them.

Far off to the northeast there were a series of brilliant orange flashes, and a plume of smoke rose from the close-knit trees.

"Blue Hare," Paula said loudly, as though she had to shout against the noise. "They've . . ." Her next words were truly drowned. The supersonic shock waves from the aircraft traveled ahead of the machines. A consuming, growling roar surrounded Paula, Bond and Trifon—a terrifying harbinger of what was to follow in the now clear dawn.

The first pair of strike aircraft came in level with the trees, crossing to the hiding trio's right, neither firing nor dropping anything.

They streaked through the cold air, little eddies of steam surrounding the wings as the subzero temperatures produced contrails even at this low level. They looked like silver darts, precision-built arrows with large boxlike air intakes, high tails, and wings folded back into a delta configuration joining the elevators to make one long, slim, lifting surface.

As if controlled by one man, the two aircraft tipped noses towards the sky and screamed upward in a terrifyingly fast climb until they were only tiny silver dots, banking away to the north.

"Fencers," Bond breathed.

"What? Fencers?" Paula scowled.

"Fencers. It's the NATO code name for them." Bond's eyes moved constantly, watching the sky for the next wave which, he knew, would bring in the first attack. "They're Su-19's. Very dangerous. Ground attack fighter-bombers. They pack a nasty punch, Paula." In the back of his head Bond could almost hear the details of the Fencer clicking through, like a computer read-out. Power: two afterburning turbofans, or jets, of the 9525-kg thrust class. Speed: Mach 1.25 at sea level; Mach 2.5 at altitude. Service Ceiling: 60,000 feet; initial climb 40,000 feet per minute. Armament: one 23-mm GSh-23 twin-barrel cannon fitted on lower centerline, and a minimum of six pylons for a variety of air-to-air and air-to-ground guided, and unguided, missiles. Combat Radius: 500 miles with full weapons.

That all added up to a most efficient, and lethal, piece of war plane. Not even the most optimistic of NATO airmen could deny it.

Having spotted their target, the two leaders would, Bond thought, call up the rest of their squadron—or even wing—and pass on the coordinates and instructions, probably tapping them out on a small keyboard.

Already they would have been briefed on the order of attack, and the fast reconnaissance assured it would come in a series of angled dives, around forty-five degrees—maybe from different directions, the pairs of aircraft vectored and controlled to come in with split-second timing, one after the other.

Bond thought of the Soviet pilots—top men to be flying the Fencers—concentrating on their electronics, speed, height, timing, and angle of dive; priming their weapons; glancing constantly at the sky, sweating under their G-suits and helmets.

The first approach growl came from their left, followed almost immediately by a second from what seemed to be directly above. "Here we go!" Bond saw Paula's head turn as he looked up, and the twin streaks came tearing out of the now clear bluish sky to their left.

He had been right. The Fencers came in pairs and with noses down in a classic ground-attack dive. Quite clearly they saw the first missiles flash away from the wings: long white flames shooting back, then the orange trails as the deadly darts ripped through the air. Two from each aircraft, all four catching the front of the bunker, boring in and exploding with wide orange blossoms of fire that reached their eyes before the heavy zoom and whump hit their ears.

As the first two aircraft whipped to the left, flick-turning away, so the second pair came down from Bond's and Paula's right. The same plumes of flame shot out, then fire bloomed from within the target area.

The missiles were digging well into the rock, steel and concrete before exploding. Bond watched, fascinated, trying to identify the weaponry.

As the third pair came in from the far right, he was able to follow the missiles through their complete trajectory—AS-7's, he thought, Kerries to NATO, and the Kerry came in several specifications, both guided and unguided. They also had changeable warheads—straight HE or armor—and rock-penetrating delayed charges.

Below, after just three attacks using twelve Kerry missiles, the Ice Palace looked ready to be broken in two. The thunder of the explosions still echoed from below, and through the inevitable pall of smoke, they could see the terrible crimson glow of fire begin to sweep out of the open main doors, up from the arms stores and vehicle parks.

Then a fourth and fifth wave of Fencers hurtled out of the cold sky, their rockets seeming to hang in the air for a moment as the aircraft turned away and lifted in a whining climb, before shooting forward. Straight as ruled lines of fire, the rockets disappeared into the smoke and flame, to explode a few seconds later with twin roars which seemed to grow successively louder.

From their grandstand view, the Lapp, Paula and Bond could not draw their eyes from this sight of deliberate destruction. The sky now seemed full of aircraft—one pair following another with the accuracy of some crack air display team. Their ears were pounded with supersonic shock waves and lightning strikes as the rockets found their marks again and again.

The bunker became almost invisible, its presence marked by the tower of black smoke and the constant crimson fists punching within the dark cloud.

The attack, which could only have taken seven or eight minutes, seemed to go on for hours. Finally, a pair of Fencers came in from their left, at an unusually low angle of attack. The aircraft had exhausted their missiles and began to rake the smoke and flame with cannon fire.

Both aircraft pulled up short, their track taking them low and directly through the rising smoke. Just as they disappeared into the black cloud there was a great rumble, followed by an almost volcanic roar.

At first Bond thought the Fencers had touched wings and collided over the target; then the black smoke turned into a huge fireball, spreading outwards, growing in size, first orange turning to white and, last, a bloody crimson. The ground shook and they could feel the snow and earth moving under them, as though an earthquake had, against all the laws of nature, suddenly been activated.

Heat scorched their faces as the fireball rose past them. Tongues of licking flame reached out for them or wound themselves around the trees. Then the updraft came like a twisting tornado, the whole engulfed by a colossal noise as the explosion sound hit them. Bond's hand shot out, banging Paula's head into the snow as he buried his face, holding his breath.

The heat receded at last. The two aircraft had gone. Disappeared. Looking up, they could see other planes gaining height and circling. It was when Bond looked down that the picture became clear.

Where the bunker had been, there was now only a huge crater surrounded by burning or bent trees. Fires spouted from deep down in the ground, and you could see the uncanny sight of odd pieces of masonry, steps and steel girders hanging free above a maze of open walls and broken passages. The wreckage looked like a bombed building that had been dropped into a chasm.

The explosions and fires caused by the constant penetration of the Kerry missiles had eventually blown all the loaded ammunition, bombs, gasoline and other war matériel in one comprehensive detonation. The result was total destruction of von Glöda's Ice Palace.

Smoke billowed up and then drifted away; there was the occasional spurt of flame, mixed with fires already well burning. Apart from the odd crackling noise, though, there was no other sound. Only the terrible smell of desolation wafted up towards their perch, above what had once been a deep and seemingly impregnable fortress.

You could even make out the remains of the main arterial passages and the occasional nest of rooms. The ground, with its tracks around the bunker, seemed to have become one giant rubbish dump, though part of the metal chain runway still snaked out from the trees, twisted and lopsided, studded with rocks.

"Kristos," breathed Paula. "Whatever else happens to Kolya, he's had his vengeance."

It was only when she spoke that they realized their own sense of hearing had returned.

Still slightly dazed by what they had witnessed, they made their way back to the former site of Paula's encampment, and Bond headed towards the point where Knut was guarding Mosolov within the woods.

He spotted it before anyone else, reacting sharply with quick gestures to the Lapps to fan out and get down. Dropping to the ground himself, he pushed Paula down with him.

"You stay here," he commanded quietly. All Bond's senses were now alert, and the P7 was heavy in his hand. "Tell your people to cover me if anything happens."

Paula nodded, her face pale.

Bond ran forward through the trees, crouching and ready for anything. The evil-faced Knut appeared even more bizarre in death. By the marks in the snow, Bond reckoned that four of them had taken him, using knives for silence. The Lapp's throat was slit, but there were other wounds, signifying this was only the final act in a struggle. Knut had fought, even though taken by surprise.

Of Kolya Mosolov there was no sign, and even the most dim-witted person would quickly realize this was not the most healthy place to linger. As he made his way back to Paula, Bond wondered if the scooters had been left intact, and whether Kolya would launch his counterattack straight away.

Paula did not take the news well. Later she was to tell Bond that Knut had worked with her for many years and had been one of her most loyal operators on the Russian side of the border. But now she passed the news to the others without even a shake in her voice. Only by looking closely could you see how badly Knut's death had hit her.

Bond issued the orders quickly and clearly. One of the Lapps was to check out the snow scooters. If they were still hidden and working, Bond decided, the party would have to go for a fast getaway. The main and obvious fear was that the men who had rescued Kolya were still nearby, and ready to pounce. "Make sure your boys're prepared to fight now—and I mean fight their way out if necessary," he told Paula.

Trifon went forward, returning in a matter of minutes with the news that the scooters were untouched, with no tracks to indicate they had been found.

Bond understood now why the Lapps had proved such a formidable enemy against the might of the Russian army in 1939. They moved through the trees with speed and cunning, leap-frogging, covering each other as they went and becoming at times almost invisible, even to Bond.

Paula stayed close, for she was to lead the party out. As Bond reached the scooters with her, the three Lapps were just starting the engines. The roar of four scooters seemed to shake the trees, and Bond expected bullets to rain in on them at any moment.

Paula was in the saddle of the big Yamaha—with Bond behind her—in a matter of seconds, and they were away, gathering speed and zigzagging through the trees, heading south. No trouble so far.

The ride took the best part of two hours, and Bond—even in the cold and uncomfortable position behind Paula—was aware of the three Lapps circling them, spreading out, covering against ambush all the way. At one point, when they slowed through some particularly rough ground, Bond imagined he could hear the sound of other engines—other scooters. Of one thing he was certain: Kolya Mosolov would not let them get away scot-free to Finland. Either he was following them, or already waiting, calculating the point where Paula intended to make the last long dash to freedom.

Finally they stopped, taking up station among trees above the great open valley separating Russia from Finland, which runs like a dry artificial river from north to south.

Bond decided they should immediately take up defensive positions. He stayed with Paula beside the big Yamaha, while the three Lapps disappeared further into the trees, forming a triangle around Paula and Bond. There they would wait until it was dark enough to make the run back into Finland.

"You're confident about making it?" Bond asked Paula, testing her own nerve and will. "I mean I'd rather not end up by going over a mine."

Paula was silent for a few seconds. "If you want to walk it by yourself . . ." she began, with an edge to her voice.

"I've every confidence in you, Paula." Behind the Yamaha, Bond leaned over and kissed her. She was trembling, but not from the cold, and James Bond knew well enough how she felt. If Kolya was going to act while they were still on the Russian side, it would be soon.

Slowly the light began to go, and Bond felt the tension starting to build within him. Trifon had settled himself into a high point among the branches of a pine tree. Bond could not see him—indeed had not even spotted him making the ascent—but knew only because the Lapp had told Paula exactly where he was going.

Try as he would, straining his eyes, Bond still could not see the man, and the fast-fading light made it constantly more difficult. Suddenly the blue moment was on them that blue green haze reflecting from the snow, changing perspective.

"Ready?" Bond turned to Paula and saw her nod. In the second his eyes left the pine in which he knew Trifon was hidden, they heard the first shot.

It came directly from the pine tree, so the Lapp had got in before Kolya's men. The sound still echoed in the air when the next shots followed. They seemed to be coming from a semicircle to the front, within the trees: single rounds followed by the lethal rip of machine gun fire.

It was impossible to tell the enemy strength, or even if they were making progress. All Bond knew was that a fire fight of some vigor appeared to be developing to their front.

Though the blue moment had not entirely dropped them to darkness, there was no point in waiting. Paula had already said that the Lapps were prepared to hold off anything Kolya sent in while they tried to make their escape. Now was the time to put the promise to the test.

"Go!" Bond shouted at Paula.

Like the professional she was, Paula did not hesitate. The Yamaha's engine fired, and Bond was up behind Paula as she slewed the machine diagonally into the open and down the bare icy slope towards the valley, naked of trees, that would lead to safety.

The gunfire was louder, and the last thing Bond saw, through a fine spray of snow, was a figure falling, toppling from the branches of the pine. It was not the right moment to tell Paula that Trifon had joined his friend Knut.

By the time they had covered half a kilometer, darkness surrounded them, and the noise of firing still came from behind them. The last two Lapps were putting up a strong fight. Bond knew, though, that it would only be a matter of time, and a great deal depended on Kolya Mosolov's strength. Would he try to follow on high-powered scooters? Or, as a tactician, would the Russian prefer to spray the valley with fire?

The answer came as they neared the valley floor, with three or four kilometers of hard riding to go before they reached the far slope and safety.

Over the engine noise Bond detected a sound high above them. Then the terrain was lighted by a parachute flare, throwing an eerie dazzling light across the packed snow and ice.

"Is it safe to zigzag?" he yelled in Paula's ear, thinking of the mine fields.

She turned her head, shouting back: "We'll soon find out!" She hauled on the handlebars so that they slewed violently sideways, just as Bond heard the ominous crack of bullets breaking the air to their left.

Again Paula heaved the handlebars, working with a strength drawn from those hidden reserves all people find in desperate moments. The scooter skidded and swerved, sometimes zigzagging, then moving broadside on, then straight with throttle wide open.

The first flare was dying but the bullets still cracked around them, and twice Bond watched the long, almost lazy lines of tracer falling in front of them—reds and greens—first left, and then to their right.

They both automatically crouched low on the scooter, and Bond felt an odd sense of mingled anger and frustration. It took him a moment to detect the cause, then he realized his instincts had been to stay on the Russian side of the ridge and fight Kolya Mosolov instead of running. His head buzzed with the old jingle, "He who fights and runs away, lives to fight another day." But it was not natural to Bond's character to run from a fight. Deep inside him, though, he was aware that it was necessary. Both Paula and he had a job to complete—to return safely—and this was their only chance.

The tracers still kept coming, even though the flare had gone out. Then another small explosion heralded a second flare, and this time the guns ceased firing. instead came the terrifying noise of a fast-approaching express train: at least that was what it sounded like until the mortar bomb landed, well behind and to their left. It made a solid, ear-ringing crump, followed by a second and third: all behind them.

Paula was taking the Yamaha to its limit, relying on the straight runs for speed. There were moments, as Bond clung to her, when he thought they would leave the ground completely. Then the screech of mortar bombs came again, this time to their right and ahead. Three violent orange flashes played havoc with their eyesight in the dark, the dazzling after-flash lingering on the retina.

The first mortars had fallen behind them, Bond realized. Now they were in front. It meant only one thing: that Kolya's men were bracketing their target. Chances were that the next bombs would fall level with them.

Unless Paula could outrun the range.

She certainly did her best. Throttle wide open, the Yamaha skimmed ice and snow; through the white gloom, the far rise—the trees and Finland—loomed like a shadow in the blackness.

There was one more bad moment when they heard the distant thump, then the hiss of falling bombs for the last time. But Paula's burst of speed had given them the lead. There were half a dozen explosions this time, but all were behind them and well off line. Now, unless they hit a mine—and there had already been plenty of opportunity to do that—they would make it.

Earlier, even as Paula and Bond made their desperate dash for the Finnish border, two men climbed from the rocks near the smashed and flaming bunker of von Glöda's ruined Ice Palace. There was no one to observe them in the gathering dusk.

Since the horrors of that morning's attack, the men had worked frantically in the only tiny fragment of the bunker that had remained, miraculously, intact—one steel and concrete pen housing a small, gray Cessna 150 Commuter, with ski attachments on its tricycle undercarriage. As the light failed, so they finally managed to swing the buckled doors free.

The aircraft seemed undamaged, though the runway ahead had been gutted and strewn with debris. The taller of the men gave a few friendly instructions to his companion, who had worked so hard. Willingly, the man trudged out onto the runway, shifting what he could, clearing a few hundred yards of makeshift pathway in front of the Cessna.

The plane's engine started with a sporadic cough, then settled down to warm into its comfortable hum.

The other figure returned, climbed in beside the taller man, and the little aircraft gingerly moved forward, as though its pilot was testing the strength of the runway beneath him.

Then the pilot turned to his companion, giving him the thumbs-up sign, and pushed down the flap control to give maximum lift. A second later, he gently opened the throttle. The engine rose to full revolutions and the Cessna bumped forward, gathering speed, the pilot craning, slewing the aircraft from side to side to avoid the worst sections of the runway. With a bump, the Cessna hit a short straight patch of ice, seemed to snatch at an extra few kph of ground speed, and began to skim the rough surface.

Trees loomed ahead of them, growing taller by the sercond. The pilot felt that moment of response from his craft as the weight transferred safely to the wings. Gently he eased back on the yoke. The Cessna's nose came up. She seemed to hesitate for a second, then thrust forward, balanced only a short distance from the ground but gaining air speed with every second.

The pilot eased back a little more, his left hand holding the throttle fully open, then winding back on the trim to give the aircraft a shade more weight in the tail.

The propeller grabbed at the sky. The nose fell slightly, then the propeller grabbed again, clawed at the air and sent it barreling back over the flying surfaces until the small plane was stable, nose up and climbing.

They cleared the top of the fir trees by a matter of inches.

Count Konrad von Glöda smiled, set a course, and headed the climbing Cessna towards his next goal. This day might have been a defeat, even a crushing one, but he was not through yet. There were legions of men waiting to come under his command. But first, there was one score to be settled. Gratefully he nodded at the craggy face of Hans Buchtman, whom Bond had known as "Bad" Brad Tirpitz.

Paula and Bond reached the Hotel Revontuli at two o'clock in the morning, and Bond went straight to the Saab to send a cipher back to M. He was particularly careful in his wording of the cipher.

When he got to Reception there was a note waiting for him. It read:

We are in suite No. 5, my darling James. Can we sleep in please, and not leave for Helsinki until the afternoon? All Love, Paula.

P.S. I'm not really all that tired at the moment, and have ordered champagne and some of this hotel's rather excellent smoked salmon.

With a certain amount of satisfaction, Bond remembered Paula's hidden delights and particular expertise. Spryly he walked to the lift.

19

LOOSE ENDS

THEY TALKED ALMOST the whole way back to Helsinki in the Saab.

"There're a lot of things I still need to know," Bond had begun soon after they left Salla, now fresh, relaxed, shaved, showered and changed into clean clothing.

"Such as?" Paula was in one of those cat-who's-licked-the-cream moods. Changed and dressed in furs, looking more like a woman than what she had called "a bundle of thermal underwear," Paula shook out her lovely blond hair and snuggled her head against Bond's shoulder.

"When did your Service—SUPO—first suspect Aarne Tudeer, or Count von Glöda as he likes to call himself?"

She smiled, looking very pleased with herself. "That was my idea. You know, James, I've never worked out why you didn't cotton on to me years ago. I know my cover was good, but you didn't even suspect."

"I was foolish enough to accept you at face value," Bond said, taking a deep breath. "I did have you checked out once. Nothing came back. It's easy to say it now, but there were times when I wondered how we managed to bump into each other so often in faraway places."

"Ah."

"And you haven't answered my question," Bond persisted.

"Well, we knew he was up to something. I mean all that business about me being a schoolfriend of Anni Tudeer is absolutely true. Her mother *did* bring her back home, and I *did* meet her. But when I heard, officially, long after SUPO had recruited me, that Anni had joined Mossad I just couldn't believe it."

"Why?"

For a second Bond's mind drifted away from the road. Any mention of Anni Tudeer was bound to bring back unpleasant memories.

"Why didn't I believe she was a genuine Mossad agent?" Paula did not hesitate. "I knew her too well. She was the apple of Aarne Tudeer's eye. She also loved him dearly. I knew as only a woman can know. Partly it was some of the things she said; partly intuition. Everyone knew about her father—of course they did—there was never any secret. Anni's secret was that she had been brainwashed by him. I think that, even as a child, he had mapped out what part she would play. Almost certainly he was in constant touch with her, advising and instructing her. He was the one person who could teach Anni how to penetrate Mossad."

"Which she did very well." Bond glanced at the pretty face next to him. "Why did you mention her name to me? That first time when I questioned you, following the knife fight at your place?"

She sighed, "Why do you think, James? I was in a very difficult situation. It was the only way I could pass on some kind of clue."

"All right. Now tell me the whole story."

Paula Vacker had been in on the entire NSAA affair from the start—even from before the first incident at Tripoli. SUPO, through informers and observation, knew that Tudeer had returned to Finland, taken on the name of von Glöda, and appeared to be up to something just over the border, in Russia. "After every possible intelligence agency was called in on the National Socialist Action Army, I suggested it could be the work of Tudeer," she told him. "For my pains, my masters ordered that I infiltrate. So I put myself in the right places and said the right things. It got back. I was a good healthy Aryan Nazi."

Eventually von Glöda had made contact. "I was finally appointed to his staff as resident in Helsinki. In other words I was doubling with the full knowledge of my superiors."

"Who refrained from passing information to my Service?" There were many things that still puzzled Bond.

"No. They were, in fact, preparing a dossier. Then the storm broke over at the Ice Palace—over Blue Hare—and there was no need to make any reports. Kolya's superiors set up Icebreaker, and I was supposed to be there for your protection. I gather your Service was put in the picture—late on—after you'd left for the Ice Palace."

Bond pondered on this for a few kilometers. Eventually he said, "I find it hard to swallow—the whole business about Icebreaker and the deal with Kolya."

"It would be difficult to believe unless you were actually there, unless you really got to know von Glöda's deviousness, and Kolya Mosolov's cunning mind." She gave her delightful laugh. "They were both egomaniacs, and power mad, though each in his own way, you understand. I did the journey from Helsinki to the Arctic and across to the bunker a dozen times, you know. I was also there, and trusted, when the balloon went up."

"What? Blue Hare?"

"Yes. That was all absolutely genuine. You have to take your hat off to Tudeer, or von Glöda. He had nerve. Incredible nerve. Mind you, I think the Soviets were keeping more of an eye on him than he imagined."

"I wonder." Bond took an icy bend a little fast, swore, left-footed the brake, came out of the skid with power, and had the car under control all in a matter of seconds. "You know, a British general has said that the Russians should be awarded the wooden spoon for ineptitude. They can do the most stupid things. Tell me about what happened with Blue Hare."

Paula was well accepted within the so-called Führer's inner circle. "He seldom let us forget how clever he was in bribing those stupid NCO's at Blue Hare. He really did pay them a pittance for the equipment; and they didn't seem to think about being caught."

"But they were."

"Indeed they were. I was there when it all happened. The fat little warrant officer came dashing up to the bunker. Like the rest of them, he was really only a peasant in uniform. Stank to high heaven, but von Glöda was terrific with him. I have to admit the man could be exceptionally cool in moments of crisis. But of course he believed in his destiny as the new Führer. Nothing could go wrong, and every man had his price. I heard him tell the Blue Hare CO to get the Army people to call in the GRU. He knew they would pass it on to the KGB. Oddly it worked. Quicker than a wink, Kolya Mosolov was there."

"And asked for my head on a charger."

Paula gave a secretive smile. "It wasn't quite like that. Kolya had no intention of ever letting von Glöda get away with it. He simply played along, gave him some rope. You know the Russians; Kolya's one chink was that he wanted to bury the problem of Blue Hare. On the other hand, I think von Glöda saw himself as the Devil tempting Christ. He actually offered Kolya his heart's desire."

"And Kolya said: J. Bond, Esquire?"

"Von Glöda's madness was power to control the world. Kolya did not think that big. All he wanted was to bury Blue Hare—which meant doing away with von Glöda's setup. He could have dealt with it all in a couple of days, on his own. But von Glöda, being the kind of man he was, set his own delusions of grandeur to work. In turn they fired Kolya's imagination."

Bond nodded. "Kolya, what do you want in all the world? Kolya thinks—*You* swept out of the way, Comrade von Glöda; and the Blue Hare business hushed up. Fame and promotion for me. Then, aloud, he says Bond—James Bond."

"That's it. The old SMERSH—Department V as they now are—wanted you. So he asked for you." She began to laugh again, finding it all very funny. "Then, von Glöda had the gall to do a deal which meant that Kolya had to work, very hard. After all, it was through Kolya that the CIA, Mossad and your Service were brought in; it was through Kolya that you, James, were asked for personally; it was Kolya who set everything up."

"Under the instructions of von Glöda? It somehow doesn't ring true."

"No. No, James, it doesn't, until you take into account the personalities involved, and their motivations. I told you, Kolya had no intention of letting von Glöda get away with it. But his own private thirst for power and advancement allowed him to use the whole of von Glöda's organization for the one purpose of luring you into Russia. It took a lot of doing—the specially printed maps, the replacement of Tirpitz . . ."

"Getting Rivke appointed to the team?" Bond suggested.

"Von Glöda suggested that Kolya should ask for her, just as he suggested Tirpitz from the Americans. Kolya, of course, wanted you—he spent hours using von Glöda's telephone, talking to Moscow Center. They were sticky about it to begin with, but Kolya concocted some kind of tale. His superiors agreed and put in their formal requests to America, Israel and Britain. Everyone was furious when you couldn't be brought in straight away. The fellow Buchtman arrived first. He was some contact of von Glöda's, and they sent him off to meet the real Tirpitz and dispose of him. Then Rivke arrived in Finland. That was very worrying. I had to keep clear most of the time. Von Glöda appointed me as liaison officer to Kolya, which was handy, and by this time Moscow Center had given Kolya a free hand. They simply thought he was clearing up some nest of dissidents on the Finnish border and wiping the slate clean of Blue Hare, using the Americans, British and Israelis as fall guys if anything went wrong. I suppose they imagined that the NSAA was only a small cell of fanatics."

She paused, took one of Bond's cigarettes, then continued. "For me, Rivke was the most difficult part. I did not dare see her, and Kolya wanted messages passed to her in Helsinki. I had to do it through a third party. Then everyone was really waiting for a chance to have you brought out. Rivke came into play when von Glöda hatched this little scheme, as a standby . . ."

"Which particular scheme?"

She sighed, "The one that made me very jealous. That Rivke should worm her way into your heart, then disappear in case von Glöda needed to use her to trap you. The business on the ski slope took one hell of a lot of organization—and not a little nerve on Anni's part. But then, she was always a good gymnast . . . As you certainly discovered," she added with a bitchy intonation.

Bond grunted. "You think von Glöda had any idea that he wasn't going to be allowed to get away with it?"

"Oh, he suspected Kolya enough. He didn't trust him. That was why I liaisoned with the Russians. Von Glöda had to know everything. Then, of course, we got to the point where our noble Führer needed to know about the man your people captured in England. You were already under sentence of death. So was Kolya. Von Glöda's plan was to get all his people out to Norway."

"Norway? That was where his new command post had been built?"

"So my chiefs tell me. But they also knew of another hiding place he had in Finland. I should imagine that was where everyone was going when Kolya's air strike was called in."

They traveled in silence for a long way, Bond going over the facts in his mind. "Well," he said finally. "My trouble is that von Glöda's the first real enemy against whom I've had to pit my wits at long range. Most of my assignments allow me to get close; to know the man I'm dealing with. Von Glöda never let me really come near him."

"It was his strength. He didn't let anyone gain his complete confidence— even that woman he toted around with him. I think Anni—Rivke—was the only one who really knew him."

"And you didn't?" Bond's voice was laced with suspicion.

"What do you mean?" Paula's tone turned cold, as though offended.

"I mean there are times I'm not completely certain of you, Paula."

Paula gave a sharp intake of breath. "After all I've done?"

"Even after all you've done. For instance, what about the pair of thugs at your place? The knife merchants?"

She nodded quietly. "I wondered when you'd get back to them." She edged away, turning her body towards him. "You think I set you up?"

"It's crossed my mind."

Paula bit her lip. "No, dear James," she sighed. "No, I didn't set you up. I let you down. How can I explain it? As I said, neither von Glöda nor Kolya were playing it straight. Everyone was in a no-win situation, as they say. I worked under SUPO's instructions, and also von Glöda's orders. The situation became impossible once I was put in charge of liaison with Kolya. He was always in and out of Helsinki. You turned up out of the blue, and my chiefs had to be told. I let you down, James. I shouldn't have said anything."

"What you're trying to say is SUPO ordered you to inform Kolya? Right?"

She nodded. "He saw a way to get you in Helsinki, then whip you up to the Arctic and into Russia all on his own. Sorry."

"And what about the snow plows?"

"What snow plows?" Her mood changed. A few moments before Paula had been on the defensive, then contrite. Now she was plain surprised. Bond told her about the trouble on the way from Helsinki to Salla.

She thought for a minute. "My guess would be Kolya again. I know he had the airport and hotels watched by his own people—Helsinki, I mean. They would know where you were heading. I think Kolya would have gone to a lot of trouble to tuck you under his arm and get you into Russia without using any of von Glöda's formulas."

By the end of the journey Bond was virtually convinced by Paula's explanations. As he had said, there had never been time for him to get really close to the autocratic, iron-haired von Glöda; and he understood from past experience the strange power clash between two determined men like von Glöda and Kolya.

"Your place or mine?" Bond asked as they reached the outskirts of Helsinki. He was almost satisfied with Paula's answers, true, but a tiny niggle of doubt remained in a corner of his mind, for nothing in Operation Icebreaker had been what it seemed. Time now to play his trump card.

"We can't go to my place." Paula gave a small cough. "It's in a hell of a mess and roughed up—it got burgled, James, for real. I didn't even have time to report it to the police."

Bond pulled the car over to the side of the road and stopped. "I know." He reached over to the glove compartment, taking out von Glöda's Knight's Cross and the Campaign Shield and dropping them on Paula's lap. "I found these on your dressing table when I called there and discovered the place wrecked, on my way to the party in the Arctic."

For a second, Paula was angry. "Then why the hell didn't you use them? You could've shown them to Anni."

Bond patted her hand. "I did. She identified them. Which made me concerned, also very suspicious. Of you. Where did you get them?"

"From von Glöda, of course. He wanted them cleaned up. The man was obsessively proud of them, just as he was obsessive about his destiny." She made a disgusted noise in the back of her throat. "Oh, hell, I might have known that bitch would turn them on to me."

Bond took the medals and threw them into the glove compartment. "Okay," he said, relieved. "You pass. Let's give ourselves a treat. We'll take the honeymoon suite at the Inter-Continental. How about that?"

"How *about* that?" She squeezed his hand, running a finger across the palm.

They had no difficulty checking in, and the Inter-Continental's twenty-four-hour room service provided food and drink with the minimum delay. The drive, the explanations, and their long relationship together seemed to have taken away all the barriers.

"I'm going to shower," Paula announced. Then we can enjoy ourselves to our heart's content. I don't know about you, but there's no need for either of our Services to realize we're back in Helsinki for at least another twenty-four hours."

"You don't think we should call in? We can always say we're still on the road," Bond suggested.

Paula thought it over. "Oh, maybe I'll dial my answering service later. If my controller has anything urgent, he leaves a number for me. What about you?"

"Have your shower, then I'll follow you. I don't honestly think M would appreciate anything from me until the morning."

She gave a dazzling smile and headed for the bathroom, lugging her one small overnight case.

20

DESTINY

J<small>AMES</small> B<small>OND</small> <small>DREAMED</small>. It was a dream he often experienced: sun, and a beach, which he recognized only too well as the seafront at Royale-les-Eaux. It was the five-mile promenade as it used to be, of course, not the garish, package-tour joint it had since become. In Bond's dream, life and time stood still, and this was the place he remembered from both childhood and his younger years.

A band played. The tricolor beds of salvia, alyssum and lobelia bloomed in a riot of color. And it was warm, and he was happy.

The dream often came when he was happy; and that night had certainly brought happiness. Together Bond and Paula had escaped from the clutches of Kolya Mosolov, made their way to Helsinki, and there—well, things had gone even better than they themselves expected.

Paula returned from the bathroom looking like several million dollars, dressed only in a see-through nightdress, her body glowing and her scent as seductive as Bond had ever known it.

Before showering, Bond tapped out a call to London—a number reserved especially for taped messages from M. If there was anything new he would hear it now, in answer to the cipher sent from the Saab at Salla.

Sure enough, M's voice was on the line: a brief doubletalk message which came quite near to congratulating Bond, and also confirmed that Paula was known to be working for SUPO. There could, Bond thought, be no more surprises.

Paula had taken the initiative, making love to him as a kind of hors d'oeuvre; then, after a short rest during which Paula talked and laughed about their brush with disaster, Bond started where she had left off.

Now there was peace, safety and warmth. Warmth, except for a cold spot developing on his neck, behind the ear. Still half-asleep, Bond brushed at the cold spot. His hand came into contact with something hard, and vaguely unpleasant. His eyes snapped open and he felt the cold object pressed against his neck. Gone was Royale-les-Eaux, replaced with uncompromising reality.

"Just sit up quietly, Mr. Bond."

Bond's head turned to see Kolya Mosolov stepping away from him. A heavy Stechkin—made even more bulky by a noise reduction system around the barrel—pointed, out of reach, at Bond's throat.

"How . . . ?" Bond began. Then, thinking of Paula, he turned to see her sound asleep beside him.

Mosolov laughed—a chuckle, almost out of character, but Kolya was a man of so many voices. "Don't worry about Paula," he said, soft and confident. "You must've both been very tired. I managed to deal with the lock, administer a small injection, and move around without disturbing either of you."

Bond cursed silently. This was so unlike him, to drop his guard and allow sleep to take over so completely. He had done everything else. He even recalled sweeping the room for electronics the moment they arrived.

"What kind of injection?" Trying not to sound concerned.

"She'll sleep peacefully for six or seven hours. Enough time for us to do what has to be done."

"Which is?"

Mosolov made a motion with the Stechkin. "Get dressed. There's a job I have to see completed. After that we're going on a little journey. I even have a brand new passport—just to be certain. We leave Helsinki by car, then helicopter, and later there'll be a jet waiting. By the time Paula can alert anyone, we'll be well on our way."

Bond shrugged. There was little he could do, though his hand moved unobtrusively to the pillow under which he had placed the P7 before finally going to sleep. Kolya Mosolov reached inside his padded jacket, which he wore open, to show Bond the P7 tucked into his waistband. "I thought it safer—for me, that is."

Bond put his feet on the floor. He looked up at the Russian. "You don't give up easily, do you, Mosolov?"

"My future rests on taking you in."

"Dead or alive it would seem." Bond got to his feet.

"Preferably alive. The business at the frontier was exceptionally worrying in that respect. But now I can finish what was started."

"I don't understand it." Bond began to move towards the chair, on which some of his clothes were folded. "Your people could have had me at any time in the past few years. Why now?"

"Just get dressed."

Bond began to do as he was told, but continued to talk. "Tell me why, Kolya. Tell me why now?"

"Because the time is right. Moscow's wanted you for years. There was a period when they wanted you for death, and death only. Now things have changed. I'm glad you survived. I admit to using bad judgment in letting our troops fire on you—the heat of the moment, you understand."

Bond grunted.

"Now, as I said, things have changed," Mosolov continued. "We simply wish to verify certain information. First we'll do a chemical interrogation to clean you out. Then we'll have a nice little asset to exchange. You've got a pair of our people who've done sterling work at General Communications Headquarters in Cheltenham. In due course an exchange will be arranged, I'm sure."

"Is that why Moscow went along with all this in the first place? The games played with von Glöda and his crazies?"

"Oh, partly." Kolya Mosolov jerked his pistol. "Look, just get on with it. There's another job to be done before we leave Helsinki."

Bond climbed into his ski pants. "*Partly*, Kolya? *Partly?* Bit of an expensive operation, wasn't it? Just to get me—and you damned near killed me doing it."

"Playing along with von Glöda's wild schemes helped get rid of other small embarrassments."

"Like Blue Hare?"

"Blue Hare, and other things. Von Glöda's death is a foregone conclusion."

"*Is?*" Bond looked up sharply.

Kolya Mosolov nodded. "Amazing really. Wasn't that some display our ground attack boys gave? You wouldn't have thought anybody could survive. Yet von Glöda managed to get out."

Bond found it difficult to believe. Certainly M had not known. He asked where the fantasy leader of the Fourth Reich was now hiding.

"He's here." Mosolov spoke as though the information was obvious. "In Helsinki. Regrouping, or so he would say. Reorganizing. Ready to start all over again, unless he is stopped. I have to do the stopping. It would be embarrassing, to say the least, if von Glöda was allowed to continue his operations."

Bond was now almost dressed. "You're taking me out—back to Russia. You also intend to deal with von Glöda?" He adjusted the collar of his rollneck.

"Oh yes. You're part of my plan, Mr. Bond. I have to get rid of friend von Glöda, or Aarne Tudeer, or whatever he wishes to call himself on his tombstone. The timing is good . . ."

"What is the time?" Bond asked.

Kolya, always the professional, did not even glance at his watch. "About seven forty-five in the morning. As I was saying, the timing is good. You see, von Glöda has some of his own people here in Helsinki. He leaves for London, via Paris, this morning. I gather the madman imagines he can stage some kind of rally in London. There's also the question of an NSAA prisoner being held by your Service, I think. Naturally, he also wants to take his revenge on you, Bond. So, I consider it best to offer you as a target. He cannot resist that."

"Hardly," Bond answered crisply. Already he had felt a tidal wave of depression sluice over him at the thought of von Glöda being still alive. Now he was to be used as bait—not for the first time since all this began Bond's whole spirit revolted against the idea. There had to be a way. If anyone was going to get von Glöda, it would be Bond.

Mosolov was still speaking. "Von Glöda's flight leaves at nine. It would be a nice touch if James Bond was seated in his own car, outside Vantaa Airport. That very fact should lure Comrade von Glöda from the departure building. He will not know that I have my own ways—old-fashioned, perhaps, of making certain that you will sit quietly in the car: handcuffs, another small injection, a little different from the one I gave to Paula." He nodded towards the bed. Paula still slept soundly.

"You're mad." Though he said it, Bond knew he was the one person whose presence could lure von Glöda. "How would you do it?"

Mosolov's smile was sly now. "Your motor car, Mr. Bond. It's fitted with a rather special telephone, I believe?"

"Not many people know about that." Bond was genuinely annoyed. Mosolov had found out about the telephone. He wondered what else the Russian knew.

"Well, I do; and I have the details. The base unit for your car telephone needs to go through an ordinary phone, linking the system to that of the country in which you operate. For instance, the base unit can be fitted to the phone in this room. All we do is wire in your base unit here, and drive out to the airport. By the time we get there you will be handcuffed and unable to move. But just before we arrive, I use the car phone, call the information desk, and ask them to page von Glöda. He will receive a message—that Mr. James Bond is outside, in the car park, alone and incapacitated. I think I could even leave the message in Paula's name, she wouldn't mind. When von Glöda comes out I shall be near him." He patted the silenced Stechkin. "With a weapon like this, people will think it's a heart attack—at least to begin with. By the time they get to the truth, we shall be well away. I already have another car standing by. It will all be very quick."

"No chance. You'll never get away with it," Bond said aloud, though he knew there was every possibility of Mosolov getting away with it. This was the audacious, impossible act which so often works. But Bond grasped at a straw. Mosolov had made one error—that of imagining the Saab's telephone required a base unit fitted to the main phone system. This would be a local call, and the electronics in the car had an operating range of around twenty-five miles. An error like this one was just what Bond needed.

"So," Kolya hefted the Stechkin in his hand. "Just give me the car keys. We'll go together. You can tell me how to get at the base unit."

Bond pretended to think for a full minute.

"You have no alternative," Mosolov repeated.

"You're right," Bond said at last, "I have no alternative. I resent coming to Moscow with you, Mosolov, but I am also anxious to see von Glöda out of the way. Getting the base unit's a tricky business. There are various routines I have to go through with the locks to the hiding place, but you can have me covered all the time. I'm ready. Why don't we do it now, straight away?"

Kolya nodded, glanced at the prostrate Paula, then thrust the Stechkin inside his jacket. He gestured for Bond to take the car key and the keys to the room, then to go on ahead of him.

All the way down the corridor, Mosolov stayed a good three paces behind Bond. In the lift, he remained in one corner—as far away as possible. The Russian was well trained, no doubt about that. One move from Bond and the Stechkin would make its muffled pop, leaving 007 with a gaping hole in his vitals.

They went down to the car park, heading for the Saab. About three paces from the car Bond turned. "I have to take the key from my pocket. Okay?"

Kolya said nothing, just nodded an affirmative, moving the big pistol inside his coat to remind Bond it was there. Bond took out the key, his eyes darting around. Nobody else was in the car park, not a soul in sight. Ice crunched under his feet, and he felt the sweat trickle down his armpits inside the warm clothing. It was fully light.

They reached the car. Bond unlocked the driver's side door, then turned back to Kolya. "I have to switch the ignition on—not fire the engine, just put on the electrics to operate the lock," he said.

Again Kolya nodded as Bond leaned across the driver's seat. He took off the custom wheel lock as he inserted the key into the ignition, and told Kolya he would have to sit in the driver's seat to open the telephone compartment.

Once more Kolya nodded. Bond felt the eye of the automatic pistol boring through the Russian's jacket, and knew that surprise and speed were his only allies now.

Almost casually, Bond pressed the square black button on the dashboard, while his left hand dropped to the right position. There was a tiny hiss of gas as the hydraulics opened the hidden compartment. A second later the big Ruger Redhawk dropped into his left hand.

Trained to use weapons with either hand, helped by the very ordinary movements, urged on by speed, Bond's body turned only slightly, the flash of the Magnum cartridge burning his trousers and jacket as he fired almost before the big revolver was clear of its hiding place.

Kolya Mosolov knew nothing. One minute he was ready to squeeze the trigger of the silenced Stechkin hidden under his coat; the next moment a blinding flash, a fractional pain, then darkness and the long oblivion.

The bullet lifted the Russian from his feet, catching him just below the throat, almost ripping head from body. His heels scraped the ice as he slid back, turning as he hit the ground, sliding a good one and a half meters after he had fallen.

But Bond saw none of that. The moment he fired, so his right hand slammed the door closed. The Redhawk went back into its compartment, and the key was fully twisted in the ignition.

The Saab burst into life, and Bond's hand moved with calm, expert confidence—pushing the button to close the compartment housing the Redhawk, sliding the stick into first, clipping on his inertia reel seatbelt, taking off the brake, and smoothly moving away as his fingers adjusted the hot air controls and the rear window heater.

As he pulled away, Bond got the merest glimpse of what remained of the Russian: a small huddle on the ice and a swelling pool of crimson. He swerved the car onto the Mannerheimintie, joining the sparse traffic heading for the Vantaa Airport road.

Once settled into the road pattern, Bond reached down and activated the radio telephone—which had proved to be Kolya Mosolov's fatal mistake. This was a simple local call, needing no base unit or special provisions, for the resident agent, under whose control Bond officially worked, should be at a number situated less than ten miles from where the Saab sped towards the airport.

He punched out the number, by feel rather than looking down, for Bond's eyes had to be everywhere now. In the handset he heard the number buzz at the distant end. The buzzing continued, unanswered. In some ways Bond was pleased. Then he remembered. Had not von Glöda told him the resident had been removed? Perhaps. Perhaps not.

He drove with care, watching his speed, for the Finnish police are distinctly trigger-happy when it comes to breaking the speed-limit. The clock on Bond's dashboard, which had been adjusted to Helsinki time, said five minutes past eight. He would be at Vantaa by eight-thirty all right—possibly just in time to catch up with von Glöda.

The airport was crowded, like any other international terminal, when Bond entered. He had parked the Saab in an easily accessible place, and now carried the awkward Ruger Redhawk inside his jacket, the long barrel pushed into the waistband of his trousers and then twisted sideways. The training schools taught never to do the trick you see in the movies and shove a gun barrel straight down inside your trouser leg; always turn it to one side. If there was an accident, straight down meant losing part of your foot, if you were lucky. An unlucky man would lose what one instructor insisted on calling your "wedding tackle"—a term Bond thought oddly vulgar. Twist the weapon sideways, by the butt, and you would get a burn, though the unfortunate beside you would catch the bullet.

The big clock in International Departures stood at two minutes to eight-thirty.

Moving very fast, elbowing through the throng, Bond made the information desk and asked about the nine o'clock flight to Paris. The girl hardly looked up. The nine o'clock was Flight AY 873 via Brussels. They would not be calling it for another fifteen minutes as there was a catering delay.

As yet there was no need to put out a call for von Glöda, Bond decided. If the man's colleagues were around to see him off, there would be a chance to corner him on this side of the terminal. If not, then Bond would simply have to bluff him back from the air side.

Keeping behind as much cover as possible, Bond edged his way past the kiosks, trying to position himself near the passage on the far left of the complex which led to passport control and the air-side lounges.

At the far end of this section of the Departure area, set in front of high windows, was a coffee shop—separated from the main complex by a low, flimsy trellis barrier covered with imitation flowers.

To the left of this, very close to where Bond now stood, was the passport control section, each of its little booths occupied by an official.

Bond started to look at faces, searching through the crowds for von Glöda. Departing passengers were constantly passing through passport control, while the coffee shop was crowded with travelers, mainly seated at low round tables.

Then quite unexpectedly—almost out of the corner of his eye—Bond saw his quarry: von Glöda rising from one of the coffee shop tables.

The would-be heir to Adolf Hitler's ruined empire appeared to be just as well organized in Helsinki as he had been at the Ice Palace. His clothes were immaculate, and even in the gray civilian greatcoat, the man had a military look about him, a straightness of back and a bearing that singled him out from the ordinary. No wonder—Bond thought momentarily—that Tudeer imagined the world was his destiny.

The once and future Führer was surrounded by six men, all smartly dressed—each one of them looking like an ex-soldier. Mercenaries perhaps? Von Glöda spoke to them in a low voice, punctuating his words with quick movements of the hands, and it took Bond a second or two before he realized that the movements were similar to those of the late Adolf Hitler himself.

The radio announcement system clicked and played its little warning jingle. They were about to announce the Paris flight, Bond was certain. Von Glöda cocked his head to listen, but he'd also apparently decided, before the jingle finished, that it was his flight. Solemnly he shook hands with each of his men in turn and looked around for his hand baggage.

Bond moved closer to the trelliswork. There were too many people in the coffee shop to risk taking von Glöda there, he decided. The best place would be as the man walked clear of the coffee shop towards passport control.

Still maintaining cover among the constantly changing throng, Bond edged to the left. Von Glöda appeared to be looking around him, as if alerted to some danger.

The jingle died away and the voice of the announcer came from the myriad speakers—unusually loud and clear, then almost unbearably so.

Bond felt his stomach churn. He stopped in his tracks, eyes never leaving von Glöda, who also stiffened, his face changing at the words:

"Would Mr. James Bond please come to the Information Desk on the second floor?"

They were on the second floor. Bond quickly looked around, eyes searching for the Information Desk, aware that von Glöda was also turning. The voice repeated in English, "Mr. James Bond, please go to the Information Desk."

Von Glöda turned fully. Both he and Bond must have spotted the figure standing by the Information Desk at roughly the same moment—Hans Buchtman, whom Bond had first known as Brad Tirpitz. As their eyes met, so Buchtman moved towards Bond, his mouth opening, words floating, lost in the general noise and bustle.

For a second, von Glöda stared at Buchtman, scowling, incredulous. Then at last he saw Bond.

The whole scene appeared to be frozen for a split second. Then von Glöda said something to his companion. They began to scatter as von Glöda grabbed for his cabin baggage and started to move quickly from the coffee shop.

Bond stepped into the open in an attempt to cut him off, aware of Buchtman elbowing his way through the crowd. Bond's hand touched the Redhawk's butt as Buchtman's words finally reached his ears: "No! No, Bond. No, we want him alive!"

I'll bet you do, Bond thought, as he hauled on the Redhawk, closing towards von Glöda who was crossing in front of him, moving rapidly. There was no stopping Bond now. "Halt, Tudeer!" he shouted. "You'll never make that flight. Stop now!" People began to scream, and Bond— only a few paces from von Glöda now—realized that the leader of the National Socialist Action Army held a Luger pistol low in his right hand, half-screened by the small case in his left.

Bond still hauled on the Redhawk, which would not come free from his waistband. Again he shouted, glancing back to see that Buchtman was bearing down on him from behind, thrusting people out of his path.

In the midst of the panic erupting around him, Bond heard von Glöda shouting hysterically as he turned full on towards Bond.

"They didn't get me yesterday," von Glöda yelled. "This is proof of my mission. Proof of my destiny."

As though in answer, the barrel of the Redhawk came free. Von Glöda's hand rose, the Luger pointing towards Bond, who dropped to one knee, extending his arm and the Redhawk. Von Glöda's hand and the Luger filled Bond's vision as he called again, "It's over, von Glöda. Don't be a fool."

Then the spurt of flame from the Luger's barrel, and Bond's own finger squeezing twice on the Redhawk's trigger.

The explosions detonated together, and a great hand seemed to fling Bond sideways. The passport control booths spun in front of him, and he sprawled across the floor while von Glöda tilted and reared like a wounded stag, still trumpeting:

"Destiny . . . Destiny . . . Destiny . . ."

Bond couldn't understand why he was on the ground. Vaguely he caught sight of a passport control officer diving for shelter behind his booth. Then, still sprawling, he had the Redhawk zeroed in on von Glöda, who seemed to be trying to aim again with his Luger. Bond squeezed off another shot and von Glöda dropped the Luger, then took one step back as his head disappeared in a thick mist.

It was only now that pain began to overtake Bond. He felt very tired. Someone held his shoulders. There was a lot of noise. Then a voice: "Couldn't be helped, James. You got the bastard. All over now. They've sent for an ambulance. You'll be okay."

The voice was saying more than that, but the light ebbed away from Bond's eyes and all sound disappeared, as though someone had deliberately turned down the volume.

21

THIS CAN'T BE HEAVEN

THE TUNNEL WAS very long; its sides white. Bond wondered if he was back in the Arctic Circle. Then he was swimming. Warm and cold by turns. Voices. Soft music. Then the face of a girl leaning over him and calling his name: "Mr. Bond . . . ? Mr. Bond . . . ?"

The voice seemed to sing, and the girl's face was truly beautiful. She had blond hair and appeared to be surrounded by a halo.

James Bond opened his eyes and looked at her. Yes, a blond angel with a shining white halo.

"Did I really make it? I couldn't have. This can't be heaven."

The girl laughed. "Not heaven, Mr. Bond. You are in a hospital."

"Where?"

"In Helsinki. And there are people here to see you."

He suddenly felt very tired. "Send them away." His voice slurred. "I'm too busy now. Heaven is great."

Then he retreated, back down the tunnel, which had turned dark and warm.

He could have been asleep for hours, weeks, or months. There were no guidelines. But when Bond finally woke, he was conscious only of the pain down the right side of his body.

The angel had gone. In her place a familiar figure sat quietly in a chair near the bed.

"Back with us, 007?" said M. "How do you feel?"

The memories returned like a series of clips from an old movie. The Arctic Circle; snow scooters; Blue Hare; the Ice Palace; Paula's observation post; the bombs; then the last hours in Helsinki. The eye of the Luger.

Bond swallowed. His mouth was very dry. "Not bad, sir," he croaked, then remembered Paula, prostrate on the bed. "Paula?"

"She's fine, 007. Right as rain."

"Good." Bond closed his eyes, recalling all that had happened. M remained silent. In spite of himself, Bond was impressed. It was rare enough for his boss to leave the safe confines of the buiding overlooking Regent's Park. Eventually, Bond opened his eyes again. "Next time, sir, I trust you'll give me a full and proper briefing."

M coughed. "We thought it better for you to find out for yourself, 007. Truth is, we weren't sure about everyone ourselves. The general idea was to put you in the field and draw the fire."

"There you appear to have been successful."

The blond angel came in. She was, of course, a nurse. "You're not to tire him," she chided M in impeccable English, then disappeared again.

"You stopped two bullets," M said, seemingly unconcerned. "Both in the upper part of the chest. No serious damage done. On your feet again in a week or two. I'll see you get a month's leave after that. Tirpitz was going to bring Tudeer to us, but you had no alternative in that situation."

Uncharacteristically, M leaned over and gave Bond's hand a fatherly pat. "Well done, 007. Good job well done."

"Kind of you, sir. But I *was* under the impression that Brad Tirpitz's real name is Hans Buchtman. He was a crony of von Glöda's."

"It was what I had to let you think, James." For the first time, Bond realized that Tirpitz was also in the room. "I'm sorry about the way it turned out. In the end everything went wrong. I had to stay with von Glöda. I guess I waited a hair too long. It was pure dumb luck that we weren't killed with the rest. The Russian Air Force did some kind of number on us, Jesus Christ Almighty. It was the worst I've ever been in."

"I know. I watched it," said Bond, feeling, in spite of his condition, an irritation with the American. "But what about the whole Buchtman business?"

Tirpitz went into a lengthy explanation. About a year before, the CIA had instructed him to make contact with Aarne Tudeer, whom they suspected of doing arms deals with the Russians. "I met him in Helsinki," Tirpitz said. "I speak German well enough, and I had a phony background all set up under Hans Buchtman; I got to know him under the name of Buchtman, insinuated myself as a possible arms source. I also dropped some pretty hints that I bore a strong physical resemblance to a CIA guy called Brad Tirpitz. That was for insurance and it paid off. I guess I'm one of the few people living who got to kill themselves, if you see what I mean."

The nurse returned with a large jug of barley water and warned them they only had another few minutes. Bond asked if he could have a martini instead. The nurse gave him an official smile.

"There wasn't a hell of a lot I could do about the torture, or getting you out any earlier," Tirpitz continued. "I couldn't even warn you about Rivke, because I knew nothing. Von Glöda didn't confide much, didn't tell me about the hospital setup until too late. And the information from my own people was pretty half-assed to say the least."

Half-assed indeed, Bond thought vaguely. Then he drifted off again, and when he came to a few moments later, only M was in the room.

"We're still rounding up the remnants, 007," M was saying. "The N-S-Double-A. We've scuttled them for good, I think." M sounded pleased. "I can't see anyone else reactivating what's left of it now—thanks to you, 007. In spite of the lack of information."

"All part of the service," Bond added sarcastically. But the remark ran off M's back like water from the proverbial duck.

After M left, the nurse returned to make sure Bond was comfortable.

"You *are* a nurse, aren't you?" Bond asked suspiciously.

"Of course. But why, Mr. Bond?"

"Just checking." Bond managed a smile. "How about dinner tonight?"

"You are on a restricted diet, but if you fancy something I'll bring you our menu . . ."

"I meant you—dinner with me."

She took a step away from the bed and looked him full in the eyes. Bond thought she was built from a mold long broken. Rarely did they make figures like that anymore. Only occasionally. Like Rivke. Or Paula.

"My name's Ingrid," the nurse said coolly. "And I'd love to have dinner with you as soon as you're fully recovered. And I mean *fully* recovered. Do you remember what you said to me when you first became conscious after you were shot?"

Bond shook his head on the pillow.

"You said, 'This can't be heaven.' Mr. Bond—James—maybe I'll show you it *is* heaven. But not until you're quite better."

"Which will not be for a very long time." The voice came from the door. "And if anyone's going to show Mr. Bond what heaven Helsinki can be, it will be me," said Paula Vacker.

"Ah." Bond smiled weakly. He had to admit that, even next to the impressive nurse Ingrid, Paula had the edge.

"Ah, indeed, James. The minute I turn my back there you are, getting shot at, flirting with nurses. This is my city, and while you're here . . ."

"But you were asleep." Bond gave a tired grin.

"Yes, but I'm wide awake now. Oh, James, you had me so worried."

"You should never worry about me."

"No? Well, I've arranged things. Your chief—he's rather cute, by the way—he says I can look after you for a couple of weeks once they let you out of here."

"Cute?" Bond said, incredulous. Then he put his head back, drifting off once more as Puala bent over to kiss him.

That night, in spite of all the memories—the Arctic, the terrors, the double and triple crosses, James Bond slept without dreams or nightmares.

He woke around dawn, then drifted into sleep again. This time, as always when content, he dreamed of Royale-les-Eaux, as it had been long ago.